Orhan Pamuk won the Nobel Prize in Literature in 2006. His novel *My Name Is Red* won the 2003 IMPAC Dublin Literary Award. His recent novel, *A Strangeness in My Mind,* was an international bestseller and was shortlisted for the Man Booker International Prize. His work has been translated into more than sixty languages.

D0253806

ORHAN PAMUK

The Black Book

Translated by
MAUREEN FREELY

FABER & FABER

This new translation first published in 2006
by Faber and Faber Limited
Bloomsbury House 74–77 Great Russell Street,
London WC1B 3DA
This paperback edition published in 2015
Originally published in Turkey in 1990 as *Kara Kitap* by Can Yayinlavi Ltd

Printed and bound by CPI Group (UK) Ltd, Croydon, CRO 4YY

Grateful acknowledgement is made for permission to extract from the following:
Madame Bovary by Gustave Flaubert, translated by Alan Russell,
© Alan Russell, 1950, by permission of Penguin Books Ltd.
The Conference of the Birds by Farid ud-Din Attar, translated by
Afkham Darbandi and Dick Davis, © Afkham Darbandi and
Dick Davis, 1984, by permission of Penguin Books Ltd.
Dante's Inferno by Dante Alighieri,
translation by Mark Musa, © Indiana University Press, 1971.
Seven Gothic Tales by Isak Dinesen, © Random House, Inc, 1980.
Remembrance of Things Past by Marcel Proust, translated by CK Scott-Moncrieff
and Terence Kilmartin, © Random House, Inc, 1982.

A CIP record for this book
is available from the British Library

ISBN 978–0–571–32609–9

FSC
www.fsc.org
MIX
Paper from
responsible sources
FSC® C013604

4 6 8 10 9 7 5

To Aylın

Ibn' Arabi writes of a friend and dervish saint who, after his soul was elevated to the heavens, arrived on Mount Kaf, the magic mountain that encircles the world; gazing around him, he saw that the mountain itself was encircled by a serpent. Now, it is a well-known fact that no such mountain encircles the world, nor is there a serpent.

—The Encyclopedia of Islam

Contents

PART ONE

Chapter One

The First Time Galip Saw Rüya

Never use epigraphs—they kill the mystery in the work!
—Adli

If that's how it has to die, go ahead and kill it; then kill the false prophets who sold you on the mystery in the first place!
—Bahti

Rüya was lying facedown on the bed, lost to the sweet warm darkness beneath the billowing folds of the blue-checked quilt. The first sounds of a winter morning seeped in from outside: the rumble of a passing car, the clatter of an old bus, the rattle of the copper kettles that the salep maker shared with the pastry cook, the whistle of the parking attendant at the *dolmuş* stop. A cold leaden light filtered through the dark blue curtains. Languid with sleep, Galip gazed at his wife's head: Rüya's chin was nestling in the down pillow. The wondrous sights playing in her mind gave her an unearthly glow that pulled him toward her even as it suffused him with fear. *Memory*, Celâl had once written in a column, *is a garden*. Rüya's gardens, Rüya's gardens . . . Galip thought. Don't think, don't think, it will make you jealous! But as he gazed at his wife's forehead, he still let himself think.

He longed to stroll among the willows, acacias, and sun-drenched climbing roses of the walled garden where Rüya had taken refuge, shutting the doors behind her. But he was indecently afraid of the faces he might find there: *Well, hello! So you're a regular here too, are you?* It was not the already identified apparitions he most dreaded but the insinuating male shadows he could never have anticipated: Excuse me, brother, when exactly did you run into my wife, or were you introduced? Three years ago at your house, inside a foreign fashion magazine from Alâaddin's shop, at middle school, outside the movie theater where you once sat hand in hand. . . . No, perhaps Rüya's memories were not so cruelly crowded; perhaps she was at this very moment basking in the one sunny corner in the dark garden of her memories, setting out with Galip in a rowboat. . . . Six months after Rüya's family moved to Istanbul, Galip and Rüya had both come down with mumps. To speed their recovery, Galip's mother and Rüya's mother, the beautiful Aunt Suzan, would take the children out to the Bosphorus; some days it would be just one mother taking them by the hand and other days it would be both; whatever bus they took, it shuddered as it rolled over the cobblestones, and wherever it took them—Bebek or Tarabya—the high point of the excursion was a tour of the bay in a rowboat. In those days it was microbes people feared and respected, not medicines, and everyone agreed that the pure air of the Bosphorus could cure children of the mumps. The sea was always calm on those mornings, and the rowboat white; it was always the same friendly boatman waiting to greet them. The mothers and aunts would sit at the back of the rowboat, Rüya and Galip side by side at the front, shielded from their mothers' gaze by the rising and falling back of the boatman. As they trailed their feet in the water, they would gaze at their matching legs and the sea swirling around their delicate ankles; the seaweed and seven-colored oil spills, the tiny, almost translucent pebbles, and the scraps of newspaper they strained to read, hoping to spot one of Celâl's columns.

The first time Galip saw Rüya, six months before coming down with the mumps, he was sitting on a stool on the dining room table while a barber cut his hair. In those days, there was a tall barber with a Douglas Fairbanks mustache who'd come to the house five days a week to give Grandfather a shave. These were the days when the coffee lines outside Alâaddin's and the Arab's grew longer every day, when the only nylon stockings you could find were the ones on the black market, when the number of '56 Chevrolets in Istanbul grew steadily larger, and Galip pored over the columns that Celâl published every weekday on page two of *Milliyet* under the name Selim Kaçmaz, but it was not when he first learned how to read, because it was Grandmother who'd taught him two years before starting school. They'd sit at the far end of the dining table. After Grandmother had hoarsely divulged the greatest mystery of all—how the letters joined up to make words—she would puff on the Bafra she'd seen no reason to remove from the side of her mouth, and as her grandson's eyes watered from the cigarette smoke, the enormous horse in his alphabet book would turn blue and come to life. A was for *at,* the Turkish word for *horse;* it was larger even than the bony horses that pulled the carts belonging to the lame water seller and the junk dealer they said was a thief. In those days, Galip would long for a magic potion to pour over the picture of this sprightly alphabet horse, to give it the strength to jump off the page; later on, when they held him back in the first year of primary school and he had to learn how to read and write all over again under the supervision of the very same alphabet horse, he would dismiss this wish as nonsense.

Earlier on, if Grandfather had kept his promise, if he'd brought home that magic potion he said they sold on the streets in vials the color of pomegranates, Galip would have wanted to pour the liquid over the World War One zeppelins, cannons, and muddy corpses littering the dusty pages of his old issues of *L'Illustration,* not to mention the postcards that Uncle Melih sent from Paris and Fez; he would also have poured it over the picture of the orangutan suckling her baby that Vasıf had cut out of *Dünya* and the strange human faces he'd clipped out of Celâl's newspaper. But by now Grandfather never went outside, not even to go to the barber's; he spent the whole day indoors. Even so, he still dressed every morning, just as he'd done in the days when he went out to the store: wrinkled trousers, cuff links, an old English jacket with wide lapels that was as gray as the stubble that grew on his cheeks on Sundays, and what Father called a silk necktie. Mother refused to call it a necktie—she called it a *cravate;* coming as she did from a family that had once prided itself on being wealthier than Father's family, she liked to put on Western airs. Later on, she and Father would discuss Grandfather as if he were one of those old unpainted wooden houses that collapsed around them almost daily; as they talked on, forgetting about Grandfather, their voices would grow gradually louder until they turned to Galip: "Go upstairs, why don't you; go find a game to play. Now." "May I take the lift?" "Don't let him take the lift by himself!" "Don't take the lift by yourself!" "Should I go and play with Vasıf, then?" "No, he gets too angry!"

Actually, he didn't get too angry. Vasıf was deaf and dumb, but when I played Secret Passage, he knew I wasn't making fun of him; when I got on all fours and headed for the far end of the cave I knew to be lurking in the shadowy outer reaches of the apartment, taking cover under beds as I ventured forward—as stealthy as a cat, as furtive as a soldier creeping though the tunnel that will lead him into enemy trenches—he understood me perfectly, but apart from Rüya, who wasn't there yet, no one else in the house knew this. Sometimes Vasıf and I would stand together at the window for ages and ages, watching the streetcar line. The world we could see from the bay window of our concrete apartment reached as far as a mosque in one direction and, in the other, as far as a girl's lycée; between them stood a police station, an enormous chestnut tree, a street corner, and Alâaddin's bustling shop. Sometimes, when we were watching the people going in and out of the shop and idly drawing each other's attention to passing cars, Vasıf would suddenly let out a hoarse and terrifying cry, the cry of a boy who is battling with the devil in his dreams; if he caught me unawares, I'd be truly frightened. This would provoke a response from the two chimneys puffing behind us. Leaning forward in his low armchair, Grandfather would try in vain to distract Grandmother from the radio. "Vasıf has scared Galip out of his wits again," he'd murmur, and then, more out of habit than curiosity, he'd turn to us and ask, "So let's see now, how many cars have you spotted so far?" But no matter what I told them about the Dodges, Packards, DeSotos, and new Chevrolets I had counted, they didn't hear a thing I said.

Although the radio was on from the first thing in the morning till the last thing at night, the thick-coated and not-at-all-Turkish-looking china dog curled up on top of it never woke from his peaceful slumber. As *alaturka* music gave way to *alafranga*—Western—music and the news faded into commercials for banks, colognes, and the national lottery, Grandmother and Grandfather kept up a steady patter. Mostly they complained about the cigarettes in their hands, but as wearily as if they'd been suffering from a toothache so long they'd accustomed themselves to the pain. They would blame each other for failing to kick the habit, and if one went into a serious coughing fit, the other would proclaim, first triumphantly and then fretfully, peevishly, that the accusations were true! But not long afterward, the needling would resume. "So I'm smok-

ing a cigarette—stop nagging!" Then there'd be a mention of something one of them had read in the paper. "Apparently, cigarettes help
calm your nerves." A silence might follow but, with the clock ticking
away on the wall in the corridor, it never lasted long. Even as they took
up their papers again and began leafing through them, even as they
played bezique in the afternoons, they kept on talking, and when the
family came together for the evening meal, they'd utter the same words
they did when it came time for everyone to gather around the radio, or
when they'd both finished reading Celâl's column. "If only they'd let
him sign his real name," Grandfather would say, "maybe he'd come to
his senses." Grandmother would sigh—"And a grown man too"—and
then, her face screwed up with worry as if she were asking this question for the very first time, she'd say, "Is it because they won't let him
sign his columns that he writes so badly, or is it because he writes so
badly that they won't give him permission to write under his own
name?" "If nothing else," Grandfather would say, grasping for the
consolation that had soothed both of them from time to time, "it's
because they haven't let him sign his columns that so few people know
how much he's disgraced us." "No, no one knows," Grandmother
would say then, but in such a way that Galip knew she didn't mean it.
"Who would know that we were the ones he's been writing about in
the newspaper?"

Later on, when Celâl was receiving hundreds of letters from his
readers every week and began to republish his old columns under his
own illustrious name— some claimed this was because his imagination
had dried up and some thought it was because women or politics took
up all his time, while others were sure it was out of simple laziness—
Grandfather would repeat a line he'd recited hundreds of times
already, in a bored and slightly affected voice that made him sound like
a second-rate actor, "For the love of God, can there be anyone in this
city who does not know that the apartment he mentions in that column is the one in which we sit?" At that, Grandmother would fall
silent.

Then Grandfather would begin to speak of the dreams that would
visit him so often as time wore on. His eyes would light up, just as they
did when he told one of those stories they repeated to each other all
day long. He'd been dreaming in blue, he'd say: the rain in his dream

was the deepest blue, midnight blue, and it was this never-ending blue rain that made his hair and his beard grow ever longer. After listening patiently, Grandmother would say, "The barber's coming very soon," but Grandfather frowned whenever the barber was mentioned. "He talks too much, he asks too many questions!" After they were done with the blue dream and the barber, there were one or two occasions when Galip heard Grandfather whisper under his breath, "We should have built another building, far away from here. This apartment has brought us bad luck."

Years later, after they'd sold off the City-of-Hearts Apartments one by one, and the building, like so many others in the area, was colonized by small clothing manufacturers, insurance offices, and gynecologists who did abortions on the sly, Galip would pause on his way to Alâaddin's shop to look up at the mean and grimy facade of the building that had once been his home and wonder what could have prompted Grandfather to make such a dark pronouncement. It had something to do with his Uncle Melih, who had gone off to Europe only to settle in Africa and who, after returning to Turkey, had lingered in Izmir for many years before returning to the apartment in Istanbul. Whenever the barber asked after him—So, when's that eldest son of yours returning from Africa?—Grandfather would bridle; seeing his reluctance to discuss the matter, Galip was aware even then that Grandfather's "bad luck" had begun when his oldest and strangest son had gone abroad, leaving his wife and their son Vasıf behind, only to return years later with a new wife and a new daughter (Rüya, which was also the Turkish word for *dream*).

As Celâl told Galip many years later, Uncle Melih was still in Istanbul—and not yet thirty—when they'd started building the apartments. Every afternoon, he would leave the law offices (where he did little other than quarrel or sketch ships and desert islands on the backs of old legal dossiers) to join his father and his brothers at the construction site in Nişantaşı. The workmen would be slacking off as the end of the workday approached; much to their annoyance, Uncle Melih would take off his jacket, roll up his sleeves, and set to work. The family owned two concerns at the time: the White Pharmacy in Karaköy and a candy shop in Sirkeci that later became a patisserie and then a restaurant. They couldn't compete with Hacı Bekir, whose *lokums* were

said to be the best in the city, though they were more optimistic about
the small jars of Grandmother's quince, fig, and cherry jam lining the
shelves on the walls. But it was around this time that Uncle Melih
began to talk about going to France or Germany: He wanted to learn
how to make European-style confitures; he would find out where to
buy gilt paper for wrapping candied chestnuts; he would see if they
could go into partnership with the French and set up a factory that
made colored bubble bath—it might be an idea to visit the factories
that were shutting down one after the other all over America and
Europe around this time, to buy up some of their machinery—and
perhaps he could also find a cut-rate grand piano for Aunt Hâle; above
all, he wanted to take poor deaf Vasıf to a good ear specialist, a neurol-
ogist who knew what he was talking about.

Two years later, Uncle Melih and Vasıf set off for Marseilles on a
Romanian ship, the *Tristana*; Galip knew it only from a photograph
he'd found when going through Grandmother's boxes. The photograph smelled of rose water; the ship itself (as Celâl would discover
when he went through Vasıf's newspaper clippings) sank after running
into a free-floating mine in the Black Sea. The apartment house was
finished by the time Uncle Melih and Vasıf set off for Europe, but no
one had yet moved in. A year later, Vasıf returned alone by train, still
deaf and dumb, *naturally* (as Aunt Hâle would say any time the subject
came up, though Galip never quite understood what her strange
emphasis was meant to imply); when he pulled into Sirkeci Station,
Vasıf was clutching an aquarium on his lap, fully stocked with the
Japanese fish whose great-great-great-great-grandchildren would still
be bringing him pleasure fifty years later. From the very beginning, he
refused to be parted from them; he spent hours on end staring at the
fish, sometimes breathless with excitement and other times tearful and
despairing.

By the time Vasıf returned, Celâl and his mother were living on
the third floor (which would later be sold to an Armenian), but to allow Uncle Melih to continue his business investigations of the Paris
streets, he needed money, so they rented out the third-floor apartment
and moved up to the small sloping attic that had once served as a store-
room; half of it was later turned into a small apartment. Uncle Melih
continued to send letters from Paris stuffed with recipes for pastries

and confitures, formulas for soap and cologne, and pictures of the actors and ballerinas who ate and used these products. There were also packages containing mint toothpaste, marron glacé samples, liqueur chocolates, toy firemen, and sailor's caps. With time, though, the letters and packages became less frequent and Celâl's mother began to wonder if she and Celâl should return to her father's house. But it wasn't until the war broke out and Uncle Melih had sent them the strangest postcard of a mosque and an airplane from Binghazi that she and Celâl returned to the wooden house in Aksaray to join her mother and her father, a petty official in one of the charitable foundations. On the back of his brown-and-white postcard, Uncle Melih had written that all routes back to Turkey had been mined.

The war was long over when he sent another postcard, this one black and white, from Fez. This was how Grandmother and Grandfather discovered that Uncle Melih had married a Turkish girl in Marrakesh. His bride had a bloodline she could trace all the way back to the Prophet Muhammed and was therefore a *seyyide*—a princess—and a very beautiful woman. On the postcard was a hand-painted picture of a colonial hotel that looked like a cream cake and had appeared in a Hollywood film about an arms dealer and a spy who had fallen in love with the same bar girl. (Years later, long after he had worked out the nationalities of the flags waving on the hotel's second floor, Galip happened to be looking at this postcard one day when, falling into the style Celâl used in his "Gangsters of Beyoğlu" stories, he decided it must have been in one of these rooms that the "first seeds of Rüya were sown.")

Six months after the Fez postcard arrived, a card arrived from Izmir, but no one believed it was Uncle Melih who had sent it, because by then they'd decided he was never coming back; there were even rumors that he and his new wife had converted to Christianity, joined a group of missionaries bound for Kenya, and built a church for a sect that sought to merge the Crescent with the Cross in a valley where lions hunted three-antlered deer. Then there was the gossip who claimed to know the bride's Izmir relatives; according to this person, Uncle Melih had spent the war in South Africa, smuggling arms and engaging in various other dark ventures, like bribing a king; though he had been well on his way to becoming a millionaire, he had allowed himself to be ruled by his whimsical wife, whose beauty was legendary; the couple planned to go to Hollywood to make her world famous, and already her picture was appearing in Arab-French magazines. But the postcard that the family passed from floor to floor for weeks on end—scratching it suspiciously, as if they suspected it of being counterfeit—merely stated that Uncle Melih and his wife had decided to return to Turkey because they missed their country so much they'd fallen ill. "Now" they were well, he said; he was working for his father-in-law, who was in tobacco and figs and keen for Uncle Melih to help him develop new products. But not long afterward yet another postcard arrived, which every floor interpreted in its own way. Although everyone claimed it to be garbled and almost impossible to decipher, this may have had something to do with the property disputes that would soon drag the entire family into silent warfare; years later, when Galip examined the same postcard, he did not find the language unduly confusing. All Uncle Melih said was that he wished to return to Istanbul, he had a daughter, and had not yet decided what to name her.

Grandmother displayed Uncle Melih's postcards along the edges of the enormous mirror in the buffet where she kept the liqueurs; there were so many that they seemed to form a second frame. It was in one of these postcards that Galip first read Rüya's name. Among the views of churches, bridges, seascapes, towers, ships, mosques, deserts, pyramids, hotels, parks, and animals that Grandfather so resented were snapshots of Rüya as an infant and a young child. But in those days, he was less interested in his uncle's daughter (or his cousin, as people were just beginning to say) than he was in his Aunt Suzan, who gazed so mournfully at the camera as she parted the mosquito net to reveal the ghostly black-and-white cave where Rüya slept. As Rüya's baby pictures made their way around the apartments, it was the mother's beauty that made everyone—man and woman alike—stop and stare in silence, but Galip would not understand why until much later. At the time the question on everyone's lips was when Uncle Melih and his new family might be coming to Istanbul and which floor they would take when they arrived. By now, Celâl's mother—she had married a lawyer, only to die young of a disease for which each doctor had another name—no longer able to bear the spider-filled house in Aksaray, had finally accepted Grandmother's insistent invitation to

return with Celâl to the attic apartment, where Celâl began his pseu-
donymous newspaper career: investigations into match-fixing; exaggerated accounts of thrilling and artfully executed murders in the bars,
nightclubs, and brothels of Beyoğlu's back streets; crossword puzzles
in which the black squares always outnumbered the white; a serial
on wrestlers (which he took over after the original author became
addicted to opiated wine); various articles with titles like DISCOVER
YOUR CHARACTER IN YOUR HANDWRITING, READ YOUR CHARACTER IN
YOUR FACE, LET US INTERPRET YOUR DREAMS, and YOUR HOROSCOPE
TODAY (according to friends and relatives, it was in his horoscopes that
he first started sending secret greetings to his lovers); he also did a
BELIEVE IT OR NOT column and spent his spare time watching the latest
American films for free and then reviewing them; impressed by his
industry, people had even begun saying that he was doing journalism to
build up his savings so he could take a wife.

Long afterward, when he was watching the cobblestones along the
streetcar line disappear under a layer of asphalt for which he could see
no reason, Galip asked himself if Grandfather's strange misgivings
about the apartment building came from his feeling out of place or if
it all went back to the day the home he'd built for his family was suddenly too small to contain it. When Uncle Melih turned up one spring
evening with his beautiful wife, his enchanting daughter, and a fleet of
trunks and suitcases, he moved straight into Celâl's attic apartment, of
course. Perhaps he did this to spite his family for failing to take him at
his word.

The next morning Galip overslept. In his dream he was sitting next
to a mysterious blue-haired girl on a city bus that seemed to be taking
them far away from the school where he should have been reading the
last page of the alphabet book. He awoke to discover that he really was
late for school and his father was late for work as well. Mother and
Father were eating breakfast, discussing the goings-on in the attic
apartment in the same tones they used for the mice that ran between
the walls of the apartment and that their maid Esma Hanım reserved
for specters and djinns; what he remembered best afterward was the
sun pouring through the window and the blue-and-white checked
tablecloth that reminded him of a checkerboard. Galip did not want to
think about why he was late for school, nor did he want to think about

why the prospect of going to school late filled him with dread: for much the same reason, he did not want to know who had moved into the attic apartment. So instead he went upstairs to listen to Grandmother and Grandfather saying the same things to each other over and over, only to find the barber quizzing a rather glum-looking Grandfather about the new arrivals in the attic. The postcards had been taken out of the buffet mirror and were now strewn all over, and everywhere were new and strange objects; there was also a mysterious new smell to which he would later become addicted. It left him feeling empty, fearful, bereft: What were they like, what were they really like, these half-colored countries he'd only seen on postcards? What of the beautiful aunt in those photographs? He wanted to grow up, become a man! When he said he wanted to have his hair cut, Grandmother was very pleased, but like so many people who talk too much, the barber did not pause to consider Galip's feelings. Instead of letting him take Grandfather's armchair, he made him sit on a stool on top of the dining table. The blue-and-white cloth he draped over Grandfather was much too big, but that did not stop the barber from tying it around Galip's neck so tight he almost strangled him, and as if that weren't enough the cloth went all the way down to his knees like a girl's skirt.

Many years later, and long after they married (by Galip's calculations, their wedding day came exactly nineteen years, nineteen months, and nineteen days after their first meeting), there were mornings when Galip woke up to see his wife sleeping next to him, her head buried in her pillow, and he would wonder if the blue in the quilt made him uneasy because it reminded him of the blue in the cloth the barber had taken off his grandfather and draped around him, but he never said a word about this to his wife; he knew she would never agree to change the quilt cover for such a whimsical reason.

Galip was sure they would have pushed the newspaper under the door by now; he rose from bed with his usual care, making no more noise than a feather. His feet did not take him to the door but to the bathroom and the kitchen. The teakettle was not in the kitchen but he did find the teapot in the sitting room. Judging by the number of cigarette ends in the overflowing copper ashtray, Rüya must have been sitting here until the early hours of the morning, perhaps reading a new detective novel, perhaps not. He found the teakettle in the bathroom.

That terrifying contraption the *chauffe-bain,* was no longer working—the water pressure was too low—but rather than buy a new one they'd fallen into the habit of heating water in the teakettle instead. Sometimes they'd do this just before making love, waiting meekly for the water to come to a boil, just as Grandfather had once done with Grandmother, and Father with Mother.

But once, when Grandfather had asked Grandmother to put out her cigarette, and Grandmother had lost her temper and accused him of ingratitude, she reminded him that there had not been a single morning during their marriage when she had risen from bed later than he had. Vasıf was watching them; Galip was listening and trying to figure out what she was trying to say. Later on, Celâl would touch on this subject in his columns, but not to convey what Grandmother had intended. *To rise before the sun is in the sky,* he wrote, *to get out of bed when it's still pitch dark—only a peasant would think to live this way, and the same can be said of women who feel they must rise before their husbands.* These were the concluding remarks in a column that also described Galip's grandparents' other unbecoming household habits (how they dropped their cigarette ashes on the quilt and kept their false teeth in the same glass as their toothbrushes; the way their eyes raced over the death announcements); he presented all this to his readers without adornment. After she had read it, Grandmother said, "So it seems we're peasants!" Whereupon Grandfather had replied, "I'm sorry we never made him eat lentil soup for breakfast. *That* would have taught him what it means to be a peasant!"

As Galip went through his usual routines—rinsing the teacups, searching for clean knives and forks, retrieving white cheese and olives that looked like plastic food from a refrigerator that stank of *pastırma,* and heating up water in the teakettle so that he could shave—he felt the urge to make a noise that might wake up Rüya, but the noise never happened. When he sat down at the table to drink his weak tea and eat unpitted olives and yesterday's bread, he turned his attention to the newspaper he had retrieved from the doormat and spread out next to his plate, and while his eyes wafted over its sleepy words—the ink was so fresh he could smell it—his mind traveled elsewhere. This evening they'd go to see Celâl, or perhaps there was something good showing at the Palace Theater. He glanced at Celâl's column and decided to read it later, when they got back from the movies, but his eyes refused to obey and went straight to the first line of the column; he rose, leaving his newspaper open on the table, put on his coat, and went out the door, only to walk right back in. Digging his hands into the tobacco, loose change, and used tickets that lined his pockets, he spent a few moments paying silent tribute to his lovely wife. Then he turned around, shut the door softly behind him, and left the house.

The newly wiped stairs smelled of damp, dust, and dirt. The air outside was cold and thick with the black soot coming from the coal- and oil-burning chimneys of Nişantaşı. Puffing out great clouds of frozen breath, picking his way through the piles of litter on the pavement, he joined the long line at the *dolmuş* stop, from which shared taxis set out to all the most popular destinations in the city.

On the pavement opposite stood an old man who'd turned up the collar of his jacket to make it more like a coat; he was going through the pastry seller's wares, separating out the cheese pastries from the ones stuffed with meat. All of a sudden, Galip left the line, running back to the corner where the newspaper seller kept his stand in a well-sheltered doorway; after he'd paid for his new copy of *Milliyet*, he folded it and tucked it under his arm. He remembered Celâl mimicking one of his matronly readers: "Oh, Celâl Bey, Muharrem and I love your columns so much that some days we can't bear the wait and buy two copies of *Milliyet* in one day!" Then all three of them—Galip, Rüya, and Celâl—would laugh. Much later, after a smattering of rain had turned into a real downpour and he'd fought his way into a *dolmuş* that stank of wet clothes and cigarettes, after it had become clear that no one in the car was in the mood to strike up a conversation and he had entertained himself as only a newspaper addict can, by folding up his newspaper into smaller and smaller segments until all he could see was the column on page two, after he had spent a few last moments gazing absently through the window, Galip began to read Celâl's latest column.

Chapter Two

When the Bosphorus Dries Up

Nothing can ever be as shocking as life. Except writing.
—Ibn Zerhani

D id you know that the Bosphorus is drying up? I don't think so. Naturally, we're all preoccupied with this frenzied killing spree going on in our streets, and since we seem to enjoy it as much as fireworks, who has time to read or to find out what's going on in the world? It's hard even to keep abreast of our columnists—we read them as we struggle across our mangled ferry landings, as we huddle together at our overcrowded bus stops, as we sit yawning in those *dolmuş* seats that make every letter tremble. I found this story in a French geological journal.

The Black Sea, we are told, is getting warmer, the Mediterranean colder. As their waters continue to empty into the great caves whose gaping holes lie in wait under the seabed, the same tectonic movements have caused Gibraltar, the Dardanelles, and the Bosphorus to rise. After one of the last remaining Bosphorus fishermen told me how his boat had run aground in a place where he had once had to throw in an anchor on a chain as long as a minaret, he asked, Isn't our prime minister at all interested in knowing why?

I didn't have an answer for him. All I know is that the water is drying up faster than ever, and soon no water will be left. What is beyond doubt is that the heavenly place we once knew as the Bosphorus will soon become a pitch-black bog, glistening with muddy shipwrecks baring their shiny teeth like ghosts. But at the end of a hot summer, it's not hard to imagine this bog drying up in some parts while remaining muddy in others, like the bed of a humble river that waters a small town in the middle of nowhere. Nor is it difficult to foresee daisies and green grass growing on slopes irrigated by thousands of leaking sewage pipes. Leander's Tower will at last become worthy of its name, terrifying us from its giddy heights; in the wild terrain beneath, a new life will begin.

I am speaking now of the new neighborhoods that will take root on this muddy wasteland that we once knew as the Bosphorus, even as city councillors rush here and there waving penalty notices: I speak of shantytowns and shacks, bars, nightclubs, and amusement arcades, of rusty horsedrawn Lunaparks, of brothels, mosques, and dervish lodges, of nests where Marxist splinter groups go to hatch their young and rogue plastics factories turn out nylon stockings for the black market. Amid the doomsday chaos, among toppled wrecks of old City Line ferries, will stretch vast fields of bottle caps and seaweed. Adorning the mossy masts of American transatlantic liners that ran aground when the last of the water receded overnight, we shall find skeletons of Celts and Ligurians, their mouths gaping open in deference to the unknown gods of prehistory. As this new civilization grows up amid mussel-encrusted Byzantine treasures, tin and silver knives and forks, thousand-year-old wine corks and soda bottles, and the sharp-nosed wrecks of galleons, I can also imagine its denizens drawing fuel for their lamps and stoves from a dilipidated Romanian oil tanker whose propeller has become lodged in the mud. But that is not the worst of it, for in this accursed cesspool watered by the dark green spray of every sewage pipe in Istanbul, we can be sure that new epidemics will break out among the armies of rats as they explore their new heaven, this drying seabed strewn with turbot and swordfish skeletons and polluted with the mysterious gases that have been bubbling beneath the surface since long before the birth of history. This I know, and this I must impress upon you: The authorities will seek to contain the epidemic behind barbed wire, but it will touch us all.

As we sit on the balconies from which we once watched the moon glitter silver on the silken waters of the Bosphorus, we'll watch instead the blue smoke rising from the corpses we've had to burn in a hurry—leisurely burials having become a thing of the past. As we sit along what once was the shore, at tables where once we drank *rakı* amid the perfume of the Judas and honeysuckle blossoms, we will struggle to accustom ourselves to the acrid stink of rotting flesh. No longer will we soothe our souls with songs about the birds of spring, the fast-flowing waters of the Bosphorus, or the fishermen lining its shores; the air will ring instead with the anguished cries of men whose fear of death has driven them to smite their foes with the knives, daggers, bullets, and rusting scimitars that their forefathers, hoping to fend off the usual thousand-year inquiries, tossed into the sea. As for the *İstanbullus* who once lived on the edge of the water, when they return to their homes exhausted of an evening they will no longer open bus windows to drink in the sea air; instead, they'll stuff newspaper and cloth in the cracks to keep the stink of rotting flesh and mud from seeping in; they'll sit there staring through the glass at the flames that rise from the fearsome black chasm gaping below. Those seaside cafés where balloon and wafer halvah vendors once wandered among us? No longer shall we sit there of an evening to feast our eyes on naval fireworks, instead, we'll watch the blood-red fireballs of exploding mines that carry with them the shattered remains of the curious children who set them off. Those men who once earned their keep by combing the sands for the Byzantine coins and empty tin cans washed in by stormy seas? They'll take to collecting the coffee grinders, the moss-covered cuckoo clocks, the black mussel-encrusted pianos that a long-ago flood plucked from the wooden houses that once lined the shore.

A night will come in this new hell when I slip through the barbed wire in search of a certain Black Cadillac. This Cadillac was the prize possession of a Beyoğlu bandit (I cannot bring myself to dignify him with the word *gangster*) whose exploits I followed some thirty years ago, when I was an apprentice reporter; I recall that in the entrance to the den of iniquity from which he ran his operations there were two paintings of Istanbul I greatly admired. There were only two other Cadillacs like it in Istanbul at the time, one owned by Dağdelen, who had made his fortune in highways, and the other by Maruf, the tobacco king. It could be said that we journalists were the ones who turned our bandit into an urban legend, for we recounted his last hours in a serial that ran for an entire week. The climax was a police chase that ended with the Cadillac leaving the road at Akıntı Point and flying into the black waters of the Bosphorus. According to some witnesses, the bandit was high on hashish; others claimed that he'd freely chosen death for himself and the mistress at his side, racing toward the point like a doomed highwayman driving his horse over a precipice. Divers spent days hunting for the Cadillac, to no avail. It wasn't long before the newspaper-reading public had forgotten it ever existed, but I have already pinpointed what I am certain will turn out to be its exact location.

It is there, at the very bottom of the new valley we once knew as the Bosphorus, below a muddy cliff littered with camel bones, bottles bearing mysterious messages for nameless lovers, lone boots that lost their mates seven hundred years ago, shoes where crabs now lay their eggs. There, behind the slopes where mussel and sponge forests still sparkle with diamonds, earrings, bottle caps, and gold bracelets, past the heroin laboratory set up so hastily in the rotting shell of a barge, just beyond the sandbar where oysters and whelks feed on the buckets of blood gushing from the donkeys and packhorses as they're ground into black-market sausages.

As I plunge into this silent darkness and make my way through the stench of rotting corpses, I shall listen to the horns of the cars passing above me—on what we once knew as the Shore Road, though it now looks more like a lane snaking through a mountain pass. I'll stumble across the palace intriguers of yesteryear, still doubled over in the sacks in which they drowned, and the long-lost skeletons of Orthodox priests, still clutching their staffs and their crosses, their ankles still weighed down by balls and chains. I shall see bluish smoke rising from what seems at first to be a stovepipe but which turns out to be the old periscope from the submarine that tried to torpedo the S.S. *Gülcemal* as it was carrying troops from Tophane Wharf to Gallipoli, only to sink to the sea floor after its propeller got tangled up in fishermen's nets and rammed into some mossy rocks; it will be immediately apparent that our own citizens are drinking tea out of Chinese porcelain cups in their new home (built so many years ago in Liverpool) as they sit in velvet officer's chairs once occupied by English skeletons gasping for air. In the darkness just beyond, there will be the rusting anchor from a warship that once belonged to Kaiser Wilhelm; here a pearly white television screen will blink at me. I shall see the remains of a looted Genoese treasure, a short-barreled cannon caked with mud, the mussel-caked idols and images of lost and forgotten peoples, and the shattered bulbs of an overturned brass chandelier. As I descend into the lower depths, watching my step, weaving my way through mud and rock, I shall see galley slaves still chained to their oars as they gaze up at the stars with a patience that seems infinite. I may not notice the necklaces, eyeglasses, and umbrellas hanging from the trees of moss, but I shall certainly pause in fearful respect before the armored Crusaders, mounted on horses whose magnificent skeletons are still stubbornly standing. As I stand before these fearsome statues to study their mussel-studded weapons and the standards they brandish in their mighty hands, I shall note with horror that it is the Black Cadillac they are guarding.

So I shall approach it slowly and respectfully, almost seeking their permission, and as I move forward a blinking light of unknown origin will cast the Cadillac in a phosphorescent glow. I shall try to turn the door handles, but the car, caked as it is with mussels and sea urchins, will not permit me to enter; neither will I manage to pry open the green-tinted windows. This is when I shall take out my ballpoint pen from my pocket and use its tip to scrape the pistachio-colored moss off the glass.

Gripped though I am by the enchanted terror of midnight, I shall light a match; in the flickering gray glow I shall see the steering wheel, the nickel-plated dials, needles, and clocks still glistening as brightly as knights in shining armor—and there, still kissing in the front seat, the skeletons of the bandit and his mistress, her bony wrists still gleaming with bracelets, her ring-clad fingers still intertwined with his. Not only are their jaws conjoined, their very skulls are locked in an eternal embrace.

Then, without pausing first to strike a second match, I shall turn around to gaze upon the lights of the city and to dwell on what I have just seen: When catastrophe strikes, there can be no happier way of facing death. So let me cry out in anguish to a distant love: My darling, my beauty, my long-suffering sweet, the disaster is fast approaching, so come to me, come to me now; wherever you happen to be at this moment—a smoke-filled office, a messy blue bedroom, an onion-scented kitchen in a house steaming with laundry—know that the time has come, so come to me; let us draw the curtains against the disaster pressing upon us; as darkness encroaches, let us lock ourselves in a last embrace and silently await the hour of our death.

Chapter Three

Send Rüya Our Love

My grandfather had named them "the family."
—Rainer Maria Rilke

As he walked up the stairs to his Babıali office on the morning of the day his wife left him, with the newspaper he'd just finished reading still tucked under his arm, Galip was thinking about the green ballpoint pen he and Rüya had dropped into the depths of the Bosphorus during one of those rowboat rides they'd taken with their mothers while convalescing from the mumps. As he stared at Rüya's letter of farewell on the evening of the day she left him, he realized that she'd used a green pen identical to the one they'd dropped into the sea some twenty-four years earlier. The original pen had belonged to Celâl: seeing Galip admiring it, he had lent it to him for a week. When they'd told him they'd lost it, after he'd listened to their story of the rowboat and the sea, he'd said, "Well, if we know which part of the Bosphorus it fell into, it's not really lost!" These words had come back to Galip as he sat in his office that morning, for he had been surprised, when reading about the "day of disaster," that it had not been this ballpoint pen Celâl planned to take from his pocket to scrape the pistachio-colored moss off the glass. Because it was one of Celâl's trademarks to mix objects dating back centuries with those from his own past; the muddy slopes of his future Bosphorus were littered with Byzantine coins and modern-day bottle caps, both bearing the name Olympos. Unless—as he'd suggested only the other evening—his memory was beginning to fail him. "When the garden of memory begins to dry up," Celâl had said, "a man cannot but dote on its lingering rosebuds, its last remaining trees. To keep them from withering away, I water them from morning until night, and I caress them too: I remember, I remember so as not to forget!"

After Uncle Melih left for Paris—a year after Vasıf returned with his aquarium balanced on his lap—Father and Grandfather had gone to Uncle Melih's Babıali law offices, loaded all his files and his furniture into the back of a horse cart, and moved it into the attic flat of the Nişantaşı apartments. Galip had heard all this from Celâl. Later on— after Uncle Melih had returned from the Maghreb with his beautiful new wife and their daughter, Rüya, after the dried fig venture he'd entered into with his father-in-law had failed, after the family had decided to keep him out of their confectionery shops and pharmacies, for fear of these failing too, and Uncle Melih had decided to practice law again—he'd moved his old furniture to his new offices, the better to impress his clients. Years later, during one of those evenings they'd spent laughing and railing against the past, Celâl had told Galip and Rüya that one of the porters they'd used that day, the porter who specialized in things like carrying refrigerators and pianos, turned out to be the same man who'd carried the same furniture up to the attic twenty-two years earlier; the only difference was that he was now bald.

Twenty-one years after Vasıf gave this porter a glass of water and a thorough examination, Uncle Melih bequeathed his law practice to Galip. According to Galip's father, this was because, instead of fighting his clients' opponents, Uncle Melih had preferred to fight with the clients themselves; according to Galip's mother, it was because Uncle Melih was so old and addled by then he could no longer distinguish court records and law briefs from restaurant menus and ferry timetables; while Rüya claimed that—although Galip was still only his nephew at that point—her beloved father had foreseen the future Galip would go on to share with her. And so it was that Galip had found himself surrounded by portraits of bald Western jurists—he had no idea what they were famous for, nor did he know their names—and fez-wearing teachers of the law school his uncle had attended a half century earlier; he was also the inheritor of dossiers of cases in which the plaintiffs, the defendants, and the judges had long since died, along with a desk that Celâl had once used in the evening and his mother had used for tracing dress patterns in the morning, and that now was home to a huge ungainly black phone that looked more like an artifact from a hopeless war than an aid to communication.

From time to time, this telephone would ring of its own accord: the bell was shrill, ear-splitting; the pitch-black receiver was as heavy as a dumbbell; when you dialed a number, it creaked to the same melody as the old turnstiles for the Karaköy–Kadıköy ferry; sometimes, instead of connecting you to the number you wanted, it connected you to whatever other number it happened to prefer.

When he dialed his home number and Rüya picked up right away, he was shocked. "You're awake already?" He was happy to hear that Rüya was no longer wandering though the garden of her memories and was back in the real world with everyone else. He could imagine the telephone table, the untidy room, even the way Rüya was standing. "Have you seen the paper I left on the table? Celâl's written something very amusing." "No, I haven't read it yet," Rüya replied. "What time is it?" "You went to bed late, didn't you?" Galip said. "It looks like you made your own breakfast," said Rüya. "I couldn't bring myself to wake you up," said Galip. "What did you see in your dream?" "Late last night, I saw a black beetle in the hallway," Rüya said. Mimicking the radio announcements about free-floating mines spotted in the Black Sea but still betraying panic, she added, "Between the kitchen door and the hallway radiator . . . at two A.M. . . . and it was huge." There was a silence. "Shall I jump into a cab and come straight home?" Galip asked. "When the curtains are drawn, this house gives me the creeps," said Rüya. "Would you like to see a film this evening?" Galip asked. "There's something good at the Palace Theater. We could stop by at Celâl's on the way home." Rüya yawned. "I'm sleepy." "Then go back to sleep," said Galip. Both fell silent. As he put down the receiver, Galip thought he could hear Rüya yawning again.

In the days that followed, as Galip went over and over that conversation in his mind, he began to wonder if he'd really heard that yawn, if he'd really heard anything they'd said. Reading new meanings into Rüya's every word, and changing her words to reflect his worst fears, he was soon telling himself, *It was as if the person I was speaking to was not Rüya at all but someone else*, and this someone else had deliberately set out to trick him. Later on, he would decide that Rüya had indeed said what he'd originally thought he heard, and that after the telephone call it had been he, and not Rüya, who had changed. This new persona had gone on to reinterpret everything he'd heard wrong, everything he'd misremembered. By now his own voice seemed to belong to someone else, for Galip was only too aware that when two people converse on the phone, they can each easily pretend to be someone other than themselves. But during the early days, he took a simpler line: He blamed it all on the telephone. Because the clumsy old monster had kept ringing all day long, he'd spent the whole day lifting and lowering the receiver.

After he'd spoken to Rüya, his first phone call was from a man who'd brought a lawsuit against his landlord. Then there was a wrong number. There were two more "wrong numbers" before İskender called. Then there was a call from someone who knew he was Celâl's relation and wanted his number. After that there was an ironmonger whose son had got mixed up in politics; he was willing to do anything to get him out of prison, but he still wanted to know why he had to bribe the judge before the decision and not after. İskender rang next, and he wanted to speak to Celâl too.

İskender and Galip had been friends at lycée but had rarely spoken since, so first İskender gave him a quick summary of what he'd been up to over the past fifteen years. He congratulated Galip on his marriage; like so many others, he claimed he'd "always had a feeling it was going to turn out like this." He now worked as a producer in an advertising company. He was looking for Celâl because a BBC team doing a program on Turkey wanted to interview him. "They want a columnist like Celâl, who's been in the thick of things for thirty years—they want to interview him on camera!" They'd also spoken with politicians, businessmen, and trade unionists, he explained, giving Galip far more detail than he needed. But the person they most wanted to meet was Celâl; he was, they'd decided, a must for their program.

"Don't worry!" Galip said. "I'll find him for you." He was pleased to have an excuse to call Celâl. "The people at the newspaper have been giving me the runaround for two days now!" said İskender. "That's why I finally rang you. Celâl hasn't been near the paper for the last two days. Something must be going on." Although he was used to Celâl disappearing for days at a time, hiding out in other parts of the city at unknown addresses with unlisted phones, Galip was still certain he'd be able to track him down. "Don't worry," he said again. "I'll find him for you right away."

By evening, he still hadn't found him, though he'd been calling his home and office numbers all day. Each time he'd change his voice, pretending to be someone else, projecting his voice the way he did whenever he and Rüya and Celâl sat around of an evening, imitating actors from their favorite radio plays. If Celâl answered, he would pretend to be one of Celâl's more pretentious readers and say, "I have read today's column, my friend, and I have gleaned its hidden meaning!" But every time he'd called the paper, it was the same secretary telling him in the same voice that Celâl Bey had not yet arrived. Only once was he left with the impression that his fake voice had actually fooled someone.

As evening fell, he called Aunt Hâle, thinking she might know where Celâl was, and she invited him to supper. When she added, "Galip and Rüya are coming too!" he realized she had mixed up their voices again and mistaken him for Celâl. "What difference does it make?" Aunt Hâle said, after she realized she'd made a mistake. "You're all my children, and all the same—you all neglect me! I was just about to ring you anyway." She berated him for ignoring her, in the same voice she used with Charcoal, her cat, when it scraped its sharp claws against the furniture, and then she asked if he could stop by Alâaddin's shop on the way over to pick up some food for Vasıf's Japanese fish: apparently, they couldn't eat the same fish food as their European cousins. And Alâaddin would only give this special food to people he knew.

"Did you read his column today?"

"Whose column?" she asked, in her usual stubborn way. "Alâaddin's column? No, of course not. We buy *Milliyet* so that your grandfather can do the crossword, and Vasıf can cut out his clippings. I certainly don't buy it so I can read Celâl's column and worry myself sick about what this boy of ours has been up to."

"Then I'd be grateful if you'd call Rüya yourself to tell her the plan for this evening," Galip said. "I'm afraid I won't have time."

"Don't forget now!" said Aunt Hâle, and reminded him of the job she'd given him and what time she expected him. She then announced the guest list, which, like the menu for such family gatherings, was set in stone; she recited the names in the same low but thrilling tones that radio announcers use when reading out the famous lineup for a soccer match that listeners have been awaiting with bated breath for days. "Your mother, your Aunt Suzan, your Uncle Melih, Celâl if we can find him, and of course your father, plus Vasıf, Charcoal, and your Aunt Hâle." The only thing she didn't do was end the list with a wheezing laugh; instead she said, "I'm making puff pastry, just for you!" and hung up.

No sooner had he replaced the receiver than the phone began to ring again, and as he gazed at it blankly, Galip thought about the man Aunt Hâle had come very close to marrying the year before Rüya and her family had come home. He could recall what this suitor looked like, and he knew he had a strange name; it was on the tip of his tongue, but he still couldn't remember it. To keep his mind sharp, he decided not to answer the phone until this name came back to him. After seven rings, the phone fell silent. When it began to ring again a few moments later, Galip was thinking about the visit the suitor had made to the house with his uncle and his older brother to ask for Aunt Hâle's hand. Again the phone fell silent. When it began to ring again, it was dark outside and he could barely see the furniture in his office. Galip still couldn't remember that man's name, but he could recall being unnerved by his shoes. He had an Aleppo boil on his face. "Are these people Arabs?" Grandfather had asked. "Hâle, are you sure you want to marry this man? How did he meet you, anyway?" By chance!

By now the office building was emptying out, but before he left for his family dinner, Galip opened up the files of a client who wished to have his name changed; he sat down to read it in the light of the streetlamp and there it was, the name he'd been looking for. As he entered the line for the Nişantaşı *dolmuş*, it occurred to him that the world was too large a place to fit into one man's head; an hour later, when he was back in Nişantaşı, heading for the apartment, he concluded that whatever meaning a person found in the world, he found by chance.

uilding where Aunt Hâle shared one apartment with Vasıf and Hanım, and where Uncle Melih lived in another apartment with ızan (and, once upon a time, Rüya), was in the back streets of

Nişantaşı. It was only three streets down from the main street, the police station, and Alâaddin's shop—a mere five minutes' walk from the center—so it was not, perhaps, a "back street," but it was for his family, because when they had first moved to Nişantaşı it was a muddy field dotted with kitchen gardens. As the neighborhood grew, it turned into a proper street, paved first with rocks and later with cobblestones, but his family had watched all this from a haughty distance. As they gazed down on the main street from the City-of-Hearts Apartments— the building that in Aunt Hâle's words "towered over all of Nişantaşı"—they felt themselves at the center of the universe; as it slowly became clear that they were going to have to sell off the apartments one by one and move to the meanest and most remote streets of the neighborhood, as they struggled to make new homes in shabby rented flats, they'd been unable to resist calling it a back street—perhaps because no one could pass up a chance to exaggerate the disaster that had befallen them and hold someone else in the family responsible for it.

Three years before his death, on the day he moved out of the City-of-Hearts Apartments and into his new home in a back street, Mehmet Sabit Bey (Grandfather) had marked the occasion by sitting down in his wobbly old armchair, which no longer faced the window as in the old apartment but still faced the radio, which still sat on the same heavy table. Perhaps thinking of the emaciated horse and the rickety cart that had dragged their furniture across the city, he had cried out, "So congratulations, everyone. We've done ourselves proud! We've climbed off the horse, and now we're on the donkey!" Then he reached across to the radio—the china dog was back on top and already asleep on its embroidered doily—and turned the dial.

Eighteen years had passed since then. It was eight o'clock, and except for Alâaddin's, the florist's, and the little place where they sold nuts and dried fruits, all the shops had pulled down their metal shutters; sleet was falling through the clouds of soot, sulfur, coal, and exhaust fumes that clogged the air. As Galip saw the old lights shining in the apartment ahead of him, he felt as he always did—that his memories of this place stretched far beyond the eighteen years his family had been here. It didn't matter how narrow the street was or what the building was called (it was very hard on the tongue, too many *o*'s and *u*'s in it, so they never referred to it by name), and neither did it matter *where* it was—in Galip's mind his family had been living here in these higgledy-piggledy apartments since the dawn of time. As he climbed the stairs (they always smelled the same; in one of his angrier columns, Celâl had claimed the smell was made up of wet cement, mold, cooking oil, onions, and the stink from the air shaft), Galip steeled himself for what lay ahead, his mind racing through the scenes with the practiced impatience of a reader leafing through a book he's already read too many times to count.

Since it is eight o'clock already, Uncle Melih will be in Grandfather's old armchair, reading the newspaper he's brought down from his own apartment, and if he's not pretending this is the first time he's ever set eyes on it, he'll mutter something about hoping he can read it from a new angle if he is sitting in a new chair, or wanting to take one last look at it before Vasıf takes to it with his scissors. But his foot won't stay still. Inside his luckless slippers his toes will be twitching with such impatience that I'll think I can hear my own childhood lament: I'm bored; I have nothing to do, nothing to do, nothing to do. . . . Esma Hanım will already have been expelled from the kitchen so that Aunt Hâle can fry her puff pastries just the way she likes them, without anyone interfering; instead, Esma Hanım will be setting the table and there will be a filterless Bafra hanging from her lips, even though she still thinks Yeni Harman cigarettes are far superior. At one point she'll turn around and ask, "How many are we this evening?" as if she didn't know the answer, as if she didn't know everyone else in the room knew the answer as well as she did. Her eyes will go to Aunt Suzan and Uncle Melih, who will have taken up positions as Grandfather and Grandmother once did, on either side of the old radio and across from Mother and Father. After a lengthy silence, Aunt Suzan will smile hopefully at Esma Hanım and ask, "Are we expecting Celâl to join us tonight?" Uncle Melih will say the usual—"That boy is never going to pull himself together, never!" Then, wishing to stand up for his nephew but also happy and proud to be more balanced and responsible than his older brother, Father will mention something amusing he read in one of Celâl's recent columns. Added to the pleasure he takes in standing up for his nephew will be the pleasure he takes in showing off in front of his son; after giving us a résumé of whatever national

issue or life-and-death matter Celâl had been discussing in said column, he'll praise his nephew in words Celâl himself would ridicule if
he heard them. Then Father will offer up some "constructive" criti-
cism, so that even Mother will start nodding her head—Mother,
please, stay out of this!—but she can't stop herself; she considers it her
duty to remind Uncle Melih that Celâl is a better man than he thinks.
When I see Mother joining in, I won't be able to stop myself; even
though I know full well they'll never find the hidden meanings I see in
his columns and never will, I shall say, to no one in particular, "Have
you read today's column?" It will be now, perhaps, that Uncle Melih
will ask, "What day is it?" or "Is he writing for them every day now?
Not that it matters; I haven't read it"—even though I can see the paper
in his hands is open to that very page. My father will say, "I don't like
his using such coarse language against the prime minister, though!"
and my mother will say, "But even if you don't respect his views, you
still have to respect his identity as a writer," and it will be hard to know
if she is defending Celâl, my father, or the prime minister; at which
point, perhaps taking courage from my mother's ambiguous remarks,
Aunt Suzan will say, "When he talks about immortality, atheism, and
tobacco, he sounds awfully French," and for a moment I'll think we're
heading for another discussion about cigarettes. Now Esma Hanım,
who still has no idea how many people are coming to supper, is laying
the tablecloth, shaking it up and down as if it were a fragrant new bed-
sheet, first from one end and then the other, and squinting at it
through her cigarette smoke as it wafts so very beautifully down to the
table. But when Uncle Melih says, "Look at all that smoke, Esma
Hanım, you're aggravating my asthma!" and she says, "If anything's
aggravating your asthma, Melih Bey, it's the cigarette you're puffing on
yourself!" I'll know what's coming next, and rather than listen to this
argument for the umpteenth time I'll leave the room. In the kitchen,
where the air smells of dough, oil, and melting cheese, will be my Aunt
Hâle, frying her puff pastries; in the scarf she's wrapped around her
head, to protect her hair from the flying fat, she could be a witch stir-
ring a cauldron. Perhaps to show that there is a special bond between
us, or perhaps hoping for a kiss, she'll pop a piping-hot pastry into my
mouth as if it were some kind of bribe. "Don't tell anyone!" she'll say,
adding, "Is it too hot?" but my eyes will be watering too much by this

point for me to answer, Yes, much too hot! From there I will go into
the room where Grandfather and Grandmother spent so many sleepless nights wrapped up in their blue quilt; it was here, on the same blue
quilt, that Rüya and I sat when they gave us our art, arithmetic, and
reading lessons; after their deaths, Vasıf moved into this room with his
beloved Japanese fish, and when I walk in tonight I'll find him sitting
here with Rüya. They'll be looking at the fish together, or they'll be
going through Vasıf's clippings. Perhaps I'll join them, and—because
neither of us wishes to advertise the fact that Vasıf is deaf and
dumb—for a while neither Rüya nor I will speak and then, using the
sign language we invented together as children, we'll tell him about an
old film we just saw on television and perhaps, because we haven't seen
any old films this week, we'll act out that scene from *Phantom of the
Opera* that always gets him so excited, in such great detail that you'd
think we'd just been to see it again. A little later, Vasıf (who always
understands far more than anyone else) will turn away and give his full
attention to his beloved fish, and Rüya and I will look at each other,
and yes, for the first time since this morning I'll see you; for the first
time since last night we'll have a chance to speak face-to-face. I'll ask,
"How are you?" and you'll say the same thing you always say, "Same as
ever! Fine!" and, as always, I'll carefully consider every possible meaning, intended and unintended, that these words might convey, and
then, to hide the emptiness of my thoughts, though I can guess how
you spent the day: reading one of those detective novels that you love
so much and that I have never once managed to read to the end—
you're always telling me you'd like to translate them into Turkish one
day, but today you just didn't get round to it, today you just wandered
around in a haze—still, I'll ask you, "What did you do today? Rüya,
what did you do?"

In yet another column, when Celâl was writing again about stairwells in
back-street apartment buildings that stank of sleep, garlic, mildew,
lime, coal, and cooking oil, he suggested there might be another, more
romantic ingredient. Before he rang the doorbell, Galip thought,
Tonight I'm going to ask Rüya if she was the one who rang me three
times at the office today!

Aunt Hâle opened the door and said, "Oh, it's you. Where's Rüya?"

"Isn't she here already?" Galip said. "Didn't you call her?"

"I tried, but no one answered," said Aunt Hâle. "I decided you must have told her."

"Maybe she's upstairs at her father's," said Galip.

"Your aunt and uncle came down here ages ago," said Aunt Hâle.

For a moment, neither spoke.

"She's at home," Galip said finally. "Let me run home and get her."

"No one's answering your phone," said Aunt Hâle. "And Esma Hanım's already frying up your puff pastries."

As Galip raced down the street, the wind driving the snow blew open his nine-year-old overcoat (another of Celâl's topics). If, instead of going via the main road, he cut through the back streets—past the shuttered grocery stores and gloomy janitors' offices, past the dimly lit advertisements for Coca-Cola and nylon stockings, past that tailor on the corner who was still hard at work—he could make it from his aunt's apartment to his own in twelve minutes. This he'd calculated long ago, and he wasn't far off. He returned via the same streets (when he passed the tailor again, he was threading a needle with the same piece of cloth still resting on his knee), and the whole trip took him twenty-six minutes. It was Aunt Suzan who opened the door, and Galip told her the same thing he said to the rest of the family at the table: Rüya had come down with a cold and gone to bed, where she'd fallen into a stupor, possibly because she'd overdosed on antibiotics (she'd taken everything she'd found in the drawer!); she'd heard the phone ringing on and off but had been too drowsy to answer; she was still feeling very groggy and not at all hungry so had decided to stay in bed but had asked Galip to send her love to everyone.

Although he knew that this ran the risk of exciting too much interest (poor Rüya, languishing in her sickbed!) he was hoping it would also prompt a discussion about the safe consumption of pharmaceuticals, and so it did; as they ran through the antibiotics, penicillins, and cough medicines sold in our pharmacies, and rattled off the names of the vasodilators and painkillers that were best for the flu, and reminded each other at top volume of the vitamins that should be taken with them, they Turkified each product by adding a few syllables to its name. At any other time, he would have taken as much pleasure from their creative pronunciation and wild medical guesswork as he would from a good poem, but he was haunted now by the image of Rüya in her sickbed; even later he would not be able to decide how innocent this image was or how much of it he'd made up. The way Rüya's foot poked out of the quilt, the hairpins scattered on the sheets—these had to be images from real life, but the picture he had of her hair spreading across the pillow, for example, or the disarray on the night table—the water glass, the pitcher, the medicine boxes, the books—these were clearly borrowed from somewhere else; they came, he thought, from one of Rüya's favorite films, from one of those detective novels she consumed as ravenously as the pistachios she bought at Alâaddin's. Later, when he was fending off their well-meaning questions and trying to keep his answers as short as he could, he made an effort to draw a line in his mind between his memories of the real Rüya and the Rüya he'd invented—in deference, perhaps, to the fictitious detectives that she loved so much and that he would later try to emulate.

Yes, he told himself, as they sat down to eat, Rüya must be back asleep by now, there was no need for Aunt Suzan to wear herself out taking over some soup, and no, she had not asked for that awful doctor—he stank of garlic, and his bag smelled like a tannery. Yes, Rüya had forgotten to go to the dentist again this month, and yes, it was true, Rüya had not been going out much lately, she'd been spending most of her time inside; no, she'd not gone out at all today; oh, really, you saw her? Then she must have gone out for a while today, but she hadn't told Galip; no, she must have mentioned it, actually; where exactly did you see her? She must have gone to the button seller, to the haberdashers, to buy some purple buttons, and she would have gone past the mosque, yes, it all comes back to me now, and it was so cold today, wasn't it, that must have been how she caught cold, and she was coughing, and smoking, too, a whole pack, yes, she had seemed unusually pale, but no, Galip had not realized how pale he looked himself, and neither could he say when he and Rüya would decide to stop living such an unhealthy life.

Overcoat. Button. Kettle. Later, after the family interrogation was over, Galip would have no energy left to ask himself why these three words popped into his head. In one of his more baroque fits of anger, Celâl had once written that the subconscious, the "dark spot" lurking in the depths of our minds, did not really exist, at least not in Turkey—it was a Western invention that we'd borrowed from those pompous Western novels, those affected film heroes we tried so hard and failed so miserably to imitate. (Celâl had probably just seen *Suddenly Last Summer*, in which Elizabeth Taylor tries but fails to locate the dark spot in the strange mind of Montgomery Clift.) Galip was not to know at the time, but Celâl was by then the author of a lengthy tract (influenced, no doubt, by a few psychology books he'd read in abridged translation, and certainly struck by their ample pornographic detail) in which he traced every misery known to man back to that dark, menacing spot lurking in the depth of our minds: This part of the story would only become clear to Galip after he'd discovered that Celâl had turned his own life into a private museum-cum-library.

Galip was just about to change the subject—just about to say, Today, in Celâl's column . . . —when, taking fright by force of habit, he blurted out something else. "Aunt Hâle, I forgot to stop by Alâaddin's!" Esma Hanım had just brought out the pumpkin pudding, with such care that you might have mistaken the orange bundle in her arms for a baby plucked from her cradle, and now they were sprinkling over it the walnuts they had crushed with the mortar they'd taken as a keepsake from the candy store the family had owned so many years ago. A quarter century earlier, Rüya and Galip had discovered that if you struck the rim of this mortar with the flat side of a spoon, it would ring like a bell: *ding-dong!* "Could you stop ringing that thing before my head explodes? What do you think this is, a church?" Dear God, how hard that was to swallow! There wasn't enough crushed walnut to go around, so Aunt Hâle made sure that the purple bowl came to her last; "Really, I'm really not in the mood," she said, but when she thought no one was looking she glanced longingly at the empty bowl. Then she laid into an old business rival who had, in her view, single-handedly brought about the decline in their fortunes, so that they couldn't even afford enough walnuts for their pumpkin pudding. She was going to drop by at the police station and report him. In fact, they regarded the police station as fearfully as a dark blue ghost. Once, after Celâl had mentioned in a column that the dark spot in our subconscious was the police station, an officer from this police station had served him a subpoena asking him to report to the prosecutor's office to make a statement. The phone rang, and Galip's father answered it in his most serious voice. They're phoning from the police station, he thought. While his father talked on the phone, it seemed as if everything and everyone in the room took on the same blank expression (even the consoling wallpaper, which was the same as in the City-of-Hearts Apartments: green buttons falling through sprigs of ivy); Uncle Melih went into a coughing fit, while poor deaf Vasıf tried to look as if he were really listening, and it was now Galip noticed that his mother's hair, which had been getting lighter and lighter, was now almost as light as beautiful Aunt Suzan's. Like the rest of them, Galip listened to his father's half of the conversation and tried to work out who it was he was speaking to.

"No, sir, I'm afraid not. . . . Yes, sir, of course we were hoping. . . . Who did you say you were?" his father asked. "Thank you. . . . I'm the uncle. . . . Yes, we're certainly sorry, too. . . ."

Someone looking for Rüya, Galip decided.

"Someone looking for Celâl," his father said, as he hung up the phone. He seemed pleased. "An old lady, a fan of his, a real lady, ringing to say how much she adored the column. She wanted to speak to Celâl; she was looking for his address, his phone number."

"Which column?" Galip asked.

"Do you know which column, Hâle?" his father asked. "It's strange, but the lady I was just speaking to sounded like you—a lot like you!"

"How strange can it be that an old lady seems to you to have a voice like mine?" said Aunt Hâle. Her lung-colored neck shot up suddenly, like a goose. "But this woman's voice doesn't sound at all like mine!"

"How do you mean?"

"The lady you just spoke to rang this morning too," said Aunt Hâle. "And she didn't sound like a lady to me, she sounded like a fishwife trying to pass herself off as a lady. Or even a man trying to sound like an older woman."

Galip's father asked, How had the old lady tracked them down to this number? Had Hâle thought to ask her?

"No," said Aunt Hâle, "I saw no reason. Ever since Celâl took over the serial about the wrestler and began to flaunt our dirty linen in the paper for all the world to see, nothing he does can surprise me, and I almost thought, I almost wondered if—well, I thought that maybe, when he was finishing off a column in which he'd ripped us to pieces, he tacked on our phone number, just in case his devoted readers wanted to have a bit more fun with us. When I remember how much your dear departed parents suffered at his expense, there's only one way Celâl could shock me, and it wouldn't be to give our phone number to his readers so they can have more fun with us. It would be to tell us what it is that's made him hate us so for the last ten years."

"He hates us because he's a Communist," said Uncle Melih, who had survived his coughing fit and was now lighting himself a victory cigarette. "When it finally sank in that they were never going to get anywhere with the workers or the Turkish people, the Communists tried to con the military into staging some sort of Janissary-type Bolshevik coup. By writing columns seething with blood and rancor, Celâl became their pawn."

"No," said Aunt Hâle. "It never went that far."

"I know this from Rüya," said Uncle Melih. He let out a laugh and managed not to cough. "Apparently they promised him that, after the coup, the new Alaturka Bolshevik Janissary Union would either make him foreign minister or ambassador to Paris, and he believed them! He was even studying French at home. At first I was happy to see that these hopeless revolutionary dreams of his had at least kindled an interest in French. He never picked up a single foreign language as a youth; he was too busy running around with his disreputable friends. But when things got out of hand, I wouldn't let Rüya see him anymore."

"Nothing like that ever happened, Melih!" Aunt Suzan cried. "Rüya and Celâl kept seeing each other; they stayed very close. You'd never know he was only her half brother. She loved him like a real brother and he loved her like a sister!"

"It happened, it happened, but I left it too late," said Uncle Melih. "He may not have been able to fool the army and the Turkish people, but he did manage to fool his sister. That's how Rüya turned into an anarchist. If our Galip hadn't rescued her from those guerrilla thugs, from that rat's nest, who knows where Rüya would be? Certainly not asleep in her own bed."

Thinking that everyone around him was suddenly thinking of Rüya in her bed, Galip stared at his nails and wondered if Uncle Melih planned to add something new to his list of grievances, as he tended to do every two or three months.

"By now Rüya might even have landed herself in prison; she's never been as cautious as Celâl," and he launched into his list with such excitement that he could barely hear the chorus crying *God forbid!* "By now, Rüya would be with Celâl and those gangster friends of his— those Beyoğlu gangsters, those heroin dealers, those nightclub bouncers and cocaine-addict White Russians, and all those other debauched creatures he spends time with in the name of *reporting*—and our poor Rüya would have been sitting there with him. Think of the company we'd have to keep to have any chance of finding her: Englishmen who've come to our city in pursuit of the vilest pleasures; homosexuals who love serials about wrestlers but crave the wrestlers themselves even more; vulgar American women looking for orgies in *hamams*; con artists; would-be starlets who'd never even rate as whores in a European country, let alone as artists; officers who were kicked out of the army for insubordination or embezzlement, even; chanteuses who look like men, whose voices have cracked from syphillis; beauties from the slums trying to pass themselves off as women of quality. . . . Tell her to take İsteropiramisin."

"Pardon?" said Galip.

"It's the best antibiotic for flu, if taken with Bekozim Fort. Every six hours. What time is it? Should she have woken up by now?"

Aunt Suzan said Rüya was probably still asleep. As Galip thought of Rüya in her bed, he imagined everyone else was too.

"I won't have it!" said Esma Hanım. She was carefully gathering up the sorry tablecloth, which they'd all used to wipe their mouths, a bad habit they'd picked up from Grandfather, much to Grandmother's distress. "No, I'm not letting anyone in this house speak ill of my Celâl. My Celâl is a very important man!"

According to Uncle Melih, it was because his fifty-five-year-old son had the same opinion of himself that he no longer bothered with his seventy-five-year-old father and never let anyone know what Istanbul apartment he was living in, so that no one—not just his father but no one in the family, not even Aunt Hâle, who had shown him such forgiveness—was able to reach him. Not only had he refused to give them his phone number, he'd even pulled his phone out of its socket. Galip was afraid that Uncle Melih was getting ready to shed a few false tears, not out of sadness but out of habit. But he didn't, he did something Galip dreaded even more: again by habit, again forgetting the twenty-year difference between them, he told everyone how he'd always longed for a son like Galip, not Celâl, someone with a head on his shoulders, like Galip, someone mature and well-behaved.

Twenty-two years earlier (in other words, when Celâl was roughly the same age Galip was now) when Galip was still growing at an embarrassing rate and his gangly limbs were always getting in his way and he heard his Uncle Melih express this wish for the first time, the words had conjured up dreams of a life in which he'd be able to eat every night with Uncle Melih, Aunt Suzan, and Rüya, thus escaping those bland and colorless meals with his parents when everyone stared into the middle distance as the four walls around the dining table closed in on them. (*Mother*: There are some stewed beans left over from lunch, would you like some? *Galip*: Mmm, I don't think so. *Mother*: How about you? *Father*: What *about* me?) This was followed by other tantalizing visions: Aunt Suzan, whom he had seen in her blue nightgown once or twice, when he'd gone upstairs on a Sunday morning to play Secret Passage or I Can't See You with Rüya, would become his mother (a big improvement); Uncle Melih, whose stories about Africa and the law so thrilled him, would be his father (even better); and, because they were both the same age, Rüya and he would become twins (he dropped this line of fantasy before he could take it to its logical conclusion).

After supper was cleared, Galip told everyone that there'd been some people from the BBC trying to find Celâl but they'd not managed to track him down; this had not ignited the usual complaints about how Celâl hid his address and phone numbers from everyone and all the rumors about the apartments he had in all four corners of the city, and where they were, and how to find them. It's snowing, someone said. So when they all got up from the table, before they had glued themselves back into their favorite armchairs, they parted the curtains with the backs of their hands and stared out into the cold night to look at the light covering of snow on the back street below. It was clean snow, silent snow (a reprise from one of Celâl's favorite tongue-in-cheek vignettes, Old Ramadan Nights)! Galip followed Vasıf into his room.

Vasıf sat down on the edge of the bed, and Galip sat down across from him. Vasıf ran his hand through his white hair and then draped it over Galip's shoulder: Rüya? Galip punched him in the chest and acted out a coughing fit; she has a bad cough! Then he joined his hands together and laid his head on the pillow; she's in bed. Vasıf took a large box out from underneath his bed: a collection of some of the clippings he'd made from newspapers over the past fifty years, the best of them, perhaps. Galip sat down next to him. He picked out a few illustrations for Galip to admire, and it was almost as if Rüya were sitting there next to them, as if they were smiling together at the things Vasıf was showing them. A once famous soccer player advertising shaving cream (the picture dated back twenty years and the star beaming at them through the foam had since died of a brain hemorrhage after countering a corner shot with a head shot); Kasım, the Iraqi leader, lying dead in his bloody uniform in the aftermath of a coup; a reconstruction of the famous Şişli Square Murder ("Upon discovering that his wife had been cuckolding him for twenty years," he could hear Rüya saying in her best radio-theater voice, "the jealous colonel would come out of retirement to trail the playboy journalist for days, finally shooting him along with the young wife traveling with him in the car"); Menderes, the prime minister, sparing the life of the camel that his loyal supporters had hoped to sacrifice in his honor, while in the background, Celâl the reporter gazes off into the distance, as does the camel. Galip was just about to get up to go home when Vasıf, who was still on automatic pilot, pulled out two of Celâl's old columns, "Alâaddin's Shop" and "The Executioner and the Weeping Face." Something to read tonight, while he tossed and turned! He did not have to do too much miming to convince Vasıf to let him borrow them. No one minded that he turned down the coffee Esma Hanım had brought him. His concern for his bedridden wife must have been etched deeply into his face. He was already at the door. Uncle Melih had even said, "Yes, let him go, let him go home!" Aunt Hâle had bent down to greet Charcoal the cat on his return from the snowy street, while the others cried out from the sitting room, "Tell her to get well soon, tell her to get well soon, send Rüya our love, send Rüya our love!"

On his way home, Galip ran into the bespectacled tailor, who was standing outside his shop, pulling down the metal shutters. The street-lamp above them was studded with little icicles. The two men greeted each other and walked on together. "I'm late," said the tailor, perhaps to break the silence the snow had brought with it. "My wife's waiting for me at home." "It's cold," Galip replied. They continued walking, but in silence, listening to the snow crunch beneath their feet; when they had reached Galip's corner, he looked up at the top floor and saw the pale lamp glowing in his bedroom. The snow kept falling and, with it, darkness.

The lights were still off in the sitting room, just as Galip had left them, but the lights were on in the hallway. He went straight into the kitchen and put the kettle on for tea. After he'd taken off his jacket and trousers and hung them up, he went into the bedroom, where, in the pale light of the bed lamp he changed out of his wet socks. Then he sat down at the dining table and reread the farewell letter Rüya had written with her green ballpoint pen. It was even shorter than he remembered: only nineteen words.

Chapter Four

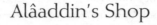

Alâaddin's Shop

If I have any fault it is digression.
—Byron Pasha

I am a *picturesque* writer. I've looked this word up in the dictionary, and I must confess that I still haven't worked out what it really means, but I still like the sound of it. I have a passion for the epic: knights on chargers; two armies standing on either side of a dark plain on a misty morning three hundred years ago, preparing for battle; luckless men downing *rakı* and exchanging unhappy love stories in *meyhanes* on a winter's night; lovers disappearing into the murky depths of the city in pursuit of a dread secret—these are the immortal tales I've always longed to tell, but all God gave me was this column, which calls for another kind of story altogether. And He gave me you, dear readers. Over the years, we've learned how to live together.

Had the garden of my memory not begun to wither, I would perhaps have no reason to complain, but every time I pick up my pen, I see you, my dear readers, and as I remember what you expect of me, as I survey my arid garden and struggle to reclaim the memories that have abandoned me, one by one, all I see are the traces they left in the dry soil. To be left with only the trace of a memory is to gaze at an armchair that's still molded to the form of a love who has left never to return: It is to grieve, dear reader, it is to weep.

So this is why I decided to have a chat with Alâaddin. When I told him I was planning to write about him in this column but wished first to interview him, he opened his black eyes wide and asked, "But Celâl Bey, won't this get me into trouble?"

I assured him it wouldn't. I told him what an important part he played in all our lives. I explained how vividly we remembered all the many thousands of products he'd sold in his little store over the years—their colors, their fragrance. I recounted how, all over Nişantaşı, there were children lying in their sickbeds, waiting impatiently for their mothers to come home with a present from Alâaddin's: a toy (a lead soldier) or a book (*The Redheaded Child*) or an adventure comic (episode seventeen, in which Kinova comes back to life to get even with the Redskins who scalped him). I told him about the thousands of children pining away in the schools nearby, longing for the bell to ring, dreaming that it rang ages ago and they are already in Alâaddin's, tearing the wrapping off a chocolate bar and pulling out a picture of a famous soccer player (Metin of Galatasaray) or a famous wrestler (Hamit Kaplan) or a film star (Jerry Lewis). I spoke of the girls noticing the pale polish on their fingernails as they set off for the Arts and Crafts Night School, and stopping off at Alâaddin's to pick up a bottle of acetone; and I told him how, years later, when these same girls were wasting away in insipid marriages and lackluster kitchens, surrounded by children and grandchildren, they would, when they recalled the early loves that caused them such pain, see Alâaddin's shop shimmering before their eyes like a fairy tale from a distant land.

So he'd come to the house and we'd sat together for some time. I told Alâaddin about the green ballpoint pen I'd bought from his shop so many years earlier, and I recounted the plot of a badly translated detective novel. I went on to tell him a second story, in which the heroine, whom I loved dearly and for whom I had bought the book as a present, was condemned to do nothing in life but read these detective novels. I told him too about the two men (one a patriotic colonel who was planning a military coup, and the other a journalist) who had held their historic first meeting in his humble shop, there to lay the foundations of a conspiracy that would change not just the course of our own history but the history of the entire East. It was evening when this momentous event took place; behind his counter, piled to the ceiling with boxes and books, Alâaddin had been its witness—utterly unsuspecting, even as he wetted his finger the better to count the newspapers and magazines to be returned the next morning. I spoke of the naked women, local and foreign, beckoning from the covers of the magazines he displayed in the windows and wrapped around the great trunk of the chestnut tree outside his door, and I spoke of the men who ambled so slowly down the street past them, and of the dreams they would have that night, dreams in which these same naked beauties proved themselves insatiable, threw themselves about like slave girls, like the sultan's wives, like houris from *The Thousand and One Nights*! But while we were on that subject, I would also tell him that the tale that bore his name had not originally featured among the stories told during the famous thousand and one nights; it was a story Antoine Galland had slipped into the book when it was published in France two hundred and fifty years ago. What's more, it was not Sheherazade who had told Galland the story but a Christian woman named Hanna. I went on to explain that this woman was actually an Aleppo scholar whose full name was Yohanna Diyab, and that it was clear from the story's descriptions of coffee that the story itself was Turkish and most probably set in Istanbul. I went on to admit, however, that it was as difficult to trace the origins of a story as it was to trace the origins of life. Because the truth of the matter was that I'd forgotten everything, everything, everything. I told him the truth, that I was old, miserable, irascible, alone, and I wanted to die. Because the traffic noise from Nişantaşı Square had merged with the human wails pouring from the radio to form an unholy chorus that brought tears to my eyes. Because my problem was this: After a lifetime telling stories, I wanted to sit back and listen to Alâaddin tell me tales about the cologne bottles, revenue stamps, illustrated matchboxes, nylon stockings, postcards, artists' drawings, sexology annuals, hairpins, and prayer books that I had seen in his shop once upon a time, only to have my memories of them vanish without a trace.

As it is with all real people who find themselves ensnared in other people's imagined tales, there was something surreal about Alâaddin, something that tugged at the boundaries of the known world and defied everyday logic. He told me he was flattered that the press was taking such an interest in him. For thirty years now, he'd been putting in fourteen-hour days in his corner shop, and on Sundays, between half past two and half past four, when everyone else in the world was listening to the football match on the radio, he was asleep at home. He told me his real name was not Alâaddin, but his customers didn't know this. He told me the only paper he read himself was *Hürriyet*. He told

me he could not permit political meetings in his shop, because the
Teşvikiye police station was just across the street and he wasn't interested in politics. It was also wrong to say he wetted his finger when he
was counting magazines, and wrong, too, to say his shop was something out of a myth or a fairy tale. He had no patience for people who
made mistakes like this. Like the elderly paupers who saw toy watches
in the window and mistook them for real watches and were so amazed
at his low prices that they came inside looking for more astounding
bargains. The ones who got angry at Alâaddin when the bet they'd
placed on the Paper Horse Race came to nothing or they'd failed, yet
again, to win the National Lottery—accusing him of fixing the game
when they had chosen their own numbers. The woman who came in to
say that her stocking had a run, the mother who came in to complain
that her child had broken out in a full body rash after eating domestic
chocolate, the reader who didn't like the political views expressed in
the newspaper he'd just bought—they all blamed Alâaddin, even
though he didn't manufacture any of these things, he just sold them. If
a customer bought brown shoe polish only to open the box and find it
was black shoe polish, Alâaddin wasn't the one responsible. Alâaddin
wasn't responsible if a domestically manufactured battery shook itself
empty before the honey-voiced Emel Sayın had finished her first song,
oozing black pitch and causing the transistor radio irreparable damage.
Alâaddin wasn't responsible if a compass that was supposed to point
north wherever you happened to be standing, always pointed instead
to the Teşvikiye police station. And neither was he responsible for the
love letter that a romantic factory girl had slipped into a pack of
Bafras, even though the painter's apprentice who opened the pack
came running back into the shop in a cloud with bells on his toes, to
kiss Alâaddin's hand and ask him to be best man and inquire after the
girl's name and address.

The shop was situated in what once had been the finest location in
the city, but his customers never failed to surprise him. He was perplexed by gentlemen who still didn't know there was a custom known
as standing in line, and sometimes he had to shout at the ones who
refused to wait as they'd been taught. He used to sell bus tickets, but he
lost patience with the handful of people who'd race into the shop the
moment a bus came around the corner, yelling like Mongolians on the

rampage, crying, "A ticket, please; a ticket, please; oh, for God's sake give me a ticket quick!" They'd create havoc and make a mess of the shop, and that was why he no longer sold bus tickets. He'd seen everything in his time—couples who'd been married for forty years arguing about lottery tickets, heavily made-up women who had to smell thirty different makes of soap before they bought a single bar, retired colonels who had to try out every whistle in the box before they found the one they wanted—but by now he was used to them; they didn't bother him anymore. The housewife who grumbled because he did not stock a back issue of a photo novel whose last issue came out eleven years ago, the fat gentleman who licked his stamps before buying them so he could find out how the glue tasted, the butcher's wife who'd come in only yesterday to return a crepe-paper carnation, complaining that it had no scent—none of these people bothered him anymore.

He'd given this shop everything he had, built it up from nothing. For years on end, he'd bound those old *Texas* and *Tom Mix* comics with his own two hands; every morning, while the city slept, he'd opened his shop, swept it out, tacked his magazines and newspapers to the door and the chestnut tree next to it, and arranged his latest novelties in the window. He'd combed the city for toy ballerinas that twirled when you brought a magnetic mirror near them, and tricolored shoelaces, and small plaster statues of Atatürk that had blue lightbulbs in their eye sockets, and pencil sharpeners shaped like Dutch windmills; signs saying FOR RENT and signs saying IN THE NAME OF GOD, THE COMPASSIONATE AND MERCIFUL; pine-flavored chewing gum that came with pictures of birds numbering from one to a hundred, and pink backgammon dice that you couldn't find anywhere but the Covered Bazaar; Tarzan and Barbarossa decals and hoods bearing the colors of soccer teams—like the blue hood he himself had been wearing for ten years—and all variety of metalware, like the gadget that doubled as a bottle opener and a shoehorn. No matter how strange a customer's request—Do you sell ink that smells of rose water? Do you have any of those singing rings in stock?—he never told them there was no such thing; if they asked for something, he assumed the item must exist somewhere, so he'd say, "We'll have it for you tomorrow." Then he'd write it down in his notebook, and the next day he'd go out on his travels, combing the shops of the city until he tracked the mystery object down. There'd been times when he'd made unimaginable sums selling photo novels and cowboy comics and pictures of blank-faced local film stars, and there'd been those cold, dull days when the only coffee and cigarettes you could find were on the black market, and you couldn't buy anything without standing in line. If you stood in this shop and looked out at the people passing by, you'd never guess that they were inclined this way or that way, but once you knew them as customers, you came to see they really were a crowd, a crowd driven by desires he could not begin to fathom.

You'd see this crowd on the pavement, a crowd in which no two people seem the same, but each and every one of them will suddenly develop a yen for musical cigarette boxes, and then they'll all want Japanese fountain pens that are no longer than your little finger, and a month later these same people will have forgotten all about them and will be yearning instead for those new revolver-shaped cigarette lighters, and Alâaddin really had to struggle to keep them in stock. Then there'd be a new craze for transparent plastic cigarette holders— for six months they'd all watch that disgusting tar building up inside them with such fascination you'd think they were perverted scientists—but then they'd lose interest and come flooding back to Alâaddin's to buy huge multicolored prayer beads—leftists and rightists alike, atheists as well as the devout and godfearing—wherever you went in the city you could hear them clacking, and when this storm blew over, leaving Alâaddin with piles of prayer beads that were suddenly impossible to move, there'd be a new craze for dreams and they'd all be lining up to buy those little booklets that claimed to interpret them. An American movie would come to town and every youth in the city wanted dark glasses; something would come out in the papers and all the women wanted lip gloss or all the men wanted skullcaps that made them look like imams; but most of the time these fads that spread through the city like a plague seemed to rise up out of nowhere. How else to explain why thousands, tens of thousands of people would suddenly decide that their every radio, radiator, rear window, room, worktable, and counter had to be adorned by the same wooden sailboat? How was a man to understand why every mother and child, man and woman, old and young, suddenly craved the same picture of an innocent child with a single tear rolling down his very European face, or why this face was suddenly staring at you from every wall and door in the city? This country was . . . these people were . . . It was I who completed his sentence—the word he was looking for was *strange*, or *incomprehensible,* or even *frightening*—for it was I, not Alâaddin, who was the wordsmith. At this juncture, we both fell silent.

It was later, as he was talking about those little nodding celluloid ducks he used to sell, and those old chocolates that came in the shape of cherry liqueur bottles and also had a cherry in the middle, and the place you needed to go to find the right strips of wood for a kite, that I began to grasp the wordless language that bound Alâaddin and his customers together. The little girl who came in with her grandmother looking for a chiming hula hoop, the pimply youth who snatched a French magazine and rushed off to a corner to make love to the naked women nestling in its pages, but quickly, before anyone noticed— Alâaddin loved them dearly. He even loved the bespectacled bank clerk who bought that racy novel and stayed up all night reading about the impossible exploits of its film-star heroes, only to return the next morning saying, "I already had this." Not to mention the old man who bought a poster of a girl reading the Koran and asked him to wrap it up in a newspaper that didn't have any pictures. But the affection he felt for his customers was guarded nonetheless. The mother and daughter who took a fashion magazine, opened up its pattern page, spread it on the floor like a map, and set about cutting material, the children who came in to buy toy tanks and were at each other's throats before they even left the shop—yes, he did think he understood why they did what they did, but when people came in asking for pencil flashlights or key chains with skulls on them, he could not but wonder if an unknown power from another planet was trying to send him a message. That strange man who had come in on a winter's day asking for a "Summer Landscape" when, as everyone else knew, it was the "Winter Landscape" students needed for their homework—what mysterious force propelled him? The two lost souls who had come in one evening, just as he was closing up the shop, and picked up two of those huge baby dolls—the ones with ready-made dresses whose arms move up and down—and cradled them as carefully, as lovingly, as if they were experienced doctors holding real-life babies, utterly entranced by the way their little pink eyelids opened and shut: They'd had Alâaddin wrap one doll up with a bottle of *rakı*, before disappearing into the night. What a fright they'd given him. After a number of similar incidents, these dolls had begun to appear in Alâaddin's dreams; he saw them standing in their boxes and plastic buckets in the dead of night, their eyelids opening and shutting oh so slowly as their hair grew ever longer. And perhaps he had been hoping to ask me what this could possibly mean, but before he could do so, he fell into that helpless, melancholy silence that falls over our compatriots when they feel they have spoken too much or imposed their troubles on the world for too long. Again we fell silent, and this time we both knew it would be a long while before either of us broke it.

Much later, as a regretful Alâaddin took his leave, he said he would leave it to me to decide how I wrote about all this, as I was far better qualified to do so than he was. And perhaps the day will come, dear reader, when I find it in me to do justice to those baby dolls, in a column so sublime it unlocks our very dreams.

Chapter Five

Perfectly Childish

*People separate for a reason. They tell you their reason. They give
you a chance to reply. They do not run away like that. No, it is
perfectly childish.*

—Marcel Proust

Rüya had written her nineteen-word goodbye letter with the green
ballpoint pen that Galip always tried to keep next to the telephone. After he saw it was no longer there, after he'd searched the
entire apartment and still not found it, he decided that Rüya must have
used it at the last moment, on her way out the door; she must have
thrown it into her bag, thinking, perhaps, she might need it later on; for
her favorite fountain pen, the fat one she used on the rare occasions
when she sat down to write a letter (she hardly ever finished them or, if
she did, she never got around to putting them into an envelope, and if
she did, she usually forgot to mail them) was still in its usual place, in a
drawer in their bedroom. Galip spent a great deal of time trying to
locate the notebook from which she'd torn the paper. He spent most
of the night going through the old chest of drawers he had (at Celâl's
suggestion) turned into a museum of his own life, checking Rüya's letter against every notebook he found: his arithmetic exercise book from
primary school, in which he'd calculated eggs to cost six kuruş a dozen,
the compulsory prayer book whose back pages he'd covered with
swastikas and caricatures of his cross-eyed teacher, and the Turkish literature notebook whose margins were decorated with sketches of
models and names of international film stars, along with Turkey's own
best-looking singers and athletes. ("They may ask about *Love and Beauty*
in the exam.") There was no faster way to shatter his illusions than to

go through these drawers, but still he carried on, digging fruitlessly to the bottom of every box he could find, checking under the beds, and then, one last time, going through every pocket of every piece of clothing Rüya had left behind—each still held her scent, each held out the empty promise that nothing had changed or ever would. It was just after the dawn call to prayers that Galip glanced over at the old chest of drawers and saw the source of the paper for her letter. She'd torn it— roughly, mercilessly—from the middle of a school notebook he'd already checked, though without paying due attention to the words or pictures inside it. (*The military coup on 27 May 1960 was provoked by concern about the government's plundering of the nation's forests. . . . The cross-section of the hydra looks just like that vase on Grandmother's buffet.*) As he stared at this notebook more closely, all the other little memories—all the other little discoveries he had made during his nightlong search—came tumbling back.

A memory: Many years ago, in middle school, when he and Rüya were in the same class, sitting in the same row, listening to their hideous history teacher with all the patience and goodwill they could muster, there'd be times when this teacher would grimace all of a sudden and yell, "Get out your pens and paper at once!" As they sat in cowering silence, dreading the test for which they all were unprepared, someone somewhere would tear a sheet of paper from a notebook, even though they all knew how she hated this sound. "Don't tear pages from your notebooks!" she'd scream in that shrill voice of hers. "I want loose sheets! People who tear up our nation's notebooks, people who destroy our nation's property—they're not Turks, they're degenerates! I'll give them zeros!" And she did.

A small discovery: in the middle of the night, during one of those strange interludes when the refrigerator motor cut off suddenly, as if to unnerve him, when he was searching the back of the wardrobe— and even he could not have said how many times he'd already done so—wedged between a pair of dark green high-heeled shoes she'd left behind, he found a detective novel in translation. There were hundreds of these lying all over the house, so normally he would not have paid it much attention, but tonight he was struck by the owl staring so treacherously from the cover, and as he leafed through this black book, it was as if his hands, well trained after a night of reaching into the backs of drawers and wardrobes and leaving nothing unturned, knew exactly where to go: There, hidden between two pages, was a picture clipped from a glossy magazine: a handsome naked man. His penis was limp, and as Galip was deciding how it compared with his own, he told himself that Rüya must have cut the picture out of a foreign magazine she'd bought at Alâaddin's.

A memory: Rüya knew Galip couldn't bear her detective novels so she was confident he'd never look through one. He detested this world where the English were parodies of Englishness and no one was fat unless they were colossally so; the murderers were as artificial as their victims, serving only as clues in a puzzle. (I'm just trying to pass the time, OK? Rüya would say, and then she'd reach into the bag of nuts she'd bought from Alâaddin before returning to her book.) Galip had once told Rüya that the only detective book he'd ever want to read would be the one in which not even the author knew the murderer's identity. Instead of decorating the story with clues and red herrings, the author would be forced to come to grips with his characters and his subject, and his characters would have a chance to become people in a book instead of just figments of their author's imagination. Rüya, who knew more about detective novels than Galip did, asked how the author was to manage all that extra detail. Because every detail in a detective novel served a purpose.

Details: Before leaving the apartment, Rüya had used that terrifying insect killer (the one with an enormous black beetle and three cockroaches pictured on the front) and sprayed it all over the bathroom, the corridor, and the kitchen. (The stink was still in the air.) She'd turned on the electric *chauffe-bain* (probably without thinking, and needlessly, because Thursdays were hot-water days in their building); she'd spent some time reading *Milliyet* (its pages were wrinkled); she'd even done a bit of the crossword with the lead pencil she must have taken with her: tomb, interval, moon, difficult, division, pious, secret, listen. She'd had breakfast (tea, white cheese, bread) and done the dishes. She'd smoked two cigarettes in the bedroom, another four in the sitting room. She'd taken with her only a few winter dresses and some of that makeup she said was bad for her skin, along with her slippers, the novel she was reading, the keyless key chain she'd hung on the chest of drawers for good luck, the pearl necklace that was her only piece of jewelry, and the hairbrush that had a mirror on its back; she'd left wearing the coat that was the same color as her hair. She must have put these things in an old medium-sized suitcase her father had brought back from the Maghreb that she had later borrowed for a trip they'd never taken. She'd shut most of the wardrobes (or, rather, kicked the doors closed); she'd shoved in the drawers, gathered up her trinkets, and put them back where they belonged, and she'd written her farewell letter in one go, without the slightest hesitation: there were no abandoned drafts in the ashtrays or wastepaper baskets.

Perhaps it was wrong even to call it a farewell letter. Although she'd not said if she would return, she'd not said she would not return either. It was almost as if she were just leaving the apartment, not leaving Galip. She'd managed, in a single four-word sentence, to enlist Galip as a co-conspirator: *You manage the mothers!* Galip was grateful she had chosen not to throw her real reason for leaving into his face, and it pleased him to be drawn into the conspiracy; whatever else it was, it was still a conspiracy with Rüya. He took comfort in the promise Rüya made next: it too was four words: *I'll be in touch.* He sat up all night, waiting in vain.

All night, the radiators and the water pipes groaned, gurgled, and sighed. There were flurries of snow. The *boza* seller wandered past at one point, hawking his millet drinks, but he never came back. For hours on end, Galip and Rüya's green signature stared at each other. Every object in the house, every shadow, took on a new personality; it was like waking up in a new home. That lamp that's been hanging from the ceiling for three years, Galip found himself thinking. It looks like a spider! Why am I only seeing that now? He tried to go to sleep, longing, perhaps, to escape into a beautiful dream, but to no avail. Instead he went over and over the search in his mind (had he looked into that box at the back of the drawer? . . . Yes, of course he'd looked, he must have looked, perhaps he hadn't looked, no, of course not, he'd forgotten to look, he was going to have to go through everything once more). Then he'd start all over again. Some way into this new bleak hunt, as he stood fingering the empty case of a long-lost pair of sunglasses, or grappling with the memories awakened by the buckle of one of Rüya's old belts, he'd see how hopeless, how pointless it all was (and how implausible the detectives in all those books, not to mention the kindly authors whispering clues into their ears!) and when that moment came, he'd return whatever object he had in his hand to its original loca- tion—with painstaking precison, like a researcher making an inventory of a museum—and lumber back to the kitchen like a sleepwalker. Looking into the refrigerator but taking nothing out, he would return to his favorite chair in the sitting room to sit for a few minutes before embarking on yet another ritual search.

Throughout their three-year marriage, it had been Rüya's chair; he would sit across from her, watching her devour her detective novels, watching her sigh with longing and tug at her hair and swing her legs with ever-growing impatience as she raced furiously from page to page. On the night she left him, whenever he sat there in her place, it was always the same scene playing before his eyes. But it did not date back to their lycée years, to the times he'd seen a gang of pimply boys who looked older than him (if only because they had taken up smok- ing earlier and managed to grow a few hairs on their upper lips) escort- ing Rüya into pastry shops where cockroaches roamed fearlessly on tabletops, and it was not that Saturday afternoon three years afterward, when he'd wandered up to Rüya's apartment (I came to ask if you hap- pened to have a blue label!) and found Rüya glancing at her watch and swinging her legs with ill-concealed impatience while her mother sat at the rickety dressing table, making herself up; and it was not more than three years after *that* when Rüya, paler and more tired than he had ever seen her, announced that she had married a young leftist firebrand much admired in her circle for his courage, his devotion to the cause, and his decision to publish political analyses—the first ever to appear in *Dawn of Labor*—under his own name. As she assured him that the marriage itself was not political in the least, Galip counted the defects that had plunged him into lonely defeat (my face is asymmetrical, my arm is crooked, I have no color in my face, my voice is too rough!). The night Rüya left him, it was a much simpler image that shimmered before his eyes, an image that reminded him of a bit of fun, an oppor- tunity, a piece of life that had slipped beyond his grasp: the light falling on the white pavement in front of Alâaddin's shop on a snowy evening.

It was a Friday evening, a year and a half after Rüya and her family moved into the attic apartment, when they were in third grade; it was

winter and already dark, and the air was thick with the noise of traffic
rising from Nişantaşı Square; they'd just taken two games they'd
invented together earlier—Silent Passage and I Didn't See It—and
combined them to make a new game: I've Disappeared! One of them
would slip into another apartment—their grandmother's or their
uncle's—and "disappear" into a corner, and the other would try to find
him. A very simple game, but because there was no time limit and
because it was against the rules to turn on the light in any room no
matter how dark it was, it tested courage and fired up the imagination.
When it was his turn to disappear, Galip went straight to a hiding place
he'd figured out two days earlier in a burst of inspiration (above the
wardrobe in Grandmother's bedroom, which he reached by stepping
first on the arm of the chair next to it and then, very carefully, its back)
and because he was sure Rüya would never find him there, he conjured
up her image in the darkness. In his daydream it was he who was
searching for Rüya, not the other way around—just so that he could
feel the pain Rüya felt at his disappearance! Rüya must be in tears, Rüya
must be bored after so much time alone, Rüya must be in a dark room
downstairs somewhere, pleading with him to come out of his hiding
place! Much later, after a wait so long it seemed as endless as childhood
itself, impatience got the better of him and—unaware that impatience
had already brought the game to a close—he climbed down from his
hiding place; after accustoming himself to the dim light, he set out to
find Rüya. After searching the entire building, he was forced to ask
Grandmother. His voice was strange and ghostly. "Goodness," she
replied. "What's all that dust on the top of your head? Where have you
been? They've been looking for you! Celâl was here," she added. "Celâl
and Rüya have gone off to Alâaddin's shop!" Galip had run straight to
the window, to the cold, shadowy, inky-blue window: It was dark outside and it was snowing, a sad, heavy snow that seemed to beckon him,
that tugged at his heart. In the distance was Alâaddin's shop: amid the
toys, magazines, balls, yo-yos, colored bottles, and tanks glimmered a
light that was just the same shade as Rüya's complexion, and he could
just see it reflected on the white pavement outside.

It was twenty-four years old, that memory, but all night long it kept
foaming up out of nowhere, as acrid as boiling milk: this piece of life
he'd missed. Where was it? He was mocked by the grandfather clock,

ticking endlessly away; it was the same clock that had stood in his grandparents' hall for so many years, awaiting their appointment with eternity. When, soon after he and Rüya had married, Galip had insisted that they move it out of Aunt Hâle's apartment and into their own new love nest, he had, in his excitement, thought it would keep their memories alive, remind them forever of the adventures they had shared as children. But throughout the three years they spent together, it was Rüya, not Galip, who'd seemed haunted by the joys and pleasures that had slipped beyond her grasp.

Every morning Galip would go to work; every evening he would head for home, fighting his way on and off buses, hopping from one shared taxi to another, plowing through an endless stream of dark anonymous faces, legs, and elbows that seemed to belong to no one. All day long, he'd look for reasons to phone Rüya; once or twice a day, he did. Though his excuses were thin and never failed to annoy her, he was still fairly confident he knew how she spent her days, just by counting the cigarettes in the ashtrays, taking note of the brands, and doing a quick check of the apartment. Had anything been moved? Was there anything new? From time to time—in a jealous moment, or a rare burst of happiness—he'd imitate those husbands in Western movies and ask her openly: What did you do all day, what did you do? His rash question would send them both tumbling into a dark and slippery world that no film—Eastern or Western—could ever hope to illuminate, face-to-face with that empty shell that statisticians and bureaucrats call "the housewife"; because Galip had never imagined Rüya bearing children and brandishing detergents, it was only after he married her that he discovered this world even existed.

But he would never know the strange herbs and ghastly flowers that engulfed this world; like the garden of Rüya's memories, it was closed to him. This forbidden realm was the common subject and target of most radio programs and color supplements, every soap and detergent ad, every photo novel, every news flash from a foreign magazine, though none came close to dispelling the mystery that surrounded it. There were times when he'd ask himself how it was that the paper scissors had ended up next to the copper bowl on the radiator in the hallway, and for what reason; or why, if they were out for a Sunday stroll and ran into a woman he'd not seen in years (though he knew Rüya still saw her frequently), Galip would stop in his tracks, sensing a sign, a clue to this silken, slippery, forbidden realm. He felt almost as if he had stumbled onto a secret cult that had once been forced underground but was now so powerful it no longer needed to conceal itself. It frightened him to see how infectious it was, how every anonymous housewife in the world was implicated, but what alarmed him more was their insistence that they had nothing to hide, that there were no esoteric rituals, no shared crimes, histories, or raptures, that everything they did, they did of their own volition. He was fascinated by their duplicity and also repelled by it. It called to mind the secrets kept by harem eunuchs, locked up and thrown away with the key. Everyone knew this world existed, so it lacked the dreadful power of a nightmare; it was, nonetheless, a mystery, never to be defined or named, and though it had been passed from generation to generation for centuries, it was tinged with sadness, for never had it been a source of pride. Never had it offered its denizens security; no victory had ever been claimed in its name. There were times when Galip thought of it as a curse, condemning every member of a family to centuries of bad luck, but because he had seen many women returning voluntarily to this accursed land—getting married, having children, leaving work for reasons that made little sense—he knew, too, that the cult exercised some sort of gravitational pull; this was most evident in women who'd gone to great lengths to break away, pursue careers, and make their mark in the world, for even they sometimes betrayed the hint of regret for the secret rites, the silken mysteries of the hidden world that would be forever closed to him. Sometimes, if Rüya shocked him by laughing too hard at one of his idiotic jokes, or if, in a moment of rapture, he dared to break all the rules he'd learned in magazines, if he passed his clumsy hands through Rüya's black silken hair to see her lips relax into a smile, Galip would suddenly want to ask his wife about her secret life—leaving aside the laundry, the dishes, the detective novels, and the trips to the store (the doctor said she wasn't going to have children, and Rüya had shown no great interest in going to work), he wanted to ask her what she had done that day, what she had done at a particular moment, but he feared the gulf that might open up between them after the question; it was so vast, and the thing he wanted to know so far beyond their shared vocabulary, he couldn't say a thing; instead, he'd hold her arms and stare at her blankly, vacantly. "You're giving me that blank look again," Rüya would say. "You're as white as a sheet," she'd say, happily repeating the words Galip's mother had said to him all through his childhood.

After the dawn call to prayer, Galip dozed off in the sitting-room chair. In his dream he was having a conversation with Vasıf and Rüya next to the aquarium; as Japanese fish swayed in water that was as green as the ink in Rüya's ballpoint pen, they agreed there'd been a mistake; it eventually emerged that it wasn't Vasıf who was deaf and dumb but Galip; this did not unduly distress them, though; whatever happened, things would soon set themselves right.

After he woke up, Galip sat down at the table and did what he guessed Rüya herself had done nineteen or twenty hours earlier: He looked for a blank piece of paper. When he, like Rüya, was unable to find one, he turned over her farewell letter and made a list of all the people and places that had occurred to him one by one over the course of the night. The more he wrote, the longer the list, the longer the list, the more names Galip was forced to add to it; he was acting like a detective in one of Rüya's novels, and this unnerved him. Rüya's old flames, her zany lycée friends, the acquaintances whose names crossed her lips from time to time, her comrades from her political days, and the mutual friends to whom Galip had decided to say nothing until he'd tracked Rüya down: As he jotted the names down, the curves and strokes of each vowel and consonant winked and waved, tantalizing Galip the apprentice detective with double meanings, mocking him with false clues. After the garbagemen had passed, knocking the sides of the truck as they emptied the enormous bins, Galip decided he should write no more, so he took his green pen and put it next to its mate in the inside pocket of the coat he was to wear that day.

He turned off all the lights in the apartment; the snow cast the shadows in a bluish glow. Galip did one last search of the trash bin and put it outside, hoping to keep the nosy janitor from asking too many questions. He brewed himself some tea, slipped a new blade into his razor and shaved, found himself clean underwear, put on a fresh but unironed shirt, and tidied up the mess he'd made while ransacking the house. While he drank his tea he leafed through the *Milliyet* that the janitor had slipped under his door while he was getting dressed; today

Celâl's column was about an *eye* he'd met many years earlier, in a dark alley in the middle of the night. Though it was a reprint of an old column, Galip still felt the terrible eye gazing down at him. At the same moment, the phone rang.

Rüya! Galip thought; by the time he picked up the receiver, he had already decided that he and she should see a film that evening—perhaps at the Palace Theater. Hope died at the sound of Aunt Suzan's voice, but he didn't miss a beat. Yes, he told her, Rüya's fever had come down and, yes, she'd had a good night's sleep, and when she woke up, she'd even told Galip about her dream. Of course she wanted to speak to her mother, could she hold on a moment? "Rüya!" Galip cried down the hallway, "It's your mother on the phone!" He imagined Rüya yawning as she rose from the bed, lazily throwing on her robe and searching for her slippers, and then the movie in his mind switched reels: Galip, the solicitous husband, strides down the hallway to find out why she has still not come to the phone; entering her room, he finds her back in bed again, fast asleep. To bring this second scene to life, to create an atmosphere strong enough for Aunt Suzan to believe it, too, he walked up and down the corridor to produce the right sound effects. He returned to the phone. "She's gone back to sleep, Aunt Suzan. When she woke up, the fever had glued her eyes shut so she got up to wash her face, but now she's gone back to sleep." "Make sure she drinks plenty of orange juice!" said Aunt Suzan, and she went on to tell him where he could find the best and cheapest fresh blood-orange juice in Nişantaşı. "We're thinking of going to the Palace Theater this evening," Galip told her in a confident voice. "Make sure she doesn't catch cold again!" said Aunt Suzan, and then, perhaps thinking she had meddled enough, moved on to a very different subject. "Do you know, you sound just like Celâl on the phone. Or have you caught cold too? Watch out for those microbes! Make sure you don't catch what Rüya has!" There the conversation ended; they both hung up, almost noiselessly, perhaps to keep Rüya from waking or perhaps in silent deference to the fragile phone.

As soon as he had hung up, Galil went back to Celâl's article, and as he read, the husband he had just impersonated came under the dreaded gaze of the eye: His mind filled with smoke, and it came to him in a flash. "Of course! Rüya's gone back to her ex-husband!" The truth could not be clearer; it shocked him to think he had failed to notice it until now. It was in the same decisive mode that he went to the phone to ring Celâl. It was time to end the confusion, time to say, I'm going out now to find them. When I find Rüya with that ex-husband of hers—it shouldn't take me long—I'm not sure if I'll be able to persuade her to come home with me. You're much better than I am at deceiving her. What should I say to get her to come home? (He wanted to say *come back to me* but the words stuck in his throat.) "First calm down!" Celâl would tell him. "When exactly did Rüya leave? Calm down! Let's think this through. Come to the paper, let's talk." But Celâl was not at home yet, and neither was he at the paper.

As he left the house, Galip considered leaving the phone off the hook, though in the end he didn't. If Aunt Suzan says, "I rang and rang, but it was always busy," I could say, Rüya must have left the phone off the hook. You know how absentminded she is, and how forgetful.

Chapter Six

Bedii Usta's Children

. . . sighs rising and trembling through the timeless air.
—Dante, *The Inferno*, Canto IV

E ver since we opened our column to the fearless examination of the things we human beings really care about, no matter who they are or where they're from, we have been inundated with letters. While it is touching to see how eager our readers are to speak openly about their own lives, and certainly they have had to wait a long time for this privilege, I regret to inform you that some of them are so impatient that they don't stop to write down their experiences. Instead, they come straight to the office, where they sit huffing and puffing until they've given us a full and unexpurgated account. Some people, seeing that we don't quite believe what they're telling us, sensing that we meet their more bizarre details with disbelief, feel compelled to draw us away from our desks to prove their stories, to prove their very lives, to take us into the muddy, mysterious darkness that our society has so long ignored and that no one has yet dared to describe in print. This, then, is how we first came across the fearsome secret history of Turkey's mannequins.

Aside from that dung-stinking piece of folkloric kitsch, the scarecrow, our society was for centuries entirely unacquainted with the art of making mannequins. Our first undisputed master, the patron saint, if you will, of Turkey's mannequins, was Bedii Usta, ordered by Abdülhamit to make mannequins for our first Naval Museum under the guidance of Prince Osman Celâlettin. It was this same Bedii Usta to whom we owe the secret history of the mannequin. It is said that the first visitors to the museum were most impressed to see the valiant youths who had sunk so many a Spanish and Italian vessel in the Mediterranean three centuries earlier standing in their full glory among the royal launches and the galleons, their handlebar mustaches still bristling. Bedii Usta created these first marvels from wood, plaster, wax, the skins of does, camels, and sheep, and hair plucked from human heads and beards. Upon first setting eyes on these magnificent creations, the narrow-minded Sheikh al-Islam went into a fury. To replicate God's creations so perfectly was to compete with the Almighty, so the mannequins were swiftly removed from view and banisters were erected between the galleons.

This is just one of thousands of examples of the prohibition fever that has raged throughout our nation's long journey westward, but it did not succeed in damping the "fever for creation" that still burned in Bedii Usta's heart. While he continued to make more mannequins in the secrecy of his home, he pleaded with the officials to allow his "children" to be returned to the museum or to find some other place where they might be displayed. No one budged, but when he gave up on the state and the authorities who spoke in its name, he did not give up on his new art. Instead, he built himself a new atelier in his basement, and it was there that he continued making his mannequins. Later, perhaps fearing that his Muslim neighbors might denounce him for "sorcery, perversion, and heresy," and also because there were by now more mannequins than could possibly fit into a humble Muslim home, he left Old Istanbul and set up house on the European side of the city, in Galata.

This strange house on Kuledibi was first described to me by a reader, who then took me to see it for myself. It was here that Bedii Usta continued to practice his exacting craft with passion and conviction, and as he worked he passed the secrets of his self-acquired art on to his son. Twenty arduous years later, in the great westernizing wave of the early years of the Republic, when gentlemen threw aside their fezzes to don panama hats and ladies discarded their scarves in favor of low-slung high heels, mannequins began to appear in the display windows of the finest clothing stores along Beyoğlu Avenue. These, however, were brought in from abroad, and when he first set eyes on these foreign mannequins, Bedii Usta was sure that the day he'd awaited for so long was upon him; ecstatic, he flew out of his atelier into the street. But on Beyoğlu Avenue, with its glittering cafés and clubs and its crowds of ostentatious shoppers, he met with a new dis-illusion that was to send him reeling back into the darkness of his base-ment atelier, there to stay until the day he died.

He took samples of his work to all the grand department stores, but (like every window dresser who visited his basement atelier and every purveyor of suits, dresses, skirts, stockings, trousers, and hats) they all turned him down. For his mannequins did not look like the European models to which we were meant to aspire; they looked like us. "Con-sider the customer," one shopkeeper advised him. "He's not going to want a coat he sees worn by someone who looks like the swarthy, bow-legged, mustachioed countrymen he sees ten thousand times a day in our city's streets. He wants a coat worn by a new beautiful creature from a distant unknown land, so he can convince himself that he, too, can change, become someone new, just by putting on this coat." One window dresser who was well versed in this game was good enough to confess, after admiring Bedii Usta's mastery, that he thought it a great shame he could not earn his keep by using "these real Turks, these real fellow citizens" in his shop windows; the reason, he said, was that Turks no longer wanted to be Turks, they wanted to be something else altogether. This was why they'd gone along with the "dress revolu-tion," shaved their beards, reformed their language and their alphabet. Another, less garrulous, shopkeeper explained that his customers didn't buy dresses but dreams. What brought them into his store was the dream of becoming "the others" who'd worn that dress.

Bedii Usta did try to make mannequins that accommodated this dream. However, he was only too aware he could never compete with the imported European mannequins with their strange and everchang-ing poses and their toothpaste smiles. So before long, he went back to realizing his own dreams, his real dreams, in his own dark atelier. He spent the last fifteen years of his life giving these terrible homespun images the semblance of flesh and blood, producing more than a hun-dred and fifty new mannequins, each one a work of art. Bedii Usta's son, who came to see me at the newspaper and then took me to see his father's basement atelier for myself, told me, as we inspected the man-nequins one by one, that "the special thing that makes us what we are" was buried inside these strange and dusty creatures.

We had come by way of a muddy alley off Kuledibi, along a filthy pavement, down a steep flight of stairs, and now here we were, in the cellar of a dark cold house. All around us were mannequins, squirming and fidgeting, hoping perhaps that by moving they might come to life. Gazing at us through the shadows of the half-lit cellar were hundreds of eyes, hundreds of faces, staring at us and at each other. Some were seated, some were talking, some were eating, some laughing, a few were at prayer. Some seemed to defy the outside world by their very existence—an existence that seemed to me at the time to be unbearable. This much was crystal clear: These mannequins were possessed of a life force stronger than anything you might see in the crowds swarming across the Galata Bridge, let alone in the display windows of Beyoğlu or Mahmutpaşa. The very complexions of this crowd of squirming, breathing mannequins were lit up with life. I was entranced. I remember approaching one mannequin (a fellow citizen, an old man buried in his troubles) with a passionate trepidation, wanting to tap into the life I sensed pulsating inside him, wanting to become part of this other world and know its secrets. But when I touched him, his thick skin was as cold and terrifying as the room itself.

"My father always said we should pay close attention to the gestures that make us who we are," the son explained, pointing proudly at the mannequins. At the end of their long and tiring workdays, he and his father would climb from their dark Kuledibi cellar to return to the earth's surface, and together they would go to Taksim, to one of those pimp coffeehouses; here they would sit down, order themselves some tea, and watch the crowds streaming by, paying special attention to gestures. In those years his father held that a nation could change its way of life, its history, its technology, its art, literature, and culture, but it would never have a real chance to change its gestures. While he was telling me this, the son showed me how a cabdriver might light a cigarette, and how and why a Beyoğlu gangster held his arms away from the body when he was walking sideways like a crab, and then he pointed to the chin of a chickpea seller's apprentice—the boy was laughing with his mouth wide open, just like the rest of us. He also explained the terror in the downcast eyes of a woman as she walked alone down the avenue with a string bag in her hands, and he explained why it was that our citizens kept their eyes on the ground when they walked through cities and their eyes on the sky when they walked through the country. . . . And he kept bringing my attention back to the mannequins that still watched over us as they awaited the hour of eternity, the hour that would bring them to life—their gestures, the thing in their pose that came "from us"—over and over, I know not how many times. Above all it was clear that these magnificent creations were perfectly equipped to model the finest fashions.

But still there was something about these mannequins, these sorry creations, that broke your heart and made you want to flee back to the daylight world above. There was something wrong about them—how can I put it?—something dark, painful, irksome, even terrifying! "In later years," the son explained, "my father stopped studying ordinary gestures," and this was when I realized what this terrible thing was. For these gestures I've been trying to describe—the way we Turks laughed, wiped our noses, walked, looked askance, washed our hands, opened bottles—over time, they began to lose their innocence, or so it seemed to this father and his son. While they were sitting in their coffeehouses, watching men and women who'd never had anyone to imitate except themselves and each other, Bedii Usta and his son could not at first figure out whom these people were imitating, whom they had taken as their models for change. Their stock of little everyday gestures was "life's great treasure," but slowly and inexorably, as if in obedience to a secret and invisible master, they were changing, disappearing, and a whole new set of gestures was taking their place. It was while the father and his son were working together on a line of child mannequins that they finally got to the bottom of the mystery. The son cried out, "It's because of those damn films!"

Yes, it was because of those damn films—brought in from the West canister by canister to play in our theaters for hours on end—that the gestures our people used in the street began to lose their innocence. They were discarding their old ways, faster than the eye could see; they'd embraced a whole new set of gestures—each and every thing they did was an imitation. Let us not dwell too long on the examples the son gave me to justify his father's anger about these fake, new, and ultimately meaningless ways of moving; suffice it to say that he covered all the new laughs our people had first seen on celluloid, not to mention the way they opened windows, kicked doors, held tea glasses, and put on their coats; these anonymous learned gestures, these new nods, winks, polite coughs, angry fits, and fistfights, the way we rolled our eyes now, the extraordinary things we did with our eyebrows, these new affectations might make us seem tougher or more elegant but they were also robbing us of our rough-hewn childishness. In the end, the father found these hybrid movements so upsetting that he could no longer bear to see them. Because he feared his "children" might also become infected by these new fake gestures, he decided to turn his back on the world and retire to his atelier: upon shutting himself into his cellar, he made it clear that he had long known "the essence of the mystery that must now unfold."

It was as I surveyed the works that Bedii Usta produced during the last fifteen years of his life that I suddenly grasped what this essence was, and with the wild surmise of a wolf child who has, at long last, discovered his true identity: for I saw much of myself in these uncles and aunts, these friends and acquaintances, these grocers and working-men; these mannequins' eyes bored right into my heart, for they were made in my image; I felt as if I too were a mannequin wasting away in this hopeless moth-eaten darkness. They were covered in a leaden dust, my mannequin compatriots (Beyoğlu gangsters numbered among them, and seamstresses; also Cevdet Bey, the famous millionaire, and Selahattin Bey, the encyclopedist; there were firemen, too, and dwarfs the likes of which you've never seen, and ancient beggars, even preg-nant women); as their shadows grew in the dim lamplight, so too did these tragic creations grow in my estimation: They were deities mourn-ing their lost innocence, they were ascetics in torment, longing but fail-ing to be someone else, hapless lovers who'd never made love, never shared a bed, who'd ended up killing each other instead. They, like me, like all of us, had, once upon a time, in a past so far away it seemed like heaven, caught by chance a glimpse of an inner essence, only to forget what it was. It was this lost memory that pained us, reduced us to ruins, though still we struggled to be ourselves. Our gestures, these things that made us who we were, the way we wiped our noses, scratched our faces, and kicked our feet and the way we let our despair, our defeat, show on our faces—in essence, these were the penalties we had to pay as we struggled to remain true to our ourselves. "My father was certain that the day would come when he'd see his own mannequins in shop windows!" So the son said, adding, "My father never stopped hoping that our people would be so happy one day that they'd stop trying to imitate other people!" But it seemed to me that this crowd of mannequins longed for the same thing as I did: to leave this airless, mildewed cellar, to walk again down sunlit streets watching other people and imitating them, to share in our happiness as we all tried so hard to become someone else.

But as I was later to discover, they hoped in vain! One day a shopkeeper with a certain interest in "curiosities" paid a visit to the atelier, taking away with him a few pieces of "merchandise," hoping perhaps to cut his costs. But in their poses and their gestures they resembled so closely the customers and the crowds filing past the shop windows, they were so ordinary, so authentic, so much "like us" that no would would even look at them. Upon which the stingy shopkeeper sawed the mannequins into pieces, thus separating their gestures from the whole that gave them meaning; their severed hands and feet, arms and legs sat in the tiny window of his tiny shop for years on end, offering gloves, boots, shoes, and umbrellas to the Beyoğlu crowds.

Chapter Seven

The Letters in Mount Kaf

"Must a name mean something?"
—Lewis Carroll,
Through the Looking Glass

When, after his sleepless night, Galip stepped out into the street to find the usual monotone grays of Nişantaşı brightened by a strange white light, he saw that it had snowed more than he'd thought. The crowds on the pavement seemed unaware of the translucent icicles hanging from the eaves of the apartment buildings. After a short visit to the local branch of the Labor Bank (which Rüya called the Vapor Bank, in homage to the bluish clowd of dust, smoke, exhaust, and coke fumes that hung over Nişantaşı Square), Galip was able to establish that Rüya had not withdrawn a particularly large sum of money from their joint account over the past ten days, that the bank's heating system had broken, but that everyone was in a good mood because one of the grotesquely made-up bank tellers had won a prize in the National Lottery. He continued down the street, past the florist's foggy window, past the covered passage where tea makers' apprentices darted to and fro with their trays, past Şişli Progressive High School, where he and Rüya had once gone to school, and under the icicles hanging from the ghostly branches of the chestnut trees, arriving finally at Alâaddin's shop. Alâaddin was wearing the same blue hood that Celâl had described in his column nine years earlier, and he was wiping his nose.

"Alâaddin, how are you—you're not ill, I hope?"

"I've caught a cold."

Rüya's ex-husband had once written for a string of political periodicals; though Galip agreed with some of them, others he opposed most vehemently, but as he asked Alâaddin if he happened to have any of them in stock, he pronounced each title with equal care. A strange look came over Alâaddin's face—fearful, suspicious, childish even, though in no way hostile—as he reminded Galip that only university students read such things. "What could you possibly want with them?"

"I want to solve their puzzles!"

After laughing to show he got the joke, Alâaddin said, "But son, you know they never have puzzles in these things!" Only a true puzzle addict could have sounded so mournful. "Here are two new ones. Would you like them too?"

"I would," said Galip, and then, whispering like an old man who's just bought a porn magazine, he said, "Would you mind wrapping them all up in newsprint?"

As he sat on the Eminönü bus, he felt the package in his lap grow strangely heavier, and, stranger still, he felt as if there were an eye hanging over him, watching everything he did. But it did not belong to a fellow passenger, for they were all gazing absently at the crowds in the snowy streets as the bus rocked back and forth, back and forth, like a steamboat in a stormy sea. Alâaddin had wrapped up his political periodicals in an old *Milliyet*, and now, as he looked down at it, he saw that Celâl's column had ended up on top; and there was Celâl, staring up at him from his picture. It was the same picture he'd seen every morning for years and years, but this was the strangest thing of all: Today it was looking at him in a new way. I understand you perfectly, the picture told him. I'm watching your every move! Galip put his thumb over the picture, hoping to save himself from this eye that could read his soul, but throughout that long bus journey he still felt its presence and its all-seeing gaze.

The moment he reached his office, he tried to call Celâl at work, but he still wasn't there. He unwrapped his package, took out the left-wing journals, and began to read them carefully. Just to leaf through them was to return to the tense but heady days when liberation, victory—the Day of Judgment!—had seemed just around the corner. When exactly had he lost faith? He could no longer remember. From time to time he'd return to the list he'd made on the back of Rüya's goodbye letter and phone a few of her old friends, and afterward more memories returned to him, and to Galip they were as beautifully implausible as the films they'd seen as children at the outdoor movies, wedged between the walls of the mosque and the coffeehouse. Those old black-and-white films from Yeşilçam Studios had never been strong on plot, and sometimes they made so little sense to Galip that he'd wonder if he'd missed the point entirely, but then it would occur to him that perhaps this *was* the point: to create a new world from nothing, a neverland populated by rich cruel fathers, gold-hearted paupers, cooks, manservants, beggars, and cars with fins (as Rüya was fond of pointing out, the license plate on the DeSoto in one film was often the same one they'd seen in another movie a week earlier); but still he would sit there sneering at their implausible theatrics, while everyone else in the audience heaved great sighs and shed great tears, until suddenly—you guessed it—he too would succumb to the sorcerer behind the screen and find himself weeping with the anguished, wilting, and oh-so-pure heroines, sharing the miseries of the sad, self-sacrificing, but still resolute heroes.

Hoping to acquaint himself further with the black-and-white fairytale world of little left-wing splinter groups that Rüya and her first husband had once inhabited, he rang an old friend who kept an archive of political journals.

"You're still collecting those journals, aren't you?" Galip asked in a confident voice. "One of my clients is in trouble, and it would help with our defense if I could take a look at your archive."

"I'd be delighted!" said Saim, as good-natured as ever, and pleased that someone had rung him about his archive. He suggested that Galip drop by that evening, at half past eight.

Galip went on working at the office until night fell. He tried Celâl a few more times but failed to get through. The secretary said either that he "wasn't in yet" or that he'd "just stepped out," and every time Galip hung up, he'd look up at the shelves that Uncle Melih had left to him, see that piece of newsprint that Alâaddin had used to wrap his journals, and there it would be again, Celâl's eye staring down at him. As he listened to the story of a dispute that had broken out among the heirs to a small shop in the Covered Bazaar—it was hard to follow, because the extraordinarily obese mother-and-son team who had come to see him kept interrupting each other, and he could not help noticing that the mother's bag was stuffed with medicines—and later, as he conversed with a policeman who hid his eyes behind dark glasses and wanted to sue the government for miscalculating his date of retirement, as he tried to explain to this policeman that, according to the current law, the two years he'd spent in a mental institution did not count as employment, he almost felt as if Celâl were there with him in the room.

One by one, he rang Rüya's friends. With each call, he came up with a new excuse. He asked her old lycée friend Macide if she could give him Gül's number—it was something to do with a case he was working on, he said. But when he got through to the beautiful home of the rose-scented Gül, whom Macide did not like at all, a well-spoken maid informed him that she had delivered her third and fourth children at the Gülbahçe Hospital only the day before, and that he could see these adorable twins (named Hüsn and Aşk, Beauty and Love) if he ran straight over to the hospital and looked through the window of the nursery between three and five. Figen told him to tell Rüya to get well soon and promised to return *What Is to Be Done?* (Chernyshevski) and that Raymond Chandler. As for Behiye, she told him that no, she had no uncle who worked for the Narcotics Branch of the Police Directorate, and Galip could tell from her voice that no, she knew nothing of Rüya's whereabouts. What Semih couldn't understand was how he'd manage to track her down to this basement sweatshop and, yes, it was true, she was working away feverishly with a group of engineers and technicians, trying to produce Turkey's first zipper, but no, she was not aware that there'd been stories in the press recently about black-market bobbins so was not in a position to help him with his case, though she did want him to pass on her very fondest (and sincere, Galip was sure of it) regards to Rüya.

But no matter how he changed his voice, no matter how many people he impersonated, he still couldn't track her down. Süleyman, who sold forty-year-old English encyclopedias door to door, told Galip (then impersonating a middle school principal) that there had to be a mistake—not only did he not have a daughter named Rüya in middle school, he didn't have any children! He was entirely convincing. It was the same with İlyas, who transported coal from the Black Sea in his father's barge—he was positive he had not left his dream book in the Rüya Theater because he hadn't been to the movies for months and didn't own a notebook like that anyway; and with Asım, who imported elevators, who said he could not possibly be responsible for the malfunctioning lift in the Rüya Apartments, because it was the first time he'd ever heard of an apartment building or a street bearing that name: When they uttered the name *Rüya* or when he asked them about dreams in general, he detected no panic, no guilt, in their voices; they were, Galip decided, speaking sincerely and utterly innocent. As for Tarık, who spent his days producing rat poison in his stepfather's laboratory and his nights writing poems about the alchemy of death, he was only too pleased that the students at the Law Faculty wished him to give a talk on his thematic treatment of dreams and the mysteries of dreams in his poetry, and he promised to meet up with them that evening in Taksim, right in front of the old pimp coffeehouses. Kemal and Bülent were traveling in Anatolia: one was putting together a calendar for Singer sewing machines and had gone to hear the reminiscences of an Izmir seamstress who, fifty years earlier, danced a waltz with Atatürk amid journalists and warm applause, only to sit right down at a pedal-operated sewing machine to complete a pair of Western-style trousers as they all sat and watched. The other was traveling by mule from village to village, coffeehouse to coffeehouse, hawking magical backgammon dice carved from the thousand-year-old thigh-bones of the old man Europeans called Papa Noel.

He didn't get through to everyone on the list—the phone connected him to several wrong numbers or the line was bad; on snowy and rainy days this happened more often—but he continued plowing through the political journals well into the evening and was soon up-to-date on the changing factions. He knew who the informers were who'd been tortured, killed, or sent to prison; who'd perished in which scuffle and who'd arranged the funeral; which letters the editors had answered, which they'd sent back, and which they'd published. He knew all the names and pen names of the cartoonists, the poets, and the editorial staff too, but nowhere could he see Rüya's ex-husband's name or any of his aliases either.

As the sky grew dark he sat sad and motionless in his chair. A crow perched on the windowsill gave him a curious, sideways glance; the sounds of a Friday evening rose up from the crowded street below.

Galip drifted off into a happy and inviting dream. When he awoke much later, night had fallen, but he could still sense the crow's eye boring into him, and Celâl's eye too. Slowly he moved about the dark room shutting drawers, felt for his overcoat, and left the office, feeling his way through the dark corridor. All the lights in the building were out. The tea boy was cleaning the toilets.

As he crossed the snow-covered Galata Bridge, he felt the cold; a harsh wind was blowing in from the Bosphorus. He stopped at a pudding shop in Karaköy, where he sat down at a marble table between a pair of mirrors that reflected each other; turning his back on them, he ordered fried eggs and a bowl of chicken and vermicelli soup. On the only wall that wasn't covered with mirrors was a mountain landscape that seemed to take its inspiration from postcards and Pan Am calendars; seeing the snow capped mountains rise up between the evergreens, behind a glassy lake, Galip was reminded not of the postcard Alps that had inspired it, but of Mount Kaf, the magic mountain he and Rüya had visited so often as children.

As he was taking the funicular to Tünel, he became embroiled in an argument with an old man he'd never met about the famous accident that had occurred in this tunnel twenty years earlier: Was it really because the cable broke that the cars flipped off the track and went crashing into Karaköy Square, breaking through walls and glass as gleefully as a herd of wild stallions? The nameless old man happened to be from Trabizon, as was the drunk machinist who had been in charge that day. The streets of Cihangir were empty. When Saim opened his door to give a warm but distracted welcome, Galip deduced that he and his wife were watching the same documentary as the janitors and the cabdrivers in the coffeehouse downstairs.

The Things We Left Behind was a catalog of Ottoman achievements in the Balkans; as the presenter talked of the old mosques, fountains, and caravansaries that had now fallen into the hands of the Greeks, the Albanians, and the Yugoslavs, he seemed close to tears. As Galip sat there on the imitation rococo sofa that long ago lost its springs, watching the sad parade of lost mosques, he felt like the neighbor's child, invited over to see a soccer match; Saim and his wife seemed to have forgotten he was even there. Saim bore a close resemblance to a now-deceased wrestler who had once won an Olympic medal and whose picture you could still see hanging at the greengrocers; his wife looked like a sweet, fat mouse. There was a dust-colored table in the room and a lamp that matched; hanging inside a gilt frame on the wall was the portrait of a grandfather who looked more like the wife (was her name Remziye? Galip asked himself lazily) than it did his friend Saim; on the buffet sat a calendar sponsored by an insurance company, an ashtray advertising a bank, a collection of liqueurs, a vase, a silver sugar bowl, and a set of coffee cups; and there, on the shelves that lined two walls, piles and piles of dusty periodicals and loose paper: the "archive" Galip had come to see.

Even years ago, when they were still at the university, it was already a joke; in a moment of rare candor Saim himself had admitted that he had not set out to compile "the definitive archive of our great revolution" (as his classmates so mockingly put it); he had been pushed into this role by his own "indecision." This was not, however, the indecision of a young man caught "between two classes" (as people liked to say in those days); he was caught, rather, between warring leftist factions, and he couldn't decide which one to choose.

He'd made sure to attend every political meeting and every student forum, spent his days racing from university to university, canteen to canteen, listening carefully to what people said, giving "every viewpoint, every political leaning" the attention it deserved, and because he was too shy to ask many questions, he became an avid reader of left-wing propaganda, desperately seeking out every mimeographed statement, brochure, and leaflet then in circulation. (Pardon me for asking, but would you happen to have a copy of that statement they were handing out at the Technical University the other day—the one calling for the Turkish language to be cleansed of foreign words?) Soon he had accumulated far more than he could ever read, but still he did not know which political line he should take, and this must have been when he began to think of the piles of unread material as a collection. With time, the urge to read lessened and, with it, the need to make up his mind; but by now his "documentary river" had grown so wide and sprouted so many tributaries that it would have been a shame to let it flow away into nothing; it cried out for a dam, Saim decided (the choice of words was his, for his degree was in engineering). He generously decided to devote the rest of his life to this noble project.

When the program was over, they turned off the set; after they'd gone through the usual polite questions, Saim and his wife fell silent and gazed at him with questioning eyes, so Galip launched straight into his story: he was defending a university student who'd been accused of a political crime he'd not committed. No, he did not mean to say there hadn't been a death: at the end of a badly planned, badly executed bank robbery, one of three young men involved had, while plowing through a crowd of shoppers on his way from the bank to the stolen taxi they were using as their getaway car, accidentally knocked over a little old lady. He bumped into her so violently that she fell to the pavement, dying the moment her head hit the scene of the crime. ("Wouldn't you know it!" said Saim's wife.) They'd only managed to catch one of the bank robbers, a quiet boy from a "good family," but he was carrying a gun. Being in thrall to his partners in crime, his young client had, of course, resolved not to give their names to the police, and the amazing thing was that he succeeded in this, despite being subjected to torture; but unfortunately, as Galip had discovered in the course of his investigations, he had done so by quietly assuming responsibility for the old lady's death. In the meantime, the boy who had actually knocked her down—an archaeology student named Mehmet Yılmaz—had been killed by unknown assailants in a volley of gunfire while writing coded slogans on the wall of a house in a new shantytown just beyond Umraniye. One might have expected the boy from the good family to name him as the true culprit at this point, but the police refused to believe that the dead Mehmet Yılmaz was the real Mehmet Yılmaz, and in another unexpected development, various members of the cell responsible for the bank robbery had come forward to confirm that the real Mehmet Yılmaz was still publishing articles in its journal, and that these articles showed all his old resolve. After explaining that he had not taken on this case at the request of the quiet boy, "now languishing in prison," but on behalf of his wealthy well-meaning father, Galip said he wanted to (1) see any articles that might establish that the new Mehmet Yılmaz and the old Mehmet Yılmaz were two different people; (2) establish the identity of the person who had assumed the identity of the dead Mehmet Yılmaz by examining his pen names; (3) inspect any materials issued by the political faction responsible for this strange incident over the past six months, for as Saim and his wife must be aware, it just so happened that Rüya's ex-husband had once been its leader; and (4) make an inventory of ghostwriters using the names of the dead and missing, with a full list of their aliases.

Saim was only too keen to help, and they began their search at once. During the first two hours, while they drank the tea and nibbled the cake that the wife (he remembered her name now, it was Rukiye) was kind enough to serve them, they looked only at the writers' names and aliases. Later, they widened the search to include the aliases used by the faction's informers, martyrs, and editorial staff; and as they perused the death notices, the warnings, the confessions, the bomb reports, the doctrinal disagreements, the poems, and the hollow slogans—things they had begun to forget even when they still lived in this shadowy underworld—they still could not stop themselves from falling under its spell.

They found aliases that did not hide the fact that they were aliases, and aliases that had been manufactured from these aliases, and aliases derived from portions of the manufactured aliases. They solved acrostics puzzles, letter games that never quite panned out, and almost transparent secret codes, though they were unable to establish if this was by design or accident. Rukiye sat down at the end of the table where the men were sitting. As Galip hunted for clues that might lead him to Rüya and pretended to look for evidence to prove the innocence of a boy unjustly charged with murder, a familiar sadness fell over the room—that mixture of boredom and impatience that he associated with those endless family gatherings on New Year's Day, when they would play lotto and race paper horses across the sitting-room floor as the radio blared in the background. Through the gap in the curtains, he saw that it had begun to snow again.

Still they searched on, Saim the patient professor, Galip his bright new protégé, both delighting in the chase as they traced their aliases' adventures, their travels from faction to faction, their rise and fall; when, from time to time, they discovered that one of them had disappeared or been caught and tortured, or if they discovered that someone whose picture had appeared in one of the early periodicals had later been gunned down by unknown assailants, they would break off their search for a few moments of sad silence, but then they would see another word game, stumble onto another curious fact, and before long they would be back on the trail, reconstructing their aliases' lives.

According to Saim, most of the names in the periodicals were invented, and so too were quite a few of the heroes whose exploits they recounted, as were many of the demonstrations, meetings, secret councils, underground party congresses, and bank robberies these same names had organized. To give an extreme example, he read aloud a story about a people's revolt alleged to have taken place twenty years earlier in the town of Küçük Çeruh, in east Anatolia, between Erzincan and Kemah, for which one of these journals had given full details, including dates; after a vase hit him on the head, the governor died and the rebels set up a provisional government; they went on to issue a pink stamp carrying the picture of a dove and produced a daily newspaper that printed nothing but poetry, while opticians and pharmacies worked together to distribute free glasses to the cross-eyed and others gathered wood for the primary school stove, but before they could finish the bridge that was to have linked them with civilization, Atatürk's armed forces arrived to take the matter in hand, and in less time than it took the cows to eat the smelly carpets that covered the earthen floor of the town mosque, the rebels were swinging from plane trees in the square. But, Saim explained—in the same calm way he had pointed out the secret signs in maps and letters—there was no such town as Küçük Çeruh, and as for this insurrection, this phoenix rising from the ashes of history, the names of those alleged to have taken part in it were likewise false. Here the trail went cold, for the secret behind the false names was buried in poetry, concealed behind an intricate web of rhymes and repetitions. They did stumble across a clue pertaining to Mehmet Yılmaz (this concerned a political murder committed in Ümraniye around the same time as Galip's story), but it was like watching one of those old black-and-white films that keeps breaking all the time, for they were unable to find a follow-up to this story in any of the later issues.

At this point, Galip rose from the table and phoned home, to tell Rüya in a gentle voice that he was probably going to be working at Saim's house until very late, so she shouldn't wait up, she should go to sleep. From the other side of the room, Saim and his wife told Galip to say hello to Rüya for them; of course, Rüya returned the compliment.

They went back to playing hunt-the-alias, to deciphering codes and creating new ones, and when every square inch of the room was covered with newspapers, periodicals, statements, and loose sheets of paper, Saim's wife left the two men to their quest and went to bed. It was long past midnight; the snow had draped the city in enchanted silence. Endlessly fascinated by these reams of pale print, all from the same ink-starved mimeograph machines, all culled from the smoke-filled university canteens, rainy strikers' tents, and remote train stations where they'd first been distributed ("But there's so much missing!" Saim would protest, ever the modest archivist), Galip searched on and on, delighting in the typesetting and spelling errors, until Saim emerged from the back room with an article he announced, in the proud voice of a true collector, as very rare: "The Case Against Ibn Zerhani, or The Story of a Sufi Traveler Whose Feet Never Left the Ground."

It was a bound copy of a typescript, and Galip leafed through its pages with care. "Our friend comes from a town near Kayseri whose name cannot be found on a medium-sized map of Turkey," Saim told him. "His father was a dervish from a small lodge who educated him in religion and Sufism throughout his childhood. Years later, he did as Lenin had done when he was reading Hegel: While reading a book entitled *The Hidden Meaning of the Lost Mystery* by the thirteenth-century Arab Sufi Ibn Zerhani, he kept a running 'materialist' commentary in the margins. He then copied out these notes, substantiating them with long and unnecessary parenthetical comments. Then he added annotations, writing a sort of treatise—as if he were musing on someone else's obscure and enigmatic document. To this he added a foreword in which he again discussed the contents as if they'd been written by other people. Then he typed the whole thing up. He prefaced all this with a thirty-page account of his own legendary adventures as a holy man and revolutionary.

"The interesting part of his legend is his account of how the writer came to see the links between the Sufi philosophy that Westerners call pantheism and the sort of materialist philosophy he himself had developed under his father's influence; the connection came to him as he was strolling one evening through the town cemetery. Years before, while strolling past the gravestones, he'd seen a crow among the grazing lambs and dozing ghosts; when, twenty years on, he gazed up at the same but now much taller cypress trees, he spotted the same crow—as you know, in Turkey crows can live longer than two hundred years. He saw at once that everything about this impudent flying beast—its legs, its head, its body, its wings—had remained exactly, but exactly, the same, and as you know, crows stand for higher thought. He even provided a likeness of the crow; it's on the cover. The book proves that every Turk aspiring to immortality must play Boswell to his own Johnson, must be his own Goethe and his own Eckermann at one and the same time. He typed six copies. I'd be surprised if you'd find a single one in the secret police archives."

The two men gazed for some time at the crow on the cover and then opened the book to read the author's autobiography. Although he had led a sad, empty, dismally provincial life, traveling back and forth between his house and the hardware store he'd inherited from his father, it still spoke to their imaginations, made them feel as if there were a third man in the room. There is only one story, Galip felt like crying out. All these words and letters, all these dreams of liberation, all these memories of torture and defeat and everything that's ever been written about them, be it in joy or sorrow—they all add up to a single story! All these years, Saim had been collecting these papers, leaflets, and periodicals, patiently casting his net in the sea of print, and somewhere along the way he'd found it, the story of stories. He knew he'd found it, but he could no longer see it; it was buried under piles and piles of paper, and he'd lost the key to the story, the only word that could unlock it.

When they came across Mehmet Yılmaz's name in a four-year-old issue, Galip said it was a coincidence and perhaps it was time for him to go home, but Saim stopped him, saying that nothing in these periodicals—he'd now begun to call them *my* periodicals—was a coincidence. For the next two hours, they embarked on the search to end all searches, racing from journal to journal, their eyes scanning each page like spotlights; they soon discovered that Mehmet Yılmaz had converted first to Ahmet Yılmaz and then, in a journal featuring a well on the cover and littered with peasants and chickens, he'd become Mete Çakmaz. It was not hard for Saim to establish that Metin Çakmaz and Ferit Çakmaz were also the same person, but by now our friend had given up on theoretical writings and turned his hand to writing lyrics for the sort of Turkish *saz* music one hears at memorials in smoky wedding halls. But it didn't stop there. For a short while he reverted to political writing (to prove that everyone except the author was a police informer); later still he became a nervous and irascible mathematically inclined economist, determined to decipher the perversities unleashed on the world by British academics, but their dark, infelicitous clichés soon proved too much for him. Saim tiptoed into his bedroom, returning with yet another batch of journals, and *presto!* there he was again, in an issue published three years and two months earlier—it was almost as if Saim had planted him there. Now his name was Ali Harikaülke: looking forward to the beautiful future when kings and queens would be obsolete and the rules of chess could change accordingly; when happy well-nourished boys named Ali would, by sitting cross-legged like good Turks with their backs against the wall, solve forever the riddle of Humpty Dumpty. On the next page it stated that Ali Harikaülke was not the author but the translator. The true author was an Albanian mathematics professor. But what shocked Galip most— after the Albanian professor's life story—was to see Rüya's ex-husband dispensing with aliases altogether, writing openly under his own name.

"Nothing's as strange as life—except writing!" cried Saim proudly, after they'd stared at it in silent shock for some time.

He tiptoed back into his bedroom, returning with two crateloads of periodicals. "These come from a splinter group with Albanian affiliations. There's a story here, a strange enigma I've spent years investigating. It has some bearing on your own investigation, as you shall see."

He brewed up more tea, pulled the documents he needed from his shelves and boxes, and spread them across the table.

"It began six years ago," he began, "one Saturday afternoon, when I was leafing through the latest issue of *People and Labor*, just to see if there was anything of interest. . . . It was one of three journals put out by splinter groups emulating Enver Hoxha and the Albanian Labor Party, but as it happened, each was bitterly opposed to the other two. . . . So anyway, I was going through this journal when suddenly I came across this photograph, this article—it was about an induction ceremony, in honor of the group's new recruits. It amazed me, not because it described a Marxist meeting in a country where Communist activity of any sort is banned, or because it talked of people reciting poetry and playing the *saz*; all the little left-wing journals ran pieces like this in every issue, because the only way to keep their heads above water was to look as if they were growing by leaps and bounds.

"The black-and-white photograph showed a hall draped with posters of Enver Hoxha and Chairman Mao. There were people reciting poems, and surrounding them was this crowd puffing on their cigarettes with extraordinary intensity, as if it were a sacred rite. But what really sparked my interest was the caption, which made pointed references to the hall's 'twelve columns.' Stranger still, all the new recruits had chosen aliases like Hasan, Hüseyin, and Ali—as you probably know, these are all Alevi names—and as I was soon to discover, they were not just Alevi names but names of famous Sufis, Bektaşi sheikhs. This wouldn't have meant a thing to me unless I'd already known how strong the Bektaşi Sufi orders had once been in Albania, but because I did, I knew at once that I was on to something, something incredible, so I really threw myself into it and over the next four years I read every book I could find on the Bektaşis, the Janissaries, and the Hurufis— you know about this sect, I'm sure, they're the ones who divine secret meanings from the works in the Koran. I also read up on Albanian communism, and when I put it all together I had unraveled a conspiracy that dates back a hundred and fifty years.

"You know what I'm talking about, don't you?" Saim said, and then he took Galip through the seven hundred years of Bektaşi history, from Hacı Bektaş Veli to the present. The order had its roots in the Sufi, Alevi, and Shamanist traditions, Saim told him; it had played a part in the inception and expansion of the Ottoman Empire, while also fostering the long tradition of revolt and revolution for which the Janissary army—a Bektaşi stronghold—became so famous. If you remembered that every Janissary belonged to the Bektaşi order, you began to see its secret imprint all over Istanbul. Though it was also the Janissaries who caused the Bektaşis to be routed from the city: in 1826, furious that his army was resisting his Western reforms, Mahmut II plastered the Janissary barracks with cannon fire, after which he shut down all the lodges offering them spiritual solace, expelling all Bektaşi sheikhs from Istanbul.

After twenty years underground, the Bektaşis returned to the city, but this time disguised as the Nakşibendi order. Over the next eighty years—until the founding of the Republic, when Atatürk shut the order down—they presented themselves to the outside world as Nakşis, but in private they lived as Bektaşis, thus pushing the secrets that bound them even deeper underground.

On the table was an engraving from a book by an English traveler depicting a Bektaşi rite that probably owed less to reality than to the artist's imagination. Galip counted the columns one by one; there were twelve of them.

"The third Bektaşi wave," Saim now said, "began fifty years after the founding of the Republic, but in a new disguise. They were no longer Nakşibendis; now they called themselves Marxist-Leninists."

After a few moments of silence, Saim set out to prove his case, illustrating his giddy recital with journals, brochures, books, clippings, photographs, and engravings: everything these Marxist-Leninists did was Bektaşi to the core, and everything they wrote; they lived their lives by the exact same code. The initiation rites were the same down to the last detail. Just as Bektaşi aspirants were obliged to prove their endurance and capacity for self-denial by going through the most punishing trials, so too were the Marxist-Leninists. Both venerated their martyrs, their saints, and those who had come before them; both paid homage in just the same way; for both the word *road* was laden with spiritual significance; both used recitation and repetition to create an atmosphere of unity; and their litanies were the same. Like the Bektaşis who had come before them, Marxist-Leninists could always identify a fellow traveler from his mustache, his beard, even his eyes; they played the same *saz* music during their ceremonies, recited poems with exactly the same meter and rhyme scheme. "The most important thing about all this," Saim said, "unless this really is just a coincidence, or unless God the Almighty has sent me these writings to play a cruel joke—I'd be blind if I didn't notice that the word and letter games you find in today's leftist periodicals are nothing other than new renditions of the games the Bektaşis borrowed from the Hurufis."

There followed a silence, broken only by the whistle of a watchman on a distant street. Saim directed Galip's attention to a word game he'd already deciphered: first the surface version, then the hidden version, complete with double meanings; he moved on to a second puzzle and then a third, reading them out in a voice that made Galip feel as if he were listening to a prayer.

In the early hours of the morning, when Galip was drifting between sleep and wakefulness, dreaming of Rüya, remembering their happy days together, Saim came to what he called "the most unique and striking aspect of this matter." Galip pricked up his ears. No, the youths who signed up for these political groups had no idea they were Bektaşis: they were unknowing pawns in a plot that the party's middle echelons cooked up with a handful of Albanian Bektaşi sheikhs; only a handful of people below that level had the slightest inkling of what was going on; so no, those well-meaning self-effacing youths who'd been joining these organizations by the thousands, changing their daily habits, turning their very lives inside out—it had never even crossed their minds that there was a band of Albanian Bektaşi sheikhs who saw them as an extension of their sect and kept abreast of their activities through careful examination of any photographs taken during their marches, secret ceremonies, and communal meals. "At first I innocently assumed I had stumbled onto a giant conspiracy, a secret that defied belief—I thought these young people had been badly taken in," said Saim. "I was beside myself, so much so that I was thinking of picking up my own pen for the first time in fifteen years and publishing my own article, but I quickly talked myself out of it." As a dark tanker rumbled down the snow-swept Bosphorus, rattling all the windows, Saim added, "Because, you see, I realized I'd change nothing by proving that the life we live is someone else's dream."

Then Saim told him the story of the Zeriban tribe, who had gone to a remote mountain in eastern Anatolia and spent two hundred years preparing for a journey to Mount Kaf. The idea came from a 320-year-old dream book, and the journey remained a dream too, but would it have done any good to tell these people that the sheikhs who'd kept the dream alive, passing it from generation to generation like a secret, had long ago come to an understanding with the Ottomans that the journey was never to be? Those soldiers you saw piling into small-town movie theaters all over Anatolia on a Sunday afternoon—if you pointed to the malicious priest who was trying to get the brave Turkish warrior to drink a chalice of poisoned wine in that historical melodrama they were watching, and told them that in real life he was a humble actor and a good Muslim, what could you achieve except deprive them of the righteous anger that was their only pleasure?

Toward morning, when Galip was dozing on the couch, Saim added a new twist: When that handful of party officials met with those old Bektaşi sheikhs in a turn-of-the-century colonial hotel somewhere in Albania, when they sat together in a ballroom that reminded them of their dreams, sobbing over those photographs, they almost certainly assumed these fine young Turks were sharing the secrets of their order and not exuberant Marxist-Leninist analyses. Not to know that their age-old quest for gold was doomed—this was not, after all, an alchemist's misfortune but his very reason for being. No matter how many times a modern illusionist insisted that what he did was a trick, there was always one happy moment when his rapt audience still believed that what they had seen was magic. There were young people who at certain times in their lives fell in love simply because of a word, a story, a book they'd both read; they married their lovers in the same excited spirit and lived happily ever after without ever seeing the illusions that guided their hearts.

As he tidied up his journals, laid the table for his wife's breakfast, and glanced through the paper that the janitor had slipped under his door, Saim remarked that at the end of the day there was nothing to be gained by reminding people that everything that had ever been written, even the greatest and most authoritative texts in the world, were about dreams, not real life, dreams conjured up by words.

Chapter Eight

The Three Musketeers

I asked him about his enemies. He began to count them. The list went on and on. . . .

—Conversations with Yahya Kemal

Thirty-two years before he died, he wrote a column about his funeral that reflected his worst fears, and his fears, it turned out, were well founded. Not counting myself and the corpse in the coffin, there were nine of us in attendance: an orderly from a small private addiction clinic in Üsküdar, an inmate from the same establishment, a retired journalist who'd been his protégé when our columnist's star was at its apex, two cross-eyed relatives who knew nothing about the deceased's life or career, an overdressed dowager with a strange veil pinned to her hat that made her look like the sultan's chief interrogator, and our honorable imam. Because the moment of interment coincided with the worst moments of yesterday's storm, the imam raced through the prayers, throwing the earth onto the coffin with what some might call unseemly haste. The moment it was over—and I cannot quite explain how—our small crowd vanished into the mist. I was the only one at Kısıklı awaiting the next streetcar. I took a motor launch across the Bosphorus; reaching the European shore, I headed straight for Beyoğlu, where Edward G. Robinson's *Scarlet Street* was playing at the Alhambra; I went in and sat down and nearly fainted from joy. The hero, an unsuccessful businessman with a second and just as unsuccessful life as an amateur artist, decides to impersonate a millionaire, hoping to impress the woman he loves. But little does he know that Joan Bennett, the object of his affections, is also playing a double game. We all watched in despair as he discovered her deception, nursed his broken heart, and succumbed to grief.

When I first met with the deceased (let me begin this second paragraph as I did the first, borrowing the words he recited so often and so lovingly in his columns), when I first met with the deceased, he was in his seventies and I in my thirties. I was on my way to Bakırköy to visit an acquaintance, and I was about to board the suburban line at Sirkeci when what did I suddenly see? The great columnist himself, at a table in the restaurant at the edge of a platform, drinking *rakı* with two other columnists I'd read and admired throughout my childhood and early youth. What shocked me was not to see these three old men—who were all over seventy and longtime residents of my literary Mount Kaf—amid the deadly, noisy crowds of Sirkeci station, but to see these three polemicists, who had been insulting each other in print since the start of their writerly careers, still sitting together at a table twenty years on, clinking their glasses like the three musketeers at Dumas *père*'s tavern. In the half century since they had taken up the pen, they had witnessed the waxing and waning of three sultans, one caliph, and three presidents, but still these three polemicists had battled on, sometimes leveling accusations with good reason, but usually seizing any opportunity to accuse one another of being atheists, Young Turks, Europeanists, nationalists, Masons, Kemalists, republicans, traitors, tinpot sultans, Westernizers, dervishes, plagiarists, Nazis, Jews, Arabs, Armenians, homosexuals, turncoats, Islamist fanatics, Communists, pro-Americans, and even—this being the epithet of the moment— existentialists. (At around that time, one of them had written a column pointing out that the greatest existentialist of all time was Ibn' Arabi, and that the Western existentialists who came onto the scene a full seven hundred years later were mere imitations who had plundered his every idea.) After I had stood there watching the three polemicists for some time, I was seized by an urge to approach their table and introduce myself; I did so carefully, making it clear that I admired them all equally.

Let me make it clear, dear readers: I was an overexcited youth, a bright, imaginative, passionate, and successful young man, but also somewhat volatile, wavering as I did between conceit and self-confidence, sincerity and cunning. I was new to the scene in those days—new enough to smell the flowers, as they say—and if I hadn't known that I already had a larger readership than they did, and received more readers' letters (and, of course, wrote better columns)—if I hadn't also known that two of them at the very least were painfully aware of all this, I doubt I would have found the courage to approach these three masters of the profession.

This was why, when they turned up their noses at me, I took it as a sign of victory. Because, of course, if I'd been an ordinary reader hanging on to their every word and not a young and successful columnist, they would have treated me far better. It was some time before they invited me to sit down with them; no sooner had they done so than they sent me to the kitchen like a waiter; then they sent me to the newsstand to buy them a weekly magazine they wanted to see; I peeled an orange for one of them; when one of the others' napkin fell to the ground, I swooped down to rescue it for him before he had a chance to do so himself; and I answered their questions in just the hesitant, self-effacing way they wanted: Yes, sir, it's a terrible shame I can't read French, but every evening I pick up a dictionary to unravel *Les fleurs du mal*. My professions of ignorance made my victory even harder for them to bear, though my constant hemming and hawing helped to mitigate my crime.

They acted as if I were of no interest to them whatsoever, but when they turned their backs on me to chat among themselves (much as I myself would do years later in the company of younger journalists) it was only too clear to me that these three masters were trying to impress me. I listened in admiring silence. What was the true nature of the forces that had compelled a German atomic scientist then causing a stir in all the newspapers to convert to Islam? Was it true that Ahmet Mithat Efendi, Turkey's greatest columnist, had, after Lastik Sait Bey got the better of him in a war of words, pushed his rival into a dark alley, beaten him to a pulp, and made him promise to abandon the war of words forever? Was Bergson a mystic, or was he a materialist? How could one prove that there was a second universe hidden inside the secret core of our own? Which poets had been criticized in the last lines of the twenty-sixth sura of the Koran for professing beliefs they did not hold and deeds they had never performed? While they were on the subject, was André Gide really a homosexual, or had he decided, like the Arab poet Ebu Novvas, to act *as if* he prefered boys to women, because he'd known it would get him attention. Had Jules Verne based his erroneous description of Mahmut II and Tophane Square in the opening paragraph of *Kéraban-le-têtu* on a Melling engraving or had he lifted it in its entirety from Lamartine's *Voyage en orient*? Had Rumi the great mystic poet included the woman who died while making love to a donkey in the fifth book of his *Mathnawi* for the story or the lesson that could be drawn from it?

It was while they were politely dissecting this last question that their eyes glided in my direction, and because they had also indicated with their white eyebrows that they were asking me the question, I added my thoughts to the discussion: The story, like all stories, stood only for itself, though Rumi had also seen fit to drape it in the veil that conveyed its lesson. Then the man whose funeral I attended yesterday turned to me and asked, "My son, do you write those columns of yours to instruct or to entertain?" To prove I could speak with authority on any subject, I gave him the first answer that came into my head. "Oh, certainly to entertain, sir." This did not please them. "You're young. You're just at the beginning of your career," they said. "Allow us to give you a few words of advice!" "Would you mind," I replied, "if I committed your advice to paper?" I raced over to the cashier in the corner, where the restaurant owner gave me a few sheets of restaurant stationery. I stacked them facedown on the table, took out my enamel fountain pen, and, as my mentors held forth, I took notes in green ink, and now, dear reader, I would like to pass their wise words on to you.

I am aware that some of my readers will be impatient to know the names of these masters, all three of them long forgotten; they will have been hoping that, having managed to conceal the names of my three polemicists thus far, I might, at the very least, whisper their names into their ears now, but I am not going to do that. This is not to leave them to sleep in peace in the cemeteries that are now their homes, but to separate those readers who deserve to know from those who do not. With this aim in mind, I shall assign to each dead columnist the pseudonym by which a different Ottoman sultan signed his poems. If those able to identify these poet sultans can also find parallels with the great masters I propose to veil with their names, they will have all they need to solve the puzzle, though I hasten to add that I do not give it much significance. The real enigma resides in this "chess game" my mentors played with me, deepening the secret with each new move and each new piece of so-called advice. Because I am still unable to grasp the beauty of this secret—and in this I am like the luckless dolt who scours chess columns in the vain hope that he might learn from the game's greatest minds—I have interspersed my masters' enigmatic words with parenthetical comments in which I offer my own humble interpretations of the text along with any piteous theories I may have drawn from it.

A: Adli. On that winter's day he was wearing a cream-colored suit made from English material (I say that because in this country we seem to call all expensive materials English) and a dark tie. He was tall and well groomed with a combed white mustache. He carried a cane. He had the look of a penniless English gentleman, though it's not for me to explain how anyone can be a gentleman when he doesn't have a penny to his name.

B: Bahti. His tie is loose and crooked like his face. His jacket is crumpled and covered with stains. In his vest pocket, connected to a chain you can see looped through the buttonhole, is a watch. He's fat and slovenly. In his hand is the cigarette he so lovingly calls his "only friend"—it will go on to betray the one-sided friendship by giving him the heart attack that will eventually kill him.

C: Cemali. He is short and irascible. Try as he might to look clean and tidy, he still looks like a retired schoolteacher, in jackets and trousers as faded as a postman's and thick rubber-soled shoes courtesy of Sümerbank National Factories. Thick glasses, severely myopic, and virulently ugly.

Here, then, is the mysterious advice my masters gave me that day, along with my own lowly efforts to crack the code.

1. *C*: To write a column purely for entertainment is to drift without a compass in the open sea.
2. *B*: That said, no columnist can be Aesop or Rumi. The lesson always rises out of the story, not the other way around.
3. *C*: Never write to the reader's level but to your own.
4. *A*: The story is the compass. (*An affectionate allusion to 1.*)
5. *C*: Those who have not cracked the secret locked inside our

history and our cemeteries cannot presume to speak about us, or indeed about the West.

6. *B*: The key to the East–West question is hidden inside these words attributed to Arif the Bearded: "Oh, you luckless creatures, staring at the West from a ship heading eastwards!" (*Arif the Bearded—a character B created for his columns—is said to be based on a real person.*)

7. *A,B,C*: Start collecting proverbs, sayings, anecdotes, jokes, aphorisms, lines of poetry, and poetry anthologies.

8. *C*: Don't wait until you've chosen your subject to hunt down the aphorism that best illustrates it; choose the aphorism first and then the subject that suits it.

9. *A*: Never sit down at your desk until you have your first line.

10. *C*: You must believe strongly in something.

11. *A*: If you don't believe strongly in anything, try to make your readers believe you do.

12. *B*: The reader is a child who wants to go to the fair.

13. *C*: The reader never forgives the writer who takes Muhammed's name in vain, and God will paralyze him too. (*This alludes to a column in which A explored Muhammed's conjugal and business affairs. Perhaps because he has decided that A was referring to him in 11, C has retaliated by referring here to the slight paralysis affecting one side of A's mouth.*)

14. *A*: Love all dwarfs, for the reader does too. (*Here A is getting even with C for 13 by making a veiled remark about how short C is.*)

15. *B*: That mysterious home for dwarfs in Üsküdar, for example; that's a good subject.

16. *C*: Wrestling is another good subject, though only when it's done, or described, for the sport. (*This is C getting back at B for 15, which he suspects is at his expense: B's strong interest in wrestling, and the serial he writes on the same subject, have led some to wonder if he's a pederast.*)

17. *A*: The reader is a married man with four children and the mentality of a twelve-year-old who has to struggle to make ends meet.

18. *C*: The reader is as ungrateful as a cat.

19. *B*: Cats are intelligent animals and not ungrateful; it's just that they know they can't trust any writer who loves dogs.

20. *A*: Forget cats and dogs and stick to national affairs.

21. *B*: Make it your business to know the addresses of all the consulates. (*This refers to rumors about the links C maintained with the German consulate and A with the British consulate during World War Two.*)

22. *B*: By all means be polemical, but only if you know how to cause injury.

23. *A*: By all means, be polemical, but only if your editor takes your side.

24. *C*: By all means be polemical, but make sure to take your coat. (*This is in reference to a famous remark B made when asked to explain why he did not take part in the War of Independence, choosing to remain instead in occupied Istanbul: "I can't bear the winters in Ankara!"*)

25. *B*: Always answer readers' letters in your column; if no one's writing to you, write letters to yourself and answer those.

26. *C*: Our teacher and master is Sheherazade; take a leaf from her book. Whenever writing about about "real life" you too can intersperse facts with stories ten to fifteen pages long.

27. *B*: Read sparingly but ardently. That way you'll look far more knowledgeable than those who read a great deal but enjoy nothing.

28. *B*: Put yourself forward; cultivate famous people so that you can write up your reminiscences after they die.

29. *A*: Don't use the words *dearly departed* at the beginning of an obituary in which you end up insulting the deceased.

30. *A,B,C*: Do whatever you can to avoid using the following sentences: (a) The dearly departed was alive only yesterday. (b) Ours is a cruel profession; what we write today will be forgotten tomorrow. (c) Did you happen to hear such-and-such a program on the radio last night? (d) How time flies! (e) If the dearly departed were alive today, what would he make of this sad state of affairs? (f) They don't do things like this in Europe. (g) The price of bread (or whatever) was only x kuruş in those days. (h) Then, when it was all over, I also remembered such-and-such.

31. *C*: *Then* is a word favored by apprentice columnists who have yet to master their art.

32. *B*: If there's anything artful in a column, it shouldn't be there; whatever else a column is, it isn't art.

33. *C*: Never flatter the intelligence of anyone who rapes poetry to satisfy his lust for art. (*A barbed comment directed at B's poetry.*)

34. *B*: Write with ease, you'll be easier to read.

35. *C*: Write in agony, you'll be easier to read.

36. *B*: Write in agony and you'll get ulcers.

37. *A*: If you get ulcers, you're an artist. (*This being the first time any of them had said anything nice to anyone else, they all burst out laughing.*)

38. *B*: And at the same time, you become an old man overnight.

39. *C*: True, but then you can put your sunset memories in writing! (*This provoked another round of affectionate grins.*)

40. *A*: The three great themes, of course, are death, love, and music.

41. *C*: But you've got to make up your mind about love; you must know what it is.

42. *B*: Search for love. (*Let me remind my readers that between all these nuggets of wisdom were long sulks, silences, and moments of stillness.*)

43. *C*: Conceal love—after all, you're a writer!

44. *B*: Love is a quest.

45. *C*: Conceal love, so that you look like you have a secret.

46. *A*: If you look like you have a secret, women will fall in love with you.

47. *A*: All women are mirrors. (*Because they opened up a new bottle of* rakı *at this point, they offered me a glass.*)

48. *B*: Remember us always. (*"I'll remember you, sir, I'll remember you all, of course!" That's what I told them and, as my readers will already know, I did indeed go on to write quite a few columns about them and relate many of their stories.*)

49. *A*: Go out into the street and look at people's faces—there's another subject for you.

50. *C*: Sense the secrets of history, even though—alas!—you'll never be able to write about them. (*At this point C told us a story; the story, which I shall tell in another column, was about a man who uttered the words "I am yours" to his beloved, and it was at this moment that I first sensed the secret that brought these three writers, who had been insulting each other in print for half a century, to sit down at the same table.*)

51. *A*: Never forget, either, that the world is against us.

52. *B*: This country loves its generals, its children, and its mothers, and so must you.

53. *A*: Never use epigraphs—they kill the mystery in the work!

54. *B*: If that's how it has to die, go ahead and kill it; then kill the false prophets who sold you on the mystery in the first place!

55. *C*: If you must use epigraphs, never quote writers or heroes from Western novels who resemble us, and never *ever* quote from books you haven't read; for when doomsday is nigh and that evil creature Deccal descends upon us, these are the deceptions he'll use against us.

56. *A*: Never forget that you're a devil and an angel, you're Deccal hiding in the shadows and He who rules the heavens. Because readers quickly tire of people who are all good or all bad.

57. *B*: But if a reader discovers that he's been tricked, that it's not the Almighty standing before him but Deccal, dressed in His clothes, the reader's anger will know no bounds; he'll push you into a dark alley and beat you up!

58. *A*: Yes, that's why you have to hide your secret; sell the secret of our profession and we're all in peril!

59. *C*: Never forget that the secret is love. The key word is love.

60. *B*: No, the key word is written on our faces. Look and listen.

61. *A*: It's love, it's love, it's love. Love!

62. *B*: Don't worry about plagiarism either, because all the secrets hidden inside the paltry books we read and write—and, indeed, all the world's secrets—are hidden inside the mirror of mysticism. Do you know Rumi's story, "The Contest between the Two Painters"? He, too, borrowed the story from someone else, though he himself—(*I know the story, sir, I said.*)

63. *C*: One day, when you're older, when you ask yourself if a man can ever be himself, you'll also ask yourself if you've ever understood this secret. Don't forget! (*I haven't.*)

64. *B*: And never forget old buses, books written in haste, and those who endure—pay as much attention to those who do not understand as to those who do!

———

A song floated across the station, or perhaps from inside the restaurant, a song that spoke of love and grief and the emptiness of life; at this point they forgot me and remembered who they were: three aging mustachioed Sheherazades, three brothers, three sad friends with stories to share. Here are a few of them:

The tragicomic tale about the luckless columnist whose life's passion was to trace Muhammed's travels through the Seven Heavens, only to lose hope when he discovered that Dante had already done something similar; the story about the crazy and perverted sultan who had spent his childhood running amok with his sister, chasing crows in a vegetable patch; the story about the reader who began to believe he was both Albertine and Proust; the story of the columnist who disguised himself as Mehmet the Conqueror, et cetera, et cetera.

Chapter Nine

Someone's Following Me

Sometimes snow fell, and sometimes darkness.
—Sheikh Galip

I t was morning by the time Galip left his friend, Saim the archivist. As he made his way through the old streets of Cihangir toward the steep steps that would take him down to Karaköy, he caught a glimpse of an old armchair; this image would come back to him again and again through the day, like the last remaining detail of a nightmare. The armchair was sitting outside a shuttered shop selling wallpaper or linoleum or cabinets or plaster moldings, in one of the Tophane back streets that Celâl had come to know so well in the days when he was tracking the heroin and hashish trade. The varnish had flaked off its arms and legs, and the rusty springs that spilled out of a great gash in the leather seat called to mind the green intestines of a cavalry horse felled in battle.

Reaching Karaköy and finding it as empty as the lonely alley in which he'd seen the armchair (though it was already past eight o'clock), Galip began to wonder if something was wrong, some catastrophe for which everyone else in the city had read the signs. The ferries that should have been plowing down the Bosphorus by then were still tied to each other on the piers; the landing stations were deserted; the street peddlers, flash photographers, and disfigured beggars—who would normally have been working on the Galata Bridge—seemed to have decided to spend their last days on earth relaxing at home. Leaning over the bridge's railings and gazing into the murky waters below, Galip remembered how, once upon a time, swarms of children had dived from this end of the bridge to retrieve the coins Christian tourists threw into the Golden Horn, and he asked himself why it was that Celâl had not mentioned these coins in his column about the Bosphorus drying up—for in future years, wouldn't they point to other hidden meanings?

Arriving at his office, he sat down at his desk to read Celâl's latest column. It was not, in fact, a new column, but a reprint of something he'd first published years earlier. While this was a clear sign that Celâl had stopped filing new material some time ago, it could also be a secret sign indicating something utterly different. The question at the heart of the column was "Do you have a hard time being yourself?" and it seemed to Galip as if the barber to whom Celâl gave this line might have voiced it for reasons other than those stated in the story; his true aim may have been to point to other secret meanings in the outside world.

Galip remembered how Celâl had once spoken to him on this very subject. "Most people," Celâl had told him, "fail to see the inner essence of the things around them, simply because these things are right under their noses, while they pay great attention to the secondary properties of things that seem just beyond them, simply because they find them in dark corners, on the edge of things, and therefore think them more obscure. This is why I never make open references to my true purpose in my columns. I mention it only in passing—hide it in a corner, as it were. But never in a particularly dark or secret corner; it's a game of hide-and-seek that any child could play. Whatever my readers happen to find in that corner they believe instantly—which is, after all, my ultimate aim. And this is the worst part: They pay no attention to the overt content of the piece, the things that are right under their noses; they ignore even the secret and accidental riddles it would take them only a little patience, an ounce of intellect, to solve—and as for the newspaper itself, it ends up gathering dust in a corner of its own."

Galip was suddenly gripped by a desire to throw his own paper into a corner; having done so, he set off to the offices of *Milliyet* to see Celâl. He knew Celâl tended to go there on the weekends, when no one was there; with a bit of luck, he'd catch him alone in his office. On his way down the alley, he decided he would just tell Celâl that Rüya was a little out of sorts, nothing more. Then he'd tell him a story about a dis-traught client whose wife had left him. How, he wondered, would Celâl respond to such a story? An industrious, successful, clear-thinking, even-tempered, good-hearted citizen, whose beloved wife, paying no heed to our history and the traditions that bind us to our past, had suddenly and inexplicably abandoned him. What signs could such a story harbor? What hidden meanings? What signs of the impending doomsday? After he had listened carefully to every detail of Galip's story, Celâl would tell him, and as Celâl spoke the world would begin to make sense again; those "secret" but self-evident truths would find their way into a beautiful story that we already knew, even if we hardly knew we knew; consoled by this story, life would be easier to bear. As Galip gazed up at the branches of the wet trees in the garden of the Iranian consulate, he thought how much better it would be if he could leave this world behind forever and live in Celâl's world instead.

Celâl was not in his office. His desk was tidy, the ashtray was empty, and there were no teacups. Galip went over to the purple armchair, as he always did when he came here, and sat down to wait. After a short while he was sure he could hear laughter coming from somewhere down the corridor.

As his certainty faded, memories came flooding in. He recalled his first ever trip to the paper, with a classmate who would later fall in love with Rüya; they'd pretended to be after tickets for a radio quiz show; he'd not told his family. ("He would have given us a tour of the office, if only he'd had the time," an embarrassed Galip had told his friend on the way home. His friend had replied, "Did you see all those photographs of women he had on his desk?") He recalled his first trip here with Rüya; this time Celâl had found the time to give them a tour of the office ("And do you hope to become a journalist when you grow up, young lady?" the old printer asked Rüya, and Rüya had asked Galip the same question on their way home); he remembered how, once upon a time, this room had been his *Thousand and One Nights*, shimmering with stories, piled high with paper dreams. . . .

Galip rummaged through Celâl's desk, perhaps to find new stories or perhaps to forget, to forget . . . and this was what he found: unopened readers' letters, pencils, and newspaper clippings (including an old story, marked in green ink, about a jealous husband who killed his wife); pictures of people cut from foreign magazines, portraits, various notes in Celâl's handwriting (don't forget: the story of the Crown

Prince), empty ink bottles, matches, an ugly tie; badly written popular books on shamanism, Hurufism, and how to improve your memory; a bottle of sleeping pills, some vasodilating medication, a few buttons, a wristwatch that was no longer running, a pair of scissors; photographs from a reader's letter that someone had opened (one showing Celâl with a bald army officer, another a pair of oiled wrestlers and a friendly sheepdog smiling into the camera outside a rustic coffeehouse); colored pencils, combs, cigarette ends, and ballpoint pens of every color.

Tucked under the blotter he found two folders, one marked USED and the other marked RESERVE. In the USED folder Galip found the typescripts of Celâl's last six columns, along with a piece for the Sunday paper that had not yet been published. Galip guessed it was here in this folder because it had already been set and illustrated for tomorrow's paper.

There were only three pieces in the RESERVE folder. All three were published pieces from years ago. If a fourth column was sitting on the typesetter's table on the ground floor, being laid out for Monday's paper, and Galip's guess was that it almost certainly was, the pieces in the RESERVE folder would last the paper through Thursday. Could he take this to mean that Celâl had gone off on a trip or a holiday without letting anyone know? But Celâl never set foot outside Istanbul.

Galip went into the big editorial room to ask after Celâl, and his legs took him to a table where two men way past their prime were having a chat. One of them, an irascible old man whom everyone knew by his pen name, Neşati, had been writing violent pieces against Celâl for years. Now they were both at the same paper, for which he wrote a column much less important and less widely read than Celâl's, in which he reminisced about the old days with a furious righteousness.

"Celâl Bey hasn't been in for days!" he said. His face was just like the picture in his column, as sullen as a bulldog. "What's your relation to him?"

When the second journalist asked him what he'd come to ask Celâl, Galip rummaged through his disordered mind, trying to remember who this man was. Yes, he had it now; he'd seen his picture in the paper too—dark glasses, nobody's fool—the Sherlock Holmes of the magazine section; he could tell you which of the film stars now flouncing around like Ottoman ladies had worked in the deluxe brothel run by a certain Beyoğlu madam, and when and for how long; as for the *vedette chanteuse* who had worked as an acrobat in French provincial towns before coming to Istanbul to pose as an Argentinian aristocrat, she was in actual fact a Muslim woman from Algiers.

"In other words, you're a relative," said the magazine writer. "It was my understanding that Celâl Bey had no relatives except for his late mother."

"Ooooh," said the polemicist. "How would Celâl have gotten where he is today if he had no relatives? He had a brother-in-law who helped him enormously, for example: a deeply religious man who taught him how to write, only to see Celâl betray him. He belonged to a Nakşi sect that still practiced its secret rites in an old soap factory in Kumkapı. After they performed their rites—these involved various chains, olive presses, candles, and soap molds—he'd sit down and write up a report about the lodge's activities for our national intelligence agency. This man was hoping he could convince the army that the men he was informing on were not, in fact, doing anything against the government. He showed his reports to his literary brother-in-law, Celâl, hoping he might read them and learn something, acquire a taste for good prose. Later on, when the winds of politics were blowing to the left and Celâl bent his views to suit the new mood, he aped the style of these reports mercilessly, lifting metaphors and similes taken straight from translations of Attar, Ebu Horasani, İbn' Arabi, and Bottfolio. Of course, some see Celâl's similes—though they are all made of the same hackneyed stuff—as serving as a bridge between tradition and modernity, but how would they know that these pastiches are in actual fact the creations of someone else altogether? This brother-in-law Celâl would rather forget was a man of many talents: He invented a pair of mirrored scissors to make barbers' lives easier, developed a circumcision device that helped avoid the grave mistakes that have blackened the futures of so many of our children, and invented a gallows in which oiled rope replaced the traditional chains and a sliding platform replaced the traditional chair, allowing a man to be hanged without causing him any pain. During the years when he still felt he needed the affection of his beloved sister and her husband, Celâl presented these inventions in his BELIEVE IT OR NOT column."

"I beg your pardon, but you've got it all wrong!" cried the magazine writer. "In the years when he was doing his BELIEVE IT OR NOT column, Celâl Bey was utterly alone. Let me tell you a story. It's not secondhand, this is something I saw personally, with my own two eyes."

The story came straight out of one of those old Yeşilçam melodramas: two impatient youths fighting their way out of poverty and destined for success. The time: New Year's Eve. The place: a ramshackle house in a ramshackle neighborhood. Celâl the starry-eyed young journalist tells his mother that he has been invited to join the festivities at the home of their rich relations in Nişantaşı. There he will enjoy a fun-packed evening with his aunts and uncles, their spirited daughters and naughty sons, after which, who knows? He may move on to enjoy other pleasures in the city. At which point his seamstress mother, who wishes only for her son's happiness, tells him she has a surprise for him; knowing he had nothing to wear to this great occasion, she has quietly taken in his father's old jacket. Celâl tries it on: it fits him perfectly. (The scene brings tears to the mother's eyes: "You look just like your father!") Hearing that a journalist friend has also been invited to the festivities, the mother relaxes into a happy smile. This journalist is the same man who witnessed this story personally, with his own eyes, and as he walks with Celâl down the cold dark stairs of his wooden house and steps into the street, he discovers that no rich relatives have invited poor Celâl to their New Year's festivities, and no one else has, either. No, Celâl must head straight back to the paper, where he is working the night shift to pay for an operation for his mother, who has been sewing in candlelight and is slowly going blind.

When Galip broke the silence that followed this sad tale to explain how unlikely this was, given the known facts about Celâl's life, the two old journalists were not unduly concerned. Yes, of course, he could have more close relatives than they'd realized, and the dates could be wrong too; if it was true that Celâl Bey's father was still alive (Are you sure of this, my boy?), it's just possible that they'd confused him with the grandmother, and the sister with the aunt, but they made it clear that they considered these inaccuracies to be of little importance. They invited Galip to sit down with them, offered him a cigarette, and after repeating the question they'd asked him earlier (Exactly how did you say you were related to him?) they began to reminisce, plucking out memories at random and then setting them down carefully on their imaginary chessboard.

Celâl's affection for his family knew no bounds, for in the days when it was forbidden to write about anything except municipal matters, he'd write long lyrical columns about the great mansion in which he had spent his childhood, recalling that every window looked out onto a different linden tree and mystifying his censors as much as he did his readers.

Celâl was so nervous about any sort of social intercourse outside journalism that whenever he had to attend a large gathering he made sure to take along a friend whose words, gestures, clothes, and table manners he knew he could imitate.

Nonsense! Here we have a young journalist who, in three short years, went from writing crossword puzzles and advice columns for women to writing a column that was not just the most widely read in Turkey but in the Balkans and the Middle East; was it not self-evident that this could never have happened—and neither could Celâl have insulted everyone of consequence in the country, from left to right— had he not enjoyed the unrequited love and undeserved protection of relations with friends in high places?

Then there was the story about the birthday party and the forward-looking statesman who, hoping to convince his countrymen to take up this charming tradition—which was, as everyone knew, a cornerstone of Western civilization—had taken it upon himself to invite a number of journalists to his eight-year-old son's birthday party, whereupon the boy, surrounded by his friends, blew out all eight candles on a strawberry cream cake while a Levantine dowager played on the piano; if Celâl made cruel pigheaded fun of the party in his column, it was not for ideological, political, or aesthetic reasons, as most people thought, but because he was only too painfully aware that he'd never known a loving father, never really known love.

Now, if no one could find him, if all the addresses he'd given out were wrong or false, this stemmed from the strange and incomprehensible hatred he felt for these close relations, whose love he could not return, though it also reflected the contempt he felt for his distant relations and indeed all human beings. (Galip had asked them where he might find Celâl.)

No, that wasn't why he had hidden himself in some unknown corner of the city and cut himself off from all humanity; the reason was
utterly different. He'd finally accepted that this disease that afflicted
him, this curse he'd worn like an unlucky halo since the day of his
birth, this relentless sense of isolation, was, in fact, incurable; so he'd
shut himself up in a room in the middle of nowhere like the hopeless
invalid he was, there to embrace his incurable loneliness with open
arms.

Galip mentioned that there was a European film crew hoping to
coax him out of his hiding place.

"In any case," said Neşati the polemicist, "Celâl Bey is about to be
fired! He hasn't sent in a new column for ten days now. Everyone
knows that the ones he's left as reserves are columns he wrote twenty
years ago; all he's done is correct the mistakes!"

The magazine writer objected, just as Galip had hoped and
expected. His columns were arousing greater interest than ever before,
his phone was ringing constantly, there were at least twenty letters for
Celâl in the post every day.

"True," said the polemicist, "but they're all propositions from prostitutes, pimps, terrorists, hedonists, drug dealers, and old gangsters he's
praised in past columns."

"So you're reading them on the sly, are you?" asked the magazine
writer.

"You do too!" the polemicist replied.

They both straightened their chairs like chess players pleased with
their opening moves. The polemicist reached into his pocket and
pulled out a small box. Staring as intently as a magician about to make
an object disappear, he offered the box to Galip. "The only thing I
have in common now with this man you say is your relation are these
stomach pills. They cut stomach acid instantly. Would you like to try
one?"

Galip had no idea what game these men were playing, or how long
it had been going on, or where it was heading, but because he wanted
to join in, he accepted one of the white pills and chewed it obediently.

"Are you enjoying our game?" the old columnist asked with a smile.

"I'm trying to work out what the rules are," Galip replied dubiously.

"Do you read my column?"

"I do."

"When you pick up the paper, whose column do you read first, Celâl's or mine?"

"Celâl Bey is my relative."

"Is that the only reason you read him first?" asked the old writer. "What draws you in, the blood tie or the beauty of the prose?"

"Celâl might be a relative, but his prose is beautiful too!" said Galip.

"Anyone could write those things, can't you see that?" said the old columnist. "Anyway, many of them are far too long to qualify as columns. They're ersatz stories. Artistic nonsense. Empty words. A few commonplace tricks, that's all. A cloying parade of honeyed reminiscences. Can't go for two lines without seizing on a paradox. Or an irony—the sort the Divan poets called *erudite ignorance*. Makes things that really happened look as if they never did, and things that didn't happen look as if they did. And if all else fails, he hides the empty shell that is his talent by dazzling his readers with those overblown sentences they mistake for good prose. He has the same sort of life, the same sort of past, the same sort of memories as everyone else. Including you. Tell me a story!"

"What sort of story?"

"Whatever comes into your mind. Any story will do."

"There was a man who came home one day to find his beautiful wife had left him," Galip said. "And so he went to look for her. Wherever he went in the city, he found traces of her, but still he couldn't find her . . ."

"And then?"

"That's all."

"No, no, there must be more to it!" said the old writer. "What does this man see in these clues his wife has left in her wake? Was she really beautiful? Into whose arms did she run?"

"When he looks at these clues, this man sees his own past, the past he shared with his beautiful wife. He doesn't know who she's run off with, or else he doesn't want to know, because wherever he goes, whenever he stumbles onto another clue that talks to him of the past he shared with his wife, he can't help thinking that the man she's run off with, and the place where she's hiding, reside somewhere in his past."

"Excellent idea," said the old columnist. "Just as Poe advised, stick with dead or lost women! But a good storyteller has to be more decisive. Readers don't trust writers who can't make up their minds. Let's end this story with a few of Celâl's tricks. . . . First, the memory trick: Adorn your stories with bittersweet recollections of a man-about-town. Style: Adorn your memories in pretentious language, adding clues that point to the void. *Erudite ignorance*: the man should pretend he cannot figure out the identity of the man who's spirited off his wife. Paradox: Therefore the man who spirited off his wife is none other than himself. But how could this be? Do you see what I mean? You could write like this. Anyone could write like this."

"But only Celâl writes like this," said Galip.

"Point taken! But from now on, you can too!" cried the old columnist, in an emphatic voice to indicate that this was his last word on the subject.

"If you want to find him, study his columns," said the magazine writer. "He's hiding somewhere inside them, that's for sure. He's always using his column to send messages to people, all sorts of people—small private messages. You catch my drift, don't you?"

By way of a reply, Galip told them how, when he was a child, Celâl had shown him how the first and last words of every paragraph in his columns combined to form a sentence. He'd also shown Galip the letter games he'd used to get past the censors and the press prosecutor, the chains he'd constructed from the first and last syllables of every sentence, the sentences he'd constructed from all the capital letters, and the word games he'd invented to "anger our aunt."

The magazine writer asked, "Is your aunt an old maid?"

"She never married," Galip replied.

Had Celâl Bey and his father stopped speaking after an argument about an apartment?

That, Galip told them, was water under the bridge.

Was it true he had a lawyer uncle who'd confused his court records, writs, and statute books with restaurant menus and ferryboat schedules?

According to Galip, this was probably just another story, like all the rest.

"Don't you see, young man?" the old writer said peevishly. "Our friend here didn't get these stories straight from Celâl. No, he got them by playing detective, using all the tricks he picked up from the Hurufis, scouring Celâl's columns for hidden letters and picking them up one by one, like a man digging out a well with a pin."

The magazine writer said that perhaps these word games carried meaning, giving voice to the great mystery, and that it was Celâl's deep intimations of that mystery that elevated him to heights other writers would never reach, though he still felt compelled to remind him of the truth in the homily: "Journalists who take themselves too seriously can look forward to funerals paid for either by donation or by the city council."

"Another possibility: He could—God forbid—be dead," said the old journalist. "Are you enjoying our game?"

"That story about him losing his memory, is it true or just a story?" asked the magazine writer.

"It's true, and it's also a story!" said Galip.

"And those houses of his, those addresses he kept secret?"

"The same goes for those."

"Maybe he's lying in one of those houses at this very moment, breathing his last breath," said the columnist. "You know, it's just the sort of guessing game he always loved."

"If that's what's going on, he would have summoned someone to whom he felt very close," said the magazine writer.

"There's no such person," said the columnist. "He doesn't feel close to anyone."

"Our young friend here seems to think differently," said the magazine writer. "You haven't even told us your name."

Galip told them his name.

"So then tell us, Galip Bey," said the magazine writer. "If Celâl Bey has gone into hiding in some hole-in-the-wall to weather some sort of crisis, there'd be someone there at his side, wouldn't there? Someone he felt close to, someone to whom he could pass on his literary secrets, his will and testament. After all, he wasn't as much of a loner as some people like to think."

Galip thought for a while. "No," he said apprehensively. "He wasn't as much of a loner as people thought."

"So who was it he called to his side?" asked the magazine writer. "Was it you?"

"It was his sister," said Galip, without thinking. "He had a stepsister twenty years younger. She was the one he called to his side." He paused to think. He remembered the armchair with the gashed seat and the rusty springs spilling out. Then he thought some more.

"It seems you are beginning to grasp the logic of our game," said the old columnist. "Now that you're getting results, you're getting a taste for it yourself. So let me be frank with you: All Hurufis come to a bad end. Fazlallah of Astarabad, the founder of Hurufism, was killed like a dog; they tied a rope around his feet and dragged his body through the market. Did you know that he first made his name—six hundred years ago—analyzing dreams, just like Celâl Bey? Not for a newspaper, though; he practiced his art outside the city, in a cave."

"If you are trying to understand someone, are such comparisons of any use at all? Can they penetrate a life's great secrets?" asked the magazine writer. "For thirty years now, I've been trying to penetrate the unseemly secrets of those sad local artists we insist on calling *stars*—as if copying the Americans ever did us any good. What I've learned is this: Those who say that people come in pairs are wrong. No two people are alike. Every one of our poor girls is poor in her own way. Each of our stars is alone in the sky, a destitute starlet like no other."

"The original Hollywood model excepted," said the old columnist. "Have I already mentioned the originals Celâl Bey draws his ideas from? Let me add another name to the list. He has stolen things not only from Dante, Dostoyevsky, and Rumi but also from Sheikh Galip."

"Each life is unique!" cried the magazine writer. "A story is a story only when it has no equal. Every writer is poor and all alone."

"I must disagree!" said the old columnist. "Let's begin with that piece so many people call a classic: 'When the Bosphorus Dries Up.' The signs of the apocalypse—aren't they all lifted from the Koran's verses on the Day of Judgment and from Ibn Khaldun and Ebu Horasani? All describe the days of destruction that will precede the arrival of the Messiah; Celâl Bey does the same by plundering their words. To this he adds a vulgar tale about a gangster. It has no artistic merit whatsoever. But that's not why a certain small band of fanatics found it so exciting, and neither does it explain why hysterical women made hundreds of phone calls that day. Inside the letters are secret messages—not for the likes of you and me but for the dervish disciples who have in their hands the wherewithal to crack the codes. These disciples are all over the country; half are prostitutes and the rest are pederasts. They take these messages as sacred orders and consider it their duty to call the paper day and night to insist that we do not punish their beloved sheikh, Celâl Bey, for writing such nonsense by showing him the door. Not to mention that there are always one or two people waiting for him outside the building. So how are we to be sure you're not one of them, Galip Bey?"

"Because we took a liking to this Galip Bey!" said the magazine writer. "We saw in him something of the young men we once were. We warmed to him—enough to tell him all these secrets. So this is how we know what's what. As the once-famous film star Samiye Samim said in the rest home where she spent her last days—the disease we call jealousy—What's wrong, young man, you aren't leaving, are you?"

"Galip Bey, if you must leave, my son, you must first answer this question!" said the old columnist. "Why is it that these English television people want to speak to Celâl and not me?"

"Because he's a better writer than you are," said Galip. He left the table for the silent corridors that led to the stairs. From behind him came the booming and still cheerful voice of the old columnist.

"Did you really think that pill you swallowed was an antacid?"

When he reached the street, Galip looked carefully around him. On the pavement opposite—the same corner where a group of youths from a religious high school had once burned a newspaper containing a column in which Celâl had, in their view, made a slur against religion—Galip saw a bald man loitering next to the man selling oranges. But there seemed to be no one waiting for Celâl. He crossed the street and bought himself an orange. As he peeled the orange, he began to feel as if he were being followed. As he made his way back to his office in Cağaloğlu, he tried in vain to figure out why what had happened at that moment made him think so; as he ambled slowly down the alley, gazing at the books in the shop windows, he wondered, too, what had made him so sure. All he knew was that he could almost feel something on the back of his neck—an "eye"—that's the only way he could put it.

When, slowing down as usual for one particular window, he saw another very particular pair of eyes gazing out at him, he was as happy as if he'd run into a close friend and understood, for the first time, how very dear he was. This was a publishing firm that specialized in the-detective novels that Rüya read so avidly. Perched as always above the books in the tiny display window was the treacherous owl he'd seen on so many book covers, training its patient gaze on Galip and the Saturday-morning crowds. Galip went into the store and picked up three books from their backlist that he thought Rüya hadn't read yet, along with a copy of their latest offering, *Women, Love, and Whiskey*. As he was waiting for the assistant to wrap them up, he saw a poster tacked to the upper shelves that said, "NO OTHER TURKISH SERIES HAS EVER REACHED ITS 126TH VOLUME. WHEN IT COMES TO THE QUALITY OF OUR DETECTIVE FICTION, THE QUANTITY IS THE GUARANTEE." There was also a LITERARY ROMANCE series and an OWL series of comic novels; so Galip took a chance and asked for a book on Hurufism. There was a coarse-looking old man sitting in the chair next to the door, positioned so he could see the pale youth behind the counter and the crowds passing by on the muddy street outside; his answer was the one Galip had expected.

"We don't have one. Try İsmail the Miser, he might have the thing you're looking for!" Then he added, "Did you know that Crown Prince Osman Celâlettin Efendi, who was himself a Hurufi, translated detective novels from French into Turkish? The typescripts passed into my hands once. Do you know how he was murdered?"

When he left the shop, Galip examined both pavements carefully but saw nothing to interest him: a woman wearing a head scarf and a boy wearing a coat that was far too big for him peering into the window of a sandwich shop, two schoolgirls wearing identical green socks, an old man in a brown coat waiting to cross the street. But as he set off for his office, he could feel that eye again, gazing down at him.

Because he had never been followed before, because he'd never even felt he was being followed, everything Galip knew on the subject came from the movies he'd seen and Rüya's detective novels. Although he'd only read a few of these novels, Galip was always taking them apart. One day, he'd say, he was going to write a novel in which the first and last chapters were identical, or a story that seemed to have no ending because the true ending was hidden inside it; or perhaps he'd write a novel in which all the characters were blind. As he went from one fantastic idea to the next and Rüya rolled her eyes, Galip also dreamed that one day he could become someone else.

Sitting in the alcove next to Galip's office was a legless beggar who now also seemed to be blind in both eyes; this was when Galip decided that this nightmare that had engulfed him was as much due to sleeplessness as it was to Rüya's disappearance. When he walked into his office, he went straight to the window, opened it, and looked down at the street. After studying it carefully, he sat down at his desk; he watched his hand reach for the folder next to the telephone. He took out a sheet of clean paper. Without pausing to think, he wrote:

Places where I might find Rüya. Her ex-husband's house. My aunt and uncle's. Banu's. A safe house. A house that political fugitives sometimes use as a safe house. A house where people do nothing but talk about poetry. A house where people talk about everything under the sun. Another house in Nişantaşı. Any house at all.

Deciding that he could not think and write at the same time, he put down his pen. When he picked his pen up again, he crossed out everything except *Her ex-husband's house* and then wrote:

Places where I might find Rüya with Celâl. Rüya with Celâl in one of Celâl's houses. Rüya with Celâl in a hotel room. Rüya with Celâl, going to the movies. Rüya with Celâl? Rüya with Celâl?

Writing all this down on paper made him feel like the hero in one of those detective novels he'd dreamed of writing; it was like standing on the threshold of a new world that reminded him of Rüya, a world where he could become someone else. A world, he felt, where he could be followed but still feel at peace. If you thought you were being followed, at least you had to convince yourself that you were the sort of person who could sit down at a desk and set down all the leads that might take you to a missing person. Galip knew he bore no resemblance to the hero of a detective novel, but the pretense soothed him; the thought that he could "become" that sort of person made it just a bit easier to sit there in his cluttered office, lost inside the tangled web that was his life. By the time a boy who had parted his hair with shocking precision arrived with the food he'd ordered from a nearby restaurant, the leads Galip had jotted down on that blank piece of paper had drawn him so deeply into that other persona that it was no longer a plate of lamb with rice and carrot salad sitting on the dirty tray in front of him, but a strange dish he was seeing for the very first time.

The phone rang while he was still eating, and he answered it promptly, as if he'd been waiting for a call. Wrong number. After he'd finished eating and put the tray to one side, he rang his house in Nişantaşı in the same businesslike way. While the phone rang and rang, he conjured up an image of Rüya—she'd come home tired and gone straight to bed; she was struggling to her feet at this very moment— but when no one answered, he was not at all surprised. He dialed Aunt Hâle's number.

He knew she'd be bursting with questions—Was Rüya still ill? Why didn't she answer the phone or even come to the door? Didn't she know how worried they all were?—so he knew he had to say everything in one breath: Their phone was out of order, which was why they hadn't called; Rüya's fever had burned itself out; she was back on her feet again, looking so healthy you'd never know she'd been ill; she was now happily ensconced in the back of a taxi, a '56 Chevrolet, bundled up in her purple coat and waiting for Galip; they were off to Izmir, to see an old friend who was seriously ill; the ship was about to leave, Galip had stopped at a grocery store along the way to make this call; he thanked the grocer for letting him use the phone when there were so many people waiting to be served, so goodbye then! But that didn't stop Aunt Hâle from asking questions: Were they sure they'd shut the door properly on their way out? Had Rüya remembered to pack her green wool pullover?

When Saim rang, Galip was asking himself how much a person could change himself just by looking at a map of a city in which he'd never set foot. Saim had continued going through his archives after Galip had left, and he was calling to tell him he'd found a few more promising leads: Mehmet Yılmaz, the man responsible for the old lady's death—yes, it was true he could still be alive, but he was no longer going under the names of Ahmet Kaçer or Haldun Kara as they'd previously thought; his new alias was Muammer Ergener, which didn't even sound like an alias, and he was wandering around the city like a ghost. Saim had not been surprised to come across this name in a periodical famous for always seeing everything "from the viewpoint of the opposition"; what had shocked him was to find another piece in the same issue, written under the name of Salih Gölbaşı but containing the same style and the same spelling mistakes, sharply criticizing two of Celâl's columns. After realizing that Salih Gölbaşı rhymed with Rüya's ex-husband's name and shared the same consonants, Saim was further amazed, when leafing through a back issue of an educational journal called *The Hour of Labor*, to find Salih Gölbaşı listed as its editor in chief; and now Saim was calling him to give him the address. The journal's main offices were outside the city, in the Güntepe development: 13 Refet Bey Street, Sinanpaşa, Bakırköy.

After putting down the phone, Galip opened up the city directory to locate the Güntepe development. He was astounded, though not swept off his feet in the way he longed to be. This was the location of the shantytown where Rüya and her first husband had moved just after getting married, so that her husband could do a study on their worker neighbors; the shantytown had now disappeared to make way for this new development that covered the entire hill, and according to the map, each street in this new neighborhood was named after a hero from the War of Independence. In the far corner of the map there was what he took to be a park: a small green square decorated with a minaret and a statue of Atatürk. If Galip spent the rest of his life inventing new countries, this would be the last to enter his mind.

After he'd phoned the paper again, to be told that Celâl had still not arrived, Galip rang İskender. He told him he'd managed to track down Celâl and told him that there was an English film crew that wanted to interview him; Celâl had not exactly objected to the idea but had said he was very busy right now; as he said all this, he could hear a little girl crying in the background. İskender told him that the film crew was going to be in Istanbul for another six days. They'd heard such good things about Celâl he was sure they'd be willing to wait; if Galip wished he could contact them directly at the Pera Palas Hotel.

He locked up his office, leaving his lunch tray in front of the door, and as he walked down the alley he noticed that the sky had gone pale in a way he'd never seen before. He imagined snowflakes falling from the sky that were the color of charcoal: but if it did, this Saturday crowd would not even notice. Or perhaps they feared it too; perhaps this was why they all kept their eyes on the muddy pavements instead. He felt the calming influence of the detective novels he was carrying under his arm. Though they came from an enchanted and faraway land, though they'd been translated into "our mother tongue" by unhappy housewives who felt guilty about never completing the educations they'd begun at the city's foreign lycées, they still brought solace to us all, Galip thought; it was thanks to them that the city could go about its business as usual, that the men in pale suits standing outside office buildings selling lighter fluid, that the ragged colorless hunchbacks next to them and the silent travelers in the *dolmuş* line could carry on breathing.

He boarded a bus at Eminönü and took it as far as Harbiye; as he was stepping off the bus, he noticed a crowd in front of the Palace Theater. It was the sort of crowd you'd expect for the 2:45 showing on a Saturday afternoon. Twenty-five years ago, Galip and Rüya used to come to this matinee with groups of classmates; they'd stood in this same crowd of pimply children in raincoats, rushed down those same sawdust-covered stairs, and as they'd waited among the posters for coming attractions, each illuminated by its own little lights, Galip would quietly, patiently, wait to see who Rüya spoke to. The earlier showing would still not have ended; it seemed as if it would never end: The doors would never open, he would never sit next to Rüya, and the lights would never dim. When he found out there were still seats left for the 2:45 showing, Galip felt a rush of freedom. Inside the auditorium the air was still hot and airless and smelled of old breath. As the lights dimmed and the advertisements came on, Galip realized he was about to fall asleep.

When he awoke, he sat up straight in his seat. On the screen was a beautiful woman, an unspeakably beautiful woman, and she was as troubled as she was beautiful. Then he saw a wide calm river, then a farmhouse, and beyond it an American farm. Then the troubled beauty began to speak with a middle-aged man Galip did not think he had ever seen on screen before. Galip could tell from their faces and the way they moved across the screen—as slugglishly, as peacefully as they spoke—that their lives were full of woe. He was not just guessing, he *knew*. Life was an endless string of miseries; if one came to an end there was another waiting around the corner, and if that misfortune became easier to bear, the next would strike harder, leaving creases on our faces that made us all look alike. Even if misfortune came suddenly, we knew it had been there all along, lying in wait on the road in front of us, so we were always ready for it; when the new cloud of trouble descended on us we felt alone, hopelessly alone, inescapably alone; but still we dreamed of the happiness we might find if only we could find other people willing to share our misery. For a moment Galip convinced himself that the sorrows of the woman on the screen were the same as his own, or perhaps it wasn't a sorrow they shared but a world: an orderly world that promised little but never turned you away, where there was a clear line between meaning and meaninglessness, a world in which humility was a virtue. Later on in the film, as the woman drew water from a well, drove around in an old Ford pickup, cuddled a child in her arms, and talked to her fondly as she carried her to bed, Galip felt as close as if he were there in the room with her. It was not her beauty or her natural grace that made him want to embrace her, but the deep belief that they lived in the same world: by taking her into his arms, he would make this slim dark-haired woman believe the same. Galip felt as if he were the only one watching the film, the only one to see this scene unfurl before his eyes. Later on, when a fight broke out in a sun-baked town that had a wide highway running through it, and a strong, passionate, he-man type stepped in to take matters in hand, Galip realized that his understanding with this woman was coming to an end. He read the subtitles word by word; everyone in the theater seemed to be fidgeting. He got up to leave. Outside, the sky had already darkened; he headed home through thickly falling snow.

It was only later, while resting on top of the blue-checked quilt, wafting in and out of sleep, that he realized he'd left Rüya's detective novels in the movie theater.

Chapter Ten

The Eye

He then went through a highly productive phase, during which
his daily output was never less than five pages.
— Abdurrahman Şeref

I t was on a winter's night that I first saw it. I was going through one
of my dark phases: Though I no longer had to struggle as I'd done
during my first and most difficult years of journalism, my trials and
tribulations had left their scars, and I'd lost some of the fire I'd once
felt for my profession. On cold winter evenings, even as I reminded
myself that I was "still standing, and that's all that matters," I knew I
was talking to an empty shell. That was the winter I began to suffer
from insomnia, an affliction that dogs me to this day; the night clerk
and I would often stay at the newspaper until late at night as I struggled
to compose the columns that might have been beyond me had I waited
until the crowded chaos of morning. There was at that time a fad in
European newspapers and magazines for BELIEVE IT OR NOT columns,
and these were perfectly suited to my nocturnal habits. I'd pick up one
of the many European magazines I'd gathered together and study the
illustrations in these columns (I've never seen the need to learn a single
foreign language; it would, I'm sure, only serve to stunt my imagination); with time my eyes would light on something that would send me
into what some might call an artistic reverie, and it was then that I
would pick up my pen.

The incident I am about to describe befell me on a winter's night.
I'd been leafing through a French magazine—*L'Illustration*—when I
happened onto the picture of a grotesque monster; one of its eyes was
high on its face, the other far below. I'd hardly given it a glance before I

began to compose a small essay on the Cyclops, tracing its trajectory through the ages, from the monsters who terrified young girls in *Dede Korkut*, to the heinous creature of Homeric epics, to Deccal himself in al-Bukhari's *Lives of the Prophets* and the fiends who invade the vizier's harems in *The Thousand and One Nights*, to the apparition in the purple dress that Dante met before finding his (and my) beloved Beatrice, to the wretch that waylayed caravans in Rumi and took on the form of an African woman in *Vathek*, William Beckford's novel, of which I am so fond; I then offered my own thoughts on the secrets that might lurk behind an eye swimming alone in the center of a forehead, as dark and as deep as a well, briefly suggesting what such an eye might resemble, why it made our hair stand on end, and why we were right to fear and avoid it. By now I was so carried away that my pen could not help but add two small cautionary tales to my little monograph. There was, I wrote, a Cyclops rumored to dwell in one of the poor neighborhoods that skirt the Golden Horn, who waded every night through its muddy, oily, turgid waters, finally to reach the godforsaken lair inhabited by his twin; I went on to say that there were those who said the two Cyclopes were one and the same. There were even those who said he had noble blood running in his veins; the gentlemanly Cyclops—some even called him a count—had a taste for deluxe Pera brothels; when midnight struck, he'd remove his fur hat, and all around him girls would swoon with fear.

Knowing that my illustrator was also likely to swoon—with pleasure—when he read these lines, I jotted off a quick note to him (*no mustaches, please!*) and left the building; although it was just past midnight, I was not yet ready to return to my cold and empty home, deciding instead to walk the streets of old Istanbul. As always, I felt myself lacking, though I was pleased with my writing and the stories I'd invented. If I celebrated my small victory with a long walk, if I thought of nothing else from start to finish, I would, I hope, escape the melancholy that pulsed through my veins like an incurable disease, if only for a few short hours.

I kept to the back streets; they curved and crossed over one another at angles that seemed to defy the laws of nature, and each seemed darker and narrower than the last. Hemmed in by dark houses with crooked balconies that seemed to be collapsing into each other before my very eyes, and watched over by their black and impenetrable windows, I could hear nothing other than the sound of my own footsteps. On and on I walked, through forgotten streets forsaken even by the city's ghosts and addicts, its sleep-starved watchmen and its barking dogs.

When I first became aware there was an eye gazing down on me, I was not unduly concerned. It must be an illusion, I told myself—an echo of the phantom I'd just sketched in my column—for there was nothing ogling me from the crooked side window of these houses lurching over me, no eye hovering in the darkness of these empty lots. This watchful presence was a figment of my imagination, and I did not wish to give it importance. But as I walked on through these streets where the silence is never broken but for the watchman's whistle and the howls of fighting dogs in distant neighborhoods, this imaginary eye kept bearing down on me with ever greater force: I knew I could not escape its stifling and oppressive gaze simply by pretending that it wasn't there.

This all-knowing, all-seeing eye was gazing down at me now without even trying to conceal itself! But no, it bore no relation to the creatures I'd depicted in my stories. There was nothing frightening, ugly, or comical about this eye; nor was it alien or cold; there was something— yes—something rather familiar about it: The eye knew me, and I knew the eye. What's more, we'd known each other for quite some time, but to acknowledge each other this openly we first had to share that midnight hour in the street where I first sensed the phantom eye hanging over me.

I shall refrain from naming the street in question, for it will mean nothing to readers who do not know Istanbul well; suffice it to say that it is is located in the hills above the Golden Horn. Imagine a street lined with the dark wooden houses I can still see standing here and there, thirty years after the "metaphysical experience" I have just described; imagine the shadows these dark houses throw onto the cobblestones and the crooked branches that block the pale light of the streetlamps—that is all you need! The pavements were narrow and filthy. The wall enclosing the small neighborhood mosque stretched into a darkness that knew no end. It was there, in that darkness, at that point just before the wall and the street—and perspective—disappeared, that this absurd (would any other word do?) eye awaited me. By then we understood each other, I would say: Its intentions were not evil; it had not come to, say, scare me, strangle me, plunge a knife into me, or bring about my death; this eye was there to ease my passage into this "metaphysical experiment," which I would later decide bore the hallmarks of a dream; it was there, above all, to be my guide.

Utter silence. I knew at once that the experiment on which I was about to embark had something to do with that thing my profession had taken from me and everything to do with that emptiness I felt inside me. A man's nightmares are never so real as when he's starved of sleep! But this was not a nightmare; it was sharper, clearer, almost mathematical in its precision. *I know I'm empty inside.* This was what I was thinking. As I leaned against the mosque wall, I thought, *The eye knows too!* It knew what I thought, and what I'd done, and now it was pointing at another fact that was entirely obvious. The eye was my creation, just as I was the eye's! When this thought came to me, I imagined it would be fleeting—it would stay with me no longer than those absurd words that swoop into my mind sometimes when I put pen to paper, only to disappear a moment later—but no, the thought lingered. Inside it was an open door; I walked toward it, and like the English girl who followed the rabbit through a gap in the hedge, I soon found myself falling into a new world.

In the beginning, it was I who created the eye. My aim: I created it, of course, so that it could see me, watch me. I had no desire to escape its gaze. It was under its gaze that I made myself—made myself in its image—and I basked happily in its warm glow. It was because I was under the eye's constant surveillance that I knew I existed. If the eye didn't see me, I would cease to exist at all! This seemed so clear to me that I soon forgot I was the one who had created the eye in the first place and began to thank it for allowing me to exist. I longed to obey its every order! If I did, another and more beautiful existence awaited me, but this was difficult to achieve; the difficulty of the enterprise did not (like so much in life) stem from pain; it had more to do with achieving calm, accepting that which we have come to see as natural. So the thought world into which I fell while leaning on the mosque wall was nothing like a nightmare; it was a happy realm woven from memory, conjured from images, just like the bizarreries that rose like smoke from the works of the imaginary painters I noted in my BELIEVE IT OR NOT columns.

And there I was, at the center of this garden of bliss; I was leaning against the mosque wall, watching my own thoughts.

As for this person I saw at the center of my thoughts—or, if you prefer, at the center of this illusory universe that existed only in my mind's eye—I knew at once he was not my double; we were one and the same, he and I. I knew, too, that the gaze I'd sensed only moments earlier was my own gaze. I'd transformed myself into that eye and was now watching myself from the outside. But there was nothing weird or alien about this sensation, and nothing to fear. The moment I saw myself from the outside, I remembered—or, rather, I understood—that I had long been in the habit of doing so. For years now, I had been stepping outside myself to see how I measured up. Seeing myself from the outside, I'd say, *Yes, it's all in good order,* seeing myself from the out- side, I'd say, *I don't look good enough,* and then, *I don't look enough like the per- son I want to resemble.* Or, *I do look something like that person, but I need to try harder,* and when, after saying that to myself for years on end, I stepped outside myself for yet another inspection, I'd say, *Yes, I finally do look like that person I want to be!* happily adding, *Yes, I have arrived, I am he!*

But who was He? It was at this point in my journey through the wondrous gardens that I realized why it was that He had made Himself known to me. It was because there had been no moment during my long midnight walk when I had tried to be like Him—to remake myself in His or indeed anyone else's image. Please don't misunderstand me: Imitation is a formative art. Unless we were always trying to be like others, and wishing to become people other than ourselves, life, I think, would quickly become impossible. What I am trying to say is that I was so tired that night, and the emptiness inside me so over- whelming, that—after years of obeying His every order, I'd lost the last vestige of my desire to do so, and at that same moment I became His equal. Our equality was, I knew, only relative; I had only to look at the illusory garden I had entered at His behest. I still felt His gaze, but on that beautiful winter's night I was also free. I had not willed my lib- eration—I had triumphed over nothing—it was defeat and fatigue that had brought me to this place where I felt not just free, not just equal, but at one with Him. (The certainty of my conviction in this regard should be clear from my style.) For the first time in years, *He* saw fit to divulge His secrets to me, just as I was able to divulge mine to Him. Yes, it's true, I was speaking to myself, but don't we all? We all have a second person buried inside us, a dear friend to whom we whisper to our heart's content; and some of us even have a third.

My more discerning readers will already have shifted around the letters and figured this out, but let me say it again: He was, of course, the eye. The eye was the man I wished to be. What I created first was not the eye, first I created Him, the man I wished to be. It was He—the man I wished to be—who stepped back to cast His stifling and terrifying gaze upon me. His eye curbed my freedom; nothing I did escaped his merciless, accusing gaze, wherever I went, He was there, hanging over me, like an accursed sun. But please don't take this as a complaint. For I was enchanted by the brilliant landscape the eye had spread before me.

As I watched myself enjoy the geometric clarity of this landscape (this being the thing I admired most about it), it was, as I have said, immediately clear to me that I was his creator, but I had yet to understand exactly how this had come to pass. Certain clues suggested that I had drawn him from life, from memory. Perhaps because I wanted so much to be like Him, there was something in His manner that called to mind various heroes from the comic books of my childhood and the pensive authors I'd seen in foreign magazines, posing in front of the study, desk, or other sacred site where these illustrious figures had entertained their "deep and meaningful thoughts." Of course I wanted to be like them, but how much? As I surveyed the metaphysical landscape, asking myself what other materials from my past I might have used when first creating Him, I discovered several other disheartening clues: a rich and industrious neighbor whose praises my mother was always singing; the cloud cast by a westernized pasha who'd devoted his life to saving his homeland; the ghost of a hero from a book I'd read five times from cover to cover; a teacher who'd punished us with silence; a classmate who addressed his parents as sir and madam and was so rich he wore a clean pair of socks every day; various smart, successful, fast-talking heroes from the foreign films they show at the Şehzadebaşı and Beyoğlu theaters; the way these same heroes held their drinks; this ability they had to be so relaxed, witty, and quietly confident around women, particularly beautiful women; the famous writers, philosophers, scientists, explorers, and inventors whose lives I'd read about in encyclopedias and book prefaces; a handful of soldiers; the hero of that book I once read—the one who, because he couldn't sleep, was able to save an entire city from a catastrophic flood—I saw them all as I leaned against the mosque wall in the dark of midnight, surveying the wondrous empire of my thoughts; one by one they greeted me, lighting up like familiar names on a map. Indeed, I was as amazed as a child who is standing for the first time before a map of the streets where he has spent his entire life. Then I too felt the unpleasant aftertaste: all these buildings, streets, and parks, all these houses laden with a lifetime of memories, reduced to a system of lines and points, lines and points that seem so small, so insignificant, so meaningless inside the vast network of lines and points around them.

It was from these memories I'd made Him. But inside His gaze, this crowded collage of people, places, and images from my past, there lurked a monster's soul. For His gaze was my own now; I saw myself and my entire life through His eyes. I was happy to live under His gaze, and to subject myself to His scrutiny, for I lived to imitate Him and to come closer to Him through imitation; I lived in the belief that one day I might become one with Him, or at the very least, learn to live as He did. No, it would be wrong to say I lived in hope: My hope was that one day I might become someone other than myself—become Him. I would warn my readers against seeing my "metaphysical experiment" as some sort of awakening; this is not an exemplary tale about a man whose eyes suddenly open. The garden of wonders I'd explored while leaning on the mosque wall sparkled with geometrical clarity because it had been washed clean of guilt and sin, pleasure and punishment. Once in a dream I'd watched a full moon hanging at exactly the same angle over the same street in the same midnight sky turn slowly into the shiny face of a clock. The tableau now before me was as clear and limpid and symmetrical as that dream. How I longed to linger here, drinking in the scene, pointing out its delights and arresting details one by one.

This is not to say I didn't, as it were, imagine three stones on a dark blue slab of marble, or that I did not go on to imagine myself divining their true meaning. The I leaning on the mosque wall longs to be Him.

This man envies Him, longs to be closer to Him, while He contrives to forget that He is the creation of the I who is trying to imitate him. This, in effect, is why the eye seems so confident. He has also forgotten that the man leaning on the mosque wall created the eye in the hope that this would bring him closer to Him, but the man leaning on the wall still remembers, if only glancingly. If the man makes his move and manages to reach Him, then the eye would be in a difficult position—or, precisely speaking, a vacuum. . . . Et cetera, et cetera.

I thought all this as I watched myself from the outside. Then the I I'd been watching walked back along the mosque wall and down the street past the ever-repeating patterns of its wooden houses, empty lots, fountains, and shuttered shops, and then he walked the length of the cemetery and onward in the direction of his own house and his bed.

If we happen to be walking along a crowded avenue, glancing at the other faces that quickly pass us by, and we catch a glimpse of ourselves in the reflection of a shop window or in the great mirror behind the mannequins on display, there is always that moment of shocked recognition, and it was the same when I saw myself from the outside. But as I watched this person from the outside, as if in a dream, I was, in fact, not at all surprised to see that this person was none other than myself. What surprised me was the strength, the implausible tenderness, of my affection for him. I could see at once how fragile and pitiful he was, how miserable, hopeless, and melancholy. Only I knew that this person was not as he seemed, and I longed to take this unfortunate creature— this mere mortal, this temperamental child—under my wing, be his father or perhaps his god. Meanwhile he went on walking (while all the while I asked myself, *What is he thinking? Why is he so sad? Why is he so tired and so cowed?*) until finally he reached the main road. But still he walked, slowing down from time to time to look languidly into the unlit windows of the pudding shops and grocery stores along the way. He dug his hands deep into his pockets. Sometime later, he turned to look straight ahead. He walked all the way from Şehzadebaşı to Unkapanı without once turning his head to see the stray cars and empty taxis that passed him along the way. Perhaps he had no money.

While crossing Unkapanı Bridge, he paused for a moment to look into the waters of the Golden Horn. A tugboat was about to pass under the bridge, and though it was still pitch dark he could just make out the crew tugging at a rope tied to its slender smokestack. As he climbed an alley in Şişhane, he exchanged a few words with a drunk. Only one of the brilliantly lit shop windows on İstiklâl Avenue drew his eyes; it was a silversmith's and he stood in front of it for some time. What was going on in his mind? As I watched in trembling and affectionate apprehension, I could not help wondering.

At Taksim he stopped at a stand to buy cigarettes and matches, tearing open his new pack with those slow gestures that we see so often among our troubled citizens, and as he lit up—oh, the thin and painful wreath of smoke that rose from his mouth!—I was, for all my omiscience, as nervous as if he were the first person I'd ever met. Take care, my child! I longed to say; every street he walked, every step he took, I wanted to thank the skies that no ill had befallen him, and wherever I looked—in the street, in the apartment entrances, in the dark windows above—I saw catastrophe in the making.

Thanks be to God, he managed to get himself all the way to Nişantaşı without coming to any harm; stopping outside a building (named City-of-Hearts Apartments), he went inside! When he'd reached his attic flat, I was sure he'd had enough of those troubles of which I had so longed to unburden him. But no, instead of going to bed, he sat down on a chair, smoking and leafing through a paper. Then he stood up to pace the floor; up and down the room he went, past his tired old chairs, his dilapidated desk, his faded curtains, his papers, and his books. Suddenly he sat down at his desk, and as his creaky chair shuddered beneath him, he picked up his pen and leaned over a blank piece of paper to jot down some notes.

I stood right next to him, so close I was practically standing on the messy desk; I got as close to him as I could. He wrote with childish concentration, taking calm pleasure in his words, as if he were watching his favorite movie, but his eyes were turned inward. Still I watched him, as proud as a father watching his son write his first letter. Each time he finished a sentence, he pursed his lips, and as he wrote his eyes bumped along the page from word to word. When he'd filled a page, I read what he had written, whereupon I plunged into a deep despair.

I had hoped to read this page and find his soul stripped bare, but instead of giving me the answers to the questions I so longed to know, all I found were the same sentences you see before you. This is not his world but mine, not his words but my words—the words your eyes are racing across at this very moment (please, slow down!). I longed to stand up to him, tell him to write in his own words, but—as in a dream—I seemed unable to do anything other than stand there and watch. As sentence followed sentence, each word brought me sorrow more bitter than the last.

He paused briefly at the beginning of a paragraph. He glanced at me, almost as if he saw me, as if we were eye to eye. You know those scenes you find sometimes in old books and magazines, when authors engage in long, tender conversations with their muses, while in the margins playful illustrations show an absentminded man sharing a joke with an adorable muse who is as tiny as a pen? Well, that's just how we were smiling at each other. At long last we'd acknowledged each other; illumination, I happily assured myself, was sure to follow. He'd see what the situation called for, write down the stories about this world of his I was so curious to know, and once he'd set himself down on paper I would sit down to read through him with undiluted pleasure.

But no, it was not to be. He gave me a quick beatific smile, as if to say that everything I longed for him to illuminate was already as bright as day; then he paused, as elated as a man about to make a brilliant chess move, plunging me into the impenetrable darkness of the unknown as he wrote his last words.

Chapter Eleven

We Lost Our Memories at the Movies

Films do not just ruin children's eyes;
they ruin their minds.

—Ulunay

When Galip woke up, he was somehow aware that more snow had fallen. Perhaps he'd seen it in the dream he still half remembered upon waking but forgot the moment he reached the window, the din of traffic fading as the city settled under the silence of snow. It had been dark for some time. After washing himself with water that the *chauffe-bain* had not quite managed to heat, he quickly got dressed. He sat down at the table with pencil and paper and worked for a while on his clues. Then he shaved and put on the herringbone jacket that Rüya said looked so good on him; Celâl had one exactly like it. Throwing on his thick, coarse overcoat, he stepped outside.

By now it had stopped snowing. The cars and the pavements were covered with a new blanket several inches thick. The streets were crowded with Saturday evening shoppers returning home, laden with packages and walking gingerly through the new-fallen snow, like visitors to a planet not quite accustomed to its spongy surface.

When he reached Nişantaşı Square, he was glad to see that traffic was still moving on the main thoroughfare. He went across to the newspaper stand, which had moved into the entrance of a grocery store for the evening; among the magazines featuring naked women and scandals, he found a copy of yesterday's *Milliyet*. He then went into the restaurant across the street, taking a table in the corner so no one in the street could see him, ordering a bowl of tomato soup and a plate of grilled meatballs. While waiting for his food, he spread his newspaper over the table and slowly, carefully, went over Celâl's Sunday column.

It was a piece he'd first published years ago, and because Galip had also read it that morning, there were sentences he now knew by heart. While he drank his coffee, he marked up the text. When he left the restaurant, he hailed a taxi and asked the driver to take him to Bakırköy, to Sinanpaşa.

During the long journey, Galip began thinking it was not Istanbul he saw flowing past his window but another city altogether. Three buses had plowed into one another at the turning from Gümüşsuyu to Dolmabahçe, and now a crowd had gathered around them. The bus and taxi stops were deserted. The snow made the city seem more desolate than ever; the lamps were dimmer and he saw none of the normal nighttime activities that made the city what it was; with its closed doors and empty pavements, it looked like the empty set for a medieval city. The snow covering the warehouses, the hastily built shanties, and the domes of the mosques was not white but blue. Loitering in the streets around Aksaray he saw prostitutes with purple lips and blue faces; he saw youths sledding on ladders in front of the old city walls; as buses left the depot, their passengers stared fearfully at the blue lights of the police cars stationed outside. His elderly cabdriver told him a long and outlandish story dating back to that long-ago freak winter when the Golden Horn had frozen over. The interior light in the '59 Plymouth was just bright enough for Galip to see Celâl's Sunday column; as he pored over it, he covered it with more digits, letters, and signs, but still no answer emerged. At Sinanpaşa, the driver told him he could go no farther, so Galip got out of the taxi and went the rest of the way on foot.

The Güntepe development was closer to the main road than he remembered. The houses he passed along the way (mostly two-story concrete buildings built on the foundations of shanties) had their curtains drawn, and the shops along the street were dark; after walking up a small slope, he found himself in the little square he'd noted that morning in the City Directory. In the middle was a bust (not a statue) of Atatürk. Confident that he could remember the map well enough to find his way, he headed down the street next to the mosque, which was larger than he expected and whose walls were covered with political slogans.

It pained Galip to think of Rüya living in a place like this—in a house whose stovepipe poked right through the middle of a window, whose balcony sloped gently to the street—but ten years earlier, when he had come here to see her—again, in the middle of the night—he had seen the unthinkable and had turned on his heel at once: peering through the open window on that hot August evening, he'd found Rüya in a sleeveless cotton dress, sitting at a table piled high with papers, twirling a curl in her hair as she worked, while her husband, who had his back to Galip, stirred his tea, and above them a moth made ever more erratic circles around a naked lightbulb. Sitting between husband and wife was a plate of figs, and next to it was a canister of mosquito spray. Galip could still hear the tinkling of the spoon inside the tea glass and the chirping of the cicadas outside, but now, when he arrived at a corner and saw a sign attached to a snow-covered electricity pole that said REFET BEY STREET, nothing looked familiar.

He walked up and down the street twice; at one end was a group of children throwing snowballs, at the other a huge illuminated movie billboard showing a nondescript woman whose eyes had been blacked out, blinded. All the houses were two stories and none had numbers on their doors. The first time he came to the house he was looking for, he casually passed it by without recognizing it, but the second time around he reluctantly remembered the window, the dull and plasterless walls, the door handle he'd not wanted to touch ten years earlier. They'd added a second story. The garden now had a wall. Where there had been grass there was now concrete. The ground floor was dark. There was a separate entrance for the second story, and through the curtains he could see the bluish light of a television set; poking out of the wall was a stovepipe that looked like a cannon, puffing the sulfur-yellow smoke of lignite coal, bearing the good news that any unexpected guest that God might send would be greeted with a hot meal, a hot stove, and a roomful of good-hearted people staring stupidly at a television.

As Galip made his cautious way up the snow-covered stairs, the dog in the garden next door let out a few hopeless barks. I'm not going to say too much to Rüya, he told himself, or perhaps this was addressed to the ex-husband who still stalked his imagination. First he would ask her to explain what she hadn't explained in her goodbye letter—why she had left—then he would ask her to return to the house immediately to collect all her things—her books, her cigarettes; her single socks, empty pill bottles, hairpins, glasses' cases, half-eaten bars of chocolate, and hair clips; the wooden ducks she had played with as a child. *Everything that reminds me of you makes me unbearably sad.* Of course, he wouldn't be able to say any of this in front of that hulking brute, so it would be better to suggest that he and Rüya go somewhere where they could discuss all this sensibly. Once they had arrived in this place and come to the subject they were to discuss "sensibly," it would be perfectly easy to suggest a number of other things to Rüya, but where could he take her in a neighborhood like this, except to an all-male coffeehouse? By now he had rung the bell.

First he heard a child's voice (*Mother, someone's at the door!*) and then a woman's voice, just as worried, that bore no resemblance to his wife's, and Galip knew at that moment what an idiot he'd been to think he could come here and find the woman who'd been his friend for three decades and the love of his life for twenty-five years. For a moment he considered slipping away, but then the door opened. Galip immediately recognized the ex-husband, but he did not recognize Galip. He was middle-aged and of middling build; he was just as Galip had imagined him, and as he would never imagine him again.

As Galip stood there, waiting for the ex-husband's eyes to adjust to the darkness of the dangerous outside world and remember who he was, he saw the new wife peering out at him, and then a child, and then a second child. "Who is it, Father?" When Father finally had the answer, he froze for a moment, and Galip, thinking it was his only chance to escape from this place and avoid going into this house, blurted out his story in one breath.

He apologized for disturbing him in the middle of the night, but he was in a tight spot; he'd come back another time for a relaxed and friendly visit (with Rüya, even), but tonight there was an emergency—he'd come looking for information about a certain person, or perhaps about a name. He'd taken on a client—a university student—who'd been unjustly accused of murder. No, this was not to say there'd been no death, but the real murderer was still at large, and was wandering the city under an alias, like a ghost who once upon a time. . . .

After he'd told his story, they whisked him inside, invited him to take off his shoes, gave him a pair of slippers that were too small for him, and pressed a cup of coffee into his hands, saying that the tea was still brewing. After Galip had rounded off his story by repeating this person's name—he'd invented a new one, just to be on the safe side—Rüya's ex-husband began to speak. The longer he spoke, the more numbing his voice; anesthetized by his stories, Galip began to wonder if he'd ever find the strength to leave. He would later recall that he consoled himself at one point by reminding himself that, at the very least, he was hearing things that had to do with Rüya, things that might later serve as clues—but this was like a dying patient trying to delude himself with cheerful thoughts as he was wheeled into the operating room. It was like watching a dam burst—the flood of stories seemed to have no end—but three hours later, when he staggered out the door he had feared would never open, he knew the following:

We thought we knew a lot, but really we knew nothing.

We knew, for example, that most of the Jews in America and Western Europe were descended from the Jewish kingdom of the Khazars, which had ruled the area between the Volga and the Caucasus a thousand years ago. We also knew that the Khazars were really Turks who had converted to Judaism. But what we did not know was that Turks were as Jewish as Jews were Turkish. And wasn't it amazing, just amazing, to watch these two peoples travel through the twentieth century swaying to the rhythm of the same secret music, never meeting, always at a tangent, but forever linked, forever condemned, like a pair of hopeless twins.

Then a map floated into the room like a magic carpet; Galip woke in a flash and sprang to his feet; he walked across the overheated room, trying to pump some life back into his tired legs, and there, on the table, was the map of a storybook planet. It was covered with arrows, and—wasn't it amazing?—they'd been drawn with a green ballpoint pen.

Their first step would be to establish a new state along the Bosphorus and the Dardanelles. But instead of bringing in new settlers to populate this new state, as their predecessors had done a thousand years ago, they would turn the old inhabitants into "new people" tailored to serve their purposes. No need to read Ibn Khaldun; those charged with this task would quickly guess that the only way forward was to rip away our memories, our past, our history, leaving us with nothing to share but our misfortunes. It was known that Turkish children attending the shadowy missionary schools in the back streets of Beyoğlu and the hills overlooking the Bosphorus had once been made to drink a certain lilac-colored liquid (remember that color, said Mother, who was drinking in her husband's every word). But later on, the Western bloc's "humanitarian wing" had declared this reckless initiative too dangerous on chemical grounds and switched to a gentler approach that promised longer-lasting results: the new plan was to erode our collective memory with movie music.

Church organs, pounding out chords of a fearful symmetry, women as beautiful as icons, the hymnlike repetition of images, and those arresting scenes sparkling with drinks, weapons, airplanes, designer clothes—put these all together and it was clear that the movie method proved far more radical and effective than anything missionaries had attempted in Africa and Latin America. (These long sentences of his were well-rehearsed, Galip decided. Who else had had to hear them, his neighbors? His colleagues at work? His mother-in-law? The people sitting next to him in a *dolmuş*?) It was in the Şehzadebaşı and Beyoğlu movie theaters that they set their plan into action; before long, hundreds of people had gone utterly blind. Viewers who sensed the terrible plot that was being perpetrated on them and rebelled with angry cries were quickly silenced by policemen and mad doctors. When the children of today showed a similar reaction—when they were blinded by the proliferation of new images—they were fobbed off with free prescription glasses. But there were always a few who refused to go away quietly. A while ago, he'd been walking through another neighborhood not far from here around midnight when he'd seen a sixteen-year-old boy pumping futile bullets into a movie billboard—and immediately he'd understood why. Another time, he'd seen a man at the entrance to a theater with two cans of gasoline swinging from his hands; as the bouncers roughed him up, he kept demanding that they give him his eyes back—yes, the eyes that could see the *old* images. Then there was that peasant boy from Malatya who'd fallen into the habit of going to the movies once a week, and who realized, on the way home, that he'd lost his memory, along with everything he'd ever learned—he'd written to the papers; had Galip read his letters? He could go on for days telling Galip sad tales about people so entranced by the streets and clothes and women they'd seen on the silver screen that they'd been unable to go on living as before, and now they were poorer and more wretched than ever. As for those who identified with the stars they saw on the screen—our new masters refused to see them as "sick" or "in the wrong," enlisting them instead as partners in the project. We'd all been blinded, every last one of us, every last one. . . .

Assuming his role as head of household, Rüya's ex-husband asked, Why had not a single official in the state bureaucracy noticed that the rise of moviegoing was in inverse proportion to Istanbul's decline? Was it a coincidence that theaters were always located on the same streets as brothels? he asked. Why did movie theaters have to be dark; why were they *all* dark?

Ten years ago, he and Rüya Hanım had moved here, into this very house, hoping to serve a cause they believed in with all their hearts; this had meant taking on pseudonyms and false identities. (Galip kept glancing at his nails.) They'd devoted their lives to the propagation of ideas; this had meant taking manifestos from a distant country they'd never visited and translating them into the mother tongue while still remaining faithful to the foreign original; it had meant taking political forecasts from people they had never seen and recasting them in this "new language" for other people they would never see; it had meant a life of typing and duplicating. Though of course all they'd wanted all along was to be someone other than the people they were. When they heard of a new acquaintance who took his alias seriously, how happy they were! The fatigue of those long hours at the battery factory would suddenly lift, and he'd forget about all those unwritten articles, all those manifestos waiting to be stuffed into envelopes; he'd sit there staring, staring, at the new identity card in his hand. "I've changed!" he'd cry with joyous, youthful innocence. "I'm a completely new person!" He couldn't say it often enough, and those around him never tired of hearing it. Equipped with his new identity, he could now read meanings into the world around him that he had never before suspected: The world was a brand new encyclopedia, waiting to be read from start to finish; as they read this new tome, it would change before their eyes, and so too would its readers; so when they'd read it right to the end, they could return to the first page of their encyclopedia world and read the whole thing all over again, finally to disappear between the pages, lost even to themselves in the drunken profusion of assumed names. (While the head of household was himself vanishing into the pages of his encyclopedia metaphor—not, Galip suspected, for the first time—he noticed a stack of newspaper supplements on one of the shelves in the buffet: *Tree of Knowledge*, in weekly install-ments.) With the passage of time, however, his host had come to real-ize that this was in fact a ruse "they" had devised to distract them. For after becoming a new person, and then another and another and another, there was less and less hope of returning to the happiness they had known as the people they'd been at the beginning. A moment had arrived when, hemmed in by the signs they'd never managed to decipher—the letters, manifestos, pictures, faces, and guns—this man and his wife had been forced to admit that they had lost their way. This house stood all alone then, on a hill in the middle of a wasteland. One evening, Rüya had packed a few belongings into her little bag and returned to her old family, to her old house, where she felt safe.

Whenever the force of his own words overtook him, the host would jump from his chair to pace the room, grimacing like Bugs Bunny, or so Galip thought as his foggy mind struggled to keep pace. His host was now explaining why it was essential to go right back to the beginning if we were ever to beat "them" at their own game. As Galip Bey could see, his house defined him as petit bourgeois, a mem-ber of the middle class; everything about this place said he was a "tra-ditional citizen." All the props were there: the old easy chairs with their floral cotton slipcovers, the synthetic curtains, the enameled plates with butterflies around the rims, the ugly buffet with the candy dish they only used on holidays when guests came to call and the never-touched assortment of liqueurs, the carpets that had faded to a shabby brown. His wife was not a glamorous well-educated woman like Rüya, and she knew it too; like his own dear mother, she was plain, simple, and modest (here the wife gave him a smile Galip could not decipher); she was, in fact, his uncle's daughter. Their children resembled her too. This was the life his father would have made for himself, if he'd lived, if he hadn't changed. To have deliberately chosen this life as he himself had done, to live it in full consciousness, was to say no to a conspiracy that dated back two thousand years; it meant being true to the person you really were and refusing to become someone else.

All the things Galip Bey had assumed were here by chance were in truth here to serve this single purpose. The clock on the wall? They'd chosen it because a house like this had to have a clock like that ticking on its walls. Because there was always a television on in such houses all night long, they too kept their television on all night long, glowing in its corner like a streetlamp; they'd put a hand-crocheted doily on top of it because houses like this always had them. It was all by design: the clutter on the table, the old newspapers that they tossed aside after clipping out the coupons, the jam smear on the side of the box of chocolates someone had brought as a gift and someone else had turned into a sewing box; even the things he hadn't expressly designed, like the handle that one of the children had broken off a coffee cup—the one that looked like an ear—and the clothes that were drying near the fearsome stove. Sometimes, when he was talking with his wife or his children, his host would sit back to watch the scene, watch it like a film, and when he saw that everything they did and said was in perfect keeping with the sort of family who lived in this kind of house, how he rejoiced! If happiness was to live the way you wished, and to do so in full consciousness, then, yes, he was happy. But, above all, his happiness derived from the knowledge that he had, by living this happy life, "foiled a conspiracy dating back two millennia."

Galip, seeing his chance, chose to take this as the closing statement; saying it had begun to snow again, he lurched toward the door, feeling faint despite the ten teas and coffees he had downed during his stay. But before he could take his coat off the hook, his host blocked the way to say one more thing.

He pitied Galip Bey because he was going back to Istanbul, the very place where this disintegration had begun. Istanbul was the touchstone; forget about living there. Just to set foot in this city was to bow to "their" will, to admit defeat. What had begun in a handful of darkened movie houses had now spread far beyond; the frightful city was now awash with images of decay: hopeless crowds, old cars, bridges sinking slowly into the sea, piles of tin cans, roads riddled with potholes, billboards with giant letters that no one stopped to read, ripped wall panels signifying nothing, graffiti that made no sense because half

the paint had washed away, advertisements for bottled drinks and cigarettes, minarets from which no one ever made the call to prayer, piles
of rubble, dust, mud, et cetera, et cetera. Nothing would come of this
decay. If they were ever to see a resurgence—and Galip's host was certain there were others like him, resisting the decay all day, every day, in
every way possible—it could only begin here, in one of these districts
the high and mighty dismissed as "concrete shantytowns," for it was
only here that our true essence was still preserved. He was proud to be
this community's founder and main spokesman; he would be happy to
welcome Galip into the fold this very minute. He could spend the
night here if he wished; if nothing else, to talk it over. . . .

Galip had his coat on by now; he'd said his goodbyes to the silent
wife and the comotose children and was on his way out the door. The
host took a long look at the snow and said, "How white!" in a way that
even Galip found pleasing. He went on to tell Galip about a sheikh
he'd once known, who dressed all in white; after meeting him, he'd had
a dream all in white too. In his pure white dream, he'd found himself
sitting in a pure white Cadillac next to Muhammed. In the front, next
to a driver whose face he couldn't see, were Muhammed's two little
grandsons, Hasan and Hüseyin. As the white Cadillac rolled past the
posters, billboards, movies, and brothels of Beyoğlu, they kept turning
around to grimace at their grandfather.

As Galip headed for the snow-covered stairs, the host continued.
Galip was not to think he read too much into dreams. He'd just learned
how to pick out a few sacred signs. He wanted to share them with
Galip; he might find them useful. Rüya too. Others already did.

It had been gratifying to hear the prime minister repeating word for
word the "global analyses" he himself had written under a pseudonym
three years earlier, when his political activities were at their height. It
was beyond doubt: "these men" drew upon a vast network of intelligence agencies that even scoured the country's smallest periodicals,
and when they happened on something of worth, they sent it straight
upstairs. Not long ago, he'd caught sight of an article by Celâl Salik,
who seemed to have acquired the same material by the same means,
but this was a hopeless case: Celâl had gone in search of the wrong
answer, in vain pursuit of a lost cause, and somewhere along the way
he'd sold his soul.

But what was interesting about both cases is that, however they'd acquired them, these two men—the prime minister and the famous columnist—had felt compelled to mimic the thoughts of a true believer everyone else ignored and dismissed. For a time he'd considered going to the press and exposing these two men for their brazen plagiarism, showing word for word how they'd lifted expressions and even whole sentences from an article first published in a left-wing splinter-group publication that no one ever read, but the conditions weren't right for such a bold frontal attack. He knew as well as he knew his own name that patience was his byword: one day he would open his door, and they too would be standing on his doorstep. If Galip Bey had come all the way out to the back of beyond on a snowy evening in pursuit of an alias that was entirely improbable—this was a sign. He wanted Galip Bey to know how well he had read this and all the other signs, and as Galip finally began to walk down the steps, he whispered his last questions.

Would Galip Bey find it in him to read our history with new eyes? Since there was a danger of his taking the wrong turn, might his host accompany him back to the main road? When did Galip think he might come for another visit? Very well, then, could he send his very best regards to Rüya?

Chapter Twelve

The Kiss

*The habit of perusing periodical works may be properly added to
Averroës' catalogue of Anti-Mnemonics, or weakeners of the
memory.*

—Coleridge, *Biographia Literaria*

A man sent you his regards—a week ago, to be exact. I agreed to
pass them on, but I'd already forgotten by the time I got into the
car. Not the greeting but the man. And I can't say I'm too sorry about
that, either. In my view, an intelligent husband makes a point of forgetting every man who sends his regards to his wife. Because—well, just
in case. Especially if the woman in question is a housewife. If you rule
out relatives and shopkeepers, that luckless creature we call the housewife is unlikely, after all, to meet any man other than her own tedious
husband. So if a gentleman does take the trouble to send her his
regards, it will make her think, and she has plenty of time for that too.
This is not to fault the man for his excellent manners. For the love of
God, where do his manners come from? In the good old days, the best
a gentleman could do was send his regards to a shadowy and anonymous harem. The old streetcars were better.

Now my readers are well aware that I've never been married, that I
never will marry, and that I'll never be able to marry because I'm a
journalist, so they will know by now that my puzzling opening lines are
just that: the opening lines of a puzzle. Who's this woman I addressed
so intimately? Hocus-pocus! The aging columnist will speak now of
his slowly vanishing memory: Please, come and join me, let us walk
together through the garden, delighting in the fragrance of my fading
roses—if you catch my drift. But don't come too close; stand back so

that I can perform my simple trick without your seeing my hands move.

This is how it was thirty years ago, when I first entered journalism: I reported on Beyoğlu in those days and would go from door to door in search of news. Had there been a new murder in one of those cheap nightclubs, perhaps involving gangsters or drug dealers? Or a love affair that had ended in suicide? I'd scour the hotel registers, looking for a foreign celebrity, or at least find out if an interesting Westerner I could present to my readers as a foreign celebrity had decided to visit our city—a privilege for which I'd have to pay the desk clerks two and a half liras a month. In those days the world was not so weighed down with celebrities as it is today—and none of them came to Istanbul. From time to time I'd write up "celebrities" not yet known in their own countries, implying the opposite to be the case, but they were invariably shocked and appalled when they saw their pictures in the paper. From time to time, someone for whom I'd foreseen fame and fortune would, in fact, take their countries by storm many years later: I would dash off a few lines about "a famous French woman designer who paid a visit to our city yesterday" and discover twenty years later that, lo and behold, she'd become a famous French *existentialist* woman designer—but for this I received no thanks. That's Western gratitude for you.

But returning to that time in my life when I earned my keep chasing lackluster celebrities and home-grown gangsters (whom we now describe as the mafia): One day I happened onto an old pharmacist who, I thought, might turn out to be an interesting story. This man was suffering from insomnia and memory loss, the two ailments that afflict me today. When they both hit at the same time, there is a doomed tendency to hope that it might be possible to use the former (e.g., the extra hours of wakefulness that insomniacs must endure) to cure the latter (e.g., use that time to recultivate the drying garden of memory) when in fact the extra hours of wakefulness serve only to make it drier still. This old man found, just as I have, that sleepless nights erased his mind of all memory; he'd find himself caught inside a nameless, featureless, odorless, colorless world where time itself had stopped; it was, he said, something akin to what foreign magazines call "the other side of the moon."

The old man's solution was to retire to his laboratory, where soon he had invented the drug he hoped would cure him of his affliction; I would later invent a prose style to the same end. And it did—at a press conference attended by myself and a drug-addict colleague (including the pharmacist, there were only three of us in the room). After making a great show of his amazing pink liquid, he downed several glasses and fell into the sleep that had eluded him for so many years. This caused a certain furor—naturally, people were excited at the news that a Turk had finally invented something—but we were never to know if, having cured himself of insomnia, he also found his way back to the heavenly garden of memory, for the old pharmacist slept on and on, never to wake again.

Two days later, as I stood at his funeral contemplating the darkening sky, I couldn't help but wonder what this man had been trying to remember. I'm still wondering. As we grow older and begin to feel like beasts of burden weighed down by a surfeit of memories, which ones do we throw off first: the least felicitous memories, the heaviest, or the ones that fall most easily by the wayside?

I've forgotten what it's like to sit in little rooms in the most beautiful corners of Istanbul, watching the sun pour through the tulle curtains to bring us warmth. I've forgotten which movie theater it was where the scalper fell in love with the pale Greek girl at the ticket window, only to lose his mind. I've forgotten the names of the dear readers who wrote to me back in the days when I analyzed dreams for this newspaper, to tell me that my dreams and theirs were one and the same—just as I long ago lost the secret I went on to share with them in my letters.

One sleepless night years later, our aging columnist was thinking back on those lost days, and desperately seeking for some branch to which he might cling, when he suddenly remembered a fearsome wish that had once come over him while walking the Istanbul streets: the wish—and I could feel it with my whole body, my entire soul!—was for a kiss.

It was, I think, in one of the old theaters that I'd seen it, most likely at a Saturday matinee: a kissing scene that probably didn't last very long in an old American detective film (*Scarlet Street*) that was probably older than the building itself. It was no different from kissing scenes in other black-and-white movies, and thanks to the guidelines enforced by the censors of the day, it is unlikely to have lasted more than four seconds, but for whatever reason I suddenly found myself longing, yearning, to press my lips against the lips of a woman just like that and kiss her with all my might, and the urge was so strong that I feared I might choke on my own misery. I was twenty-four years old, but I had never kissed a woman on the lips. This is not to say I hadn't slept with women in brothels, but women like that never kiss, and I would never have wanted to kiss them anyway.

I'd left the theater before the end of the film: Trembling with impatience, I told myself that there must be some woman somewhere in the city who would want me to kiss her. I walked—ran—all the way to Tünel, and then I rushed all the way back to Galatasaray Palace, where I looked hopelessly into the darkness that surrounded me, searching, if my memory serves me, for a familiar face, a smile, an image of a woman I might kiss. I had no friends or relatives to call on and no hope of finding myself a lover—I didn't even know anyone who might one day become my lover! There I was, in the middle of a crowded city but desperately alone.

Somehow I got myself to Taksim and onto a bus. I had some distant relatives on my mother's side who had taken an interest in us after we were abandoned by my father; they had a daughter two years younger than I and from time to time we'd played jacks together. An hour later, by which time I'd made it out to Fındıkzade and was standing outside their house, ringing their bell, I remembered that the girl I'd dreamed of kissing had married years ago. So it was her parents, both retired, who welcomed me into the house. They were a bit surprised to see me; they couldn't understand why I'd suddenly decided to visit them again after so many years. We talked about this and that (they weren't even interested to hear I was a journalist; I might as well have said I wrote a gossip column; in their eyes it was the lowliest of professions); we drank tea, nibbled on sesame rolls, and listened to the football match on the radio. They were kind enough to invite me to stay for supper, but I mumbled something about prior engagements and made a quick getaway.

When I stepped out into the cold, the desire for a kiss had by no means abated: my skin was ice, and yet my blood was still boiling, my flesh still aflame, my despair so deep I found it almost impossible to bear. At Eminönü I boarded a ferry for Kadıköy. An old friend of mine from my lycée days lived there; I remembered him telling me that there was a "kissable" girl (an unmarried girl, I mean) who lived in his neighborhood. As I walked to his house in Fenerbahçe, I told myself that, even if she'd moved away, this friend of mine was bound to know another girl like her. When I got to my friend's neighborhood, I did a full tour of its dark wooden mansions and cypress trees but failed to locate his house. As I wandered among those same wooden mansions—most of which have since been destroyed—I spied, here and there, a light in a window, and whenever I did I imagined a girl who'd be willing to give a man a kiss before she married. I'd look up at the window and think, There she is, the girl who'll kiss me on the lips! There was not much distance between us—a garden wall, a door, a wooden staircase—but still I couldn't reach her, couldn't kiss her; that strange, secret, magical thing that we all long for, as alien and impossible as a dream, that fearsome wish—how near it seemed at that moment and yet how far!

Returning to the European shore, I remember wondering what would happen if I went over and kissed one of the women on the ferry—perhaps by force, perhaps by pretending I'd mistaken her for someone else—but I was only too aware that I was not in any state to finesse such a difficult maneuver, and when I surveyed the crowd I could not, in any event, find the sort of face I was looking for. There have been other times in my life when I've walked through the crowds of Istanbul, growing more hopeless and despairing with every breath and seeing emptiness, emptiness, everywhere I look, but I've never again felt it as intensely as on the day I am describing.

For hours on end, I pounded the city's damp pavements. I told myself that one day, after I'd made my fortune and won my fame, I would return to these empty, empty streets and find what I wanted. As for now I had no choice but to return to the house your faithful columnist shared with his mother, to take what consolation there was from Balzac—or, rather, from what poor Rastignac said in my Turkish translation. In those days I never read books for pleasure; like most Turks, I saw reading as a duty, a way of acquiring knowledge that might one day prove useful. But how could it help me get what I wanted now? This was why, after I had shut myself up in my room, my impatience soon drove me out again. As I was looking at myself in the bathroom mirror, it occurred to me that if all else failed, a man could at least kiss himself, and I stared into the mirror, conjuring up the memory of the couple in the film. I couldn't get the image of their lips (Joan Bennett's and Dan Duryea's) out of my mind. But by now I'd realized I'd not even be kissing myself; I'd be kissing the mirror.

My mother was sitting at the table, surrounded by patterns and pieces of silk chiffon; she was struggling to finish an evening gown in time for God knows which rich relative of which distant relation to wear to a wedding. We chatted about this and that. Most of it would have been stories and dreams—the things I hoped to do one day, my hopes, my aspirations—but I could tell my mother wasn't really listening. I realized that it didn't matter what I said; whatever I said, the important thing was that I was here at home on a Saturday night, keeping my mother company. A bolt of anger flashed through me. As I sat there glowering at her, I noticed that her hair looked neater and more carefully arranged than usual this evening; she'd even put the thinnest coat of lipstick on her lips; the shade—and I can see it to this day—was firehouse red.

"Why are you looking at me like that?" she asked fearfully.

There was a long silence. I walked toward my mother, but I had taken no more than two steps when I stopped; my legs were trembling. Before I could get any closer, I began to shout. I can no longer remember exactly what I said, only that we were soon embroiled in one of those bitter arguments we fell into so often in those days. It was one of those liberating moments of fury when a man suddenly finds himself able to speak his mind, perhaps even breaking a coffee cup or kicking the stove to drive home his point.

Eventually I was able to tear myself away and storm outside, leaving my poor mother surrounded by her silk chiffon, her spools of thread, and her imported dressmaker pins (the first Turkish dressmaker pins, manufactured by Atlı, did not appear on the market until 1976). I wandered the streets until midnight. I went into the courtyard of Süleymaniye Mosque, crossed the Atatürk Bridge, and went up to Beyoğlu. I was not myself, and a specter that could speak only of anger and revenge was fast on my heels; it was as if the person I was meant to be was chasing me.

I went into a pudding shop in Beyoğlu and found myself a table, just to be among people, but so dreadful was the thought of coming eye to eye with someone else who'd come here to wait out the empty hours of a Saturday night that I dared look at no one; people like us can recognize each other instantly, and oh, how we despise each other! I had not been sitting there long when a couple approached me. The man began to speak. I ransacked my memory—who was this white-haired ghost I saw before me?

It was none other than the friend whose house I'd tried to find in Fenerbahçe. He was married now and working for the State Railway Company, and his hair had gone prematurely white, and yes, he remembered the old days very well. You know how, when you run into an old friend, he'll sometimes turn your head by making a huge fuss over you—act as if you're the most interesting person in the world and allude knowingly to all the secrets you share from the old days, just to impress the wife who's standing next to him?—well, that's what this friend did, but he didn't fool me for a second. I was not about to collude in his fantastical reminiscences, nor was I about to let him know that I was still stuck in the same miserable rut that he'd long left behind.

As I dragged my spoon through my unsugared pudding, I told him I'd been married for some time; I was earning good money; you were waiting for me at home; my Chevrolet was parked in Taksim; I'd come here because you had a sweet tooth, and a sudden craving for chicken-breast pudding, and no one made it as well as they did here; we lived in Nişantaşı; could I drop them off on my way home? My friend thanked me but explained that he still lived in Fenerbahçe. He asked me a few questions about you, at first tentatively, just to satisfy his curiosity, and then—after he heard you were from a good family—to prove to his wife that he knew lots of good families: not wishing to pass up on this opportunity, I told him he must remember you. Yes, he did remember you! Yes, with pleasure! He sent you his very best regards. As I was leaving the pudding shop with your chicken-breast pudding wrapped in paper under my arm, I kissed him in the refined Western way I had picked up from the movies, and then I kissed his wife. What strange readers you are, and what a strange country we live in.

Chapter Thirteen

Look Who's Here

We should have met long ago.
—The great Turkish film star,
Türkan Şoray

After leaving Rüya's ex-husband's house, Galip made his way back to the main road. He searched in vain for a taxi; neither was he able to board any of the intercity buses that went hurtling past from time to time. He decided to walk over to the Bakırköy train station. As he trudged through the snow, he let his mind wander; over and over, he imagined running into Rüya, returning with her to the life they'd had before, forgetting even why it was that she had left in the first place—except that it was simple and made perfect sense—but whenever he returned to the beginning of the daydream, he could not quite bring himself to tell Rüya that he had gone to see her ex-husband.

Bakırköy station reminded him of one of those battered refrigerators you saw built into the front walls of grocery stores. On the train he boarded half an hour later, an old man told him a story dating back forty years, to a winter's night as cold as this one. During those dark lean years when it had looked as if we too might be dragged into the war, the old man's brigade had spent a long harsh winter marooned in a village in Thrace. One morning, a secret order came for the entire brigade to leave the village forthwith; they mounted their horses, and after riding all day they found themselves on the outskirts of Istanbul; but they had not entered the city, lingering instead in the hills overlooking the Golden Horn. When the city shut down for the night, they went down through the darkened streets, with only the ghostly light of the masked streetlamps to guide them; quietly leading their horses down the icy cobblestones, they had handed them over to the slaughterhouse at Sütlüce. He described the carnage in gory detail—the ruthless butchers, the horses falling over one by one, lying bewildered as their innards spilled out over the bloody cobblestones like springs from an old armchair, the strange similarity between the look in the horses' eyes as they waited their turn and the look in the eyes of the cavalrymen as they crept back into the city like criminals—but it was all Galip could do to hear him over the noise of the train.

There were no cabs waiting in front of Sirkeci Station. Galip considered walking over to his office and spending the night there, but then he saw a taxi making a U-turn and was sure it was coming to pick him up. Instead it stopped in front of a man who'd been waiting on the side of the road, a black-and-white man with a briefcase who looked as if he'd just stepped out of a black-and-white film. After this man stepped into the taxi, the driver stopped again in front of Galip, saying that he could take him and "the gentleman" as far as Galatasaray. Galip opened the door and got in.

When he got out of the taxi at Galatasaray, he was immediately sorry that he'd not drawn the man from the black-and-white film into conversation. While looking at the empty but brilliantly lit ferries tied to the Karaköy pier, Galip had imagined turning to the man and saying, Once upon a time many years ago, on just such a snowy night, sir. . . . Had he begun his story with these words, he'd have taken it with just such ease through to the end, and the man would have given it all the attention it deserved.

As Galip stood gazing into the window of a shoe shop just past the Atlas Theater (Rüya wore a size seven), a small slight man approached him. He was carrying one of those imitation leather briefcases Galip associated with bill collectors for the city gas company.

"Are you fond of stars?" he asked. He'd buttoned his jacket up to his neck to make it more like a coat. Galip thought he must be one of those men you found in Taksim Square on clear nights who charged you a hundred lira to see the stars through their telescope, but then the man reached into his briefcase and took out an album. He turned the pages himself. What he had to offer was a collection of photographs of some of our greatest film stars, all sensational, printed on paper of the highest quality.

Except no, of course, they weren't really pictures of famous film stars but pictures of lookalikes parading in their clothes and their jewelry and, most important, striking their poses; everything about them was the same—how they stood, smoked their cigarettes, pouted, or pursed their lips as if to blow a kiss. Pasted on each "star's" page was her name, cut from newspaper headlines, and a photograph cut from a magazine; around it were her impersonators, replicating her charms in the most alluring ways.

To pique Galip's interest, the little man beckoned him into the empty, narrow alley leading to the New Angel Theater and handed him the album so he could look through it himself. In the light of a strange shop window where disembodied arms and legs connected to the ceiling with thin string dangled next to umbrellas, bags, gloves, and stockings, Galip studied various Türkan Şorays, lighting sultry cigarettes and letting their skirts rise to infinity as they twirled around the dance floor; several Müjde Ars, peeling bananas, gazing saucily into the camera, and laughing with abandon; the Hülya Koçyiğits were putting on their glasses, taking off their bras to mend them, leaning into the sink to do the dishes, or gazing into the distance, sorrowful, weeping, disconsolate. All the time, the album's owner kept close watch on Galip; then, without warning, he snatched the album away, as smartly as a teacher who's caught a student with a forbidden book, and stuffed it back into his briefcase.

"Shall I take you to them?"

"Where are they?"

"You look like a gentleman; follow me."

As they walked down the back streets, Galip, pressed to make a choice, declared that he'd been very taken with one Türkan Şoray.

"She's the genuine article!" said the man with the briefcase, as if sharing a secret. "She'll be glad too; she's going to like you."

Next to the Beyoğlu police station was an old stone building with a sign over the door that said COMPANIONS; they walked up to the first floor, which smelled of dust and fabric. Though Galip could see neither fabric nor sewing machines in the darkened room, the words *sewing companions* sprang to his mind. Passing through a high white door, they arrived in a second room ablaze with light, where Galip remembered that the pimp was waiting to be paid.

"Türkan!" cried the man as he put the money into his pocket. "Türkan, come out and look, İzzet has come to see you!"

There were two women playing cards at the table; both turned around to smile at Galip. The room was like a set in an old broken-down theater: drowsily airless in the way rooms are when the stoves are not well ventilated, thick with soporific perfume, with a tired Turkish pop music soundtrack in the background. Lying on the sofa just like Rüya did when she was reading her detective novels (with one foot propped on the back), a woman who looked nothing like Rüya and nothing like a star was leafing through a humor magazine. He recognized her as Müjde Ar only because MÜJDE AR was emblazoned on the front of her shirt. An old man in a waiter's outfit was dozing in front of the television, where a panel was discussing the impact of the conquest of Istanbul on world history.

The woman with the permed hair and the jeans bore a vague resemblance, Galip thought, to an American actress whose name escaped him, though he couldn't be sure if this was by intent. A man stumbled through the other door, coming to a stop in front of Müjde Ar; staring at the name on her chest, he nodded incredulously, like a man unwilling to believe his own life until it hit the headlines; he then mumbled the name out loud with drunken gravity, though the first syllable got lost.

The woman in the leopardskin dress must be Türkan, Galip decided; as she ambled toward him, she looked almost graceful. She was probably the closest to her original: she had arranged her long blond hair to fall over her right shoulder.

"Do you mind if I smoke?" she asked, with a lovely smile. A filterless cigarette appeared between her fingers. "Could I trouble you for a light?"

Galip lit her cigarette; her head disappeared behind a thick cloud of smoke. The music died and in the strange silence that ensued, she emerged like a saint from the mist; staring into her huge black long-lashed eyes, Galip thought, for the first time in his life, that he might be able to sleep with a woman other than Rüya. As he pocketed his money, the man who was dressed to look like the manager called him İzzet. After they'd retired to a well-appointed room upstairs, the woman stubbed out her cigarette in an Akbank ashtray and took another cigarette out of her pack.

"Do you mind if I smoke?" she said again. Her pose and her tone of voice were exactly as before. She put the cigarette to the corner of her lips, just as before, turning to him with the same haughty smile. "Could I trouble you for a light?"

She leaned forward expectantly, making the most of her charming cleavage, and as she stood there waiting, Galip realized that she was playing a scene from a Türkan Şoray film and was expecting Galip to play İzzet Günay, the male lead. When he lit the cigarette, a new cloud of dense smoke enveloped her head and once again, he watched her huge black long-lashed eyes rise slowly from the mist. Only a studio could produce this much smoke. How did she do it, using just her mouth?

"Why are you so quiet?" asked the woman with a smile.

"I'm not," said Galip.

"You're a sly one, aren't you?" the woman said with feigned concern that might also have been anger. "Or are you just very innocent?" Then she repeated the same line, using just the same gestures. Her enormous earrings reached as far as her bare shoulders.

By now he'd gathered from the stills she'd wedged around the edges of the round mirror on her dressing table that her backless leopardskin dress was what Türkan Şoray had worn twenty years earlier when playing a bar girl in a film called *Licensed to Love*. She went on to recite other lines from the same movie. (Hanging her head like a spoiled and discontented child, joining her hands under her chin, and then spreading them wide): "But I can't go to sleep now; when I drink I want to have fun!" (Furrowing her forehead like a kindly aunt who is worried about a neighbor's child): "Stay with me, İzzet, stay until the bridge opens!" (In a sudden burst of joy): "We were fated to be together, to be together today!" (Like a lady): "So pleased to meet you, so pleased to meet you, so pleased to meet you. . . ."

Galip sat down on the chair next to the door and the woman sat down on the stool next to her dressing table, a close relative of the one in the film. The still from this very scene was wedged into the mirror. The woman's back was more beautiful than the original. For a moment she watched Galip watching her in the mirror.

"We should have met long ago."

"We did meet long ago," said Galip, looking at the woman's face in the mirror. "At school we never sat in the same row, but on warm spring days after long class discussions, when they opened the window, I'd gaze into the pane of glass that worked like a mirror because of the blackboard just behind it and see your face."

"Hmmmmm. We should have met long ago."

"We met long ago," said Galip. "The first time we met, your legs looked so thin and delicate I was afraid they'd break. You had rough skin when you were little, but when you got bigger, after we moved to middle school, you bloomed like a rose and your complexion was very fine. On hot summer days, when we couldn't bear playing inside anymore and they took us to the beach, when we stopped at Tarabya on our way home and walked along the shore with our ice cream, we'd use our fingernails to scratch out words on our salty arms. I loved the little hairs on your arms. I loved the way your legs went pink from the sun. I loved the way your hair spilled over your face when you reached for something on the shelf above my head."

"We should have met long ago."

"I loved the marks the straps that the swimsuit you borrowed from your mother made on your back, and the way you'd tug at your hair, almost without knowing, when you were nervous, and the way you used your thumb and your middle finger to pick up that speck of tobacco that got stuck on your tongue one day when you were smoking a filterless cigarette, and the way your mouth fell open when you were watching a movie, and the way you'd always have a plate of nuts and roast chickpeas when you were reading, and eat them without even noticing, and your knack for losing keys, and the way you'd screw up your eyes to see something because you refused to believe you were nearsighted. When you squinted at something far away, and I realized that you were somewhere else, thinking about something else entirely, I'd feel nervous and love you all the more. I loved what I did not know about you as much as I loved what I did know about you. Oh, God, but how I feared it!"

Glancing over at the mirror and seeing an anxious glint in Türkan Şoray's eyes, Galip fell silent. The woman stretched out on the bed next to the dressing table.

"Come to me, why don't you?" she said. "Nothing is worth that much, nothing, do you understand?" But Galip just sat there uncertainly. "Or don't you love Türkan Şoray?" the woman added, and Galip was not sure if the note of jealousy in her voice was real or part of the act.

"I do."

"You liked the way I fluttered my eyelashes, didn't you?"

"I did."

"Then come to me, darling."

"Let's talk some more first."

"What?"

Galip paused to think.

"What's your name? What do you do for a living?"

"I'm a lawyer."

"I used to have a lawyer," said the woman. "He took all my money, but he never managed to get back the car my husband took, even though it was registered in my name. The car was mine, do you understand? Mine. But now there's this prostitute driving it around. A '56 Chevrolet. Fire-engine red. If he couldn't get me my car back, what was the point of having a lawyer? Could you get my car back from my husband?"

"I could," said Galip.

"You could?" said the woman hopefully. "Yes, you could. If you could, I'd marry you, too. You could save me from this life—I mean, the film world. I'm tired of being an actress. People are so backward in this country, they don't realize acting is an art—they call us prostitutes. I'm not an actress, I'm an artist, do you understand?"

"Of course."

"Would you marry me?" cried the woman joyfully. "If you married me, we could drive around in my car. Will you marry me? But not unless you really love me."

"I'll marry you."

"No, no, you're the one who has to ask me. Ask me if I'll marry you."

"Türkan, will you marry me?"

"Not like that! Ask me with feeling, like they do in the movies! Get up on your feet first; no one pops the question sitting down."

Galip rose to his feet, as if to sing the national anthem. "Türkan, will you—will you marry me?"

"But I'm not a virgin," said the woman. "I had an accident."

"While riding a horse or sliding down the banister?"

"No, while I was ironing. You laugh, but only yesterday a little bird told me that the sultan is after your head. Are you married?"

"Yes, I'm married."

"I always end up with the married ones!" said the woman, and her voice was straight out of *License to Love*. "But it doesn't matter. The important thing is the National Railroad. Which team do you think is going to win the championship this year? Where do you think all this is going? When do you think the army is going to stop this anarchy? Do you know, you'd look a lot better if you cut your hair."

"Don't make personal remarks," said Galip. "That's rude."

"But what did I just say a moment ago?" said the woman, fluttering her eyelashes with fake surprise. "I asked if you could get me my car back if we got married. No, I said if you could get me my car back, would you marry me? Let me give you the license plate number: 34 CG 19 May 1919. The day Atatürk left Samsun to liberate Anatolia. It's a '56 Chevrolet."

"Tell me about your Chevrolet!" said Galip.

"Fine, I will, but remember they'll be knocking on the door soon. Your *visite* is almost over."

"No need to use French."

"Pardon?"

"I don't care about the money," said Galip.

"Neither do I," said the woman. "My '56 Chevrolet was the same color as my fingernails, exactly this color. One of my nails is broken, see? So maybe there's a dent in my Chevrolet now too. Until that disastrous husband of mine gave it to that prostitute, I'd drive here every evening in my car. But now I see it when it passes me in the street, I mean my car. Sometimes I see it on my way back to Taksim Square, and there'll be a different driver, and then I'll see it later when I'm waiting on the Karaköy pier, and there'll be another driver, waiting for a fare. That whore is obsessed with the car, paints it a new color every day. One day I look and it's chestnut brown, I see it again a day later and its flashing with chrome and fitted with new lights, and now it's the same color as milky coffee. A day after that it's become a wedding car, with garlands of flowers and a baby doll sitting on the hood, and then a week passes by and what do you know? This time it's painted black and there are six policemen with big mustaches riding in it; believe it or not, it's now a squad car. No doubt about it—it even has a sign that says POLICE. Of course, they change the license plate every time, hoping that might fool me."

"Of course."

"Of course," said the woman. "They're all her customers—the driver as well as the police. But can't that cuckold husband of mine see what goes on right under his nose? He up and left me one day, just like that. Has anyone ever done that to you? What day of the month is it?"

"The twelfth."

"How time flies. Look how you're making me talk. Or is it something special you're after? Just tell me. I've taken a liking to you: You're a gentleman; what's the harm in it? Do you really have a pile of money with you; are you really rich? Or are you a greengrocer, like İzzet? No, of course not. You're a lawyer. Tell me a riddle, Mr. Lawyer. . . . OK then, I'll tell one to you. What's the difference between the sultan and the Bosphorus Bridge?"

"I don't know."

"Or between Atatürk and Muhammed?"

"I don't know."

"You give up too easily!" said the woman. She took one last look at herself in the mirror, stood up, and whispered the answers into his ear. Then she wrapped her arms around Galip's neck. "Let's get married," she mumbled. "Let's go to Mount Kaf. Let's belong to each other. Let's become different people. Take me, take me, take me."

They kissed in the spirit of the game. Was there anything about this woman that reminded him of Rüya? There wasn't, but Galip was still pleased with himself. When they fell into bed, the woman did something that reminded him of Rüya, though not in exactly the same way. Rüya had an unnerving way of pulling back her tongue, and it made Galip feel as if she were someone else, but the fake Türkan Şoray's tongue was bigger and thicker than Rüya's and also more forceful; when she pushed it gently, but also playfully, into his mouth it was not the woman in his arms but he who became someone else, and this aroused him. Inspired by the woman's theatrics, they tossed and turned and rolled from one end of the bed to the other like they did in those preposterous kissing scenes in Turkish movies; first he was on top and then she was, and then he was back on top again. "You're making me dizzy!" said the woman, imitating a ghost no longer in the room, and shaking her head as if it were really spinning. They could see themselves in the dressing table mirror at this end of the bed—the woman watched in the mirror as they both undressed—and during the love scene that followed, there were moments when Galip felt as if there was a third person in the mirror watching them, or an entire jury, sent to judge them as if in an athletics competition and rather pleased to see a gymnast performing her tricks with such panache. Later, at a moment when they were bouncing gently on the bed and Galip wasn't looking into the mirror, the woman murmured, "We've both become different people." Then she asked, "Who am I, who am I , who am I?" but Galip was too far gone to give her the answer she wanted to hear. The woman said, "Two times two is four," and murmured, "Listen, listen, listen!" and she whispered into his ear a story about a sultan and an unlucky crown prince, as if it were a fairy tale, as if it might never have happened.

"If I am you, then you are me," the woman said, as she was getting dressed. "How does it all add up, if I am you and you are me?" She shot him a sly smile. "So, did you like your Türkan Şoray?"

"I did."

"Then save me from this life, save me, get me out of here, take me with you; let's go somewhere else together, let's run away, let's get married, let's start a new life."

What scene was this, then, and from what film? Galip couldn't tell. Perhaps this was what the woman really wanted. She told Galip she didn't believe he was married: because she knew her married men, she could tell. If they got married, if Galip managed to retrieve her '56 Chevrolet, they could go out for a drive along the Bosphorus, stop in Emirgân to buy wafer halvah, spend some time in Tarabya too, looking at the sea, and then they could find a place to eat in Büyükdere.

"I don't like Büyükdere," said Galip.

"In that case, you'll wait in vain for Him to come to you," said the woman. "He'll never come to you, ever."

"I'm not in any hurry."

"I am," she said stubbornly. "But I'm afraid I won't recognize Him when he comes. I'm afraid I'll be the last one to see Him, the very last one."

"Who is He?"

The woman laughed mysteriously. "Don't you watch any movies at all? Don't you know the rules of the game? That's classified information. Loose talk can get you killed in a country like this. I want to live."

She was telling him about a friend who had mysteriously disappeared and had probably been killed and thrown into the Bosphorus, when there was a knock on the door.

The woman fell silent. But as Galip left the room, she whispered:

"We're all waiting for Him, all of us; we're all waiting for Him."

Chapter Fourteen

We're All Waiting for Him

We're all waiting for Him. We've all been waiting for Him for centuries. When we tire of the crowds on Galata Bridge and gaze down instead at the leaden blue waters of the Golden Horn, it is Him we seek; we seek Him as we toss a few more sticks of wood into a stove too weak to heat a tiny room in Surdibi, as we climb the endless staircases of a certain old Greek building in Cihangir, as we sit in that *meyhane* in a distant Anatolian town, waiting for our friends to arrive and poring over the crossword in our Istanbul paper. Wherever our dreams take us—onto the airplane we see pictured in that same paper, into a well-lit room, there to fall into the arms of a beautiful woman— it is Him we seek. We long for Him as we stroll along muddy pavements, laden with groceries wrapped in newspapers that a hundred pairs of eyes have scanned, with plastic bags that make all the apples inside them smell synthetic, with string bags that leave purple marks on our hands and fingers. We wait for Him as we sit in movie theaters watching hairy men breaking bottles on a Saturday night and world beauties embarking on breathtaking adventures; we seek Him as we walk home from the brothels that have succeeded only in making us feel lonelier than before, as we leave the *meyhanes* where friends ridicule us for our small obsessions, as we thank our neighbor for inviting us over to hear the radio play, even though we didn't hear a word of it because his noisy children refused to go to bed. Some of us believe that it will be in the back streets—in a lonely corner where darkness has reigned ever since louts with slingslots shattered the streetlamps—

that He will make His first appearance; others of us believe it will be in front of one of those impious shops where they sell lottery tickets, girlie magazines, toys, tobacco, condoms, and untold quantities of useless trinkets. But wherever He ultimately chooses to reveal Himself, be it in the restaurant kitchens where little children mold ground meat into meatballs for twelve hours a day, or a movie theater where thousands of eyes unite in longing to become a single eye, or a green hill sitting where shepherds as pure as angels fall under the spell of the cypresses swaying in the graveyard, we are agreed at least that when the endless wait is over, when eternity vanishes in the blinking of an eye, those of us who are lucky enough to see Him first will recognize Him immediately and know, too, that deliverance is nigh.

The Koran is explicit on this point, though only for those who can divine its letters (as in the 97th verse of the Al-Isra sura and the 23rd verse of the Al-Zumar sura, which describe the holy book as being "consistent in its various parts" and "repeating," et cetera, et cetera). However, those in search of proof must make do with a line from *Origins and History*, penned 350 years after the revelation of the Koran: according to its author, Mutahhar Ibn Tahir of Jerusalem, He would "reveal the road to a man who resembles Muhammed or bears His name or whose work is consistent with my own"; and indeed this statement leads us back to the depositions of the witnesses who supplied the information for this hadith and others like it. Moving on another 350 years, we find a brief mention in Ibn Batuta's *Journeys*, wherein Shiites prepare for His coming during a ceremony in the underground passages below the shrine of Hakim-al Wakt at Samarra. In an account dictated to his scribe thirty years afterward, Firuz Shah described thousands of miserable wretches gathering in the dusty yellow streets of Delhi, so sure were they that He would soon reveal Himself, and in so doing reveal the mystery of the letters. In his more or less contemporaneous *Preface*, based on a thorough examination of extreme Shiite texts, Ibn Khaldun made this much clear: When He made His appearance on the Day of Judgment, He would have at His side the fearsome creature some call Deccal and others know as Satan—what Christians call the Antichrist—but before that day was through He would slay him.

But here's the surprising thing: Though we all await His coming, and though many claim to have foreseen it, no one—and I am speaking now of all humanity, from my dear reader Mehmet Yılmaz, who once described a vision that came to him while sitting in his home in remotest Anatolia, to the great Ibn' Arabi, who recounts being visited by the same vision seven hundred years earlier in *The Phoenix*; from the philosopher al-Kindi, who dreamed that He, and all those He had saved, would take Constantinople from the Christians, to the salesgirl who sees Him in her daydreams as she sits surrounded by bobbins, buttons, and nylon stockings in a dry-goods store in a Beyoğlu back street, centuries after al-Kindi's dream came true—there is not in this throng of humanity a single soul who saw His face.

As for Deccal, we can see him very clearly indeed: in *Lives of the Prophets*, al-Bukhari tells us he is a one-eyed creature with red hair, while in *Pilgrimage* his name is emblazoned on his face; Tayalisi describes him as having a thick neck; while Hoca Nizamettin Efendi describes the creature who came to him in a vision in Istanbul as red-eyed and thick-hewn. During my early days as a reporter, a newspaper called *Karagöz* that was very popular in the Anatolian hinterlands ran a comic strip about the adventures of a Turkish warrior, and whenever Deccal crept into the frame to perform yet another devilish trick on him and his fellow soldiers (catching them off guard, as when they were making love to the beauties of Constantinople, this despite the fact that the city had yet to be conquered), he was crooked-limbed and crooked-mouthed, with a broad forehead and a bulbous nose, and no mustache (this last detail being in compliance with the instructions I sometimes left for the illustrators). But while Deccal inspires us to imaginative excesses, our only writer to present the Almighty in all His glory was Dr. Ferit Kemal in *Le grand pacha*; written in French and published in 1870, it does not—to the regret of many—feature in our literary canon.

To exclude the only work that shows the Almighty in His true colors, simply because it was written in French, is as grievous as to allege that the Russian author Dostoyevsky stole the model for the Grand Inquisitor in *The Brothers Karamazov* from the same slim treatise—though it must be said that those who made this charge in the eastward-looking journals *Fountain* and *The Great East* did so with trepidation. Whenever I venture into the endless saga about what the West stole from the East and the East from the West, I think this: If this realm of dreams we call the world is but a house we roam like sleepwalkers, then our literary traditions are like wall clocks, there to make us feel at home. So:

1. To say that one of these wall clocks is right and another wrong is utter nonsense.
2. To say that one is five hours ahead of the other is also nonsense; by using the same logic you could just as easily say that it's seven hours behind.
3. For much the same reason, if it is 9:35 according to one clock and it just so happens that another clock also says it's 9:35, anyone who claims that the second clock is imitating the first is spouting nonsense.

A year before he attended Averröes's funeral in Córdoba, Ibn' Arabi, who would write two hundred mystical texts before his own demise, found himself in Morocco; it was during his sojourn that he penned a text inspired by the Al-Isra sura of the Koran, as mentioned above (*note to the typesetter: If we're at the top of a column, replace above with below, please!*); or more specifically, the story (the dream) in which Muhammed, having been carried to Jerusalem, climbed a ladder (*mirach* in Arabic) into the sky to explore Heaven and Hell. Now, anyone who reads Ibn' Arabi's account of his travels with his guide through the seven heavens and concludes, after noting he was thirty-five years old at the time of writing (1198), that Nizam, the girl of his dreams, was right, and Beatrice wrong, or that Ibn' Arabi was right, and Dante wrong, or that the Book of the Israelites and *Makan al-Asra* was correct, while the *Divine Comedy* is incorrect, is perpetrating the first sort of nonsense I was describing.

In the eleventh century, the Andalusian philosopher Ibn Tufeyl wrote a book about a child abandoned on a desert island; during his sojourn there he came to respect nature, the sea, the life-giving sustenance afforded to him by a doe, the certainty of death, the heavens above and the "divine truths"; but anyone who claims that *Hayy Ibn Yakzan* ("The Self-Taught Philosopher") is six hundred years "ahead" of *Robinson Crusoe*—or that Ibn Tufeyl is six hundred years "behind" Daniel Defoe because the tools and objects that feature in the latter's novel are described in greater detail—is perpetrating the second sort of nonsense I was describing.

In March 1761, Hacı Veliyyüddin Efendi, a sheikh of Islam during the reign of Mustafa III, sat down to write a long poem in couplets, taking as his inspiration a disrespectful and inopportune remark made by an indiscreet friend who'd dropped by of a Friday evening; spying a magnificent chest in the sheikh's study, he had cried, "But, sir! Your chest is as cluttered as your mind!" His poem was by means of a retort, setting out as it did to prove that everything was in its place in his mind, as in his walnut chest, and to show that each bore striking resemblances to the other. He went on to suggest that our minds, like the splendid Armenian-made chest, boast two compartments, four shelves, and twelve drawers in which we store times, places, numbers, papers, and all the odds and ends we now describe as *existence, necessity, and cause-and-effect*; and though he wrote this poem twenty years before Kant divided Pure Reason into twelve compartments, anyone who suggests that the German philosopher was "imitating" a Turk is guilty of the third sort of nonsense I described.

When Dr. Ferit Kemal was working on his vivid rendition of the Redeemer for whom we all wait, he would not have been surprised to hear that he would become the object of this sort of nonsense in a hundred years' time; ignored and forgotten, he lived in his dreams. He was never photographed, so I am left to imagine this dream traveler's ghostly visage: he was an addict. He turned a number of his patients into addicts too; we know this from Abdurrahman Şeref's derogatory opus, *The New Ottomans and Freedom*. It was 1866—yes, one year before Dostoyevsky's second European tour—that the winds of freedom and rebellion swept him off to Paris, where he wrote several pieces for two expatriate newspapers then being published in Europe, *Liberty* and *The Reporter*. With time his fellow Young Turks reconciled their differences with the Palace, returning one by one to Istanbul, while he stayed on in Paris. The trail goes cold at this point. He alludes to *Les paradis artificiels* in his preface, and perhaps he also knew of De Quincey, who is another favorite of mine, so it is possible that he was experimenting with opium; but in his passage about Him he gives us no reason to believe this is so: The signs to be found therein point instead to a powerful logic that we hunger for today.

I am writing this column to illuminate this logic and to introduce the powerful thinking behind *Le grand pacha* to the patriotic officers serving in today's armed forces. But to do so I must first give some sense of the book as an object. So imagine a slender volume bound in blue, printed on paper made from straw, and published by Poulet-Malassis in Paris in the year 1861. It is only ninety-six pages long. Imagine illustrations (by the French artist de Tennielle) that call to mind not the Istanbul of his time but the stone buildings, pavements, and cobblestone streets we see today; the dungeons and primitive instruments of torture in use in the mid-nineteenth century are likewise nowhere to be found; instead, we see the concrete rat holes we have come to know so well in recent years, rooms where you can imagine a man suspended from a ceiling, an interrogator in the shadows, a magneto.

The book begins with a description of an Istanbul back street at midnight. Except for the watchmen beating their sticks against the pavement and the dogs barking in a distant neighborhood, all is silent. No lights are burning behind the grilled windows of the wooden houses. A thin column of smoke rises from a stovepipe to disappear into the mist that sits over the city's domes and rooftops as the neighborhood settles into sleep. Then suddenly footsteps ring out on the empty pavement. How strange, how unexpected—but the people know at once that these new footsteps bring good tidings, even those who are putting on layer after layer as they brace themselves for their cold beds, even those who are already dreaming under seven quilts.

The next day is sunny, joyous—no sign of the previous night's gloom. Everyone recognized Him; they recognized Him from His very footsteps; knowing that the sorrowful eternity they'd thought would never end is drawing to a close, they all rejoice. And He is among them, riding the merry-go-rounds; embracing enemies-turned-friends; delighting in the music, the laughing crowds of dancers, the children with their candied apples and their chewing gum. Hard to see Him now as the Redeemer who will lead them to a better place, urging the downtrodden from one victory to the next; today He is an older brother, walking among beloved siblings. But on His face there is the shadow of a doubt—a misgiving, a premonition. It is now, as He walks lost in thought through the city streets, that the Grand Pasha's men arrest Him and throw Him into a stone dungeon. The Grand Pasha himself arrives at midnight, candle in hand, to pay Him a visit; whereupon they talk until the break of dawn.

Who is this Grand Pasha? Like the author, I would prefer my readers to decide for themselves, so I shall refrain from giving you the full Turkish translation of his name. As he is a pasha, we might think of him as a great statesman, a great soldier, or simply a man of high rank. As he speaks with decisive logic, we might assume he's a philosopher, an eminence possessed of the kind of wisdom we attribute to those who put their country's interests before their own. In the dungeon that night, it will be the Grand Pasha who does the talking, and He who does the listening. Here, then, is the Grand Pasha's line of reasoning, and the words render Him speechless.

1. Like everyone else, I too knew at once that You were He (the Grand Pasha began). There was, however, no need for me to glean this secret from words and numbers, or look for signs in the Koran and the sky above, or study the predictions made in Your name over the past thousand years. I knew it was You from the moment I saw the joy and triumph in people's faces. Now they expect You to throw off their melancholy and erase their pain and all memory of their losses; most of all, they expect to follow You from victory to victory, but do You really think You can do this for them? Muhammed may have managed to instill hope in the hearts of the miserable all those centuries ago, but that was because he was indeed able to lead them from victory to victory with his sword. But today—never mind how devout we are—there is no getting around the fact that the weapons of the enemies of Islam are stronger than ours. There is simply no hope of a military victory! While it is true that certain false messiahs made serious trouble for the French and the English in India and Africa, is it not also the case that they were later crushed and banished, thus paving the way for catastrophes on an even larger scale? (These pages abound with military and economic comparisons that demonstrate not just Western dominance over Islam but over the East as a whole: as the Grand Pasha describes the wealthy West and the ruined East, he takes the direct tone of a politician who is determined to be realistic,

while He, who is not a charlatan, who really is the One we've been waiting for, can do no more than confirm the bleak picture the pasha has drawn.)

2. But this is not to say that there is nothing in this bleak picture that might awaken the hope for victory in the hearts of the downtrodden (continues the Grand Pasha until long past midnight). However, it would be pointless to take up arms only against the enemy outside. What about the enemies within? Might it not be the case that the authors of our suffering are none other than the sinners, usurers, blood drinkers, and tyrants who walk among us, parading as godfearing men? The only way we can rekindle the hope for happiness and victory in the hearts of our long-suffering brothers is by waging war on the enemy within—surely You see that too, don't You? If this is so, You must also agree that this is not a war for great generals and heroic soldiers but for informers and executioners, police officers and torturers. If You show our hopeless brothers the men responsible for their misery, You can easily convince them that these same men must be crushed before they can climb up to Heaven in the sky above. This in effect is what we've been doing for the past three hundred years. We expose the enemy within to give our brothers hope. And they believe us, for they need hope just as desperately as they need bread. Before these culprits are sentenced, the brightest and most steadfast among them—those who understand the logic of the enterprise—will often admit to more crimes, exaggerating even the smallest, for they know that this will bring more hope into the hearts of the downtrodden. We even pardon a few of them now and again, so they can help us hunt down other enemies within. Like the Koran, hope underpins our success in the real world as much as it does our spiritual happiness: We expect the hand that feeds us to bring us hope and freedom too.

3. Now I know that You have the resolve that is needed to achieve this mighty task, that You will pluck the guilty from the crowds without batting an eyelid, that You will remain steadfast, see that justice is done—even if, alas, this means subjecting them to torture—for You are He. But once You have rekindled hope in the hearts of the downtrodden, how to keep the flickering flames

alive? With time they will see that things are no better than they were before. When they see that their daily bread is the same as ever, their hopes will begin to die. They will lose faith in the Book, lose faith both in the real world and that other world shimmering in the heavens above, and surrender once again to darkness, dissolution, and the spiritual void. Even worse, they'll begin to doubt You, hate You. The informers will begin to suffer pangs of conscience about the culprits they handed over so lovingly to Your torturers and executioners; the guards and policemen will tire of torture and begin to question its purpose, so much so that nothing will work on them anymore; the latest methods will cease to beguile them, and the hope You once brought to them will be similarly tarnished. Before long they will decide that all the luckless creatures they strung up on their gallows like bunches of grapes were hanged for nothing. So by the Day of Judgment, as You will see, they will no longer believe in You or in the stories You've told them. But You can already see, I'm sure, that this is not the worst of it. For when they are no longer able to all believe in the same story, each one will begin to believe in his own story; indeed, they will all *become* their own story, and each and every one of them will also want to tell it. Millions of wretches will wander like sleepwalkers through the city's filthy streets, its muddy and eternally disordered squares, wearing their sad stories like halos of woe. By now they will no longer see You as Him but as Deccal— yes, You! Now they will put their faith in Deccal's stories instead of Yours. Deccal will return victorious, and he will be me or someone like me. And this person will tell the people You've been deceiving them for years, that instead of bringing them hope You've fed them lies, that You yourself *are* Deccal. Perhaps there will be no need for this, for by now either Deccal or some malcontent who has decided You've been lying to him for years will surely have followed You into a dark alley after midnight to empty his gun into that mortal body they once proclaimed impervious to bullets. So this is how it will all end up, after years of bringing the people hope, years of deceiving them. One night they will be walking down the muddy streets You have come to know and love, and there, on the filthy pavement, they will find You dead.

Chapter Fifteen

Love Stories on a Snowy Evening

Idle men, chasing after fairy tales. . . .
—Rumi

Only moments after leaving the Türkan Şoray look-alike's room, Galip ran into the man with whom he'd shared a taxi—the one who seemed to have walked straight out of an old black-and-white film. Galip was standing in front of the Beyoğlu police station, trying to decide where to go, when a police car pulled up smartly to the curb, its blue light flashing. The door flew open and out came two policemen with a third man he recognized at once, though his face had now lost its black-and-white glamour and taken on the dark blue sheen of the criminal. As the man moved into the floodlights that protected the police station from all manner of attack, a bloodstain formed at the corner of his mouth, but he made no attempt to wipe it away. The briefcase that he'd hugged to his chest in the taxi was now in the hands of one of the policemen; though he walked with resignation, daring only to look straight ahead, he seemed strangely elated. When he saw Galip in front of the stairs leading up to the station, he gave him a ghastly smile.

"Good evening, sir!"

"Good evening," Galip replied uncertainly.

"Who's that?" one of the policemen asked, pointing at Galip.

By now they had pushed him through the doors into the station, so Galip did not hear the end of the conversation.

When he reached the main road, just after one in the morning, there were still people walking up and down the snowy pavements. On one of the streets that runs parallel with the British consulate, thought

Galip, there's a place that stays open all night that's frequented not just by nouveau-riche peasants from Anatolia but by intellectuals too. It was Rüya who picked up this sort of information, usually from arts journals that alluded to such places only to make fun of them.

He was just passing the building that had once housed the Tokatlıyan Hotel when he bumped into İskender. It was clear from his breath that he'd drunk a great deal of *rakı*; he'd picked up the BBC film crew from the Pera Palas Hotel earlier that evening to do what he called "the thousand-and-one-nights tour of Istanbul" (dogs knocking over rubbish bins, carpet and hashish merchants, potbellied belly dancers, nightclub lowlifes) and they'd ended up in a dive in the back streets. Then an odd-looking man with a briefcase had taken offense at something inaudible someone—not in his own party, someone sitting nearby—had said to him; eventually the police had come and dragged him off by the collar and someone else had escaped through the window; but then other people had come to fill the empty tables and it had turned into a fun evening, and would Galip like to join them? After Galip and İskender had walked the length of İstiklâl Avenue in search of filterless cigarettes, they turned into a side street; the door they entered had a sign over it that said NIGHTCLUB.

Inside, Galip was greeted with joy, noise, and indifference. One of the English journalists, a beautiful woman, was telling a story. The classical Turkish music ensemble was packing up for the night and the magician was performing a trick, taking boxes out of boxes, and then taking more boxes out of those. His female assistant had bowlegs and, just below her belly, a cesarean scar. It was hard to imagine her giving birth to any child other than the sleepy rabbit she held in her hands. Although he was able to hold the audience's attention with Zati Sungur's famous vanishing-radio trick, their interest fell off again when he went back to taking boxes out of boxes.

As the Englishwoman told her story at the other end of the table, İskender translated it into Turkish. Galip listened, hoping that the woman's expressive face would help him catch the gist of the story, even though he'd missed the beginning. It was about "a woman" (Galip was sure it was the woman telling the story) trying to get a man who had known and loved her since the age of nine to accept a sign she'd read on the face of a Byzantine coin that a diver had brought up from the bottom of the sea; though the woman saw the sign as self-evident, the man was so blinded by passion that he refused to see it altogether; all he could do was to write her love poems. "So the two cousins were married," said İskender in Turkish, "and all because of a Byzantine coin scooped up from the sea floor by a diver. But while the magic sign on its face had changed this woman's life forever, the man had no inkling of it." The woman had been forced to live out her life alone, in a tower. (Galip assumed from this that she had left the man in question.) When the story came to an end, the table fell respectfully (and in Galip's opinion, stupidly) silent. Perhaps it was wrong to expect them to be as pleased as Galip to hear that a beautiful woman had left her dolt of a husband, and perhaps he would have felt differently had he heard the story from the beginning, but the "tragic ending" (and the pretentious response to it) made him want to laugh. The only thing that moved him about the story was the beauty of the woman who had told it, though by this point he felt like downgrading her from beautiful to fairly attractive.

The tall man who now launched into another story was (he gathered from İskender) a writer whose name he'd heard before. Adjusting his glasses, he told his audience that while his story concerned a writer, they were not to assume he was speaking about himself. He smiled oddly as he spoke—he seemed embarrassed, but at the same time eager to please—and Galip was unable to read the writer's motives.

The story was about a man who, according to this writer, spent many long years at home alone writing novels that he showed to no one, and that no one would ever have published, even if he had. So completely had he surrendered himself to his work (which wasn't even considered work at the time) that the man soon came to like living behind closed doors—not because he didn't enjoy the company of others or because he was critical of the way they lived—it was simply that he could not bear to drag himself from his desk. But because he spent so much of his time at that desk, the writer lost whatever social skills he'd ever had, so that on the very rare occasions when he did go out, he'd be so bewildered by the social swirl that he'd retreat to a table in a corner to count the minutes until he could return to his desk. He'd work for fourteen hours at a stretch, retiring to bed as the dawn call to prayer wafted from one minaret after another to echo in the hills, apparently to dream of the woman he loved, whom he only saw once a year, and even then only by chance, but what he felt for this woman was neither romantic nor sexual; it was the yearning for an imaginary companion, an antidote to solitude.

Though he claimed to know nothing of "love" but what he read in books and didn't think sex was too exciting either, this writer did end up marrying an extraordinarily beautiful woman. At about the same time, his books began to be published, but neither this nor his marriage had much effect on his daily routine. The writer still put in fourteen-hour days at his desk, constructing his sentences as painstakingly as before or dreaming up details for new stories as he stared at the blank page in front of him. The only change was the link he sensed between the dreams his beautiful and silent wife was dreaming, as he came to bed at dawn, and the daydreams he conjured up while listening to the call to prayer. He could feel their reveries spilling into each other, rising and falling, as he lay there next to her. They were breathing in harmony, to the same silent song. The writer was happy with his new life; after so many years alone, he did not find it difficult to sleep at someone else's side; he loved to daydream as he listened to his wife's breathing, loved believing that her dreams flowed into his, and his into hers.

After his wife left him—on a winter's morning, and without giving him much of a reason—the writer went through hard times. No longer could he daydream as he listened to the dawn call to prayer. The reveries he'd conjured up so easily before and during his marriage, to ease himself into sleep—if they came to him at all—were now lackluster and unconvincing. It was like writing a novel that was refusing to go according to plan: It was as if there were a secret locked inside his dream that refused to reveal itself, that kept luring him into cul-de-sacs to confirm his incompetence, compound his confusion. During the first days after his wife left him, his daydreams were so weak and thin that this writer who had always gone to sleep at dawn would still be lying awake after the first birdsongs had floated from the treetops, and the seagulls had flown away from the rooftops where they spent their nights, and the garbage truck had rumbled past, and the first city bus of the morning. Even worse, the dearth of dreams and sleep affected his writing. Even if he wrote the same sentence twenty times over, the writer could not breathe life into even the simplest sentence.

To escape his depression before it suffocated him, he set himself a strict regime, forcing himself to remember each and every one of the dreams he'd once had, hoping they might bring him back into harmony. Weeks later, after drifting off into a peaceful sleep during the dawn call to prayer, he had risen from his bed still fogged with sleep and gone straight to his desk, and when he saw the life and beauty in the sentences rolling from his pen he knew his depression had finally lifted, and at the same time he realized that he had, without knowing it, played a strange trick on himself.

The man whose wife had left him, this writer who could no longer invent his own dreams, had cured himself of his affliction by dreaming of the man he once was, the man who shared his bed with no one, whose dreams never intertwined with the dreams of a beautiful woman. He conjured up this forgotten self with such force and intensity that he was soon inhabiting his skin; by dreaming his dreams, he was able to lull himself to sleep. Before long he had grown so accustomed to his double life that it seemed like second nature; no longer did he have to force himself to dream or to write. When he wrote, he became someone else, filling his ashtray with the same cigarettes, drinking coffee from the same cup, drifting off to sleep at the same time in the same bed with the ghost of his own past.

When his wife came back to him (or the house, as she herself put it) on yet another winter's morning, without giving him much of a reason, the writer again went through hard times. He just couldn't get used to it: The same uncertainty that had troubled him during the early days of his abandonment came back to haunt him. If, after hours of tossing and turning, he managed to get himself to sleep, he'd be awakened by his nightmares; restlessly turning from his old self to new self, drifting aimlessly like a drunk who cannot find his way home. On one such sleepless morning, the writer rose from his bed, tucked his pillow under his arm, crossed over to his study, which smelled like dust and paper, and, curling up on the divan in the corner, fell at last into a deep sleep. From that morning onward, the writer never slept next to his silent wife, dreaming her mysterious dreams; instead he slept in his study, next to his desk and his papers. The moment he rose, before the fog of sleep had dissipated, he would sit down to write, and he could almost feel his dreams flowing into the stories he now wrote with such ease; but now he had another problem, and it terrified him.

Just before his wife left him, he'd written a novel (his readers called it "historical") about a man who changed places with his double. Later, after his wife left him and he forced himself to become the man he'd once been so as to sleep in peace, he became the man who had written that novel, and when he became the man he'd once been, he was blind both to his future and his own, and he found himself writing his novel about the doubles all over again! It was not long before this world— where everything was a copy of something else, where people were at once themselves and their own imitations, and all stories opened out into other stories—grew to look so real that the writer, thinking no one would want to read a story in a place this "realistic," decided to invent another, surreal world that might be more fun to write about, and that his readers might also enjoy more. From then on, while his beautiful mysterious wife lay sleeping in her bed, the writer spent his nights roaming the city's dark alleys under the shadow of smashed streetlamps, exploring underground passages from the days of Byzantium and the coffeehouses, *meyhanes,* and clubs where the dregs of humanity gathered to give themselves to their addictions. The more he saw, the more he realized that everything he ever dreamed about "our city" was actually real; this fact alone told him that the world was a book. Entranced by the book of life, he spent ever longer hours wandering around its streets, delighting in the new faces, new signs, and new stories he found before him with every turn of the page, but the longer this went on, the more he feared returning to his beautiful wife in her bed and the unfinished story that lay neglected on his desk.

So ended the writer's story. It was met with silence, possibly because it was more about loneliness than love and more about storytelling than it was about people. And because everyone can remember being "abandoned for no reason," Galip imagined they were all curious to know why this particular writer's wife had left him.

The next storyteller was a bar girl who began by telling her listeners several times that her story was true. She wanted to be absolutely sure that "our tourist friends" had been set straight on this very important point, because she wanted this story to serve as an example not just for

Turkey but for the entire world. Her story was set in the recent past, and in the very club where they now sat. Two cousins met by chance after a separation of many years, and their childhood passion for each other was rekindled. Seeing as the girl was a bar girl and the boy a tout ("In other words," said the woman, turning to the women tourists, "he was a pimp") there was no danger of an honor killing. In those days, it was peaceful in the club, as it was in the country as a whole; there were no youths killing each other in the streets, and on holidays people sent each other packages with candy in them, not bombs. The girl and the boy were happy and in love. After the girl's father died rather suddenly, they were able to live under the same roof, though they still slept in separate beds, waiting eagerly ("with four eyes, as we say in Turkish") for their wedding day.

On the very day they were to marry, while the girl and all the other such girls in Beyoğlu were busy perfecting their makeup and dousing themselves with perfume, the boy went first to the barber for his nuptial shave and then out for a stroll along the avenue, whereupon he fell into the clutches of a woman of astounding beauty. A moment was all it took for him to lose his reason; it was only after she had taken him back to her room at the Pera Palas Hotel and made passionate love to him that she revealed her secret: this luckless woman was the bastard child of the Queen of England and the Shah of Iran. Her visit to Turkey was part of a grand revenge she'd planned against the parents who had abandoned her after their one night stand. She now came to the point: She wanted this young man to find her a map; it was divided into halves, she said; one was in the hands of the National Security Bureau and the other with MİT, the secret police.

Still aflame with passion, the boy excused himself and ran off to the club where the wedding was to have taken place; the guests had dispersed by now but the girl was crying in the corner. After he'd consoled her, he explained that he'd been recruited into "a national cause." They postponed their nuptials and sent word out to every bar girl, belly dancer, madam, and Sulukule Gypsy in Beyoğlu, asking them to find out whatever they could from each and every one of the crooked policemen who frequented the dens of iniquity in which they earned their daily bread. But by the time they'd got hold of the two halves of the map and put them together, the girl had also worked out that her beloved cousin had duped her—and all the other hardworking girls of Istanbul—for he had fallen in love with the daughter of the Queen of England and the Shah of Iran. Slipping the map into the left cup of her bra, she gathered up the pieces of her broken heart and banished herself to a room in a Kuledibi brothel, fabled for the depravity of its women and frequented by the city's most unscrupulous men.

Under orders from the shrewish princess, the cousin searched the city for her. But as he went from street to street, he realized it was not the hunter he truly loved but the hunted, not the princess but the cousin he had known since childhood. Arriving finally at the Kuledibi brothel, he caught a glimpse of her in a mirror through a peephole; she was with a rich man wearing a bow tie, and when he saw the tricks his childhood love was playing to "preserve her innocence" he kicked in the door and rescued her. But now, a huge mole suddenly appeared in the eye he'd pressed to the peephole (to see his half-naked sweetheart "playing the flute") and like the jealousy burning in his heart, it refused to go away. An identical love mark appeared on the girl's left breast. Later, when the boy went with the police to the Pera Palas Hotel to arrest the shrew who had led him astray, he opened a drawer to find photographs of ten thousand innocent youths the man-eating princess had seduced and then photographed naked in compromising poses. She had been intending to use this collection for political blackmail, and that was not all; she was also in possession of hundreds of books you saw next to mug shots of anarchists on television, not to mention manifestos emblazoned with hammers and sickles, and the last testament of that queer, the last sultan, and a plan to partition Turkey on a manuscript overlaid with a Byzantine cross. The secret police were well aware that this woman had come to Turkey to infect it with anarchy, and that her methods were no different from those before her who had come to infect it with syphillis, but unfortunately her blackmail album included quite a few policemen posing in their birthday suits and waving their "nightsticks," so the whole thing was hushed up before the papers could get their hands on the incriminating pictures. The only picture they released to the press was the one that accompanied the cousin's wedding announcement. The bar girl then produced the clipping she claimed to have cut from the paper with her own two hands and passed it around the table for all to see: It was the bar girl herself, wearing a stylish coat with a fox collar and the same pearl earrings as tonight.

Seeing that some of her listeners had doubts about her story while others had found it funny, the woman lost her temper; insisting again that everything she'd said was true; she called for reinforcements, for it just so happened that the photographer who'd worked on this shameless project with the princess was in the club tonight. When this grayhaired photographer approached the table, the bar girl told him that "our guests" would be willing to have their pictures taken, and also leave him a fat tip, if he could tell them a good love story. He obliged with this one.

It must have been at least thirty years ago when a servant came to his small studio to call him to a residence on the Şişli streetcar line. He couldn't understand why anyone who lived at such an address would choose a nightclub photographer rather than one of his many colleagues who specialized in society parties, but he was curious, so off he went, to be met by a beautiful young widow who made him a "business proposition": She would pay him a substantial sum of money if he agreed to make copies of every photograph he took in the clubs of Beyoğlu and bring them over to her the following morning.

The photographer agreed, partly out of curiosity. Sensing a love story behind her business proposition, he decided to keep a close eye on the comely though cast-eyed brunette, but by the end of their second year together, he was sure that she was not searching for a man she knew, or even a man she recognized. Every morning, she'd pick out a handful of photographs from the hundred he showed her, either to ask if he had the same man in another pose or to ask for an enlargement, but it was never the same man. It was several years later that the woman—perhaps because their collaboration had brought with it a certain intimacy, or perhaps because she had grown to trust him—began to confide in our photographer:

"Such empty faces," she'd say. "Such meaningless expressions! I can't read anything into them! Don't bring me any more pictures like this—they're useless," she said. "I see no meaning in them, no letters at all!" He'd show her the same faces in other poses, but she found them almost impossible to *read* (she put great emphasis on this word). "How sorrowful they look!" she'd cry. "How dejected! If this is all a nightclub or a *meyhane* can do for them, then dear God! Just imagine how empty their faces must be when they return to their offices, their dreary counters, their manager's desks!"

This was not to say they didn't come across a few specimens that gave them both some hope. Once the woman thought she could read something in the wrinkled face of an old man they later discovered was a jeweler, but the meaning was ancient, stagnant. Though there was much to read in the wrinkles that covered his forehead and the richness of letters in the pockets under his eyes, they were but the final refrains of a closed book that was doomed to repeat itself forever and cast no light on the world of today. There was another man—an accountant, they later discovered—whose worried forehead was riddled with letters that did point to the world of today; one overcast morning, when they were examining an enlargement of his stormy face with considerable excitement, the lady passed him another large photograph that had appeared in that day's paper, along with the headline MAN MILKS BANK OF TWENTY MILLION. As he stood between two mustachioed policemen, looking calmly into the camera, he seemed relaxed; now that the excitement of guilt and lawlessness was over, his face was as vacant as a henna-stained sacrificial lamb.

By now, of course, people at the table had decided, after much whispering and raising of eyebrows, that the real love story was between the photographer and the lady, but as the photographer brought his story to a close, a new hero emerged. On a cool summer morning, as he was showing her a photograph of a crowded nightclub table, she looked among the blank stares, saw a shining face, and knew at once that she had not searched these eleven years in vain. That same evening, he went back to the same nightclub, where he was able, without much trouble, to take many more snaps of the same superb young face into which the lady was able to read a meaning that was as simple and clear as it was pure: The meaning was love. Though the sentence on his clean and open face was written in the Latin alphabet, which had only just been introduced, the lady could read the four new letters so clearly, she could not believe the photographer saw nothing in this man (whom they later discovered was thirty-three years old and repaired watches in a small shop in Karagümrük). If this face said nothing to him, she said, the photographer must be blind. She spent the days that followed trembling like a bride on her first visit to the matchmakers, sighing as painfully as a lover who knows from the start that her heart will be broken, and, when she felt the tiniest flickering of hope, entertaining elaborately detailed fantasies of future happiness. By the end of the week, by which time the photographer had had to resort to all manner of tricks to secure his quarry, every wall in the lady's house was covered with the pictures of the young watch repairman.

One night, after he'd managed to get close-ups more detailed than any he had taken before, the angel-faced watch repairman left the nightclub never to return; the lady was beside herself. She sent the photographer to Karagümrük to find him, but he was not in his shop, and when he went to the neighborhood where they said he lived, he was not at the address they'd given him. When he returned a week later, the shop was for sale as a "going concern" and the house was empty. Though the photographer continued to supply the lady with pictures, "for love, not money," she took no interest in them; even the most interesting face said nothing to her, unless it was the face of the watch repairman. Autumn came early that year, and it was on an usually windy morning that the photographer went over to the lady's house with an interesting "specimen," only to have the nosy janitor tell him, a bit too smugly, that the lady had moved to another address he was not at liberty to divulge. The photographer sadly told himself that this was the end of the story, though it might also be the beginning of the story he would build for himself from his memories.

But the real end of the story came to him many years afterward, as he was perusing a newspaper, only to come across the following headline: SHE THREW NITRIC ACID IN HIS FACE! The jealous woman who had thrown nitric acid into her lover's face did not have the same name as his Şişli lady, did not in any way resemble her, and was not even the same age, and the husband whose face she had disfigured with nitric acid was not a watch repairman but a public prosecutor in the small Anatolian town mentioned in the byline. There was, in fact, not a single detail in the article that chimed with anything he remembered about the lady and her beautiful watch repairman, but the moment he saw the words *nitric acid* our photographer knew in his heart they were indeed "his couple," together for all those years. They'd played this trick on him so they could elope and thus escape the many unhappy men who—like the photographer himself—might have come between them.

Here the photographer paused to study the foreign journalists in his audience; seeing that they approved of his story and thought it interesting, he capped his triumph by supplying a final detail in a voice that implied he was sharing a military secret: When (again, many years later) this photograph of the same ruined face appeared in the same disgraceful paper, purporting to be the last victim of a long and drawn-out Middle Eastern war, the caption read, *And they say that in the end it was all for love.*

Then everyone at the table smiled for his camera. Galip knew a few of the journalists and ad executives among them; there was also a bald man who looked somewhat familiar and, huddled at the far end of the table, the foreigners. They seemed all to be enjoying their accidental intimacy: like travelers who've ended up in the same country lodge for the evening, perhaps after facing some minor mishap, they shared some sort of bond and were curious to know more about one another.

By now Galip was quite sure they'd shot *License to Love* here, the film in which Türkan Şoray had played the bar girl, so he called over the elderly waiter and asked him if this was true. Everyone at the table turned to look at him, and—perhaps inspired by the other tales he'd overheard that evening—the waiter now added a small story of his own.

No, it was not about the movie Galip had mentioned, it was about another movie that had in fact been filmed here, and the week it showed at the Dream Theater he'd seen it fourteen times. The producer and the beautiful woman in the lead had both asked him to appear in a few scenes, and he'd been more than happy to oblige. Two months later, when he went to see the finished product, he recognized the face and hands in those scenes as his, but when he was shot from a different angle in another scene, he had a most delicious fright: his back, shoulders, and neck were not, in fact, his own. Then there was the voice: it too belonged to someone else; what's more, it belonged to a man he would later hear in many other films. But none of his friends and relatives seemed too interested in these confusing, spine-tingling, dreamlike substitutions; nor did they notice the trick photography; above all, they failed to see how easy it was for someone else to assume a man's identity, for a man to pass himself off as someone else.

His listeners were no doubt aware that the theaters of Beyoğlu ran double features in the summer and that most of the movies were old; for years the waiter had lived in the vain hope that he might catch another glimpse of himself. Not to remember how he'd looked when he was young, his dream had been to embark on a new life; though his friends and relations had failed to grasp the "obvious reason," he was sure this would not be the case for the distinguished guests gathered here tonight.

Once the waiter was out of earshot, the distinguished guests spent a long time trying to work out what this "obvious reason" might be. Most were convinced it was love: the waiter's love for himself, or for the world in which he saw himself, or for cinematic art. The bar girl put an end to their speculation by announcing that the waiter was (along with every wrestler she'd ever heard of) a homosexual; he'd been caught defiling himself in front of the mirror and molesting the bus-boys in the kitchen.

The bald old man whom Galip vaguely recognized took issue with the bar girl's "unfounded allegations" against "our national sport"; it just so happened that he had followed the lives of several leading wrestlers when he was based in Thrace, and these exceptional people had, he insisted, led model family lives. As he rattled through a long list of examples, İskender leaned over and told Galip who this man was. He'd found him in the lobby of the Pera Palas Hotel—around the time he was running around frantically trying to fix interviews for the English film crew, and most particularly trying to track down Celâl—so, yes, it was probably on the evening of the day he'd phoned Galip that he'd run into this bald old man. The man had told him he knew Celâl, and just happened to be trying to find him too, to settle a personal matter—which is why they'd decided to join forces. Over the days that followed, he had bumped into him several times and he'd proved very helpful, not just in the search for Celâl but in other small matters, by tapping into his large network of friends—it turned out he was a retired army officer. He saw it as a chance to practice his few words of English, and he was obviously enjoying it. Clearly, he was one of those pensioners with time on their hands who like to be useful; he just wanted people to be happy, and he knew Istanbul like the back of his hand. After he had said his piece about the wrestlers of Thrace, he went on to relate his own story—though it was more a riddle.

During an eclipse of the sun, a confused flock of sheep returns to the village of its own accord, and after the shepherd puts them back into their pen, he returns home to find his beloved wife in bed with her lover. After a moment of indecision, he picks up a knife and kills them both. When he hands himself in and goes before the judge, his defense is simple: The woman he found in his bed with her lover was not his wife but someone he'd never before laid eyes on. The woman with whom he'd shared his life all these years, the woman he knew and trusted—she would never have done this to him; it therefore followed that she was not the woman in the bed, and he was not "himself." Under normal circumstances, this startling switch of identities would be unheard of, but this was not a normal day—there had just been an eclipse of the sun. The shepherd was willing to take responsibility for the crime committed by this other person who had taken over his body; he still insisted that the couple he had killed be seen as two thieves who'd broken into his house and made shameless use of his bed. When he'd served his time—however long it was—he was going off in search of this wife he'd not seen since the sun's eclipse, and when he found her, she would, he hoped, help him find his own lost self. So what punishment did the judge mete out to the shepherd?

As the others gave the retired colonel their answers, Galip remembered that he'd heard the story before, or perhaps he'd read it, but he couldn't quite remember when or where. As he gazed at one of the pictures the photographer had just brought back from the bathroom, it almost came back to him, and during the same fleeting moment, he thought he remembered where he'd seen this bald old man before; in a moment, he thought, I'll be able to tell this man who he really is; his face might be as hard to read as the faces in the photographer's story, but I'll break the code. When it was his turn to speak, and Galip said that the judge had no choice but to pardon the shepherd, he did think he saw the key to the retired colonel's secret written all over his face: it was almost as if he had been one person when he began telling his story, but someone else entirely by the time he finished it. What had happened to him as he told his story? What was it about the story that had changed him?

When it was his turn to speak, Galip chose a love story that an old and lonely columnist had once told him, claiming he'd heard it years earlier, from another columnist. This man had spent his whole life sitting in newspaper offices in Babıali, translating foreign magazines and reviewing the latest films and plays. He'd never married—being more interested in women's clothes and women's jewelry than he was in women—choosing instead to live alone in a two-room flat in the back streets of Beyoğlu, his only company a tabby who looked even older and lonelier than he did. The only tremor in his quiet life was when Marcel Proust enticed him into reading À la recherche du temps perdu; reaching the end of the book, he went straight back to the beginning to read through to the end again; this he continued to do for the rest of his life.

The old journalist was so enamored of this book that, in the beginnning, he talked of it to everyone he met, but he found no one willing to take the trouble to savor it in the original French, no one with whom to share his excitement. So he turned in on himself, took the story he had by then read God only knew how many times, and began to tell it to himself, scene by scene. All day long, whenever something upset him, whenever he had to deal with rudeness or cruelty from coarse, insensitive, greedy, uncultured philistines, he'd console himself by thinking, Who cares? I'm not really here anyway. I'm at home, in my bed, dreaming of Albertine asleep in the next room, dreaming of what she'll do when she finally opens her eyes in a moment; I hear her sweet, soft footsteps as she roams about the house, and I rejoice! When strolling sadly through the city streets like Proust's narrator, he would dream of a woman named Albertine, a woman so young and beautiful that just to be introduced to her one day had once seemed a dream beyond his reach, and he would dream that she was at home waiting for him, dream of what she did in the house as she waited. Returning to his apartment and the stove that never managed to give up much heat, the old journalist would sadly recall the pages in the other volume, where Proust talks of Albertine leaving him, and he'd feel the empty chill of the house in his very bones as he remembered how he and Albertine had once sat here laughing and talking and drinking coffee, how she always insisted on ringing the bell when she visited, how he'd succumbed so often to fits of jealousy; one by one he'd conjure up his memories of the trip they'd taken to Venice together, first pretending to be Proust, then pretending to be his mistress, Albertine, until his face streamed with tears of pain and joy.

On Sunday mornings, as he sat in his apartment with his tabby cat, fuming at the coarseness of the stories in the paper or the taunts of nosy neighbors, insensitive distant relations, and disrespectful children, he'd pretend he'd found a ring in one of the drawers in his old cupboard, and he'd tell himself that Françoise the maid had found this ring in a drawer in a rosewood table, and that it belonged to Albertine, who had forgotten to take it with her, and he'd turn to his imaginary maid and say, "No, Françoise"—loud enough for his tabby to hear him—"Albertine did not forget to take this ring with her, and there's no point in sending it on, as she's going to be coming back to this house very soon."

It was because no one here knew who Albertine was, or even knew who Proust was, that this country was in such a sorry wretched state, or so the old journalist had convinced himself. But one day, if this country ever produced people capable of understanding Albertine and Proust, yes, maybe then these poor mustachioed men he saw roaming the streets would begin to enjoy a better life; maybe then they'd stop knifing each other the moment jealousy overtook them and devote themselves instead to conjuring up their lovers in dreams more colorful than life itself. As for all those writers and translators who managed to get work at newspapers by passing themselves off as educated, it was because they didn't read Proust, didn't know Albertine, didn't even know that the old journalist himself read Proust—that he *was* Proust, and Albertine too—that they were so evil and thickheaded.

But the most striking thing about this story was not that the old journalist came to identify with Proust's hero so deeply that he came to believe he was Proust himself; like all Turks who come to love Western authors that no one else reads, he went from loving Proust's words to believing that he himself had written them. With time, he came to despise those around him not just because he loved a book they'd never read but because he'd written a book they could never have written. So the really striking thing was not that the old journalist spent years pretending to be Proust and Albertine but that he had, after years of hiding this secret from all and sundry, decided to entrust it to another columnist.

Perhaps he'd done so because he had a special place in his heart for this young columnist, for there was something about the boy that reminded him of Proust and the beautiful Albertine: just the hint of a mustache on his upper lip, a strong and classical build, good hips, long lashes; like Proust and Albertine he was dark and not too tall, with the soft, silky, radiant complexion of a Pakistani. But that was as far as the resemblance went: the beautiful young columnist's interest in European literature only went as far as Paul de Kock and Pitigrilli; on hearing the old columnist's story, his first response had been laughter and then he said he would use this interesting story one day in a column.

Seeing his mistake, the old journalist begged his handsome young colleague to forget everything he'd said, but he pretended he hadn't heard and went on laughing. Returning home that night, the old man saw in an instant that his life was in ruins: no longer could he sit in this empty house thinking about Proust's jealous fits, or the good times he'd shared with Albertine, or wondering where Albertine was now. To know that extraordinary and bewitching love he and he alone felt for her—to know that no other person in Istanbul felt the same—this had been his only source of pride. To think that his pure and lofty love was soon to be reduced to pap for hundreds of thousands of insensitive readers—it was like hearing that Albertine, the woman he had worshiped for so many years, was to be raped. These brainless readers read papers to learn how the prime minister had defrauded them or to find out what mistakes they'd made on the radio recently, and then they wrapped fish in them or used them to line their garbage cans. Oh, his beloved Albertine, who had caused him such jealous anguish, who had left him a broken man, who could forever shimmer in his dreams just as she did the days he set eyes on her, mounting that bicycle at Baalbec! The thought that her name should be so much as mentioned in a vile newspaper made him want to die.

This was what gave him the courage and determination to phone the downy-lipped, silken-skinned young columnist; saying that "he and only he" would ever be able to do justice to his unique and eternal love, his human suffering, his helpless, boundless jealousy, he begged him never to mention Proust and Albertine in a column, never to mention them anywhere, ever. He found the courage to add, "Especially bearing in mind that you yourself have never read Proust's book!" "Whose book?" he was asked. "What book? Why?"—because the young columnist had by now forgotten all about his older colleague's love. The old man told him the whole story again from the beginning, and again the young columnist met it with laughter, saying, Yes, yes, he was going to have to write this up, he really was. Perhaps he even thought this was what the old columnist wanted him to do.

And write it he did. It was less a column than a story, and it described the old columnist in much the same terms as the story you have just heard: an old and unhappy *İstanbullu* who falls in love with a hero in a Western novel, eventually convincing himself that he *is* that hero, and his author too. Like the real journalist on whom he was based, the old journalist in the story had a tabby cat. And the old journalist in the column is also shaken when he sees his story mocked in a column. In the story inside that story, he too wants to die when he sees Proust's and Albertine's names in the paper. In the nightmares that the old journalist suffered during the last unhappy nights of his life, he saw Prousts, Albertines, and old journalists endlessly repeating one another, and a bottomless well of stories inside stories inside stories. Waking in the middle of the night, the old journalist realized that his love had vanished; no longer could he find happiness in his dreams of her, for his dreams had depended on no one else even knowing of her existence. Three days after the cruel column was published, they broke down the door to find the columnist had died quietly in his sleep, asphyxiated by smoke from the stove that had never managed to put out any heat. Though the cat had not eaten in two days, it had not found the courage to eat its master.

Though Galip's story was sad, it seemed to him to bring the company together, just as the other stories had done. As music floated into the room from an invisible radio, several people—including a few of the foreign journalists—stood up to dance with the bar girls, and they went on dancing, joking, and laughing until the nightclub had to close.

Chapter Sixteen

I Must Be Myself

"If you wanted to be cheerful, or melancholic, or wistful, or thoughtful, or courteous, you simply had to act those things with every gesture."

—Patricia Highsmith,
The Talented Mr. Ripley

I have already written briefly in this column about the metaphysical experiment that befell me on a winter's night twenty-six years ago. This is going back eleven or twelve years; I can't be more exact than that (what a pity I can no longer avail myself of my "secret archive," now that my memory is failing me). Anyway, after I wrote in depth about the matter, I was deluged with readers' letters. Though many expressed anger that I had deviated from my customary subjects, thus failing to live up to their expectations—why wasn't I writing about matters of national importance like I always did; why wasn't I writing, like I always did, about the melancholy of the rainy streets of Istanbul?—there emerged from this sea of anodyne complaints one letter from a reader who "sensed" that we were in agreement on "another very important subject." He promised to pay me a visit in the near future, to discuss several "deep" and "unique" matters on which we were certain to agree.

He also told me he was a barber (this I found rather odd), but I'd just about forgotten him when he turned up in the flesh one afternoon. We were close to the deadline and were all rushing to meet our word limits; I really had no time for him. Besides, I could just see him sitting down, going on about his troubles for hours on end and then pestering me because he wanted to know why I hadn't given him as much space in the column as he thought he deserved. Just to get rid of him, I asked him to come back another time. He reminded me that he'd written in advance to tell me he'd be coming in, adding that, in any event, he had no time to "come back another time"; all he wanted was to ask me two questions he was sure I could answer instantly, while I was still on my feet. Impressed by the speed with which the barber got to the point, I told him to ask me his questions forthwith.

"Do you have trouble being yourself?"

A small crowd had gathered around the table, hoping, perhaps, to witness something strange, something amusing they could all laugh about later: a handful of the younger journalists I'd taken under my wing, a fat and noisy football correspondent well loved for his jokes. So when I answered the question, I did what they expected from me— I told him one of my own "clever" jokes. The barber listened to this joke as carefully as if it were the answer he'd wanted, and then he asked me his second question.

"Is there a way a man can be only himself?"

He asked this question in a way that suggested that he was not asking it to satisfy his own curiosity but on behalf of someone else. What was crystal clear was that he'd memorized the question. The laughter from the first joke was still hovering in the air; others, hoping for some fun, had joined the crowd, so, rather than launch into an ontological oration about a man's "need to be himself," what could be more natural than to nail him with the second joke our audience was so breathlessly awaiting? What's more, a second joke would, I hoped, add to the first and turn this little incident into an elegant story people would tell in my absence. After I'd told this second joke (which, alas, I can no longer recall) the barber cried, "I just knew it!" And left the building.

We in this country rarely appreciate double entendres unless the second meaning is rude or derogatory, so I didn't spend too much time worrying that I might have offended this barber. I would even go so far as to say that I gave him as much of my time as I would if an overexcited reader approached me in a public toilet and asked me, as he fastened his trousers, if I believed in God or if I could tell him the meaning of life.

But as time went on. . . . There will no doubt be those who, having read that unfinished sentence, will already have assumed that I came to regret my insolence, for the barber had asked the great question of our time; there may even be those who are expecting me to say that my guilt was so great that I was having nightmares, waking up in the middle of the night, but these are the readers who have yet to know me for who I am. The barber didn't even cross my mind—except once. And that one time it was while I was thinking about something else. What I was thinking was a continuation of a thought I'd had before I met him—many years before I met him. In the beginning it was hardly even a thought; it was more a refrain that had been coming into my mind on and off since childhood, something that would ring in my ears—no, in my mind—something that would spring up suddenly from the very depths of my soul to intone the same words over and over: *I must be myself, I must be myself, I must be myself.*

One midnight, after a day crowded with relatives and "friends" from work but still not ready to go to bed, I sat down in the old armchair in my other room, propped my feet on the stool, lit a cigarette, and stared at the ceiling. All the people I'd had to see that day were still buzzing inside my head; their words, their little noises, their endless stream of demands had blended into a single sound that preyed on my ears like a nasty, tiresome headache or, even more insidious, a toothache. This was when I first heard the refrain I just refrained from calling a "thought"; it was—how shall I put it?—in counterpoint to the ringing in my ears. It promised to save me from the madding crowd, to show me the road back to my inner voice, my own peace, my own happiness, even my own smell. *You must be yourself, you must be yourself, you must be yourself!*

So that midnight, I finally came to see how glad I was to live apart from that madding crowd, from the vile and muddy chaos into which everyone (teachers, politicians, imams in their Friday sermons, my aunts, my father, my uncles, everyone) is always commanding me, commanding us all, to immerse ourselves. To leave them to their tasteless and pedestrian stories, to wander alone in my own garden of memories—it felt so sweet that before long I was even gazing with love at the thin legs and the wretched feet stretched out on the stool in front of me; I even found it in me to tolerate the ugly, clumsy hand that brought my cigarette to my lips so I could blow smoke at the ceiling. For once I was myself! Because I was myself for once, I could at last *like* myself! It was at this happy moment that the refrain changed its colors. I became like the village idiot who says the same word with each new stone he passes as he walks along the mosque wall, like the old man who counts the telephone poles as he watches from a train window; as I recited my mantra over and over, it spread beyond me to envelop my pitiful old room, and everything in it, with a furious intensity. As I continued my similarly furious recitation, I felt the bliss of anger swelling up in me.

I must be myself, I said over and over. I must forget these people buzzing inside my head, I must forget their voices, their smells, their demands, their love, their hate, and be myself, *I must be myself,* I told myself, as I gazed down at the legs resting so happily on the stool, and I told myself again as I looked up to watch the smoke I'd blown up to the ceiling; I must be myself, because if I failed to be myself, I became the person *they* wanted me to be, and I can't bear the person they want me to be; if I had to be that insufferable person, I'd rather be nothing at all. It would be better if I didn't even exist, because when I was young, my uncles and aunts were always saying, "What a shame he's doing journalism, but he does work hard, so perhaps, God willing, he might see some success," and then I'd become the person they saw me to be; after years and years of trying to escape that person, I—a grown man now—went back to that house, where my father lived with his new wife; I became the person who "after many years of hard work had, at least, seen just a bit of success," and what was worse, even I could not see myself any other way; this person clung to me like an ugly skin I couldn't shed, and afterward, whenever I was with them, I would catch myself saying this other person's words and not my own, and in the evening, when I returned home, I would torment myself by remembering all the things this other person had said, mimicking him mercilessly, spouting trite sentences like "I touched on this subject in this week's long column" or "I took this matter up in my column last Sunday" or "I shall return to this question in my next column" or "This Tuesday, I shall delve into this other matter too," repeating them to myself over and over until I thought I was going to suffocate in my own misery.

My life is full of unhappy memories of this order. I'd sit in my chair and stretch out my legs, and before I could even remember who I was I was remembering all the times when I'd been pretending to be some-one else.

I remembered, for example, that—simply because the other con-scripts decided on the first day what sort of person I was—I spent my entire military service being the "sort of man who, even when the chips are down, can't resist making a joke." There was a time when I went to see a bad film, not to pass the time so much as to be alone in a cool dark place, and as I was smoking my cigarette during the five-minute intermission I could tell from the way the idle crowd was look-ing at me that they considered me to be "a worthy young man destined to do important work" and that's all it took; from then on I was a "young man lost in deep, even sacred, contemplation." During the days when we were busy planning a military coup and dreaming of the moment when our hands seized the instruments of power, I remem-ber becoming a patriot so full of love for his people that he couldn't sleep at night, for fear of delaying the coup and thus prolonging their suffering. I remember that when I scuttled off to one of those broth-els I visited in secret, making sure no one saw me, I would, because I knew the whores treated people like this more kindly, act like a man bereft of hope after a recent romantic tragedy. If I couldn't cross the street in time, I'd try to look like a decent godfearing citizen whenever I walked past a police station. When I went to my grandparents for New Year's Eve, but only because I lacked the courage to weather that dreadful ritual on my own, I would pretend to enjoy myself while play-ing lotto, just to look like I was joining in. Whenever I was around women I found attractive, I would, rather than be myself, adapt the persona most likely to make them warm to me—so for some I was the sort of man who thought of nothing but marriage and the struggle to earn a living, while for others I was a resolute creature who had no time in his life for anything but the liberation of our country, or I became a man who was tired, tired, tired of the insensitivity, the stu-pidity you saw everywhere in our country; there were even times when I pretended to be that awful cliché, a "secret poet." Later still (yes, at last) when I was sitting at the barber's, as I did once every two months, I remember not being myself: instead I was imitating the man who was nothing more than the sum total of all those people I was imitating.

I'd gone to the barber to take my mind off things (not—of

course!—the same barber who appeared at the beginning of this story!). But as the barber and I discussed how to cut my hair, as we looked into the mirror to look at the head beneath the hair, and the shoulders and the chest beneath it, I immediately knew that this person sitting in the chair looking at his reflection in the mirror was someone else. When the barber asked, "How much should we take off the front?" the head he touched, like the neck that carried it, and those shoulders, and that chest—they did not belong to me, but to the columnist, Celâl Bey.

I had nothing to do with this man. This was so clear to me that I was sure the barber would see it too, but he paid no attention. It was almost as if he was going out of his way to make me forget myself and really feel like a columnist—questions like "If war breaks out, can we defeat the Greeks?" "Is it true that the prime minister's wife is a prostitute?" "Is it the vegetable sellers who are driving up prices?" I am at a loss to describe the oppressive genie that kept me from sharing my own thoughts on these matters, insisting instead that this gruesome columnist staring back at me from the mirror mumble the usual smart-alecky nonsense: "Peace is a good thing." "It's important to realize that you can't bring the prices down just by hanging a few men!" And so on.

Oh, how I hated this columnist who thought he knew everything, who knew even when and what he didn't know, who had learned to turn even his defects and shortcomings into clever little jokes! How I hated this barber whose every question made me more like "Celâl Bey the columnist"! It was at this point in my unhappy meanderings that I recalled the barber who'd come to the paper to ask me those strange questions.

But now, in the dead of night, as I sat in the old armchair that let me be the man I really was, with my feet propped on the stool, my head swirling with bad memories, and that old refrain ringing furiously in my ears, I knew what to say. "Yes, my dear barber!" I said to myself. "It's true. There is no way they'll give people the permission to be themselves; they don't let them be themselves and they never will!" My words had the same insistent beat as my refrain, but they plunged me deeper into that haven of peace I wished to share with no one. It was at this moment that I saw the link between the barber who came to the paper to see me at the beginning of this story and the other barber who caused me to remember him at the end; these twinned mirror images belonged to a grand design—a system of meaning that my more devoted readers will remember from earlier columns—what I can only describe as a "secret symmetry." It was, in effect, a sign pointing to my future; at the end of a long day, and a crowded evening, to be able to sit alone in your armchair and be yourself. . . . It was like returning from a long journey crowded with adventure . . . like coming home.

Chapter Seventeen

Do You Remember Me?

*"Though I look back on those days in search of solace, I am left
only with the vague impression of a crowd moving through
darkness."*

—Ahmet Rasim

When the storytellers left the nightclub, they did not immediately disperse; instead they lingered in the street, watching the snow flurries and looking at one another as if they expected something fun to happen, even though they had no idea what it would turn out to be; as if they'd just witnessed a fire or a murder and had decided to linger at the scene of the crime in case there was a second one. The bald man, now wearing a fedora, was saying, "But we can't all go there, İskender Bey. They can't accommodate this many people. I want to take our English friends, that's all. They might as well see this side of our country also; if nothing else, it will be a lesson to them." He turned to Galip. "You can come too." But as they made their way to Tepebaşı, they were joined by two others who refused to be shaken off as easily as the rest of the group: a woman antiques dealer and a middle-aged architect with a mustache that looked like a brush.

They were just passing the American consulate when the bald man, in the fedora, asked, "Have you ever been to Celâl Bey's houses in Nişantaşı and Şişli?" *Why do you ask?* asked Galip, gazing closely at his face but unable to read its meaning. "İskender Bey told me you were Celâl Sadik's nephew. Aren't you looking for him? Wouldn't you like him to explain our country to our English guests? Look, the world is finally taking some interest in us." *Yes, of course,* said Galip. "So do you have his addresses?" asked the man in the fedora. *No, I don't,* said

Galip, *He doesn't give them out to anyone.* "Is he true that he shuts himself up in those places with women?" *No,* Galip replied. "Please don't take offense," said the man. "It's only gossip, that's all. The things people say! Who can stop them? Especially if you're a larger-than-life legend like Celâl Bey! I know him personally." *Is that so?* "It is indeed. He once invited me to one of his houses in Nişantaşı. *Where exactly was it?* Galip asked. "A place that was torn down ages ago. A two-story stone house, and he spent the whole evening complaining about how lonely he was. He told me I could visit him any time I wished." *But he's the one who wanted to live alone,* said Galip. "Perhaps you don't know him as well as you think," said the man. "There's a voice inside me, telling me that he needs my help. Are you absolutely sure you don't have his address?" *Absolutely sure,* said Galip, *but it's not for nothing that people identify with him.* "He's an exceptional man!" concluded the man in the fedora hat. This was how they came around to the subject of Celâl's latest columns.

They were walking down a side street in the direction of Tünel; hearing what sounded like a watchman's whistle, they all turned around to gaze at the narrow alley, at the snowy pavement lit only by a purple neon light; when they turned down one of the streets leading off from the Galata Tower, it seemed to Galip that the top floors of the buildings on either side were slowly closing in on him like curtains in a theater. The lights at the top of the Galata Tower were red; there'd be more snow tomorrow. It was two in the morning; from somewhere not far away came the sound of a shop's shutters descending.

After walking around the tower, they went into a side street Galip had never seen before and continued down its icy pavement. The man with the fedora knocked on the old door of a tiny two-story house. After some time, a light went on upstairs and a bluish head appeared at the window. "Open the door, it's me," said the man in the fedora. "We have English guests with us." He turned to give his English companions a bashful, guilty smile.

On the door was a sign that said, MARS MANNEQUIN ATELIER; a pale, unshaven man in his thirties opened it. His eyes were fogged with sleep. He was wearing a blue-striped pajama top with black pajama trousers. He shook everyone's hand, gazing into each pair of eyes as if they were all brothers enlisted in the same secret cause and led them into a brilliantly lit room piled high with boxes, molds, cans, and various body parts and smelling of paint. As he passed around the brochures he'd picked up on his way in, he explained in a monotone: "Our establishment is the oldest mannequin-making enterprise in the whole of the Balkans and the Middle East. Our hundred-year history offers us an inspirational example of Turkey's achievements as a modernizing and industrializing nation. Not only are our arms, legs, and hips now one-hundred-percent Turkish—"

"Cebbar Bey," said the bald man with annoyance, "these people have not come to see the showroom; they would like, with your guidance, to see what you keep downstairs, underground: the malcontents, our history, the things that make us who we are."

Scowling, the guide turned a knob, and as the room and its hundreds of arms, legs, heads, and trunks plunged into darkness, a naked lightbulb went on in the small landing that led to a flight of stairs. As they were making their way down the iron staircase, Galip stopped suddenly to sniff the damp air. Cebbar Bey came to his side, with surprising ease.

"You'll find what you're looking for here, don't worry!" he said knowingly. "I'm here at His behest. He doesn't want you wandering into cul-de-sacs and getting lost."

Did he speak this enigmatically to everyone? Arriving in the first room, their guide gestured at the mannequins around them and said, "My father's first creations." In the second room, where another naked lightbulb illuminated an assortment of Ottoman seamen, corsairs, and scribes watching over a group of peasants squatting around a meal set out on a tablecloth, the guide continued his mysterious whispering. It was only when they came to a third room, this one inhabited by a washerwoman, a beheaded atheist, and an executioner with the tools of his trade, that Galip could catch what the guide was saying.

"A hundred years ago, when those works you viewed in the first room were first created, no one, not even my grandfather, had more in mind than this one simple ambition: to ensure that the mannequins in shop windows were based on our own people—that's all my grandfather wanted. But he was prevented from doing so by a powerful cabal, who were themselves the victims of an international conspiracy dating back two hundred years."

They went down more stairs, passing through doors that led to more steps, until they had arrived at a room where the ceiling glistened with water and a string of naked lightbulbs dangled from what looked to be a clothesline; in the room below were hundreds of mannequins.

Among them they saw Field Marshal Fevzi Çakmak, who for thirty years had served as chief of staff; fearing that the populace might collude with the enemy, he had contemplated blowing up not just all the bridges in the country but also (lest the Russians use them as landmarks) all the minarets; he had, in addition, wanted to evacuate Istanbul and turn it into a ghost town, a labyrinth that would swallow their enemies whole if they ever got their hands on it. Farther on, they saw peasants from Konya so inbred they all—mothers, fathers, daughters, grandfathers, uncles—looked identical, and the junk dealers who cart from door to door all the old discarded objects that (though we don't know it) make us who we are. They saw movie actors who couldn't be themselves or anyone else, playing heroes who couldn't be themselves either, and Turkish superstars who simply played themselves; and those poor bewildered creatures who dedicated their lives to translation and adaptation so they could bring the best of Western art and science to Turkish audiences; and the dreamers whose gravestones are long vanished, whose dreams have yet to come true, whose days were spent poring over maps with a magnifying glass, imagining the jumbled streets of Istanbul giving way to a magnificent new network of avenues, lined with linden trees as in Berlin, in the shape of a star as in Paris, overarched with bridges like St. Petersburg, and graced with modern pavements so that our generals, like their European counterparts, could take their dogs out on a leash of an evening and watch them shit; and they saw erstwhile secret agents, formerly of MİT, who had taken early retirement because they wanted to continue torturing their suspects using local and traditional methods rather than change them to meet international standards, and the peddlers who carried great yokes over their shoulders, as they went from street to street selling yogurt, *boza*, and bonito. Among the Coffeehouse Scenes—which the guide introduced as "a line begun by my grandfather that my father went on to develop and I have now taken over"—they saw unemployed men with their heads sunk to their shoulders, and the lucky ones who could, when they played backgammon or checkers, forget what century they lived in and who they were; and compatriots sitting with a glass of tea in one hand and in the other a cheap cigarette, staring into infinity as if trying to remember the reason for their existence; and others who were feeling great pain; and yet others who had managed to escape that pain by abusing cards, dice, and friends.

"When my grandfather was on his deathbed, he knew full well what a powerful international conspiracy he was up against," said their guide. "These historical powers did not want to give our people the chance to be themselves, and because they wanted to deprive us of the everyday activities and gestures that are our greatest treasure, they kicked my grandfather out of the shops of Beyoğlu, the display windows of İstiklâl. When my father found out that my grandfather's only legacy was the underground—yes, the underground—he did not yet know that, since the beginning of its history, Istanbul has been an underground city. This only emerged later on, when he was digging through the mud to make more room for his mannequins and came across a number of underground passages."

As they walked down the staircases leading to these underground passages, from landing to landing, through muddy caves that could hardly qualify as rooms, they saw crowds of hopeless mannequins. As they stood under the naked lightbulbs, covered with mud and dust, they sometimes reminded Galip of people waiting at a forgotten bus stop for a bus that never came, and sometimes they recalled an illusion that would come to Galip as he walked the city's streets—that the unhappy people of the world all belonged to the same brotherhood. He saw lotto men with their sacks. He saw nervous and sarcastic students. He saw apprentice nut sellers, birdwatchers, treasure hunters. He saw mannequins reading Dante to prove that all Western science and art came from the East, mannequins making maps to prove that those things called minarets were transmitting signs to other planets, and mannequins dressed as divinity students who, after being struck by a high tension cable and turning blue with electric shock, had begun to recall events from two hundred years ago. The mannequins were grouped by type, with some areas for swindlers and others for sinners, for people who could not be themselves and people who had become other people. There were rooms for the unhappily married, for restless ghosts, for war heroes risen from their graves. They saw the people who had mysterious letters written on their foreheads, and the sages who had read these signs, and even the illustrious sages who were carrying on the tradition to this day.

In one corner, among Turkey's most famous writers and artists, there was even a mannequin of Celâl wearing the raincoat that had been his trademark twenty years earlier. The guide explained that his father, who had had high hopes for Celâl, had confided to him "the mystery of the letters," only to see this man abuse them just to achieve a few cheap victories. A framed copy of the column that Celâl had written about the guide's father and grandfather twenty years later was hanging around the mannequin's neck like an execution order. Like many shopkeepers, the family had dug out their caverns without getting the necessary permits, and as Galip followed his guide, trying not to choke from the mold and damp oozing from the walls, the guide told him how, after countless betrayals, he had put all his hope into the secret letters he had collected during his Anatolian journeys, how he had engraved these secret letters on his unhappy mannequins' foreheads, and how, all the while, he'd continued to dig out, one by one, these underground passageways that made Istanbul the city it was. For a long while Galip stood still in front of Celâl's mannequin, studying his great fat form, his soft gaze, his small hands. It's thanks to you I can't be myself! he felt like saying. It's because of you that I believed all those stories that turned me into you. For a long time he stared at Celâl's mannequin, like a son studying a high-quality photograph of his father. He remembered that Celâl had bought the material for the trousers on sale, at a shop owned by a distant relative in Sirkeci, that Celâl had loved this raincoat because he thought it made him look like the sleuth in an English detective novel, that the seams had unraveled around the pockets because of the way Celâl jammed his hands into them, that he'd seen no razor cuts on his lower lip or his Adam's apple for some years now, and that the fountain pen in the pocket was the same one Celâl used to this day. Galip loved and feared this man: He wanted to be in Celâl's place and also to escape him; he wanted to find him and he wanted to forget him. He took Celâl's jacket by the lapels, as if to demand, once and for all, the key to this secret he'd never managed to decipher, this other world Celâl knew about, which he'd always kept hidden, the way out of this game that had turned into a nightmare. From a distance he could hear his guide, still reciting his set piece, though in a voice that betrayed his excitement.

"With time, my father was using his knowledge of the letters to etch meanings onto the faces of his mannequins that were no longer to be seen in our streets, our homes, or anywhere in society, and he was doing this at such speed that we ran out of space in the rooms we'd dug out of the mud. So in this sense, it was not really an accident that we happened onto the passageways at around the same time. My father quickly realized that our history could only survive underground, that life underground was itself a sign of the imminent collapse above, that these passageways leading to our house, these underground roads strewn with skeletons, provided us with a historical opportunity, a chance to create citizens who carried their histories, their meanings, on their faces."

When Galip let go of Celâl's lapels, the figure rocked back and forth like a lead soldier. Thinking he would remember this strange, terrifying, but also comic image forever, he took two steps backward and lit a cigarette. With some reluctance, he followed the group down to the threshold of the underground city where "mannequins will one day mingle with the skeletons."

Once they were there, the guide pointed into the underground passage, one of the many passages that the Byzantines, fearing that Attila might attack them, had dug under the Golden Horn 1,536 years earlier; if you went in there with a lamp, he told them angrily, you'd see skeletons sitting on chairs and tables covered with cobwebs, standing guard over the treasures they'd hidden from their Venetian invaders 775 years earlier, and as he did so Galip remembered Celâl writing a column long ago about the puzzle that these same images, this same story, signified. While the guide was explaining how his father, reading these powerful signs of an approaching collapse, had decided to decamp to the underworld, he mentioned that each incarnation of this city—Byzantium, Vizant, Nova Roma, Anthusa, Tsargrad, Miklagrad, Constantinople, Cospoli, Istin-Polin—had beneath it the underground passages in which the previous civilization had taken refuge. This had led to an extraordinary sort of double city, the guide explained heatedly, with the underground city ultimately wreaking revenge on the overground city that had supplanted it; as he listened, Galip remembered how Celâl had once suggested in a column that today's ugly apartment buildings were proof that this was still going on. His voice growing louder with rage, the guide went on to say how his father, convinced as he was that the world was coming to an end, had thrown himself into the doomsday spirit, dreaming of populating each and every one of these rat- and spider-infested, skeleton-strewn, and treasure-clogged passages with his mannequins; it was this dream that had given his father's life meaning, and now the guide himself was following in his footsteps, engraving on each mannequin's forehead the letters that give it meaning.

Galip was already beginning to wonder if this man got up early every morning to be the first to buy a copy of *Milliyet*, to read Celâl's column with a jealous and furious impatience, when the guide announced that they could, if they wished, proceed into this amazing passage, to look, if they dared, through the veil of gold necklaces and bracelets that dangled from the ceiling, to see skeletons of the Byzantines who had been driven underground by the Abbasites, and Jews clinging to each other as they hid from the Crusaders; this told Galip that their guide had indeed read Celâl's latest columns very carefully. The guide went on to say that they would find 700-year-old skeletons of the Genoan, Amalfian, and Pisan merchants who had fled the city after the Byzantines massacred six thousand of their number, sitting with 600-year-old skeletons who'd fled the Black Death—brought to the city by a ship from the Sea of Asov—leaning against each other at tables brought underground during the siege of the Avars and all waiting so patiently for the Day of Judgment. On and on he went, until Galip was sure he was as patient as Celâl. The guide pointed out the passageways where the Byzantines had hidden from the invading Ottomans—these extended from Haghia Sofia to Haghia Eirene and the Pantocrator and, when that was not enough, all the way to this side of the Golden Horn. Four hundred years later, when Murat IV had banned coffee, tobacco, and opium, there had been another influx: you could see these skeletons too, clutching their coffee grinders, coffee pots, pipes, opium and tobacco pouches, and cups, waiting for the mannequins to deliver them, and as he did so, Galip imagined a silken coat of dust settling over Celâl's mannequin. The guide told them that—in addition to the skeleton of Ahmet III's heir apparent, who had decamped, after a failed palace coup, to the passageways dug by Jews trying to escape the Byzantines, and the skeleton of the Georgian slave girl who had escaped the palace with her lover seven hundred years later—they'd also be able to see modern-day counterfeiters holding up wet banknotes to check them for color, and if not that, then they'd certainly see the Muslim Lady Macbeth descending from her little theater into the cavern she used as her dressing room, to dip her hands into a bowl of contraband buffalo blood, dyeing them to a shade of red so authentic its like had never been seen on any other stage; or, if not that, they would see inspired young chemists distilling in glass globes top-quality heroin that they hoped to export to America on rusty Bulgarian ships; and as he heard this, Galip felt as if he could read all these meanings in Celâl's face as well as his columns.

Later, after the guide had drawn his lecture to a close, after he had spoken of that future day that had been his father's greatest dream and was his dream too: that on a warm summer day, when all of overground Istanbul was roasting in the sun, dozing amid flies, piles of garbage, and clouds of dust, the skeletons that had been waiting so patiently in these dark and mildewed passages would start to twitch and come to life, and there would follow a great celebration, a blessing of life and death that took them beyond time, history, and the rule of law. After he had conjured up such visions of this joyous day that Galip no longer needed his voice to guide him—for he could already imagine the mannequins and the skeletons dancing, and the music fading into silence, and the silence giving way to the clacking of copulating bones, and he could see the pain etched on the faces of his "fellow citizens" and the broken cups and goblets strewn at their feet—as they began their climb upward, Galip still felt their sadness pressing down on him. It was not the steep stairs, the narrow passages, or his long day that made him feel weak in the legs. It was the faces he passed as he struggled up slippery steps lit only by naked lightbulbs, the weariness he read in the faces of the mannequins, his brothers. It was as if their bowed heads, bent spines, hunched backs, and crooked legs were extensions of his own body. Their faces were his face, their despair was his despair; they seemed to be inching toward him, and Galip did not want to look at them, did not dare to look them in the eye, but he could no more resist them than he could tear himself away from an identical twin. What he wanted to believe—what he *had* believed, when he'd read Celâl's column as a teenager—was that, if he ever solved the puzzle, if he ever uncovered the secret hiding behind the visible world, the truth would be simple—a secret recipe offering liberation to those who found the key—but (just as he felt whenever he read Celâl's column) he'd end up losing his bearings, so that whenever he tried to solve the puzzle, he'd feel his memory slipping away from him, until he felt as helpless as a child: He had no idea what the mannequins signified and no idea what business he had here; he did not know the meanings written in the letters on these faces, and neither did he know the secret of his own existence. The higher they climbed, the closer they came to the surface, the harder it was for Galip to recall the secret underworld he'd just witnessed; he could feel it slipping away from him already.

As they passed through one of the upper rooms, inhabited by mannequins too ordinary for the guide to mention, he looked into their faces and knew at once that they thought the same thoughts, shared the same fate: Once upon a time, they had all lived together, and their lives had had meaning, but then, for some unknown reason, they had lost that meaning, just as they'd also lost their memories. Every time they tried to recover that meaning, every time they ventured into that spider-infested labyrinth of memory, they got lost; as they wandered about the blind alleys of their minds, searching in vain for a way back, the key to their new life fell into the bottomless well of their memories; knowing it was lost to them forever, they felt the helpless pain known only by those who have lost their homes, their countries, their past, their history. The pain they felt at being lost and far from home was so intense, and so hard to bear, that their only hope was to stop trying to remember the secret, the lost meaning they'd come here to seek, and, instead, hand themselves over to God, to wait in patient silence for the hour of eternity. But as he approached the surface, Galip knew he could never join them in their stifling wait; he would never know peace until he'd found what he was seeking. To be a bad imitation of someone else, wasn't that better than being someone who'd lost his past, his memory, his dreams?

Arriving at the iron staircase, he put himself in Celâl's shoes; now he despised these mannequins and the concept that had brought them into being: a piece of nonsense, an obsession that betrayed its very origins, a malevolent caricature, a chilling joke, a wretched piece of foolishness that simply did not add up! Just look at this guide, this self-made caricature: To justify his concept he is saying that his father did not hold with Islam's so-called prohibition against figurative art, for the thing we called a *concept* was nothing more than one's own figure, and that's all they saw here—a series of figures. And now, as we return to the first room, our guide takes it upon himself to explain that it was to support this "great concept" that he was in the mannequin business, and to urge his guests to help keep it going by leaving whatever they could in the green donation box.

After Galip had thrown a thousand liras into the green box, he came face-to-face with the woman antiques dealer.

"Do you remember me?" she asked. She looked as if she'd just woken from a dream; her expression was childish, playful. "All those stories my grandmother told me—it seems they were true." In the dimly lit room, her eyes sparkled like a cat's.

"Pardon?" Galip asked, in an embarrassed voice.

"So you can't remember who I am," said the woman. "We were in the same class in middle school. My name is Belkıs."

"Belkıs," said Galip, and at the same moment he realized that he couldn't conjure up any face from that class except for Rüya's.

"I have a car," said the woman. "I live in Nişantaşı too. I can drop you off."

Restored to the fresh air of the street, the group took some time to disperse. The English journalists headed back to the Pera Palas Hotel; the man in the fedora gave Galip his card, passed on his regards to Celâl, and vanished into a back street heading toward Cihangir; İskender stepped into a taxi; and the architect with the brush mustache walked on with Galip and Belkıs. Just beyond the Atlas Theater they bought a plate of pilaf from a street vendor. Near Taksim, they stopped in front of a watchmaker's to gaze at the watches glistening like bewitched toys behind the icy window. As Galip gazed at a torn film poster that was the same inky blue as the sky, and into the window of the photography shop next door, displaying the portrait of a former prime minister who had been executed years before, the architect suggested taking them to Süleymaniye Mosque: he had something to show them that was much more interesting than the "mannequin hell" they'd just visited; the four-hundred-year-old mosque was slowly shifting ground! They went to retrieve Belkıs's car from its parking place on a Talimhane back street and headed off in silence. As he watched the dark and dreary two-story houses slipping past them, Galip wanted to cry out, Too dreary for words! A flurry of snow was falling from the sky, and the whole city slept.

After a long drive, they arrived at the entrance to the mosque, where the architect explained himself; he had come across the passageways under the mosque while doing restoration and repair work, and he knew the imam would be happy to open all doors in exchange for a small consideration. When Belkıs turned off the ignition, Galip said he would wait for them in the car.

"If you stay in the car, you'll freeze!" Belkıs said.

Galip noticed first that this woman was taking a very familiar tone with him and then that—despite her beauty, but because of her heavy coat and the scarf on her head—she reminded him of a distant relative, one of his great-aunts. They'd visit her on holidays, and her marzipan was so sweet that Galip would have to drink a glass of water before accepting the next piece she pressed upon him. Why hadn't Rüya ever gone along on those visits?

"I don't want to come!" Galip said firmly.

"But why?" said the woman. "Afterward we can climb a minaret." She turned to the architect. "Can we climb a minaret?"

There was a short silence. A dog was barking, not far away. Galip could just hear the hum of the city under the snow. "My heart can't take the stairs," said the architect. "You two can go by yourselves."

Pleased at the prospect of climbing a minaret, Galip got out of the car. Passing through the first courtyard, where naked lightbulbs lit up the snow-covered branches of the trees, they entered the inner courtyard. From here the great stone mass looked smaller than it was; it became a familiar building that could not hide its secrets. The icy snow covering the marble was dark and pockmarked, like the face of the moon in advertisements for foreign watches.

In the place where the arcade formed a corner was a metal door; the architect began to fiddle officiously with the padlock. As he did so, he explained that for centuries now—partly due to its weight but also to the incline of the hill on which it stood—the mosque was sliding toward the Golden Horn at a rate of two inches a year; in fact, its descent to the shore would have been much faster, had it not been for "these great stone walls" that circled the building (though its secret had yet to be understood); "this sewage system" (so sophisticated it had yet to be rivaled by modern technology), "this water table" (so subtly conceived, so brilliantly balanced), and "this complex of underground passageways" dating back four hundred years. When he had unlocked the door and ushered them into a dark passage, Galip saw the woman's eyes come alive with curiosity. She might not be all that beautiful, this Belkıs, but you still wanted to know what she was going to do next. "This is one mystery the West never solved!" said the architect, sounding like a drunk, and like a drunk he headed into the passage. Galip stayed outside.

As the imam emerged from the shadows of the icy columns, Galip could hear voices coming from the passage. The imam did not seem at all put out to be awoken so early in the morning. After he too had listened to the voices coming from the passage, he asked, "Is the woman a tourist?" *No,* Galip replied, noticing that the beard made the imam look older than he really was. "Are you a teacher too?" asked the imam. *Yes, I am.* "You're a professor, then, like Fikret Bey!" *Yes.* "Is it true that the mosque is moving?" *It's true, that's why we're here.* "May God be pleased." He seemed suspicious. "Did the woman have a child with her?" *No,* said Galip. "There's a child hiding in there, in the deepest depths." *The mosque has been moving for centuries,* said Galip uncertainly. "I know that," said the imam. "And it's forbidden to go in there, but this tourist woman went in anyway, with her child, I saw her. When she came out, she was alone. The child stayed inside." *You should have told the police,* said Galip. "There was no need," said the imam. "Because their pictures were in the papers—the woman's and the child's. The child was the grandson of the King of Ethiopia. It's about time they came and got him out." *What was on the child's face?* asked Galip. "Look, don't you see?" said the imam suspiciously. "You know all this already. You couldn't even look this child in the eye." *What was written on his face?* asked Galip insistently. "There were many things written on his face," said the imam, beginning to falter. *Do you know how to read faces?* The imam fell silent. *When a man goes off in search of the face he's lost, do you think it's enough to chase its meaning?* Galip asked. "You know more about this than I do," said the imam anxiously. *Is the mosque open?* "I've just opened the door," said the imam. "They'll be here soon for the morning prayers. Go ahead."

There was no one inside the mosque. Neon lights illuminated the bare walls but not the purple carpets that stretched out before him like a sea. Galip could feel his feet turning to ice inside his socks. He surveyed the dome, the columns, the great stone structures above his head, longing to be moved but feeling stuck. There was the vaguest of premonitions . . . but this great edifice was as impenetrable as stone itself. It did not welcome a man in, nor did it transport him to a better place. But if nothing signified nothing, then anything could signify anything. For a moment he thought he saw a flash of blue light, and then he heard the flutter of what sounded like the wings of a pigeon, but then he returned to his old stagnant silence, waiting for the illumination than never came. Then it occurred to him that the things around him, the stones in the walls, were more "naked" than they seemed to be; they seemed to be crying out to him, crying, *Give us meaning!* But later, as two whispering old men crossed the floor, stopping to kneel in front of the mihrab, Galip could no longer hear their call.

Perhaps this is why, as he climbed the minaret, Galip had no sense of anticipation whatsoever. When the architect informed him that Belkıs Hanım had started up without him, Galip went racing up the steps, but before long he could feel his heart beating in his temples, so he stopped for a rest. His legs began to ache, and his hips, so he sat down. He'd sit down on each step, look up at the naked lightbulb, and move on to the next step. When he heard a woman's footsteps some-where above him, he sped up again, but it was only when he stepped out onto the balcony that he caught up with her. For the longest time they stood there in silence, gazing down on the dark city, its dim lights blinking, its shadows flickering with snow.

Though the sky was slowly brightening, the city was still in shadow, more so, Galip thought, than the dark side of the moon; the night was far from over. Later, as he stood there shivering, it seemed to him that the mosque and the concrete hovels below him and even the smoke rising from their chimneys were illuminated from within. He could almost believe that he was looking at the surface of a planet that had yet to find its final shape. The domes of the city and these vast stretches of concrete, stone, tile, wood, and Plexiglas were coming apart, and in the cracks you could just see the underworld's molten glow—but not for long. Soon the city was sketching in its details; among the walls, chimneys, and rooftops they could now see billboards advertising banks and cigarettes, and as their giant letters emerged from the mist, the imam's tinny voice came bursting through the loudspeaker right next to them.

As they headed down the stairs, Belkıs asked after Rüya. Galip said his wife was waiting for him at home; today he'd bought her three new detective novels; Rüya liked to stay up all night reading detective novels.

The next time Belkıs brought up Rüya, they were back in her anodyne Murat; they had just dropped off the architect on Cihangir Avenue—deserted as always—and were heading up to Taksim. Galip explained that Rüya had no job; she spent her days reading detective novels, and very occasionally she translated them too. As they drove around Taksim Square, Belkıs asked how Rüya did her translations, and Galip told her that she did them very slowly: every morning, Galip would go to his office, and Rüya would clear their breakfast things off the table and go to work; but because he'd never once seen Rüya working at that table, he couldn't imagine it either. In response to another question, Galip, as vague now as if he were walking in his sleep, explained that on some mornings, he left home while Rüya was still in bed. He said they went to their aunts' for supper once a week, and they sometimes went to the Palace Theater in the evening.

"I know," said Belkıs. "I've seen you there. Looking at the posters in the lobby, moving up the stairs to the balcony with the crowd, always keeping a gentle hand on your wife's arm—I could see you were happy with your life—but when your wife looked into the crowd, when she looked at those posters, she was searching for a face that might open up a door to another world. Even at a distance, I could tell that she could read the secret meanings in faces."

Galip stayed silent.

"During the five-minute intermission, you did what any happy well-behaved husband would do: You decided to buy a chocolate bar with a coconut filling, or a Penguin ice cream, just to please your wife; so you signaled for the vendor, who was standing under those dim house-lights in the aisle, knocking a coin against the underside of his wooden tray, and you dug into your pockets for change while your wife gazed miserably at the screen, and it seemed to me that even when she was watching advertisements for vacuum cleaners and orange squeezers, she was still looking for clues, waiting for the magic signal to usher her into another country."

Still Galip said nothing.

"Just before midnight, when all the other couples were leaving the theater arm in arm and nestling into each others' coats, I saw the two of you walking home, arm in arm and staring straight in front of you."

"So all you are telling me," Galip snapped, "is that you saw us at the movies—once."

"Not just once. I saw you at the movies on twelve separate occa-sions, and I must have seen you more than sixty times on the street, and three times in restaurants, and six times in shops. When I got home, I did just what I'd done when we were little: I'd pretend it wasn't Rüya at your side but me."

Another silence.

"In middle school," continued the woman, as her car drove past the Palace Theater, "during recess, Rüya would spend all her time laughing with those boys who hung key chains from their belt buckles, whose idea of a good time was to get their hair wet and slick it down with those combs they kept in their back pockets; while she was laughing at their stories, and you were sitting at your desk pretending to read a book, I would pretend it wasn't Rüya but me you were watching. On winter mornings, I'd see that happy girl next to you, who could cross the street without checking for traffic because you were there to do so for her, and I'd pretend it was me, not Rüya. Sometimes, on Saturday afternoons, I'd see you walking toward the Taksim *dolmuş* stop with some uncle who was making you laugh, and I'd imagine that you were taking me to Beyoğlu with you."

"How long did this game last?" asked Galip, as he turned on the car radio.

"It wasn't a game," said the woman, and as she sped past his street without slowing down, she added, "I'm not turning into your street."

"I recognize this song," said Galip, looking back at his street as if it were a postcard from a distant country. "Trini Lopez used to sing it."

There was nothing about the street or the apartment to suggest that Rüya had come home. Anxious to find some use for his hands, Galip began to fiddle with the dials on the radio. A man with a kindly cultivated voice was offering farmers advice on rat control.

"Didn't you ever marry?" asked Galip as the car turned into the back streets of Nişantaşı.

"I'm a widow," said Belkıs. "My husband died."

"I can't remember you at all," said Galip, with a brutality he couldn't understand. "But there's something about you that reminds me of another classmate. A very sweet, very shy Jewish girl: Meri Tavaşi; her father was the owner of Vogue Hosiery, and every new year there would always be a few boys, and even some teachers, who'd ask her to bring in the latest Vogue calendar, which had pictures of women putting on Vogue stockings, and she'd do as they asked, even though it made her horribly embarrassed."

"When Nihat and I were first married, we were very happy," said the woman, after a silence. "He was very refined, very quiet, and he smoked a lot. He'd spend Sundays reading the paper and listening to the soccer match on the radio; someone had given him a flute and he'd practice on that, too. He drank very little, but he was as sad as the saddest drunk you've ever seen. When he started complaining about headaches, he almost sounded embarrassed. But all that time, he was patiently growing a huge tumor in the back of his brain. You know those children who won't show you what they're hiding in the palm of their hands, no matter how hard you try; well, that's how he hid this tumor that he'd been growing so stubbornly in his brain; and you know how children will smile sometimes, just as they finally open their palms to show you the bead they've been hiding? Well, he gave me that same happy smile as they wheeled him into the operating room, where he passed away without saying another word."

Parking her car on a street near Aunt Hâle's that he didn't visit very often but still knew as well as his own, she led Galip into an apartment building that—from the outside, at least—bore a shocking similarity to the City-of-Hearts Apartments.

"I knew his death was some sort of revenge," said the woman, as they stepped into the old elevator. "If I was an imitation of Rüya, he had to be an imitation of you. He knew this—because there were a few evenings when the cognac got the better of me, and I couldn't stop myself from speaking about you and Rüya for a very long time."

There was another silence as they entered her apartment, which was furnished in much the same way as his own; as he sat down, he turned to her apologetically and in an anxious voice he said, "Nihat was in our class too, wasn't he?"

"Do you think he looked like you?"

Galip scoured his memory for images, and a few finally surfaced: Galip and Nihat standing with notes from their parents giving them permission to skip gym class, while the teacher denounced them as laggards; Galip and Nihat, drinking water from the taps in the boys' toilet, which stank like a corpse; he remembered him as fat, clumsy, serious, slow, and not particularly bright. No matter how hard he tried, he could not remember much about his double and could feel no affinity.

"Yes," said Galip. "I suppose Nihat did look a bit like me."

"He didn't look like you at all," said Belkıs. Her eyes sparkled dangerously, just as they had done when Galip had first noticed her. "I knew he never would. But we were in the same class. I could make him look at me the same way you looked at Rüya. During the lunch break, when Rüya and I were smoking cigarettes with the boys in the Sütiş pudding shop, I'd see him passing by on the pavement, glancing anxiously at the happy crowd inside because he knew I was there in the middle of it. On those sad autumn evenings when the sun sets so early and the branches look so bare in the harsh light of the apartments, I knew he'd be looking at them just like you did, but thinking of me, not Rüya."

When they sat down to eat breakfast, sunlight was pouring in through the curtains.

"I know how hard it is for a person to be himself," said Belkıs, changing the subject as someone can only do who knows the other person is obsessed with the same story. "But I didn't know this until I was in my thirties. Until then, I just thought of it simply as a question of wanting to be someone else, as simple jealousy. At night, when I lay on my back in bed, gazing at the shadows on the ceiling, I so longed to be that other person, I thought I could slip off my own skin as easily as a glove; my desire was so fierce that I thought it would ease me into this other person's skin and let me begin a new life. Sometimes, I'd be sitting in a theater, or standing in a crowded store, watching people look right through me because they were so lost in their own worlds, and my longing to become this person, to live her life, became so intense, and the pain I felt was so overwhelming, that tears would slip from my eyes."

The woman picked up a thin slice of toast and scraped her clean knife over its brittle surface, as if to butter it.

"Even after all these years, I still can't understand why someone would want to live someone else's life and not their own," she continued. "I can't even explain why it was Rüya's life I wanted, rather than someone else's. All I can say is that for many years I saw it as an illness, an illness I had to hide from the world. I was ashamed of the soul that had contracted this disease, just as I was ashamed of the body condemned to carry it. My life was not real life but an imitation, and like all imitations I thought of myself as a wretched and pitiful creature, doomed to be forgotten. In those days, I thought the only way to escape my despair was to imitate my "true self" more faithfully. At one point, I considered changing schools, moving to a new neighborhood, making new friends, but I knew that putting a distance between us would only mean that I thought about you all the more. On stormy autumn afternoons, I would sit listlessly in my armchair, watching the raindrops on the window, for hour after hour; I'd be thinking of you: Rüya and Galip. I'd go over whatever clues I had handy and imagine what Rüya and Galip were doing at that moment; and if, after an hour or two I had managed to convince myself that it was Rüya sitting in that armchair in that dark room, this fearsome thought would bring me exquisite pleasure."

Because she kept rushing back and forth from the kitchen with tea and toast as she spoke, smiling as easily as if she were telling an amusing story about a distant acquaintance, Galip was not unduly troubled by what she said.

"I continued to suffer from this illness until my husband's death. I still suffer from it, though I no longer see it as an illness; after my husband died, when I was alone with my guilt, I finally accepted that no one in this world can ever hope to be themselves. The overwhelming regret I felt was but another variation of the same disease, and so was my new passion: to relive the life I had shared with Nihat, relive it exactly, but now as myself. One dark midnight, as I warned myself that regret could ruin what time was left to me, I had an eerie thought: I had not been myself during the first half of my life because I wanted to be someone else, and now I was going to spend the second half of my life being someone else who regretted all those years she had spent not being herself. I couldn't help but laugh, and when I did, the terror and misery I had thought to be my past and my future became a fate I shared with everyone, and a fate I had no need to dwell on. For by now I knew beyond the shadow of a doubt that none of us can ever hope to be ourselves: that the troubled old man standing in that long line, waiting for the bus—he too has ghosts living inside him, ghosts of the 'real' people he once longed to become. That rosy-cheeked mother who's taken her children to the park on a winter's morning to soak in some sunlight—she too has sacrificed herself, she too is a copy of some other mother. The melancholy men straggling out of movie theaters, the wretches I saw roaming along crowded avenues or fidgeting in noisy coffeehouses—they too are haunted day and night by the ghosts of the 'true selves' they longed to become."

They were still sitting at the breakfast table, smoking cigarettes. The room was warm, and as the woman spoke, Galip felt waves of sleep rolling over him with promises of innocence: Relax, they said, this is only a dream. When he asked if he could stretch out on the divan next to the radiator for a quick nap, Belkıs began to tell him the story of the Crown Prince; it was, she said, pertinent to "everything we've been discussing."

Yes, once upon a time there lived a prince who'd discovered that there was one question in life that mattered more than any other: to be or not to be oneself—but before Galip could conjure up the story, he could feel himself turning into someone else, and then into someone else who fell asleep.

Chapter Eighteen

The Dark Air Shaft

"The aspect of the venerable mansion has always affected me like a human countenance."

—Nathaniel Hawthorne,
The House of the Seven Gables

One afternoon years later, I went to look at that building. This is not to say I'd avoided the street in the interim, for of course I'd walked along these pavements on many an occasion—at noon to push against a tide of lycée students in sloppy jackets and loosened ties, swinging bulky bags; in the evening to mingle with men rushing home from work and women prancing home from tea parties—but never before had I gone back just to look at the building that had once meant so much to me.

It was winter, and the afternoon was drawing to a close. The sky was darkening and the soot from the chimneys hung so heavily over the narrow avenue that it already felt like night. I could see lights in only two apartments; the dim and soulless glow coming through their windows told me they were not homes but offices, full of bent heads working late. No other sign of life from the front of the building; the other floors were pitch black. The curtains were drawn at each and every window, and they all stared down at me, as empty and as frightening as blind men's eyes. How cold this building looked, how forlorn and insipid! How hard to imagine that this same building had once hummed with the hustle and bustle of one big unhappy family.

It was almost as if the building were being punished for the sins of its youth, and it pleased me to witness its ruin. I knew this was so only because I had never been able to enjoy my rightful share of its sinful pleasures—so to see the building in decay was to taste revenge—but I had something else on my mind at that moment: What happened to the secret inside the pit that later became the gap? When it turned into the gap, what happened to the pit and everything in it?

I thought back to the pit that had once sat next to the building, a bottomless pit that made me shiver at night—and not just me but every girl and boy in the building, and the grown-ups too. It was of mythic proportions, thick with bats, rats, scorpions, and poisonous snakes. It was, I was sure, the same pit Sheikh Galip described in *Love and Beauty* and Rumi in *Mathnawi*. Lower a pail into it, and something cut the rope; they told us there was an ogre lurking in its darkest depths, a black ogre as big as our building! *Never go anywhere near it, children!* That's what they'd say. Once they tied a rope to the janitor's belt and lowered him into the pit; when he emerged from the black and timeless void, his lungs were caked with cigarette tar for all eternity and his eyes were brimming with tears. I already knew that the venomous desert witch who guarded the well could sometimes assume the form of the janitor's moon-faced wife and that the secret of the pit was buried in the memories of everyone who lived in the apartments. It haunted us all, casting shadows over our lives like a secret sin that could not hide in the past forever. So—just as animals will fling dirt over anything that shames them—it was eventually decided that the time had come to suppress that pit and the creatures swirling inside it. One morning, when I awoke from a nightmare drenched in the colors of night, my head swirling with faces I couldn't read, I saw that the pit had been covered over. But my nightmare was not yet ended; the terror had only just begun, for the pit had turned on its axis to rise high into the sky. How to describe this dread funnel bringing mystery and death to our windows? Some called it the gap. Others called it the dark air shaft. . . .

Of course, there were those who insisted these new spaces let in light, not darkness, though most of us hated them: hence our derogatory terms. When the apartment house was first built, there were empty lots on either side, and in no way did the building itself resemble the ugly concrete affairs that would soon line the avenue like a filthy wall. In the early days, you could look out any of the kitchen windows and see the mosque, the streetcar line, the girls' lycée, and Alâaddin's shop; the view was the same from the long thin corridors that ran the length of each apartment and from the spare rooms we used to store furniture, maids, babies, ironing boards, great-aunts, and poor relations. But then the empty lot next door was sold to a builder, and soon there was a huge apartment house standing between us and the world, leaving nothing to contemplate but a row of new windows three yards away. This was how the gap into the well was formed, a dark dead space hemmed in by dirty, discolored, concrete walls, between windows reflecting other windows into infinity, not to mention the lower floors.

It was not long before the pigeons had claimed this space; the gloom now had its own special scent. They roosted with their ever-multiplying young on concrete ledges, on windowsills that broke off of their own accord, and in the elbows of inaccessible rainspouts that were soon overflowing with their filth. From time to time they'd be joined by insolent flocks of seagulls, auguring not just meteorological disasters but evils of all kinds, and then there were the black crows that lost their way in the dead of night who'd fling themselves against the blind windows of the bottomless pit . . . There was a low iron door leading to the janitor's airless and low-ceilinged lodgings; a novice might mistake it for the entrance to a prison cell (its creaking hinges called to mind a dungeon); those venturing through it with bowed heads would, as they surveyed the yawning shadow that was the floor, see winged rat-nibbled corpses strewn across it. There was all variety of ordure in these basement passageways, things so disgusting they cried out for their own words: the shells of pigeon eggs stolen by rats who used the spouts to penetrate the upper stories, unlucky forks and knives shaken into the petroleum void from the folds of flowered tablecloths, orphaned socks shaken from the folds of sleepy bed-sheets, dustcloths, cigarette ends, shards of glass from broken windows, crushed lightbulbs, shattered mirrors, rusty bedsprings, the armless torsos of pink baby dolls whose long-lashed eyes continued to open and close with hopeless obstinacy, deflated balls, soiled children's underwear, the carefully shredded remains of suspect magazines, dubious newspapers, and photographs too fearsome to contemplate. . . .

From time to time, the janitor would retrieve one of these objects and wander from floor to floor, holding the piece of filth far in front of him, like a policeman who's just collared a criminal, but no residents ever owned up to the dubious objects he dragged from the muddy underworld: "It's not ours," they would say. "It fell all the way down *there*, did it?"

They uttered the word *there* as if it were a fear they were desperate to escape and forget forevermore, even as they resigned themselves to its eternal grip; they spoke of the air shaft as one might speak of an ugly and contagious disease; the void was a cesspool into which they too might fall if they didn't watch their step; it was the crucible of evil, insinuated by sly unknown hands into the very heart of their lives. Those microbes they mentioned in the papers—no one doubted that this was where they incubated; this was why their children were always ill and why they were haunted from such a young age by ghosts and intimations of death. It was the breeding ground, too, for the strange smells that sometimes engulfed the building like a ring of fear; our hopelessness and ill fortune emanated, no doubt, from the same source. Many misfortunes had befallen us after the gap sprang from the lower depths to darken our lives—debt, divorce, and bankruptcy, jealousy, infidelity, incest, and death—and though we jumbled the pages of our family history, pushing them to the darkest recesses of memory, the cloud of blue-black smoke swirling past our windows was always there to remind us.

But, God be thanked, there is always someone willing to rummage through the forbidden pages of the past in search of treasure, and so it was in the long hallways (kept dark to save on electricity) when children (ah, children!) squirmed between the tightly drawn curtains and pressed their little foreheads against the window to stare into the air shaft; on the days when the entire family was invited to Grandfather's, the servant girl would call into the gap to let the people downstairs (and the people next door) know that the food was on the table; on the occasions when they did not think to include the mother who'd been banished to the attic with her son, she'd open her kitchen window to find out what they were eating and what plots they were hatching around the table; a deaf mute would spend long evenings standing at the window, staring out into the black hole, stopping only when his aged mother caught sight of him standing there and sent him to bed;

on rainy days, the servant girl would stand at the window and day-dream as she watched the water spilling past her; so also did the victo-rious young man who would later return to the building as the family staggered on to crumble into nothingness.

Let's take a quick inventory of the treasures they found there: the fading images of unheard girls and women on frosted kitchen win-dows; a dim room inhabited by the ghostly shadow of a back rising and falling in prayer; a magazine lying on a quilt on a bed and, next to it, an old lady's leg (if you wait long enough, you'll see a hand stretch out to turn the pages and then slowly scratch the leg); pressed against the cold windowpanes, the forehead of a young man who refuses to let his family cover up the truth, who has resolved to return one day in victory to unearth the mystery of the bottomless pit. (From time to time, this same young man would look into the window opposite and see the enchanting reflection of his beautiful stepmother, lost in dreams, just as he was.)

Let us not forget the heads and breasts of pigeons nestling in the darkness, or the blue-black shadows, the twitching curtains, the lamps that turn off only to go on again a moment later, the orange lines on the windows of rooms where the lights are still burning, and the sad, guilty memories that these lines come to signify: How short our lives are, how little we see, how little we know; so let us dream, at least. My dear readers, I wish you all a happy Sunday.

Chapter Nineteen

Signs of the City

*"Was I the same when I got up this morning? I almost think I
can remember feeling a little different. But if I'm not the same,
the next question is 'Who in the world am I?'"*

—Lewis Carroll,
Alice in Wonderland

Galip woke up to find an unfamiliar figure standing over him.
Belkıs had changed and was now wearing a tar-colored skirt that
told him he was in a strange house with a strange woman. Her face and
hair had changed too. She had combed her hair back in the style of Ava
Gardner in *55 Days at Peking* and painted her lips with the same
Supertechnirama Red. As he stared into her new face, Galip realized
that people had been playing games with him for some time.

A few minutes later, Galip went over to the wardrobe where the
woman had neatly hung his overcoat; taking the newspaper out of the
pocket, he spread it out on the now also neat and tidy breakfast table.
As he reread Celâl's column, the notes he'd made in the margins and
the words and syllables he'd underlined in the text made no sense to
him at all. He could see at once that the words he'd marked were not
keys to the mystery, so much so that he wondered in passing if there
was any mystery at all; it was as if the words signified themselves and,
at the same time, something else. Every sentence of the story Celâl had
told in his Sunday column—about an amazing discovery he could no
longer announce to the world now that his memory was failing him—
seemed to come from another story about some other human tragedy
that everyone else in the world knew and understood. This was so clear
and so real that there was no need to extract certain letters, syllables,

and words to arrange them in another order. To extract the hidden "secret" meaning, all he had to do was hold on to that conviction as he read the column. As his eyes traveled from word to word, he told himself that, while his first object was to locate Celâl and Rüya's hiding place (and also make sense of it), these lines would also reveal to him all the secrets of the city, all the secrets of life itself, but whenever he glanced up from the page to see Belkıs's new face, his good intentions vanished. To keep himself in check, he tried keeping his eyes on the page, reading the column over and over, but he was still not able to extract the meaning he had been sure he would find so easily. He felt happy, on the verge of a revelation—the secret of life, the meaning of the world, shimmering just beyond his grasp—but when he tried to put this secret into words, all he could see was the face of the woman who was sitting in the corner watching him. After struggling for some time, he decided that faith and intuition were getting him nowhere; his only hope was to use his mind, and to this end he began making new notes in the margins and underlining new syllables and words. He was deep in thought when Belkıs came over to the table.

"That's Celâl Salik's column," she said. "I knew he was your uncle. Did you see how frightened I was when we saw that mannequin of him in the underground passages?"

"I did," said Galip. "But he's not my uncle, he's my uncle's son."

"It's because the mannequin looked so much like him," said Belkıs. "When I'd wander around Nişantaşı hoping to run into you and Rüya, I'd run into him instead sometimes, wearing exactly the same outfit."

"Yes, that was the raincoat he wore in those days," said Galip. "He wore it a lot."

"He still wanders all over Nişantaşı, like a ghost," said Belkıs. "What are these notes you've written in the margins?"

"They have nothing to do with the column," said Galip, as he folded up the paper. "They're about a polar explorer who disappears. So another explorer steps in and then he disappears too. The mystery surrounding the second explorer deepens the mystery surrounding the first, who by now is living in a forgotten city under an alias, but one day he's murdered. At which point the murdered man who's been living in a forgotten city under an alias is . . ."

When Galip got to the end of the story, he knew he was going to have to go right back to the beginning and tell it again. As he did so, he thought hateful thoughts about people who made you tell the same stories over and over. If people would only just be themselves, he felt like saying. If only they would stop telling stories! As he told the story for the second time, he rose from the table and put the folded newspaper back into the pocket of his old overcoat.

"Are you leaving?" Belkıs asked bashfully.

"I haven't finished my story," Galip snapped.

When he'd finished his story, he looked at Belkıs again, and it seemed as if she were wearing a mask. If he took that mask by its Supertechnirama lips and pulled it off, he'd have no trouble reading the face underneath, but he still had no idea what it would mean. There was a game he'd played as a child when he was bored out of his skull: Why Are We Here? He could continue with whatever else he was doing and still keep the game going, and it was the same now; as he retold his story, his mind was able to wander. There was a time when he'd wondered if that's what had made Celâl so attractive to women, this knack he had of pursuing his own thoughts even as he told a story, but then Belkıs did not look like the sort of woman who'd listen to Celâl tell a story; she looked like someone incapable of hiding the meaning on her face.

"Won't Rüya be wondering where you are?" asked Belkıs.

"Not at all," said Galip. "She's used to me coming home at all hours. I can't even remember how many nights I've lost chasing down clients. I handle all sorts: missing political activists, swindlers who've taken out loans under false names, tenants who've run off without paying the rent, luckless men who use forged identity cards to take on second wives. . . . Sometimes I don't surface till morning."

"But it's past noon," said Belkıs. "If I were Rüya and I were waiting for you at home, I'd want you to call me immediately."

"I don't want to call her."

"If I were the one waiting for you, I would have dropped onto my bed by now from worry," Belkıs continued. "I'd be watching the window, listening for the phone. I'd be thinking that even though you knew how worried and unhappy I was, you still hadn't called, and that would make me even more unhappy. Go on, call her. Tell her you're here; tell her you're with me."

The woman brought over the phone, cradling it like a toy, and Galip called home. No one answered.

"No one's at home."

"Where is she then?" asked the woman in a voice that was playful rather than curious.

"I don't know," said Galip.

He took the newspaper from his coat pocket, returned to the table, and read Celâl's column over again. He read it over so many times that the words lost their meaning and turned into shapes. Sometime later, it occurred to Galip that he could have written this column himself—he could write like Celâl. Soon after this thought came to him, he retrieved his overcoat from the wardrobe, carefully folded up his newspaper, tore out the column, and put it into his pocket.

"Are you going?" said Belkıs. "Don't go."

It took him some time to find a taxi, and as he turned to the window to take one last look at this familiar street, he feared he would never get her face out of his mind; he could still see her, pleading with him to stay; how he wished he could remember her with another face, in another story! He turned to the driver, wanting to say, Avenue Such and Such, and fast! like a hero in one of Rüya's detective novels; instead he asked to be taken to the Galata Bridge.

As he walked across the bridge, gazing idly into the Sunday crowds, he was suddenly certain that he was on the verge of solving a riddle that had been vexing him for years without his even being aware of it. In some deep and dreamlike way he was also aware that this was an illusion, but he was able to hold the contradictory thoughts in his mind with ease. He passed soldiers on leave, men throwing fishing lines into the sea, families rushing for ferries. Though they didn't know it, they all resided inside the mystery he was about to solve. This father he could see in front of him—he was off on a Sunday visit, with the baby in his arms and his older son skipping along next to him in his new gym shoes. This mother he could see on the bus—she was wearing a head scarf, and so was the daughter sitting next to her. The moment Galip solved the mystery, they too would see the thing that had shaped their lives for so very long.

He was still on the bridge—on the side overlooking the Sea of Marmara—when he started rushing at the people, almost running into them, and it seemed to him as if the meanings that had long ago faded from their faces suddenly returned to illuminate them, if only for a split second. They were startled—why was this man rushing toward them?—their eyes lit up and widened, and when Galip looked into them he could read all their secrets.

Their coats and jackets were old, old and faded. Nothing in the world surprised them; everything was as ordinary as the pavement beneath their feet, and yet they were not at home in this world. They were lost in their thoughts, and yet, if you provoked them just a little, their eyes lit up and their masks fell away and for a moment you could almost see it: the past, the soul, the key. If only I could startle them again, Galip thought. If only I could tell them the story of the Crown Prince! As the story came back into his head, it seemed brand new; it was as if he had lived this story, had just remembered it.

Almost everyone on the bridge was carrying plastic bags. They were bulging with paper sacks and newspapers and plastic and metal. He stared at them as if he were seeing them for the first time, carefully reading their logos. For a moment it seemed to him that *these* were the words and letters that would lead him to the other world, the true world, and his heart leaped. Their bright promise never lasted longer than a moment: like the faces, they would light up only to fade away. But still Galip went on reading them: PUDDING SHOP . . . ATAKÖY . . . TÜRKSAN . . . DRIED FRUITS . . . TIME FOR . . . PALACES.

When his eyes lit on an old fisherman—when he saw that there were no letters on his plastic bag, just the picture of a stork—it occurred to him that he could read pictures just as easily as letters. On one bag he saw a happy family—a perfect family, with a mother, a father, a daughter, and a son—smiling hopefully out at the world; on another he saw two fish; he saw pictures of shoes, maps of Turkey, silhouettes of buildings, packs of cigarettes, pieces of baklava, black cats, roosters, horseshoes, minarets, and trees. All contained the key to the mystery, but what was the mystery? On the bag next to the old woman selling bird feed for the pigeons in front of the New Mosque he saw the picture of an owl. It was when he deduced that this was either the same owl as the one he'd seen on the front of Rüya's detective novels or his cunningly concealed brother that Galip first felt the presence of an invisible hand secretly bringing order to the world.

There it was, another hand trick crying out to be exposed, deciphered, but no one gave a damn, no one but him. Even though they were in it up to their throats, buried in this very secret!

To examine the owl more closely, Galip bought a cup of bird feed from the old woman, who reminded him of a witch. He scattered the kernels on the ground, and suddenly he was standing under a vast black umbrella of pigeon wings. Yes! He was right! The owl on the bag was the same as the owl on Rüya's novels! He looked over at a pair of proud parents, happily watching their young daughter feed the pigeons; how they made him despair. How could they ignore this owl, this shining truth, these signs? How could they stand here and see absolutely nothing? Not even the hint of a suspicion in their minds—not a clue! They'd forgotten. He imagined that Rüya was waiting at home for him, and that he was the hero of the detective novel in her hand. It was between him and the hand now, the invisible and almighty hand that had arranged the world and was now pointing him toward the heart of the mystery.

All he needed then was to see an apprentice walk past the Süley-maniye Mosque carrying a picture of that mosque in a beaded frame: if the words, letters, and pictures on plastic bags were signs, then so too were the things they signified. The garish colors in the picture were more real than the mosque itself. The invisible hand did not confine himself to words, faces, and pictures, he played with everything under the sun. Not long after this thought struck him, he found himself walking through the warren of streets known as Zindan Kapı, the Dungeon Door district—this too had a secret meaning, but only he could see it: he felt as patient as a man who has almost finished a cross-word and knows that the last words will fall easily into place.

He surveyed the ramshackle shops lining the crooked pavements: These garden shears he saw before him, these star-spangled screw-drivers, NO PARKING signs, cans of tomato paste, these calendars you saw on the walls of cheap restaurants, this Byzantine aqueduct fes-tooned with Plexiglas letters, the heavy padlocks hanging from the metal shop shutters—they were all signs crying out to be read. He could, if he wished, read them like faces. Thus the pliers signified *vigi-lance* while the olives in that small jar signified *patience*; the happy driver in an ad for car tires stood for *almost there*; together they told him that he was almost there and should be vigilant and patient as he proceeded to his destination. But he was surrounded by other signs that refused to divulge their meanings: telephone wires, traffic signs, detergent boxes, shovels without handles, a sign advertising circumcisions, illegible political slogans, numbered electric service designations, shards of ice, traffic arrows, blank sheets of paper. . . . Maybe if he waited, all would be clear, but it was so confused, wearisome, noisy. How different from the cosy world of Rüya's detective novels, where authors never vexed a hero with more signs than he needed.

Even so, he was consoled by the Mosque of Ahi Çelebi, for it signified a story he could understand. Years before, Celâl had written of a dream in which he'd found himself in this small mosque with Muhammed and a number of his saints. He'd later paid a visit to a dream reader in Kasımpaşa who'd told him what it meant: He would keep on writing until the end of his life. He would imagine so many things in his writing that he would think back on his life as a long journey, even if he never left the house. It was only much later that Galip realized that Celâl had borrowed the story from the seventeenth-century travel writer, Evliya Çelebi.

Passing in front of a food market, Galip told himself, *This is why the story meant one thing the first time I read it and something else altogether when I read it for the second time.* He was in no doubt that if he read Celâl's column for a third and a fourth time, it would again reveal new meanings; even if it did, Galip was still sure he was on course; it was like one of those puzzles he'd loved so much as a child; he was going through a series of doors, getting closer and closer to the heart of the mystery. With this thought in mind, Galip began to tire of the tangled streets around the fruit and vegetable market; he longed for a place where he could sit and read through every column Celâl had ever written.

Heading out of the market, his head still spinning from the noise and the stench, he saw a junk dealer: At his feet, spread out on a large cloth on an empty stretch of pavement, was a selection of objects that soon had Galip transfixed: two elbow-shaped pipes, assorted records, a pair of black shoes, a broken pair of pliers, a lamp base, a black phone, two bedsprings, a mother-of-pearl cigarette holder, a broken wall clock, a stack of White Russian banknotes, a brass faucet, a figurine of a Roman huntress—the goddess Diana?—an empty picture frame, an old radio, a pair of doorknobs, a sugar bowl.

He named them all, enunciating each word with care, and studied them closely. It was not the objects that bewitched him, it was the order in which they'd been arranged. Nothing on this cloth was unusual—junk dealers across the city sold the same things—but this old man had arranged his wares in a pattern that called to mind a checkerboard. Four perfect columns, four perfect rows: this could not be by chance but by design. It reminded him of the vocabulary tests when he was studying English and French: sixteen familiar objects, waiting to be renamed in a new language. Galip wanted to call out the answers: Pipe, record, telephone, shoes, pliers. . . .

But they made no secret of their other meanings; that's what Galip found shocking. He'd look at the brass faucet and, thinking this was a vocabulary test, he'd tell himself it was a brass faucet, nothing more and nothing less, but when he looked at it again, he'd feel the thrill of its other meaning. He'd look at the black phone, an exact replica of every telephone he'd seen in those foreign language textbooks; marveling at its overt purpose—to link a caller with other voices—but he'd sense a second, greater, hidden purpose.

How to enter the secret world of second meanings, how to break the code? He was standing on the threshold—joyful and expectant—but he had no idea how to cross it. In Rüya's detective novels, when the puzzle was solved and the murky second world revealed itself, it would burn bright for a few seconds, only to recede into the shadows of the first world for lack of interest. When, in the middle the night, still nibbling on the roasted chickpeas she bought at Alâaddin's store, Rüya would turn to him and say, "So it turns out that the murderer was the retired colonel; it seems the victim once insulted him: The motive was revenge!" he'd know that his wife had already forgotten the English butlers, cigarette lighters, dinner tables, porcelain cups, guns, and all the other details that had littered the text; the only thing still lingering in her mind was this secret new world that these people and these objects signified. But when she reached the end of these vile translations, these same objects did transport Rüya and her detective to a new world, whereas all Galip could do was entertain the hope that he might one day see it. Desperate for more clues, Galip now turned to the old man who had spread his wares so mysteriously; looking him straight in the eye, he tried to read his face.

"How much is the black phone?"

"Are you a buyer?" asked the junk dealer, ready to bargain but suspicious too.

Galip was thrown by his question; he had not expected this man to ask him who he was. So this is what it's come to, he thought. Now they see *me* as signifying something else! But this was not the world he wanted to enter; the world he longed for was the one Celâl had conjured out of words. By naming the objects in this world and peopling it with stories, he'd made himself a hiding place and hidden the key. The junk dealer's eyes had now lost their shine; no longer sure of a sale, they had sunk back into their old gloom.

"What's this for?" Galip asked, pointing at the small and simple lamp base.

"That's a table leg," said the man. "But some people put them on the ends of curtain cornices. Or use them as doorknobs."

When he stepped onto Atatürk Bridge, Galip had resolved to look only at faces. Watching each face brighten at his gaze, he could almost see question marks bubbling from their heads—the way they did in the Turkish versions of Spanish and Italian photo novels—but they vanished into the air without leaving a trace. Gazing across the bridge at the skyline, he thought he saw each and every one of their faces shimmering behind its dull gray veil, but this too was an illusion. It was perhaps possible to look into the faces of his fellow citizens and see in them the city's long history—its misfortunes, its lost magnificence, its melancholy and pain—but these were not carefully arranged clues pointing to a secret world; they came from a shared defeat, a shared history, a shared shame. As they churned across the gray-blue waters of the Golden Horn, they left a trail of ugly brown bubbles in their wake.

By the time he walked into a coffeehouse in one of the streets behind Tünel, Galip had studied seventy-three new faces. Pleased with his progress, he sat down at a table. After ordering tea from the boy, he took Celâl's column out of his coat pocket and began to read it again from the beginning. The letters, words, and sentences had not changed in any way, but as his eyes traveled over them, they suggested ideas that Galip had never before entertained; these were not Celâl's ideas but his own, though in some odd way he saw them reflected in the text. Seeing the parallel between his ideas and Celâl's, a wave of pleasure passed over him, much as it had done when he was a child and had managed to do a perfect impersonation of the man he longed to become.

On the table was a piece of paper that had been shaped into a cone; around it were the hulls of sunflower seeds. From this he deduced that the man who'd sat here before him had brought in a packet of sunflower seeds that he'd probably purchased from a street vendor. Looking at the edges of the cone, Galip now saw it had been fashioned from a piece of paper torn from a school notebook. He studied the childish handwriting on the other side:

6 November 1972. Unit 12. Assignment: our home, our garden. In the garden behind our house there are four trees. Two of them are poplars and the others are willows. One of the willow trees is large and the other is small. Around our garden is a wall. My father made the wall with stones and chicken wire. A house is a shelter that protects us from the winter cold and the summer heat. Our house is a place that protects us from evil. Our house has one door, six windows, and two chimneys.

At the bottom of the page was a colored pencil drawing of a house inside a walled garden. Each tile had its own careful outline, though the roof as a whole was a sloppily filled-in red. Seeing that the number of doors, windows, and chimneys in the picture corresponded exactly with the number of doors, windows, and chimneys in the text, Galip felt another wave of happiness passing through him.

Still feeling its traces, he turned the sheet of paper over and began to jot down notes. He knew without a doubt that the words he set down between the lines signified things as real as the ones the schoolchild had described in his homework. It felt like finding his voice again, the language he'd thought he'd lost forever. He listed all his clues in tiny letters, and when he came to the end of the page, he thought, How easy that was! and then, Since I am now certain that Celâl and I think alike, I must study more faces!

After studying the faces of the tea drinkers around him, Galip returned to the cold street. In one of the streets behind Galatasaray, he saw an old woman in a head scarf who was talking to herself. Looking into the face of a girl who was coming out of a grocery shop, ducking under its half-closed shutters, he read that all lives resembled each other. In the face of a young girl in a faded dress who stared at her rubber shoes as she slipped over the ice, he could read that she knew what it meant to suffer from anxiety.

After Galip had sat down in another coffeehouse, he took out the child's assignment and read through it quickly, just as he'd done with Celâl's column. By now he knew that if he read Celâl's columns over and over, he would gain access to Celâl's memory, and once he had infiltrated Celâl's memory, he would know where he was hiding. This meant that he had first to locate the archive where Celâl kept his complete works. It was already clear to Galip that this archive had to be a house, *a place that protects us from evil.* As he reread the homework, he felt as innocent as a child who feels no fear in naming objects by their true names, so much so that he expected the words on the pages to tell him exactly where Rüya and Celâl were hiding, where they were sitting waiting for him even now. Every time this happy thought came to him, he'd jot down a few more clues, but they told him nothing.

By the time he returned to the street, Galip had eliminated some clues and emphasized others: they could not be outside the city, because Celâl could not write anywhere else. They couldn't be on the Asian side of the city, because he'd always looked down on it; there wasn't enough "history" there. Rüya and Celâl could not be hiding at one of his friends' houses, because he didn't have that sort of friend. They couldn't be hiding at one of Rüya's friends' houses, because Celâl would never go to a house like that. They couldn't be hiding out in an anonymous hotel room either; even if they were brother and sister, a woman sharing a room with a man always aroused suspicion.

By the time he entered the next coffeehouse, he was at least certain he was on the right track. He was walking through the back streets of Beyoğlu now, heading for Taksim and from there to Şişli, to Nişantaşı, to the heart of his own past. He remembered how Celâl had once written at length about the names of Istanbul streets. Glancing into a shop, he saw on the wall a portrait of a now-deceased wrestler, an Olympic medalist, about whom Celâl had once written a great deal. You could see this same framed picture in barbershops and tailor shops and produce stores all over the city: a black-and-white portrait torn from the pages of *Hayat* magazine. He was standing with his hands on his hips, smiling modestly at the camera, and as Galip studied his face he remembered that the man had died in a car crash. Not for the first time, he saw a connection between this man's modest smile and the accident that had killed him some seventeen years earlier; this accident, he now realized, was a sign.

It meant that coincidence had a part to play, if he was to fuse fact with fiction to create a new set of signs pointing to a new story. For instance, Galip thought when he'd left the coffeehouse and turned toward Taksim, when I look at the tired old horse pulling that cart to the edge of the narrow pavement on Hasnun Galip Street, I remember the horse in the primer my grandmother used when she was teaching me to read and write. The moment I remember the picture of that giant alphabet horse, I think of that little attic apartment on Teşvikiye Avenue where Celâl lived by himself for so many years, surrounded by objects that reflected his personality and harked back to his past. This in turn signals the importance this apartment holds in my own life.

But Celâl had left that apartment years ago. Thinking he might have read the signs wrong, Galip paused. If he began to believe that his feelings could mislead him, the city would soon swallow him up; of this he had no doubt: It was stories that kept him going, and he found these stories by feeling his way through the darkness, searching for familiar objects like a blind man. He was still on his feet because, after three days of wandering bereft through the streets of the city, he had been able to construct a story out of all the faces he had passed along the way. He was sure it was the same for all these other faces he could see around him: It was stories that kept them going.

His confidence restored, Galip went into another coffeehouse to assess his progress so far. The words on his list of clues, written on the back of the school assignment, looked clear and simple. At the far end of the coffeehouse was a black-and-white television showing a soccer match on a snow-covered field. The lines had been drawn with ash and the ball was black with mud. Aside from one or two groups of men playing cards on bare tables, everyone in the coffeehouse was watching this black ball.

As he left the coffeehouse, Galip told himself that the secret he was searching for was as clean and spare as that black-and-white soccer match. All he had to do was pay close attention to the images and faces streaming past him, and his feet would take him where they wished. Istanbul was full of coffeehouses; a man could walk the length and breadth of the city and step into a coffeehouse every two hundred yards.

Near Taksim he suddenly found himself inside a crowd of people leaving a movie theater. They were staring straight ahead, as if in a trance, walking down the stairs arm in arm or with their hands plunged in their pockets, and Galip was so overwhelmed by what he read in their faces that his own nightmare faded into the background. What he read in their faces was peace: These people had been able to forget their own sadness by immersing themselves in a story. They were here, on this wretched street, but at the same time they were there, inside that story to which they'd so eagerly given themselves over. They had gone into the theater with minds sucked dry by pain and defeat, but now their minds were full again with this rich story that gave meaning to their memories and their melancholy. They can believe they're someone else! thought Galip longingly. For a moment he was tempted to go in to watch the film they'd just seen, to lose himself in the same story and become someone else. As they wandered down the street, stopping now and again to gaze into boring shop windows, Galip watched them return to the dull and dreary world they knew so well. They don't make much effort! thought Galip.

On the other hand, to become someone else you had to use all your strength. By the time he reached Taksim Square, Galip knew that he had—at last—the strength and determination to make his dream come true. I'm someone else! he told himself. How good it felt! He felt the world around him changing—not just the icy pavement beneath his feet, not just the billboards for Coca-Cola and Tamek Preserves, but his own body, from head to toe. If he put his mind to it, if he recited these words over and over, a man could change the entire universe, but there was no need to go to such extremes. I'm someone else, Galip told himself again. Though he could not bring himself to name this someone else; he could feel his memories, his sadness, rising up in him like a dirge. As the music grew louder, he watched Taksim Square—the center of his universe—slowly change shape; soon the buses struggling through the traffic like giant turkeys and the trolleys crawling behind them like stunned lobsters had faded into the misty street corners that had never seen the light of day. All at once he was stepping into a poor, forgotten country he had never seen before, beholding the brash modern square at its center. Its landmarks were the same, but now, when Galip looked at the snow-covered Statue of the Republic, at the wide Greek staircase leading nowhere, at the "opera" house he'd so blithely watched burn to the ground ten years earlier, he knew that they too belonged to the imaginary country they signified. As he jostled with the crowds at the bus stop, as he watched them pushing and shoving their way into buses and *dolmuşes*, he did not see a single mysterious face; not a single plastic bag offered veiled promises of a second world.

So he walked on, toward Harbiye and Nişantaşı, not once feeling the urge to stop off at a coffeehouse to read faces. Much later, when he was sure he'd found the place he'd been searching for, he could not quite define who he'd been during that last stretch. I was not quite convinced I was Celâl yet! he told himself, and as he rummaged through the old columns, notebooks, and newspaper clippings that illuminated the entirety of Celâl's past, he added, I'd not yet stopped being myself! He'd walked through the streets like a tourist whose plane has been delayed, who finds himself with a half a day to kill in a city he'd never thought to visit. The statue of Atatürk told him that a soldier had played an important role in this country's history; the crowd idling in front of the bright muddy lights of the movie theater told him that on Sunday afternoons people in this country escaped boredom by watching dreams imported from abroad; the sandwich and pastry vendors waving their knives, as their eyes darted back and forth between the display windows and the pavement, told him that their sad dreams and sadder memories were fast fading from their minds; the line of dark bare trees running down the center of the avenue told him that they would grow darker still as evening fell, to signify the sorrow of an entire nation. Dear God, what is there to do at a time like this, on an avenue this dreary, in a city this lost? Galip had mumbled, but he knew at the same time that this was a phrase borrowed from one of Celâl's old columns.

The sky was dark by the time he reached Nişantaşı. The narrow pavements were thick with soot from the chimneys of the apartment buildings and exhaust fumes from the evening traffic. But the air had its own odd pungency, and as Galip breathed it in he felt at peace. Arriving at the crossroads that was the heart of Nişantaşı, the desire to be someone else rose up in him so powerfully that, though he'd seen them ten thousand times before, the apartment fronts and shop windows and bank panels and neon letters seemed new, transformed. He felt lighthearted, ready for adventure. It was, he knew, his mood that made the streets where he'd spent all his life look so different, but he knew at the same time that it was more than a mood, it was a state of mind that would be his forever.

Instead of crossing the street and heading home, he turned left on Teşvikiye Avenue. He was beside himself with happiness and so in thrall to the person he had now become that he could not see anything without marveling at its newness; it was as if he'd just been cured of an illness that had kept him locked inside his house, as if he were seeing the outside world for the first time in years. So it seems this pudding shop I've been passing every day for who knows how long really does have a display window as bright as any jewelers! he felt like saying. So the street was always this narrow, and the pavements this crooked!

As a child he'd often imagined himself shedding his body and his soul to become someone new, but this had never stopped him from seeing this new person from the outside; and now, as Galip did the same, he caught a glimpse of its ghost. He's walking past the Ottoman Bank now, he said to himself. And now he's passing the City-of-Hearts Apartments—where he lived for so many years with his mother and his father and his grandfather—without giving it so much as a glance. Now he's stopped in front of the pharmacy, and when he looks in at the man at the cash register, he sees it's the son of the woman who gave him his injections. Now he's passing fearlessly in front of the police station; now he's moving on to smile at the mannequins standing among the Singer machines as if they're all old friends. Now he's taking one last breath, gathering up his strength and resolve before plunging into the heart of a secret conspiracy that is the fruit of many long years of scheming.

He crossed the street and doubled back, crossing the street again to walk once more under the linden trees that dotted the avenue here and there and the billboards that seemed to hang from every balcony. Then he started all over again. Each time he went a little farther up the avenue and a little farther down, thus enlarging his field of research; as he went he memorized the details that his hapless former self had neglected to notice: In Alâaddin's window, nestling among the old newspapers, toy guns, and nylon stockings, was a switchblade; the MUST TURN sign pointing traffic into Teşvikiye Avenue really pointed at the City-of-Hearts Apartments; despite the cold, the bread crumbs people had left for the birds on top of the low wall around the mosque had gotten moldy; some of the words in the political slogans on the walls of the girls' lycée had double meanings; in that classroom where the lights were still burning, there was a portrait of Atatürk on the wall and through the grimy window Galip could see that he too was looking straight into the City-of-Hearts Apartments; a hand that worked in mysterious ways had seen fit to attach petals to the roses in the florist window with safety pins; the flashy mannequins in the window of the new leather shop were looking up at the attic apartment where Celâl had once lived, and where Rüya had later lived with her mother and father.

For a long while Galip looked up with them. Forcing himself into the mold of a never-erring hero from one of Rüya's foreign detective novels, he reminded himself that Rüya—like these novels and these mannequins—had been conceived abroad; it seemed reasonable to follow the mannequins' upward gaze and conclude that Celâl and Rüya were hiding in the attic flat.

He averted his eyes and rushed back toward the mosque, but it took all his strength to do so. It was as if his legs did not want to leave the City-of-Hearts Apartments; they wanted to go straight inside and run up the steps they knew so well, all the way to the top floor; they wanted to take him inside and, having breached its dark and fearsome center, they wanted to show him something. Galip did not even want to imagine this scene. Using all his strength, he kept walking away from the apartment building, struggling to read the old meanings back into the pavements, shops, billboards, and traffic signs he passed along the way. The moment it had come to him—the moment he'd guessed they might be up there—he'd been overcome by intimations of an impending disaster. The longer he walked, the more his dread grew, perhaps because he'd come to Alâaddin's shop by now and was approaching the police station, perhaps because he'd noticed that the MUST TURN sign on the corner did not actually point to the City-of-Hearts Apartments after all. By now he was so confused and exhausted he knew he had to find a place where he could sit and think.

He went into the cafeteria next to the Teşvikiye–Eminönü *dolmuş* stop and ordered himself a plate of pastries and a glass of tea. Wouldn't it be the most natural thing in the world for Celâl—obsessed as he was with his past and his vanishing memory—to rent or buy the apartment where he'd spent so much of his childhood and youth? Considering that the relatives who'd forced him out had now lost all their money and retreated to a dusty building in the back streets, reclaiming this flat for himself would be a personal victory. It would, Galip thought, be entirely in character for Celâl to conceal his victory from everyone in the family except Rüya; and even though it was on the main thoroughfare, he'd have had no trouble covering his tracks.

In the minutes that followed, Galip gave his full attention to a family that had just walked into the cafeteria: a mother and a father with their son and daughter, here for supper after spending their Sunday afternoon at the movies. The parents were the same age as Galip. The father was leafing through the paper he'd brought out of his pocket; the mother was supervising their squabbling children with her eyebrows, and as she acceded to her family's many and varied requests, her hands flew in and out of her small bag as fast as a magician pulling rabbits from a hat: first it was a handkerchief for her son, whose nose was running; then it was a red pill for the father's outstretched hand, a clip for her daughter's hair, a lighter for the father (who was reading Celâl's column now), the same handkerchief for her son again, and so on.

Galip had eaten his pastry and finished his tea when he realized that the father was another old classmate from lycée and middle school. As he was going out the door, he was overcome by an urge to tell him so, and as he noticed the frightful burn scar running down the man's right cheek all the way down to his throat, he recognized the wife as the clever chatterbox who'd been in his and Rüya's class at Şişli Progressive High School. As the adults went through the usual motions, remembering the old days, bringing each other up-to-date and, to make the picture complete, speaking fondly of Rüya, the two children profited from their parents' inattention to settle scores. Galip explained that he and Rüya had no children, that Rüya was sitting at home reading a detective novel, awaiting his return, that they were planning to see something at the Palace Theater this evening, that he'd come out just now to buy the tickets, and that he'd just run into Belkıs too: Belkıs— did they remember her? dark hair, medium height—that Belkıs.

But that was impossible, the tedious couple tediously insisted. "There was no one in our class called Belkıs!" From time to time they took out their leather-bound yearbooks to reminisce about each and every classmate; that's why they were so sure.

Returning to the street, Galip rushed back to Nişantaşı Square. Convinced that Rüya and Celâl were going to the 7:15 performance at the Palace Theater, he ran straight to the theater, but he couldn't see them on the pavement, nor could he see them in the crowd gathered at the door. Glancing at the photograph of the woman he'd seen in the film yesterday afternoon, when he was waiting for them to come back, he again longed to be in her place.

He wandered up and down the street, gazing into shop windows and reading the faces of the people flowing past him, and it was some time before he found himself standing once again before the City-of-Hearts Apartments. By eight in the evening, the windows of every building on the avenue except the City-of-Hearts Apartments glowed with the blue light of television. Staring up at its dark windows, Galip noticed a dark blue cloth hanging from the balcony on the top floor. Thirty years ago, when they'd all lived here as a family, they'd hung identical cloths from their balconies as a signal for the water carrier, so when he and his horse dragged his cartload of enamel containers down the avenue, he'd know which floors had run out of drinking water and take the water right up.

Deciding that this cloth, too, must be a signal, Galip ran through the possibilities. It could be Rüya and Celâl's way of telling him they were there. Or it could signal that Celâl had embarked on yet another excursion into his cherished past. He stood there thinking until half past eight, and then he headed home.

It made him unbearably sad to see the lamplight in the sitting room where he and Rüya had shared their evenings, smoking and reading their books and their papers; it seemed so long ago, though it was not very long ago at all; he might have been looking at the picture of a lost paradise in the travel supplement. Nowhere could he see a sign that Rüya had come back to the house or even called; returning to the nest, the tired husband met the same smells, the same shadows. Leaving his silent furniture to sit under the melancholy lamplight, Galip went down the dark hall to the dark bedroom. Taking off his coat, he felt his way to the bed and lay down on his back. A faint light coming from the sitting room and the streetlight shining into the corridor threw shadows on the ceiling, fashioning them into finely etched devil's faces.

When he rose from his bed, Galip knew exactly what he had to do. He picked up the paper and read through the television listings, and then he looked to see which movies were playing in the area, taking care to note that the showing times were the same as ever. He took one last look at Celâl's column. Opening the refrigerator, he found a container of olives, picked out a few that had not yet spoiled, broke off a piece of white cheese that still looked edible, found himself a heel of dry bread, and sat down to eat. He left the house at a quarter past ten and walked back to the City-of-Hearts Apartments, stopping across the street, just a few paces back from the place where he'd stood before.

He had not been there long when the hall light went on, and there in the door was İsmail Efendi, who had been the building's janitor since time began; with his usual cigarette dangling from his mouth, he was taking out the trash, emptying the cans into the big barrel next to the enormous chestnut tree. Galip crossed the street.

"Hello, İsmail Efendi, how are you? I came to leave an envelope for Celâl."

"Aaah, Galip!" said the old man, glad to see him after all these years but—like a headmaster who's just been accosted by an old pupil—not quite sure what to make of him. "But Celâl's not here."

"Listen, I know. I know he's here but, listen, I'm not telling anyone either." As he spoke, Galip stepped decisively into the building. "Whatever you do, please don't mention this to anyone else. He gave me express instructions: Leave this envelope downstairs with İsmail Efendi. That's what he said!"

Galip marched down the stairs leading to the janitor's apartment. The corridor smelled of propane gas and cooking oil, just as it had when he was a child. And there was İsmail's wife Kamer, sitting in the same armchair, watching the television that stood on the stand that had once been home to their radio.

"Kamer, look's who's here," said Galip.

"Aaaah," said the woman. She stood up to embrace him. "You forgot us!"

"How could we ever forget you?"

"You all walk past the building all the time, but you never come in to say hello!"

"I brought this for Celâl!" said Galip, showing her the envelope.

"Did İsmail tell you?"

"No, Celâl told me himself," said Galip. "I know he's here, but please, on no account should you tell anyone else."

"We're keeping our mouths shut, aren't we?" said the woman. "He gave us strict orders, after all."

"I know," said Galip. "Are they up there now?"

"We have no idea. He comes back in the middle of the night when we're already asleep, and he goes out again before we wake up. We take out his trash and leave him his newspaper. Sometimes there are piles of newspapers waiting outside his door."

"I won't go up," said Galip. He looked around the apartment, as if to find a place to leave the envelope: the same dining table, covered in the same blue-checked oilcloth, the same pale curtains veiling their view of pedestrians' legs and the muddy tires of passing cars, a sewing basket, an iron, a sugar bowl, a propane stove, a sooty radiator. . . . Hanging from a nail on the shelf above the radiator, Galip saw a key. The woman settled back into her chair.

"Let me make you some tea," she said. "Sit down on the edge of the bed over there and make yourself comfortable." She still had one eye on the television. "And how is Rüya Hanım? Why don't you have any children yet?"

By now she was giving her full attention to the television screen; though she was very far away, the beautiful girl they could see there looked something like Rüya: It was not clear what color her hair was, but it was ruffled, as if by sleep, her skin was fair, and in her eyes was the same childish indifference to the outside world. She was putting on lipstick and looking rather pleased.

"A beautiful woman," Galip murmured.

"Rüya Hanım's even more beautiful," said Kamer Hanım in the same soft voice.

But her fearful and admiring eyes were still on the woman on the screen. Galip stretched out his hand and slipped the key off the nail and dropped it into his pocket, pressing it against the homework assignment and its list of clues. He looked over at Kamer Hanım; she hadn't seen.

"Where shall I put this envelope?"

"You can give it to me," she said.

Through the little window that looked out to the street, Galip could see İsmail Efendi bringing the empty trash cans back into the building. They listened to him getting into the elevator; when it began to move, the picture on the television screen flickered and went fuzzy, and Galip took this opportunity to say his goodbyes. Slowly, quietly, he crept back upstairs to the building's main entrance. He opened the door and then slammed it shut again, remaining inside. He returned quietly to the stairwell and went up two flights, his heart beating so wildly by now he could feel it in his fingers. Sitting down on the flight between the second and third floors, he waited for İsmail Efendi to leave the empty cans on the floors above him and go downstairs. Suddenly the lights went off. "Automatic!" murmured Galip, remembering how alien and bewitching this word had sounded to him as a child. The lights went on again. The janitor got back into the elevator, and as it began its descent, Galip slowly crept upstairs. On the door of the apartment where he and his parents had once lived he saw a brass plaque bearing the name of a lawyer. Outside his grandparents' old apartment he saw a brass plaque bearing the name of a gynecologist and an empty trash can.

He found no sign on Celâl's door and no name either. Galip rang the bell with the confidence of a bill collector from the gas company. With his second ring, the light went off in the stairwell. As he rang the bell for the third and fourth times, he dug his free hand into his bottomless pocket and searched for the key; even after he'd found it, he still kept his finger pressed down on the bell. They're in there hiding! he told himself. They're sitting in those armchairs in the sitting room, saying nothing, staring at each other, waiting! First he couldn't fit the key into the lock; he'd almost decided he had the wrong one, but then—just as a confused mind can, in a moment of brilliance, suddenly understand itself and see order in the confounding muddle that is the world—the key slipped into the lock, and how wondrous, how blissfully simple, to see the strange symmetry of life so neatly confirmed. First Galip noticed that the apartment was dark and then that somewhere inside the dark apartment a telephone was ringing.

PART
TWO

Chapter Twenty

The Ghost House

He felt as dreary as an empty house. . . .
—Gustave Flaubert,
Madame Bovary

Although the phone had begun ringing a good three or four seconds after Galip opened the door, it was as raucous and insistent as an alarm bell in a gangster film, and—thinking that there must be some sort of mechanical connection between the phone and the door—Galip panicked. By the third ring, Galip had imagined an agitated Celâl bumping into him as he raced through the dark house to the phone; by the fourth ring, he'd decided that there was nobody home; by the fifth, he'd concluded there had to be someone in the apartment, because no caller would let a phone ring so long unless he was sure the house wasn't empty. By the sixth ring, Galip was struggling to remember the layout of this ghostly apartment he had last visited fifteen years earlier, and as he fumbled for the light switch, he walked into what turned out to be the phone itself—though how he'd found his way to it across the dark and cluttered room was beyond him. As he struggled with the receiver, his body found itself an armchair and sat down.

"Hello?"

"So you've finally come back!" said a voice he did not recognize at all.

"Yes."

"Celâl Bey, I've been trying to track you down for days. I apologize for ringing you at such a late hour, but I need to see you urgently."

"I can't place your voice."

"We met once, years ago, at a ball on Republic Day. I did introduce myself, Celâl Bey, but chances are you won't remember. Later on, I sent you two letters under assumed names—once to suggest a theory that might have unlocked the secret of Sultan Abdülhamit's death; the other had to do with the infamous university student conspiracy known as the trunk murder. It was I who suggested to you that there was a secret agent involved; you then applied your sharp mind to the matter, and when you got to the bottom of the mystery you wrote it up in your column."

"Yes."

"I now have a new dossier in front of me."

"Leave it for me at the paper."

"I know you've not been in to the paper for several days. Besides, I'm not sure I can trust the people there with a matter this urgent."

"Fine, then. Leave it with the janitor."

"I don't have your address. Directory assistance only gives out the telephone number, never the address. You must have registered this phone under another name. There's no one in the directory by the name of Celâl Salik. But there's an entry for Celâlettin Rumi, which has to be an alias."

"Didn't whoever gave you my number also give you my address?"

"No."

"Who gave you my number?"

"A mutual friend. I'd like to talk to you about this part too, when we meet. I've been looking for you for days. I've left no stone unturned. I rang your family. I spoke to your aunt, who's very fond of you. I went to all the places you've mentioned so fondly in your columns—the back streets of Kurtuluş, and Cihangir, the Palace Theater—I kept hoping I'd bump into you. Somewhere along the way I heard about an English film crew at the Pera Palas that wants to interview you— they're looking for you too. Did you know about this?"

"Tell me about this dossier."

"I don't want to talk about it on the phone. Give me your address, it's not that late, I could come right over. It's in Nişantaşı, isn't it?"

"Yes," said Galip, trying to sound cold and offhand, "but I'm not interested in things like this anymore."

"What do you mean?"

"If you read my columns carefully, you'd already know why subjects like this no longer interest me."

"No, no, this is just the sort of thing that interests you, something you'll be sure to want to write about. You can tell the English film crew about it too. Give me your address."

"I beg your pardon," said Galip, in an elated voice that even he found shocking, "but I no longer have any time for literature buffs."

Feeling rather pleased with himself, he hung up the phone. Reaching confidently into the darkness, his hand located the switch on the base of the table lamp and flipped it on. As it swamped the room with its pale orange light, Galip was presented with a scene that left him feeling so shocked and confused that he would later describe it as a mirage.

The room was exactly as it had been a quarter century earlier, when Celâl the young unmarried journalist had lived here. Everything—the furniture, the curtains, the placement of the lamps, the colors, the shadows, the smells—exactly replicated the room of twenty-five years ago. If there was anything new, it was a simulation of something old; Galip had to ask himself if this was part of the game, as if these things were meant to trick him into thinking the last quarter century had never happened. But then, as he looked more closely, he decided that nothing in this room was playing a game with him; he felt instead as if everything he'd lived through since the time he was a child had melted away and vanished. The objects emerging from the terrible darkness were not new. They radiated the enchantment of newness only because they were things Galip would have expected to have aged, fallen apart, vanished, gone the way of his own memories, yet here they were, just where he'd last seen and forgotten them. It was as if the old tables, faded curtains, dirty ashtrays, and worn-out armchairs had refused to bow to the fate Galip had assigned them, as if they had decided (on the day Uncle Melih returned from Izmir and moved in with his new family) to escape that fate by taking refuge in a new world of their own creation. As Galip fearfully reminded himself, the young journalist living here twenty-five years ago had arranged things in the exact same way as they'd been arranged forty years ago, when Celâl first lived here with his mother.

The same walnut table with the lion-claw legs, standing at the same distance from the window with the same pistachio-green curtains; the same human-shaped oil and brilliantine stain on the headrest of the armchair still upholstered with the same fabric from Sümerbank National Factories (and, twenty-five years on, the same hungry, vicious greyhounds were still chasing doomed gazelles though a forest of purple leaves); the English setter that seemed to have wandered off the set of an English film still sitting in the copper bowl inside the dusty china cabinet, gazing patiently at the same old world; the same broken watches, cups, and nail clippers on the radiator—in the pale orange lamplight, they looked just as they had when Galip had left them, never to think of them again. "Some things we don't remember," Celâl had written in one of his last columns. "Other things we don't even remember we don't remember—and these are the things we need to look for." Galip remembered that after Rüya and her parents had moved into this flat and Celâl had been moved out, these furnishings had slowly shifted their location, or they'd worn out and been replaced, vanished into a netherworld without leaving a trace. When the phone began to ring again and Galip, still in the old armchair and still wearing his coat, reached out to pick up his old friend the receiver, he knew— though he did not know this to be his intention—that he would have no trouble imitating Celâl's voice.

It was the same voice on the phone. At Galip's request, this time he identified himself not by shared memories but by his name: Mahir İkinci. But Galip was unable to connect the name with a face.

"There's going to be a coup. A little band inside the army. A very religious little band, too, a brand-new order. They believe in the Mehdi, the Messiah. They believe His time has come—thanks largely to your column."

"I've never had any dealings with anyone peddling that sort of nonsense."

"Oh, but you did, Celâl Bey, you did. It's just that—as you yourself have admitted in your column—you've either lost or destroyed your memory, or perhaps you don't want to remember. Take a look at your old columns, read a few of them while you're at it—then you'll remember."

"No, I won't."

"You will. Because as far as I know you, you're not the sort of person who can sit comfortably in his armchair after hearing that there's going to be a military coup."

"You're right, I'm not. In fact, I'm not even myself these days."

"I'm coming right over. I'll remind you of your past, bring back all those lost memories. You'll soon see how right I am and give this everything you have."

"I'm sure you're right, but I still refuse to see you."

"I will see you, you can count on it."

"Then you'll have to find my address. I never leave the house."

"Look: there are three hundred ten thousand entries in the Istanbul phone book. I've already guessed the first digit, and I know I can scan five thousand numbers an hour. At the very most, it would take me five days to find your address and this alias I'm so curious about."

"Don't wear yourself out for nothing!" said Galip, trying to sound confident. "This number is unlisted."

"You're just crazy about pseudonyms. I've been reading you for years, so I know how much you love aliases, and playing the imposter, and all those games that let you take someone else's place. You'd have far more fun coming up with a false name than you would filling out a form to get your real name kept out of the directory. I even have a list of the false names I think you might have gone for."

"What are they?"

The man rattled them off. After Galip had hung up and unplugged the phone, he recited the names back to himself. Fearing they would soon vanish from his memory without leaving a trace, he retrieved the piece of paper in his pocket and jotted them down. It unnerved Galip so much to know that there was someone else on Celâl's trail—someone who read his columns even more carefully than Galip did and remembered them better too—that he began to doubt his own reality. Although he found this reader's diligence repellent, he could still feel a certain brotherhood with him. If the two of them could sit down together to discuss Celâl's old columns, he would, he was sure, be able to read even deeper meanings into this armchair he was sitting in and this surreal room.

He was six years old—and Rüya's family had not yet moved back in—when he'd begun to sneak out of his grandparents' apartment to go upstairs to Celâl the bachelor's attic flat—of which his parents did not quite approve—to listen to the Sunday-afternoon soccer match on the radio. (Vasıf would come too, and he'd sit there nodding as if he could hear the match as well as they could.) As he watched Celâl working on the wrestling serial that his delicate boss had been forced to abandon midway, typing away at an extraordinary speed with a burning cigarette hanging from the side of his mouth, Galip would sit in this same chair. Before Celâl was pushed out of the flat, when he was sharing it with Uncle Melih and his family, and Galip got permission from his parents to come up here on cold winter evenings, ostensibly to listen to Uncle Melih's African stories but really to admire Aunt Suzan and Rüya, who was, he had only just discovered, every bit as entrancing as her mother, Galip would sit in this same chair and watch Celâl make fun of Uncle Melih's tall tales by doing strange things with his eyes and his eyebrows. A few months later, after Celâl vanished into thin air, when Uncle Melih and Galip's father started quarreling and making Grandmother cry, when the adults would gather in Grandmother's apartment to argue about who owned what and which of them was entitled to live on which floor, someone would say, "Send the children upstairs," and when they came up here to this silent room, Rüya would sit down and dangle her legs from this armchair, and Galip would watch her, mute with respect. This was twenty-five years ago.

For a long time, Galip just sat there, silent, in the armchair. Then, hoping to find a clue that might tell him where Celâl and Rüya might be hiding, he subjected the other rooms in the flat to an exhaustive search—these, too, Celâl had furnished with memories of his childhood and youth. But two hours later (by which time he felt less like a detective in forced pursuit of his missing wife than a man who has just gained entry to the first museum ever to exhibit his primary passion in life and is strolling from room to marvelous room in openmouthed awe) he had drawn the following conclusions:

From the two cups on the table he'd bumped into on his way to the phone, he deduced that Celâl had entertained other people in this flat. But the fragile cups had shattered, so he was unable to draw any definitive conclusions even after tasting the thin coating of coffee on several fragments (Rüya drank her coffee very sweet). Judging by the date on the oldest of the *Milliyet*s in the pile by the door, Celâl had visited the flat on the day Rüya had disappeared. A copy of that day's column—"When the Bosphorus Dries Up"—was sitting next to the Remington, its mistakes corrected with a green ballpoint pen in Celâl's usual angry scrawl. There was nothing about the wardrobes in the bedroom and in the hall next to the front door to indicate that Celâl had gone on a trip or that he planned to stay away from this apartment for any length of time. Everything he owned seemed to be here—from his blue-striped army pajamas to the fresh mud on his shoes, from the dark blue overcoat he'd worn all winter to his cold-weather vests and the dirty socks in his laundry basket and his vast supplies of underwear (in one of his old columns, Celâl had confessed that, like so many middle-aged men who come into money after an impoverished childhood, he was addicted to buying underwear, and owned far more than any man could ever use); everything suggested that he could be back any minute to resume his everyday life.

Though it was hard to tell from the towels and the bedsheets just how meticulously Celâl had gone about replicating the decor of his childhood home, it was clear that he had repeated the sitting room's ghost-house motif throughout the apartment. So the walls of Rüya's childhood bedroom were the same childish blue, and in the same room was the skeletal replica of the bed where Celâl's mother had once laid out her sewing materials with the dress patterns, imported fabrics, fashion magazines, and clipped photographs that the Şişli and Nişantaşı socialites brought over for her. As for the smells, they were easy to understand, for wherever there was a strong fragrance harking back to times lost, there was also a visual cue that rendered the return complete. Galip found he could remember a smell just by recognizing the objects he associated with it; thus, when he approached the beautiful divan that had been Rüya's bed, he could smell a mixture of Puro (once the only soap on the market) and Uncle Melih's old cologne (Yorgi Tomatis, no longer for sale anywhere). But in actual fact there was no drawer full of all the colored books and dolls and hairpins and colored pencils Rüya had brought back from Izmir or Beyoğlu or Alâaddin's shop, nor could he see gathered around the bed any of the soaps, peppermint Chicklets, or imitation Pe-Re-Ja cologne bottles that might have produced this heady aroma.

The ghost-house motif made it difficult for Galip to establish just how often Celâl came here or how much time he spent here when he did. As he inspected the Yeni Harman and Gelincik cigarette ends in the ashtrays that Celâl had scattered throughout the apartment, and the clean plates in the kitchen cupboards, and the uncrusted tube of İpana toothpaste that Celâl had squeezed from the top with the same fury he'd vented in a column attacking the İpana brand many years earlier, he felt as if he were viewing permanent fixtures in a museum so carefully tended it verged on madness. One could almost imagine that the dust in the globe lamps had been arranged to replicate the shadows they had cast on the pale walls twenty-five years ago—shadows in which two small children had seen African jungles and Central Asian deserts and the weasels, wolves, witches, and demons from their aunts' and grandmother's stories (or so Galip thought as he struggled to swallow). This was why it was impossible to tell how much this house was in use from the little pools of water around the edges of the tightly shut door to the balcony, or the silky gray balls of dust that had gathered in the corners, or the brittle squeak of the parquet panels that had buckled from the heat of the radiators. The ostentatious clock on the wall outside the kitchen was a replica of the one that still chimed every hour on the hour at the millionaire Cevdet Bey's (this man came from old money, as Aunt Hâle was always so proudly reminding them), but this clock had been stopped at 9:35, making Galip think at once of those Atatürk museums where you saw the same sick attention to detail, with all the clocks stopped at 9:05, the time of the great man's death; it didn't occur to Galip to ask himself if this clock in front of him might point to another death, or who it was who might die at 9:35.

By now the ghostly past was pressing down on him so hard his mind was spinning. To think of what had happened to the original furnishings: sold to a junk dealer for lack of space, carted off to who knew what distant land to be sold off and forgotten! So Galip went into the hallway to rummage through the only piece of furniture in the house that he thought might be new, the glass-fronted elm cabinet that ran the length of the wall between the bathroom and the kitchen. A short search of the shelves—all arranged with the same sick attention to period detail—yielded the following:

Clippings from news pieces Celâl had written as an apprentice reporter; clippings of all the articles in which Celâl had ever been mentioned, favorably or unfavorably; every column and story Celâl had

ever published under an assumed name; every column Celâl had published under his own name; clippings of every BELIEVE IT OR NOT column Celâl had ever written and a full collection of every piece he had
written for columns named "Your Dreams Explained," "Today in History," "Incredible Moments," "Your Signature Analyzed," "Your Face,
Your Personality," and "Puzzles and Crosswords"; clippings of every
interview Celâl had ever given; rough drafts of every column which,
for one reason or another, had never been published; special notes;
tens of thousands of articles and photographs clipped from papers
over a period of many years; notebooks in which he'd written down his
dreams, his reveries, and details he didn't want to forget; thousands of
readers' letters, stored in shoe boxes, nut boxes, dried fruit boxes, and
marron glacé boxes; clippings of the serials Celâl had either half written or written single-handedly and published under a pseudonym;
copies of hundreds of letters Celâl had written himself; hundreds of
bizarre magazines, pamphlets, books, brochures, school yearbooks,
and army yearbooks; boxes and boxes of photographs—portraits,
pornography, pictures of strange-looking bugs and animals; two big
boxes of articles on Hurufism and the science of letters; the stubs of
old bus tickets and soccer tickets and movie tickets, with the signs, letters, and symbols underlined; the prizes he'd been awarded by the
Association of Journalists; old Turkish and White Russian banknotes
long out of circulation; and three telephone and address books.

Upon finding the three address books, Galip returned to his armchair in the sitting room and read through them, one by one. After a
search lasting forty minutes, he had established that the people named
inside them had been part of Celâl's life during the fifties and sixties,
that most of them would have moved since the end of the latter
decade, and that the phone numbers listed were unlikely to lead him to
Celâl and Rüya. After a second very brief search of clutter inside the
glass cabinet, he located the letter Mahir İkinci had said he'd sent Celâl
about the trunk murder; hoping to find the columns Celâl had written
on this subject, Galip sat down to read through Celâl's columns and
readers' letters from the early seventies.

Galip was drawn to the political murder that the papers had dubbed
the trunk murder because he'd been acquainted with some of those
involved during his lycée years. But Celâl was drawn to it because, this

being a country where everything was a copy of something else, the splinter group charged with the murder had, without even realizing it, replicated the plot of a Dostoyevsky novel (*The Possessed*) down to the last detail. As he rummaged through the readers' letters from that period, he recalled that Celâl had alluded to this in one or two of their late-night conversations. Those were the cold, sad, sunless days he had so needed to forget—and indeed, until this very moment, forgotten—when Rüya had married that "nice boy" whose name was always slipping Galip's mind as he struggled to decide whether he respected him for his triumph or found him utterly unworthy of it; when Galip, led astray by his shameful jealousy, had paid careful attention to every bit of gossip that came his way, and, though he went to great lengths to find out just how happy or unhappy the newlyweds might be, ended up finding out far more about what was going on politically. . . . One winter's evening, as Vasıf was quietly feeding his fish (red *wakins* and *watonais* whose ruffled fins had diminished through interbreeding) and Aunt Hâle was doing the *Milliyet* crossword, glancing up from time to time at the television, Grandmother took one last look at the cold ceiling of her cold bedroom and died. Rüya came to the funeral in a faded coat and an even more faded scarf—and alone (so much the better, said Uncle Melih, who hated his provincial son-in-law and whose words echoed Galip's secret thoughts); after the funeral, she disappeared without a trace. After the funeral, he and Celâl had spent a few evenings together in one of the family apartments; Celâl had asked Galip if he knew anything about this trunk murder and then, more pointedly, if any of these student revolutionaries Galip said he knew had ever read "the book by that Russian author." "Because all murders," Celâl had said that same evening, "are copies of other murders, just as all books are copies of other books. That's why I'd never think of publishing a book under my own name." The next night, when they were again sitting up with the mourners—it was very late by then, and it was just the two of them—he'd added, "But even in the worst murders, there's some small aspect that's always unique, and you could never say the same about a bad book." It was a thought Celâl had continued to develop over the years, and as he watched him descend step by step into its depths, Galip felt as though they were embarking on an actual journey. "So in other words, it's books, not murders, that are perfect imitations. But what we love most of all are imitations of imitations; murders that explain books and books that explain murders have a universal appeal, because it is only when a man believes himself to be someone else that he can bring the cudgel down on the victim's head. (Because who can bear to think of himself as a murderer?) Creativity rises out of anger, the kind of anger that erases all memory, but we can only express anger in ways we've learned from others. As for the knives we use—and the guns, the poisons, the literary techniques, genres, and metrical schemes: even the immortal words uttered by so-called 'public enemies,' 'I wasn't myself, your honor!'—they all betray the selfsame truth: that we learn all the rituals and telling details of murder from others, in other words, from legends, stories, reminiscences, and newspapers. In short, we learn about murder from literature. Even the simplest murder—say, a murder committed in error and provoked by jealousy—is an imitation, a literary imitation, even if its perpetrator doesn't know it. I really should write this up, don't you think?" He never did.

Long after midnight, as Galip was reading the old columns he'd retrieved from the hall cabinet, the lamps in the sitting room slowly dimmed like footlights, and as the refrigerator motor groaned mournfully, like an old heavy truck changing gears halfway up a steep and muddy alley, the apartment was plunged into darkness. Accustomed, like other *İstanbullus*, to the vicissitudes of power cuts, Galip stayed put in his chair, with the folders of clippings balanced on his lap, just in case it came right back on. For a long time he listened to the apartment's long-forgotten inner workings: the rattling of the radiators, the silence of the walls, the crackling of the parquet floor, the hissing faucets and waterpipes, the ticking of an unknown clock, and a strange moan wafting in from the air shaft. A great deal of time passed before he felt his way into Celâl's bedroom. As he took off his clothes and stepped into Celâl's pajamas, he thought of the tall novelist he'd met in the club the night before, remembering how, in the historical novel he'd described, the hero had also stretched out on his double's dark and silent empty bed. He got into Celâl's bed, but he did not immediately fall asleep.

Chapter Twenty-one

Can't You Sleep?

Our dreams are a second life.
—Gérard de Nerval, *Aurelia*

Y ou've just gone to bed. You're in familiar surroundings, nestling inside sheets and blankets that are steeped in your own smells and memories; your head has found that pocket of softness in the middle of your pillow; you're lying on your side, and as you curl your legs up against your stomach, your forehead tilts forward, and the cold side of the pillow cools your face: soon, very soon, you'll fall asleep and, in the darkness that engulfs you, you'll forget everything—everything.

You'll forget it all: the cruel power of your superiors, the thoughtless things you wish you'd never said, the stupidities, the unfinished work, the lack of consideration, the betrayals, the injustices, the indifference, those who've blamed you, those who *will* blame you, your financial troubles, the rush of time, the endless waits, the things and people forever beyond your reach, your loneliness, your shame, your defeats, your wretchedness, your pain, and the catastrophes—all those catastrophes—in just a few minutes you'll forget them all. The prospect comforts you. Patiently you wait.

Waiting with you in the darkness, or the half-light, are all those ordinary and oh-so-familiar wardrobes, chests of drawers, radiators, tables, trays, chairs, tightly shut curtains, discarded clothes, and cigarette packs—the matches are in the pocket of that jacket, and next to it is your handbag and your watch—all waiting, waiting.

As you wait, you listen to the familiar sounds of night: a car passing through the neighborhood, swishing through the puddles at the side of the street and over the cobblestones you know so well; a street door closing, somewhere nearby; the hum of the old refrigerator motor; dogs barking in the distance; a foghorn wafting in from the sea; the sudden clatter of the pudding shop's metal shutters. With these sounds come memories of sleep and dreams, memories of oblivion, of being ushered into another world; they remind you that it won't be long now, soon they'll vanish from your mind along with everything around you, even your beloved bed, as you slip into the enchanted world of sleep. You are ready.

You are ready: it feels as if you're wafting away from your own body, wafting away from your beloved legs, your hands, your arms. You are ready, and this so pleases you that you no longer feel the need for these limbs you're leaving behind; you know you'll be forgetting them soon too, as you close your eyes.

A soft twitch of the lids reminds you that your pupils are safely shielded from the light. It is as if your eyes have themselves absorbed the happy sights and smells that augur sleep, as if the vague light now shining comes not from the room but from your mind; as it slowly opens to the peaceful deep, this dim sputtering light explodes into the night like a fireworks display; you see pools of blue and blue thunderbolts; purple smoke and purple domes; and trembling waves of midnight blue, and the shadows of lavender-colored waterfalls, and magenta rivers of lava flowing from the mouths of volcanoes, and the silent sparkle of Prussian-blue stars. As the shapes and colors silently repeat themselves, fading into the darkness only to burst forth yet again and slowly take on new forms, you see your memories parading before you in all their pomp and colorful circumstance—and forgotten scenes—and scenes that never happened at all.

But still you can't sleep.

Isn't it too soon to confess the truth? Better to invite back the thoughts that have helped you fall asleep in the past. No, you are not allowed to think about what you did today or what you're going to do tomorrow; call back the sweet memories that have eased you into the sea of oblivion so many times before. Look! They've all been waiting for you, and now you're back, and they're overjoyed; No! You're never going back, and you're sitting on a train traveling between two long rows of snow-covered telephone poles, and in your arms is a bag packed with all your favorite things. Yes! That was a very clever answer you shot back at them, and to think you conjured up those beautiful words from nowhere, and they've all fallen silent, for they see their mistake and secretly admire you; you've wrapped your arms around your lover and you're pressing her beautiful body against yours, as she does the same against you; you've returned to the garden you never forgot to pluck ripe cherries from the branches; summer is coming, winter is on its way, it will be autumn soon; soon it will be morning, a morning of bright blue skies, a beautiful morning, a sunny morning, an utterly delightful morning. . . . But no, you still can't sleep.

So do as I do: turn gently to one side, but without moving your arms or legs; let your head sink into the other end of the pillow, and let your cheek feel the cool. Then think of Princess Maria Paleologina, who was sent away from Byzantium seven hundred years ago to marry Hulagu, the Khan of the Moguls. Forced to leave her childhood home—Constantinople, the city that is your home too—she was dispatched to Iran to marry Hulagu, but he died before she got there, so she was married instead to his son, Abaka, who then rose to the throne; after she had spent fifteen years in the Mogul palace, her husband was killed and she returned at last to the hills where you are now struggling to find a peaceful night's sleep. So put yourself in Maria's shoes, imagine her sorrow as she left the city behind, and imagine her last days, shut up in the church she built for herself on the shores of the Golden Horn after her return. Or think of the dwarfs that Handan Sultan so adored. To bring her beloved friends some happiness, this mother of Ahmet I built them a dwarf house in Üsküdar; after living there for many years, they—again with Handan Sultan's help—built a galleon to take them away to another land, a paradise to be found on no map; and off they sailed, never to return to Istanbul again. Imagine Handan Sultan's sadness as her friends depart, and the grief of the dwarfs as they wave their handkerchiefs from the galleon; feel the depths of their emotion as strongly as if it were you embarking on a journey and watching Istanbul fade into the distance, taking with it everything you love.

If that doesn't send me to sleep, dear readers, I think of a troubled man pacing up and down the platform of a desolate station in the dead of night, waiting for a train that never comes; by the time I've figured out that man's destination, I have become him. I think about the men digging the passageway underneath the city walls at Silivrikapı to get to the Greeks who occupied the city seven hundred years ago. I imagine the amazement of the man who discovered that all the things in the world have second meanings. I imagine a parallel universe, hidden inside the one we inhabit, and I imagine myself wandering intoxicated about its new and sparkling streets, as the objects around me open like flowers to reveal their interior selves. I imagine the amazement of a man who has lost his memory. I imagine I've been abandoned in a ghost city I've never seen before, where everything, but everything—the neighborhoods that once were home to millions, the avenues, mosques, bridges, and ships—is empty; as I roam about its haunted spaces I remember my own past and my own city, and as tears roll down my cheeks I make my slow and painful way back to my own neighborhood, my own house, and the bed where I am now tossing and turning and trying to put myself to sleep. I imagine I am François Champollion, rising from my bed at night to decipher the hieroglyphics on the Rosetta Stone, wandering like a sleepwalker through the dark streets of my mind to lose himself in the cul-de-sacs of lost memory. I imagine I am Murat IV, changing into commoner's clothes in the palace one night so I can see with my own eyes if my ban on drink has had the desired effect; setting out with my armed guards, who are also in disguise but still confident that they can protect me from harm, I wander about my city, gazing fondly at my subjects as they loiter around the mosques, and the stores I can see here and there, still open for business, and those dark lairs in hidden passageways where the idle while away their nights.

Then I become a quilt maker's apprentice, wandering from door to door, whispering the first and last syllables of a secret code word, preparing the shopkeepers of the city for one of the last Janissary rebellions of the nineteenth century. Or else I am a messenger, sent out from the *medrese*, to awaken the drowsy dervishes of an outlawed order from years of silent sleep.

If I'm not asleep by now, dear readers, I'll become an unhappy lover searching for an exact copy of a lost sweetheart but losing all trace of her in my memories; I shall roam about the city, searching for my beloved, searching for my very past behind every door I open, every opium den I visit, and every gathering of storytellers, every house I find where songs are sung. If my memory, my powers of imagination, and my bedraggled dreams do not cave in from exhaustion in the course of my long travels, I'll keep on drifting through that gray land between wakefulness and sleep until my eyes light on a place I know— the home of a distant acquaintance, the abandoned mansion of a close relative—whatever it is, I'll go inside, and after opening every door and searching every room as if the house itself were the lost recesses of my own memory, I'll go into the last room, blow out the candle, stretch out on the bed, and, surrounded by strange and alien objects, fall asleep.

Chapter Twenty-two

Who Killed Shams of Tabriz?

How much longer do I seek you, house by house, door to door?
How much longer, corner to corner, street by street?

—Rumi

In the morning, Galip awoke from a long and peaceful sleep to find the fifty-year-old overhead light still glowing parchment yellow. Still wearing Celâl's pajamas, Galip went through the apartment turning off all the other lights he'd left on; picking up the *Milliyet* at the door, he sat down at Celâl's desk and began to read. Today's column was the one he'd seen on Saturday morning, while he was at the newspaper, and when he saw an error (they'd printed "being ourselves" instead of "being yourselves") his hand reached out of its own volition to pick up a green ballpoint pen and correct it. When he reached the end of the column, he remembered that when Celâl sat down at this desk wearing his blue striped pajamas to correct his copy with the same green ballpoint pen, he also smoked a cigarette.

He had a gut feeling that things were going well. He made himself a cup of coffee with the happy confidence of a man who has had a good night's sleep and who is even looking forward to the difficult day ahead, so much so that he almost sees no need to be someone else.

When he'd drunk his coffee, he removed several boxes of columns, letters, and clippings from the cabinet in the hall and set them on the desk. If he read all this with conviction, if he gave it his full attention, he would find what he was looking for in the end, of this he was certain.

As he read of the savage lives of the faceless children who lived on the pontoons of Galata Bridge, of the city's monstrous and stuttering orphanage directors, of the aerial competitions of winged scholars who jumped into the air in just the same way as they jumped into the water from the Galata Bridge, and of the history of pederasty and its "modern" merchants, Galip was able to give each new column the patient attention it deserved. As he perused the reminiscences of the Beşiktaş mechanic's apprentice who had been first to drive a Model T Ford in Istanbul, as he found out why every neighborhood in the city needed its own musical clock tower, as he discovered the historical significance of the Egyptian ban on all scenes in *The Thousand and One Nights* in which the women of the harem made assignations with their black slaves, and pondered the advantages of being able to board a horse-drawn streetcar while it was still in motion, and established why it was that the parrots had left Istanbul and the crows had taken over, and why and how the crows were responsible for all the snow that now fell over the city each winter, he remained as confident and optimistic as before.

As he read, he recalled the days when he'd first read these same pieces; from time to time, he paused to jot down a few notes, or a sentence, or a paragraph, or he would stop to read a few words again; when he finished a column he would put it back into its box and lovingly pull out another.

The sun shone on the window ledges but no rays came into the room. The curtains were open. Water was dripping from the icicles on the building next door and from its filthy snow-caked gutters. There were patches of blackened snow on the red-tiled roof, and through the black teeth of its towering chimney rose a column of lignite smoke; wedged between the triangle of the roof and the rectangle of the chimney was a bright blue sky. When Galip tired of reading and gazed at this small space between the triangle and the rectangle, the blue was crisscrossed with the black arcs of flying crows. Galip realized that when Celâl sat here editing his columns, he too would rest his eyes by watching crows flying through this same patch of sky.

Much later, when the sun was shining on the tightly shut curtains of the windows next door, Galip felt his optimism ebbing away. Though he was fairly sure that every object, word, and meaning was now in its proper place, the deeper truth that held them all together was still, he sadly admitted, beyond his reach. By now he was reading a series of columns Celâl had written on messiahs, false prophets, and pretenders to the throne; these led to an account of Rumi's friendship with a certain Shams of Tabriz; he also wrote about a jeweler named Selâhaddin, who became intimate with "the great Sufi poet" after Shams's death, and about Çelebi Hüsmettin, who took Selâhaddin's place after he too passed away. Finding them distasteful and hoping to bolster up his spirits, he turned instead to a pile of BELIEVE IT OR NOT columns, but he failed to be diverted by the stories about the poet Figani, who after writing an insulting couplet about Sultan Ibrahim's grand vizier, was tied to a donkey and paraded all across the city, and about Sheikh Eflâki, who married all his sisters one by one only to inadvertently precipitate their deaths. When he moved to the box of readers' letters, he could not help marveling at the sheer variety of the people who took an interest in Celâl, who were as much in awe of Celâl as he himself had been as a child, but as he plowed through the mountain of correspondence— some readers wanted him to send them money; others wanted him to take their side in a dispute or to hate or love the same people they loved and hated; others wanted him to know that the wife of another columnist with whom he was involved in a war of words was a prostitute, that a secret sect was hatching a conspiracy, and that the local monopoly director was taking bribes—he felt increasingly hopeless.

He was aware that ever since he'd sat down at this desk his mental image of Celâl had been changing shape. Surrounded as he was by familiar objects from a familiar world, he was able to see Celâl through the same prism —as a man whose columns he'd been reading for many years, whose "darker side" he'd understood, if only from a distance, and described with those same words. In the afternoon, as the elevator carried a steady stream of ailing or pregnant women to the gynecologist's office directly beneath him, and as Galip's mental image of Celâl lost its heroic sheen to become a man who was "strangely lacking," he slowly became aware that this room and its contents were changing too. No longer did they welcome him; they were danger signs, pointing to a world that kept its secrets buried deep.

Sensing that this alarming new development was closely linked with what Celâl had written on Rumi, Galip decided to go straight to the heart of the matter. He quickly assembled all the pieces Celâl had ever written on Rumi and began to read them as fast as he could.

What interested Celâl most about the greatest mystical poet of all time was not the verse he wrote in Persian while living in Konya during the thirteenth century, nor was he particularly drawn to the stock lines extracted from these verses by middle school ethics teachers to illustrate the concept of virtue. Neither was he interested in the "pearls of wisdom" that generations of mediocre writers had extracted from his work to adorn their first pages, or in the skirted barefoot whirling dervishes whose ceremonies so delighted tourists and postcard manufacturers. Though Rumi and the order that had established itself after his death had been the subject of tens of thousands of treatises in the seven hundred years since he had walked this earth, Celâl was interested in Rumi only as a useful point of reference for his columns. What Celâl found most interesting about Rumi was the "sexual and mystical" intimacy he enjoyed with certain men.

At the age of forty-five, when Rumi was, like his father before him, a sheikh in Konya, loved and admired not just by his devoted disciples but by the entire city, he fell under the influence of Shams of Tabriz, an itinerant dervish whose values, outlook, and learning had little in common with his own. In Celâl's view, nothing about this association made any sense. The fact that scholars had been struggling to "interpret" it for seven hundred years was proof in itself. After Shams of Tabriz disappeared (or was killed), Rumi—in the face of fierce resistance from his other disciples—appointed an ignorant jeweler with no redeeming features to serve in his place. This was not, Celâl insisted, proof that his new assistant induced in him the same "mystical rapture" that generations of scholars claimed he had felt in the presence of Shams of Tabriz; rather, it pointed to a man plagued by sexual and spiritual anxiety. When, after the death of this assistant, Rumi chose a third, he was every bit as dull and anodyne as the second.

Though scholars had been sifting through the evidence for centuries, shifting the facts around to make the implausible look plausible and attributing impossible (and unsubstantiated) virtues to these three assistants—even, in some cases, falsifying their lineage so as to claim they were descendents of Ali or Muhammed—they'd all overlooked the one thing above all others that set Rumi apart. In a Sunday column timed to coincide with the memorial ceremony still performed in Konya every year, Celâl set out his ideas on the subject, which was also, he claimed, reflected in Rumi's verse. Galip remembered how, when he'd first read this column twenty-two years ago, it had, like all religious writing, bored him stiff; the only reason he remembered it at all was because of the Rumi stamp series that had come out that same year (the fifteen-kuruş stamps were pink, the thirty-kuruş stamps blue, and the much rarer sixty-kuruş stamps were green); as he thought all this, Galip felt the objects in the room changing yet again.

According to Celâl, it was true that Rumi had (as already related in ten thousand treatises over the centuries) fallen under Shams of Tabriz's influence the very moment he'd set eyes on him. But it was not because—as so many had claimed—Rumi had decided, after Shams had asked him his famous question and the two had plunged into their famous dialogue, that the man must be a sage. What they'd discussed that day was an ordinary Sufi parable about modesty, of the type you could find in any of the thousands of vapid books on Sufism you found on sale outside mosques. If Rumi were as wise as he was meant to be, he would never have been impressed by a parable so pedestrian; he would have just pretended to be impressed.

This was exactly what he had done. He had acted as if he'd seen in Shams a man of depth and powerful spirituality. In Celâl's view, all this proved was that the forty-five-year-old Rumi longed on that rainy day to find just such a "soul mate"; what he longed for was to look into a man's face and see a replica of his own. So the moment he set eyes on this man, he convinced himself that this was the man he'd been seeking, and of course it had not taken him much effort to convince Shams himself that he was this august person. Immediately following their meeting—23 October 1244—they retreated to a cell in the back of the *medrese*, not to emerge until six months later. What went on in that cell during those six long months? The Mevlevi order had never shown much interest in addressing this question, deeming it too "secular," and Celâl, not wishing to annoy his readers unduly, had chosen his own words carefully and then moved on to what he saw as the heart of the matter.

All his life, Rumi had been searching for his "other," the double who might move him and light up his heart, the mirror who might reflect his face and his very soul. So whatever they'd done or said in that cell, they were best seen as the words and deeds of a multitude masquerading as a single person, or of one person masquerading as a multitude. Because to endure this suffocating thirteenth-century Anatolian town and the devotion of his brainless disciples (whom he just couldn't bring himself to give up), Rumi needed to be able to draw from a storehouse of alternative identities, just as poets over the ages have availed themselves of disguises for much the same reason—to enjoy a few moments' peace. To add to the elegance of this deep desire, Celâl threw in an image plundered from one of his own earlier columns: "In much the same way, the ruler of a benighted country, tired of looking down at the tyrants, sycophants, and paupers who populate his realm, might keep hidden in a trunk the peasant garb that he dons from time to time to roam the streets in comfort."

As Galip expected, this column had earned Celâl death threats from a number of religious readers and letters of congratulation from readers who saw themselves as secularist republicans; though the editor of the newspaper had asked him never to touch on the subject again, he had returned to it a month later.

Celâl began his new column by running through the facts on which all Mevlevis agreed: Rumi's other disciples, outraged by Rumi's intimate relations with a dervish of no distinction, had made life hell for Shams and indeed threatened him with death. Whereupon Shams had disappeared from Konya on a snowy winter day—15 February 1246, to be precise. (Galip was charmed by Celâl's passion for chronological precision: it reminded him of his lycée textbooks and their multitude of typographical errors.) Unable to bear life without his beloved double, Rumi, who had by now received a letter informing him that Shams was in Damascus, brought his "beloved" back to Konya (Celâl had put *beloved* in quotation marks to avoid offending his readers more than necessary), whereupon he married him off to one of his daughters. But it wasn't long before the noose of jealousy began to tighten around his neck again, and on the fifth Thursday in December 1247, Shams was ambushed by a rabble, including Rumi's own son Alâaddin, and knifed to death; as a cold dirty rain pelted from the night sky, his body was thrown into the well right next to Rumi's house.

As he read about the well into which Shams's body had been thrown, Galip came across details that were not at all unfamiliar. If he saw the strange and fearsome scene—the well, the body, the lonely misery of the corpse—as vividly as if he himself had been standing there watching it on that cold dark night seven hundred years ago, it was because he literally recognized the stone wall and the Horasan plasterwork. After reading the column several times over and glancing at a few other columns dating from the same period, Galip discovered that Cclâl had lifted several sentences word for word from his own column about the apartment's pit, entitled "The Dark Air Shaft," and he'd somehow managed to do so without in any way altering the column's style.

Though he would have made less of this little trick had he read Celâl's columns on Hurufism, it prompted him to read with new eyes the pile of columns sitting on the desk. This, then, was when he discovered why it was that, as he read Celâl's columns, the objects surrounding him kept changing—why all these tables, curtains, lamps, ashtrays, chairs, and even that pair of scissors on the radiator had been drained of the meaning and goodwill that had once bound them together.

Celâl spoke of Rumi as if he were the man himself; somewhere between the lines, he had retreated into the shadows without anyone's noticing and exchanged his identity for Rumi's. When Galip returned to other, earlier columns and found that Celâl had used the same sentences, paragraphs, and even the same mournful voice in the columns he'd written about his own life as he did in his "historical" columns about Rumi, he became all the more certain that the two men were one and the same. And that was not all; he'd even gone so far as to continue this strange game in his private journal, the rough drafts of unpublished columns, his "historical conversations," the essays he'd written on another Mevlevi poet (Shcikh Galip, the author of *Beauty and Love*), his dream interpretations, and countless columns.

In his BELIEVE IT OR NOT pieces he had written hundreds of stories about kings who thought they were someone else, Chinese emperors who had burned down their palaces to become someone else, and sultans so addicted to leaving the palace in disguise by night to roam among their people that they would leave urgent matters of state behind for days on end. In a notebook filled with half-finished stories that looked to be autobiographical, Galip read that in the course of one ordinary summer day Celâl had imagined himself to be Leibniz, the famous tycoon Cevdet Bey, Muhammed, the owner of a news-paper, Anatole France, a successful chef, an imam much admired for his sermons, Robinson Crusoe, Balzac, and six other people whose names he'd crossed out in embarrassment. Glancing through the caricatures inspired by the drawings of Rumi on so many stamps and posters, he happened onto a clumsily drawn picture of a casket on which were written the words *Rumi Celâl*. Then he found an unpublished column that began, "Rumi's greatest work, *Mathnawi*, is plagiarism from start to finish!"

In highly stylized sentences that wavered between genuine anxiety and the fear that he might say something to provoke mockery from genuine scholars, Celâl listed (and exaggerated) the offending passages. Such and such a story had been lifted from "Kelile and Dimne"; another story from Attar's "Mantik-ut Tayr"; the aforementioned anecdote had been copied word for word from "Leyla and Mecnun," while "Menakibi" had been stolen from Evliya. As he surveyed the list of sources, he saw mentions of "Kisas-I Enbiya," *The Thousand and One Nights*, and Ibn Zerhani. Celâl ended his list with Rumi's own thoughts on stealing stories from others. As he read on in the darkening room, made darker still by the black thoughts before his eyes, he felt as if they came not just from Rumi but from Celâl, the man who had taken his place.

Celâl went on to explain that, like so many others who cannot bear to be alone and can only find solace by pretending to be someone else, Rumi could only begin to tell a story if he could say that he'd heard it elsewhere. After all, for those unhappy souls who burn to become someone else, storytelling is a ruse, the best way they've discovered to escape the bodies and souls that so oppress them. He told one story only to gain access to another. Like *The Thousand and One Nights*, the *Mathnawi* was of a strange and complex composition, with the second story beginning before the first was finished, and a third story beginning before the second was finished—endless stories, begun only to be discarded, like the identities their tellers so longed to escape. As he leafed through Celâl's copy of *Mathnawi*, Galip saw pornographic passages underlined in green pen and various other passages peppered with angry green question and exclamation marks or scribbled out in their entirety. As he raced through the stories on these filthy ink-stained pages, Galip realized that, of Celâl's columns, many he had assumed to be entirely original when he'd first read them had been lifted from the *Mathnawi* and then adapted to modern-day Istanbul.

Galip recalled how Celâl had often talked for hours into the night about the fine art of the *nazire*, a poem that sets out to imitate an existing poem in both form and content; it was, he'd said, the only skill he had. As Rüya nibbled on the cakes they'd bought along the way, Celâl would confess that he'd written many—perhaps all—of his columns with the help of others; the important thing was not to create something, but to draw instead from the marvels created over thousands of years by the many thousands of great minds who'd come before us, to change here and there and turn it into something new; this, he said, was why he always drew his columns from other sources. But if Galip had by then begun to wonder if the room and its many objects, the desk and its piles of paper, had any basis in reality whatsoever, it was not because he knew now that many stories he'd long attributed to Celâl were actually the work of someone else. What unnerved him were the other possibilities this suggested.

For it now occurred to him that there might be yet another room in some other part of the city that had been furnished and arranged to look exactly as it had twenty-five years ago. If Celâl was not sitting in that room at this very moment—sitting at the same desk as Galip, telling stories, with Rüya hanging on his every word—then the man who was sitting at that other desk, poring through his archives and hunting for some clue that might lead him to his lost wife, was Galip's luckless double. If objects and images and the symbols on plastic carrier bags could be signs of something else, if Celâl's columns could suggest new meanings with every new reading, it followed that his own life would take on a new meaning every time he thought about it, and as he contemplated this endless freight train of meanings mercilessly multiplying itself into infinity, he feared he might lose himself inside it forever. It was growing dark outside and the almost palpable gray mist seeping into the room called to mind a spider-infested cellar thick with mold and the odor of death. Galip knew there was only one way out of this ghostly realm, this nightmare into which he had accidentally fallen, and that was to force his tired eyes to keep on reading; with this in mind, he turned on the lamp.

So this was how he went back to pick up where he'd left off—the moment when Shams's murderers threw his corpse into the spider-infested well. Upon learning he had lost his "friend and beloved," the poet was beside himself with grief. He simply could not believe that Shams had been murdered and his corpse thrown into a well; what's more, he was furious when those around him pointed to the well that was just under his nose; he looked instead for excuses to search else-where for his beloved: Could Shams not have gone back to Damascus, as he'd done the first time he was missing?

This is how it came to pass that Rumi set out for Damascus, and this was why he searched every street in that city for some sign. Up and down every street he went, entering every room, every tavern, peering into every corner and under every stone; he visited each and every one of his beloved's old friends, and every acquaintance they had in com-mon, and all the places in the city he'd most loved, every mosque and lodge he'd ever been known to frequent, until the moment arrived when the search itself became more important than the answer he'd come to seek. At this point in the column, the reader found himself lost amid the bats, rose water, and opium smoke of a mystical pantheist universe where the searcher and the object of his desire changed places, where it was less important to reach a goal than to keep walking toward it, and where it was not the lost love who counted but the rap-ture that used love as its pretext. There followed a brief summary of the adventures that befell the poet as he wandered the streets of the city, and they replicated the stages every traveler on the Sufi path must pass through as he strives for enlightenment: so if the scene of confu-sion following his love's disappearance was "negation," it followed that the scenes in which the poet meets with his beloved's friends and ene-mies, visits the streets he onced walked, and goes through the belong-ings laden with painful memories could be seen as a series of "ordeals." If the scene in the brothel signified "dissolving into love," then the ciphered letters discovered in al-Hallaj Mansur's home after his death—and all the other writings in this cache that cloaked their true meaning with pseudonyms, literary tricks, and word games—described "being lost in heaven and hell" or, as Attar described it, "being lost in the valley of mystery." The scene in which storytellers gathered in a tavern in the middle of the night, each to tell a "love story," had been lifted from Attar's *Conference of the Birds*, as was the scene in which the poet, roaming about the city and drunk with the mystery rising from its streets, shops, and windows, finally understands that he is in Mount Kaf, seeking none other than himself; this last scene stood for the stage when the Sufi traveler achieved "absolute union with God" (or dissolving into the absolute), as described in the same book.

Celâl had adorned his column with flashy versifications in the classical mode, ostensibly to establish the long Sufi tradition of seekers who became one with those they sought, but when he came to the words Rumi had uttered in exhaustion as his many months of searching came to an end, he felt compelled to paraphrase them, for he hated poetry in translation. "If I am He," exclaimed the poet one day as he wandered lost inside the mysteries of the city, "then why am I still searching?" This was where the column reached its climax, and Celâl topped it off with the literary fact that all Mevlevis are prone to repeat with such pride: After reaching this stage in his journey, Rumi gathered up all the poems he had written along the way, but instead of putting his own name to them, he signed them as Shams of Tabriz.

What Galip found most interesting about this column—and what had interested him most when he'd first read it as a child—was the way in which the search followed the stages of a police investigation. Here Celâl offered up the conclusion that would so annoy religious readers whom he'd managed to lull into complacency with his weighty discussions of the Sufi path, but that would delight the republican secularists: "Because, of course, the man who wanted Shams of Tabriz murdered and thrown into the well was none other than Rumi himself!" Celâl then proved his case with a ploy often used by the Turkish police, not to mention the prosecutor he had grown to know so well during the 1950s, when he was a reporter assigned to the Beyoğlu district court. Mimicking the pompous tones of a small-town official, he reminded his readers that the person who most benefited from Shams's death was Rumi, for it turned him from a theology teacher of no distinction into the great Sufi poet of all time; if anyone had a motivation, it was he. Although there was, of course, a difference between wanting someone dead and actually murdering him, this was a tiny legal distinction that mattered only in Christian novels, so Celâl was disinclined to dwell on it too long, preferring to move on to look at

Rumi's strange behavior following the murder: the signs of guilt and all the little tricks novice murderers tend to play, like pretending they can't believe the person is really dead, and babbling like madmen, and refusing to look at the corpse in the well. And after Celâl had proven his case to his satisfaction, he moved on to a new subject that plunged Galip into the deepest despair: If Rumi was the murderer, then how to understand the many months he'd spent combing the streets of Damascus? He walked the length and breadth of the city time and time again; what did this signify?

Celâl had devoted more time to this subject than the column suggested; Galip knew this from notes he'd found, jotted down in various notebooks, and from the map of Damascus he'd found in a box under a pile of old ticket stubs for soccer games (Turkey 3–Hungary 1) and movies (*Woman in the Window, Coming Home*). He had traced Rumi's trajectory through the city in his usual green ink. Since Rumi knew he had murdered Shams, he could not have been looking for him; it therefore followed that Rumi was in the city for another reason, but what was it? He'd marked every corner of the city the poet had visited, and on the back of the map he had listed the names of all the neighborhoods, inns, caravansaries, and taverns Rumi had searched along the way. He'd shuffled their letters and syllables in search of a hidden meaning, a secret symmetry.

Long after nightfall, Galip happened onto a map of Cairo and the 1934 Istanbul Directory: they were in a box filled with odds and ends Celâl had accumulated around the time he'd written a column about "Mercury Ali," "The Clever Thief," and various other stories from *The Thousand and One Nights* that bore a close resemblance to detective fiction. As expected, he found the story lines indicated with arrows drawn in green ink. On the maps of the Istanbul directory he found more arrows—in the same green ink, if not from the same pen. Though the maps of the city were in a terrible jumble, it still seemed to him as if the green arrows followed the same adventure-strewn path as he himself had followed during the days he'd spent wandering through the city. Desperate to prove himself wrong, he reminded himself that the arrows pointed to office buildings he'd never set foot in, mosques he'd never visited, and alleys he'd never once passed through, but then he was forced to admit to himself that he'd gone into the building next door, visited the mosque down the road, climbed up another alley that led to the same hilltop—which meant that, whatever the map said, the city of Istanbul was swarming with people who had set out on the same journey!

So then he spread out the maps of Damascus, Cairo, and Istanbul side by side, just as Celâl had foreseen in a column inspired by Edgar Allan Poe. He cut the maps out of the Istanbul directory with a razor blade he found in the bathroom—a razor blade that had once cut the contours of Celâl's beard, as the wiry hairs still clinging to it attested. When he first put the maps together, he saw that their arrows and line fragments were different sizes, so he was at first unsure how to proceed. Then he pressed them together against the glass pane of the sitting-room door, just as he and Rüya had done as children when they'd wanted to trace a picture out of a magazine, and let the light from the other side of the door shine through it. Then he spread them out on the same table where Celâl's mother had once spread out her dress patterns and tried to view them as the last pieces in a puzzle, for all he had seen when he'd pressed them together against the door— and this seemed more by chance than by design—was the wrinkled countenance of an old man.

The longer he stared at this face, the more convinced he was that he'd been long acquainted with it. Soothed by this thought and by the silence of the night, he felt his confidence growing and, with it, the sense that the cloak of serenity now protecting him had been carefully sewn together and preordained for someone else. Galip was now certain that it was Celâl guiding him. Although Celâl had written a great number of columns about the meanings concealed in faces, what Galip remembered now were a few lines Celâl had written about the "inner peace" he'd felt when contemplating the faces of foreign female film stars. This was how he came to take out the box in which Celâl had stored his movie reviews from the early years of his career.

In these reviews, Celâl described the pain and longing that the faces of certain film stars evoked in him, in words that likened them to translucent marble sculptures, the silken faces of planets that are forever turned away from the sun, the whispers of a dream from a far-away land. As he read these lines, it seemed to Galip that the love interest he and Celâl shared was not Rüya or the art of storytelling but the enchanting harmonies, the barely audible music, of longing itself: He loved the thing he and Celâl had discovered in these maps, these faces, these words, and yet at the same time he feared it. He wanted to go deeper into these reviews, immerse himself in the heavenly harmonies beneath their surface, but something stopped him. Celâl had never described the faces of Turkish actors in this style; *their* faces reminded him of fifty-year-old telegrams whose codes and meanings were long lost and forgotten.

By now Galip knew only too well why it was that the optimism he'd felt after breakfast, when he'd first sat at this desk, had abandoned him: during the eight hours he'd spent reading, his image of Celâl had undergone a radical change, and he too had become someone else. When he'd sat down that morning—at peace with the world, and certain, in his innocence, that if he kept working, kept his patience, this world would reveal its secret essence—he'd felt no longing to be someone else. But now, as the world drew away from him, its secrets still intact, as the objects surrounding him lost their aura of familiarity to become alien signs from an alien planet, as he stared into maps to find faces he could not recognize, all Galip wanted was to escape from the body that had brought him to this hopeless vista. By the time he returned to the columns in which Celâl spoke of his own past, to hunt for some last clue that might explain to him Celâl's interest in Rumi and the Mevlevi order, it was suppertime in the city, and the blue glow of its television sets had settled over Teşvikiye Avenue.

Celâl had been drawn to the Mevlevis not just because he knew it would speak to his readers' devoted if never quite articulated interest in the subject but because his own stepfather had been a Mevlevi. After his real father flew off to Europe and South Africa and his mother, despairing of his return, was forced to divorce him, after she had found herself unable to support herself and her son by working as a seamstress, his mother had married a "hunchback lawyer who spoke through his nose"; it later emerged that this man belonged to a secret Mevlevi lodge located next to a Byzantine cistern in the back streets of Yavuz Sultan; with a savage secular wit Galip thought worthy of Voltaire, Celâl had described its secret rituals. Reading on, Galip learned that, while he had lived under the same roof with this man, Celâl had worked as an usher in a movie theater, where he'd been drawn into many fights, sometimes as the perpetrator and sometimes as the victim; that he'd sold fizzy drinks during the intermissions; and that he'd arranged for the *çörek* maker to increase the amount of salt and pepper in his braided buns so that people would buy more fizzy drinks from him; and as he read, he identified first with the usher, then with the brawling audience, then with the *çörek* maker, and finally—good reader that he was—with Celâl.

As he moved on to the next column, in which Celâl described the job he took after leaving the theater in Şehzadebaşı—with a bookbinder whose shop smelled of glue and paper—Galip's eyes hit on a sentence that seemed to prefigure the predicament in which he now found himself. It was one of those lazy sentences all writers fall into when they are inventing sad but worthy pasts for themselves: *I read whatever I could get my hands on,* wrote Celâl, and Galip, engaged as he was in reading whatever he could get his hands on that might tell him more about Celâl, was left feeling that Celâl was no longer speaking about his days at the bookbinders but about Galip himself.

Until he left the house at midnight, Celâl's sentence continued to reverberate in his thoughts, and every time it came into his mind he saw it as proof that Celâl knew what he was doing at that very moment. His five-day ordeal had changed its meaning. No longer did he believe he had been searching the city for Celâl and Rüya but that he was a pawn in a game that Celâl (and perhaps Rüya) had devised for him. Celâl, after all, was obsessed with the little tricks, ambiguities, and fictions that allowed him to manipulate others from a distance; so it was not beyond the realm of possibility that his investigations in this room had pointed not to his own liberation but to Celâl's.

This suffocating thought—and the pain behind his eyes after so many hours of reading—made him want to leave the house at once; he couldn't find anything to eat in the kitchen either. He took Celâl's dark blue overcoat out of the wardrobe next to the door, so that—just in case the janitor and his wife had not yet gone to bed and happened to glance sleepily out the window—they would see the familiar overcoat and think he was Celâl. He went down the stairs without turning on the light, and when he went past the low window that looked out on the front door from the janitor's apartment, he saw no lights burning inside. Since he didn't have the key to the front door, he left it ajar. As he stepped out onto the pavement, a shiver went through him: that man on the phone: He'd forgotten all about him, but he now half expected him to step out of the shadows. This man, he imagined, would not be at all unfamiliar to him, and he would be holding something far more deadly, far more terrifying, than a dossier proving that a secret cadre was busy planning a new military coup—but he was wrong, for there was no one else in the street. He imagined himself as the voice from the telephone, following him down the street. But no, tonight he could not imagine himself in anyone's shoes but his own. I see life just as it is, he told himself as he walked past the police station. The policemen standing guard with their submachine guns outside the police station gazed at him with sleepy suspicion. To stop himself from reading the letters in the posters and political graffiti on the walls and the sizzling neon signs, he kept his eyes on the ground. All the restaurants and cafeterias in Nişantaşı were closed.

Much later, after walking for hours down empty pavements under the horse chestnuts and the cypresses and the plane trees, and listening to the mournful sighs of melting snow slipping down the rainspouts, and the buzz from neighborhood coffeehouses, and the sound of his own footsteps—after stopping at a simple restaurant in Karaköy and filling his stomach with soup, chicken, and bread pudding and buying some fruit at a stand and some bread and cheese from a cafeteria—he returned to the City-of-Hearts Apartments.

Chapter Twenty-three

A Story About People
Who Can't Tell Stories

"Aye!" (quoth the delighted reader). "This is sense, this is genius!
This I understand and admire! I have thought the very same a
hundred times myself!" In other words, this man has reminded
me of my own cleverness, and therefore I admire him.
—Coleridge, *Essays on His Own Times*

No, my greatest ever masterpiece—the column in which I deciphered for once and for all the secret that engulfs us throughout our lives without our ever knowing—was not the investigation I wrote sixteen years and four months ago, setting out the extraordinary similarities between the maps of Damascus, Cairo, and Istanbul. (Those who wish to do so can, however, return to this column to see that the Darb-al Mustakim, the Halili Market, and our own Covered Bazaar are all in the shape of an M—an M that will, when they see it, suggest a certain face.)

No, my most profound work is not another column I wrote in a similar burst of enthusiasm many moons ago about the two hundred and twenty years of remorse suffered by poor Sheikh Mahmut after giving up the secrets of his order to a French spy in return for immortality. (However, readers interested in finding out more can, if they return to this column, find out how this same sheikh roamed the battlefields, hoping to escape the curse of immortality by fooling a hero into assuming his identity as he lay bleeding to death.)

As I recall all the pieces I've written about Beyoğlu bandits, poets who lose their memories, magicians, songstresses with double identities, and lovers whose hearts never mend, I can see how I never quite got to the point, how I was forever gliding around the haunted edges of the subject I now consider to be the most important question of them all. But I'm hardly the only one to have done so! I have been writing for thirty years now, and though I may not have been an avid reader for quite that long, I know of no other writer, in the East or in the West, who has illuminated the truth I am about to unveil to you here.

Now, as you read what I have to say, please try and imagine the faces I describe to you. (For what is reading but the animating of a writer's words on the silent film strip in our minds?) Project onto this silver screen a simple general store in eastern Anatolia. It's a cold winter's afternoon and the sky is already growing dark, and because business is slow, the barber across the way has left his apprentice to mind the store, and now he is here, sitting around the stove with his younger brother and a retired old man and a visitor who's come to town, more for the company than to do the shopping. To pass the time, they make idle conversation, sharing stories about their days in the army and flipping through the newspaper and exchanging gossip, and they laugh from time to time, but sitting among them is one troubled man who speaks very little and has a hard time getting anyone to listen to him when he does: the barber's brother. He has stories he wants to share, and jokes too, but much as he longs to tell them, he just doesn't have the knack, he just can't make himself shine. The one time all afternoon he tried to begin telling a story, the others cut him off without even realizing it. Please imagine the expression on this barber's brother's face when the others interrupted his story.

Now imagine an engagement party in the home of a westernized but not unusually wealthy Istanbul doctor. At one point, a handful of the guests who have invaded his house happen to find themselves in his daughter's room, around a bed piled high with coats. Among them is a charming young girl and two men who long to impress her; one is not particularly good-looking or intelligent, but he's chatty and gregarious. So the girl, like the older men in the room, listens to his stories; everyone present gives him their full attention. Now please try to picture the face of the other young man, who is so much brighter and more sensitive than his prattling friend but who can get no one to pay him any attention whatsoever.

Now please imagine three sisters who have all been married over the past two years; they've gathered at their mother's house two months after the youngest sister's wedding. The huge clock ticking on the wall and the impatient canary clucking in the cage tell us that we are in the home of a moderately successful merchant. As the four women sit sipping their tea in the leaden light of the wintry afternoon, the youngest daughter, who's always been the vivacious one, tells such amusing stories about her two months of married life that her eldest and most beautiful sister, though she knows so much more about married life, sadly asks herself if perhaps there is something lacking in her husband, something missing in her life. So now please bring this melancholy face before your eyes!

Have you seen all these faces? Have you noticed that, in some strange way, they all look alike? Is there not something that makes them all resemble each other, an invisible thread that joins their souls? When you look into the faces of these quiet creatures who don't know how to tell stories—who are mute, who can't make themselves heard, who fade into the woodwork, who only think of the perfect answer after the fact, after they're back at home, who can never think of a story that anyone else will find interesting—is there not more depth and more meaning in them? You can see every letter of every untold story swimming on their faces, and all the signs of silence, dejection, and even defeat. You can even imagine your own face in those faces, can't you? How many we are, how much anguish we all carry, and how helpless most of us are in the face of the world!

But I have no wish to deceive you again; I am not one of you. Anyone who can pick up a pen and scribble something down—and somehow manage to convince others to read it—has been cured of this ailment, at least to some degree. This may well explain why I have yet to come across an author who can write with authority on this, the essence of the human condition. But now, whenever I pick up my pen, I am finally aware that there is no other subject: From now on I shall devote myself utterly to the hidden poetry of our faces, the terrifying secret that lurks inside our human gaze. So be prepared.

Chapter Twenty-four

Riddles in Faces

The face is what one goes by, generally.
—Lewis Carroll,
Through the Looking Glass

When he sat down at the desk on Tuesday morning and surveyed the piles of columns before him, Galip did not feel as optimistic as he'd done the morning before. In the course of one day's work, his image of Celâl had changed, almost of its own volition, so much so that he was no longer clear what it was he was trying to find. But he took some comfort in the one thing he still felt sure about: In his present predicament he had no choice but to continue reading through the columns and notebooks he'd taken from the cabinet in the hall and come up with some sort of hypothesis as to where Celâl and Rüya might be hiding. In any event, it was far more pleasant to sit in this room full of sweet childhood memories, reading Celâl's columns, than it was to sit in his dusty Sirkeci office, poring over dossiers about iron and rug merchants who were swindling each other and rental agreements that might or might not protect tenants from unscrupulous landlords. His life might have fallen apart, but he still felt the contentment of a government official who's been promoted to a more interesting job at a better desk.

His elation stayed with him as he drank his second coffee and ran through all the clues he had amassed so far. Picking up the *Milliyet* that the janitor had left at the door, and seeing a reprint of "Excuses and Insults," a column Celâl had first published many years earlier, Galip deduced that Celâl had failed to file a new column on Sunday. This was the sixth reprint that the paper had run in as many days. There was only one column left. Unless Celâl sent in a new column in the next thirty-six hours, his Thursday column would be a blank space. After thirty-five years of reading Celâl's column the first thing every morning—for unlike other columnists, Celâl had never once gone on leave or fallen so ill he'd failed to file—just to think of opening the paper to page two one morning to find a blank space was to feel as if the world were coming to an end. As if the very waters of the Bosphorus were drying up.

Needing to make sure that he was open to any clues that might be trying to reach him, Galip plugged in the phone he'd disconnected shortly after his arrival two nights earlier. He spent a few moments thinking about the man who'd rung him that night, the voice that had introduced itself as Mahir İkinci. Recalling what the voice had said about a trunk murder and an impending military coup, Galip decided to go back to a number of Celâl's old columns. After he had retrieved them from their boxes and read them with care, he remembered various other passages in which Celâl had written about messiahs. Mostly these were passing references and asides in columns that purported to be about something else, and it took Galip so much time and effort to track them down that he soon felt as tired as if he'd done a full day's work.

In the early 1960s, when Celâl was writing columns aimed at provoking a military coup, he would have borne in mind what he himself had seen as one of Rumi's principles: A columnist wishing to win a wide readership over to an idea must dive down to salvage it from the very dregs of their memories, for it was there, dozing away, like the wrecked galleons that have lain for centuries at the bottom of the Black Sea! As Galip read through Celâl's historical perambulations, he waited meekly for an idea to rise up from the dregs of his own memory, but all the words did was churn up his imagination.

As he read about the Twelfth Imam, who stalked the passages of the Covered Bazaar, striking terror in the hearts of its price-rigging merchants, and of the sheikh's son who, after being proclaimed Messiah by his father and attracting a band of Kurdish peasants and master ironsmiths to his cause, had launched attacks on a number of forts (as detailed in *The History of Weaponry*), and of the dishwasher's assistant who, after dreaming that he had seen Muhammed passing over the sewage-strewn cobblestones of Beyoğlu in a white Cadillac convertible, had proclaimed himself Messiah to incite the city's prostitutes, Gypsies, paupers, tramps, pickpockets, cigarette boys, and shoeshine men to rise up against the pimps and gangster lords who ruled their lives, Galip infused each and every scene with the brick-red dawn-orange glow of his own dreams and memories. But there was one story that did more than provoke his imagination. As he read of Hunter Ahmet, who, after falsely proclaiming himself crown prince and then sultan, had claimed himself to be the Prophet, he suddenly remembered an evening when—as Rüya smiled with her usual sleepy innocence—Celâl had spoken at length about what a "False Celâl" might need to write his columns in his place (curiously enough, he had said that all the person would need was access to his memory). A wave of fear went through Galip as he recalled these words: This was a dangerous game he'd been dragged into, a deadly trap.

He went through the address books again, checking the names and numbers against the ones in the telephone directory. He dialed a few numbers that aroused his suspicions: the first connected him to a plastics manufacturer in Lâleli; they specialized in dishpans, laundry baskets, and buckets; so long as they had a model for the mold, they could produce any object in any color in the hundreds and deliver them in a week. When he dialed the second number, a child answered; after he'd told Galip that he lived with his mother, his father, and his grandfather, and that his father wasn't at home, his elder brother—whom he'd *not* mentioned—interrupted to say that they didn't give their name out to strangers, at which point the suspicious mother grabbed the phone. "May I have your name, please? Would you please tell me who you are?" she asked in a guarded, frightened voice. "You must have the wrong number."

It was noon by the time Galip began to rummage through the annotated bus and movie tickets. In his careful handwriting, Celâl had noted his thoughts on various films, along with the names of some of the actors. Some had been underlined, and Galip tried to work out why. He'd jotted down words and names on the bus tickets, too: on one was a face drawn from letters of the Latin alphabet. (The ticket had cost fifteen kuruş, which meant it was from the early sixties.) After examining the letters on the tickets, he read a few of Celâl's movie reviews, a

handful of celebrity interviews from the early days of his career
("Mary Marlowe, the famous American movie star, paid a visit to our
city yesterday!"), a few rough drafts of crossword puzzles, a number of
readers' letters chosen at random, and various news items about various Beyoğlu murders that Celâl had cut out of the paper with a view to
writing a column about them. The killings had all been perpetrated
after midnight, when both the assailant and his victim were drunk, and
the weapon was always a sharp kitchen knife; each story was in the
same macho style, driving home the same hard-boiled moral—"This is
what happens to people who involve themselves in shady dealings!"—
and most of the murders did seem to be imitations of previous ones.
Celâl had also drawn from news clippings about Istanbul's Most Exciting Neighborhoods (Cihangir, Taksim, Lâleli, Kurtuluş) in the
columns in which he'd retold the stories of these same murders. In the
same box Galip found a serial entitled "Historical Firsts"; it reminded
Galip that one Kasım Bey, the owner of the Education Library Press,
had published the first Turkish book to use the Latin alphabet in 1928.
For decades thereafter, the same man had produced the *Daily Almanac
with Prayer Times*. These had a page for every day of the year, and
though they'd always torn each one off in turn and thrown it away,
Galip could still remember them clearly: Each offered a "menu of the
day" (Rüya had loved these), an aphorism from Atatürk or an important Islamic authority or a famous foreigner like Benjamin Franklin or
Bottfolio, a tasteful joke, and clock faces indicating the prayer times for
that day. When Galip found discarded pages from these almanacs on
which Celâl fiddled with the hands of the clock faces, turning them
into human faces with drooping mustaches and hooked noses, he jotted down some notes on a clean sheet of paper, hoping to convince
himself that he had stumbled onto an important clue. While he was
eating the bread, cheese, and apples he had bought himself for lunch,
he stared at his notes with a strange fascination.

On the last pages of a notebook in which Celâl had summarized the
plots of two foreign detective novels (*The Golden Scarab* and *The Seventh
Letter*) and the keys to secret codes he'd gleaned from books about
German spies and the Maginot Line, he found the shaky trail of a
green ballpoint pen. The lines were vaguely reminiscent of the ones he
had found on the maps of Cairo, Damascus, and Istanbul, though they

sometimes called to mind a face, a bouquet of flowers, or a slender river snaking across a plain. After puzzling over the meaningless asymmetries of the first four pages, Galip solved the puzzle on the fifth. The green line traced the last uncertain meanderings of an ant; as it circled each blank page, the green pen had chased behind it; it had dropped in exhaustion in the middle of the fifth page, where its dried corpse still lay pressed into the page. Wondering how many years had passed since the unhappy ant had been so severely punished for failing to produce results, Galip decided to find out if Rumi could cast any light on this strange experiment. In the fourth volume of *Mathnawi* he found a passage in which Rumi described an ant walking over his manuscript: First the creature sees the jonquils and lilies in the Arab script; then it sees the pen that has created this garden of words; then it sees the hand that directs the pen and the intelligence that directs the hand, "And then," as Celâl once added in a column, "the ant saw that there was a higher intelligence directing that intelligence." Once again, Celâl's dreams had merged with the imaginings of the Sufi poet. Though Galip had hoped to find some sort of correlation between the columns and the dates in the journal, all he found on the final pages were the dates and locations of the great Istanbul fires and the number of wooden houses each had destroyed.

Galip next read of the ruses perpetrated by a secondhand bookseller's apprentice who had sold his wares from door to door at the beginning of the century. Each day he had taken a ferry to a different Istanbul neighborhood, there to target the rich in their mansions, selling the bargain books in his satchel to harem ladies, and men too old to leave the house, and overworked clerks, and dreamy-eyed children. But his real customers were the pashas, the ministers of state who had been grounded by Abdülhamit and did not dare leave their ministries and mansions, for the sultan's spies were everywhere. As he read how the bookseller's apprentice taught his pashas (his *readers*, as Celâl preferred to call them) the Hurufi secrets that would help them decipher the messages he had inserted into the text of the books he sold them, Galip slowly felt himself slipping away, just as he had hoped, to become someone else. For he knew these Hurufi secrets were as simple and as childish as the signs and key letters he'd once seen on the last page of an abridged version of an American adventure that took place on the high seas of some distant ocean. Celâl had given this book to Rüya one Saturday afternoon when they were still very young: You became someone else when you read a story—that was the key to the mystery. That was when the phone rang, and of course it was the same voice at the end of the line.

"I'm glad you've reconnected your phone, Celâl Bey!" It was the voice of a man well past middle age. "At a time like this, when disaster looms, for a man of your importance to be cut off from the entire city, the entire nation—it hardly bears thinking about!"

"How much of the phone book have you managed to get through?"

"I'm working hard, but it's slower than I expected. When you spend hour after hour looking at numbers, your mind begins to wander and you find yourself thinking the unthinkable. I've begun to see magic formulas, symmetrical groupings, repetitions, matrices, shapes. They slow me down."

"Do you see faces too?"

"Yes, but these faces of yours only emerge after I've noticed a symmetrical grouping. These numbers don't always speak; sometimes they remain silent. I tell myself that the fours are trying to tell me something, because I'm seeing so many of them, one after the other. I notice they're coming in twos, and then suddenly they're shifting into symmetrical columns, and lo and behold, they've become sixteen. Then you see sevens pouring in to fill the gap, whispering to the same tune. I'd like to tell you that it's just a lot of silly coincidences, but when you see that the number for a man named Timur Yıldırımoğlu is 140 22 40, don't you immediately think of the Battle of Ankara, which took place in 1402, in which Timur the Barbarian crossed swords with Beyazid, the great lightning-footed warrior we also know as Yıldırım? And did not Timur seize Beyazid's wife after his victory and take her into his harem? The phone directory is shimmering with fragments of our history! It pulls me in, slows me down, keeps me from getting to you, but I still know you are the only one who can stop this great conspiracy. You are the one whose arrow pointed them in this direction, and Celâl Bey, you are the only one who can stop it!"

"Why?"

"When we last spoke, I neglected to mention to you that they are waiting for the Messiah but waiting in vain. A handful of soldiers got this idea from a column you wrote, years and years ago. Not only did they read it, they believed it—just like me. I beg you to take your mind back to those columns you wrote in early 1961—that *nazire* you wrote about the Grand Inquisitor, for example, and that snide conclusion to the piece in which you found so unconvincing the picture of the happy family on the National Lottery tickets (the mother knitting, the father reading the paper, maybe even reading your column, the son doing his homework on the floor, the cat and the grandmother dozing next to the stove)—you should take another look at these pieces, and some of your movie reviews too! Why did you write such cruel things about Turkish movies in the early sixties? These films brought pleasure to millions, they expressed the way we really felt, but all you ever saw were the sets: the cologne bottles on the chest next to the bed, the spiderwebs gathering around the photographs sitting atop pianos no one ever played, the postcards stuck into the sides of mirrors, the dog figurine sleeping on top of the family radio—now why is that?"

"I don't know."

"Oh, you don't, do you? You show these as signs of our misery and collapse. You talk about them the same way you talk about the vile things we throw into our air shafts; and the families who live huddled together in the same apartment building, so close together that the cousins end up marrying each other; and the slipcovers we put on our armchairs so they don't wear out: These, too, are painful signs pointing to our irreversible decay, our descent into mediocrity. But not long after all that, in your so-called historical essays, you start hinting that liberation might be just around the corner; at our darkest hour, someone might emerge to deliver us from wretchedness. A savior who's walked this earth before, perhaps centuries before, will come back to life as someone else; five hundred years after his death, He'll come back to Istanbul as Mevlana Celâlettin or Sheikh Galip or perhaps even a newspaper columnist! While you were busy spinning these fine thoughts, and rhapsodizing about the sadness of women waiting at the city's public water fountains and the sad love laments carved into the wooden frames of the seats on the old streetcars, there was a band of young officers who took you at your word. They came to believe that one day a Messiah would come to deliver them from all this wretchedness and misery, that in an instant everything would be put to rights. You were the one who put this idea into their heads! You know who they are! You wrote those pieces with these very men in mind!"

"So what exactly do you want from me now?"

"Just let me see you. That's enough."

"What for? This nonsense about a dossier—you made that up, didn't you?"

"If you will just let me see you, I can explain everything."

"You've given me a false name, too!" said Galip.

"I want to see you!" cried the voice, using the same pretentious inflections, the same strangely touching tones, of a dubbing artist saying *I love you!* "I want to see you. When we meet, you'll see at once why I wanted to see you. No one knows you as well as I do, no one. I know how many teas and coffees you drink as you sit up all night, smoking the Maltepes that you've left to dry out on the radiator, dreaming your dreams. I know that you correct your typescripts with a green ballpoint pen, that you are happy with neither your life nor yourself. I know that though you've paced up and down the room night after night from dusk till dawn, yearning to be someone else, you still can't decide who this other person is you so long to become."

"I've written about all this many times!" said Galip.

"I also know that your father has never loved you, and that after he returned from Africa with his new wife, he kicked you out of the attic flat where you'd taken refuge. I know of your trials and tribulations after you moved back in with your mother. O, brother of mine, when you were a struggling and impoverished Beyoğlu reporter, you invented murders that had never happened, just to attract attention! You went to the Pera Palas to do interviews with nonexistent film stars, to talk about American films that were never made! To write the confessions of a Turkish opium addict, you smoked opium! To finish a wrestling serial you published under an assumed name, you went on a trip through Anatolia and got the beating of your life! You wrote tearful accounts of your life in your BELIEVE IT OR NOT column, but still people didn't understand! I know you have sweaty hands, that you've been in two traffic accidents, that you still haven't found a good pair of waterproof shoes, that though you fear loneliness more than anything, you spend most of your time alone. You like climbing minarets, reading pornographic magazines, wandering around Alâaddin's store, and spending time with your stepsister. Who else but me knows all this?"

"Quite a few people, in fact," said Galip. "They can read it in my columns. Can you please give me the real reason why you want to see me?"

"The military coup!"

"I'm hanging up—"

"I swear to you!" said the voice, sounding hopeless and panic-stricken. "If I could just see you, I could tell you everything."

Galip unplugged the phone. Returning to the cabinet in the hall, he took out a yearbook that had caught his eye the day before and sat down in the same chair where Celâl would sit when he returned, dead tired, at the end of each day. It was a handsomely bound copy of the 1947 War College Yearbook; though the opening pages featured pictures of (and aphorisms by) Atatürk, the president, the joint chiefs of staff, the commander, and the college faculty, most of the pages contained carefully posed photographs of the students; there was a sheet of onionskin protecting each page. As he leafed through the yearbook, Galip was not quite able to explain to himself why it was that he had thought to pick up this yearbook immediately after hanging up the phone, but he did find the students' faces strikingly similar; like the hats on their heads and the bars on their collars, they were almost identical. For a moment he thought he was looking through one of those old numismatics journals he'd sometimes come across on those dusty tables you find outside secondhand bookstores, in which the pictures of the silver coins look so much alike that only an expert could distinguish the figures imprinted on them. But still his spirits lifted, just as they did when he walked the streets or sat in the waiting rooms of ferry stations: He liked looking at faces.

As he turned the pages of the yearbook, he remembered how he'd felt as a child when he opened up a new and long-awaited comic book and smelled the paper, the ink. Of course—as books were always telling us—everything was connected to everything else. Looking into these faces, he saw the same momentary brightness he'd seen in faces in the streets. It was as if the eyes had as much to say to him as the faces.

If he excluded the high-ranking officers who might have encouraged the conspirators from a distance without jeopardizing their own careers, Galip was sure that most of the architects of the failed coup in the early sixties were pictured in these pages. But though Celâl had doodled all over the onionskin, childishly giving some photographs beards and mustaches and shading in others under the nose or the cheekbones, there was no mention of a military coup. He'd lined a number of their foreheads with meaningless letters from the Latin alphabet and reshaped the bags under their eyes to form nicely rounded Cs and Os; other faces he'd decorated with stars, horns, and spectacles. He'd outlined the young officers' chin bones, and the bones in their foreheads and their noses, and on some faces he'd drawn lines from the forehead to the chin, from the nose to the lips, and from side to side, as if to measure their proportions. Underneath some photographs were references to photographs on other pages. To many faces he'd added pimples, moles, liver spots, Aleppo boils, birthmarks, bruises, and burn marks. Next to a face too bright and clean to be disfigured with lines or letters, he'd written, *To retouch a photograph is to kill the soul!*

Galip ran across the same sentence in other yearbooks he retrieved from the same corner: Celâl had also doodled on the photographs of the students at the School of Engineering, the faculty of the Medical School, the deputies elected to the National Assembly in 1950, the engineers and administrators working on the Sivas–Kayseri railroad, the members of the Bursa Beautification Association, and the veterans of the Korean War from the Alsancak district of Izmir. He'd drawn thick lines down the middle of their faces, dividing them in two, as if to make the letters on each side more visible. Galip alternated between flipping through the pages very quickly and stopping to gaze at one particular face for a long time; whenever he paused, it felt like trying to catch a distant hard-won memory before it flew away again into oblivion, like trying to work out the address of a house to which you had been taken in the dark. Some faces did not yield anything other than what was immediately apparent; other faces looked calm and quiet when he first set eyes on them and then, when he least expected it, launched into stories. That was when Galip saw the colors: Years ago, he'd seen this same melancholy gaze in a waitress in a foreign film, but only fleetingly, because no sooner had she appeared onscreen than she'd vanished; he'd felt this way once when listening to a beautiful song on the radio, a song everyone around him knew by heart but that he had somehow missed, and knowing it was playing for the very last time.

As afternoon turned into evening, Galip returned to the cabinet in the hall and took out all the yearbooks, all the albums, and all the boxes of pictures and photographs cut from newspapers and magazines; carrying them out to the sitting room, he began to rummage through them like a drunk. Many depicted young girls, fedora-wearing gentlemen, ladies in head scarves, clean-faced youths, bedraggled wretches; there was no indication as to who they were or where or how their photographs had been taken. Others depicted unhappy faces who made no secret of it: two citizens anxiously watching their alderman present a petition to the prime minister under the kindly gaze of the security police and a handful of cabinet ministers; a mother who'd managed to rescue her bedroll and her child from a fire that had ravaged Dereboyu Avenue in Beşiktaş; women lining up for tickets outside the Alhambra to see a movie starring the celebrated Egyptian actor Abdul-Wahab; a famous belly dancer and film star being escorted by police into Beyoğlu police station after being picked up for possession of hashish; the accountant whose face went blank the moment he was caught embezzling. He could almost hear these faces telling him why they existed, why they'd been saved. Can there be anything more profound, more satisfying, more curious, Galip thought, than a photograph that captures the expression on a person's face?

Even the pictures that had been retouched or otherwise enhanced by trick photography, even in the ones whose blank expressions hid their meaning—they exuded a melancholy, a story heavy with terror and memory—expressed with their eyes a buried secret that could never be put into words; as they gazed now into Galip's eyes, he felt unspeakably sad. Tears came into his eyes as he looked into the happy but bewildered face of a quilter's apprentice who had just won the jackpot in the National Lottery, as he inspected an insurance broker who'd knifed his wife and a Turkish beauty queen who'd proved herself "an excellent ambassador for our country" by being chosen as second runner-up for Miss Europe.

In some faces he saw the traces of a melancholy that Celâl had expressed so often in his columns; he decided Celâl must have written these particular columns while gazing at these same photographs: the inspiration for his piece about the laundry hanging in the gardens of tenements overlooking factory warehouses must have been this portrait of "our" amateur boxing champion (weight 126 pounds) that Galip now held in his hand; and he was sure Celâl had written that piece about the crooked streets of Galata (which he argued were not really crooked at all, except in the eyes of foreigners) while looking at the photograph of the purplish-white face of "our" famous 111-year-old singer and remembering how proudly she had insinuated that she had slept with Atatürk. When Galip gazed into the faces of dead pilgrims lying by the side of the road, their caps still on their heads, after the bus taking them home from Mecca was involved in a traffic accident, he immediately remembered a column Celâl had once written about maps and engravings of old Istanbul. This was the column in which he had claimed that some old maps of the city had signs pointing to hidden treasure, while some European engravings had signs pointing to crazed enemies of the state who had come to Istanbul to assassinate "our" sultan. As he imagined Celâl sitting down to write this article after he'd spent weeks in hiding in some other corner of Istanbul, in some other secret apartment, he decided it must be connected in some way with the maps he'd marked up in green ink.

He began to sound out the names of neighborhoods on the Istanbul map. Because he'd uttered many of these names thousands of times in the course of his everyday life, they were so heavy with memory as to be meaningless, as meaningless as all-purpose words like *water* or *thing*. But when he repeated the names of areas beyond his normal range in a very loud voice, they were powerfully evocative. Galip now remembered that Celâl had written a series about the forgotten neighborhoods of Istanbul. Returning to the cabinet, he found several pieces with the headline THE CORNERS OF OUR CITY THAT ARE STILL VEILED IN SECRECY, but it soon became clear that they were intended more as vehicles for Celâl's short fictions than as descriptions of Istanbul's least-known districts. Under other circumstances, this might have made him laugh, but now it made him angry to see his hopes so cruelly dashed: it was not just his readers Celâl had been fooling all these years; he'd also been conning himself. As he read about a small fight that had broken out on the Fatih–Harbiye streetcar, and the little boy from Feriköy who'd been sent out to the grocery store, never to return, and the music of ticking clocks at a watchmaker's shop in Tophane, Galip muttered to himself that he "wasn't going to let this man" fool him ever again.

But moments later, his mind had gone back of its own accord to wondering if Celâl might be hiding in some house in Harbiye, or Feriköy, or even Tophane, and he was no longer angry at Celâl for luring him into a trap; instead, he was furious at his own mind for seeking clues in everything Celâl wrote. He just could not bear to live without stories but he hated himself for it, just as he hated children who could not live without constant entertainment. He decided then and there that there was no room in this world for signs, clues, second and third meanings, secrets, or mysteries; they were nothing more than figments of his imagination—he'd seen these signs only because his hungry and inquiring mind had wanted to see them, had grasped at any straw that hinted at some higher meaning. A desire rose up in him to live in a world where things meant themselves and nothing else: a world in which letters, texts, faces, and streetlamps stood only for themselves, where Celâl's desk, Uncle Melih's old armchair, the scissors, and the ballpoint pen did not, even if they carried Rüya's fingerprints, shimmer suspiciously with secrets. How to find his way into this world where green ballpoint pens were nothing but green ballpoint pens and he would never again long to be someone else? Like a child dreaming of a distant land he has only seen on film, Galip looked down at the map spread out on the desk and tried to convince himself that he was already there. For a moment he could almost see the wrinkled forehead of an old man, and then the faces of all the sultans, all merged into one, and then, perhaps, the face of a prince, but no sooner had they suggested themselves than they vanished.

After a time, he decided that these faces Celâl had been collecting for thirty years might offer him glimpses of this other realm to which he longed to escape, and with this in mind he settled into an armchair. Taking photographs out of the boxes at random, he tried to look into the faces without seeking either signs or secrets. Soon they became as anonymous as the physical descriptions on identity cards: random arrangements of noses, eyes, and mouths. From time to time, he'd catch sight of an unusually sad and beautiful woman on a photograph affixed to an insurance document, but before he could sink into her sad mystery, he'd quickly turn his attention to another face that harbored no pain, no untold story. To keep himself from getting pulled into these faces' stories, he avoided reading the captions and ignored the letters Celâl had written in the margins and across their faces. Though he pored over these photographs for the longest time, struggling to see them as simple maps of human faces, listening to the traffic in the street below grow steadily heavier, while tears rolled down his cheeks, he managed to skim only the surface of Celâl's thirty-year-old collection.

Chapter Twenty-five

The Executioner
and the Weeping Face

"Don't cry, don't cry, oh, please don't cry."
—Halit Ziya

Why does the sight of a man in tears upset us so? It's not every day we see a woman crying, but when we do it's a painful, touching scene and our hearts go out to her. But if it's a man crying, we feel helpless. We assume that something terrible has happened—the death of a loved one, perhaps, or the end of the world; as we watch him stand there, bereft, resourceless, all his courage spent, we cannot help but feel disquiet, and as we ask ourselves if he was ever really one of us we can feel the chill finger of terror crawling down our spines. For we all know, the dread surprise occasioned by a familiar face—a map we think we know by heart—that has suddenly and without warning taken on the contours of a foreign land. I once happened on a story about this very subject in the fourth volume of Naima's *History*; it can also be found in Mehmet Halife's *History for Royal Pages* and *The History of Executioners* by Kadri of Edirne.

One spring evening in the not-too-distant past—three hundred years ago at the very most—Black Ömer, the most renowned executioner of the age, was approaching Erzurum Castle on horseback. He had in his possession an edict from the sultan, handed to him twelve days earlier in Istanbul by the chief of the palace guard; it called for the execution of Abdi Pasha, the fort's commander. He was pleased to have taken only twelve days to cover a distance that would take any ordinary traveler a month at this time of year; so sweet was the spring night that he forgot how tired he was, but at the same time he felt a sudden and unusual misgiving about the task ahead: the shadow of a curse, the hint of a suspicion, the looming prospect of an uncertainty that might keep him from discharging his duties in the proper way.

The job was fraught with difficulties: He had never set eyes on this pasha and did not know what he looked like; he would be going alone into a garrison full of men who were loyal to their master; when he presented the edict, his towering presence would be enough, he hoped, to convince the pasha and his entourage that there was no point in opposing the sultan's will, but if by any chance the pasha was slow to appreciate the gravity of the situation, he was going to have to kill him then and there, before the pasha's men had time to get the upper hand. But the executioner was so experienced in this sort of work he knew it couldn't be the source of his disquiet: During his thirty-year career, he had executed almost twenty princes, two grand viziers, six viziers, and twenty-three pashas. If you added all the others—the honest and the crooked, the innocent and the guilty, the men and the women, the young and the elderly, the Christians and the Muslims—he had terminated more than six hundred lives; from the beginning of his apprenticeship, he had also subjected thousands of people to torture.

Before he entered the city on that spring morning, the executioner stopped by a spring; descending from his horse, he did his ablutions and knelt to pray. Only rarely did he appeal to God to help him stay on course. But, as always, the good Lord acceded to the prayers of His humble, hardworking slave.

So everything went according to plan. The moment the pasha set eyes on his visitor, he knew—from the conical red-felt hat on the man's shaven head and the greased noose in his sash—that his executioner had arrived, but he made no unusual effort to resist him. Perhaps, knowing his crime, he had long since prepared himself for his fate.

First, he read the edict from start to finish at least ten times, each time giving it his full attention (a sign of true obedience). After he had finished, he kissed the edict and, with a pretentious flourish, raised it to his forehead (though Black Ömer was not impressed by this gesture; it was a common ploy in a man who still needed to impress those around him). He then announced that he wished to read the Koran and say his prayers (a standard request from true believers as well as those hoping to buy time). After he finished his prayers, he removed all his valuables—his rings, necklaces, and decorations—and distributed them among his men, murmuring, "Something to remember me by," thus ensuring that there would be nothing left for his visitor (this, too, is a common ploy, especially among those so worldly and superficial that they bear a personal grudge against their executioner). He then did what all condemned men do if they have already run through all the tricks described above: As the executioner went to slip the noose over his head, he tried to fight him off, shouting and cursing as he used his fists. But one good blow to his chin and he crumbled. He prepared for his death. He was in tears.

It was normal for his victims to cry at this stage, but something he saw in the pasha's weeping face made the executioner doubt himself for the first time in his thirty-year career. So he did something he'd never yet done: Before he strangled his victim, he covered his head with a piece of cloth. He'd always been severely critical of colleagues who did this, for he believed that any executioner who was worthy of his title should be able to stare straight into his victim's eyes from start to finish without his technique faltering.

After he was sure the pasha had breathed his last, he took out his sharpest, straightest blade (sometimes called a *cipher*) and quickly separated the pasha's head from the body; while it was still steaming he threw the head into the honey-filled mohair sack that would preserve it during the long journey back to Istanbul. It was while he was arranging the head in the honey-filled mohair sack that he had his final terrifying glimpse of the weeping face that would both haunt and perplex him until his own (not-so-distant) death.

He mounted his horse forthwith and left the city, the head safe in its sack. He wanted the pasha's head to be at least two days' distance from the city when his wailing mourners carried the rest of his body to its final resting place. After riding nonstop for a day and a half, he arrived at another fort: Kemah Castle. After supping at the caravansary, he went with his sack into his cell and fell into a deep sleep.

He slept for half a day, slipping out of one dream only to fall into another, and as he drifted back into wakefulness, his last dream took him back to the Edirne of his childhood. There before him was a huge jar full of preserved figs. He recalled how, when his mother was boiling them in their syrup, the fragrance of figs would spread throughout the house, the garden, and the entire neighborhood, but now, as he approached the jar, he realized that the little green globes he'd thought were figs were the eyeballs of a weeping head. A pang of guilt went through him as he screwed open the lid, not because it was forbidden to do so but because he could barely contain his fear of its ghostly contents, and when the sobs of a grown man rose up from the jar, he was speechless with terror and unable to move.

The next night, as he slept in another bed in another caravansary, his dreams took him back to an evening in his youth; it was just before nightfall, in one of the back streets of Edirne. A friend—but who was he?—had just called to him, asking him to look at the sky: There, at one end, was the setting sun and, at the other, the pale white face of the rising moon. Later, after the sun had set and the sky had darkened and the moon's round face had turned a sparkling gold, he suddenly realized that it was a human face, gazing down on him and weeping. But no, it was not the sadness of the weeping face that troubled the Edirne night and gave its streets the ghostly aura of an alien land, it was the enigma.

The next morning, when the executioner recalled the vision that had come to him in his sleep, he realized he'd drawn it from memory. In the course of his career, he'd seen men's weeping faces in the thousands, but none had made him feel so ruthless, fearful, and guilty. Although it was not widely known, he pitied his sad victims; he had, however, never wavered in his conviction that justice must be done. For as he prepared to strangle his victims or break their necks or sever their heads, he knew that they knew far more about the chain of events that led them to their crime than did their executioner. Though a man might approach the hour of his death wailing and sobbing and choking and begging as snot ran from his nose, he could do nothing to shake the executioner's resolve. He was not like those idiots who thought condemned men should exit the world with famous last words or some grand flourish that would live forever in history and legend— or despised them if they didn't—nor was he immobilized by pity upon seeing their histrionics, like those other idiots who had yet to comprehend life's random ruthlessness.

So what was it in his dreams that plunged him into this strange paralysis? One sunny sparkling morning, as he rode with his horse and his mohair sack through deep and rocky chasms, the executioner decided it must have something to do with the indecision he'd felt on the outskirts of Erzurum and his vague intimations of a looming curse; he had stared at the mystery in the pasha's face and this was why he had sought to cover it, why he had been so desperate to consign this face to oblivion. For the rest of that long day, as the executioner rode with his horse past rocky precipices that took on ever-more-arresting shapes (a potbellied sailboat, a fig-headed lion), past long rows of pines and beeches that seemed as alien, as shocking, as if he were seeing them for the first time, and along icy rivers whose banks were covered with the strangest—the very strangest—pebbles he had ever laid eyes on, he didn't think once about the face lurking inside the mohair sack dangling from the back of his horse. For now the truly shocking thing was the world itself. It was a new world, and he'd just discovered it, just noticed it for the first time.

He noticed for the first time that the trees resembled the dark shadows he saw winking between the memories that came to him on sleepless nights. He saw that the sinless shepherds tending their sheep on the greening slopes carried their heads on their shoulders as if these heads belonged to someone else. Passing the little villages that dotted the foothills of the mountains—ten small houses all in a row—he saw for the first time that they looked like empty shoes lined up at the door of a mosque. Two days later, as he rode through the purple mountains of the western provinces, under clouds that looked as if they'd been plucked straight from a miniature painting, he knew for the first time what they signified: the world stripped bare, stripped to its very essence. As he gazed upon the plants and timid animals and rocks and stones around him, he was suddenly aware of the realm of horror to which they pointed: It was as plain as the helplessness that now engulfed him and as old as memory. As he continued traveling westward and the lengthening shadows took new meanings, the executioner saw signs and clues oozing from every new vista, like blood seeping through the cracks of an earthenware bowl, but still he could not fathom their mystery.

When night fell, he retired to a caravansary and filled his stomach, but he knew it was pointless to shut himself up in a cell with his mohair sack and try to sleep. He feared the dream that would engulf him in the middle of the night, oozing in all directions like pus from a burst wound; he could not bear to see that helpless weeping face he now knew would return to him every night, and each night in the guise of a different memory. So after he had lingered for some time in the caravansary, and gazed with amazement at the variety of faces in the crowd, he set out into the night to continue his journey.

The night was cold and silent—not the hint of a breeze, not a single branch moving—and the tired horse found his own way. He traveled for some time without incident—happy to see nothing of interest, as had once been his wont. No unanswered question plagued his mind; later, he would decide that this must have been because it was dark. Because as soon as the moon peeked through the clouds, the trees and shadows and stones around him slowly began to point again to a mystery that could never be solved. What unnerved him were not the sorrowful tombstones or the lonely cypresses or the howling of wolves in the desolate night. What shocked and horrified the executioner was his own longing to turn all this into a story. It was as if the world were trying to tell him something, lay itself bare, but its voice was lost in a mist he could barely see, had only seen before in his dreams. Toward daybreak, the executioner heard sobbing in his ears.

As the sun rose in the sky, the executioner told himself he was mistaken: It wasn't sobbing he heard but the rustling of branches in the newly risen wind. By noon, the sobs coming from the mohair sack were so distinct that—like a man who has risen from his warm bed to stop a window from squeaking—he stopped his horses and climbed down to secure the mohair sack to the pillion more firmly. But later that same day, as he rode on through a cruel rainstorm, it was not just the sobs; he could feel tears pouring from the weeping face onto his own skin.

When the sun came out again, he decided that the mystery of the world was linked in some way with the enigma of the weeping face. For now it seemed clear to him that the world he knew—the world he'd thought he'd understood—was made familiar through the ordinary meanings expressed by ordinary faces; so from the moment he'd first seen that eerie look in the weeping face, the meaning of the world itself had shattered; what he gazed upon in his desolation were the shattered pieces of an enchanted bowl, a magic crystal cracked beyond repair, a world turned upside down. As he dried his wet clothes in the sun, he realized that there was only one way to restore order: He was going to have to deprive the head of its mask, wipe this expression off its face. But his guild was a strict one, and he was honor-bound to return to Istanbul with the head untouched and still perfectly preserved in its bath of honey inside the mohair sack.

He spent a sleepless night on horseback, trying but failing to ignore the ever more insistent and exasperating sobs rising from the sack behind him; when dawn broke, the world seemed so changed that he could hardly remember who he was. The pines and the plane trees, the muddy roads, the crowds around the village fountains that dispersed in horror at the very sight of him—he'd never seen sights quite like these. When he stopped at a town he did not recognize to wolf down his midday meal, he could barely identify the food on his plate. When he stopped outside the village to rest his horse and stretched out under a tree, he noticed that the sky was not a sky at all but a strange and vast blue dome he'd never seen before and would never understand. At sunset, he mounted his horse and continued on his way, but he still had six more days to reach his destination. By now it had become clear to him that—unless he performed the magical task that would stop the sobbing in the sack, change the weeping face's expression, and return the world to its own self—he would never again see Istanbul.

After nightfall, he ventured into a village where he heard dogs barking and chanced onto a well. Jumping off his horse, he removed the mohair sack. Untying the strings that bound it and dipping into the honey, he took the head by the hair and carefully lifted it out. He then cleansed it with bucketfuls of water from the well, washing it as carefully as a baby. After he had dried it thoroughly from top to bottom with a piece of cloth, he gazed at the head in the light of the moon; it was weeping still, and on its face was the same unbearable and unforgettable look of woe.

He left the head at the side of the well and went back to the horse to retrieve the tools of his trade: a pair of special knives and a few of the blunt steel rods he used for torture. First he tried using one of the knives to change the sides of the mouth, to separate the skin from the bone. After working for some time, he had, despite making a great mess of the lips, managed to create the hint of a crooked and ambiguous smile. Then he began the more delicate task of lifting the eyelids, still squeezed shut in pain. It was only after he'd been hacking away at them for the longest time that a smile began to radiate across the entire face; as much as the effort had exhausted him, he still felt relieved. And it pleased him to see the purple mark from the fist he'd brought down on the side of Abdi Pasha's chin before he'd smothered him. With childish optimism, and certain that he'd put the world to rights, he rushed back to the horse to pack his tools into their sack.

When he returned to the well, the head was gone. At first he thought the smiling head was playing games with him, but when he realized it had fallen into the well, he knew at once what he had to do. Running over to the nearest house, he pounded on the door until he had woken up everyone inside. One look at the fearsome executioner was all it took for the old man and his son to obey his every order. The trio worked until morning to pull the head from the well, which was not, they assured him, as deep as it seemed. They fixed the greased noose around the son's waist and lowered him into it; it was just before dawn that they pulled him out, screaming with horror and holding the head by the hair. The head was smashed and broken, but it was no longer weeping. With peace in his heart, the executioner dried the head once again, returned it to the honey-filled mohair sack, thanked the old man and his son, pressed a few coins into their hands, and happily left the village to continue his journey westward.

As the sun rose, and the birds chirped in the flowering trees of spring, he gazed around him with a joy as wide as the sky and saw that the world had gone back to its old self. There were no more sobs rising from the sack behind him. Just before noon, arriving at a lake surrounded by hills of pine trees, he climbed from his horse and lay down to drift into the deep and blissful sleep that had eluded him for so very long. Before falling asleep, he'd risen happily from his resting place and walked to the lake's edge: seeing his own reflection in the water, he knew he'd put the world in order.

When he arrived in Istanbul five days later, those who knew his victim well insisted that the head he plucked out of the honey-filled mohair sack could not possibly belong to Abdi Pasha, for none of them had ever seen him smile, but when the executioner gazed into the face, he saw in it the happy reflection he'd seen that day in the lake. He

knew that it was pointless to refute the charges made against him—
that Abdi Pasha had bribed him to take someone else's head, the head
of a sinless shepherd perhaps, and that he'd disfigured the face to
make identification impossible—for he had already noted the arrival of
the executioner who would soon be severing his own head.

As for the rumors that the head belonged to an innocent shepherd
and not Abdi Pasha, they spread so fast that when the second executioner to be dispatched to Erzurum walked into his fort, Abdi Pasha
was ready for him and killed him at once. So began the insurrection
that lasted twenty years and cost six thousand five hundred heads—
though the identity of its true leader was uncertain, for those who read
the letters in the pasha's face would later claim him to be an impostor.

Chapter Twenty-six

The Mystery of the Letters
and the Loss of Mystery

A hundred thousand secrets will be known
When that surprising face is unveiled and shown.
—Attar,
The Conference of the Birds

B y suppertime, when the traffic in Nişantaşı Square had eased and
the air no longer rang with the shrill, insistent whistle of the
policeman on the corner, Galip had been looking at the photographs
for so long that they had ceased to move him: Faces that might once
have spoken of pain, misery, and melancholy now said nothing; no
tears spilled from his eyes. No longer could his fellow citizens inspire
joy, affection, or excitement; life had nothing more to offer him. As he
gazed at the photographs, he felt the indifference of a man who has
been divested of his memories, his hopes, his very future. At the back
of his mind he sensed the gathering silence that would soon, he was
sure, seep into every corner of his body. As he ate the bread and
cheese he'd brought in from the kitchen and sipped his stale tea, he
continued to look through the photographs, now speckled with bread
crumbs. The insistent clamor of daytime had given way to the sounds
of night: the hum of the refrigerator, the rattle of descending shutters
from a shop at the far end of the street, a peal of laughter near Alaâd-
din's shop. From time to time, he'd hear high heels clicking down the
pavement; now and again a face would suddenly gaze up at him, in
fear, horror, or preposterous amazement, and drown the silence out.

It was now that he began to think there might be a link between the
mystery of letters and the meanings in faces—but this had less to do
with wanting to decipher the signs Celâl had made on the photographs

than it did with wanting to imitate the heroes in Rüya's detective novels. To be like a hero in a detective novel, Galip thought wearily, to apprehend an endless string of clues in everything you see, all you need to do is convince yourself that every object that surrounds you is hiding a secret. He went back to the cabinet, and after he had located the box in which Celâl had stored his books, treatises, and clippings on Hurufism—along with many thousands of photographs—he took it back to his desk and went straight to work.

He found faces formed from letters from the Arabic alphabet: the eyes were *wâw*s and *'ayn*s, the eyebrows *zây*s and *râ*s, and the noses *alif*s. Celâl had drawn the letters so carefully he might have been a good-natured schoolboy struggling to master old Turkish. In one lithograph he saw weeping eyes made of *wâw*s and *jîm*s; the dots in the *jîm*s were fashioned to look like tears rolling down the page. In a black-and-white photograph that had not been retouched he had no trouble reading the same letters in the eyes, eyebrows, noses, and lips; Celâl had written out the name of a Bektaşi sheikh in legible script below. He saw inscriptions that read *Ah, sigh of love!* and letters shaped to resemble galleons in peril on stormy seas; he saw, descending from the heavens, lettered lightning bolts that looked like eyes—eyes opened wide with horror—and he saw lettered faces caught inside lettered tangles that looked like tree branches and beards, each one fashioned from a different letter. He saw pale portraits whose eyes Celâl had gouged out with his pen, and innocents into whose lips Celâl had carved the signs that marked them as guilty, and sinners whose fearsome fates he had engraved on their foreheads. He saw the listlessness of bandits and prime ministers as they dangled from the gallows in their white execution robes, oblivious to the placards on their chests listing their crimes for all to see, staring instead at the ground their feet could not reach; he saw the faded color photographs of movie stars in whose eyes Celâl's readers had read the lettered shame of a life of prostitution; and he saw pictures sent by readers who considered themselves to be exact replicas of sultans and famous pashas, Rudolph Valentino and Mussolini, who had decorated their own faces with letters and signs. Celâl had once written a column in which he'd suggested there was a reason why the word *Allah* ended in an *h*; those readers who had divined a secret message in said column had written to him at length; as he delved deeper into the box, Galip found the signs of the secret letter games Celâl had found in these readers' letters and explications of the secret symmetries in Celâl's use of the words *morning, face,* and *sun* over a given week or month or year, as well as complaints from people who held that letter games were on a par with idol worship. He found pictures of Fazlallah of Astarabad, the founder of Hurufism, copied from miniatures and crawling with letters from both the Arabic and the Latin alphabets; he found a collection of the picture cards of soccer players and movie stars that came with the chocolate wafers he used to buy from Alâaddin, and with those sticks of colored bubble gum that were as hard as the sole of a gym shoe—these too were covered with letters and words; he also found photographs of murderers, sinners, and sheikhs, all sent in by readers. There were hundreds, thousands, tens of thousands of pictures of "our fellow citizens"—with letters swarming over each face—and photographs that Celâl's reader compatriots had sent in from every corner of Anatolia over the past thirty years: from dusty little villages and remote towns where the summer sunlight leaves cracks in the earth, where the blankets of snow that fall on the first day of winter remain for four months, keeping away all visitors except for hungry wolves; from smugglers' villages on the Syrian border where half the men were lame; from mountain villages that were still waiting for a road, forty years after it was first promised; from bars and cheap nightclubs of all Anatolia's great cities and from caves serving as illicit slaughterhouses, or the secret headquarters of drug traffickers and cigarette smugglers; from the lonely control rooms of remote train stations; from the lobbies of hotels frequented by cattle dealers; and from the brothels of Soğukoluk. He saw thousands of prints taken by the street photographers you found in front of every government office and municipal building, next to the men who typed up petitions for the illiterate; they all used Leica cameras, which they set up on tripods from which they always dangled an evil eye, and when they took their pictures, they dove behind a black curtain like an alchemist or a fortune-teller to fiddle with the pumps and bellows, the black lens covers and the glass plates. It was not hard to imagine how these fellow citizens of his had felt as they gazed into the camera, as their wish for immortality was slowly eaten away by intimations of death. But Galip saw at once how deeply they wished for it, and how this wish was related to the signs of death, defeat, and ruin he had found on so many of their faces. Once upon a time they had been happy, and then calamity had struck; a volcano had blown its top and now all lay buried in ash and dust, and if he was to uncover the mystery that lay beneath, if he was to recapture their lost memories, Galip had no choice but to decipher the tangle of letters on each face.

There were notes jotted on the backs of some photographs: these had later made their way into YOUR FACE, YOUR PERSONALITY, a column Celâl had taken on during the fifties, when he was also churning out puzzles and film reviews and BELIEVE IT OR NOT. Some photographs had been sent in at Celâl's request (*We would like to view our readers' photographs with a view to publishing them in our column*); others had been sent in for more tenuous reasons. As these people stared into the camera, they looked as if they had just remembered something from the distant past; as if they had just glimpsed, in the green afterimage of a lightning bolt, the vague hint of a black spot on the horizon; as if they were amnesiacs, long resigned to the certainty that their memories would never return to them, watching their destinies sinking yet again into a dark swamp. As Galip stared into these faces and felt the silence in their eyes, he knew at last why Celâl had spent so many years covering these pictures, clippings, faces, and expressions with letters, but when he tried to apply this insight to his own case—when he tried to divine the way in which his own life was intertwined with Celâl's and Rüya's, or to imagine his way out of this ghost house, or to use his newfound understanding as a key that might lead him to the story of his life—he would pause, just like the faces in the picture; even as he forced his mind to link one event with another, to create a story that meant something, it got lost in the mist of letters and faces. So it was that he slowly began to draw closer to the horror in these faces, the horror that was soon to seep into his own life.

In lithographs and pamphlets riddled with spelling mistakes, he read about the life of Fazlallah, the prophet and founder of the Hurufi sect. He was born in 1339 in Horasan, in a town called Astarabad, near the shores of the Caspian Sea. At the age of eighteen, he embarked on the Sufi path, and after undertaking a pilgrimage to Mecca he became the disciple of one Sheikh Hasan. As Galip read what he learned of the world and its ways while traveling from city to city in Azerbaijan and Iran, and what he had discussed with the sheikhs he had met along the way, in Tabriz, Shirvan, and Baku, there rose up in him an irrepressible urge to learn from his example—as the lithographs put it, to "begin anew." The predictions Fazlallah had made about the life and death that awaited him—all later proven to be correct—seemed to Galip to describe events that anyone embarking on the "new life" he so desired would consider ordinary. Fazlallah first became famous for his dream interpretations. In one of his own dreams he saw himself with the Prophet Solomon and two *hudhud* birds; as the birds gazed down from their tree at the two men slumbering underneath, Fazlallah's dreams mixed in with the Prophet's, causing the two *hudhud* birds to merge into one. In another dream, he was visited by a dervish who'd come to visit him in the cave where he'd secluded himself; later, when the same dervish actually came to visit, Fazlallah learned that the dervish had dreamed of him too: as they sat together in the cave, leafing through a book, they saw their faces in the letters; when they looked up, they saw the letters of the book in each other's faces.

According to Fazlallah, the dividing line between Being and Nothingness was sound, because everything that passed from the spiritual to the material world had its own sound; even the "most silent" objects made a distinct sound when knocked together. The most advanced sounds were, of course, words; words were the magic building blocks of the exalted thing we called *speech* and they were made up of letters. Those wishing to understand the meaning of existence and the sanctity of life and see God's manifestations here on earth had only to read the letters hidden in the faces of men. We were all born with two brow lines, four eyelash lines, and one hairline—seven lines in all. At puberty, when our "late-arriving" noses divided our faces into two, the number of letters engraved on them increased to fourteen. When we took into account the more poetic real and imaginary lines, the number doubled again, to prove beyond all shadow of a doubt that it was not by coincidence that the Prophet Muhammed had spoken in a language with twenty-eight letters, or that it was this language that had brought the Koran into being. But Persian, Fazlallah's native tongue and the language in which he wrote *The Book of Eternal Life*, uses thirty-two letters, so Fazlallah, wishing to see all the letters of the alphabet in every face, found the four extra characters by looking more carefully at the hair and chin lines and dividing them into two. When he read this, Galip realized why some of the photographs in the box showed men with their hair parted in the middle, like the brilliantined Hollywood movie stars from the 1930s. It all seemed so straightforward, so childishly simple that Galip was once again able to see what it was that Celâl so liked in word games.

Fazlallah proclaimed himself a savior, a prophet—the Messiah whose descent from the skies was awaited by both Jews and Christians, the Mehdi heralded by Muhammed, and the august personage Celâl refused to name in his columns, referring to him as "He." After finding himself seven disciples in Isfahan, Fazlallah went forth to spread the word. As Galip read how Fazlallah went from town to town, preaching that the world was not a place that yielded its secrets easily—that it was awash with secrets and that the only way to penetrate these secrets was to penetrate the mystery of the letters—a great wave of peace rolled over him. It was as he had expected, as he had desired for so long; it was proof that his own world was awash with secrets too. What reassured him most, he thought, was the simplicity of the proof. For if it was true that the world was awash with secrets, it was also true that everything he could see on the table in front of him—the coffee cup, the ashtray, the letter opener, and even his own hand as it rested like a drowsy crab alongside the letter opener—were not just signs pointing to another world; they themselves belonged to it. Rüya was in this other world. Galip stood on its threshold. Soon he would penetrate the mystery of the letters.

To do so, he would have to read more carefully. He returned to the accounts of Fazlallah's life and death. It was clear to him that Fazlallah had dreamed of his own death and had walked into it as if in a dream. Accused of heresy—for worshiping letters, people, and idols instead of God, for proclaiming himself the Messiah, for believing in his own dreams, for using his dreams to read secret and invisible meanings of the Koran, thus ignoring its real and visible essence—he had been arrested, tried, and hanged.

After Fazlallah and his associates had been killed, the Hurufis no longer felt safe in Iran, so they followed the poet Nesimi, who was now in charge of the sect, to Anatolia. Loading Fazlallah's books and manuscripts into a green trunk that would become one of the Hurufis' abiding legends, he wandered from city to city, preaching in remote *medreses* where even the spiders were drowsy and sleepy dervish lodges where even the lizards could hardly bring themselves to move. To demonstrate to his new disciples that it was not just the Koran that was awash with secrets but the entire world, he taught them letter and word games that were inspired by his own favorite game in the world, chess. In one of his most famous couplets, he likened a feature and a beauty spot on his lover's face to a letter and a full stop, and the letter and the full stop to a sponge and a pearl at the bottom of the sea, only to suggest that he himself was like a man who dove into the deep for the pearl only to die for it, and that this man who had so willingly plunged to his death was like a lover seeking God, and finally, coming full circle, that his lover was like God. The poet Nesimi's own life ended after he was arrested in Aleppo, subjected to a lengthy trial, and flayed to death; after his body had been strung up for all the city to see, it was cut into seven pieces and each piece sent off to be buried in one of the seven cities where adherents still recited his poems.

This did little to stem Nesimi's influence, and Hurufism continued to spread rapidly among the Bektaşis throughout the Ottoman world; fifteen years after the conquest of Istanbul, it even found its way to Mehmet the Conqueror. But soon it came to the attention of the theologians in his entourage that the sultan was walking around with Fazlallah's writings, talking of the mystery of the world, the enigma of lettters, and the Byzantine secrets winking from every corner of his new palace; pointing to each and every chimney, dome, and tree he had begun to claim that any of them could be the key that unlocked the mystery of the great underground realm that sat beneath their feet. The anxious clerics quickly banded together to entrap those Hurufis who were close to the sultan, and once they had done so they burned them all alive.

While leafing through one little book (a handwritten note on its last page claimed that it had been printed secretly in Horasan, near Erzurum, at the beginning of World War Two, though perhaps it had just been made to look as if this were so), Galip found pictures of Hurufis being burned and beheaded after their failed assassination attempt on Beyazid II, the Conqueror's son. On another page, the artist had used the same childish style to depict expressions of great horror on the faces of Hurufis as they were burned at the stake for failing to accede to Süleyman the Magnificent's deportation order. When he studied the sinuous flames licking up against their bodies, he could easily make out the *alif*s and *lam*s that made up the first four letters of the word *Allah*; but stranger still—as these men were consumed by the flames of the Arab alphabet, the tears falling from their eyes resembled the O's, U's, and C's in the Latin alphabet. This was the first time Galip had come across a Hurufi response to the 1928 Alphabet Revolution, when the country moved from the Arabic to the Latin alphabet, but because he was still bent on finding a formula that would help him solve the enigma of the letters, he did not pause to examine it carefully before returning to the box.

He went on to read a great many pages attesting that God's main attribute was a hidden treasure, a *kenz-i mahfi*, a mystery. All that remained was to find a way in. All that remained was to see how the mystery was reflected in the world. All that remained was to see how the mystery was present in every object, every person in the world. The world was a sea of clues; every drop bore the salty trace of the mystery behind it.

As his tired and inflamed eyes traveled from one page to the next, Galip became more and more certain that he would soon be diving into this ocean's secrets. Because if signs were everywhere, if they resided in everything, then the mystery was also everywhere and residing in everything. The longer he read, the more clearly he saw that the objects surrounding him were—like the pearls, roses, wine goblets, nightingales, golden hair, nights, flames, and lovers' faces in the poems he was reading—both signs of themselves and of the mystery he was slowly entering. The curtain in the weak light of the lamp, the chairs in which he could read so many memories of Rüya, the shadows on the wall, and the fearsome telephone receiver were all so heavy with memories and stories that Galip could not help wondering, as he had often done as a child, if he had stumbled into something unaware; but he continued on, disregarding his own vague premonitions about this scary game in which everyone was impersonating someone else and everything was a replica of an absent original, and convincing himself, as he had done so often as a child, that he would come through it in one piece by entering into the spirit of the game and becoming someone else too. "If you're afraid, I'll turn on the lamp," he'd said to Rüya when he sensed the same fear overtaking her. "No, don't," Rüya would reply, because she loved games, loved scaring herself.

Galip read on. At the beginning of the seventeenth century, when Anatolia was being torn asunder by the Celâli uprisings, the Hurufis took advantage of the confusion to settle in various remote villages that the peasants had abandoned, fleeing from the wrath of pashas, judges, bandits, and imams. As Galip struggled to make sense of a rather long poem describing the happy and meaningful lives they had enjoyed in these villages, his mind went back to the happy life he had enjoyed with Rüya as a child.

In the poem's distant golden age, action and meaning were one and the same. Heaven was on earth, and the things we kept in our houses were one with our dreams. Those were the happy, happy days when everything we held in our hands—our tools, our cups, our daggers, our pens—was but an extension of our souls. A poet could say *tree* and everyone who heard him would conjure up the same perfect tree— could see the word and the tree it signified, and the garden the tree signified, and the life the garden signified—without wasting any time on counting the leaves and branches. For words were so close to the things they described that, on mornings when the mist swept down from the mountains into the ghost villages below, poetry mixed with life and words with the objects they signified. No one waking up on misty mornings could tell their dreams apart from reality, or poems apart from life, or names apart from people. No one ever asked if a story was real, because stories were as real as the lives they described. They lived their dreams and interpreted their lives. Those were the days when faces, like everything else in the world, were so laden with meaning that even the illiterate—even the man who could not tell an alpha from a piece of fruit, an *a* from a hat, or an *alif* from a stick— could read them with ease.

To evoke those happy, distant, timeless days, the poet described an orange sun hanging motionless in the evening sky, and galleons standing still on oceans that glinted ash and glass, surging forward as their sails filled with a wind that never came, and as Galip read of white mosques and whiter minarets rising over that sea, each one a shimmering mirage but also everlasting, he realized that the teachings of the

Hurufis, secret since the seventeenth century, had embraced all of Istanbul. For once upon a time, storks and albatrosses and simurghs and phoenixes had risen from the white three-tiered minarets to fly off into the horizon, only to stop over the domes of Istanbul to sway in the sky for centuries, and a man could wander aimlessly about the streets of Istanbul without once crossing another traveler's path at right angles but everywhere enjoying the dizzy diversions of a holiday in eternity. When these journeys came to an end, and the traveler took out a map to trace his path with his finger, he could see his own face in the picture that stared back at him, and on that face the letters that revealed to him the mystery of life; on warm moonlit summer nights, when those same travelers dipped buckets into wells, they pulled out not just ice-cold water but pailfuls of mysterious signs and stars; and they would stay up all night long, reciting verses that illuminated the meaning of signs and the signs of meaning—and as he read all this, Galip became more and more certain of two things: the golden age of Hurufism had taken place in Istanbul, and his own golden age with Rüya was gone, never to return.

He opened a book of verse that had been gnawed around the edges by mice; he leafed through its damp and fragrant pages, admiring the bright greens and turquoises of the mildew flowering in their corners; and when he reached the last page he found a note directing those seeking more detailed information to a particular pamphlet published in the town of Horasan, near the city of Erzurum. On the last page of said pamphlet, between the last lines of a poem and the book's identifying details—the publisher's and printer's addresses, the dates of publication and printing—the typesetter had inserted a long and ungrammatical sentence directing interested readers to the seventh volume in the same series; *The Mystery of the Letters and the Loss of Mystery* and its author, F. M. Üçüncü, had, it said, been roundly praised by the Istanbul journalist Selim Kaçmaz.

Dizzy from lack of sleep, his mind swirling with word games and dreams of Rüya, Galip thought back to the early years of Celâl's career, when his interest in word games had not extended beyond the secret messages he sent to friends, colleagues, relatives, and lovers. He rummaged furiously through the teetering mountains of paper. After an exhaustive search, he went back halfheartedly to one of the first boxes, in which Celâl had filed his clippings from the sixties, and there it was—but by now it was long past midnight, and the eerie silence that had fallen over the street outside spoke to him of curfews, military coups, and the death of hope.

As is so often the case with "works" whose publications are announced too soon, *The Mystery of the Letters and the Loss of Mystery* had not come out at the advertised time; it was not until 1962 that the 200-page book was finally published—and not in Horasan but in Gördes, a town in which Galip would not have expected to find a publishing house. On its yellowing cover was a dark picture printed from a crude plate in bad ink: a road lined with chestnut trees, vanishing into the horizon. But behind every tree were letters, gruesome, bloodcurdling letters.

On first inspection, the book resembled something that an idealistic military officer might write: "Two hundred years on: Why have we still not caught up with the West? How can we foster progress?" It began with the sort of dedication that you'd expect to see in a book printed in a remote Anatolian village at the author's expense. "O War College Cadet! It is you who will save our country!" But as Galip began to rifle through its pages, he soon saw it was another type of book altogether. He rose from his chair, walked over to Celâl's desk, and, propping his elbows on either side of the book, began to read it very carefully.

The Mystery of the Letters and the Loss of Mystery had three sections, two of which appeared in the title. The first, *The Mystery of the Letters*, began with an account of the life of Fazlallah, the founder of the Hurufis. F. M. Üçüncü, had given the story a secular slant, downplaying Fazlallah's Sufi principles and his mystical writings and describing him instead as an intellectual, a philosopher, a linguist, and a mathematician. Yes, he might also have been a prophet, a Messiah, martyr of Islam, a holy man, a saint, but he was first and foremost a thinker, a genius: at the same time he was "unique to us." So to do as some Western Orientalists had done—to describe him as a pantheist or as a thinker influenced by Plotinus, Pythagoras, and the Kabbalah—was to smother Fazlallah under the Western traditions he had opposed so vehemently throughout his life. For their Fazlallah was a pure man of the East.

According to F. M. Üçüncü, the world was divided into two opposing halves; the East and the West were as different from each other as good and evil, white and black, the angels and the devils. The fantasies of idle dreamers notwithstanding, the chances of these two worlds living peacefully together were nil. One or the other always had the upper hand; if one was the master, the other was its slave. They were, and had always been, warring twins, as his brief survey of recent millennia made abundantly clear. He began with Alexander cutting the Gordian knot (or as the author described it, "the cypher"); he then moved on to the Crusades, and the book Haroun al-Rashid had sent to Charlemagne, featuring a magic clock covered with letters and numbers with double meanings, and Hannibal's passage across the Alps and the Islamic victories in Andalusia (here he spent a whole page counting the columns in the Córdoba mosque); moving on to Mehmet the Conqueror's triumphant entry into Constantinople, he declared this same sultan to be a Hurufi; he finished with the collapse of the Khazars and the Ottoman defeats at Doppio (or White Castle, as it was also known) and Venice.

According to F. M. Üçüncü, all these great historical events illustrated a truth to which Fazlallah had made frequent veiled allusions in his writing. It was not chance that determined which world had the upper hand or how long its dominance lasted, it was logic. In "any given historical period," the winning side was the one that succeeded in seeing the world as a mysterious place awash with secrets and double meanings. Whereas the side that saw the world as a simple place, devoid of mystery and ambiguity, was doomed to defeat and its inevitable consequence, slavery.

In the second section of his book, F. M. Üçüncü offered up a detailed analysis of the loss of mystery. In his view, there existed in both Eastern and Western traditions the idea of a center hidden from the world: the idea in ancient Greek philosophy, the Deity in Neoplatonic Christianity, the Hindu's Nirvana, Attar's simurgh, Rumi's beloved, the Hurufi's secret treasure, Kant's noumenon, the detective novel's culprit. In F. M. Üçüncü's view, a civilization that lost its notion of such a center could not help but go out of kilter.

There followed a cryptic passage in which F. M. Üçüncü purported to explain why Rumi had been obliged to have his beloved Shams murdered, why he then had to travel to Damascus to protect the mystery he had "established" with Shams's death, why he had been unable to sustain his "secret" thought during his long days spent searching the city, and why, whenever he felt his mind spinning out of control, he had stopped at certain places along the way to rediscover his center. Galip found the passage impossible to follow. The author went on to suggest two ways of reestablishing the mystery that had been lost: one was to commit the perfect murder, and the other was to vanish without a trace.

F. M. Üçüncü now moved on to the central concern of all Hurufis: the relationship between letters and faces. Following the same line of argument that Fazlallah set out in *The Book of Eternal Life*, he explained that God, though his own face was hidden, manifested himself in human faces; after subjecting the lines common to all faces to detailed analysis, he demonstrated the ways in which these were reflected in the Arabic alphabet. After an overly long and rather childish discussion of various lines from the greatest Hurufi poets—Nesimi, Rafi, Misali, Ruhi of Baghdad, and Gül Baba—he offered up a formula: In times of happiness and victory, our faces were full of meaning, as indeed was the world in which we lived. This was thanks to the Hurufis, for it was the Hurufis who could see the mystery in the world and the letters in our faces. But now Hurufism had vanished from the earth and the world had lost its mystery, just as our faces had lost their letters. Our faces had emptied of all meaning, and with it, the art of reading faces; our eyebrows, our eyes, our noses, our gazes, our expressions, our faces were blank. Reading this, Galip suddenly wanted to stand up and go look at himself in the mirror, but he continued reading, as carefully as he could.

There was a link between the emptiness of faces and the dark art of photography—as anyone looking into the faces of Turkish, Arab, and Indian movie stars could see, for their strange topography called to mind the dark side of the moon. It was because our faces were empty that the huddled masses roamed the streets of Istanbul, Damascus, and Cairo like moaning ghosts at midnight—the men all wearing the same frowns and mustaches, the women all wearing the same head scarves, and all of them, all of them, staring at the ground. There was only one way forward, and that was to vanquish this emptiness, give new meaning to our faces, by devising a new system that linked the lines in faces to the letters in the Latin alphabet. In the last line of the second section, the author promised that in the book's final section he would do just that.

By now Galip had grown to like F. M. Üçüncü, with his penchant for words with double meanings and his childish love of word games. There was something about him that reminded him of Celâl.

Chapter Twenty-seven

A Very Long Chess Game

*Haroun al-Rashid would at times go around Baghdad in
disguise, wishing to find out what his subjects thought about him
and his rule. So, yet another night. . . .*

—The Thousand and One Nights

There is a dark moment in recent history that some call "the road
to democracy," and a letter shedding light on the mysteries at its
center fell into the hands of a reader who wishes to keep his identity
secret, while also asking (and with good reason) that not a word be said
about the strange chain of coincidence, compulsion, and betrayal that
brought said letter into his possession. The letter's author is none other
than the dictator who once presided over us, and the letter itself seems
to be addressed to a son or a daughter residing abroad; what you see
below is an exact replica of the original, for I have made no effort to
water down the pasha-like grandiosity of its style.

"It was exactly six weeks ago, on an August night, and it was so suf-
focatingly hot in the room where the Founder of the Republic had
taken his last breath that one could almost imagine that time had
stopped—and not just the famous golden ormulu clock whose hands
had remained at five minutes past nine since the moment of his
death—do you remember how it frightened your dear departed
mother, and how, seeing her fright, you were driven to laugh? No, it
was so hot on that August night that one could easily imagine that all
the clocks in Dolmabahçe Palace, all the clocks in Istanbul, had
groaned to a halt, arresting all movement, arresting even our thoughts.
There was not even the hint of a breeze coming in from the Bosphorus; the curtains stood limp and still; the sentries lined up along the

shore were as still as mannequins—not, it seemed to me, because I had commanded them to do so but because time itself had stopped. The moment had come, I decided, to pursue that plan that had been on my mind for so many years, though I had never before found it in myself to fulfill it; off to my trunk I went to don the peasant clothes I had secreted in its depths. As I slipped unnoticed through the never-used Harem Gate, I tried to bolster up my courage by reminding myself how many other sultans and great leaders had slipped out through this same back gate, and the back gates of all the other great Istanbul palaces—Topkapı, Beylerbey, Yıldız—over the past five hundred years, lost themselves inside the shadows of the night, become one with this great city, and returned to their palaces safe and sound.

"How Istanbul had changed! It seemed that the windows of my bulletproof Chevrolet had shielded me not just from gunfire but from the everyday rhythms of my beloved city. Having breached the palace walls and set out in the direction of Karaköy, I purchased some halvah from a street vendor; it tasted of burnt sugar. Passing coffeehouses that spilled out over the pavement, I exchanged words with the men who were idling at their tables, listening to the radio, playing cards and backgammon. I saw prostitutes sitting in pudding shops waiting for their customers, and children begging outside restaurants, pointing at the kebabs displayed in their windows. I entered into the courtyards of mosques to mingle with the crowds emerging from the evening prayer; venturing into the back streets, I sat down in the gardens of family tea-houses to nibble on roasted sunflower seeds as I sipped my tea. As I walked down one back street paved with enormous cobblestones, I spied a young family returning home from an evening with the neighbors: and oh, if you could see how trustfully the mother—who wore a head scarf—clung to her husband's arm, and how lovingly the father carried his drowsy child on his shoulders. Tears rolled from my eyes.

"But no, it was not my fellow citizens' joys and miseries that moved me; what moved me—even as I savored the night of freedom for which I had longed for so long—was to see them living their real lives, however humble, for it rekindled the dread and misery I'd felt so often in my dreams, upon leaving reality far behind. I struggled to deliver myself from my fears by taking in the sights of the city. But as I looked into the display windows of the pastry shops, as I watched the crowds spilling from a city ferry just returned from its last journey of the evening, as the last wisps of smoke rose from its handsome funnel, I could not help myself, no, I could not stop myself from shedding more tears.

"Very soon now the curfew I had imposed on the city would come into effect. Longing to partake of the cool of the sea on my way home, I approached a boatman in Eminönü; handing him fifty kuruş, I asked him to row me to the other side of the Golden Horn and drop me off in Karaköy or Kabataş. 'What's wrong with you, man?' he cried. 'Did you eat your brain with your bread and cheese? Don't you know that our Pasha President goes out in his launch at this time every night, arresting anyone he finds along the way and throwing them into the dungeon?' Reaching through the darkness and handing him a clutch of the pink banknotes that bore my likeness (I was well aware of the rumors that my enemies, enraged that this should be so, had been circulating since their first appearance) I said, 'If we go out in your rowboat anyway, would you be so kind as to point out the Pasha President's launch?' 'Crawl under the tarpaulin, then,' he said, gesturing at the prow of the rowboat with the hand clutching the cash, 'and don't move a muscle!' Then he added, 'May God protect us!' and began to row.

"The sea was so dark that I cannot tell you where we went—it could have been the Bosphorus, or the Marmara, or the Golden Horn. The sea was still, and as silent as the black shadow that was the city. As I lay under the tarpaulin, I caught the tiniest whiff of mist rising from its surface. As the sound of a distant speedboat reached us, the boatman whispered, 'Here he comes! Same as always! Right on time!' Once we were safely concealed behind the mussel-encrusted barges of the port, I was unable to take my eyes off the searchlight moving left and right across the water, mercilessly probing every quarter of the city and every inch of the sea, penetrating the darkest recesses of the mosques and buildings that lined the shore. Then I watched the slow approach of the great white vessel itself. Standing to attention along the railing was a row of bodyguards, each wearing a life jacket and holding a gun; above them, on the captain's bridge, I could see a small crowd of passengers, and there, on the top deck, was the Pasha President Imposter! It was difficult for me to make him out in the half-light, but despite the mist and the shadows I could see that he was wearing my clothes. I asked the boatman to follow him, but in vain. Reminding me that the curfew was soon to begin, he dropped me off in Kabataş. I walked back to the palace through the city's dark and deserted streets.

"I spent the rest of the night thinking about him—my look-alike, the Imposter—but not because I was curious to know who he was and what he was doing, roaming the city's seas; I thought about him because this allowed me to think about myself. The following morning I instructed the generals of the martial law command to put the curfew back an hour, so that I would have more time to follow him: they broadcast an announcement to this effect immediately after my address to the nation. I then ordered that a number of detainees be set free, thus giving the impression that a relaxation of martial law was imminent; in no time at all, they were walking free.

"Was Istanbul in higher spirits the next night? No! This is proof that the thick cloak of melancholy sitting over our people is not, as my superficial enemies claim, a by-product of political oppression; its source is far deeper, far more hopeless. That next night, they were still smoking and drinking, still eating the same ice cream and roasted sunflower seeds, and as they sat in their coffeehouses listening to me reduce the curfew, they seemed as drowsy and as melancholy as ever—but at the same time, how real they were! As I walked among them, I felt as sad as a sleepwalker who knows himself to be barred forever from the waking world. For some reason, the boatman was waiting for me in Eminönü. We set out at once.

"Tonight there was a wind and the sea was rough; perhaps the Pasha President had seen some sign alerting him to trouble, for he kept us waiting. As we hid ourselves behind another barge to watch the motor launch pass in front of Kabataş, I took a good long look at the Pasha Imposter, and he seemed to me to be a creature of great beauty; and he was, if you can put the two words together, as real as he was beautiful; could this be possible? As he stood alone on the top deck—for again, the other passengers were huddled on the bridge below—his eyes seemed like searchlights, scanning the city and its people and history itself. What did he see?

"I pressed a roll of banknotes into the boatman's hands, and he went back to his oars. After rolling our way over the waves, we caught up with the launch near the boatyards of Kasımpaşa, but we were only able to observe them from a distance. They were stepping into a fleet of black and dark blue limousines, but among them was my very own Chevrolet. The boatman warned me that time was running out. The curfew was soon to begin.

"After rolling in the waves for so long, I had a hard time finding my balance once I was back on shore but, as I was soon to discover, this was not what made my surroundings so surreal. For it was very late by now, as the boatman had warned, and the city was deserted, its avenues emptied by the curfew I myself had imposed, and as I made my way back to the palace, overwhelmed by the otherworldly pallor of the streets through which I walked, I was visited by an apparition that I had heretofore assumed to belong only to the world I visited in my dreams. The avenue from Fındıklı to Dolmabahçe was deserted, but for the packs of roaming dogs and the corn vendor who was pushing his cart twenty paces ahead of me and could not put one foot in front of the other without turning back to look at me. I could tell from his expression that he feared me and was running away from me, and I longed to tell him that he should be worrying instead about that thing lurking behind the chestnut trees that lined the avenue. But—as in a dream—I couldn't open my mouth to tell him so, and—as in a dream—my unwilled silence frightened me, or perhaps I was too frightened to speak. The faster I walked, and the more I tried to distance myself from the frightening thing moving slowly through the shadows, the more frightened the corn seller became too, and the faster he walked; though I had no idea what this thing was, I knew one thing for certain—and this was what I found most frightening: it was not a dream.

"The next morning, not wishing to subject myself to such horrors again, I pushed the curfew back even more and released another group of detainees. I didn't bother to make a new announcement; instead, they used one of my old speeches.

"Armed as I was with the wisdom only age can bring, I knew I would find the city unchanged that evening, and I wasn't wrong: A few open-air theaters had extended their hours, but that was all. The hands of the cotton candy vendors were still the same shade of pink; and though they had not been so brash as to venture into the streets without their guides, the faces of Western tourists were just as white.

"I found my boatman waiting for me in the usual place. I can say the same of the Pasha President. We were not far from shore when we found him. The sea was as calm as it had been on the first night, but without that hint of mist. In the mirror that was the dark sea, there shimmered the lights and minarets of the city, and I could just make out the shape of the Imposter standing, as before, on the deck above the bridge. He was real. Ablaze with light as the city was, he could see us as well as we could see him.

"We began rowing toward him, catching up with him at the Kasım-paşa docks. I quietly stepped ashore, only to have the Pasha's men—who looked more like nightclub bouncers than soldiers—spring from the shadows to grab me by the arms. What was I doing here at this time of night? In a shaky voice I reminded them that the curfew had not yet begun; I was a poor unfortunate peasant staying in a Sirkeci hotel; I'd just wanted to go out on the Bosphorus in a rowboat before going home to my village. I'd heard nothing of the Pasha's curfew. But when the Pasha President came forward with his men, the terrified boatman confessed everything. Though he was in civilian clothes this evening, the Pasha looked more like me than ever, and I looked more like a peasant. After giving us another hearing, he issued his orders: The boatman was free to leave, and I was to go with him.

"Before I knew it, the Pasha and I were sitting alone in the back of the bulletproof Chevrolet and leaving the harbor. The soundproof glass partition between us and the driver—a feature I did not have in my own Chevrolet—made it possible for us to speak in perfect privacy.

"'We've both been looking forward to this day for years!' said the Pasha, in a voice that didn't sound to me like mine at all. 'Though I've known it all along, and you have not. But neither of us could have known that we'd meet under these circumstances.'

"And so he launched into his story, the fatigue in his voice fired by a waning obsession, as if his excitement at finally being able to do so was muted by the peace he felt at knowing the story was soon to reach its end. Apparently, we'd been in the same class at the War College. We'd taken the same classes, he informed me, with the same teachers. We would go out on the same training exercises on the same cold winter nights; in the hottest days of summer we would line up in front of the taps in our stone barracks and wait for the water to trickle out; when we were granted leave, we would set out together for the streets of our beloved Istanbul. That was when he had his first inkling that things would turn out as they had, though of course he could not have known exactly how it would come to pass.

"For he had known even then—even as we secretly competed to get the best grade in mathematics, to get perfect marks in target practice, to become the most popular cadet in the college, with the highest average—that I would know more success in life: I would be the one who ended up living in the palace surrounded by the clocks that frightened your mother so because they were stopped at five past nine. I reminded him that the competition between us must have been very secret indeed, as I did not remember being in competition with a fellow cadet at the War College—you will know what I think about that sort of thing, from the lectures I gave you so often when you were children—and neither did I remember him as a friend. He was not at all surprised. He had been quick to realize that my self-confidence was too great for me to notice my competitor; my achievements had already put me far ahead of all my peers, and even those cadets who were ahead of me in years, not to mention the lieutenants and captains that were meant to be our superiors; not wishing to be my imitation, my second-class shadow, he had withdrawn from the competition altogether. There was no future in shadows; he wanted to be 'real.' As he told me all this, I gazed through the windows as the streets emptied of people, though I paused from time to time to examine the Chevrolet; which I was slowly coming to see was not in fact the exact replica of my own; and when I looked at our four legs, stretched out motionless in front of us, and our four feet, lined up along the floor, I could not help but notice they were identical.

"After much time had passed, he told me that chance had played no part in our drama. You didn't have to be an oracle to predict that, forty years after we went out into the world, our destitute nation would bow to yet another dictator and hand over the entire city of Istanbul, or that this dictator would turn out to be a career soldier about our age, and neither had it been difficult to predict that this dictator soldier would turn out to be me. So before we had even left the War College, he had mapped out the future, simply by extending the logic of what he already knew. He had two choices: He could spend his life wavering

between authenticity and falseness, between the damning present and
the dreams of glory past and future—like everyone else in the ghostly
city over which I would preside as President Pasha; or he could give his
life to finding a new way of becoming real. Having chosen the latter,
his first step was to commit a crime that was great enough to get him
expelled from the War College but not so great as to land him in
prison, and it was while he was telling me how he'd donned the uniform of the War College commander, gone out to inspect the night
guard, and succeeded in being caught red-handed that I finally remembered this lackluster cadet. He'd gone straight into business after his
expulsion. 'Everyone knows that in a poor country like ours, it's the
easiest thing in the world to get rich!' he said proudly. It might sound
paradoxical, but if we were a poor country, it was because we didn't
encourage the entrepreneurial spirit; instead, we taught our people to
accept their lot. After a silence, he added that I was the one who had
taught him how to be authentic. 'You!' he said, talking to me as if I
were his inferior. 'After all these years, I can finally see that you are less
real than I am. You poor peasant, you!'

"There followed a very long silence. How silly I felt as I sat there in
the 'authentic' Kayseri peasant garb that my assistant had procured for
me—no, it was worse than that. I felt unreal, as if I had been dragged
against my will into a dream. It was during this same silence that I realized where this dream came from; it rose out of the dark Istanbul
scenes rolling past the windows like a slow-motion film—the empty
streets and pavements, the vacant lots—for my curfew had begun by
now and everyone had fled, leaving the city to its ghosts.

"By now I knew that the thing my proud classmate had demonstrated to me was none other than the dream city I had myself created.
The Chevrolet moved on, taking us past wooden houses dwarfed and
sometimes even erased by the giant cypresses hanging over them, and
through neighborhoods so poor they had spilled into their cemeteries,
arriving finally at the threshold of our dreams. We traveled down cobblestone streets that had been abandoned to their packs of warring
dogs and up hard narrow lanes whose sallow streetlamps cast more
shadows on the ground than light. We passed things I had heretofore
seen only in my dreams—crumbling walls, broken chimneys, fountains
that had gone dry, sleepy mosques that suddenly looked more like

sleeping giants and left me trembling with fear and thinking that it was not just in the palace that time had stopped but in all of Istanbul—and as we passed through our great public squares with their empty pools, forgotten statues, and broken clocks, I paid no attention to my imitator as he bragged about his towering successes in the world of business, nor did I listen to the stories he told me because they echoed the situation in which we now found ourselves. (These included a story about an old man who caught his wife with her lover, and the story from *The Thousand and One Nights* in which Haroun al-Rashid disappears.) As daylight approached, the avenue that bears my last name—and yours—had, like all the other avenues, streets, and squares of the city, drained off all reality, become extensions of a dream.

"It was while my vainglorious imitator was telling me of the dream Rumi calls "The Contest between the Two Painters" that I drafted the proclamation that would be broadcast to the nation later that day, bringing to an end not just the curfew but lifting martial law—it was, of course, this same proclamation that would prompt our Western friends to interrogate you behind closed doors. As my sleepless night drew to a close, as I lay tossing and turning in my bed, I imagined myself in a world where empty squares would again swarm with happy crowds, and the frozen hands of broken clocks would again begin to move, and the people sitting in coffeehouses nibbling on roasted seeds, the crowds walking across bridges and milling at the entrances of movie theaters, would embark on new lives in which they were more real than their ghosts and their dreams. Have my dreams come true? Is our Istanbul finally graced with a landscape in which I can be real? I have no answers, though I hear from my aides that freedom has as always—afforded my enemies more opportunities than it has the world's dreamers. Already they're getting organized, gathering in teahouses, in hotel rooms, and under bridges, wherever they meet, plotting our downfall; already the night is teeming with opportunists who deface our walls with slogans that no one can ever hope to decipher, but none of this is important: The days are over when a sultan or a pasha can expect to wander among his people in disguise; it is a thing we can expect to encounter only in the world of books.

"It just so happens I came across this story in one such book only recently. In his *History of the Ottoman Empire*, Hammer writes of Yavuz

Sultan Selim visiting Tabriz as a young prince and venturing out into its streets disguised as a dervish. After Prince Selim gained a reputation as a fine chess player, Shah İsmail, also an aficionado of the game, called him to the palace. At the end of a very long game, Prince Selim beat the Shah of Persia. It was only after the Battle of Chalderon, when Selim, now the Ottoman sultan, took the city of Tabriz, that the Shah finally realized who it was who had beat him at chess so many years before; I can't help but ask myself if he was still able, so many years later, to remember all the moves in that game. For my conceited pretender must surely remember all the moves in our own game. By the way, my subscription to the chess journal, *King and Pawn*, seems to have run out; they stopped sending it months ago; I'll be transferring some money to your account at the embassy. When it arrives, would you please renew my subscription."

Chapter Twenty-eight

The Discovery of Mystery

. . . the section you are reading interprets the text of your face.
—Niyazi of Egypt

B efore he launched into the third section of *The Mystery of the Letters and the Loss of Mystery*, Galip went to make himself a cup of strong coffee. Hoping it might help him stay awake, he went into the bathroom and threw cold water on his face, but he was able to hold himself back so he did not look at his face in the mirror. When he returned with his coffee to sit down again at Celâl's desk, he felt as excited as a lycée student on the verge of solving an impossibly difficult math problem.

According to F. M. Üçüncü, it was on Turkish soil that the Messiah who would become the savior of all the East would make His appearance, and it therefore followed that, in preparation for that day, if they were to recover the lost mystery, His future followers should begin by establishing the correspondences between faces and the new Latin alphabet that Turkey adapted in 1928. To this end—and drawing from forgotten Hurufi pamphlets, Bektaşi poems, Anatolian folk art, the ghostly ruins of pristine Hurufi villages, the figures etched on the walls of dervish lodges and pashas' mansions, and thousands of calligraphic inscriptions—he demonstrated the "values" accorded to various sounds when they were translated from Arabic and Persian into Turkish, after which he went on to show, with a terrifying precision, where each individual letter could be found on human faces. As he gazed at the faces in the pictures on the pages that followed—faces whose meanings were so clear that you could read them easily, the author claimed, even if you couldn't see any Latin letters in them—Galip felt the same dread chill he had felt when looking through the photographs he had pulled from Celâl's cabinet. The captions under these badly reproduced photographs identified the faces as belonging to Fazlallah, his two successors, "a portrait of Rumi copied from a miniature," and "our Olympic champion wrestler" Hamit Kaplan, but when he turned a page to find a picture of Celâl from the late fifties, his heart missed a beat. Like the others, it was marked up with letters, each indicated by an arrow. F. M. Üçüncü had located a U on Celâl's nose, Z's on his eyes, and a sideways H that covered his entire face. Flipping through the pages that followed, Galip found—mixed in with the portraits of various Hurufi sheikhs and famous imams who had died and journeyed into the other world, only to return to this one—photographs of various Hollywood stars (Greta Garbo, Humphrey Bogart, Edward G. Robinson, and Bette Davis) whose faces were laden with "exceptional meaning"; there were pictures, too, of famous executioners and various Beyoğlu gangsters whose exploits Celâl had related during the early years of his career. The author went on to say that every letter found on every face carried a double meaning: the plain and self-evident meaning carried by the letter itself and the secret meaning carried by the face.

If every letter in every face had a hidden meaning, and if each signified a concept, it followed that every word composed of those letters must also carry a second, hidden meaning, or so F. M. Üçüncü went on to claim. The same could be said of sentences and paragraphs—in short, all written texts carried second, hidden meanings. But if one bore in mind that these meanings could also be expressed in other sentences or other words—other letters, finally—one could, "through interpretation," glean a third meaning from the second, and a fourth from the third, ad infinitum—so there were, in fact, an infinite number of possible interpretations of any given text. It was like an unending maze of city streets, with each street leading to another: maps resembling human faces. So a reader who set out to solve the mystery in his own way, following his own logic, was no different from a traveler who finds the mystery of a city slowly unfurling before him as he wanders through streets on that map: The more he discovers, the more the mystery spreads; the more the mystery spreads, the more is revealed and the more clearly he sees the mystery in the streets he himself has chosen, the roads he's walked down and the alleys he's walked up; for the mystery resides in his own journey, his own life. It would be at that very moment when the woeful reader, weakened by the pull of the story, sank so deep into it as to lose his bearings, that our long-awaited savior, the Messiah some dared only name as He, would finally manifest Himself. It would be here—in the thick of life, in the maze that was the text, at the point where faces merged with maps—that the traveler (like all those who have embarked on the Sufi path before him) would at last receive the Mehdi's long-awaited signal and, armed with his letter keys and his ciphers, begin to find his way. All he had to do, said F. M. Üçüncü with childish joy, was follow the signposts. It was simply, he said, a question of seeing the signs the Mehdi has left us, not just in the real world but in texts.

To solve this, the ultimate puzzle, F. M. Üçüncü believed it was incumbent upon us to put ourselves in the Mehdi's shoes from this day onward and foresee what He might do; we had to think like chess players, in other word, and anticipate His next moves. After inviting his readers to join the game, he asked them to imagine a man who could reach a wide audience at any time, under any circumstances. "For example," he added quickly, "we might imagine a columnist." A columnist read by hundreds of thousands of people every day, in every corner of the country, on every ferry, bus, and shared taxi and in every barbershop, and every corner of every coffeehouse, would, he said, be an excellent conduit for the propagation of information about the secret signs by which the Messiah would show the way. For those unaware of the mystery, his columns would carry only a single meaning, the surface meaning. But those awaiting the Messiah, those who knew something of ciphers and secret formulas, would glean a second meaning, the text's hidden message, from the letters. So, for example, if the Messiah inserted into the text a phrase like "these were my thoughts as I observed myself from the outside"—leaving the ordinary reader perplexed by the odd turn of phrase—those readers who were conversant with the mystery of letters would immediately know that the phrase contained the secret message for which they had been waiting; armed with their ciphers, they would embrace the great adventure that awaited them and set off down the path that would lead them to a bright new life.

So—as he had implied by entitling the third section of his book "The Discovery of Mystery"—it was not enough to recover the *idea* of mystery, though the loss of this idea was what had turned the East into the slave of the West; the urgent task was to discover the sentences that the Messiah had concealed in His texts.

F. M. Üçüncü now turned to Edgar Allan Poe's essay, "A Few Words on Secret Writing," paying particular attention to the cipher formulas proposed therein; the reshuffling of the alphabet was, he said, the method closest to the one used by the Sufi mystic al-Hallaj; having asserted that the Messiah was sure to use the same code, he brought his book to an abrupt close with a passage that summed up all that had come before: The starting point for all ciphers and formulas must always be the letters to be found on each traveler's face. No one could embark on the great journey, and no dreamer could begin to create a new world, without first seeing the letters in his own face. The reader was to see the humble book he now held in his hands as a guide that might help him find the letters in all human faces. It was, however, no more than an introduction to the study of the ciphers and formulas that would lead him to the heart of the mystery. For this was the preserve of the Messiah, who was soon to rise like the sun to suffuse us with His divine light—it was He and only He who could insert them into the text.

But now Galip saw something in that last sentence that made him throw down the book: for the Arabic word for *sun* was *shams*, and Shams was Rumi's murdered lover. Racing into the bathroom to look at his face in the mirror, gripped by a fearful thought that had been lurking in the back of his mind for some time, he cried out, "Celâl read the meaning in my face ages ago!" He felt doomed, marked, exposed—as guilty as a child who's just done something wrong, or become someone else, or stumbled onto someone else's secret—for this was the end of the road, and there was no turning back, no escape from the catastrophe he saw ahead. "From now on, I really am someone else!" Galip told himself, and though there was something childish in this thought, he knew he had embarked on a journey from which there would be no return.

It was twelve minutes past three, and the city was buried in the silence that only the early hours of the morning can bring, though it was more an intimation of silence, because there was still the faint whir of a nearby furnace or the distant generator of a ship passing through the Bosphorus. Though he had known for some time what he now had to do, he managed to restrain himself for just a little longer.

A thought he had been holding at bay for three days came back into his mind: Unless Celâl had sent something in, tomorrow's column would be a blank space. Never once in all these years had he let this happen, and Galip could not even bear to think of it, for if a new column failed to appear in tomorrow's paper, he would no longer be able to tell himself that Celâl and Rüya were hiding somewhere in the city, laughing and chatting and waiting for him to find them. Rifling through the old columns he had taken at random from the cabinet, he thought, I could have written any of these! After all, he had the recipe—not the recipe that old columnist had given him three days earlier, during his visit to the newspaper but something else. *I've read everything you've ever written, I know everything about you, read everything there is to know.* Though he was speaking to himself, he nearly said the last words out loud. He picked up another old column at random and read that too. But it could hardly be called reading, because even as he heard the words in his head, he was looking for the second meanings that might be lurking inside them, and the better he grasped these second meanings, the closer he felt to Celâl. For what did it mean to read a text if it did not mean entering into the garden of its author's memory?

He was ready now to go back to the mirror and read the letters in his face. He went back into the bathroom and gazed into the mirror. After that, things happened very fast.

Much later—months later—whenever Galip sat down at this same desk, surrounded by the silent objects that so soothingly replicated the world he'd known thirty years before, he would recall the moment when he had first looked into the mirror and the same word would come into his mind: terror. Yet when he had rushed to the mirror that day, to stare at his reflection, he had felt no fear. What he felt instead was an emptiness—as if something he could no longer remember was missing, as if he'd lost even the capacity to feel. Because as he stood there under the naked lightbulb, he studied his face with the cold interest he might give the photograph of a prime minister or a movie star in a newspaper. No longer did he feel he was on the verge of solving a mystery or cracking a secret code that had been eluding him for days; he looked into his face as if it were a faded overcoat, a dreary old umbrella, a winter morning so drab and ordinary that nothing struck the eye. Later on, when his mind went back to that moment, he would think, I was so used to living with myself back then that I was hardly aware of my own face. But his indifference was short-lived. Because when he started to look at the face in the mirror in the way he'd looked at the faces in the photographs and pictures he'd retrieved from Celâl's cabinet, letters began to take shape in its shadows.

It seemed to him that his face was a sheet of paper covered with writing, an inscription riddled with secret signs for other faces, other eyes; odd as this sensation was, he did not dwell on it for long, because now he could see distinct letters rising from the shadows between his eyes and his eyebrows. Before long, they were so clear that he could hardly believe he'd never noticed them before. It had, of course, occurred to him that they might be no more than afterimages—optical illusions produced by the long hours he'd spent looking at the thousands of pictures Celâl had marked with letters—or perhaps this was just the next stage in a game of illusions he had been tricked into taking too seriously. But when he took his eyes off the mirror, only to glance back a moment later, the letters were still there; they didn't come and go like the figures-and-ground pictures in the magazines he'd so loved as a child—first all you see are the branches of a tree but then you look again and see the thief hiding among them—the letters were firmly planted in the same landscape he gazed upon so absentmindedly every morning as he shaved—in his eyes, below his eyebrows, on his nose—where all Hurufis saw an *alif*, on the round plane they called the "facial circle." Not to read these letters would be more difficult than reading them. But Galip tried to do just that—hoping to liberate himself of this loathsome mask, he summoned up all the disparaging thoughts he'd accumulated from his long days of studying Hurufi art and literature, tried to breathe new life into his old skepticism, to convince himself that it was childish and arbitrary nonsense even to entertain the notion that you could read letters in faces—but the letters in the lines and curves of his own face were so emphatic, so clear to the naked eye, that he was unable to pull away from the mirror.

That was when the terror overtook him. But it had all happened very quickly—first the letters had appeared and then, almost in the same instant, the words those letters signified—so that when he thought about it later, he was unable to decide if the terror had come from seeing his face transformed into a mask swarming with signs or from reading the dreadful message that the letters conveyed. Later, when he picked up a pen and tried to write this message down—tried to convey this truth that he had known for so many years but struggled to forget, had remembered but never acknowledged, studied but never accepted—he would express it in entirely different words. But that morning, when he first read the letters in his face, it seemed to him that the truth couldn't have been plainer, for he already knew the thing he saw written on his face; he could not pretend to be surprised. Perhaps the thing he would later call terror came from his surprise that the truth could be so simple, for he was struck with the same awe one might feel upon glancing at a slender tea glass sitting on a table and seeing it as a thing of incredible beauty, while at the same time seeing it as a familiar object of no special interest.

When Galip decided that the thing he had read in his face was not an illusion but the truth, he withdrew from the mirror and went back into the hall. By now the thing he would later call terror had less to do with seeing his face transformed into a mask, a face belonging to someone else, an inscription riddled with signs, than with the thing this inscription signified. Because at the end of the day, the rules of this beautiful game dictated that you could find these same letters in all faces. He was sure of this, and his certainty consoled him, but as he scanned the shelves of the cabinet in the hall, he felt such a deep pain inside him, and he missed Celâl and Rüya so desperately, that he could hardly stay on his feet. It was as if his body and his soul had abandoned him to pay for crimes he'd not committed; as if a secret defeat, an untold misery, had taken over his mind, squeezing out all other thought; as if a sorrowful history happily discarded by everyone around him had been left for him to bear alone.

Later on, when he tried to reconstruct what he had done during the four or five minutes after leaving the mirror—because all this happened in a very short space of time—he would remember the moment when he found himself halfway between the cabinet in the hallway and the window that looked out onto the air shaft; drenched in terror, hardly able to breathe, longing to put a great distance between himself and the dark mirror, with cold beads of sweat forming on his forehead. For a moment he imagined going back to that mirror, tearing this papery mask from his face like a scab from a wound, and being no more able to read the signs and letters on the new face that emerged behind the mask than the ones he'd found on billboards, plastic bags, and the city's tangled streets. To escape his pain, he tried to read another column he'd plucked from the cabinet, but by now he knew everything Celâl had ever written as well as if he'd written it himself. He tried to imagine—as he would do so often in the months and years to come—that he was blind or that his eyes were made of marble, with dark holes instead of pupils, that there was an oven door where his mouth should have been and rusting bolt holes where there should have been nostrils. Every time he thought of his face, he remembered that Celâl had also seen the letters written on it, that Celâl had known all along that one day he would see them too, that Galip had been colluding with him from the very beginning, but he was later unable to be sure if he'd been able to think about it with such clarity only minutes after the fact. He wanted to cry but no tears came; he was still having trouble breathing; a moan of pain rose unwilled from his throat; his hand reached out of its own accord to grasp the handle on the window; he wanted to look at it, at the air shaft, the place where once there had been a well. He felt like a child trying to impersonate someone he didn't even know.

He opened the window and leaned out into the darkness, propped his elbows on the window ledge, pressed his face into the bottomless well: an ugly odor wafted up to him, the stink of a half century of pigeon droppings, discarded belongings, apartment dust, city soot, mud, tar, and hopelessness. This was where people got rid of the things they wanted to forget. He was seized by the urge to throw himself into its bottomless depths too—to plunge into the discarded memories of all those who had once lived here, into the dark hole that Celâl had been constructing so patiently, and for so many years, from the wells and fears and mysteries of old poetry—but all he could do was stare into the abyss like a drunk.

The smell brought back memories of the days he and Rüya had spent in this apartment as children: the innocent child he had once been, the good-natured teenager, the devoted husband, the ordinary citizen teetering on the brink of the unknown—they were all made from this smell. The desire to be with Celâl and Rüya rose so powerfully inside him that he felt like crying out; it was as if he were dreaming, as if half his body had been ripped away from him and dispatched to a dark and distant place, as if his only hope of ever escaping this trap was to kick and shout until someone rescued him. But all he could do was stare into the bottomless darkness, as the damp of the cold snowy night pressed against his face. Only by staring into the dark void could he share the pain he had felt during his days of searching the city, and understand the terror, and see the thing he would later call the mystery of defeat, misery, and ruin—the whole of Celâl's life, the fully furnished trap that Celâl had been so lovingly preparing for him all these years. He stayed there for the longest time, hanging out the window, staring into the air shaft. Only when the bitter cold had eaten into his face and neck did he pull himself back inside and shut the window.

What happened next was clear, well-illuminated, and easy to understand. Later, when he recalled what he had done during the last hours of the night, his every movement seemed logical, necessary, and appropriate, and he remembered, too, that he'd felt calm and in control. He went back into the sitting room and threw himself into a chair. Then he straightened out Celâl's desk, returning the papers, clippings, and photographs to their boxes and the boxes to the cabinet. He tidied up the rest of the apartment—not just the messes he'd made himself during his two-day stay but all the clutter Celâl had left behind too, emptying the ashtrays, washing the cups and glasses, cracking open the windows to air the place out. He washed his face, made himself another cup of strong coffee, transferred Celâl's old Remington to his now clear and tidy desk, and sat down. In the drawer was a ream of the paper Celâl had been using for many years; taking out a clean sheet, he rolled it into the typewriter and immediately began to write.

He wrote for close to two hours without once leaving the desk. Everything was falling into place now; even the smell of fresh paper was invigorating, and the words were pouring out. As his fingers hit the keys, singing their old familiar song, it was clear to him that he'd composed these words in his head a long time ago. Perhaps, from time to time, he had to pause to find the right word, but he let himself be directed by the flow of his thoughts—in Celâl's words, never forcing them.

He began his first column with the words, *I gazed into the mirror and read my face.* He began the second with the words, *I dreamed that I had at last become the person I've always longed to become.* And in the third, he retold famous tales from old Beyoğlu. Each was as effortless as the last, but the longer he wrote, the deeper and more hopeless was the ache in his heart. What he wrote was exactly, he told himself, what Celâl's readers would want and expect. He signed all three pieces with Celâl's own signature; after the years he had spent practicing in the backs of his lycée notebooks, he was not surprised to see how easily he could replicate it.

After daybreak, as the garbage truck, its bins clattering against its sides, made its way down the street below, Galip went back to take a closer look at Celâl's photograph in F. M. Üçüncü's book. On another page he found an uncaptioned photograph of a pale and listless man and decided this must be the book's author. He went back to the author's biography and read it with care, calculating how old F. M. Üçüncü would have been when he was implicated in the failed 1962 military coup. If he had seen Hamit Kaplan at the start of his wrestling career, during his own first assignment in Anatolia—in other words, when he was a lieutenant—that would make him the same age as Celâl. Galip went back to comb through the rows of graduates in the 1944, 1945, and 1946 War College yearbooks. Though he found a number of faces that could be younger versions of the anonymous face in "The Discovery of Mystery," his most notable feature—baldness—would have been concealed by his military cap.

At half past eight, Galip slipped out of the City-of-Hearts Apartments, and as he dashed across the street—his coat flying behind him, his three columns folded up in his jacket pocket—he looked just like a family man rushing off to the office. No one saw him or, if they did, they did not call after him. It was a fine morning, the sky a wintry blue; the pavements were caked with snow, ice, and mud. He darted into a passageway, racing past the Venus Barbershop—these were the people who'd come to shave Grandfather every morning, and in later years Galip had often come here with Celâl—and stopping at the locksmith's while they made a copy of Celâl's key. He bought himself a *Mil-*

liyet from the vendor on the corner. Then he went into the Sütiş pudding shop, where Celâl had often eaten breakfast, and ordered himself fried eggs, clotted cream, honey, and tea. As he ate his breakfast, he read Celâl's column and, as he did, he wondered if the heroes in Rüya's detective novels felt like this when they'd conjured up a meaningful story from a handful of clues. He felt like a detective who had just found the key to a mystery, who would now be using the same key to open new doors.

Today's column was the final piece from the reserve folder Galip had found on Celâl's desk when he'd visited the newspaper the previous Saturday, but Galip did not even try to work out the second meanings in the letters. After he'd finished his breakfast, as he was waiting in the *dolmuş* line, he thought about the man he'd once been and the life this man had led until so very recently: He'd sit in the shared taxi every morning, read the paper, and think about going home in the evening, dream about his wife asleep in their bed. Tears gathered in his eyes.

"So that's all it takes," mused Galip, as the *dolmuş* drove along the Dolmabahçe Palace walls. "If you want to turn your world upside down, all you have to do is somehow convince yourself you might be someone else." The city he saw through the taxi windows was not the Istanbul he'd known all his life but another city whose mystery he'd just unlocked and would later put in writing.

At the newspaper the editors were in a meeting with the department heads. Tapping on the door to Celâl's office, he waited a few moments before stepping inside. Celâl's desk was just as he had found it before; nothing had been moved. Sitting down in Celâl's chair, he quickly searched the desk drawers. Old invitations to launches and openings, various statements from left- and right-wing splinter groups, the same clippings he'd seen on his earlier visit, a few buttons, a tie, a wristwatch, several empty ink bottles, assorted medicines, and a pair of dark glasses he'd somehow missed the time before. . . . He put on the dark glasses and left Celâl's office. As he entered the large editorial room, he caught sight of the old polemicist Neşati bent over his desk. Pulled up right next to it was the chair where the magazine writer had been sitting on his last visit, but this morning the chair was empty. Galip went straight over and sat down. After waiting a few moments, he turned to the old man and asked, "Do you remember me?"

"Of course I do! You're a flower in the garden of my memory too," said Neşati, without lifting his eyes from the page he was reading. "The garden is a memory—whose words are these?"

"Celâl Salik's."

"No, they're Bottfolio's," said the old columnist, as he raised his eyes. "From his classic translation of Ibn Zerhani. In his usual way, Celâl Salik just lifted them. Just like you've lifted Celâl's glasses."

"These glasses belong to me," said Galip.

"Which must mean they make glasses in identical pairs, just like people. Hand them over!"

Galip took off the glasses and passed them to the columnist. After the old man had looked them over, he tried them on, and suddenly he looked just like one of the gangsters whose exploits had so preoccupied Celâl during the fifties: the café-brothel-nightclub owner who had plunged with his Cadillac into the Bosphorus. He turned to Galip with a mysterious smile.

"It's not for nothing that they say it's important to see the world through someone else's eyes from time to time. Because that's really when you can start to understand the mystery of life, not to mention other people's secrets. Can you tell me who said that?"

"F. M. Üçüncü," said Galip.

"He had nothing to do with it. He's the king of idiots, nothing more," said the old man. "A piteous creature, a hopeless wreck. . . . Who gave you his name?"

"Celâl once told me it was one of his favorite pseudonyms. He used it for years."

"Which means that when a man's mind really begins to go, it's not enough for him to deny his own past and repudiate his own writings; no, he has to steal other people's lives and works and claim them as his own. But I can't really imagine our crafty Celâl Bey going quite that senile. He must have had a score to settle, or he wouldn't have told such a bald-faced lie. F. M. Üçüncü was a real-life person. A reader, no less—an army officer who bombarded our office with letters going on twenty-five years ago. After we printed one or two of them—just out of politeness, you understand—he started coming to the office, swaggering around as if he were a member of the permanent staff. Then suddenly he vanished, and no one saw him again for another twenty years. Then only last week he turned up again, as bald as an egg—came right across to see me, said he was an admirer. But he was not in a good way; he kept babbling about signs and omens."

"What signs were those?"

"Come on, you know that already—you must! Didn't Celâl ever mention any of this? *The time is ripe, the omens are there for all to see, so take to the streets,* and so on and so on—every trick in the book. The Day of Judgment. Revolution. The Liberation of the East. You've heard all this before, haven't you?"

"Yes, Celâl and I were talking about it only the other day—and about your connection with it."

"So where's he hiding?"

"I've forgotten."

"The editors are in a meeting just over there," said the old columnist. "They're about to sack your Uncle Celâl because he's still not sent in any new columns. Tell him that they're going to offer me that space on page two—and I'll be turning it down."

"The other day, when we were discussing that military coup you got mixed up in, in the early 1960s, Celâl spoke of you with great affection."

"Lies. He betrayed us, which is why he hates me and everyone else involved in that coup," said the old columnist. Though he was still wearing the dark glasses, he looked less like a Beyoğlu gangster of yesteryear and more like a leader. "He sold us out. Naturally he'd tell you it was the opposite; he'd tell you he was the mastermind, but as always your Uncle Celâl did not get involved until everyone was beginning to believe that our coup would succeed. Before then—while the rest of us were organizing readers' networks the length and breadth of Anatolia—whispering about pyramids, minarets, Cyclopes, mysterious compasses, Freemason's symbols, pictures of lizards, Selçuk domes, and White Russian banknotes with special marks on them—all Celâl did was invite his readers to send in their pictures and add these to his film star collection; you'd have thought he was a child. One day he made up that story about the mannequin museum; another day he started babbling about an eye that followed him down narrow streets in the dead of night. We took all this as meaning he wanted to join us, so we obliged. We thought he would use his column to help our cause; we hoped he might draw in more officers. Fat chance! There were a lot of madmen around in those days, parasites like your friend F. M. Üçüncü; the first thing Celâl did was put the headlock on them. Then—thanks to all his cyphers, formulas, and acrostics—he linked up with another, even worse, band of shady characters. But in his mind these were astonishing achievements, so he would come to us demanding that we give him a place in the cabinet once we'd seized power. To add to his bargaining power, he made large boasts about his links with the last surviving dregs of the old dervish orders, and secret sects still awaiting the Mehdi, and people who claimed to be in touch with the various Ottoman princes still twiddling their fingers in France and Portugal; and if that were not enough, he claimed to have received letters from people who didn't exist—he would promise to bring them in so that we could see for ourselves, but did he ever?—and he told us he'd been visited in his own home by the grandchildren of pashas and sheikhs who had left in his safekeeping their august ancestors' handwritten memoirs and testaments—each and every one bursting with secrets!— and people were always coming to visit him here at the newspaper offices in the middle of the night. Every last one of these people was an invention.

"It was around this time, when this man who could barely string two words of French together started spreading rumors that he was to become foreign minister after the Revolution, that I suggested the time had come to burst a few of his bubbles. These were the days when he was writing endless columns based on what he claimed to be the last living testament of a dark creature from the legendary past: lots of nonsense about prophets, and the Messiah, and the apocalypse, and dark hints about a conspiracy that would, when he exposed it, reveal a truth of great historical consequence. So I sat down and wrote a column in which I set out the facts, quoting from Ibn Zerhani and Bottfolio as needed. And the coward backed down! He immediately broke off from us and joined other factions. His new friends were said to have even closer ties to young officers, and there were rumors that Celâl was so eager to prove to them that the people I'd said he'd invented were real that he would go out after dark in disguise and impersonate his pathetic heroes. One night he turned up at some theater entrance dressed up either as the Messiah or Mehmet the Conqueror, to proclaim to the astonished crowd gathered outside that the time had come for the entire nation to change their clothes and step into new lives; that American movies were as hopeless as Turkish movies; that it was no longer worth our while even to try to imitate them. He thought that if he could turn the moviegoing public against the producers of Yeşilçam Studios, they'd join his cause. Because the 'miserable petty bourgeoisie' he was always mentioning in his columns—the people who lived in those old wooden houses in the city's outlying neighborhoods—they were all waiting for a 'savior,' as was the rest of the city in those days—as they are even today. Then, as now, they sincerely believed that if the army stepped in, the price of bread would go down; that if sinners were tortured, the gates of Heaven would fly open. But because Celâl was greedy for power and willing to go to any lengths to hold people in his thrall, he managed to set the different factions inside the conspiracy against one another, and the coup came to nothing; instead of going to the radio station that night as planned, they rolled right back to their barracks. The result? As you can see for yourself, we're still crawling, still cowering in the shameful shadow of Europe, even if we manage to cast a few votes now and again so we can stand tall in front of foreign news correspondents and claim we are just like them. Isn't this the same as saying we have no hope of salvation? But there is a way out. If that English television crew had asked to speak to me and not Celâl, I could have told them about the really important secret—how the East will continue to be the East for tens of happy thousands of years to come.

"Galip Bey—my son—let me tell you something about this cousin of yours, Celâl Bey: He's a pathetic emotional cripple. To become ourselves there's no need to stuff our wardrobes with wigs, fake beards, and historical costumes like he did. Yes, it's true, Mahmut I did wander the city in disguise some evenings, but do you know what he wore? He replaced his sultan's turban with a fez and took a walking stick—that's all! None of this spending hours on makeup, like Celâl did, and decking himself out in strange gaudy costumes or tattered beggar's rags! Our world is a living whole; it has not fallen apart. Inside this realm there does indeed exist another, but it's not a secret world of phantoms and stage sets, as in the West; no need to pull away the veil, cry *Eureka!* and expose the truth. Our modest realm is everywhere, it has no center; you will find it on no maps. But that, in actual fact, is our secret; and it is very, very hard to comprehend. It would take a huge effort. Tell me, how many intrepid heroes are there out there who know that they themselves are the universe whose mystery they are seeking, and that the universe is he who is seeking the mystery? Only those who have achieved this enlightenment have the right to disguise themselves and become someone else. I share only one sentiment with your Uncle Celâl: I pity those poor film stars of ours who can be neither themselves nor someone else. I feel even greater pity for those compatriots of ours who see themselves in those film stars. These people could have been saved—the entire East could have been saved—had not this Uncle Celâl of yours, this cousin, sold us out for his own gain. But now he's running in fear from his own creation, running away from the entire nation, taking his wardrobe of tricks and strange disguises with him. Tell me, what is he hiding from?"

"You know already," said Galip. "Every day, out there on those streets, there are between ten and fifteen political murders."

"Those aren't political murders, they're crimes of the heart. And besides, if there are pseudo-Sufis out there killing pseudo-Marxists, and pseudo-Marxists killing pseudo-Fascists, what's it to Celâl? No one's interested in him anymore. By going into hiding, he's just drawing attention to himself—even inviting someone to kill him, just to convince us he's important enough to warrant an assassination. In the days of the Democratic Party, there was a nice well-behaved writer who was a bit of a coward; he got into the habit of writing to the press prosecutor under an alias, denouncing himself. He hoped that by doing this, he'd get prosecuted and earn himself a reptutation. Then, as if this weren't enough, he claimed that we were the ones writing the incriminating letters. Do you see what I'm driving at? It's not just his memory Celâl Bey has lost, it's his past—and this was his last link with his country. It's no accident he can no longer write."

"He's the one who sent me here," said Galip. He took the columns out of his pocket. "He asked me come here to drop off his new columns."

"Hand them over, let me take a look."

As the old columnist (still wearing dark glasses) read through the pieces, Galip noticed that the open volume on his desk was an old

Turkish translation of Chateaubriand's *Mémoires d'outre-tombe*. When a tall man emerged from the editor's office, the old writer gestured for him to come over.

"Celâl Bey's latest columns," he said. "Still showing off."

"Send them right downstairs to the typesetters," the tall man said. "We'd been planning to run another old column."

"I'll be the one bringing in his columns for the time being," said Galip.

"Why hasn't he been around?" the tall man asked. "Lots of people have been looking for him."

"Apparently, the two of them have been going out at night in disguise," said the old writer, pointing his nose at Galip. The tall man smiled and turned away, and the old man turned to Galip. "You've been wandering around the ghost streets, haven't you? Seeking out shady deals, strange mysteries, phantoms, people who've been dead for a hundred and twenty years, combing through mosques with broken minarets, ruins, condemned houses, abandoned dervish lodges, consorting with swindlers and heroin dealers, decking yourselves out in gruesome disguises, masks, these glasses . . . am I right? Because Galip Bey—my son—you've changed so much since I last saw you. Your face is pale and your eyes have sunk way back in your skull; you've become someone else. Istanbul nights are endless; a ghost with a guilty conscience cannot sleep. What did you just say?"

"May I please have my glasses, sir, so I can leave?"

Chapter Twenty-nine

It Seems I Was the Hero

"On the subject of personal style: the apprentice writer always begins by imitating those who came before him. This is born of necessity. Do not children also learn to speak by imitating others?"

—Tahir-ül Mevlevi

I gazed into the mirror and read my face. The mirror was a silent sea, my face a pale sheet of paper, written over in sea-green ink. "You poor dear!" your beautiful mother—or, rather, my uncle's wife—used to say, whenever I gave her a blank look. "Your face is as white as paper!" I gave her blank looks because—even without knowing it—I was afraid of what was written on my face: I'd give her blank looks because I was afraid I'd not be able to find you where I'd left you—among those old tables, those tired chairs, pale lamps, newspapers, curtains, and cigarettes. In the winter, evening came in one dark swoop. As the sky went black, as the doors swung shut and the lights came on, I'd think of you, sitting there in your corner: on separate floors when we were younger, and behind the same door when we grew up.

Reader, dear reader, you who have already guessed that I am speaking of a relation—a young woman—who once lived under the same roof, as you read, be sure to put yourself in my place and pay close attention to the signs, because when I am talking of myself, I know I am also talking of you, and when I am telling your story you know full well that I am also giving voice to my own recollections.

I gazed into the mirror and read my face. My face was the Rosetta Stone I had deciphered in my dream. My face was a tombstone from which the turban had fallen. My face was a mirror made of skin in which the reader beheld himself. We breathed together through the same pores, you and I; your beloved detective novels piled high on the floor, and the air thick with the smoke from our cigarettes, the refrigerator humming sadly in the dark kitchen, while above us a lampshade the color of a paperback cover sent a light the color of your skin spilling onto my guilty fingers and your long legs.

For I was the sad resourceful hero of the book you are reading; I was the traveler who, with his guide, went slipping around the marble stones, giant columns, and black rocks among the fretful souls banished to the underground, who climbed the staircase to the skies to visit the seven starry heavens, who gazed at his love at the far end of the bridge leading over the chasm and cried, "I am you!" I was the hard-boiled detective who, led on by his kindly author, found traces of poison in the ashtray and knew what they signified . . . while you impatiently—wordlessly—turned the pages. I committed crimes of passion, crossed the Euphrates on horseback, buried myself under pyramids, assassinated cardinals. "What's that book about, darling?" You were a contented housewife, I was a husband who came home every night. "Oh, nothing, really." When the last bus, the emptiest bus, passed by in all its emptiness, our armchairs would tremble together. In your hands a paperback, in mine the newspaper I couldn't manage to read. I'd ask, "If I were the hero, would you love me?" "Stop talking nonsense!" The books you read talked of the night's cruel silence. I knew just how cruel silence could be.

Her mother was right, I'd think: because my face stayed white. Five letters are written across it. On our old alphabet-book horse there was an **A. A** stood for *at*, and the word *at* meant horse. **D** stood for *dal* and meant branch. **DD** stood for *dede*—grandfather. **BB** stood for *baba*—father. In French it was **PP**—*papa*. Mother, uncle, aunt, family. There was no magic mountain, no Mount Kaf, and it was not encircled by a snake. I raced over the commas, stopped at periods, cried out in surprise at the exclamation points! Tom Mix, the ranger, lived in Nevada. Here's one about Pecos Bill, the hero of Texas, set in Boston; and another, about Karaoğlan, in Central Asia. The Man of a Thousand and One Faces, Brandyman, Roddy, Batman. Alâaddin—oh, Alâaddin, is Issue 125 of *Texas* out yet? *Wait!* Grandmother would say as she snatched our comics from our hands. Wait! If we can't find the latest issue of that horrid piece of nonsense, *I'll tell you a story instead*. She'd tell us her story with her cigarette hanging from her mouth. The two of us—you and I—would climb to the top of Mount Kaf, pick the apple from the tree, slide down the beanstalk, slip down chimneys, follow clues. We were the best detectives in the world, then came Sherlock Holmes, Pecos Bill's sidekick White Feather, and Memet My Hawk's enemy, Lame Ali. Reader, oh, reader, are you keeping track of my letters? Because I knew nothing of this, I had no idea, but it seems my face was a map all along. "And then?" you'd ask, as you sat there in your chair across from Grandmother, swinging your legs. "And then?"

And then, much later, years later, after I'd become the husband who'd come home tired from work every evening, when I took the new magazine I'd just bought at Alâaddin's out of my bag, you'd take it from my hands, sit down in that same chair, and—dear Lord—swing your legs just as insistently. I'd give you that blank look of mine and, too afraid to ask out loud, I'd wonder, What's going on in your mind? What's the secret, what's the mystery behind the locked doors of your secret garden? I'd study your shoulders, your long hair, the colored photographs in your magazine; gathering up my clues, I'd try to solve the puzzle of your swinging legs, to penetrate the secret of the garden in your mind: skyscrapers in New York, fireworks in Paris, handsome revolutionaries, resolute millionaires. (*Turn the page.*) Airplanes with swimming pools, superstars with pink ties, global geniuses, and the latest bulletins. (*Turn the page.*) Hollywood's new young stars, rebel singers, globe-trotting princesses and princes. (*Turn the page.*) Some local news: two poets and three critics meet to discuss the benefits of reading.

Still the mystery would elude me, but you'd keep turning the pages, hour after hour, late into the night, until the streets below were swarming with hungry packs of dogs, until finally you'd solved the puzzle. Sumerian goddess of health: Bo. Italian valley: Po. Symbol for telerium: Te. Musical note: Re. River that flows upward: Alphabet? Imaginary mountain in the valley of letters: Mount Kaf. Magic word: Listen. Theater of the mind: Rüya. Rüya, my dream. The handsome hero in the adjacent picture: You'd know all the answers, and I could never figure out a single one. In the silence of the night, you'd lift your head from your magazine, and half your face would be brilliantly lit, the other half a dark mirror, and when you asked, "Do you think I should have my hair cut?" I was never sure if you were asking me or the handsome, famous hero hiding inside the puzzle. For a moment, dear reader, I'd stare at her blankly—very blankly indeed!

I could never convince you that I believed in a world without heroes. I could never convince you that the poor writers who invented heroes were no heroes themselves. I could never convince you that the people whose photos you saw in those magazines belonged to another breed. I could never convince you to be content with an ordinary life. And never could I convince you that I, too, could play a part in it.

Chapter Thirty

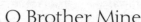

O Brother Mine

Of all the monarchs of whom I have ever heard, the one who comes to my mind, nearest to the true spirit of God, was the Caliph Haroun of Baghdad, who as you know had a taste for disguise.

—Isak Dinesen,
"The Deluge at Norderney,"
Seven Gothic Tales

When he stepped out of the newspaper building, Galip was wearing dark glasses; instead of going to his office, he headed straight for the Covered Bazaar. As he walked past the tourist shops and across the courtyard of Nuruosmaniye Mosque, he was hit by a wave of fatigue that made Istanbul look like a city he was seeing for the first time. The leather bags, meerschaum pipes, and coffee grinders he saw in the Covered Bazaar no longer bore testament to the world its inhabitants had created over thousands of years; these objects had become signs of an alien land to which millions had been exiled. The strangest thing of all, thought Galip, as he lost himself in the bazaar's tangled streets, is that once I've read the letters on my face, I am absolutely certain I can really be myself.

As he turned into the Street of the Slipper Makers, he was almost ready to believe that it was he who had changed and not the city, but— now he'd solved the mystery at its center—he couldn't quite convince himself that this was so. As he looked into the window of a carpet store, he was suddenly certain that he'd seen these carpets before, that he had stepped on them with his own muddy shoes and his own worn slippers, that he knew this carpet dealer who was sipping coffee on his stool outside the door and eyeing him so suspiciously, that he knew every little trick, every little swindle in the shop's dusty history—every chapter in the book—as well as he knew his own. The same thoughts came to him when he looked into the jeweler's, the antique dealer's, and the shoe store. Choosing another arcade two streets away, he was soon convinced that he knew everything that had ever been sold in this place, from the copper pitchers to the scales and weights, from the sales clerks loitering in the street to the crowds following past them. Istanbul was an open book to him now; it harbored no secrets.

He felt at peace with the world; he walked the streets as if in a dream. For the first time in his life, Galip could see the gaudy profusion in the windows, the faces in the passing crowds, as figments in a dream that were, nonetheless, as familiar and reassuring as a family sitting down for supper. As he walked past the long row of glittering jewel shops, he told himself that the peace he now felt in his heart came from the secret he'd read in the letters in his face—the secret that had brought him such terror—but now he'd read the letters, now he'd left behind that piteous creature he'd been before reading the letters; he didn't want to think about him. What made the world mysterious was the second person each of us hid inside ourselves, the twin with whom we shared our lives. After he had walked down the Street of the Cobblers, past the clerks idling in their doorways, as he glanced at the cityscapes on the brightly colored postcards outside a small shop at the end, Galip decided that he'd left that twin behind long ago; the Istanbul on these postcards was so very familiar, he thought, so crude and trite. As he inspected the ferries nearing Galata Bridge, the chimneys of Topkapı, the lonely Leander's Tower, and the Bosphorus Bridge, he told himself again that the city no longer had any mystery for him. But he lost this feeling the moment he stepped into the Bedestan, the heart of the old market, where the bottle-green windows reflected each other as ominously as ever.

Though there was no one in these tiny passages who aroused his suspicions, Galip had a strong premonition of disaster. He began to walk quickly. When he reached the Street of the Fur Hat Makers, he turned right and headed out of the bazaar as quickly as he could. He kept the same pace as he walked through the secondhand book market, but when he found himself in front of the Alif Bookstore, he

stopped abruptly; although he had passed this store for years without
noticing it, it now seemed like an omen. But it was not the shop's name
that struck him as significant—though *alif* was the first letter of Allah
and, according to the Hurufis, the source of both the alphabet and the
universe—what electrified him was that the letter *alif* had been written
out in Latin letters over the door, just as F. M. Üçüncü had foreseen.
Even as he tried to tell himself that there was nothing special about
this and it could not therefore be a sign, the dark windows of Sheikh
Muammer Efendi's shop suggested otherwise. Once upon a time, poor
widows with aching hearts had come here from all the outlying neighborhoods of the city—long-suffering American billionaires too—but
today the Zamani sheikh had shut his doors, and it could not be
because he had decided to stay at home that day, out of the bitter
cold, nor could he have died; these doors were closed, Galip decided,
because they were trying to tell him that there was yet another mystery
lurking inside the city's heart. If I'm still seeing signs in the city, he told
himself, as he passed the great piles of translated detective novels and
Koran interpretations that stood outside the other shops' doors, that
means I still haven't grasped what the letters on my face were trying to
teach me. But it wasn't the real reason; every time it occurred to him
that someone might be following him, his legs would go faster of their
own accord, and every time he speeded up, the city ceased to be a quiet
place where all signs and objects looked familiar and turned into a
realm of horror, shimmering with mystery and danger. Galip decided
that if he walked faster, if he could leave this shadow behind him, he'd
shed this disquiet, escape this encroaching mystery too.

  At Beyazıt Square, he turned into Tentmakers' Avenue, and then,
because he liked the name, Samovar Street. From here he went into
Water Pipe Street, which ran parallel to it, walking all the way down to
the Golden Horn. Then he turned into the Street of the Mortar Makers and climbed uphill again. He walked past little restaurants, copper-
smiths, locksmiths, and ateliers where they made plastics. So it looks as
if I was meant to pass these shops as I launch into my new life, he
thought innocently. He saw shops that sold pails, basics, beads, glittering sequins, army and police uniforms. For a while he walked in the
direction of Beyazıt Tower, just to give himself a destination, and then
he walked back the same way, passing trucks, orange sellers, horse

carts, old refrigerators, moving vans, rubbish dumps, and the graffiti-covered walls of the university, arriving finally at the courtyard of Süleymaniye Mosque. Entering the courtyard, he walked along the line of cypress trees; when his shoes were muddy, he went out to the street next to the *medrese*, where he found long rows of unpainted wooden houses, each one propping up another. As he looked up at the stovepipes coming out through the first-floor windows of these dilapidated houses, he noticed that they looked like sawed-off shotguns, like rusting periscopes, like the yawning mouths of fearsome cannons, but since he was no longer in the mood to link anything with anything, he didn't even want to dwell on the word *like*.

To reach Young Blade Street, he turned into the Street of the Dwarf Fountain, which he could not help but take as another sign. Deciding that these old cobblestoned streets were riddled with signs that might lead him into a trap, he turned into the Avenue of the Princes. He saw *simit* sellers, and minibus drivers drinking tea, and university students looking at the posters outside a movie theater as they munched on *lahmacuns*: there were three films playing simultaneously. Two were karate films, both staring Bruce Lee; torn posters and faded billboards indicated that the third starred Cüneyt Arkın as a Selçuk warlord who beat up Byzantine Greeks and slept with their women. Fearing that he might go blind if he lingered in the lobby looking at these posters, in which every actor had an orange face, Galip walked on. As he walked past the Prince's Mosque, he was reminded of the story of the Crown Prince, though he tried not to think about it. But everywhere he looked now, he saw secret signs: traffic signs rusting at the edges, crooked graffiti, the Plexiglas signs of dirty restaurants and hotels, posters advertising "arabesque" singers and detergents. Though he did everything he could to ignore all these signs, he still could not walk along the Aqueduct of Valens without remembering the red-bearded Greek Orthodox priests he'd once seen in a historical film as a child, and when he walked past the Vefa Boza Shop he could not help but remember the holiday when Uncle Melih, drunk from all the liqueurs he'd downed at lunch, had brought the entire family here in taxis so they could all taste its famous fermented millet drink, but it wasn't long before these remembered images turned into signs of a mystery still locked in the past.

Racing across Atatürk Avenue, he decided yet again that if he walked fast, very fast, he'd soon be able to see the city's letters and images the way he wanted to see them—not as fragments of a mystery but as themselves. He turned quickly into the Street of the Store Clerks, and from there into the Street of the Lumber Sellers, after which he walked for some time without looking at the street names. He walked past old wooden houses squeezed in between ramshackle apartment houses with rusting balconies, long-nosed fifties trucks, tires that now served as children's toys, bent electricity posts, pavements that had been torn up and abandoned, cats crawling through rubbish bins, old women in head scarves smoking cigarettes at their windows, traveling yogurt sellers, sewage diggers, and quilt makers.

After going down the Avenue of the Carpet Sellers, he made a quick left turn just before the Avenue of the Nation, crossing to the other side of the street and then back again; when he stopped at a small grocery for an *ayran*, he tried to tell himself that it was only in Rüya's detective novels that people were followed, but he knew he could no more rid his mind of the thought than he could escape this impenetrable secret at the heart of the city. He turned into the Street of the Pair of Doves, making another left at the next corner, stepping up his pace as he walked along the Street of the Educated Man, until he had almost broken into a run. When the lights turned red, he crossed Fevzi Pasha Avenue, darting among the minibuses. When he looked up at the next street sign to see that he was on the Street of the Lion's Den, he immediately took fright; if the invisible hand whose presence he'd felt three days earlier on the Galata Bridge was still placing signs across the city, this mystery he sensed so intensely must still be far away from him.

He walked through the crowded marketplace, past fish stalls selling mackerel, lamprey eel, and turbot, and into the courtyard of the Mosque of the Conqueror, where all roads converged. There was no one in this enormous courtyard except for a crowlike man with a black beard and a black coat. The little graveyard was empty too. The door to the Conqueror's *tekke* was locked too; as Galip peered through the windows, he listened to the city's roar. The din of the market, the beeping horns, the shouts and cries coming from the playground of a distant school, the knocking of hammers, the hum of engines, the screeches of sparrows and crows in the courtyard trees, the passing minibuses, the growling motorcycles, the opening and shutting of nearby windows and doors, the rattling of office buildings, houses, trees, and parks, and the ships moving through the sea, entire neighborhoods, the entire city. Mehmet the Conqueror, the man whose sarcophagus he could only just see through the dusty window, the man he longed to be, had used Hurufi texts to unlock the mystery of the city he'd conquered five hundred years before Galip's birth; slowly but surely, he'd penetrated that realm in which every door, chimney, street, aqueduct, and plane tree signified something other than itself.

If only they'd not detected that conspiracy, thought Galip. If only they'd not burned all those Hurufis and their writings too. Turning from the Street of İzzat the Calligrapher into Zeyrek, he added, And if the sultan had been able to unlock the city's mystery, what would he have seen as he walked the streets of vanquished Byzantium—if he were walking past these crumbling walls and centuries-old plane trees, these dusty streets and empty lots that I see before me, what would he have understood? As he approached the old and frightening tobacco warehouses of Cibali, he gave himself the answer he'd known ever since he'd read the letters on his face: When he saw the city for the first time, it would have been as if he'd seen it thousands of times before. But that was the oddest thing of all: Istanbul looked like it had only just been conquered. These muddy streets, these broken pavements, these crumbling walls, these sad lead-gray trees, these decrepit cars and even more decrepit buses, this never-ending stream of sad and identical faces, these starving dogs—it was as if he'd never seen them before, never even known they existed.

By now he had realized that he was never going to get rid of this thing—real or imagined—that was following him, but he kept on walking, past the small factories that lined the shore of the Golden Horn, the empty industrial barrels, the crumbling Byzantine aqueducts, the workmen eating meatballs and bread for lunch or playing soccer in muddy fields, still in their overalls, until his desire to see the city as a tranquil and familiar place was so overwhelming that he had to imagine himself as someone else—as Mehmet the Conqueror. After he had amused himself for some time with this childish fantasy—which did not seem to him to be mad or even ridiculous—he remembered a column Celâl had written many years earlier, to mark some anniversary of the conquest, in which he'd said that of the 120 men who had ruled Istanbul during the 1,650 years from Constantine I to the present, Mehmet the Conqueror was the only one who had felt the need to roam through the city by night in disguise. As he swayed back and forth with all the other passengers on the Sirkeci–Eyüp bus, Galip remembered Celâl's knowing aside: "Our readers will be well aware of his reasons." From Unkapanı he boarded the bus to Taksim; it amazed him how the person following him had managed to change buses so far. He could feel his gaze—feel it on the back of his neck. After he had changed buses again in Taksim, he decided that if he talked to the old man who took the seat next to him, he could transform himself into someone else and escape the shadow that was chasing him.

"Do you think this snow is going to continue?" Galip asked, still looking out the window.

"Who knows?" said the old man, and perhaps he would have said more, had Galip not blurted out his next question.

"What does this snow signify?" he asked. "What does it augur? Do you know the great Mevlana's story about the key? Last night I was granted a dream on the same subject. Everything around me was white, pure white, as white as the snow around us. Then suddenly I awoke to a terrible, cold, ice-cold pain in my chest. It felt as if there were a snowball pressing against my heart—a ball of ice, a crystal ball—but there wasn't; it was Rumi Mevlana's diamond key that was sitting on my heart. I took it into my hand and rose from my bed, thinking I could use it to open my bedroom door, and I did, but I was in some other room, and there, on the bed, was someone who looked like me but he wasn't me. Taking the key that lay on the sleeping man's heart and leaving my key in its place, I opened his room's door: the next room was the same, another sleeping man who looked like me—though his shape was more pleasing—and lying on his heart was another diamond key. The next room was the same, and the next room after that. What's more, I now saw that there were others in these rooms, too: other shadows like me, other sleepless ghosts, all brandishing keys. In every room a bed, and in every bed a dreaming man like me! I knew then that I was in the marketplace of Paradise. But there was no buying or selling there, no money and no stamps—just faces and shapes. Whatever you liked, you became—you simply put on the

new face like a mask and began your new life—but I knew that the
shape I longed to become was in the last of the thousand and one
rooms, and when I turned the last key in that last lock, the door did not
open. It was then that I realized that the only key that could open that
door was the ice-cold key I'd found on my chest on first waking, but I
had no way of knowing where that key was now or who it was who
held it—if it was on the bed I'd abandoned or in one of the thousand
and one rooms I'd passed through—and as guilty tears poured from
my eyes, I knew I was condemned to walk from room to room with all
those other hopeless waifs, exchanging one key for the next, looking
aghast into each sleeping face, forever and ever—"

"Look!" said the old man. "Look!"

Galip, still wearing dark glasses, looked at where the old man was
pointing. Just in front of the radio station there was a dead man lying
on the pavement; one or two people were standing over him, shouting
and quickly attracting a crowd of curious onlookers. As the traffic
slowed, both the seated and the standing passengers on the bus leaned
over as far as they could to watch the bleeding corpse in silent horror.

When the road opened up again, the silence persisted for quite
some time. Galip got off the bus in front of the Palace Theater. From
there he went into the Ankara Pazar Market on the corner; after buying
himself salted fish, fish roe salad, sliced tongue, a bunch of bananas
and a few apples, he raced back to the City-of-Hearts Apartments. By
now, he felt so much like someone else that he was beginning to wish
he didn't. He went straight down to the janitor's apartment: he found
İsmail Efendi and Kamer Hanım sitting at the table with their little
grandchildren, eating potatoes fried with minced meat, on the same
blue oilcloth—a family so happy it seemed to Galip to be a scene from
the distant past.

"Please, don't let me disturb your meal," said Galip. After a silence,
he added, "I gather you never got that envelope to Celâl."

"We knocked and knocked, but he wasn't there," said the janitor's
wife.

"He's up there now," said Galip. "Where's the envelope?"

"Celâl's upstairs?" said İsmail Efendi. "If you're going up, you can
take him this electricity bill too."

Rising from the table, he rummaged through the pile of bills on top of the television set, peering myopically at each one. Galip quickly slipped the key out of his pocket and hung it back on the empty hook on the side of the shelf over the radiator. They hadn't noticed. Taking the envelope and the bill, he left them to finish their meal.

"Tell Celâl not to worry, I'm not telling anyone anything!" Kamer Hanım called after him. The gaiety in her voice was worrying.

For the first time in many years, Galip had the pleasure of riding in the old apartment elevator, which still smelled of wood polish and machine oil and still moaned like an old man with lumbago as it rose. Though the mirror was the same one he and Rüya had once used to check their heights against each other, Galip did not dare look into it, for fear of the terrifying letters he might read in his face.

He'd been in the apartment only just long enough to hang up his jacket and his coat when the phone rang. But he wanted to be prepared for whatever lay ahead, so before he answered it, he rushed to the bathroom and—for three, four, five seconds—gazed into his face: desirously, courageously, decisively. Chance had played no part in this; the letters were all still in place, as was the universe, and the mystery at its core. I know, Galip thought as he picked up the phone. I know. Even before he heard the voice, he knew how it would sound—as joyous as if it were bringing glad tidings of the military cleanup so long awaited by the nation's pure-hearted patriots.

"Hello."

"What should your name be this time?" said Galip. "There are so many false names flying about now, I'm losing track."

"A very clever opening," said the voice. He sounded more confident than Galip had expected. "Celâl Bey, you can give me whatever name you like."

"Mehmet, then."

"As in Mehmet the Conqueror?"

"Exactly."

"Good. My name is Mehmet. I have not, I'm afraid, managed to find your name in the phone book. So give me your address and I'll come right over."

"Why would I give you an address I've kept secret from everyone I know?"

"I am an ordinary and well-meaning citizen trying to pass on documents to a famous journalist that attest to the bloody coup that is soon to befall this country, that's why."

"You know too much about me to qualify as an ordinary citizen," said Galip.

"Six years ago, I ran into a fellow citizen at the train station in Kars," said the voice now named Mehmet. "A very ordinary citizen, one Attar, a simple shopkeeper, just like Farid od-Din Attar, the twelfth-century poet. That day he was on his way to Erzurum to buy more wares. We talked about you throughout our short journey together. He knew why you had begun the first column you ever wrote under your own name with the word *listen—bishnov* in Persian—which is, no less, the first word in Rumi's *Mathnawi*. In a column you wrote in July 1956, you likened life to a serialized novel, and exactly one year later you wrote a second column in which you likened a serialized novel to life—but by then he was well aware of your work's hidden symmetries and the strong utilitarian streak that also runs through it, because he had already guessed that it was you who had finished that serial about wrestlers that the original writer had abandoned in the middle after a fight with the publisher— you used a false name, of course, but this man had guessed from the style that it was you. Around the same time, you began another column by telling your readers that they should stop scowling at the beautiful women they passed in the street and smile at them warmly instead—like Europeans—and this same man knew, when you described one woman of your acquaintance who was unhappy about the uncouth scowls men in this country gave her, that the beautiful woman you described with such love, compassion, and admiration was your own stepmother. In another piece, in which you satirized an extended family that all lived together in a dusty Istanbul apartment house and went so far as to liken them to an aquarium full of luckless Japanese fish, he knew that these same fish happened to belong to your deaf-mute uncle and the family in the piece was your own. This man had never been as far as Erzurum, let alone Istanbul, but he knew all these relatives you hadn't named by name, and the exact location of your Nişantaşı apartment house, and all the streets in the neighborhood, and the police station on the corner, and Alâaddin's shop just across the street, and the Teşvikiye Mosque with the reflecting pool in the courtyard, and the last remaining gardens, and the Sütiş pudding shop, and the chestnut and linden trees lining the

pavement—he knew these places as well as he knew his own neighborhood on the slopes of Kars Castle, where he sold, in his little shop, all
the same things as Alâaddin, everything from perfume to shoelaces,
from tobacco to needles and thread. Those were the days when we had
not yet managed to tame the accents of our radio broadcasters so that
they could speak to the nation with one voice, but this simple shopkeeper remembered that just three weeks after you wrote a column
making fun of the Eleven Question Quiz on Istanbul Radio—sponsored, as you no doubt remember, by İpana Toothpaste—they made
your name the answer to the twelve-hundred-lira question—hoping
that flattery might shut you up—but as this man had predicted, you
rejected this small bribe, and in your very next column you were advis-
ing your readers to stop using American toothpaste and rub their teeth
instead with mint soap they could make with their own clean hands. Of
course, there would be no way of your knowing that our good-natured
shopkeeper followed the recipe you gave in the same column and went
on rubbing this 'soap' over his teeth for years and years, as they fell out
one by one. But let me tell you, for the rest of our journey we devised a
diverting quiz game for ourselves, 'Subject: Our Renowned Columnist,
Celâl Salik!' Though my opponent was gripped by a single fear—that he
might forget to get off the train at Erzurum—I had a hard time beating
him. He was a man who'd aged early and had never been able to afford
to replace those teeth he'd lost; aside from your columns, his only pleasure in life was spending time with the various birds he kept in cages, and
he had lots of stories to tell about birds too. Yes, he was just an ordinary
citizen. So do you see what I'm driving at, Celâl Bey? Even ordinary citizens—and please, don't make any attempt to belittle them—even ordinary citizens know you. But I know you even better than an ordinary
citizen. That's why we'll be talking all night!"

"Four months after my second column on toothpaste," Galip said,
"I wrote another. Why was that?"

"In the evenings, before going to bed, lovely little girls and boys giving their mothers and fathers and uncles and aunts and stepbrothers
good-night kisses, their lovely little mouths fragrant with mint toothpaste. To put it mildly, not a very lovely piece."

"A few more examples of those Japanese fish I mentioned?"

"I remember you mentioning them six years ago, in a column you wrote about your longing for silence and death, and one month after that, in a column you wrote about your quest for order and sleep. You often compared our televisions with aquariums. You also passed on various facts about the terrible things that happen to *wakin* fish when they're inbred—all lifted from the *Encyclopedia Britannica*. Who did the translation for you, your sister or your nephew?"

"The police station?"

"So many associations: midnight blue, darkness, beatings, identity cards, the woes of being a citizen, rusting waterpipes, black shoes, starless nights, scowling faces, metaphysical inertia, misfortune, being a Turk, leaking faucets, and, of course, death."

"Did the shopkeeper know all this too?"

"All this and more."

"What did the shopkeeper quiz you about?"

"This was a man, you remember, who'd never seen a streetcar in his life and was unlikely ever to see one, but his first question was whether the horse-drawn streetcars had a different smell from the horseless variety. I told him there was more to it than sweat and horse fumes; it was the smell of motors, oil, and electricity. He asked me if Istanbul electricity had a special smell. You hadn't mentioned this, but he'd deduced it from your column. He asked me to describe how newsprint smelled just after it had rolled off the press. The answer was the one you gave in a column you wrote in the winter of 1958: quinine infused with damp cellars, sulfur, and wine—a heady mixture, in other words. (Newspapers take three days to get to Kars, it seems, by which time they've lost their fragrance.) But the shopkeeper's most difficult question was about lilacs. I had no memory of your ever showing this flower any interest. But according to this shopkeeper—and how his eyes twinkled when he told me this; oh, he was a picture, like an old man recalling sweet memories of youth—according to this shopkeeper, you alluded to their fragrance on three separate occasions over a period of twenty-five years. Once, when you were telling the story of the strange and solitary prince who terrified his entourage as he waited to ascend the throne, you said the woman he loved smelled of lilacs. Twice—and here we see a pattern emerging—you wrote about a little girl, almost certainly a relation, returning to primary school at the end of her summer holidays, on one of those sad, sunny, late-autumn mornings, wearing a freshly ironed smock and a bright new ribbon in her hair; the first time it was her hair that smelled of lilacs, the second time it was her head. Was this life repeating itself or a writer repeating himself, a writer reduced to stealing from his own work?"

For a few moments, Galip remained silent. "I don't remember," he said finally, as if he'd just woken from a dream. "I know I considered writing about the prince, but I don't remember actually writing it."

"The shopkeeper certainly remembered. His sense of place was as good as his sense of smell. Through his close reading of your columns, he had conjured up an Istanbul that was more than a cornucopia of smells: He knew every corner of the city that you had visited, grown to love it—love it secretly, without telling a soul—for its mystery, but just as he was unable to imagine certain odors, he had no idea where these places were in relation to one another. I myself had, thanks to you, visited these places from time to time—when I've needed to find you—though I've not done so on this occasion, as I can tell from your number that you're hiding somewhere in the Nişantaşı–Şişli area. I know you'll be curious about this, so let me tell you: I told the shopkeeper to write to you. But it turned out that the nephew who read him your columns did not know how to write. The shopkeeper himself, of course, could neither read nor write. You once wrote in a column that letters, once recognized, stunted the memory. Shall I tell you how our quiz game ended—how I was able to beat this man who had heard your columns but never read them—as our steam train went chug-chug-chugging into Erzurum station?"

"I'd rather you didn't."

"Although this man could remember every single abstract concept you'd ever mentioned in your columns, he just couldn't seem to see what they meant. For example, he had no idea what plagiarism meant, or literary appropriation. You see, he'd never had his nephew read him anything but your columns, nor was he in any way curious about writing by anyone else. It was almost as if he thought a single person had produced all the writing in the world in a single instant. I asked him why you were always going on about the Mevlana, the poet Rumi. He fell silent. I then asked the shopkeeper about a column you wrote in 1961 entitled 'The Mystery of Hidden Texts'—how much of it was you and how much Edgar Allan Poe? This time he spoke: It was all you, he said. I went on to quiz him about the dilemma that proved so problematic in your famous dispute with the columnist Neşati about Bottfolio and Ibn Zerhani—or your fight, as the shopkeeper recalled it—the dilemma sometimes described as 'the source of the story versus the story's source.' He told me, in all sincerity, that letters were the source of everything. He'd understood nothing, so I won."

"Going back to that dispute you mentioned," said Galip. "When I answered Neşati's charges, that was the basis of my argument—that letters were the source of everything."

"But those aren't Ibn Zerhani's words, they're Fazlallah's. After writing that copycat *nazire* of yours on 'The Grand Inquisitor,' you had to think about your safety, didn't you? So you used Ibn Zerhani as a smokescreen. You had one and only one thing in mind when you wrote those pieces, and that was to make Neşati look bad in front of the boss—get him kicked off the paper. You lured him into your trap by asking, 'Is it translation or plagiarism?' You knew how much he envied you, so it did not take much to trick him into accusing you of plagiarism. Then you pounced, accused him of insulting the Turkish people—implying that the East could not create anything original—because hadn't Neşati argued that you had plagiarized Ibn Zerhani, who had himself plagiarized Bottfolio? You then set yourself up as the great defender of our glorious history and 'our culture' and urged your readers to write to the owner of the newspaper to complain. You knew what you were doing—there is, after all, nothing the wretched newspaper-reading public loves more than to declare some New Crusade against those who would seek to defile our glorious history; just remember what they did to those perverts who claimed that Sinan, 'Turkey's greatest-ever architect,' was really an Armenian from Kayseri—so naturally they were not going to pass up on this new opportunity; they deluged the owner of the newspaper with letters denouncing this degenerate Neşati, who was so drunk with pleasure right then from having caught you plagiarizing that he had forgotten to watch his back, and before he knew it he had lost his column and his job. Later on, of course, he ended up working on the same paper with you, but in a lesser position—though I hear you could fill a well with the rumors he's been spreading about you. Did you know this?"

"What have I written about wells?"

"How to begin but to say that it would be rude to ask a reader as loyal as myself even to attempt an answer—you are so lucid on this subject, after all, and so endlessly wordy—one might even say you were a bottomless well. So let me pass quickly over the wells of Divan poetry, and the well into which Rumi threw the body of his beloved Shams, or the wells of his *The Thousand and One Nights*, which you've plundered so mercilessly, or the wells said to be inhabited by witches and giants, or the wells lurking in the gaps between apartment houses, or the dark and bottomless pits in which you claim we lost our souls—you've written enough about all this already. So what about this instead? In the autumn of 1957, you wrote an angry, mournful, but carefully worded column about the mosques going up in the new suburbs of our fast-expanding city; what bothered you most were their concrete minarets—the emphasis being on the concrete, because apparently you had no problem with minarets made from stone—and on their location, because your point was that these new suburbs were laying siege to the city proper and surrounding us on all sides, and to see those concrete minarets pressed against the sky was to gaze upon a forest of hostile lances. But—and isn't this always the case for anything that does not speak directly to the news and scandals of the day?—the vast majority of your readers paid little attention to the undistinguished mosque you mentioned in your final lines: a small mosque in a poor neighborhood with a single squat minaret and a back garden choked by symmetrical ferns and asymetrical thorns that concealed a dry and bottomless well. It was immediately clear to me that you had chosen to describe this real-life well to suggest, in the most elegant way, that—rather than raise our eyes to the sky to look at concrete minarets—we should look instead into the dark, dry, snake- and soul-infested wells of our submerged and forgotten past. Ten years later, you wrote a column in which you managed to insert the entire history of the Cyclops into the tale of your own unhappy past; you began by describing a lonely night—and such a lonely night it was!—when, condemned to sleeplessness and beset by the ghosts of your uneasy conscience, you took to the city's dark streets, only to find yourself followed by an eye that would go on to haunt you for years, reminding you, wherever you went, of the sins of your past; it was not by accident but by design that you chose to describe this visual organ as looking 'like a dark well in the middle of the forehead.'"

What did the voice look like? Galip imagined a man with a white collar, a faded jacket, and the face of a ghost; was he pulling these sentences out of his own teeming memory or was he reading from a script? Galip paused to think. And it was almost as if the voice read a sign in his silence, for now there was a peal of victorious laughter coming down the line. Galip imagined its long journey beneath the city's hills, down underground passages littered with Byzantine coins and Ottoman skulls, through cables strung as tightly as clotheslines between plane trees and chestnut trees and rusting poles, and clinging like black ivy to the crumbling plaster walls of aging apartment buildings; and all the while the voice grew warmer, more brotherly, more loving, as if it were not a phone wire connecting them but an umbilical cord that attached them to the same mother; he had such deep affection for Celâl, he thought so much of Celâl, he knew Celâl so very well: Celâl was no longer in any doubt of this, was he?

"I wouldn't know," said Galip.

"Then let's get rid of these black phones that are keeping us apart," said the voice. Because sometimes they rang of their own accord, to frighten one unnecessarily; because their receivers were black as pitch and heavy as dumbbells; because every time you dialed a number, they moaned like the old turnstiles for the Karaköy–Kadıköy ferry; because sometimes, instead of connecting you to the number you'd dialed, they connected you to the number of their choice. "Do you see what I'm driving at, Celâl Bey? Give me your address and I'll be right over."

For a moment, Galip hesitated, like a teacher rendered speechless by a genius student. Then—amazed by the flowers that opened in the garden of his memory with each answer, intrigued by the seeming endlessness of the garden from which his opponent plucked his questions but still cognizant of the trap into which he was slowly walking—he asked, "What about nylon stockings?"

"In a column you wrote in 1958, you harked back to a summer's day two years earlier—when you were not yet writing under your own name, in other words, and everything you wrote came out under one or another of your dismal pseudonyms. It was unbearably hot, and you were aching from overwork and loneliness, so to escape the noonday sun you dipped into a Beyoğlu theater (the Rüya Dream Theater), arriving halfway through the first film in the double bill; though it was set in Chicago, it had been dubbed into Turkish, and though the air rang with machine-gun fire, crashing bottles, smashing glass, and the very Turkish-sounding laughter of Beyoğlu's most piteous dubbing artists, you could still hear a woman's long fingernails scratching her legs through her nylon stockings. When the first film came to an end and the lights went up, you saw a beautiful and elegant mother sitting with her bright and beautifully behaved eleven-year-old son; they were chatting together like friends. How long and how longingly you watched them, and how closely you eavesdropped on their conversation. In another piece you wrote two years after this, you described how, when the second feature began, you could barely hear the clashing swords and raging seastorms on the soundtrack, so intent were you on those restless fingernails as they traveled up and down those legs that would be feeding the mosquitoes of Istanbul again that night; neither could you follow the plotting corsairs as they bounded across the screen, for all you could think about was the warmth you sensed between this mother and her son. As you explained in a third column, which you wrote twelve years later, your nylon-stocking column earned you a dressing down from the owner of your newspaper. Did you not know that it was dangerous, very dangerous, to describe a wife and mother as a sexual being? That the Turkish reading public was just not going to tolerate this slur on its honor? And did you not realize that, if you wished to survive as a columnist, you had to watch what you said about married women and, above all, watch your style?"

"What have I had to say on style? Keep your answer brief, please."

"For you, style was life. Style, for you, was voice. Style was your way of thinking. Style was your true self, but there was more than one of these, there were two, even three—"

"These are?"

"The first voice is the one you call your 'simple persona,' the voice you'll use with anyone, the voice you'd use if you were sitting at the table at the end of family dinner, puffing away at a cigarette and gossiping through the clouds of smoke. This is the voice that brings you news of everyday life in all its rich detail. The second voice belongs to the man you'd like to be, the mask you've stolen from those you most admire: those creatures who, unable to find peace in this world, have entered another world to lose themselves in its mystery. If it were not for the solace this hero has brought you, if he were not teasing, needling, soothing you with the puzzles and word games he is forever whispering into your ear, and if you had not trained yourself to repeat his little refrains back to yourself, over and over, like a senile old man— if it weren't for this hero, whom you first merely imitated but whom you later became, you would have turned away from life a long time ago, like all the other unhappy people on this earth, retreating to some god-forsaken corner to await your death—or so I remember reading in a column you wrote once, as tears rolled down my cheeks. So, to summarize, your first style is your objective voice, the second is the subjective, but it is the third that can take us into realms that are closed to the first two: the dark self, the dark style! What you wrote on nights when masks and imitations were not enough to stem your misery—this I know better than you know yourself—but as for the dark acts you perpetrated on those same nights—o brother mine, only you could say! So you see we understand each other, and we shall find each other; together we will go out into the night in disguise. Give me your address."

"Tell me what I've said about addresses."

"That cities are made from addresses, addresses from letters, and letters from faces. On Monday October twelfth—and of all the columns you've written over the years about Istanbul, this is one of my all-time favorites—you talked about Kurtuluş, the old Armenian quarter formerly known as Tatavla. I read it with great pleasure."

"What have I said about reading?"

"Once—in February 1962, if you'd like the date, and I'm sure you will have no trouble remembering those tense days when you were busy preparing for the military coup that might have rescued this country from destitution—on a wintry evening, in one of the darkest streets of Beyoğlu, you were walking past one of those cheap night-clubs where belly dancers and magicians take turns on the stage, when suddenly what should come out through the door but an enormous gilt-framed mirror, on its way, apparently, to a similar nightclub, though who could say why; and then, as you stood there gaping—and perhaps it was the cold that did it—it burst into smithereens, causing you to note that it was no coincidence that the Turkish word for the preparation that turns a piece of glass into a mirror is the same as the Turkish word for *secret*. After describing this flash of insight in a column, you went on to say this: 'To read was to gaze into a mirror; those who know the "secret" behind the looking glass are able to travel to the other side; but those who have no knowledge of the mystery of the letters will see nothing but their own dull faces.'"

"What's the secret?"

"You're the only one who knows the secret—aside from myself. You know, too, that it's not the sort of thing that should be discussed over the phone. Give me your address."

"What's the secret?"

"Don't you understand that a reader has to devote his whole life to you to penetrate this secret? That's what I did; I gave you my life. All these years of sitting in unheated state libraries, shaking from the cold even though I was still wearing my coat, my hat, and my gloves, reading everything I thought you might have written before you began publishing under your own name: the serials you wrote in someone else's name, the puzzles, the profiles, the political reportage, the sentimental journeys. For more than thirty years, you've averaged eight pages a day—that's a hundred thousand pages or three hundred volumes running to three hundred thirty-three pages apiece. The nation should reward you with a statue for this alone!"

"And another for you," said Galip, "for reading it. Statues?"

"During one of my Anatolian journeys, in a town whose name I've since forgotten, I was standing in the central square, killing time until my bus was due to leave, whereupon one of the young men of the town sat down next to me, wanting to talk. First we discussed the statue of Atatürk, who was pointing at the bus depot, as if to indicate that there was only one thing worth doing in this wretched town and that was to leave it. Then I happened to mention a column you'd written, in which you'd mentioned that there were more than ten thousand statues of Atatürk in the country as a whole. You'd gone on to say that on the day of the apocalypse, when thunder and lightning ripped across the dark sky and the earth rolled beneath our feet, all ten thousand of those fearsome statues would come back to life. Whatever their poses, whatever their attire—be they dressed in European clothes speckled with pigeon droppings or in the fully decorated uniform of a field marshal, wearing top hats and ghostly capes, or atop rearing stallions with large male organs—they would, you said, begin to turn on their pedestals, and how beautifully you described these pedestals and the countless flowers, wreaths, flies, dusty buses, and horse carts that had encircled them over the years, and the soldiers wearing uniforms that stank of sweat, and the schoolgirls, whose uniforms stank of mothballs, gazing up at these stone Atatürks, year in and year out, as they sang the national anthem—but come the apocalypse they would begin to move; one by one they would step off their pedestals, crushing the flowers and wreaths beneath their feet to vanish into the night. This passionate youth had, it now emerged, read the selfsame column, and how it had fired him up to read of our wretched citizens, quaking behind their shuttered windows, cowering to the roar of the apocalypse as the earth swayed and the sky split in two, and hearing the rumble of bronze boots and marble hooves in the street outside. So impatient was he that he wrote to you at once, asking if you could tell him exactly when this day would come. If what he told me was true, you sent him a short letter asking him to send in a small photograph of himself; after you'd received it, you'd written to him again to tell him a 'secret' that would, you said, 'serve as an omen' of the 'Day' that would soon be upon us. But never fear, the secret you told this youth was not that secret—perhaps it was the disappointment he felt after so many years of waiting in this park with its paltry patches of grass and its waterless pool that he decided to tell me what this secret was—and a very personal one it was, too. You explained the second meanings of various letters, and you told him that he was to look out for a certain sentence in your columns, that when he saw it, he should read it as a sign. When he saw that sentence, this teenager of ours was to decipher the column and go straight into action."

"What was the sentence?"

"'My life is full of unhappy memories of this order.' That was the sentence. I cannot tell you if he made it up or if you really wrote this in your letter, but here's the coincidence—though you can't seem to write two lines these days without complaining that your memory is drying up or lost altogether—it just so happens that I read this very sentence and a number of others in one of those old columns they reprinted last week. Give me your address, and I can come over at once and tell you what it all means."

"What were the other sentences?"

"Give me your address! Give me your address—because you can't fool me, you have no interest in those other sentences or in any other stories I have to tell you. You care so little for your country you don't even want to hear about it. All you want to do is fester away in that rat hole you're hiding out in—hiding from your friends and your colleagues, hating the world, hating your solitude even more. Give me your address, and I'll tell you which secondhand bookstores to go to if you want to see boys from religious high schools trading photographs of you—and which to go to if you want to find wrestling umpires with a taste for young boys. Give me your address, and I'll show you engravings of eighteen sultans cavorting with loose women who are really wives from their own harem, sent out to secret meeting points all over Istanbul, disguised as Western whores. Did you know that, in the most sought-after dressmakers' salons and brothels of Paris, the affliction that drives us to deck ourselves from head to toe with garish clothes and gaudy jewelry is known as the 'Turkish disease'? Do you know of the engraving that shows Mahmut II copulating in disguise in a dark Istanbul street, his legs naked but for his boots, which are the same boots Napoleon wore during his Egyptian campaign? Or that his favorite wife, Bezm-I Alem, the Queen Mother—who had a ship named after her; who would go on to become the grandmother of the prince whose story you like so much—appears in the same engraving, looking as if she hasn't a worry in the world and wearing a cross made of diamonds and rubies?"

"Tell me what I've said about crosses," Galip cried, and there was joy in his voice. For the first time since his wife had left him—the first time in six days and four hours—he was taking pleasure in life.

"The cross is the inversion of the crescent, its repudiation and negation—or so you said in a column of the eighteenth of January, 1958, in which you proved your case by drawing from early Egyptian geometry, Arab algebra, and Syriac Neoplatonism. It was no coincidence, methinks, that on the same day—just below your column, in fact—they ran a piece on the marriage between Edward G. Robinson—that 'cigar-chomping tough guy beloved of stage and screen audiences alike' (he's my favorite too)—and the New York dress designer Jane Adler; the photograph, you will recall, shows the newlyweds standing in the shadow of a crucifix. Give me your address. A week later, you wrote that in our zeal to teach our children to hate the cross and love the crescent, our youth was no longer able to decipher the enchanted faces of Hollywood and that this same pedagogical practice caused them sexual confusion, as they were also unable to see any moon-faced woman as anything but a mother or an aunt; then, to prove your point, you claimed that if we raided the state boarding schools for the poor on the night after they'd studied the Crusades in history class, we would find that hundreds of the poor creatures had wet their beds. But these are just odds and ends. Give me your address, and I'll bring you all the stories about crosses you could ever want, every mention I found in provincial newspapers during those long days searching those libraries for your work. I'll tell you about the crosses one convict saw on his trip to Hell, after a stroke of good fortune returned him to the land of living: the headline, I recall, was CON-VICT ESCAPES GALLOWS AS OILED NOOSE AROUND HIS NECK SNAPS. That was in the *Erciyas Post*, in Kayseri, in 1962. Here's another from *Green Konya*, from 1951: *.oday our edi.or in chief sen. a .elegraph .o .he Presiden., poin.ing ou. i. would be more pa.rio.ic and more in keeping wi.h .he .urkish na.ional charac.er if we banished .his so obviously cross-shaped le..er from .he alphabe. and replaced i. w.th (.).* If you give me your address, I can bring over many more. . . . I'm not saying that you'd want to use these things as material; I know how much you detest other columnists who draw their material from real life. But let me bring over all these files that are sitting in their boxes here, right in front of me; we can read through them together, laugh together, cry together! Come on, give me your address, and I'll bring over a serial I clipped from an İskenderun paper about the latest local cure for stuttering; when those afflicted go to prostitutes and tell them how much they hate their fathers, they find themselves cured! Give me your address, and I'll bring you the story of the waiter who can read your love line and your lifeline; he might be illiterate and he might not even speak proper Turkish, let alone Persian, but he can recite Omar Khayyam's undiscovered poems—you know why? Because their souls are twinned. Give me your address, and I'll bring you the dreams of a journalist and printer from Bayburt: When he saw his memory was leaving him, he ran a serial on the last page of his newspaper in which he set down all that he still remembered about his life and times, and he continued to do this until the night of his death. In his last dream, he describes a large garden, and I am sure you will find your own story among its faded roses, its fallen leaves, its dry well, o brother mine. I know that you take medication to thin your blood, that you spend hours every day lying down with your feet propped against the wall to force blood back into your brain, and that as you lie there you pull your memories out of that same dry ungrateful well. 'Sixteenth March 1957,' you say to yourself—and your face is beet-red by now, after hanging so long over the side of your sofa or your bed or wherever it is you've been lying. 'On sixteenth March,' you say again, forcing yourself to remember, 'I went to the Provincial Meat Restaurant with my friends from the newspaper, and when I was wolf-ing down my lunch I spoke about the masks we're forced to wear when we're eaten up with jealousy!' Then you push yourself a bit more. You say, 'Yes, yes, of course. In May 1962 I woke up in a back street in Kur-tuluş after a bout of ferocious lovemaking and told the naked woman lying next to me that her large beauty spots reminded me of my step-mother's!' But then, a moment later, you're gripped by a doubt you will later describe as 'cruel.' Did you really say this to this woman? Or was it to that ivory-skinned woman in the stone house with the windows that didn't close properly, thus failing to shut out the never-ending din of the Beşiktaş Market? Or did you say it to the misty-eyed woman who, because she loved you so dearly, went all the way to Beyoğlu to find you the cigarette lighter you'd insisted you could not live without (you could no longer recall why by the time you wrote about it, though you did know she shouldn't have gone all the way to Beyoğlu, because she had put her own life at risk by returning late to the single-room house overlooking the naked trees of Cihangir Park that she shared with her husband and children). Give me your address, and I'll bring you the lat-est European cure—mnemonics. It cuts right though the nicotine and bitter memories that clog the vessels in our brains, takes us right back to our lost paradise. You put twenty drops of this lavender liquid in your morning tea—not ten, like the package tells you—and before you know it, memories you thought you'd lost forever come flooding back into your mind—memories you'd forgotten you forgot—it's like being a child again, and pulling out an old cabinet to find behind it all those colored pencils, combs, and lavender marbles you'd forgotten you lost. If you give me your address, you'll finally be able to remember the col-

umn you wrote about the maps to be found in all our faces, maps that
are alive with signs—signs pointing to certain significant locations in
our very own city. Not only will you remember this column, you'll
remember why you wrote it. If you give me your address, you'll
remember why it was you wrote that column in which you felt compelled to repeat Rumi's story about the competition between the two
famous painters. If you give me your address, you'll remember why
you wrote that obscure column to explain why it was impossible to be
hopelessly alone, because even at our loneliest moments we have the
women of our daydreams to keep us company; and not only that, these
women we see in our fantasies can somehow read our minds, so they
wait for us, look for us, sometimes even find us. Give me your
address—let me remind you of all the things you've forgotten—for
the Heavens and Hells you've lived and dreamed are slowly seeping
away from you, o brother mine. Give me your address, and let me save
you before your entire memory sinks into the bottomless well of
oblivion. I know everything about you. I've read everything you've
ever written. No one else can help you re-create that realm from which
your magic texts rise up to glide like bloodthirsty eagles by day and
cunning ghosts by night. Once I've come to your side, you too will rise
once again to churn out columns that kindle the hearts of young men
idling their lives away in the most forlorn coffeehouses of Anatolia,
columns that cause tears to roll down the cheeks of primary teachers
consigned to its wildest outer reaches, and down their pupils' cheeks
too, columns that can even bring joy back into the lives of mothers sitting in the back streets of small towns, leafing through photo novels as
they wait for death. Give me your address. Let us talk till dawn and
you'll remember that, as much as you love your lost memory, you also
love your country and your people. Think of the hopeless souls who
write to you from snowy mountain villages where the postman calls
only once in a fortnight; think of the bewildered souls who write to
you for advice before they break off their engagements, go on pilgrim-
ages to Mecca, or cast their votes. Think of the unhappy schoolchild-
ren who sit in the back row in geography class so they can read your
pieces, and the long-suffering dispatch clerks who scan your column as
they sit waiting for retirement in dark corners where someone more
important has shoved their desks, and the luckless hordes who,

deprived of your column, would have nothing to discuss during their evening visit to the coffeehouse but the programs they'd heard on the radio. Think of all the people reading you at unshaded bus stops, in the waiting rooms of sad, dirty movie theaters, and in remote train stations all over the country. They're all waiting for you to perform a miracle— all of them! You have to give them their miracle; you have no other choice. Give me your address. We can do this better if we work together. You must write to them. Tell them that the day of redemption is nigh, tell them that their days of waiting in line at the neighborhood fountain to fill their plastic jugs with water will soon be over, tell them that lycée girls who run away from home really can avoid ending up in Galata brothels and really can become film stars, tell them that— after the miracle has come to pass—every ticket for the National Lottery will be guaranteed to win a prize, and husbands who come home drunk late at night will no longer beat their wives, and all commuter trains will have extra cars added, and bands will play in all the town squares of the country just like they do in Europe. Tell them that one day everyone will be a famous hero; one day they'll be able to sleep with whichever woman they want, including their mothers, and afterward, as if by magic, go back to looking at these same women as virgin sisters. Write and tell them about the secret documents that will unravel the historic mystery that sent us into misery so many centuries ago; give them the key, tell them the mystery is solved! Tell them that there is already a network connecting the entirety of Anatolia, a popular movement of true believers that is ready to spring into action at a moment's notice; tell them we know the names of the queers, priests, bankers, and whores who organized the international conspiracy that sent us reeling into poverty—and we know the names of their local collaborators too. Show them their enemies, so they can take comfort in knowing who's to blame for their desperate lot; let them understand what they must do to rid themselves of these enemies, so that even as they tremble with their sorrow and their rage, they can imagine the day when they achieve true greatness; conjure up their loathsome foes and paint their dastardly acts so vividly that they may find the peace of mind that can only come to those who heap their own sins onto others. O brother mine, I know you are possessed of a mighty pen, a pen that can realize all these dreams—and tales far more implausible than

these—and miracles others might deem impossible. With your beautiful words, and with the astonishing memories you will soon be pulling
from the bottomless well that is your mind, you can bring these dreams
to life. If our shopkeeper from Kars could see the colors of the streets
in which you spent your childhood, it's because he could glimpse these
dreams between your lines— so give him back his dreams. Once upon
a time you wrote words that sent chills down the spines of readers the
length and breadth of Anatolia by harking back to the swings and
merry-go-rounds they remembered from their own childhood holidays, not just to stir up their memories but to console them with
visions of the days to come. Give me your address and you can do it
again. In this wretched land of ours, what other path is open to us
except to write? I know you write because it is the only thing you can
do, because you're helpless. Oh, how long I've agonized over these
terrible bouts of helplessness you suffer! I know how you despaired as
you gazed upon the pictures of pashas and fruits in the produce stores,
how you worried about the piteous fierce-eyed brothers you've spied
in dirty back-street coffeehouses, dealing each other cards damp with
sweat. Whenever I see a mother and her son lining up in front of the
State Meat and Fish Foundation at the crack of dawn and hoping for
bargains, whenever I see fathers sitting with their families in brown
and treeless parks of a Sunday, smoking their way through the endless
tedium of the afternoon, I always wonder what *you* would have to say
about them. Had you witnessed these scenes, you would—I know—
have gone home to your little room in the evening, to sit down at that
desk that is as shabby and old as our forgotten country, and watch the
white paper sucking in your ink as you composed these people's stories. I'd see your head bent over your paper until long after midnight,
when you'd rise from your desk in hopeless misery to shuffle over to
the refrigerator; there you'd stand, staring through the open door but
taking nothing, turning back into the apartment, to wander from room
to room like a sleepwalker; I could almost see you circling around your
desk. O brother mine, you were so sad, so very lonely, and in such pain.
How I loved you! All those years I spent reading your work, I thought
only of you. Please, give me your address—if nothing else, give me
your answer. Let me tell you what I saw on the Yalova ferry: War College cadets, their faces crawling with letters—large dead spiders, that's

what they looked like—and let me tell you what a delicious childish panic these handsome strapping boys went into when they found themselves alone with me in that same ferry's filthy toilet. Let me tell you about the blind lottery-ticket seller who sent you a letter and who, when you replied, went straight to his favorite tavern and, after knocking back a flask of *rakı*, took your letter out of his pocket and asked his friends to read it aloud to him, stopping them from time to time to point proudly between the lines at the secret you'd shared with him, who made his son read him *Milliyet* every morning thereafter to listen for the sentence that would bring the mystery out into the open. There was a Teşvikiye post office stamp on the letter you sent him. Hello— are you still listening? Answer me, tell me you're still there; that's all I ask. Dear God! I can hear you breathing, I can hear your breath. Listen. These are sentences I prepared very carefully in advance, so listen carefully to what I have to say. It was when you wrote that column explaining why it was that the sad funnels of smoke rising from the smokestacks of the old Bosphorus ferries looked so elegant, and so fragile, that I knew I understood you. I knew I understood you when you wrote about the torpor that overcame you when you walked the back streets among the old wooden houses that are slowly spilling into cemeteries, when you explained why you'd go home from these rambles with tears in your eyes. I knew I understood you when you wrote about that movie you saw one afternoon—about Hercules, or Samson, or the Romans—at one of those theaters where you will find small children standing at the entrance, selling secondhand copies of *Texas* and *Tom Mix*; about that moment when the long-legged sad-faced third-rate Hollywood starlet who was playing the beautiful slave strutted across the screen, and every man in the pulsating audience fell silent and you wanted to die. How about that? Do you understand me? Answer me, you shameless man! At least once in his life, a writer should have a chance to meet his perfect reader—I am that person! Give me your address and I'll bring you photographs of lycée girls who adore you, one hundred and twenty-seven in all; some have addresses on the back, others come with excerpts from the lovely things they've said about you in their journals. Thirty-three of them wear glasses, eleven have braces, six have necks as long as swans, and twenty-four have those little ponytails you love so much. They all

adore you; they practically faint when they hear your name. I swear to
you. Give me your address, and I'll bring you a list of all the women
who were absolutely convinced that you were speaking to them personally, and only to them, when you began that chatty column you
wrote at some point during the sixties with the words 'Did you listen to
the radio last night? What agony it was, listening to *The Hour of the
Lover and the Beloved*; I could think of only one thing.' Did you know
that you have as many admirers in high society as you have in middle-
class neighborhoods and provincial towns, as many army wives who
long for you as high-strung impressionable students? If you can let me
have your address, I'll bring over all my photographs of women who
go out in disguise—but not just in the night, not just to the ball—these
are women who are never *not* in disguise, who must wear disguises just
to get through a normal day. You once wrote that we do not have private lives in this country—and how right you were—that, though we'd
seen it mentioned in translated novels and foreign magazines, we can
hardly even grasp the *idea* of a private life; but when I show you these
photographs of certain someones in their high-heeled boots and
devil's masks, you may want to change your mind. . . . For goodness'
sake, just give me your address, I beg of you: I can bring over my amazing twenty-year collection of citizens' faces. I have mug shots of jealous lovers, just after they've doused each other's faces with nitric acid,
and mug shots of fundamentalists, some clean-shaven, some bearded,
all still in shock after being caught conducting secret rites for which
they've drawn Arabic letters on their faces. I have Kurdish rebels, who
used to have letters on their faces, before they were burned off by
napalm; I have pictures of rapists, hanged by provincial mobs—and
what bribes I had to pay, to worm my way into the official files! They
look nothing like the broken-necked men you see swinging from the
oiled ropes in cartoons: you never see their tongues hanging out. All
that happens is that you can see the letters on their faces more clearly.
So I understand the secret desire that drove you to confess—this was
in one of your earliest columns—that you preferred the old executioners and the old ways of putting men to death. Just as I know how much
you love ciphers, word games, and cryptograms, so too do I know how
much you love to wander among us after midnight in disguises
designed to restore our lost mystery. I know the games you've played

on your lawyer nephew, just so you can stay up all night with your step-sister, make fun of everyone and everything around you, and amuse her with the purest, simplest stories—the stories that make us who we are. Those pieces you wrote making fun of lawyers: when their angry wives wrote in to complain and you wrote back to assure them that the lawyer you had in mind was most certainly not their husband, you were telling the truth, of that I have no doubt. This has gone on long enough; give me your address. I can interpret your dreams for you, give you a detailed reading of each and every cavorting dog, skull, horse, and witch; I can tell you which of those tiny pictures of women, guns, skulls, soccer players, flags, and flowers that you see hanging from the rearview mirrors in taxis made their way into your love letters. I know a fair number of the 'coded sentences' you fob off on your readers just to get rid of them, and I also know that you never, ever, go anywhere without the notebook in which you record those same sentences—or without your historical costumes. . . ."

Much later, after Galip had quietly pulled the phone from the wall, after he had gone through all of Celâl's notebooks and closets and old clothes, after he had wandered off to bed like a sleepwalker searching for his memories, after he had lain in bed for some time, wearing Celâl's pajamas, listening to the noises of the Nişantaşı night as he drifted off, he remembered what it was he so treasured in a deep long sleep: He could forget the awful yawning gap between the person he was and the person he longed to become. As he sank peacefully into the abyss, life came together in a single swirling mist—all he'd heard and all he hadn't heard, all he'd seen and all he hadn't seen, all he knew and all that would be forever dark.

Chapter Thirty-one

In Which the Story Goes
Through the Looking Glass

The two together
The reflection and its reflection entered the mirror.
—Sheikh Galip

I dreamed that I had at last become the person I've always longed to
become. In the midst of life, wandering through the muddy concrete forest that is our city, in a dark street swarming with darker faces:
my dream, my Rüya. Drained by sorrow, I fell asleep and found you.
In my dream, in the story my dream brought me, I knew you'd still
love me, even if I failed to become someone else; I knew I must resign
myself, look at the person staring back at me in my picture, and accept
myself just as I was; there was, I knew, no point in fighting it any longer
and nothing to be gained by stepping into someone else's shoes. The
streets were dark; the dread houses bent over our heads; but they
seemed to open up for us, and as we walked we seemed to bring meaning to every shop we passed, every pavement we crossed.

How many years ago was it, when exactly did you and I stumble
onto that magic game of ours for the very first time? It was the day
before a religious holiday—our mothers had taken us to the children's
department of a clothing store (these being the happy days before they
decided that girls' clothing should be separate from boys')—and it was
there, in the darkest corner of this boring store (more boring even
than the most boring religion class) that we found ourselves caught
between two full-length mirrors. We stood there stunned, watching
our reflections multiply, watching them grow smaller and smaller and
vanish into infinity.

Two years after this, we were having a laugh about various children of our acquaintance who had sent their pictures in to *Children's Week* in the hope of appearing on their Animal Lovers page, though as always we fell silent when we got to the Great Inventors column. After we'd read it, we turned to the back page to find a picture of a redheaded girl reading the same magazine we held in our hands: she too was looking at the redheaded girl on the back cover, who was looking at a smaller version of the same back cover, on which a smaller redheaded girl was looking at a back cover on which was an even smaller redheaded girl. . . .

Later, when we had grown taller and drifted away from each other, I saw the same thing on a jar of olive paste that had just come on the market, which, because we never ate it in our house, I only ever saw when I joined you at your breakfast table on Sunday mornings. "Oooh! I see you're eating caviar!" "It's not caviar, it's Ender Olive Paste!" That was the routine in the radio ads, and the label on the jar itself featured a perfect father sitting at a table with his happy wife and beaming children. I was the one who pointed out the jar of Ender Olive Paste on their table, and the smaller family on its label, on which there was an even smaller family, and as we traced the chain of families to the vanishing point, we both divined the beginning of the story I am about to tell you—though not its end.

There were once two cousins, a boy and a girl. They grew up in the same apartment house, walking up and down the same staircase, gobbling up the same *lokums*, lion-shaped candies, and Turkish delights. They did their homework together, they came down with the same illnesses, they scared each other playing hide-and-seek. They were the same age, too. They went to the same school, and every morning they walked to school together, and in the evenings they would listen to the same radio programs. They liked the same records and read the same books and *Children's Week*s; they'd rummage through the same trunks and closets, and out would come the same fezzes, the same silk covers, the same boots. They had an older cousin they both adored, and one day, when he came to visit, they grabbed his book from his hands and began to read it.

At first the boy and the girl were amused by its ancient vocabulary, its lofty language, and its strange Persian figures of speech; when laughter gave way to boredom, they tossed the book into a corner, but then—thinking there might be a torture scene among the illustrations, or a naked body, or a submarine—they picked it up again and began to flip through the pages, and before long they were reading it in earnest. Though the book was terribly long, there was a love story early on in which the boy wished he could be the hero. So beautiful were the book's descriptions of love that the boy wished he too could be in love. So when he read on to discover that he shared the hero's other symptoms (impatience with food, inventing reasons to see the girl, not being able to drink a whole glass of water, even if he was thirsty), it dawned on him that he'd fallen in love with the girl at that magic moment when they had sat down together with the book open before him, his hand on the edge of one page and hers on the other.

So what was this story they were reading? It was a very old story, about a boy and a girl born into the same tribe. The girl's name was Beauty, the boy's name Love; born on the same day, they had taken their lessons from the same teacher, wandered along the edges of the same pool, and fallen in love. Years later, when the boy asked for the girl's hand, the elders set him a task: If he wished to marry Beauty, he was to travel to the Land of the Hearts and return with a certain alchemical formula. So the boy set out on his journey, which was long and arduous: He fell down a well and was enslaved by a painted witch; the thousands of faces and images he found swirling inside a second well reduced him to a strange drunkenness; he became infatuated with the daughter of the emperor of China, because she looked like his true love; he climbed out of wells to be locked up in castles; he followed and was followed; he struggled through bitter winters, traveled great distances, seizing upon every sign and clue he found along the way; he immersed himself in the mystery of letters; he listened to other people's stories and told others his own. At long last, Poetry, who had been following him all along in disguise, came to him and said, "You are your beloved, and your beloved is you; can't you see this?" That is when the boy in the story remembered how he had fallen in love with the girl— when they were studying with the same teacher and reading from the same book.

The book *they* had read together told the story of a sultan named King Jubilant and a young beauty named Eternal, and though the sultan was utterly bewildered, you have already guessed that the lovers in this story too would turn out to have fallen in love while reading a third love story. The lovers in the third story would have fallen in love while reading a fourth, and the lovers in the fourth story while reading a fifth.

But it was not until much later, years after we'd paid our visit to the clothing store, and read *Children's Week* together, and studied the picture on the jar of olive paste—after you had run away from home, after I had given my life over to stories, and tried at last to tell my own—that I realized the gardens of our memories were linked in the same way: Each story led to another story in an infinite chain, with each door leading to another door that led to another. No matter where they were set—in Damascus or the Arabian Desert, in Horasan overlooking the Asian steppes, in Verona in the foothills of the Alps, or in Baghdad on the shores of the Tigris—the love stories were sad and moving. The saddest and most moving thing about these stories was the way they lingered in your mind, the ease with which you could put yourself in even the saddest, purest, most selfless of their heroes.

If someone sits down one day to write this story of ours, this story whose end I am still unable to foresee—and perhaps this task will fall to me—I cannot be sure our readers will be able to identify with us so easily, or if our story will linger in their minds, but since I've noticed that there are always certain passages that set the lovers apart from each other, and others that set apart their stories, I have written the following in preparation.

Once we went out together on a visit. Long past midnight, as we sat in a room so thick with cigarette smoke that the air was blue, listening to someone three paces away from you telling a long involved story, I watched the strangest expression come over your face; I could read it clearly. *I'm not there*, it said—and I loved you. Once, at the end of a long lazy week, you were looking rather listlessly for a belt among your shirts and green jumpers and all those old nightgowns you couldn't bring yourself to throw away, and as you stood before your wardrobe, daunted by your own mess, I loved you. Once, when you were still a child and flirting with the idea of becoming an artist, you sat down at a

table with Grandfather to learn how to draw a tree, and when he teased
you, you didn't mind, you laughed—I loved you then too. Once you
slammed the *dolmuş* door on the hem of your purple coat, and when
the five-lira coin flew out of your hand to make a perfect arc before it
flew into the grate in the gutter, I loved the playful surprise on your
face, and I loved you. On a beautiful April day, you went to see if the
handkerchief you'd left on our tiny balcony that morning was dry yet,
and finding it still wet you realized the sun had fooled you, and just
after that, as you stood there listening to the children playing in the
vacant lot and looking so mournful, I loved you. Once, I listened to
you telling someone about a movie we'd seen together, and, oh, how it
unnerved me to realize how differently you remembered it, and how
different my memory must be from yours, but still I loved you. I loved
you. Once, when you had retired to a corner to a read a sumptuously
illustrated newspaper article—it didn't matter to me that it was a
learned professor, railing against intermarriage among close relations,
because I loved seeing how you pushed out your upper lip when you
were reading, just like a character in a Tolstoy novel. I loved the way
you looked at your reflection in the mirrors of elevators, as if the face
staring back at you belonged to someone else, and then, right afterward, you'd dig into your handbag, as if you were hunting for something you'd only just remembered. I loved the way you kept your
high-heeled shoes waiting side by side for hours on end—one resting
on its side like a narrow sailboat, the other crouching like a hunch-
backed cat—only to slip into them so very quickly, and then, many
hours later, I loved watching your hips, legs, and feet sway into action
of their own accord, to flick off the muddied shoes and send them
back into asymmetrical retirement. When I saw you looking so sadly at
the hopeless blackened matches and cigarette ends in your overflowing
ashtray, as your thoughts went who knew where, I loved you; and I
loved you when a street we'd known all our lives suddenly looked different, as if a new light were shining on it, as if the sun that morning
had risen in the west, but it wasn't the street I loved, it was you. On
winter days, when a wind blew in from the south to melt the snow and
chase away the dirty clouds that had been hanging over the city, when
you pointed across the sea at the shadow rising above the minarets, the
antennae, and the Prince's Islands, it wasn't Uludağ I loved but the way

you tucked your head into your shoulders as you shivered; and I loved the wistful way you looked at the tired old horse pulling the water seller's cart, loaded down with enamel canisters; I loved the way you made fun of people who said people should never give money to beggars because they were actually quite rich, and the happy way you laughed if you had found us a quick way out of the movies, and got us back to the street when everyone else was still who knew how far down beneath us, shuffling up the labyrinthine stairs. I loved the solemn way you'd tear a sheet off the *Daily Almanac with Prayer Times*, bringing us one day closer to our death, and your mournful tones when you went straight to the very last sheet to its suggested menu of the day—meat with chickpeas, pilaf, pickles, and mixed fruit compote—and your patience when you taught me how to open the tube of Eagle anchovy paste—first remove the disk, then turn the cap, but don't forget to read the label, "with best wishes of the manufacturer, Monsieur Trellidis"; on winter mornings, when I noticed that your face was the same color as the pale white sky, and when we were children and I saw you dashing madly between the cars streaming down the avenue, I was worried for you, and I loved you: I loved the smile that lit up your face as you studied the crow perched on the coffin laid out in the courtyard of the mosque; I loved it when you pretended to be a radio announcer, giving the latest news about our parents' arguments; when I held your head in my hands and looked into your eyes and saw where life was taking us, I loved you; when you left your ring next to the vase one day, and several days later left it there again, I didn't understand why, but still I loved you; when I was making love to you, and we were slowly, arduously, taking flight, like immense mythical birds, you brightened our solemn rites with a joke, with a surprise, and I loved you; I loved you when you showed me the perfect star in the heart of an apple when you cut it crosswise, not from top to bottom; I loved you when I glanced across my desk at midday and saw a single strand of your hair and could not for the life of me understand how it had got there; once, when we were on an outing, and I was looking at our hands, side by side, grasping the overhead bar of the crowded city bus and noticing how very different they were, I loved you as I loved my own body, as if you were my lost soul, and even as I felt the joyous pain of knowing I had changed my skin, I loved you; as we watched a train passing before us, bound for who knows where, and a shadow passed across your face; when the same shadow crossed your face again that evening, as you watched a passing flock of madly screeching crows; as the same strange melancholy returned to your face after the power cut that evening, as darkness filled our apartment, and the sky glowed with evening light—my heart ached with helpless jealousy, but still I loved you.

Chapter Thirty-two

I'm Not a Madman,
Just a Loyal Reader

"I fashioned your likeness into a mirror."
—Süleyman Çelebi

Galip slept well on Wednesday night—he had, after all, gone for two days without any sleep at all—but when he rose from his bed on Thursday morning, he was not really awake. Later, when he tried to reconstruct the earlier hours of that morning—not just what he had done but the places he had visited in his mind between 4 A.M., when he had first woken up, and the 7 A.M. prayer, when he crawled back into bed to drift back off to sleep—he would decide that he had spent these hours wandering amid what Celâl had once called "the wondrous mythic land between sleep and wakefulness."

As is so common to those who, after prolonged sleeplessness, fall into a deep slumber only to awaken in the middle of the night—and it is the same for those luckless souls who wake up to find themselves in someone else's bed—Galip had no idea where he was at first; not only did he fail to recognize the bed, the room, and the apartment, he could not even remember how it was he had gotten here, but rather than find his bearings he chose to remain bewildered and enchanted.

So when Galip went out to the desk where he'd been working until he went to bed, he was not at all surprised to see Celâl's box of disguises sitting next to it, and the things he then pulled out of the box did not surprise him either: a melon hat, assorted sultan's turbans, caftans, canes, boots, stained silk shirts, fake beards in various colors and sizes, wigs, pocket watches, glassless glasses, caps, fezzes, silk cummerbunds, daggers, Janissary medals, wristbands, and any number of other odds and ends from Erol Bey, owner of the famous Beyoğlu shop that supplied costumes and equipment for all domestically produced historic films. He tried to imagine Celâl wandering about the same district, dressed in these costumes; it was like plucking a memory from the back of his own mind. The images playing before his eyes were no less mysterious, no less real, than the blue-tinged rooftops, crooked streets, and phantom beings in the dream from which he'd just awoken; they were marvels, impossible to explain though at the same time not quite defying explanation. In his dream he'd been searching for an address in a district of Damascus, thought it was also located in Istanbul, and on the slopes of Kars Castle, and it had all felt quite effortless, like doing the easiest clues in a crossword puzzle at the back of a Sunday supplement.

Though he was now awake, he was still under the dream's spell, so when he looked over at the desk to see a notebook filled with names and addresses, it seemed the happiest of coincidences: It was, he thought, a sign specially placed there by an invisible hand, a playful deity who liked playing hide-and-seek. So pleased was Galip to find himself in this sort of world, he could not help but smile as he cast his eyes on the addresses listed inside and the sentences he found next to them. To think of all the faithful readers all across the city—all across Anatolia—who scanned Celâl's columns day after day, waiting for these sentences to appear; perhaps some of them had appeared already. Still drifting in his mist of dreams, Galip struggled to remember: Had he seen these sentences before? Hadn't he read some of them years and years ago? Even if he could not remember reading these sentences, he knew he'd heard them from Celâl's own lips: "A true marvel has a touch of the ordinary, just as a truly ordinary thing has a touch of the marvelous."

Though there were some sentences he'd never read or heard, he felt as if he remembered them from somewhere else—like Sheikh Galip's two-hundred-year-old warning, in his story about the schooldays of two children named Beauty and Love: "Mystery is sovereign, so treat it with respect."

There were other sentences he knew he'd never read in Celâl's work, or in anyone else's either, but still they felt as familiar as if he'd read them many times over, inside and outside Celâl's columns. Like the sentence that was to serve as a signal for the Beşiktaş resident on Serencebey, Fahrettin Dalkıran: "Most of us entertain only the crudest dreams of Judgment Day—for them it was merely the day when, at long last, they could beat their teachers to a pulp, or, to simplify matters even further, they could kill their fathers; but this particular gentleman had the good sense to foresee it as the day when his long-lost twin sister would return to him in the guise of death, and it was with this in mind that he withdrew himself from sight, taking himself to a house where no one could find him, and which he never left." Who could this gentleman be?

As the first light appeared in the sky, Galip decided on impulse to plug in the phone again; then he washed himself, helped himself to whatever he found in the refrigerator, and—after the morning prayer—made his way back to bed. As he drifted off into the land between sleep and wakefulness, daydreams and night dreams, he was suddenly a child again, sitting next to Rüya in a rowboat on the Bosphorus. There were no mothers with them, or aunts, or boatmen; it was just himself and Rüya, and Galip found this strangely unnerving.

When he woke up, the phone was ringing. By the time he reached it, he was sure it would be the persistent voice again, not Rüya; he was startled to hear the voice of a woman.

"Celâl? Celâl—is that you?"

It was not a young voice, and not a voice Galip had ever heard before.

"Yes."

"Darling! Darling, where have you been? Where have you been? I've been looking everywhere for you, for days, for days, looking everywhere, oh, dear me, everywhere, oh—"

Her last syllable turned into a sob and then into a crying jag.

"I can't place your voice," Galip said.

"You can't place my voice?" said the woman, imitating his tone. "How refined you are suddenly. You're telling me—*me*—you can't place my voice? So I'm just a voice now, am I?" After a silence she put her cards on the table, haughty but at the same time rejoicing over her winning hand. "This is Emine."

This meant nothing to Galip. "Yes."

"Yes? All you have to say is yes?"

"After so many years . . ." Galip murmured.

"Yes, my darling, after so, so many years. Can you imagine how I felt when—at long last—you called out to me in your column? I've been waiting for twenty years. Can you imagine how I felt when I read that sentence I've spent the last twenty years waiting for? I wanted to shout out to the whole world, to the whole world, I tell you. I almost lost my mind; it was all I could do to keep hold of myself. I wept. As you know, they forced Mehmet into retirement after he got mixed up in that revolution business. But he still goes out every morning, always has things to do. As soon as he left the house, I rushed out too. I ran straight to Kurtuluş—to our old side street—but there was nothing there, nothing. Everything had changed. They'd torn it all down; nothing was where it should have been. Our little house was gone. I burst into tears: there, in the middle of the street. Someone came out and offered me a glass of water. I went straight home after that, packed my bag, and left before Mehmet came back again. Celâl—my darling—tell me how I can find you. For seven days now, I've been on the road, going from hotel room to hotel room, staying with distant relations who make no secret they don't want me there, and how could I hope to hide my shame? I can't tell you how many times I called the paper, but all I got was 'We don't know where he is.' I called your relatives too—they don't know anything either. I rang this number, but no one answered. I hardly took anything with me, but I don't care; what else could I need? Mehmet's been hunting for me everywhere. I left him a short letter, explaining nothing. He has no idea why I left home. No one knows— I've told no one; no one knows about you, my love; you're my secret, my only pride in life. What's going to happen now? I'm afraid. I'm all alone! I no longer have any responsibilities. Your plump little bunny will never have to get home to her husband before supper; you can breathe free. My children are grown—one's in Germany, the other's in the army. I'm all yours—I can give you all my time: my life, everything. I can do your ironing. I'll clear up—oh, yes, I will—that desk of yours, I'll change your pillowcases; I've never seen you anywhere except in that bare place where we met. I can't tell you how curious I am about your real house, your furniture, your books. My darling, where are you? How am I going to find you? Why didn't you code your address in that column? Give me your address. You've been thinking of me too, haven't you? You've been thinking of me all these years, am I right?

We're going to be alone again, in that one-room stone house of ours; we'll sit there with our teas, and the sun will pour down on us through the linden leaves, on our faces, and our hands, our hands that know each other so well. But Celâl—that house is gone now; they tore it down, there's nothing there, and the Armenians are gone too, and all the old shops. . . . Didn't you know this? Did you really want me to go there and cry my eyes out? Why didn't you ever put this into a column? You who can write anything, you could have written this. Speak to me. I've been waiting twenty years, so speak to me! Do your hands still perspire when you're feeling shame, do you still get that childish look on your face when you're asleep? Tell me, call me, darling. . . . How am I going to see you?"

"Madam," said Galip carefully, "My dear lady—I've lost my memory. There must have been a mistake. I haven't sent a column in to the paper for days, so they've just been printing things from thirty years ago. Do you understand what I'm saying to you?"

"No."

"I never intended to send you or anyone else a coded sentence, or indeed any message at all. I no longer write. The people at the paper are just reprinting my old columns. My guess is that the sentence comes from one of those old pieces."

"That's a lie!" the woman cried. "You're lying to me! You love me. You loved me with all your heart. Everything you wrote, you wrote to me. When you wrote about the most beautiful places in Istanbul, you described the street where we met to make love—our Kurtuluş, our little love nest—it was not your usual *garçonnière*, was it? You described the view from the window, our linden trees. When you described Rumi's moon-faced beauty, it wasn't poetry; it was your own moon-faced love you were describing. It was me! You talked about my cherry lips, too, and my crescent eyebrows; all this time I've been the one inspiring you. When the Americans landed on the moon, when you wrote about the dark spots on the moon's face, I knew you were really describing the beauty spots on mine. My darling, don't you ever dare deny it! When you wrote about the 'dark and fearsome mysteries of bottomless wells' you were talking about my own black eyes—and yes, thank you, you brought tears to them, yes, you did! You wrote, 'I went back to that apartment!' and of course you meant our own two-story

house, but since you didn't want anyone to know of our secret and forbidden love, you had to turn it into a six-story house with an elevator—I know. Because you and I, we met in Kurtuluş, in that little
house, eighteen long years ago. Met five times. Please—don't deny it—
I know you loved me."

"My dear lady—as you've said yourself, all this happened a very
long time ago," said Galip. "I no longer remember any of it, I'm losing
my memories, one by one."

"My darling Celâl, my sweet little Celâl, this cannot be you. I don't
believe it is. Is there somebody in the room with you—someone keeping you hostage, making you say these things? Are you alone? Just tell
me the truth, tell me you've loved me all these years. That will be
enough. I've waited eighteen years, I can wait for another eighteen if I
have to. Just say it once, one little sentence, that's all I ask; tell me you
love me. . . . All right, then at least tell me you loved me then. Tell me 'I
loved you then,' and I'll hang up the phone."

"I loved you."

"Call me darling."

"Darling."

"Not like that! Say it with feeling!"

"Madam, please! Let the past stay in the past. I've aged, and perhaps
you are not as young as you once were, either. I am not the person
you've been dreaming about, not at all. So please, let's put this behind
us—this is all due to a simple printing error. Let's accept that someone's playing a nasty joke on us, just by failing to pay attention."

"Dear God! So what is to become of me then?"

"Go home, go back to your husband. If he loves you, he'll forgive
you. You can think of a story; if he loves you, he'll believe you right
away. So go back to your house, back to your loyal husband, before you
break his heart."

"After waiting eighteen years, I want to see you—if only once."

"Madam, I am no longer the man I was eighteen years ago."

"No, you *are* that man. I read your columns. I know everything
about you. I think about you always; you have no idea how much I
think about you. Tell me: Is the day of our liberation coming soon?
Who will our Savior be? I'm waiting for Him, too. You are He. Plenty
of people know this. You alone hold the secret. But you're not going to

gallop in on a white horse, you'll be riding in a white Cadillac. Everyone sees this dream. My darling Celâl, how much I've loved you. Let me see you once, just once—if I can just see you from afar, that's enough—at a park; come to Maçka Park at five. Let me see you from afar just once at Maçka Park; come."

"Madam, please excuse me, I'm going to have to hang up. But first I hope you'll forgive an old man for taking advantage of the love you have so undeservedly lavished on him and let me ask a favor. Please, would you mind telling me how you found my number? Do you have any of my addresses? These are very important to me."

"If I tell you, will you give me permission to see you, at least once?"

Galip fell silent.

"Yes, I will," he said finally.

Another silence.

"But first you have to give me *your* address," said the woman cunningly. "The truth is, after all these years, I don't really trust you anymore."

Galip paused to think. He could hear the woman breathing nervously, like a tired steam engine, at the other end of the line. He had a feeling it might be two women—somewhere, in the background, he thought he heard a radio—but it didn't sound like the wailing laments about love, pain, and abandonment that passed for Turkish popular music; it sounded more like the music he associated with Grandfather, Grandmother, and their cigarettes. Galip tried to conjure up an image of a room with a large old radio sitting at one end and, in the other, a weeping, wheezing matron sitting in a shabby armchair, clutching a phone, but the only room he could see was the one two floors below the flat in which he was now standing, where Grandfather and Grandmother had once sat smoking their cigarettes, where he and Rüya had once played "Now you see it, now you don't."

"Your addresses—" Galip began, but then the woman cried out with all her might.

"No! No! Don't tell me! He's listening too. He's here. He's the one who's been making me say all this. Celâl, darling, don't give him your address! He's coming to kill you! Ah, oh, ah!"

As the last moan died away, Galip heard a strange and terrifying metal crunch; as he pressed the receiver against his ear, trying to make sense of the clatter that followed, he imagined a scuffle. Then there was a loud noise: a gunshot, or perhaps they'd been fighting over the receiver and dropped it. A silence followed, but not a real silence. Galip could hear Behiye Aksoy crooning "You bad boy you, oh, you bad bad boy" on a distant radio, and—just as distant—a woman sobbing. Someone had grabbed the receiver; Galip could hear his heavy breathing, but he didn't say a word. These sound effects continued for some time. A new song started on the radio, but the breathing remained the same; and so, too, did the woman's droning sobs.

"Hello?" said Galip, feeling very angry now. "Hello! Hello?"

"It's me, it's me," a male voice said finally, and it was the voice he'd been hearing for days now, the usual voice. He spoke with cool confidence, as if to calm Galip down, bring some sort of unpleasantness to a close. "Yesterday Emine confessed everything. I found her and brought her home. Celâl Efendi, you disgust me. I'm going to destroy you." Then, in the indifferent voice of an umpire summing up a dull game that lost everyone's interest hours ago, he added, "I'm going to kill you."

There was a silence.

"Perhaps you could let me explain my side of the story," said Galip, falling back into his lawyerly habits. "The column was published by mistake. It was a column from years ago."

"Let's forget all that, just drop it," said Mehmet. What was his surname? "I've heard it already; I've heard all I need to hear. That's not why I'm going to kill you anyway, even though you deserve to be killed for that too. Do you know why I'm going to kill you?" But he wasn't asking because he wanted Celâl—or Galip—to give him an answer; he knew the answer already. Out of lawyerly habit, Galip listened. "It's not because you betrayed the coup that might have got this miserable country back on its feet, or because you ridiculed the upstanding officers and other brave patriots whose futures you ruined, and it's not because of these insidious daydreams you conjured up in your favorite armchair, while *they* were putting their lives on the line, or because of the conniving way you gained the trust of simple patriots all over the country, infecting their dreams; it's not even because you deceived my wife, who—I'll be brief—had a bit of a breakdown when the rest of us were caught up in revolutionary fever. No, I'm going to kill you because you deceived us all, deceived the entire nation with your bold lies, scandalous dreams, paranoid obsessions, insinuating refinements, elegant turns of phrase, and endearing antics—for years and years, you fooled even me. But now at long last my eyes are open. So now let everyone else open their eyes too. That shopkeeper whose story you once heard, only to mock it? This man you laughed at and forgot—I'm avenging him too. I've thought of nothing else all week, as I've been combing the city for you; I've come to see that there is only one way forward. Because now I must forget all I've learned, and so too must the entire nation. After all, it was you who wrote that by the first autumn following their funerals, we lose all memory of our writers— consign them to the bottomless well of oblivion, to sleep for ever-more."

"I couldn't agree more," said Galip. "Did I already tell you that my memory has dried up almost entirely? That I plan to get out of this writing business for good, once I've written these last few columns, and rid myself of the few little fragments I have left? Which reminds me—would you mind telling me what you made of today's column?"

"You rotten bastard, have you no sense of responsibility? Do you have any idea what commitment means? Or honesty? Or altruism? These amusing little signs you sent out to your poor deceived readers, just to make fun of them—are you trying to tell me that they remind you of nothing else? Do you know what brotherhood means?"

Galip wanted to say, I do!—not to defend Celâl but because he liked the question. He had no chance, though, for now the voice that called himself Mehmet—which Mehmet was this Muhammed?—began to pelt him with furiously inspired curses.

As the tirade came to an end, Mehmet said, "Shut up! I've had enough!" He was, Galip decided, talking to the woman crying in the background, for now she became quiet. Then he heard her explaining something; then someone in the room turned off the radio.

"You knew she was my cousin, didn't you? That's why you wrote all those clever pieces making fun of people who married their relations," continued the voice who said he was Mehmet. "Even though you knew full well that half our of nation's youth marry their uncle's daughters, and the other half their aunt's sons, you still went ahead and wrote those disgraceful things about the perils of inbreeding. But let me just make it clear, my dear Celâl Bey. I did not marry her because I had never had occasion to meet any other girls, or because I was afraid of all women who did not happen to be relations, or because I did not believe that any woman other than my mother, my aunts, and their children could love me truly or find the patience to put up with me: I married this woman because I loved her. Do you have any idea—any idea at all—what it means to love a girl who was your playmate from early childhood? Have you any idea what it means to love one woman all your life? This woman you hear crying for you: I've loved her for fifty years. I've loved her since I was a child—do you understand?— and I love her still. Do you know what it means to look at a woman who is your other half? It's like seeing yourself in a dream. Do you know what love is? Have words like this served only as means to an end—to play disgraceful tricks on backward readers who are all too ready to believe any story you tell them? Oh, how I pity you, despise you, grieve for you. Have you done anything in life but turn phrases and play with words? Answer me!"

"My dear friend!" said Galip. "This is my profession."

"He says it's his profession!" bellowed the voice at the other end of the line. "You seduced us, deceived us, degraded us all! Oh, when I think how much faith I put in you! How I let you convince me that life was one long parade of misery, a string of asinine delusions, a hell of nightmares, a masterpiece of mediocrity in which all the world was vulgar, mean, and pitiful. You rotten bastard! I admired you so much, I even believed you when you told me that I had only my own cowardice to blame for my misfortunes, that every misfortune our nation has ever suffered stemmed from the same source. Oh, the time I wasted trying to pinpoint my mistakes! Aching to identify what it was that had turned me into a coward, and why, and all the while seeing you— whom I know now to be the greatest coward of them all—as the source of all courage! I worshiped you so much. I read every column you wrote, even the ones in which you went on and on about your utterly ordinary childhood, writing about things we'd all done—not that you would have known, because you didn't have the least interest in us; yes, I even read the ones about that dark apartment house with the murky stairwells that stank of fried onions, where you lived for some time as a child, and the ones about ghosts and witches and meta-

physical experiments that made no sense at all; but still I was convinced that there were secret miracles shimmering under the surface,
so I never read them just once but hundreds of times over. I'd have my
wife read them too, and we'd spend hours every evening talking them
over, until I'd convinced myself that there was only one thing I could
believe—that these columns contained the signs that would lead me to
life's secret meaning. I even came to think I'd divined this secret meaning, only to discover that the secret meant nothing."

"I never asked my readers to admire me so slavishly," Galip inter-
jected.

"That's a lie! From the very beginning of your career, you've gone
out of your way to con people like me. You answered readers' letters,
asked them for their photographs, studied their handwriting, pretended to pass on secrets, passwords, coded sentences. . . ."

"But only to serve the revolution, to advertise the Day of Judgment, the coming of the Messiah, the hour of liberation—"

"And then what? After you stop writing, then what?"

"Well, at least I gave my readers something to believe in."

"They believed in *you*, and didn't you ever love that! Listen, I
worshiped you so fervently that if I read a particularly brilliant column
of yours, I'd jump up and down in my chair and tears would roll down
my cheeks. I couldn't stay still; I'd pace the room, pace the streets; I'd
dream about you. But that was just the beginning. I thought and
dreamed about you so much that a moment arrived when the line
between us faded into the mists of my imagination, and I could no
longer see where you ended and I began. No, I was never so far gone
that I actually imagined myself to be the author of your work. Do not
forget that I'm not a madman, just a loyal reader. But it did seem to me
that in some strange way, by a circuitous route that would be difficult
to trace, I had played some part in the making of these brilliant sentences, these elegant ideas. That if it were not for me, these inspired
inventions would never have come to you. Don't take this the wrong
way. I'm not talking about the countless ideas you stole from me, without once bothering to ask my permisssion. I'm not talking about the
myriad ways in which I found inspiration in Hurufism, nor am I referring to the discoveries I made at the end of the book I had such difficulty publishing. Those were yours, anyway. What I'm trying to explain

is this sense I had that we were thinking the same things at the same time, this sense I had that I shared in your success. Do you understand?"

"I understand," said Galip. "In fact, I once wrote something along just those lines."

"Yes, in that infamous piece that they reprinted by mistake. But you still don't understand, because if you had you would have gone along with me then and there. That's why I'm going to kill you—that's exactly why! Because you pretended to understand when in fact you didn't! Because you insinuated yourself into our souls and our dreams, even though you were never with us! All those years I spent devouring your words and thinking I myself had contributed to their brilliance, I'd try to conjure up memories from those happy years when we were friends—convince myself that there must have been a time we had entertained these same thoughts. So often did I succeed, so often did you figure in my daydreams, that when I met another fan of yours, and he showered you with praise, I felt as if he were praising *me*; I felt as if I were just as famous as you were. Those rumors they spread about your murky secret life—they were proof that I was not as ordinary as I looked, that I too had been touched by your divine secret; I felt as if I too were a living legend. I'd feel inspired; through your intercession, I became a new person. In the early years, whenever I was sitting on a city ferry and saw two fellow citizens holding newspapers in their hands and discussing you, how I'd long to say, I know Celâl Salik personally—even intimately, you might say! How I'd long to share our secrets with them, as they watched me in awe and amazement! Later on, this urge grew even stronger. The moment I saw two people reading you or discussing you, I'd want to say, Gentlemen, you are closer to Celâl Salik than you could ever imagine—for I am he! But I found this thought so intoxicating, so jarring, that every time I was tempted to speak out, every time I imagined the astonished admiration my words would cause, my heart would start thumping, and beads of sweat would form on my forehead, and I would almost faint from pleasure. So I never did declare myself in public, and if I kept my joy and triumph well hidden, it was because it was enough to have the thought flit through my mind. Do you understand?"

"I understand."

"When I read your pieces, I felt as intelligent, as triumphant, as if I had written them myself. They were not just applauding you, they were applauding me too—of that I was certain. Because you and I were together, far from the madding crowd, on another plane. I understood you so very well. Just like you, I hated those crowds you saw filing into movies, soccer matches, fairs, and festivals. Doomed never to become full-fledged human beings, they were always falling for the same old stupidities, the same old stories. Even at the moments when they looked their most innocent, even when they were victims of tragedies that broke your heart, you still knew they were the culprits too, or, at the very least, collaborators. I too was sick and tired of their false messiahs, their blundering presidents, their military coups, their democracies, their torture, their films. For years, whenever I came to the end of one of your columns, I'd tell myself, Yes! This is why I love Celâl Salik so much! and such would be my elation that tears would stream from my eyes. As they did yesterday, when I sang for you like a nightingale, recalling each column, one by one. Before yesterday, could you ever have imagined a reader like me?"

"Perhaps, to a degree—"

"Then listen. I'm harking back now to a distant moment in my own piteous past, a moment that anyone dwelling in our insipid, mediocre disaster of a city will immediately recognize. Some animal, some uncultivated lout, had slammed a *dolmuş* door on my finger, and there I was, trying to pull together the papers to request a pitifully small increase in my pension, while this worthless smart aleck behind the desk took his own sweet time—yes, there I was, mired in misfortune— when suddenly a thought came to me that I seized like a life buoy: What would Celâl Salik have done if he were in my shoes? What would he have said? Am I acting the way he would act? Over the past twenty years, that last question turned into something like an illness. I'd be joining the circle to dance the *halay* with all the other guests at a relation's wedding—but only because I did not want to ruin everyone else's fun—or I'd be sitting in a coffeehouse where I'd gone to play cards just to kill time, and laughing because I'd just won a hand of sixty-six, when suddenly I'd think, Would Celâl Salik ever do something like this? This would be enough to ruin the whole evening, enough to ruin my whole life. I spent my whole life asking what Celâl

Salik would do right now, and what he was doing right now, what he was thinking at that precise moment. But if it had stopped there, I wouldn't have minded. But then another question would flash into my mind: I wonder what Celâl Salik thinks of me? If Celâl Salik saw me smoking a cigarette after breakfast, when I was still in my pajamas, what would he say? What would Celâl Salik think if he saw me scolding the imbecile who bothered the married lady sitting next to me on the ferry, just because she was wearing a miniskirt? How would Celâl Salik feel if he knew I cut out all his columns and stored them in Onka brand binders? If he knew all I thought about him, if he knew all I thought about life, what, I wondered, would Celâl Salik have to say?"

"My esteemed reader, my faithful friend," said Galip, "just tell me why, during all these years, did you not once try to get in touch with me?"

"Do you think I never thought of it? I was afraid. Don't get me wrong—I wasn't worried that you might misunderstand me or that I might belittle myself in your august presence and flatter you in the way people always do in such circumstances, nor was I worried that I might find great miracles in even the most ordinary things you said, nor was I bothered by the thought that you might wish me to do so, or afraid that I might burst into laughter at the wrong moment and annoy you. Of course, I'd imagined all these scenarios a thousand times but I'd moved beyond them."

"You are more intelligent than those scenarios suggest," Galip said kindly.

"What I feared was that—once we'd met, once I'd expressed my admiration and showered you with praise in the way I described—neither of us would have anything left to say to each other."

"But as you can see, it wasn't like that at all," said Galip. "Look how nicely we've been talking the night away."

There was a silence.

"I'm going to kill you," said the voice. "I'm going to kill you! Because of you, I've never had a chance to be myself."

"No one can ever be himself."

"So you're always saying, but you could never feel like I do, you could never understand what I mean. . . . The thing you call *mystery*— you knew this truth without understanding it, described it without knowing it. Because no one can hope to discover this truth unless he is truly himself. But if he does discover it, this too means that he has not become himself. If one of the above is true, the other cannot be. Do you see the paradox?"

"I am both myself and someone else," said Galip.

"No. You can't say that and mean it," said the man at the other end of the line. "So that's why you're going to die. It's just like your columns: You make other people believe things without believing them yourself; it's precisely because you don't believe them that you're so convincing. But these people you've deceived—when they find out you've made them believe things you don't believe yourself, they're terrified."

"Terrified?"

"Don't you understand? What terrifies me is that thing you call *mystery*, that vast gray area, that imposter's game called writing, and the dark faces of words. For years, whenever I was reading your columns, I felt that I was both over there, sitting at the table or sitting in my chair, and in some other place, sitting next to the writer who was telling me these stories. Do you know how it feels to find out that you've been made to believe something by a nonbeliever? To know that the man who has converted you does not believe his own words? My complaint is not that you have kept me from becoming myself. You enriched my poor, pathetic life—by becoming you, I was able to escape the dark cloud of self-loathing that has pursued me always—but at the same time I was never sure of this magical thing I called *you*. I didn't know this, but I knew without knowing. Can this be called knowing? It seems that I did know where my wife of thirty years went after leaving a letter of farewell explaining nothing on the kitchen table, but it also seems that I had no idea I knew. Because I didn't know what I knew, I searched the entire city thinking I was looking for her, not you. But even as I was searching for her, I was looking for you without knowing it, because even as I went from street to street, struggling to solve the mystery of Istanbul, there was this terrifying question in my mind: If he knew that my wife had up and left me, what would Celâl Salik say? I'd already decided that my predicament was 'classic Celâl Salik.' I longed to tell you all about it. Here, at last, was the thing I'd been looking for all these years: something you and I could talk about. The prospect so excited me, I finally found the courage to get in touch with you, but I couldn't find you anywhere; you'd vanished. I knew, but I didn't know. Over the years, I'd collected a few of your phone numbers; just in case I ever found the nerve. I tried them all but couldn't find you. I called your family—that aunt of yours who's so fond of you; your stepmother, who adores you; your father, who cannot control his feelings for you at all; your uncle—they all expressed concern for you, but you yourself weren't there. I went to the offices of *Milliyet*, but you weren't there either. There were other people looking for you at the paper too: your uncle's son, your sister's husband, Galip; he was trying to find you because some English journalists wanted to interview you. Something told me I should follow him. Something about this dreamy sleepwalking young man told me he'd know where to find Celâl. He must know, I told myself—what's more, he must know he knows. I followed him all over Istanbul like a shadow. We walked all the streets of the city—he in front, myself just far enough behind—together we explored handsome stone office buildings, old shops, glass-covered arcades, and filthy theaters and wandered all over the Covered Bazaar; we crossed bridges, venturing into dark streets and neighborhoods no one in Istanbul has ever heard of and other neighborhoods so poor they have no pavements, stepping through the dust, the mud, the filth. We never arrived but we never stopped moving. We walked as if we knew every last inch of the city, and yet we recognized nothing we saw. I lost him, only to find him again, and in the end he found me, in a run-down nightclub. Here we sat around a big table and everyone present told a story. I love telling stories, but I have a hard time finding people willing to listen. But this time they did listen. So there I was, in the middle of my story, watching the curious and impatient faces all around me try to guess the ending from my face, and fearful—as people tend to be in such situations—that they might actually succeed, and as my mind traveled back and forth between the story and this other train of thought, it suddenly came to me: My wife had run away to be with you. I must have known all along that she'd run off to Celâl, I told myself. I must have known, yet not known that I knew. This, I decided, was the state of mind I'd been seeking. At last I had opened the door at the back of my soul and entered a new realm. After so many years of trying and failing, it seemed that I had finally

succeeded in being myself and someone else at the same time. I
wanted to tell a lie—to say *I read this story in a column once*—but at the
same time I felt a peace I had been seeking for longer than I could
remember. While walking the streets of Istanbul, trudging down its
jumbled pavements, past muddy shops, watching the gloom in our
compatriots' faces and reading your columns to try and figure out
where you were, I'd had terrifying intimations of this accursed peace I
am describing. But now I'd finished my story; I knew where my wife
was. Even before then—while I was listening to the waiter and the tall
writer tell their stories—I'd sensed this terrible denouement looming.
I'd been deceived all my life; I'd been taken in from the very beginning!
My God! My God! Do these words mean anything to you at all?"

"They do."

"Then listen. This mystery, this truth you've been making us run
after for all these years—here's what I think it is, just as you yourself
have written, without knowing or understanding what it means: No
one in this country can ever be himself. To live in an oppressed,
defeated country is to be someone else. I am someone else, therefore I
am! But what if this person I want to become is himself someone else?
This is the crux, the heart of the deception! Because the man I
believed in, the man I read so faithfully, would never have stolen the
wife of a man who was his most ardent fan. That night at the nightclub, I looked around the table at all those whores, waiters, photographers, and cuckolded husbands telling stories, and I wanted to shout
out, Oh, you wretched and defeated creatures! You little, lost, forgotten souls! Do not fear. No one is ever himself, no one! Not even the
kings, sultans, celebrities, film stars, and happy creatures with whom
you long to change places! So walk away from them. Set yourselves
free! It's only when they're gone that you'll discover the story they pretend is secret. Kill them all off! Invent your own secrets, solve your
own mysteries on your own! Do you understand? I have no wish to
avenge myself—I am not your typical cuckolded husband wishing to
vent his rage—it is because I do not want to be pulled into this new
world of yours that I am going to kill you. When I kill you, the entirety
of Istanbul and all the letters in the alphabet will merge with all those
signs and faces you placed in your columns to reveal the true mystery.
CELÂL SALIK HAS BEEN SHOT! the newspapers will proclaim. A MURDER

SHROUDED IN MYSTERY. A MURDER THAT MAKES NO SENSE, they'll say, and with reason—for no one will ever be able to solve it. On this Judgment Day you're always harping on, it may well happen that the world will lose the meaning it never really had, and it may well be that Istanbul will descend into anarchy during the days preceding the Messiah's arrival, but for me, and for many others, this will be the moment when we rediscover life's lost mystery. Because no one will ever know the secret behind this business. You know what secret I'm referring to, for it is the one I discussed in the humble book you so very kindly helped me publish—is it not evident that the mystery at its center will once again be laid bare?"

"That's not the way it's going to happen," said Galip. "You can commit the most mysterious murder the world has ever known, but it won't stop there. They—the privileged and the downtrodden, the brainless and the forgotten—will band together to concoct a story to prove that there's no mystery in this whatsover. They'll make me out to be a colorless pawn in a lackluster conspiracy, and everyone will believe them. Before my funeral is over, they'll all be convinced that I was the victim of either a crime of passion or a conspiracy that put our national integrity at risk. As for my murderer, if he's not acting on behalf of a drug cartel or a group of officers plotting to overthrow the government, he'll have links with a Nakşibendi sect, or a confederation of politicized pimps, or the flag-burning grandsons of the last sultan, or the sworn enemies of democracy and our Republic, or an association of Christian sympathizers laying down plans for the Last Crusade."

"In the middle of Istanbul, on a muddy pavement, lying in a rubbish heap, surrounded by vegetable peelings, dog corpses, and discarded National Lottery tickets, a famous columnist is found under mysterious circumstances . . . so now it is for us to find the secret that is still walking among us in disguise, on the edge of oblivion, in the deepest depths, in our past, in the dregs of our memories, lost amid words and sentences that are not as they seem—how else to convince these lazy wretches that the mystery persists and now must be found?"

"Speaking as a man who has been writing for thirty years," said Galip, "I don't think they can remember anything—anything at all. Anyway, there's no guarantee you'd be able to pull this murder off.

Most likely you'd shoot me but fail to kill me; but why wound me for no reason? All you'd get for that would be a good beating at the police station—let's not even utter the word *torture*—and meanwhile I'd be the hero, just the sort of hero you never wanted me to be; while you languished in your cell, I'd be sitting with that brainless president of ours, who's come to tell me to get well soon. Mark my words, it's just not worth it! Times have changed; people today have no desire to believe there is an insoluble mystery lurking behind the material world."

"So who is going to prove to me that my life has not been one long deception, a cold and bitter joke from start to finish?"

"I am!" said Galip. "Listen . . ."

"*Bishnov?*" he said, repeating the word in Persian. "No, I don't want this."

"Believe me. I believed all this as sincerely as you did."

"I'll believe you!" cried Mehmet ardently, "if you can put meaning back into my life, I'll believe you—but what about all those apprentice quilt makers, struggling to find their lives' lost meanings in those coded sentences you've fobbed off on them? Those workers who will never return from Germany, who will never be able to bring over their fiancées, either—those dewy-eyed virgins dreaming of the furniture, orange squeezers, fish-shaped lamps, and lace sheets you've promised them in Paradise? The retired ticket takers who, following your instructions, have looked into the mirror and seen in their faces the floor plans of the apartments they'll be deeded in Paradise; and what about the surveyors, gas bill collectors, sesame roll sellers, junk dealers, and beggars—you see, even now I can't stop myself from using your words—yes, what about all the poor souls who've counted up the numerical values of your letters to calculate the day when the Messiah will appear on our cobblestone streets, to save our piteous nation, to save us all? What of our shopkeeper from Kars, and your readers, your poor readers, who now know, thanks to you, that the mythical bird they await is none other than themselves?"

"Forget all this," said Galip, fearing that the voice on the phone might be launching into yet another of his endless lists. "Forget these people; put them all out of your mind. Think instead about those last Ottoman sultans who went out in the night in disguise. Think of the

tradition-bound gangsters of Beyoğlu, who ritually torture their victims before they kill them, just in case they have a last few pieces of
gold stashed away, or a last few secrets. Think of the pictures you find
hanging on the walls of the city's twenty-five hundred barber shops—
those pictures of mosques, dancers, bridges, Turkish beauties, and soccer players clipped from the pages of magazines like *Life*, *Voice*, *Sunday
Post*, *Seven Days*, *Fan*, *Nymph*, *Review*, and *This Week* that were originally
black and white, and that some artist has painted over, so that all the
skies are Prussian blue, and our muddy lawns look as green as the ones
in England. Think of all the Turkish dictionaries you'd have to go
through to find the words to describe the thousand and one smells in
the dark, narrow, haunted stairwells of our apartment buildings, and
their origins, and the tens of thousands of ways in which these smells
mix."

"You bastard writer, you!"

"Consider the mystery of the first steamboat the Turks ever bought
from the English; why did they name it *Swift*? Think of the left-handed
calligrapher—who so loved reading fortunes in coffee grounds that he
felt driven to produce a three-hundred-page manuscript in which he
reproduced the fortunes he had found in the grounds of the many
thousands of cups of coffee he had drunk in his lifetime, writing out
the fortunes they illuminated in his beautiful handwriting in the margins—what to make of his obsession with order and symmetry?"

"But this time you are not going to deceive me."

"Remember how, when our contemporaries blocked up all the wells
that our forebears had dug in their gardens over a period of two and a
half thousand years—filled them with cement and stone to build foundations for apartment houses—they also blocked up the scorpions,
frogs, and grasshoppers who made their homes in them, and all variety
of bright and shining Ligurian, Phrygian, Byzantine, and Ottoman
gold coins, rubies, diamonds, crosses, portraits, outlawed icons, books
and treatises, treasure maps, and the sad skulls of men and women
murdered by persons unknown. . . ."

"Which brings us back to Shams of Tabriz and the corpse tossed by
persons unknown into a well, am I right?"

"Think of all the things these foundations support: the concrete,
the steel, the apartments, doors, aging janitors, the parquet floors

whose cracks become as black as dirty fingernails, the worried mothers, the angry fathers, the refrigerators whose doors never stay closed, the sisters, the stepsisters . . ."

"So are you Shams of Tabriz now? Are you Deccal? The Messiah?"

". . . the stepsisters, the married uncle, the hydraulic elevator, the mirror inside it . . ."

"Yes, yes, you've written about all this."

". . . the secret corners that the children found for themselves, and the games they played in them, the bedspreads they saved for their trousseaus, the silk cloth that Grandfather's grandfather bought from a Chinese merchant when he was governor of Damascus and that no one has ever dared cut . . ."

"You're throwing me a line, aren't you?"

"Think of the mystery that lurks beneath our very lives. Think of the sharp razor that the old executioners used to sever the heads of their victims after hanging them, so that they could display them on pedestrals and thus strike fear into the hearts of all who saw them—it was known as the *cipher*—why? Think of the retired colonel who renamed all his chess pieces, calling the king *mother*, the queen *father*, the rook *uncle*, the knight *aunt*; why did he call the pawns *jackals* instead of *children?*"

"Do you know, after you betrayed us, I only saw you once in all the years since; you were wearing some strange Hurufi costume, as Mehmet the Conqueror, I think—"

"Consider the infinite patience of the man who goes home on an evening no different from any other to spend the evening at his table, solving the enigmas in Divan poetry and the crossword in the paper. The lamplight illuminates the papers he has spread before him and the letters on those papers, but all the other objects in the room—the ashtrays, the curtains, the clocks, the regrets, the memories, the lost times, the sadness, the anger, the defeat—oh, our defeats!—are plunged in darkness. Remember the mysterious vacuum at the heart of every crossword puzzle—and the weightlessness you feel as you sail back and forth between DOWN and ACROSS—remember, too, that there is only one other way to achieve such heights, and that is through the endless fascination afforded to those who wander a city in disguise."

"Listen here, my friend," said the voice at the other end of the line, and his no-nonsense tone took Galip by surprise. "I've had it with end-less fascination, so let's forget all these games, letters, and twins; we've gone beyond all this now and they no longer concern us. Yes, I set a trap for you, but it didn't work. You know this, so let me say it openly once again. Your name is not in the phone book, nor was it ever; like-wise, there was no coup, no dossier! We love you, we think about you day and night; we're both your most ardent fans, we really are. We've lived with you all our lives, and we'll keep on doing so. So for now, let's just forget what we need to forget. Why don't Emine and I pay you a visit this evening. Let's pretend nothing happened; let's sit and talk as if there's nothing bothering us at all. You can continue this monologue you've been giving me; you can go on for as long as you like. Oh, please, say yes! Believe me—I'll do anything you want, bring anything you ask for!"

Galip thought for a long while.

"What I want is that list you say you have, of my phone numbers and my addresses."

"I can give them to you now—but don't expect me to forget them."

The man went to look for his address book, and his wife picked up the phone.

"Believe him," she said in a whisper. "He's truly sorry now, truly. He loves you so much. He was ready to do something crazy, but he's talked himself out of it. If he's going to do anything, it will be to me, not you—he's a coward, I assure you. Everything's been put to rights, thank God. When we come to you this evening, I'll wear that blue-checked skirt you like so much. My darling, I'll do anything you want, and he will too—both of us will—whatever you want! And let me say this: he looks up to you so much he even goes out some nights dis-guised as the Hurufi Mehmet the Conqueror; he collects pictures of your family and reads the letters in their faces—" When she heard her husband's footsteps approaching, she fell silent.

Her husband took the phone and began reading out Celâl's other numbers and addresses. Galip pulled a book at random off the shelf next to him (*Les caractères*, by La Bruyère) and turned to the last page, writing down each number and each address very carefully and then making the man repeat them several times just to be sure he had them right. Once he was done, he planned to tell them that he'd changed his mind, that he had no wish to see them, that his time was too precious to waste on readers who didn't have the grace to leave him alone. But at the last minute, he decided not to. He had a new idea in his head. Much later, when he was struggling to remember exactly what had happened that night, he'd say, "I must have been curious. I must have been curious to take a look at this couple, if only from a distance. Now that I had the numbers and addresses that would lead me to Celâl and Rüya, I may have been thinking ahead—thinking how to improve this incredible story I had to tell them, because it would be so much better if I had more than these telephone conversations to go on, if I could also describe how this couple looked, how they walked, what they wore."

"I'm not going to give you my home address," he said. "But we can meet somewhere else. Tonight at nine o'clock, for example, in Nişantaşı, in front of Alâaddin's shop."

Galip did not think he was offering much, so the gratitude he felt coming down the line made him feel uneasy. Did Celâl Bey want them to bring an almond cake with them this evening, or a box of petits fours from the Long Life Pastry Shop, or—since they would probably go on talking for many hours—pistachios, hazelnuts, and a bottle of cognac? When the tired husband added, "I'll bring along my photograph collection too, and the mug shots, and all those pictures of lycée girls!" Mehmet let out a strange, fearsome laugh, and Galip realized that an open bottle of cognac had been sitting between this man and his wife for quite some time. It was with great enthusiasm that they confirmed the time and place of their planned meeting, and after they had done so they hung up.

Chapter Thirty-three

Mysterious Paintings

"The mystery I took from the Mathnawi.*"*
—Sheikh Galip

It was early summer of 1952 (if an exact date is required, on the first Saturday in June) that Istanbul's greatest ever den of iniquity—and it had no rival in all of Turkey, the Balkans, and the Middle East—opened its doors in the heart of Beyoğlu's red-light district, in one of the streets leading up to the British consulate. This happy occasion also marked the culmination of a hotly contested painting competition that had been the talk of the town for six months. For the owner—the Beyoğlu gangster who would later turn himself into an urban legend by driving his Cadillac into the Bosphorus—had decided that the walls of his new establishment's spacious lobby should be decorated with scenes of the city.

No, his aim was not to become a patron of an art form prohibited by Islam and therefore somewhat neglected in our part of the world (I am referring here to figurative painting, not prostitution); our gangster simply wanted to offer the best of everything to his illustrious clients, who flocked to his pleasure palace from all four corners of Istanbul and, indeed, all four corners of Anatolia; as keen as he was to delight them with music, drugs, alcohol, and girls, he was keener still to enchant them with the beauties of the city. Off he went to the great painters of the Academy, but they turned him down, saying they only accepted commissions from banks (and perhaps with good reason, enslaved as they were by the tenets of Western cubism, armed as they were with protractors and triangles, intent as they were to make the village beauties in their paintings look like diamond-shaped baklavas);

instead, he appealed to the artisans who painted the ceilings of provincial mansions, the walls of summer theaters, and the vans, horse carts, and snake-swallower tents you saw at fairs. When, after some months, two artisans stepped forward, each—in the time-honored way of all artists—claiming that he was the better craftsman, the gangster, taking his inspiration from the banking sector, dispatched the ambitious rivals to opposite walls in the lobby of his pleasure palace and announced to the world that the one who did the better painting of Istanbul would win a large cash prize.

The first thing the artists did was to put a thick curtain between them, for they mistrusted each other deeply. A hundred and eighty days later, when the pleasure palace opened its doors, that same patched curtain still ran down the center of the lobby, in stark contrast to its lavish furnishings: gilt chairs upholstered in piped red velvet, Holbein carpets, silver candelabras, crystal vases, portraits of Atatürk, porcelain plates, and tables inlaid with mother-of-pearl. There was a distinguished crowd in attendance that evening—even the governor was there, though only in an official capacity, for the club was formally registered as the Society for the Preservation of Classical Turkish Art—and when the proud owner pulled back the sackcloth curtain, they saw a splendid view of Istanbul running along one wall and, running along the wall opposite, a mirror that reflected the same scene, though in the silver light of the candelabras it seemed brighter, finer, and more beautiful than the original.

The prize went to the artist who'd installed the mirror, of course. But for years it was the amazing doubleness of the lobby's views that entranced the guests who ended up in this palace of sin; after contemplating each wall at length, they would wander back and forth between them for hours as they struggled to give a name to the intense and mysterious pleasure that the twin views afforded them.

The gloomy, wretched stray dog in the painting looked just as gloomy in the reflection, but he also had an air of cunning; when you went back to the painting, you saw that this dog, too, had something cunning about him, and you could not help feeling a certain disquiet, for now the dog looked as if he were about to spring into action; crossing the room yet again to reexamine the dog's reflection, you noticed other strange stirrings; by now your head would be spinning, but still you could hardly stop yourself from returning to the painting on the first wall.

One nervous elderly customer spent so long examining this gloomy dog—and the street the dog patrolled, and the square into which this street led—that a moment arrived when it seemed to him that the fountain in the center of that same square, though dry in the picture, was gushing out water in the reflection. He rushed back to the first wall—as agitated as an old man who has just remembered he left home without turning off his taps—and when he saw that the fountain in the picture was still dry, he went back to the reflection, only to see that the water was gushing forth more abundantly than before; so amazed was he that he could not stop himself from sharing his amazing discovery with the bar girls who worked there, but he was met with indifference (they had long since tired of this mirror's little tricks), thus leaving the sad old man to return to his shell and with it the one certainty he had ever known in life—that he was doomed forever to be misunderstood.

But in fact, the women who worked in this pleasure palace were not as indifferent as he'd assumed; when they lolled around the lobby on snowy winter nights, passing the time by telling each other the same old stories, they used the mirror almost as a touchstone, for the strange interplay between the walls gave them interesting insights into their clients' characters. There were the rushed, anxious, insensitive customers who did not even notice the strange discrepancies between the painting and its reflection: these men either wanted to go on and on about their own troubles or they wanted one thing and one thing only from these women, and of course this was the only thing that any man could ever want from a bar girl if he failed to see anything in her that set her apart from the others. Then there were the customers who did see the play between the mirror and the reflection but gave it no importance; these were men who'd been through so much in love that nothing touched them, fearless men who were to be feared. And then there were the ones who saw the discrepancies between the painting and the mirror and found them deeply upsetting—the bar girls and the waiters and the gangsters dreaded these the most, because what were they to say when these childish creatures demanded that someone bring the two back into perfect symmetry at once? These men tended to be stingy and short of funds: Drink couldn't make them forget the

world, and neither could women; their obsession with order and symmetry made them poor friends and poorer lovers.

Sometime later, when most regulars had grown immune to the
games the painting played with its reflection, the Beyoğlu chief of
police—himself a regular, and loved less for the power of his purse
than for the umbrella of protection he provided—happened to be
gazing into the mirror when he came face-to-face with a shady-looking
bald character, standing in a dark alley, holding a gun; at that same
moment, he decided that this must be the killer in the great unsolved
mystery of the age, the Şişli Square Murder; certain that the artist
who'd installed the mirror would be able to shed some new light on the
case, he'd launched an investigation to establish his identity.

There was another night—a hot and sticky summer night when
the dirty water trickling down the pavements could not make it as far
as the grate on the corner without going up in steam—when a
landowner's son, having parked his father's Mercedes in front of a NO
PARKING sign, looked into the mirror and saw the image of a dutiful
daughter who wove carpets for a living in her home in the back streets
of the city and knew at once that she was the secret love he'd been
seeking all his life, but when he turned back to the painting, all he saw
was a sad and colorless girl who was no different from those who lived
in his father's villages.

As for the owner—who would go on to ride his Cadillac like a stal-
lion into the fast-running currents of the Bosphorus, there to discover
that other world hidden inside this one—he was under no illusion that
these lovely little jokes and coincidences had anything to do with the
painting or its tricky reflection, or indeed with the mystery of the
world; it was simply that his drugs and his *rakı* had briefly freed his customers from their cloud of habitual misery and returned them to the
happy world of their imagination. So ecstatic were they to rediscover
this lost paradise that they confused the enigmas in their dreams with
the images in the mirror. Despite his admirable realism, the famous
gangster had been seen sitting with the bar girls' children on Sunday
mornings, going through the puzzle pages in the Sunday supplements
and happily helping the children with "Find the Seven Differences
Between These Two Pictures" as they waited for their tired mothers to
take them to the movies.

But there were more than seven differences between the painting in the lobby and its reflection—there was no end to them, just as there was no limit to the number of meanings they could carry and the shocking ways in which they changed before your very eyes. For the painting on the first wall—though it was technically no different from the ones you saw on the sides of horse carts and on tents at fairs—had the dark and eerie soul of shadowy engraving, and it was as rich in subject matter as a fresco. The enormous bird in the fresco became, in the mirror, a creature of legend, slowly and languorously opening its wings; in the mirror, simple fronts of old wooden mansions became terrified faces; fairgrounds and merry-go-rounds became brighter, more animated; every streetcar, horse cart, minaret, bridge, murderer, pudding shop, park, seaside café, ferryboat, inscription, and trunk was a sign pointing to a better place. A black book that the first artist had slyly placed in the hands of a blind beggar became in the mirror a book of two parts, two meanings and two stories; but when you returned to the first wall, you saw that it still held together as a single book, and that its mystery was lost somewhere inside it. Just as he must have done in so many fairground paintings, the first artist had included a certain doe-eyed, red-lipped, long-lashed Turkish film star in his mural; in the mirror she became the large-breasted impoverished mother who consoles the entire nation, but one more clouded glance at the first wall and you saw—with as much horror as pleasure—that she was not the national emblem of motherhood but the wife with whom you'd been sharing a bed for so many years.

But what visitors to the pleasure palace found most terrifying were the crowds; the painting was seething with them, and in the mirror the sea of faces surging across the city's bridges radiated new meanings, strange signs, unknown worlds. Looking into the painting, they'd see an ordinary troubled citizen or an industrious and contented-looking man in a fedora, but in the mirror these same faces were crawling with signs and letters that turned them into maps, into the last fragments of a long-lost story, and as they traveled back and forth between the velvet chairs, there would form in the clouded minds of some viewers the illusion that they had been initiated into a mystery that was open only to a tiny elite. The bar girls treated them like pashas, for they knew these men would never rest until they had grasped the secret behind the painting and its reflection; they would travel to the ends of the earth and face any danger, to solve its enigma.

Years later—after the owner had vanished into the enigma that is the Bosphorus and the pleasure palace had fallen into disrepute—the older bar girls looked into the mournful face of the Beyoğlu chief of police as he walked through the door and recognized him instantly as one such unquiet soul.

The man had still not solved the infamous Şişli Square Murder; hoping to find the clue he'd missed earlier, he had come to take another look at the mirror. He was too late, they told him. The previous week a brawl had broken out in the lobby—not a serious brawl, nothing involving women or money; if it was motivated by anything, it was boredom—but as the bouncers entered the fray, the huge mirror crashed down on them and smashed into a thousand pieces. As he stood amid the shards of glass, the soon-to-retire police chief could see no sign of the murderer, nor could he find the mirror's secret.

Chapter Thirty-four

Not the Storyteller, but the Story

"My way of writing is rather to think aloud, and follow my own
humours, than much to inquire who is listening to me."
—Thomas de Quincey,
Confessions of an English Opium eater

Before they agreed to meet in front of Alâaddin's shop, the voice
on the phone had given Galip seven of Celâl's phone numbers.
Galip was so certain that one of them would lead him to the place
where Celâl and Rüya were hiding that he could already imagine the
streets, the doorsteps, the apartment houses they would see together.
He knew that as soon as he saw them, as soon as they explained to him
why they had gone into hiding, he would accept their reasons as reasonable and entirely justified. This, he knew, was what Celâl and Rüya
would say to him: *Galip, we were looking everywhere for you too, but you weren't*
at home and you weren't at the office either. Where on earth have you been?

Galip rose from the armchair where he'd been sitting for many
hours. He took off Celâl's pajamas, washed and shaved, and got
dressed. When he looked at the letters in his face, they no longer spoke
of mad riddles or dark conspiracies, nor did they trick his eyes in a way
that made him doubt his identity. Like the old razor lying next to the
mirror, like the bar of pink soap whose twin Sylvana Mangano had
once brandished in an advertisement, these letters belonged to the real
world.

Picking up the *Milliyet* that the janitor had pushed under the door,
Galip turned to Celâl's column and read his own words as if they'd
been written by someone else. Appearing as they did under Celâl's picture, it was easier to think of Celâl as their author. At the same time,

Galip could not quite forget that these words were his own. This did not strike him as a contradiction; on the contrary, it was an extension of the known world. He imagined Celâl sitting at one of the seven addresses he now had in his possession, reading the column that some-one else had written in his name, but Galip guessed that he would not see this as an affront or the true author as an imposter. Most likely, he would not even realize that the column was not one of his own retreads.

He cut himself a few slices of bread, took the *tarama* and the sliced tongue out of the refrigerator, peeled himself a banana, and sat down to eat. Then, wanting to strengthen his ties with the real world even further, he decided to see to various legal matters he'd left hanging, so he called a colleague who'd worked together with him on various polit-ical cases, explaining that he'd been dealing with an emergency and had been out of the city for days. One case was progressing as slowly as ever, he now heard, but another political case had been decided, and their clients had been sentenced to six years apiece for harboring the founders of an underground Communist organization. He had, he now remembered, skimmed a news item about that same trial in the paper he'd only just finished reading, but without recognizing the case as one of his own. He suddenly felt angry, though he had no idea what he was angry about or why. Then he phoned home—as if it were the most natural thing in the world. If Rüya answers, he told himself, I'm going to play a trick on her too. He would change his voice, pretend to be someone looking for Galip. But no one answered the phone.

He rang İskender and asked how much longer the English film crew planned to stay in Istanbul. "This is their last night," said İskender. "They're leaving early tomorrow morning for London." Galip said he was on the verge of finding Celâl, and Celâl was eager to meet up with the English crew; he had important things to say to them; this inter-view meant as much to him as it did to them. "In that case," said İsk-ender, "I should try and track them down this evening. Because they really want to see him too." Galip read off the number on the phone receiver and said this was where İskender could reach him.

He dialed Aunt Hâle's number; deepening his voice, he announced that he was a loyal reader and ardent fan who had rung to congratulate Celâl on today's column. As he spoke, questions came pouring into his mind: after hearing nothing from either Rüya or himself for so many days, had they gone to the police? Or were they still waiting for their return from Izmir? Or had Rüya rung them to explain everything? Had there been any word from Celâl in all this time? Aunt Hâle's sober response—Celâl Bey wasn't there, so best to try him at the paper—told him nothing. At twenty minutes past two, Galip opened *Les caractères* to the last page and dialed the seven numbers, one by one.

The first connected him to a family he'd never heard of, the second to the sort of overtalkative child that everyone knows, the third to a shrill and coarse-sounding old man, the fourth to a kebab restaurant, the fifth to a supercilious real estate agent who had absolutely no interest in the people who'd had this number before him, and the sixth to a soft-spoken seamstress who had been at the same number for forty years; by the time he'd established that the seventh number belonged to a newlywed couple who'd returned home late, it was seven in the evening. At some point between these calls, he rummaged through the bottom shelf in the elm cabinet, where—at the bottom of a box of postcards he'd overlooked until now—he found ten photographs.

A family outing to the Bosphorus—the café under the famous Emirgân plane tree, Uncle Melih in a coat and tie with a young and beautiful Aunt Suzan, looking very much like Rüya does now; a strange man, either one of Celâl's friends or the imam of Emirgân Mosque; and there, staring curiously into the camera, which Galip now understands to be in Celâl's hands, is Rüya herself. . . . Next, Rüya in the strapped dress she wore the summer between second and third grade, standing in front of the aquarium with Vasıf, holding Aunt Hâle's two-month-old kitten, Charcoal, to show it the fish, and next to them, Esma Hanım, her eyes narrowed because of the cigarette hanging from her mouth, who tries to keep her face out of the picture by adjusting her scarf, although she is not quite sure if she is really in the frame. . . . Rüya, grown-up, fast asleep on Grandmother's bed after a holiday feast, her knees pulled to her chest and her face buried in a pillow, just as he last saw her, seven days and eleven hours ago—but this picture is dated the first year of her first marriage, when she was a revolutionary and didn't look after her appearance and rarely asked after her mother, her uncles, and her aunts; she'd turned up that winter morning alone and unannounced. . . . The entire family standing in front of the City-of-Hearts Apartments with İsmail the janitor and Kamer Hanım, his wife; Celâl has Rüya in his arms, and she has ribbons in her hair, and she's looking down at the pavement at a stray dog that must have died years ago. . . . Aunt Suzan, Esma Hanım, and Rüya, standing with the crowds lining both sides of Teşvikiye Avenue, from the girls' lycée all the way to Alâaddin's store, waving at Charles de Gaulle, who does not appear in the photograph, though the nose of his car does. . . . Rüya, sitting at her mother's vanity table, surrounded by pots of powder, tubes of Pertev cold cream, and bottles of rose water and cologne, perfume atomizers, nail files and hair clips, pressing her little bobbed head between the wings of the mirror so she can see three, five, nine, seventeen, thirty-three Rüyas. . . . Sun pouring through a window on Rüya, age fifteen, who is wearing a sleeveless cotton dress and leaning over a newspaper, tugging at her hair and chewing on her pencil as she does the crossword; she does not know she's being photographed and is not looking at the bowl of chickpeas at her side, and the expression on her face makes Galip feel left out and afraid. . . . Rüya laughing in the same armchair where Galip is sitting now, next to the phone on which he's only just spoken, in the room he's been pacing for so many hours; she is wearing the Hittite Sun necklace he gave her on her last birthday, which means the picture has been taken sometime during the past five months. . . . Rüya with her parents at a country restaurant Galip doesn't recognize, looking very glum, because her mother and her father had terrible arguments whenever they went out on day trips. . . . Rüya, trying to look happy, but even as she smiles, exuding a melancholy that her husband despairs of ever understanding; she's at Kilyos Beach, the year she finished lycée; behind her, waves roll in from the Black Sea; her beautiful arm is leaning on the carrier of a bicycle as if she owns it, though she does not; she is wearing a bikini so small you can see her appendicitis scar, and between the scar and her navel are two tiny lentil-shaped moles, and you can almost see the shadows of her ribs on her silken skin; she is holding a magazine but Galip cannot make out which one it is, not because the picture is unfocused but because his eyes are brimming with tears.

He was weeping inside the mystery now. He felt himself in a place he knew but hadn't known he knew; he felt as if he were buried in a book he'd read before that still excited him because he had no memory of reading it. This sense of doom, this utter devastation: he knew he'd felt it before, but at the same time he knew that no person could withstand a pain this strong more than once in a lifetime. He'd been deceived, he'd lost everything, his illusions were smashed, and though he knew his tragedy to be utterly unique, he still felt like a pawn on a chessboard, still feared he had walked into a carefully planned trap.

He did not wipe away the tears that fell onto Rüya's photographs; he was having a hard time breathing through his nose; he sat in his chair without moving. The sounds of Friday night rose up from Nişantaşı Square: every window, every object in the room, reverberated with the tired engines of crowded buses, the horns honking in the traffic jam, the policeman in the corner nervously blowing his whistle, the song blaring from the loudspeakers in front of the music shop at the front of the arcade, the humming crowds on the pavements. When he noticed every object in the room trembling, Galip remembered that furnishings and other inanimate objects belonged to their own private world—a world far removed from the one he shared with them. *To be deceived is to be deceived*, he told himself. He repeated these words over and over, until they had ceased to carry any meaning at all; they became sounds and letters signifying nothing.

He let himself daydream: He was not here in this room but with Rüya, in the home they shared; it was evening, and they were getting ready to go out; they were going to the Palace to see a movie, and they'd stop along the way for something to eat. On the way back, they'd buy the early edition of tomorrow's paper, and when they got home, they'd curl up with their books and their papers in their usual chairs. In the next daydream, a ghostlike man was saying, "I've known who you are for years, but you didn't even recognize me." When he remembered who this ghostlike man was, he realized that the man had been keeping a watch on him for years. Then he realized the man wasn't keeping a watch on him but on Rüya. Once or twice, he'd watched Rüya and Celâl without their knowing it, and what he'd seen had frightened and surprised him. *It was as if I'd died, as if I had been condemned to stand on the sidelines of my old life and watch what happened after I was gone.* He sat down at Celâl's desk and wrote a column that began with that same sentence, and at the bottom of the last page, he signed Celâl's name. He was certain now that someone was watching him—if not a real person, then at least one eye.

The noise from Nişantaşı Square was fading now to make way for the televisions blaring in the next building. When he heard the signal tune for the eight o'clock news, he imagined six million *İstanbullus* gathering around their dining tables to watch. He longed to masturbate, but he still sensed that eye hanging over him. His longing to be himself and no one but himself was so great by now that he felt like breaking every object in the room and killing everyone who had conspired to bring him to this terrible place. He was thinking about pulling the phone from the wall and throwing it out the window when it began to ring.

It was İskender. He'd located the film crew, and they were very excited about the proposed meeting; they'd set up a room in the Pera Palas Hotel so they could tape the interview this evening. Had Galip been able to reach Celâl?

"Yes, yes, yes!" cried Galip, surprised by his own fury. "Celâl is ready. He's going to make a number of important revelations. We'll be at the Pera Palas by ten."

After he hung up, he was seized by an excitement that wavered between terror and bliss, disquiet and calm, revenge and brotherly love. He rummaged through the piles of notebooks, papers, old columns, and newspaper clippings as if he were looking for something in particular, though in fact he had no idea what he was looking for. Was it proof of the letters on his face? But the letters and their meanings were so clear they needed no further proof. Was he looking for some line of reasoning that would help him choose the stories he would be telling? But he was too far gone to trust in anything but his anger and his excitement. Was he looking for some sort of example, something that illustrated the beauty of the mystery? But he knew all he needed to do was to believe his story as he told it. He went back to rummage through the cabinet, ran his eyes over the address books, spelled out the "key sentences," looked over the maps, and shuffled through the mug shots. He was going through the box of disguises when he glanced at the clock and saw it was three minutes to nine; guiltily aware that he had made himself late on purpose, he raced out of the house.

At two minutes past nine, he stepped into the dark entrance of the apartment building just opposite Alâaddin's shop, but when he looked across the street he saw no one on the pavement who resembled the bald storyteller or his wife. He was still angry at them for giving him those dud phone numbers: Who was deceiving whom? Who was the puppeteer and who the puppet?

The window of Alâaddin's well-lit store was crammed with objects, but Galip could only see a few of them. Toy pistols hanging on strings, rubber balls in net bags, orangutan and Frankenstein masks, board games, bottles of *raki* and liqueur, brightly colored gossip and sports magazines taped to the window, baby dolls in boxes, and, wandering in and out of view among them, Alâaddin bending over or bobbing his head: He was counting up the newspapers to be returned. He was alone in the store. He'd been there at his counter since early morning; his wife would be at home in their kitchen, waiting for his return. Someone walked into the shop, and Alâaddin went back behind the counter, and then, as Galip's heart jumped into his throat, he saw an elderly couple entering the store. The first man left the shop—he was dressed in a strange outfit—and when the couple came out after him, arm in arm and carrying a huge bottle, he knew at once that they were not the couple he was waiting for; they were too immersed in their own world. A gentleman in a fur-collared overcoat stepped into the shop; as he and Alâaddin began to talk, he tried to imagine what they might be saying.

He trained his eyes on Nişantaşı Square, on the pavement in front of the mosque, and on the street coming up from İhlamur, but he saw no one unusual: just people lost in thought, and coatless sales clerks walking as fast as they could, and lonely men whose shapes were barely visible in the gray-blue of night. An instant later, the streets emptied out, and Galip could almost hear the hum of the neon sign over the sewing machine store across the street. Apart from the guard cradling his submachine gun outside the police station, there was not a soul to be seen. Galip gazed over at the trunk of the great chestnut tree— Alâaddin used it to display his magazines, pinning them to underwear elastic; lifting his eyes to the bare branches, Galip began to feel afraid. He was being watched, he'd been located, he was in danger. There was a noise. A '54 Dodge coming up from İhlamur almost collided with an old Skoda municipal bus on its way to Nişantaşı. The bus driver slammed on the brakes, and after the bus had shuddered to a stop, Galip watched the passengers pulling themselves up; their heads all turned to the other side of the street. In the bus's pale headlights, only one yard away from him, Galip came face-to-face with a tired man who seemed to have taken no interest in what was going on around him; he was in his sixties and seemed utterly exhausted; his eyes were strangely dull and brimming with pain and sorrow. Had he seen this man before? Was he a retired lawyer, a teacher awaiting death? Were they both thinking the same thing as they took advantage of this chance encounter to stare each other down? After the bus began moving again, and as it accelerated down the road, the two men parted company, perhaps never to meet again. Gazing through the purple exhaust fumes at the pavement opposite, Galip could now see something moving. Two young men were standing in front of Alâaddin's store, lighting each other's cigarettes, waiting perhaps for a third friend with whom they planned to go to the movies. There were several people inside Alâaddin's store: three people looking at magazines and a night watchman. An orange seller with a huge mustache had suddenly appeared; as he pushed his cart toward the corner, Galip wondered if he'd been there all along without his noticing. Galip saw a couple walking past the mosque, carrying packages, and a father carrying his child. At the same moment, he saw the old Greek lady who owned the cake shop next door turning off her lights; wrapping her old coat around her, she came out into the street. She gave Galip a polite smile as she raised her hook; then there was an unholy screech as she pulled down her metal shutters. Now suddenly Alâaddin's shop was empty again, and so too were the streets. The neighborhood lunatic came strolling down the pavement from the direction of the girls' lycée; he thought he was a famous soccer star, was dressed in a blue and yellow soccer uniform, and was pushing a baby carriage. He sold newspapers out of this baby carriage, just outside the Pearl Theater in Pangaltı; when the wheels moved, it played a music that Galip liked. A light wind was blowing. Galip felt the chill. It was twenty past nine. I'll wait for three more people to pass, he thought. Now he couldn't even see Alâaddin in his shop, and the guard in front of the police station had disappeared too. The door to a tiny balcony on the apartment building across the street opened and Galip saw the ember of a cigarette; after tossing the cigarette away, the man went back inside. The wet pavements had a metallic sheen to them, as did the billboards and neon signs, and everywhere he looked he saw balled-up paper, piles of rubbish, cigarette ends, plastic bags. . . . He had lived here all his life, memorized it down to the last detail, witnessed every little change, but for a moment the distant chimneys of the tall apartment buildings he saw pressed against the dull night sky seemed as alien as dinosaurs in a children's book. Suddenly he felt as if he'd become the hero he'd so longed to be as a child, the man with the X-ray eyes: he could see the world's secret meaning. The signs hanging over the restaurant, the carpet store, and the pastry shop, the cakes in the window, the crescent buns, the sewing machines, the newspapers—they shimmered with their second meanings, beckoning him into the second realm; but the sleepwalkers passing by on the pavement had lost all memory of this second realm, lost all knowledge of its mysteries, so they were forced to subsist on the shallow certainties of the first world—they were, Galip now decided, like people who, having lost all knowledge of love, brotherhood, and heroism, found solace in movies that championed those virtues. He walked toward Teşvikiye Square and hailed a taxi.

As the taxi passed in front of Alâaddin's shop, Galip imagined the bald man lurking, just like him, in a dark apartment entrance, waiting for Celâl. When they passed the sewing store, and Galip noticed how eerie the mannequin seamstresses looked as they bent over their machines in the neon light, he wondered if the oddly dressed, and oddly terrifying shadow he saw lurking among them was yet another figment of his imagination. For a moment, he wasn't sure. When they reached Nişantaşı Square, he had the taxi stop so that he could buy the early edition of the next day's paper. As he read his own column, it surprised him and played on his senses in much the same way that Celâl's columns had always done, but when he tried to imagine Celâl picking up the same paper and reading someone else's words under his picture and byline, he could not guess his reaction. A wave of anger went through him—he was furious with both of them, Rüya as well as Celâl. He felt like crying out, You'll get what you deserve! but he still didn't know what it was they deserved—was it retribution or was it a reward? At the back of his mind, he still nurtured the fanciful hope that he would bump into them at the Pera Palas. As the taxi bumped its way through the crooked streets of Tarlabaşi, past dark hotels and wretched bare-walled coffeehouses packed to the rafters with men, it seemed to Galip that all of Istanbul was waiting for something to happen. Looking out at the cars, the buses, and the trucks, he was surprised at how old they all looked; it was as if he were noticing this for the first time.

The entrance to the Pera Palas was warm and brilliantly lit. In the spacious lobby to the right, he saw İskender sitting on one of the old divans. Like the tourists around him, he was watching a crowd at the other end of the room: It was a local film crew, taking advantage of the rich nineteenth-century decor to make a historical movie. The mood among the onlookers was light and cheery.

"Celâl's not with me, I'm afraid. In the end, he couldn't make it," Galip told İskender. "Something very important came up. Something top secret—which is why he went into hiding in the first place. For reasons I can't go into—except that it's related to what I've just told you—he's asked me to do the interview in his place. I know everything he wanted to say to them. I'll stand in for him."

"I'm not sure these people will go along with that!"

"What if you told them I was Celâl Salik?" The anger in his voice surprised him.

"Why would I want to do that?"

"Because what matters is not the storyteller but the story. We have a story to tell now."

"But these people already know you," said İskender. "You even told a story at the club that night."

"You think they know me?" Galip said, sitting down. "I'm not sure that's the right word. They saw me, that's all. Anyway, I'm a different person tonight. Essentially, they know nothing about the person they saw that night, and nothing about the person they'll see today. They probably even think all Turks look alike."

"Listen," said İskender. "Even if we tell them that the man they saw the other night was someone else, they'll still be expecting someone a lot older than you are."

"How much do they know about Celâl?" Galip asked. "My guess is that someone told them there was a famous columnist they should speak to, someone who'd be *just terrific* for a program on Turkey. So they jotted down his name. But I doubt if they stopped to ask how old he was or what he looked like."

At that moment, they heard laughter coming from the corner where they were making the historical film. They turned around to look.

"Why are they laughing?" Galip asked.

"I'm not sure," said İskender, although he was smiling as if he were.

"No one is ever himself," Galip whispered, as if divulging a secret. "None of us can ever be ourselves. Don't you wonder if other people see you as someone other than the person you really are? Are you so very sure you are your own person? If you are, are you sure that the person you are sure you are is really you? What do these people want? Let me tell you what sort of person I think they're looking for: a foreigner who will appeal to the after-dinner audience, a man whose troubles will trouble them and whose sadness will touch their hearts. And I have just the story for them! No one even needs to see my face. They could keep my face dark when they shoot the film. A celebrated columnist whose life is veiled in mystery—a Muslim, don't forget how much that adds to the allure—fearing assassination, sensing an imminent coup, mindful, too, of the brutal way his government treats its critics, has agreed to give an interview to the BBC, providing his identity is kept secret. What could be better than that?"

"All right, then," said İskender, "I'll call up to the room. They'll be expecting us."

Galip watched the filming at the other end of the large lobby. An Ottoman pasha in a crisp uniform resplendent with sashes, orders, and medals was speaking to his dutiful daughter, and though she was giving her father her full attention, she was looking into the camera, as were the waiters and bellboys standing in respectful silence to either side.

"No one will come to our assistance, we can't defend ourselves, we've run out of hope, we've lost everything, and the whole world has turned against the Turk," said the pasha. "Only God knows, but it would not surprise me if we were forced to abandon this fort too."

"But my darling father, look; look at what we still have." The daughter held out the book in her hand, more for the benefit of her audience than her father, but Galip could not make out what it was. When they stopped to do a retake, Galip tried again, but still he couldn't see the title; it was not the Koran, though, and that made him all the more curious.

Later, as İskender took him up to Room 212 in the old elevator, Galip felt an emptiness inside him, as if he'd forgotten the name of someone he knew very well.

In the room were the three English journalists he'd met in the nightclub. The two men were arranging the lights and the cameras, their *rakı* glasses still in their hands. The woman looked up from the magazine she'd been reading.

"Our famous journalist—our columnist Celâl Salik—stands before you in person!" said İskender in an English that struck Galip as stilted, though—good student that he was—he translated it straight back into Turkish.

"Pleased to meet you!" said the woman, with the men chiming in like twins in a comic book. Then the woman added, "But haven't we already met?"

"She said, 'but didn't we already meet?'" said İskender to Galip.

"Where?" said Galip to İskender.

İskender turned to the woman and repeated Galip's question.

"At that club," said the woman.

"I've not been to a nightclub for many years, nor do I have any plans to do so in future," Galip said with conviction. "In fact, I don't think I've been to a nightclub ever. That kind of social occasion, that sort of crowd—it pulls me down, robs me of the solitude I need to do my work. So I hide myself away, as I must; my intense literary endeavors leave me with no choice, and now, with the state trying to crush us, with political assassinations happening almost daily, to go out and join the fray is positively dangerous. At the same time, I am well aware that there are godfearing citizens all over Istanbul—indeed, all over Turkey—who think of themselves as Celâl Salik and who go around introducing themselves as Celâl Salik, for reasons I can fully endorse. I have crossed paths with a good number of them on those nights when I roam the city in disguise—yes, as I've wandered from one wretched den of iniquity to the next, penetrating ever deeper into the darkness, into the very heart of the mystery that subsumes us, I've even had occasion to befriend a number of these wretched creatures, who are so much like me it takes my breath away."

As İskender translated his words, Galip turned to the open window to gaze out at the Golden Horn and the pale lights of old Istanbul: because half its lights had been stolen, the Yavuz Sultan Selim Mosque had lost its famous silhouette; this strange forbidding heap of stones and shadows now looked more like an old man's gap-toothed smile. When İskender had finished translating, the woman apologized most courteously for having confused Celâl Bey with the tall bespectacled novelist who had told a story there that night, and though she kept a straight face, she did not give the impression she believed what she said. But she was clearly amused—here was yet another charming Turkish eccentricity, a cultural enigma she could respect without ever hoping to understand it. She knew the cards were rigged, but she was still willing to go ahead with the game, and Galip liked her all the better for it. Wasn't she a little like Rüya?

With the lights behind him, surrounded by cameras and black cables, Galip felt as if he were sitting in an electric chair facing execution. Noticing his unease, one of the men offered him a glass of *rakı*, smiling politely as he watered it down. Smiling even more broadly now, the woman slipped a video cassette into the player, pushing the button as provocatively as if she were about to treat him to a porn film. Though what appeared on the small screen were the rushes from the eight days the crew had spent in Turkey, there was still something about the silence that fell over them, something about their amused detachment that made him feel as if they really *were* watching a porn film: an acrobatic beggar, joyfully displaying his broken arms and dislocated legs; an angry demonstration and a fervent spokesman making a statement just afterward; two old men playing backgammon; scenes from *meyhanes* and nightclubs; a carpet seller gazing proudly into his own display window; nomads on camels, riding up a hill; a steam train, puffing up great white clouds as it shuttled down the track; street children, waving at the camera, women in head scarves, examining oranges at a fruit and vegetable stand; the victim of a political assassination (lying under a blanket of newsprint) and the events that followed; an old porter pulling a grand piano on a horse cart—

"I know that porter!" Galip cried out. "That was the man who moved us twenty-three years ago, when we left the City-of-Hearts Apartments for that place in the back streets!"

Nodding earnestly but still enjoying the game, they all looked at the old porter. He seemed to be in on the game too, as he pulled his cart into the front garden of an old apartment building.

"The Prince's piano, at long last returning home." He had no idea whose voice he was using—or even who he was—but it still felt right. "Right where that apartment house is now, there was once a hunting lodge, and I am going to tell you the story of the Prince who once lived there!"

As they quickly prepared to film, İskender reminded them that the famous columnist had come here to make a statement of great historical import. Nodding knowingly, the woman launched into an animated and far-ranging introduction that included references to the last Ottoman sultans, the clandestine Turkish Communist Party, Atatürk's secret and unknowable legacy, the recent rise of political Islam, and the current wave of political assassinations.

"Once upon a time," began Galip, "there lived in our city a Prince who discovered that the most important question in life was whether to be, or not to be, oneself." As he spoke, he felt the Prince's anger rise up in him and transport him to some other body. Who was this other person? As he described the Prince's childhood, he was returned to the Galip he had been during his own childhood. When he went on to describe how the Prince had struggled with his books, he felt as if he were the authors of those books. When he spoke of the days the Prince spent alone in his hunting lodge, he saw himself as the hero in the Prince's own stories. When he described how the Prince dictated his thoughts to his Scribe, he felt himself the author of those thoughts. Because he was telling the Prince's story in the same way he told Celâl's stories, he felt himself to be one of Celâl's heroes. As he described the Prince's last months, he told himself, This is just how Celâl would have told this story—and he hated the others in the room for not knowing this. His fury was eloquent, for the English film crew seemed to understand what he was saying before İskender translated it. After describing the Prince's end, he went straight back to the beginning: "Once upon a time, there lived in our city a Prince who discovered that the most important question in life was whether to be, or not to be, oneself." His voice had lost none of its conviction.

It was only four hours later, when he was back in the City-of-Hearts

Apartments, that he realized what set the two tellings apart: The first time he'd told the Prince's story, Celâl had still been alive; the second time he'd told it, Celâl was lying dead on the floor of the Teşvikiye police station, just a little way down the road from Alâaddin's shop, under a blanket of newsprint. When he was telling the story the second time, he stressed sections he had failed to notice the first time; when he told the story for the third time, it became clear to him that he could be a different person each time he told it. *Like the Prince, I tell stories to become myself.* Furiously angry at all those who had prevented him from being himself, and certain that it was only by telling stories that he would come to know the mystery of the city and the mystery of life itself, he brought the story to a close for the third and final time, to be met with a white silence that spoke to him of death. Quickly, İskender and the English journalists began clapping—and their applause was as genuine as if one of the world's great actors had just given the performance of his life.

Chapter Thirty-five

The Story of the Crown Prince

"The streetcars we had in those days were so much nicer."
—Ahmet Rasim

Once upon a time, there lived in our city a prince who discovered that the most important question in life was whether to be, or not to be, oneself. It took him his whole life to discover who he was, and what he discovered was his whole life. It was the Prince himself who made a short statement to this effect at the end of his short life; he dictated it to a scribe he had hired for no other purpose than to put his discovery into words. For his last six years, the Prince spoke and the Scribe wrote.

In those days—a hundred years ago—our city was not yet swarming with millions of unemployed men flapping down the streets like bewildered chickens; our alleyways were not yet choked with garbage, and sewage did not yet flow under our bridges; our ferries' funnels did not yet spew out great clouds of tar-black smoke, and people never elbowed each other rudely at bus stops. In those days, the horse-drawn streetcars went at such a leisurely pace that you could step on and off while they were still moving; the ferries were so slow that passengers could step off at one station, amble down the shore among the linden trees, laughing and talking as they went, and relax for a few minutes at the teahouse outside the next ferry station before boarding the same ferry they had left and continuing along their way. Where we now see electricity poles plastered with posters advertising circumcisers and tailors, in those days we saw chestnut and walnut trees. Where the city ended, we did not see bare garbage hills bristling with electricity and telephone poles but the groves, meadows, and woodlands that our sad and merciless sultans used as their hunting grounds. It was on one of these green hills, later to be crisscrossed with sewage pipes, apartment buildings, and cobblestone lanes, that the Prince had his hunting lodge, and it was here that he lived for twenty-two years and three months.

The Prince dictated his thoughts in order to feel he was himself. To feel he was himself, the Scribe had to be sitting at his mahogany desk, and the Prince had to be dictating to him. Only when he was dictating to his Scribe did his ears stopping ringing with other people's voices—except that when he was dictating his mind was full of their stories as he paced the floors of the hunting lodge; even when he was safe inside the high walls of his garden, he still couldn't escape their thoughts. "To be oneself," said the Prince, "a person must hear only his own voice, his own stories, his own thoughts!" and the Scribe wrote down his every word.

But this is not to say that the Prince heard only his own voice when he was dictating. No, even as he began a story, he was thinking about someone else's story; just as he began to develop an idea, someone else's idea ensnared him; even as he succumbed to anger, he felt someone else's anger rising up inside him. Yet he knew that the only way to find one's own voice was to produce a voice that could shout all the other voices down—a voice, in the Prince's words, that "went right for their snarling throats." So to dictate his thoughts was to create a battlefield in which he held the advantage—or so he thought.

As he struggled on said battlefield, pitting word against word, story against story, thought against thought, the Prince would pace up and down the rooms of his hunting lodge. He would utter one sentence as he walked up one side of his twin staircase; as he returned to the same landing by the other route, he would change it; then he went back up the first set of stairs; or he would lie down to rest on the divan across from the Scribe's desk, and he would say, "Now read that back to me," and the Scribe would read out the Prince's last few sentences in a solemn monotone.

"Prince Osman Celâlettin Efendi believed that there was one question that we in this land, this sewage-strewn land, must ask above all others: How to be oneself? Only by solving this mystery can we hope to save our people from destruction, enslavement, and defeat. In the view of Osman Celâlettin Efendi, it was because they had failed to find a way to be themselves that whole peoples had been dragged into slavery, whole races into degeneracy, and entire nations into nothingness, nothingness."

"There's a word missing. You should have written nothingness three times over!" the Prince would say, and he would walk up a flight of stairs, or down a flight of stairs, or around the Scribe's table. He would say this with such force and confidence that he was at once reminded of Monsieur François, who had taught him French in his early youth; suddenly aware that he was imitating his old teacher's every mannerism, pacing up and down the room as Monsieur had done during his dictation exercises and affecting the same didactic tone, he would suffer a crisis of nerves that would "arrest all intellectual activity" and "drain his imagination of all color." The Scribe, whose long years of experience had accustomed him to such fits, would put down his pen, erase all expression from his face, listen impassively to his master's anguish for having failed yet again to be himself, and patiently wait for the histrionics to come to an end.

Prince Osman Celâlettin Efendi was of two minds about his childhood and early youth. The Scribe remembered writing at length about the Prince's early years in various Ottoman palaces, lodges, and mansions, and he recalled the Prince describing himself as a lively, entertaining, and fun-loving young man, but those writings were now stored away in old notebooks. "Because my mother, Nurucihan Kadın Efendi, was his favorite wife, my father, Sultan Abdülmecit Han, loved me the most of all his thirty children," the Prince had told him many years later. During the same years, he had also told the Scribe that "because my father, Sultan Abdülmecit Han, loved me most of all his thirty children, he loved my mother, Nurucihan Kadın Efendi, his second wife, more than all the other wives in the harem."

The Scribe had also written about the day when the little Prince had been racing around the harem, bursting through doors, slamming them behind them, with his older brother Reşat in fast pursuit, when he had slammed a door in the face of the black eunuch who guarded over the harem and caused him to faint. He had also written about the night the Prince's fourteen-year-old sister, Princess Münire, was married off to a foolish, arrogant forty-five-year-old pasha: taking her sweet young brother onto her lap, she told him that the only, only reason she was sad was because she would no longer be with him; she had shed so many tears that the little boy's white collar was soaking. The Scribe had written about a party held in honor of the French and the English whom the Crimean War had brought to Istanbul; with his mother's permission, the Prince had danced with an eleven-year-old English girl and spent long hours with her perusing a book full of illustrations of locomotives, penguins, and corsairs. The Scribe had written about the day a ship was named after his grandmother, Bezmiâlem Sultan: during the ceremony, his brother had dared him to eat exactly four pounds of the rose and pistachio *lokum*; having done so, he'd had the pleasure of slapping the nape of his idiotic brother's neck. The Scribe had written about the time when the princes and princesses got punished for taking the royal carriage out to a Beyoğlu department store and, instead of choosing from its vast array of handkerchiefs, cologne bottles, fans, gloves, umbrellas, and hats, made the salesboy take off his apron and sell it to them, because they were always making up their own plays in the palace and needed an apron for their costume chest. The Scribe had written about how the Prince, during his childhood and early youth, had imitated everyone and everything that had caught his eye—doctors, British ambassadors, ships sailing past the windows, grand viziers, the creaking doors of the palace and the high-pitched voices of the harem eunuchs; his father, horse carts, the sound of rain pelting the windows, characters in books, the mourners crying at his father's funeral, waves, and his Italian piano teacher Guateli Pasha; in later years, the Prince would recall the same details of all the same memories, but in a seething and accusing voice; he would go on to say that it was impossible to think about them without also thinking of the cakes, mirrors, music boxes, and countless books and toys, and those kisses, all those kisses, he had received from girls and women ages seven to seventy.

After he had hired the Scribe to record his thoughts and memories, the Prince would say, "My happy childhood years lasted a very long time. So very long did my foolish childhood happiness last that I lived as foolishly and as happily as a child until my thirtieth year. If an empire can permit a prince destined for the throne to live like a foolish, happy child until he is twenty-nine years old, it is doomed to be crushed, dissolved, annihilated." Until his thirtieth year, the Prince, who was fifth in line to the throne, lived like all the other princes of that era: he had fun, made love with many women, read books, acquired property and possessions, and took a passing interest in music and painting and a fleeting interest in military science: He married and had three children, two of them boys; like everyone else, he made some friends and enemies along the way. Later he would say, "It was perhaps necessary for me to reach my thirtieth year before I could free myself of these many burdens—the possessions, the women, the friends, and those foolish thoughts."

When he was in his thirtieth year, a series of historical accidents resulted in his going from fifth to third in line for the throne. But according to the Prince, only a fool would see them as accidents, for it was only natural that his soulless, spineless, addled uncle, Sultan Abdülaziz, should die, only natural that his eldest brother should go mad shortly after ascending to the throne and find himself deposed. After he had dictated these words to the Scribe—as he was climbing up the hunting lodge stairs—the Prince would declare that Abdülhamit, his successor, was every bit as mad as their eldest brother; as he walked down the other side of the twin staircase, he would add that the other Prince who was sitting in another hunting lodge and waiting, as he was, to be called to the throne, was an even greater lunatic than their two older brothers; after he had dictated these dangerous words for perhaps the thousandth time and the Scribe had written them down, he would record the Prince's speculations as to why his elder brothers had gone mad, why they'd been made to go mad, why Ottoman princes had no choice but to go mad.

Because to spend an entire life waiting to become the ruler of an empire would drive anyone mad; because to watch one's elder brothers dream the same dreams and then succumb to madness, one by one, was to court the same dilemma; because the dilemma—to go mad or not to go mad—was a false one; because they went mad by trying to fight madness off; because the memory of their ancestors weighed heavily on them; because they could not help going mad, if they recalled—if only briefly, if only once during their interminable wait—that their forefathers had, upon ascending to the throne, traditionally had all their younger brothers strangled. His illustrious ancestor Mehmet III was a case in point—upon becoming sultan, he'd ordered the deaths of nineteen younger brothers, some of whom were still at their mothers' breasts—and seeing as anyone could read about that incident in any historical account of the era, seeing as it was his duty as a prince to acquaint himself with the history of the empire over which he might one day rule, just to read about a sultan killing his younger brothers was enough to drive a prince mad; because if, after years of wondering if or when he might be poisoned or strangled or killed in a way that was later made to look like a suicide, a prince went mad, it was his way of saying, "Count me out of the race"; because waiting for the throne was like waiting for death, and madness, the easiest escape route, was also the perfect expression of his deepest and most secret desires; because going mad saved princes from the sultan's informers, who kept all the brothers under constant surveillance, and from the traps and conspiracies set by political intriguers seeking the sultan's favor via the same same web of informers, and—last but not least— from their own nightmares about ascending to the throne; because any prince glancing at the map of the empire over which he dreamed of presiding one day could not help but see that the many countries he alone might soon rule were so large and far-flung as to be almost boundless; this alone was enough to push him to the brink of madness, and any prince who could contemplate such a map without being undone by its boundlessness must be mad already. After rattling off this long list, Prince Osman Celâlettin Efendi would say, "If I am saner than all the fools, lunatics, and idiots who have ruled the Ottoman Empire, it is precisely because I understand its boundless madness! For when I contemplated the boundlessness of the empire over which I might one day preside, I did not go mad like all those aforementioned weak-willed wretches; no—quite the opposite—I brought myself back to myself by thinking deeply about the boundless feeling that had engulfed me; and it was because I remained resolute, kept hold of myself, and subjected my intimations of boundlessness to deep and careful consideration that I was able to discover life's ultimate question: to be, or not to be, oneself."

It was when he went from being fifth to third in line for the throne that the Prince began to read seriously. Every prince who has a real chance of becoming sultan will aim to equip himself for the awesome task, and he too innocently believed that he might succeed in that aim through study. He read with impatience, hungrily turning from page to page in search of ideas that might prove useful; soon he had convinced himself that he might be able to use these ideas in his future reign and so restore the Ottoman Empire to glory, and it was this dream that kept him sane; wishing now to rid himself of all that reminded him of his old, foolish, childish life, he abandoned his Bosphorus mansion—and with it his wife, his children, his possessions, and his habits—and moved to the small hunting lodge where he would spend the next twenty-two years and three months. The hunting lodge was situated on a hill where, a hundred years later, we would find a cobblestone road lined with streetcar rails; dark and eerie apartment buildings built in imitation of assorted Western styles, boys' and girls' lycées, a police station, a mosque, a dress shop, a florist, a carpet seller, and a dry cleaner. Protecting the Prince from the foolish world that surrounded him were the high walls the sultan had had built, the better to contain his dangerous brother; rising above them were the great chestnut and plane trees whose branches and trunks would, in a hundred years' time, be festooned with black telephone wires and magazines of naked women. The only sound to be heard in the hunting lodge were the cries of the crows that were still to be heard on this hill a century later; on days when the wind blew from the land to the sea, one could just hear soldiers drilling and music playing outside the barracks on the neighboring hills. As the Prince would dictate many times over, his first six years in the hunting lodge were the happiest he ever knew.

"Because all I did was read," he'd say. "Because my only dreams came from the books I read. Because I spent those six years alone with their authors' thoughts and voices." He would add, "But throughout those six years, I was unable to become myself." Whenever the Prince recalled that six-year period, he would dictate this sentence in painful longing: "I was not myself, and perhaps that was why I was happy, but a sultan's duty is not to be happy—it is to be himself!" Then he would add the other sentence that the Scribe had written down in his notebook perhaps a thousand times before: "This is not just a sultan's duty, it is everyone's duty—everyone's."

As he would go on to dictate to his Scribe, this truth that he described as "life's greatest discovery, and its very aim" had come to him one evening during his sixth year in the lodge. "I was imagining—

as I had done so often during this, the happiest chapter of my life—that I was sitting on the Ottoman throne, scolding some fool over a matter of state. In my daydream I had just dignified my haughty speech with the words *As Voltaire says* . . . when suddenly I saw where I had landed myself in so doing. It suddenly seemed to me that the man I imagined as the thirty-fifth Ottoman sultan was not me but Voltaire—not me but a Voltaire impersonator. Oh, the horror I felt, when I realized that this sultan who would preside over the lives of millions, this man whose empire knew no bounds, was not himself but someone else altogether!"

Later, when he related this story in a darker mood, the Prince would tell a number of other stories that shed some light on this moment of discovery, but the Scribe knew full well that in all of them the moment of discovery evoked the same response: Was it right for a sultan who ruled over the lives of millions to be walking around with another man's sentences wafting around in his head? Wasn't it essential for a prince destined to rule over the greatest empire in the world to answer to his own will, and his own will alone? If a man's head was a nightmarish swarm of other people's thoughts, was he a sultan or a shadow?

"As I wished to be a real sultan, and not a shadow, it was now clear to me that I should resolve to be myself and not someone else; whereupon I decided to free my mind of books—not just the ones I had read over the previous six years but everything I'd ever read in my life." So said the Prince as he began to describe the decade that followed. "To be myself, and not someone else, it was incumbent on me to free myself from all those books, all those writers, all those stories, all those voices. This took me ten years."

The Prince proceeded to tell the scribe what he had done, whereupon the Scribe would write about how the Prince gathered up all the volumes of Voltaire in his lodge and burned them, because whenever he read this author, whenever he so much as thought about him, he believed himself to be cleverer than he really was; he became a godless humorist—a witty Frenchman!—and so failed to be himself. He went on to remove all volumes of Schopenhauer from the lodge, because these volumes had caused the Prince to waste hours, even days, contemplating his will; he'd identified with its pessimistic author to such a degree that the man who ascended to the Ottoman throne would not have been the Prince but a German philosopher. As for his volumes of Rousseau, though they had cost him a small fortune, he had them torn to bits before removing them from the lodge, because they had, he now decided, turned him into a savage who had turned in on himself, a savage who had become his own policeman. "As for those French thinkers—Deltour, De Passet, Morelli, who believed the world to be a realm of reason, and Brichot, who believed the opposite—I had them all burned, because when I read them I no longer faced the world as I needed to face it—as myself, a future sultan; instead I faced it like a mocking professor-polemicist whose greatest dream is to discount all thinkers who came before him." He had *The Thousand and One Nights* burned, for though he had identified with all those sultans wandering around their cities in disguise, they were not, he now saw, the sort of sultan he should aspire to become. He had *Macbeth* burned, not because it made him feel like a spineless coward willing to spill blood to win the crown but because, instead of feeling shame at his moral turpitude, he felt poetically proud. He had Rumi's *Mathnawi* removed from the lodge, because every time he leafed through the stories in this utterly disorganized book, he found himself identifying with a dervish saint who believed disorganization to be the very essence of life. "I burned Sheikh Galip because he turned me into a melancholic lover," the Prince declared. "I had Bottfolio burned because he made me see myself as a Westerner who longed to be an Easterner, and I had Ibn Zerhani burned because he made me see myself as an Easterner who longed to become a Westerner, and because I had no wish to see myself as an Easterner, a Westerner, an obsessive, a madman, an adventurer, *or* a character from a book." After the Prince uttered these words, the Scribe would write down the same refrain that he recorded for six years in countless notebooks: *All I wanted was to be myself; all I wanted was to be myself; I wanted to be myself, that was all.*

But he knew this was no easy task. Having rid himself of a particular series of books, their stories would continue to resonate in his mind; when enough time had passed and even these residual voices had faded away, the silence in his mind grew so unbearable that the Prince would reluctantly dispatch one of his men to the city to buy him more books. The moment they arrived, he would tear open the packages and devour each and every one; having mocked their authors, he would proceed to burn the books with ritual fury, but he could still hear their stories, and no matter how hard he tried not to do so, he would find himself imitating their authors; and, though he was painfully aware of the dangers of fighting fire with fire, he would decide that the only way to erase them from his mind was to read other books, and he would send his man back to the foreign booksellers of Babıali, who were, of course, eagerly awaiting his arrival. *After resolving to become himself, Prince Osman Celâlettin Efendi spent the next ten years of his life waging war with books*, wrote the Scribe one day, and the Prince corrected him: "Don't write *waging war*! Write *going for their throats*!" After battling with books and the voices inside them for ten long years, Prince Osman Celâlettin Efendi finally realized he would only become himself if he could speak in his own voice, and speak forcefully enough to drown out the voices in those books. That was when, with this in mind, he engaged the Scribe.

"Thoughout these ten years, Prince Osman Celâlettin Efendi did not just go for the throats of all those books and stories, he also went for the throat of anything that stopped him from being himself!" The Prince would shout these words from the top of the stairs, and though the Scribe had written them down a thousand times before, he would record them for the thousand and first time just as diligently; and the Prince would go on to utter the next familiar sentences with the same conviction, excitement, and determination as he had done a thousand times before. The Scribe would record how, over the same ten years that the Prince was waging war against books, he was also waging war with any object around him that influenced him the ways books did, because—be it comfort these pieces of furniture provided or discomfort, be they necessary or expendable—these tables, chairs, and trays had a way of distracting a man from the life of the mind, because all those ashtrays and chandeliers had a way of catching his eye and thus distracting him from the thoughts that might lead him to become himself; because the oil paintings on the walls, the vases on the trays, and the puff cushions on the divans sent the Prince into mental states that he was most anxious to avoid; because all those clocks, bowls, pens, and antique chairs were laden with memories and associations that kept the Prince from becoming himself.

The Scribe would then write how, even as the Prince was getting rid of his furniture—breaking some things, burning or discarding others—he was also going for the throats of all the memories that made him into someone else. "I would be lost in thought, in the midst of a daydream," the Prince would say, "when a tiny unimportant detail from a memory many years old would rise up from nowhere to drive me to distraction—pursue me like a merciless killer, or a lunatic fired up by a murky age-old desire to wreak revenge." Because if one was a man who would, upon ascending to the throne, find himself obliged to consider the wretched lives of the millions, the many, many millions, under his rule, it was terrifying, absolutely terrifying, to have one's thoughts interrupted by the memory of a bowl of strawberries one had eaten as a child or by some nonsense once uttered in one's presence by a worthless harem eunuch. A sultan who was himself—but the same could be said of anyone, everyone—anyone who was full to the brim with thoughts that were his and no one else's, who had reached his conclusions through the exercise of his own will and determination, must, by necessity, resist the haphazard drift of random memories that might keep him from remaining himself. One day the Scribe recorded that *having resolved to go for the throats of all memories that robbed his thoughts and his will of their purity, Prince Osman Celâlettin Efendi had his lodge cleansed of all smells and rid of all familiar objects and articles of clothing, forswearing also the soporific art of music, cutting off all links with his never-played white piano, and having the walls of the lodge painted white.*

"Most pernicious of all—worse than memories, possessions, or books—were people," the Prince would add, reclining on the divan he had not yet found the will to throw away, to hear the Scribe read his words back to him. People came in all shapes and sizes, dropping in at the worst and most inappropriate moments with worthless rumors and disgusting gossip. If they came hoping to do a good deed, they succeeded only in disturbing the peace. Their affections failed to calm; they simply smothered. They spoke only to prove they had thoughts. To convince you they were interesting, they told you stories. To show you that they loved you, they robbed you of your peace of mind. Though most might not see any of this as important, they were devastating for the Prince, who would have shed blood to become himself, who wanted nothing more than to be alone with his thoughts; after every visit from these bloodless gossips, these foolish, inane superfluities, he would for a very long time find himself unable to be himself. *Prince Osman Celâlettin Efendi was of the view that the greatest obstacles to a man hoping to become himself were the people who surrounded him*, the Scribe once wrote. *Man's greatest joy is to make others resemble him*, wrote the Scribe on another occasion. The Prince once declared that his greatest fear was that he might have to establish relationships with these same people once he became their ruler. "A man cannot help but pity the wretched, the destitute, and the long-suffering," the Prince would say. "And he cannot help but be influenced by them, but having involved himself with ordinary people of no distinction, he achieves nothing except to become as ordinary and featureless as they are." He would add, "By the same token, we cannot help but be similarly influenced by men of distinction, and feel great respect for them, too, and find ourselves beginning to imitate them, this being the most dangerous outcome of all. So write that I sent every one of them packing—washed my hands of every last one!" the Prince would cry. "Write that I embarked on this long struggle not just for myself, and not just to become myself, but to liberate millions of others too!"

In the sixteenth year of his struggle against outside influences—on an evening he'd spent fighting to free himself of the possessions he most prized, the smells he most loved, and the books that imprinted themselves on his mind—the Prince peered through the slats of his oh-so-Western venetian blinds to watch the moonlight play on his large snow-covered garden and understood for the first time that he had been waging this war not just on his own behalf but for the many millions who had bound their fates to the crumbling empire over which he might one day rule. So—as the Scribe recorded perhaps ten thousand times during the last six years of the Prince's life—*all peoples who are unable to be themselves, all civilizations that imitate other civilizations, all those nations who find happiness in other people's stories* were doomed to be crushed, destroyed, and forgotten. And so it was that, sixteen years after he had retired to the hunting lodge to await his ascent to the throne, when he had come to understand that he would only vanquish the stories he heard inside his head if he proclaimed his own stories in his own voice, and was on the brink of engaging the Scribe, did the Prince finally realize that his long spiritual battle had not just been a personal struggle but "a struggle to the death with history, . . . the final scene of a battle that comes but once every thousand years, the crux of which is to shed, or not to shed, one's shell," and "the lull before the storm, the transformation that historians in later centuries would rightly see as the turning point in our history."

Not long after that evening he spent watching the moonlight play upon his snow-covered garden—and whenever he recalled it, the moonlight in his memories would speak to him of the endless horror of eternity—the Prince had retained the Scribe; every morning thereafter, this patient, loyal, aged man would sit down at his mahogany desk and the Prince would dictate his own story, his own discovery; a moment would always arrive when the Prince would remember that, in fact, he'd discovered "the most historically significant aspect" of his story many years before. Before shutting himself up in his lodge, had the Prince not watched the streets of Istanbul change before his eyes, the better to imitate the ghost city of a foreign land that did not even exist? Had he not seen his wretched, luckless subjects change their very clothing, in slavish imitation of Westerners they saw in photographs and the Western visitors they saw roaming their streets? Had he not seen the miserable inhabitants of the city's poor neighborhoods gather around the stoves of coffeehouses, not to tell the stories that had been passed down to them by their fathers but to edify one another with stories written by second-class columnists who'd lifted them wholesale from *The Three Musketeers* and *The Count of Monte Cristo*, changing only the names, so that the heroes looked to be Muslim? Had he himself not been driven by boredom to seek out the Armenian booksellers who brought out collections of these loathsome tales in book form? Before he had found the resolve and the will to shut himself up in his lodge, as he was drawn into banality along with the wretched, long-suffering, and luckless multitudes, had the Prince not felt, upon looking into the mirror every morning, that the face staring back at him was slowly, oh, so slowly, voiding itself of its mysterious and ancient meaning? *Yes, he did*, the Scribe would write after these questions, for he knew the Prince would wish him to do so. *Yes, the Prince did feel as if his own face were changing.*

After working with the Scribe—and it *was* work, the Prince was adamant about that—after dictating his thoughts to the Scribe for almost two years, the Prince had dictated his past in exhaustive detail, describing the ship horns he'd imitated and the Turkish delights he'd gobbled as a boy; the full catalog of the nightmares that haunted him, the books that had captivated him, the clothing he had worn happily or unhappily, and the illnesses he had suffered during his forty-seven years on earth, along with everything he knew about animals; over and over, the Scribe recorded the guiding principle that the Prince reiterated just as many times: *I subjected each sentence, each word, to careful scrutiny, examining it in the light of my great discovery.* And as the Scribe took up his place at the mahogany desk every morning and the Prince sat back on the divan opposite, or paced the floor, or walked up one side of the twin staircase and down the other, perhaps they both knew that the Prince had no new story to dictate. But this was the very silence that both men sought. Because it was only when a man had run out of stories to tell that he came close to being himself, the Prince would say. "Only when a man has run out of things to say, only when he has lost all memory of his past, his books, and memory itself, only when he has plunged into that deep silence will he hear—rising from the depths of his soul, from the infinitely dark labyrinths of his being—the true voice that will allow him to become himself."

One day, as he wafted inside a bottomless well of stories, waiting for that voice to rise slowly from the deep, the Prince found it in himself to broach two topics he had heretofore mentioned only fleetingly, for women and love were, in his view, "the most perilous subjects of all." For almost six months, he spoke of his old loves, and the various affairs that couldn't count as love, and the "intimacy" he had enjoyed with various women of the harem—apart from one or two, he remembered them with pity and sorrow—and he also spoke of his wife.

In the Prince's view, the most frightening aspect of intimacy was that—without your even knowing, and even when the woman in question was utterly ordinary—she could still invade your thoughts, to the point that it was difficult to think of anything else. In his early youth, and during the years of his marriage, and even during the first few years after he had left his wife and his children in their Bosphorus *yalı* to take up residence at the lodge—in other words, until he was thirty-five years of age—the Prince had not been unduly concerned by this; he had, after all, not yet resolved to "become only himself" by "freeing himself of all outside influence." Moreover, "living as we do in a slavish culture of imitation," to lose yourself in the love of a woman, or a boy, or the Almighty himself—"to dissolve into love" was a virtue to be admired and aspired to; so the Prince too, like the multitudes swarming the streets, had taken pride in being "in love."

After retreating to his lodge, reading voraciously for six long years, and discovering that the greatest question in life was to be, or not to be, oneself, the Prince knew he must begin at once to practice extreme caution vis-à-vis women. It was true that without women he felt as if a part of himself were missing. But it was also true that every woman with whom he became intimate would disrupt his thoughts and take up residence in his dreams, robbing both of the purity he now so craved. For a while, he had thought that the only antidote for that poison called love was to be intimate with as many woman as possible, but because he embarked on this course in a purely utilitarian frame of mind, seeking only to inure himself to love, to overindulge himself in love to the point where he became sickened by it, he didn't find any of these women at all interesting. The woman who was (as he dictated to the Scribe) the "most colorless, harmless, innocent, and undistinguished" of the lot was named Leyla Hanım; certain that there was no danger of his falling in love with her, he began to see her most of all. "Prince Osman Celâlettin Efendi, believing that he could never fall in love with her, believed he could open his heart to her without fear," the Prince declared one night; because by now they had begun to work nights as well as days. "But because she was the only woman to whom I could open my heart, I quickly fell in love with her," said the Prince, adding, "It was one of the most terrifying times in my life."

The Scribe went on to record the Prince's descriptions of the days when the Prince and Leyla Hanım would meet at the lodge and quarrel. Leyla Hanım and her manservants would leave her father's mansion in a horse-drawn carriage, arriving at the lodge after a half day's journey; the two would sit down for a meal that was just like the meals they had read about in French novels, and—like the delicate and refined characters in those same novels—they would talk about poetry and music as they ate; when the meal was over, when the time had come for Leyla Hanım to leave for home, they would launch into a quarrel that the cooks, manservants, and coachmen listening at the doors found most upsetting. "It was never quite clear what we were arguing about," the

Prince once explained. "It was simply that I felt angry at her: because she had kept me from being myself, because she had robbed my thoughts of their purity, because she had made it impossible for me to hear the voice rising up from the depths of my being. This went on until she died, following a mishap for which I will never know if I should, or should not, be held responsible."

After Leyla Hanım's death, the Prince declared, he was overcome with grief but also liberated. The Scribe, who throughout his years of service had maintained a respectful silence, did something he had never done before—he tried to get the Prince to speak at greater length on this love and this death—but the Prince refused to be drawn out; he would only return to these subjects on his own terms and in his own good time.

One night, about sixteen months before his death, the Prince explained that if he had still not succeeded in being himself, if his fifteen-year struggle in this lodge was doomed to fail, then the very streets of Istanbul would vanish to become the streets of a luckless city that could never be itself; as for the hapless people roaming among squares, parks, and pavements that were but imitations of the squares, parks, and pavements of other cities, they too would be unable to be themselves; and though he'd not ventured beyond the garden for many years, every street, pavement, streetlamp, and shop of his beloved Istanbul was still alive in his imagination and as clear as if he passed them every day; here his voice lost its usual angry edge as he admitted in a hoarse whisper that, during the time Leyla Hanım was coming to his lodge in her horse-drawn carriage every day, he had spent most of his days, and most of his nights, imagining a horse-drawn carriage making its way through the city streets. *During the days when Prince Osman Celâlettin Efendi was struggling to be himself, he spent half the day imagining a carriage drawn by two horses—one black, one bay—for half the day he would imagine this carriage making its way from Kuruçeşme to our lodge, and then after the usual meal, and the quarrel that inevitably followed, he would spend the rest of the day imagining the carriage returning a tearful Leyla Hanım to her pasha father's mansion, along most of the same streets.* So the Scribe wrote, in his usual neat and careful hand.

On another occasion, hoping to silence the other voices and other stories that began to crowd his mind during the last hundred days of his life, the Prince offered up an angry list of all the other selves he had knowingly or unknowingly carried inside him since birth; together they weighed him down as heavily as a second soul, he said; he might as well have been one of those sultans who went out into the city streets every night in a new disguise. His voice suddenly went quiet as he told the Scribe that—of all the guises he had ever assumed—he loved only one, the man who had loved a woman whose hair smelled of lilacs. Because he was in the habit of reading, and then carefully rereading, every line and sentence that the Prince dictated to him, and since, over his six years of service, he had come to know and own the Prince's every memory and, indeed, his entire past, the Scribe knew it was Leyla Hanım who had smelled of lilacs, because on another occasion he had written down a love story about a man who was never able to become himself, because he could not rid his mind of the fragrance of lilacs after a certain woman who smelled of lilacs had died due to an accident or a mistake for which he would never know if he was to blame.

During his last months with the Scribe, the Prince had a burst of energy that so often precedes an illness, describing it as a period of "intense labor, hope, and faith." These were the days when the Prince could truly hear the voice inside his head that dictated his words, and the more he dictated, the more he told his own stories, the stronger it became. They'd work late into the night, and when they were done, no matter how late it was, the Scribe would climb into the carriage that awaited him and go home to sleep, returning early in the morning to take his place at the mahogany desk.

The Prince would tell him stories about kingdoms that had failed to be themselves and so vanished into nothingness, about whole races that had imitated others so assiduously they'd ceased to exist, about distant lands where people had forgotten who they were and had, as a consequence, been forgotten by all others too. He spoke of the Illyrians, who after struggling for two centuries to find a king strong enough to teach them to be themselves, had abandoned the world's stage. The Tower of Babel had not, he said, collapsed because King Nimrod had challenged God but because, in his zeal to build the tower, he had exhausted the very sources that might have allowed Babel to become itself. The nomads of Lapitia had, he said, been on the verge of setting down roots when they fell under the spell of the

Aitipal people, with whom they traded; so completely did they emulate the Aitipal, that they themselves had soon ceased to exist. As Tabari's *History* made abundantly clear, the Sassanids had suffered a similar fate because their last three rulers (Hormizd, Khosru, and Yazgard) had been so fascinated by the civilizations of the Byzantines, the Arabs, and the Hebrews that they had failed to be themselves for a single day. As for the Lydians, it was after they built their first temple under Susian influence in their capital, the city of Sardis, that they began their fifty-year descent from the stage of history. Today, even historians knew nothing of the Serberians, but it was not just because they'd lost their memories; the truth was that, just as they embarked on the building of a great Asian empire, they'd forgotten the mystery that made them who they were and had begun, instead, to adorn themselves with Sarmatian clothes and ornaments; they'd even taken to reciting Sarmatian verse; it was as if the entire populace had succumbed to an epidemic. "The Medes, the Paphlagonians, the Celts"—the Prince would say, and the Scribe would set down the next words without waiting for his master to say them—*They all disappeared because they were unable to be themselves.* Late at night, when exhaustion overtook them, when they had run through all the tales of death and collapse they had to tell, they'd hear a cicada chirping steadily in the summer night outside.

One windy autumn day, when the red leaves of the chestnut tree were falling into the lily pond at the end of his garden, the Prince caught a cold and retired to his bed, but neither man was particularly concerned. The Prince was more concerned about the fate that awaited the crumbling streets of Istanbul, should he fail to become himself or should he, having become himself, fail to ascend to the Ottoman throne; the city's bewildered inhabitants would be condemned, he said, to "seeing their lives through the eyes of others, and favoring other people's stories over their own, and, instead of seeing the mysteries in their own faces, live in thrall to the faces of others." They made themselves tea from the blossoms of their own linden trees and worked late into the night.

The next day the Scribe went upstairs to fetch another quilt for his master, who was lying on the divan downstairs, running a high fever, and suddenly he saw the lodge with new eyes: with its chairs and tables demolished, its doors ripped from their hinges, its furnishings ban-

ished. It looked so bare, so very bare. The rooms, the walls, the staircase—their bare whiteness was the stuff of dreams. In one of the bare
rooms stood the white Steinway piano, unique in all of Istanbul, a last
remnant from the Prince's childhood, forgotten and never played. The
white and otherworldly light streaming in through the windows made
the Scribe wonder if the past had retreated forever, if memory had
faded into nothingness, if all the smells and sounds of life had receded
and time itself had stopped. As he walked down the stairs with a white
and odorless quilt under his arm, he looked at the mahogany desk
where he had worked for the past six years, and at his white paper and
the windows, and they seemed to him as fragile and unreal as the furnishings in a doll house. As he laid the quilt over his master, the Scribe
noticed the white stubble on the Prince's face. On the table next to his
head, he saw half a glass of water and several white pills.

"Last night in my dream, as I was wandering in a dense, dark forest,
in a strange and distant land, I saw my mother waiting for me," said the
Prince, still lying on his divan. "Water was pouring from a pitcher, but
slowly, as slowly as syrup," said the Prince. "That was when I realized it
was because I had insisted throughout my life on being myself that I
had survived," said the Prince. *Prince Osman Celâlettin Efendi spent his
entire life waiting for the silence that would allow him to hear his own voice and his
own stories*, wrote the Scribe. "When waiting for the silence," the Prince
repeated, "there is no need for the clocks of Istanbul to stop. When I
looked at the clocks in my dream," the Prince began, and the Scribe
continued: *He kept thinking they were telling other people's stories*. There was a
silence. "I envy the stones of empty deserts, for they are only themselves, and for the same reason I envy the rocks of mountains where
no man has set foot, and the trees in valleys no man has ever seen."
The Prince's voice was strong now, and full of passion. "In my dream,
as I was wandering through the garden of my memories—" he began.
"Nothing," he added, after a pause. *Nothing*, wrote the Scribe in his
careful hand. There followed a long, long silence. Then the Scribe rose
from his table, approached the divan on which the Prince was lying,
studied his master carefully, and returned to his desk in silence. *After
dictating this sentence in his hunting lodge on the hills of Teşvikiye at 3:15 in the
morning on Thursday, the 7th of Shaban, Prince Osman Celâlettin Efendi passed
away,* he wrote. Twenty years later, he added, in the same careful hand,

Seven years after his demise, the throne for which he had spent his life preparing went to his older brother, Mehmet Reşat Efendi, whose neck he had slapped when he was young, and it was under his rule that the Ottoman Empire, having entered the First World War, collapsed.

It was a relative of the Scribe who had brought Celâl Salik this notebook; the article it inspired was found in our columnist's papers following his death.

Chapter Thirty-six

But I Who Write

Ye who read are still among the living;
But I who write
shall have long since gone my way
into the region of shadows.

—Edgar Allan Poe,
"Shadow—A Parable"

Yes, yes, I am myself! thought Galip, as he finished the Prince's story. Yes, I am myself! Now that he had told the story, he was so certain he could become himself, and so pleased to be able to be himself, that he wanted nothing more than to rush right back to the City-of-Hearts Apartments and dash off more new columns.

He left the hotel and hailed a taxi; as they set off, the driver launched into a story. Because he now knew that it was only by telling stories that a man could be himself, Galip was happy to indulge him.

On a hot summer's day a hundred years earlier, the German and Turkish engineers in charge of building Haydarpaşa station were sitting at their tables, busy with their computations, when a boy who'd been diving nearby approached them with a coin. Embossed on the coin was the image of a woman. She had a strange face, this woman, a bewitching face that spoke of a mystery he could not begin to fathom. Hoping that he might be able to unlock this mystery, perhaps by reading the letters on the coin, the diver walked over to a Turkish engineer, who was, like his colleagues, standing under a black umbrella. But it was not the letters that affected the young engineer, it was the enchanting expression on the face of this Byzantine empress; so great was his awe and amazement that even the diver was taken aback. Though her face was covered with the same Latin and Arab letters that the engineer had been using to make his own calculations, what struck him was her close resemblance to a beloved cousin he had long hoped to marry. But her family was just about to marry her off to someone else.

"Yes," said the driver in answer to Galip's question. "The road in front of Teşvikiye police station has been blocked off. It seems they've shot someone again."

Galip paid the driver, got out of the taxi, and set off down the short and narrow street connecting Emlâk Avenue with Teşvikiye Avenue. The blinking blue lights of the police car blocking the intersection gave a sad neon pallor to the wet asphalt. The lights of Alâaddin's shop were still burning, and in the little square in front, silence reigned; never in his life had Galip seen such stillness, and never again would he see it, except in his dreams.

The traffic had been diverted. The trees were still. There was no wind. The little square looked as fake and contrived as a stage set. The mannequins standing among the Singer sewing machines in the shop window were gazing out at the cluster of officials and curious bystanders who had gathered outside the police station and seemed about to join them. A camera flashed, and in its silvery blue light, Galip saw, but without quite seeing it—for he felt as vague as if he had been wandering inside a half-forgotten dream and happened onto a key that had been lost for twenty years—a face he did not wish to recognize: There on the pavement, two paces from the Singer sewing machine display window, was a white blot. A man: Celâl. They'd covered him with newsprint. Where was Rüya? Galip moved closer.

They'd covered every part of his body with newsprint except for his head, which was resting on the muddy pavement as if it were a pillow. His eyes were open, but they were clouded, dreamy; he looked tired, lost in thought; at the same time, there was something peaceful about him, as if he were trying to say, I'm just relaxing with my memories. Where was Rüya? The game goes on, Galip told himself, but even as he assured himself that this was just a joke, a wave of regret came over him. There was no sign of blood. How had he known that this was Celâl's corpse before he'd even seen it? Didn't you know? he felt like asking. Didn't you know that, all along, I had no idea I knew everything? Inside your mind, my mind, our mind, there was a well; a button, a purple button; coins, bottle caps, buttons, lost behind the cabinet. We're gazing up at the stars, the stars nestling among the branches. *Cover me with a quilt, keep me warm*, the corpse seemed to be telling him. *I am myself!* He looked more closely at the sheets of newspaper they'd draped over the body: They were from *Milliyet* and *Tercüman*, covered with rainbow blotches of diesel oil. Newspapers they'd once scanned for Celâl's columns. *Cover yourself up. It's cold.*

From inside the police van, he heard a voice on the walkie-talkie asking for the inspector. Please, sir, where is Rüya, where is she? Where is she? The traffic lights at the corner kept changing needlessly: green, then red. Then green again. Then red. In the Greek lady's cake shop, too. Now green. Now red. I remember, I remember, I remember, Celâl was saying. Alâaddin's shutters had been rolled down, but the lights inside his shop were still burning. Could this be a clue? Please, sir, Galip longed to say to the inspector, I'm writing Turkey's first ever detective novel, and look, here's our first clue. The lights inside his shop were still burning. On the ground outside were cigarette ends, pieces of paper, rubbish. Galip caught sight of a young policeman and went over to ask him what had happened.

The incident took place between half past nine and ten. The assailant was not known. The poor man died the moment he was shot. Yes, he was a famous journalist. No, he had no one with him. No, thank you, he didn't smoke. Yes, police work was difficult. No, there was definitely no one with the victim, of this the officer was certain. And why was the gentleman asking these questions? What sort of work did the gentleman do? What was he doing here, so late at night? Would the gentleman mind showing him his identity card?

As the officer examined his identity card, Galip looked at the blanket of newsprint over Celâl's body. From this distance the light from the mannequins' display window gave it a pinkish glow. He thought, Perhaps I should explain, sir, this was just the sort of tiny detail that the deceased liked to notice. I am the one in the picture, and the face is my face. Here you are, take it. It's my pleasure. I'd better be going. My wife's at home, waiting up for me. It looks like I've managed to smooth things over.

Leaving Nişantaşı Square as fast as his legs could take him, he walked straight past the City-of-Hearts Apartments and turned into his own street, where, for the first time in years, a stray dog—a mud-colored mongrel—barked at him as ferociously as if he were about to attack him. What did this mean? He crossed over to the other pavement. Were the sitting room lights burning? As he stepped into the elevator, he asked himself, How had he failed to notice this?

There was no one at home. He could see no sign of Rüya; she had not even dropped by. Everything he touched—the doorknobs, the scissors and spoons, the ashtrays where Rüya had once stubbed out her cigarettes, the dining table where they had once eaten their meals, their sad, empty armchairs—every piece of furniture in this apartment brought him unspeakable pain, unbearable melancholy. He left as quickly as he had come.

He took a walk. He walked from Nişantaşı to Şişli, along the same streets he and Rüya had walked so happily as children as they raced up to the City Theater, but now they were empty, except for the dogs rummaging through the garbage cans. How many columns did you write about these dogs? How many columns did *I* write about them? Later, making his way back, he circumvented Teşvikiye Square by taking the street behind the mosque, and—as he had expected—his feet took him back to the corner where Celâl's body had been lying forty-five minutes earlier. But now there was no one. The police car, the reporters, the crowd, the body—they'd all gone. The mannequins were still standing among the sewing machines in the display window, and the light streaming past them still lit up the pavement, but Galip could see no trace of Celâl's body. The blanket of newspapers had been tidied up and thrown away. Standing in front of the police station was the usual lone guard.

As he walked into the City-of-Hearts Apartments, he felt more tired than he'd ever felt before. Entering Celâl's apartment and seeing Celâl's past so faithfully replicated, he felt as surprised and as soothed as a soldier returning home after years of war and adventure. How distant this past was! Though it was not even four hours since he'd left. How inviting the past looked, as inviting as sleep! As innocent as a child—and as guilty—he crawled into Celâl's bed; closing his eyes, hoping for blameless dreams about columns, lamplight, photographs, mysteries, Rüya, and that which he had been seeking for so very long, he fell asleep.

When he woke up, he thought, Saturday morning. In fact, it was Saturday afternoon. So no need to go to the office, no need to go to court.

Without pausing to find his slippers, he went to the door to pick up the *Milliyet*. CELÂL SALIK MURDERED. The headline was over the masthead. There was a picture of the body, before it was covered with newsprint. The story covered the entire front page and included statements from the prime minister and other important officials as well as celebrities. Inside a black frame was Galip's column; presented as Celâl's last work, it was headed COME HOME. Their picture of Celâl was recent and flattering. The celebrities all agreed that the bullets had been aimed at democracy, freedom of speech, peace, and all the other lovely things that they seized every opportunity to mention. There was a hunt under way for the assailant.

He sat down at the table and smoked a cigarette and stared at the piles of paper and newspaper clippings strewn across it. For a long time, he just sat there, in his pajamas, smoking. When the doorbell rang, he felt as if he'd been sitting there for an hour, smoking the same cigarette. It was Kamer Hanım. At first she just stood there, the key in her hand, staring at Galip as if he were a ghost; then she walked inside, but she had hardly made it to the chair before she burst into tears. They'd all thought Galip was dead too. Everyone had been looking for him for days. The moment she'd read the news in the paper, she'd gone running to Aunt Hâle's. She'd seen the crowd that had gathered in front of Alâaddin's. That was when she found out that Rüya had been found dead inside the shop that morning. When he'd opened up the shop that morning, Alâaddin had found her, lying among the dolls, looking for all the world as if she'd just fallen asleep.

Reader, dear reader, throughout the writing of this book I have tried— if not always successfully—to keep its narrator separate from its hero, its columns separate from the pages that advance its story, as I am sure you will have noticed; but please allow me to intervene just once before I send these pages off to the typesetter. There are pages in some books that affect us so deeply that they remain imprinted in our minds forever, not because the author has displayed extraordinary skill but because "the stories seem to write themselves." Because they flow by their own logic. If these pages remain in our minds or our hearts— whatever you want to call it—we do not remember them as miracles of craftsmanship but as little fragments of Heaven and Hell that are every bit as real to us, every bit as tender and heartbreaking, as our own memories. So if I were an illustrious author and not the parvenu columnist I really am, I'd simply assume this to be yet another page in my great work, *Rüya and Galip*; I'd know, too, that its fine words would be delighting my more sensitive and intelligent readers for years to come. But because I am a realist when it comes to judging my writerly talents, I can do no such thing. That, dear reader, is why I would prefer to leave you alone on this page—alone, that is, with your memories. It would be best, I think, if I asked the printer to submerge all the words on the pages that follow with a blanket of printer's ink. This would allow you to use your own imaginations to create that which my prose can never hope to achieve. This would do justice to the black dream that descends upon us at this point in the story—to the silence in my mind, as I wander like a sleepwalker through its hidden world. For the pages that follow—the black pages that follow—are the memoirs of a sleepwalker, nothing more and nothing less.

It seems that Kamer Hanım ran all the way from Alâaddin's shop to Aunt Hâle's. She found everyone in tears, convinced that Galip was dead too. At long last, Kamer Hanım spilled Celâl's secret: for years Celâl had been living secretly in the attic flat of the City-of-Hearts Apartments; she went on to tell them that for the past week Rüya and Galip had been hiding there too. That's when everyone decided Galip must be dead also. Later, when Kamer Hanım had returned to the City-of-Hearts Apartments, İsmail Efendi had told her, "Go upstairs, and see for yourself!" So she'd taken the key and gone upstairs. As she stood there in front of the door, the strangest fear overtook her, but then something told her that Galip was still alive. She was wearing a pistachio-green skirt Galip had seen her wear many times before, and over it was a soiled apron.

Later, when he himself went over to Aunt Hâle's, he looked at the great purple flowers on her dress and saw they were printed on a background that was the exact same shade of pistachio green. Was this a coincidence, or a strange leftover from thirty-five years ago, or a reminder that the world, like the gardens of memory, still shimmered with magic? Galip sat down with his sobbing relatives—his mother, his father, Uncle Melih, Aunt Suzan, Aunt Hâle, Vasıf—and told them that he and Rüya had returned from Izmir five days earlier: since then they had been spending most of their time in the City-of-Hearts Apartments, sometimes even staying overnight. He explained that Celâl had bought the attic flat years earlier but kept it secret from everyone. People had been making threats against him, so he'd gone into hiding.

Late that afternoon, when Galip was being interviewed by the MİT agent and the man who'd come from the prosecutor's office to take his deposition, he spoke at length about the voice on the phone. But the two men just looked at him, as if to say, We know everything already, expressing no interest in his story. He felt helpless—unable to escape a nightmare that no one else could see. He felt his mind falling into a long, deep silence.

Toward evening, he found himself in Vasıf's room. Perhaps because it was the only room in the house where no one was weeping, he found in it living traces of the happy family that was no longer: the Japanese goldfish, degenerated "after generations of intermarriage," were swimming peacefully in their aquarium. Aunt Hâle's cat, another Charcoal, was stretched out on the edge of the carpet, lazily peering over at Vasıf. Vasıf was sitting on the side of the bed, going through the pile of papers in his hand. These were hundreds of telegrams of condolence—one from the prime minister, others from ordinary readers. On Vasıf's face was the same playful and admiring look as when he'd sit here with Rüya and Galip, going through his box of clippings. The room was lit by the same weak light as when they'd sit here, waiting for Grandmother and, later, Aunt Hâle, to call them to supper. How tired the old furniture looked under the naked low-watt lightbulb, how sleepy the faded wallpaper; it took him back to a sadness he'd shared with Rüya—took him over, like an incurable disease. But how he cherished that sadness; now it counted as a good memory. Galip had Vasıf stand up. He turned off the lights. He felt like a child who wanted to cry before bedtime. Without taking off his clothes, he stretched out on the bed and slept for twelve hours.

The next day, at the funeral, which was held at Teşvikiye Mosque, Galip found himself standing next to the editor of Celâl's paper; he

told him there were many boxes of unpublished pieces in Celâl's apartment and went on to tell him that—although Celâl had sent in only a
handful of new pieces in recent weeks—he had been working tire-
lessly, finishing off all the rough drafts that had accumulated in his bottom drawer and taking up a host of new subjects he'd never before
touched upon but writing them up in the same playful manner that had
been his trademark. The editor said that he would, of course, want to
run all these pieces in Celâl's old space. So this was how Galip launched
himself into a literary career that he would continue for many years, in
Celâl's space, under Celâl's name. As the mourners filed out of
Teşvikiye Mosque and made their way to Nişantaşı Square, where the
hearse was waiting, Galip saw Alâaddin gazing dreamily from his shop
door. In his hand was a doll he was about to wrap up in newspaper.

The night after he took his first batch of Celâl's new pieces into the
Milliyet offices, he had the first of many dreams in which he saw Rüya
with this same doll. After he'd handed in the pieces, Celâl's friends and
enemies—the old columnist Neşati among them—had crowded
around him to offer their condolences and offer theories about the
murder; later he'd gone into Celâl's office, where he found a pile of
newspapers from the previous five days; he began to read them.
Depending on their political leanings, the other columnists in the city
had blamed Celâl's murder on the Armenians, the Turkish mafia (no,
the Beyoğlu gangsters, Galip longed to write in green ink), the Communists, cigarette smugglers, the Greeks, the Islamists, the rightists,
the Russians, and the Nakşibendis; as he leafed through their tearful
and excessive eulogies and the accounts of all the other murders in
Turkish history that this murder resembled, he found one interesting
piece by a young journalist about the investigation into the murder
itself. This piece had come out in *Cumhuriyet* on the same day as the
funeral; although it was short and concise, the style was far from eloquent; instead of naming the victim, it identified him by profession.

On Friday, at seven in the evening, the Famous Columnist had left
his Nişantaşı home in the company of his sister. They'd gone to the
Palace Theater. The film, *Coming Home*, had finished at twenty past
nine. Still accompanied by his sister, who was married to a lawyer (even
if it was in parentheses, it was still the first time Galip had ever seen
himself mentioned in a newspaper), the Famous Columnist had filed

back into the street with the rest of the crowd. The snow that had been falling over Istanbul for ten days by then had begun to dissipate, but it was still very cold. Crossing Valikonak Avenue, they had walked down Emlâk Avenue to Teşvikiye. At 9:35, when they were just in front of the police station, they met with death. The killer, who had used a Kırıkkale gun of the sort issued to retired military personnel, had in all probability been aiming at the Columnist, but he had managed to hit them both; perhaps the trigger was stiff. Three of the five bullets fired had hit the Columnist, while the fourth had hit the sister, and the fifth the wall of Teşvikiye Mosque. Because one of the three bullets went into his heart, the Columnist had died on the spot. Another bullet had gone into the pen in the Columnist's shirt pocket, which was why (and the other columnists went wild over this strange little fluke) there was more green ink on his white shirt than there was blood. The sister, who had been shot in the lung and severely wounded, had staggered to the little shop on the corner that sold cigarettes and newspapers, about the same distance from the scene of the murder as the police station. The reporter described her last moments as meticulously as a detective who'd watched the key scene of a film many times over: the sister, drifting slowly toward the shop, known in the vicinity as Alâaddin's; Alâaddin, having taken cover behind the tree trunk, failing to see her. There was something about this scene that made Galip think of ballet dancers, drenched in a deep blue light. Then the film speeded up and became absurd: the shopkeeper, who had been taking down the magazines he'd pinned to the trunk of the chestnut tree, had panicked at the sound of gunfire, and—having failed to see the sister entering the shop—had rolled down his metal shutters then and there and run home as fast as his legs could take him.

Although "the tobacconist's known in the vicinity as Alâaddin's" had its lights on all night long, none of the police officers investigating the incident, and no one among the crowd of onlookers, seemed to have noticed the dying girl, let alone gone inside to help her. The authorities were also perturbed to learn that the police guard had not simply failed to intervene, he'd failed even to notice that a second person had been shot.

The murderer had managed to escape to parts unknown. In the morning, one citizen had come forward to tell the authorities that, moments before the incident and just after he'd been to Alâaddin's to buy a lottery ticket, he had seen a shadowy apparition near the scene of the crime, a man in a strange caped outfit who seemed to have walked straight off the set of a historical film. ("For a moment I thought he was Mehmet the Conqueror.") He'd been so struck by this dark figure that he'd gone home and described him in detail to his wife and his sister-in-law—in other words, long before he'd read about the murder in the paper. The young journalist concluded his article by saying he hoped that lack of interest or general ineptitude did not condemn this new clue to the same fate as the young woman who had been found dead among the baby dolls the following morning.

That night, Galip saw Rüya among the baby dolls in Alâaddin's shop. She had not yet died. Like the dolls around her, she was blinking and she was breathing, but only just; she was waiting for Galip, but he was late; he just couldn't manage to get there; he just stood there at his window in the City-of-Hearts Apartments, staring at Alâaddin's shop in the distance, watching the light stream from its window onto the snow-covered pavement as tears rolled from his eyes.

One sunny morning in February, Galip's father told him that Uncle Melih had made inquiries at the Şişli Land Deeds Office and had now heard back from them that Celâl owned another apartment in the back streets of Nişantaşı.

Galip and his uncle went to see this apartment, taking with them a hunchback locksmith, arriving at an old, narrow, cobblestone side street along pavements riddled with potholes. Looking up at the blackened facades of the three- and four-story buildings that lined each side and seeing how the paint was peeling off the balconies and window frames like skin from a dying man, Galip could not help but wonder why the rich would ever have wanted to live in such miserable surroundings, or why anyone who did live in such miserable surroundings could be said to be rich. Celâl's other secret apartment was on the top floor of one of these buildings; there was no name on the door, and the locksmith had no trouble opening its worn lock.

In the back of the apartment were two narrow bedrooms, and in each there was a single bed. In the front they found a small and sunny sitting room that looked out over the street; there were two armchairs, one on either side of a table piled high with news clippings about recent murders, photographs, film and sports magazines, new issues of *Tom Mix*, *Texas*, and other comics Galip had read as a child, detective novels, and piles of paper and newsprint. The large copper ashtray piled high with pistachio shells left Galip in no doubt that Rüya had been sitting at this table.

In a room he was sure had been Celâl's, he found aspirin, vasodilators, matches, and packages of Mnemonics, a drug that claimed to improve the memory. Rüya's almost empty bare-walled room reminded him that his wife had left home taking almost nothing with her: there, on a Thonet chair, was her makeup, her slippers, the keyless key chain she thought brought her good luck, and her hairbrush with the mirror on its back. As Galip stood there staring at these objects, unable to tear himself away, a moment arrived when he felt as if he had moved beyond enchantment, walking through his own illusions to see the second meanings they hid deep inside them; moving through these too, he was suddenly sure he had penetrated the mystery hidden inside the very heart of the world. They must have come here to tell each other stories, he told himself, and went back to join Uncle Melih, who was still out of breath from climbing all those stairs. He could tell from the way the papers were arranged on the table that Celâl had been dictating stories and Rüya writing them down, and that Celâl had been sitting in the chair on the left, where Uncle Melih was now sitting; and that the other chair, the chair that was now vacant, had been Rüya's. After Galip gathered up all the stories he might be able to use in his *Milliyet* column and put them into his pocket, he offered Uncle Melih the explanation he was clearly (though he had not put it into so many words) desperate to hear.

Quite some time ago, the famous English physician Dr. Cole Ridge had diagnosed Celâl as suffering from a terrible memory disease; he had, however, failed to find a cure. To keep his illness secret from the world, Celâl had taken refuge in this apartment, though he had depended on the constant support of Galip and Rüya. So on some nights Galip would stay here with him, and on other nights Rüya; hoping to help him recall and restore his past, they had sat here listening to Celâl's stories, sometimes even transcribing them. As the snow fell outside, Celâl would go on for hours and hours.

Uncle Melih fell silent, as if he understood everything all too well. Then he burst into tears. Then he lit up a cigarette. Then he had a small coughing fit. His elder son had led his life pursuing mad ideas, he said. Celâl had never forgiven his family for kicking him out of the City-of-Hearts Apartments, never forgiven his father for pushing Celâl and his mother to one side so he could remarry, and he'd dreamed all his life of making his family pay. Yet Uncle Melih had always loved Celâl at least as much as he had loved Rüya. Now he had no children. No. Now the only child he had left was Galip.

Tears. Silence. The noises of a strange house. Galip felt like telling Uncle Melih to buy himself his bottle of *rakı* from the store on the corner and go home. Instead, he asked himself a question that he would never ask himself again (and readers wishing to ask themselves this question are advised instead to skip the paragraph that now follows).

As they wandered together in the garden of memory, admiring the stories and recollections and legends blooming at their feet, which of these blossoms had told Rüya and Celâl that they should shut Galip out? Had they done so because Galip had no idea of how to tell a story? Was it because he wasn't as lively and vibrant as they were? Or because he just couldn't understand some stories at all? Had he been too admiring of Celâl, and had they found his idol worship tiresome? Had they wanted to escape from the heavy melancholy he carried with him everywhere, like a contagious disease?

Rüya had put an empty yogurt container under the radiator, to catch the water leaking from the valve—just as she had done at home.

By the end of that summer, finding himself unable to bear the memories their home carried—for even the furniture seemed to wince with pain—Galip left the apartment he'd shared with Rüya and moved into Celâl's flat in the City-of-Hearts Apartments. Just as he'd been unable to look at Rüya's body, he couldn't bring himself to look again at the things his father sold or gave away. He was no longer able to dream of a happy ending, as he had done so often during her first marriage, no longer able to assure himself that one day she would appear out of nowhere to resume their life together, like a book abandoned in the middle. That summer the days were hot and never-ending.

At the end of the summer, there was a military coup. The new gov-

ernment was composed of cautious patriots who had never before
ventured into that cesspool known as politics; they let it be known that
they aimed to apprehend all those responsible for the politically motivated murders committed in the period prior to their arrival. So on the
first anniversary of Celâl's murder, the newspapers—heavily censored
and so no longer able to print real news—saw fit to remind them that
the mystery surrounding this case had yet to be resolved; though they
were careful to couch their comments in the most polite and respectful
language. One newspaper—not Celâl's old paper *Milliyet*, for some reason—offered a substantial reward to any informer whose evidence led
to the apprehension of the murderer. It was enough money to buy a
truck, a small flour mill, or a good monthly stipend lasting a lifetime.
So it was that everyone in the city was suddenly all agog with the mystery behind the Celâl Salik Murder. Perhaps seeing it as their last
chance to immortalize themselves, martial law commanders stationed
in provincial towns all over the country did everything in their power
to help solve the case.

You will, no doubt, have noted from my style that it is me again telling
the story. For as the leaves grew back on the chestnut trees, I too began
the slow transformation from a melancholy man to an angry one. The
angry man I was slowly becoming had no time for the bulletins coming
in from provinces about the various investigations purported to be
going on "behind closed doors." One week he read that the killer had
been apprehended in a small town whose name he'd once heard mentioned in conjunction with a bus accident that left a busload of soccer
players and their supporters lying crushed at the foot of a ravine just
outside the town limits; the next week he read that the murderer had
been caught in a seaside town, gazing longingly at the distant hills of
the neighboring country that had given him many sackloads of money
to commit the crime. Because these first news flashes encouraged
many citizens who would not normally have had the courage to turn
informer and fostered a competitive spirit among other martial law
commanders, there was, during the early weeks of the summer, a spate
of hysterical stories claiming that the murderer had been caught. This
was when the security authorities began to haul me down to their

headquarters in the middle of the night to "pump me for information" and "identify the culprit."

By now there was a curfew, and because the city could not afford to keep their generators running all night, there were power cuts daily from midnight until morning; silence reigned, though one could almost hear the illegal butchers furiously slashing the throats of old horses under cover of darkness; terrorized, the city sank into itself; soon it too was a provincial town like any other, in thrall to religion, mindful of its cemeteries, seeing the world in black and white, and showing its enemies no mercy. Just after midnight, I would rise from my smoky desk with my latest column, knowing it to be as inspired and as imaginative as anything Celâl himself had ever written, and I'd walk down the dark stairs of the City-of-Hearts Apartments to step out onto the empty pavement to await the police car that would take me to the headquarters of MİT, looming like a castle on the hill overlooking Beşiktaş. The streets through which we drove were dark, still, and empty, but the castle would be buzzing with activity and blazing with light.

They'd present me with mug shots, endless pictures of drowsy young men with disheveled hair and purple rings under their vacant eyes. From time to time, I was reminded of the boy who'd come up to our apartments with his father, the water carrier; his black eyes would survey the room like a movie camera, and he'd have recorded every item of Uncle Melih's furniture by the time his father had filled the tank; some reminded me of the pimply boy who'd come up to Rüya during the five-minute intermission at some matinee or other, as she was nibbling on her Penguin Ice Bar, boldly introducing himself as the "friend of a friend's older brother" and paying no attention to the fact that her cousin was sitting there right next to her; others reminded me of the sloe-eyed salesboy—who couldn't have been any older than we were—who would lean against the half-open door of the old haberdashery store, to watch us streaming out of school and heading home; still others—and these were the most frightening—reminded me of no one and called nothing to mind at all. As I sat there staring at these vacant faces, these boys who'd been pushed up against unpainted police department walls that were streaked with dirt and stained with God only knew what, as I struggled to find in them some shadow that might elicit some memory still lost in the mist—in other words, when I too found myself up against the wall—the tough-guy agents standing over me would offer up a few tantalizing facts about whatever ghostly face I happened to have before me: This boy had been picked up at a right-wing coffeehouse in Sivas following a tip and had committed four previous murders; this other boy who was hardly old enough to grow a mustache had written a long piece in a political journal friendly to the views of Enver Hoxha, in which he had named Celâl as an enemy of the cause and invited readers to take appropriate action; the one whose jacket had a few buttons missing was a teacher who was being transferred from Malatya to Istanbul and who had told his nine-year-old students that Celâl deserved to die for an article he'd written fifteen years earlier in which he'd blasphemed the great Rumi; this timid middle-aged family man was a drunk who'd gone into one of our city's taverns and given a great long speech about how our nation needed to be cleansed of all its microbes, after which another citizen at a neighboring table who knew about the newspaper reward had gone to the Beyoğlu police station and denounced him, saying that he'd included Celâl in his list of microbes. Did Galip Bey recognize this groggy drunk, these hopeless layabouts, these angry wretches? If they went through all the pictures again, one by one, would Galip Bey remember seeing any of these vapid, guilty faces in Celâl's company in recent years?

In the middle of the summer, around the time they brought out the new five-thousand-lira notes with Rumi's face on them, I was reading the paper one morning when I happened onto an obituary for a retired colonel named Fatih Mehmet Üçüncü. During the same hot weeks, my enforced visits to the MİT headquarters grew more numerous, as did the mug shots they gave me to examine. I had a hard time finding the humanity in these faces, for they were sadder and more mournful than any face I'd seen in Celâl's modest collection; they belonged to bicycle repairmen, archaeology students, sewing machine operators, gas station attendants, grocery delivery boys, Yeşilçam film extras, coffeehouse owners, authors of religious tracts, bus conductors, park attendants, nightclub bouncers, young accountants, encyclopedia salesmen. . . . They'd all been either tortured, badly beaten, or knocked about; they'd forgotten about that mysterious loss, that hidden knowl-

edge, now wafting into the depths of their minds, and because they'd
forgotten it, they'd stopped searching for it too. It was better, they
seemed to be saying, if it sank to a bottomless well, never to return,
never again to haunt their memories; as they'd gazed into the cameras,
their sad and fearful expressions had said, I'm not really here, and anyway I'm really someone else.

For me (and also, I suspect, for my readers) this is an old game by
now—a game whose outcome has been clear for only too long—and
as I have no desire to dwell upon the moves I made along the way,
without ever knowing the fate awaiting me at the end, I shall not mention the letters I saw in the faces in these pictures. But during one of
my interminable visits to the castle (or would it be more accurate to call
it a fortress?), after I had again refused to find anyone I recognized
among the faces they showed me, one MİT agent (whom I later discovered was a staff colonel) came right out and asked me, "What
about the letters? Can't you even see the letters?" Seasoned profes-
sional that he was, he then added, "We also are only too aware of how
hard it is for a man to be himself in this country. But why can't you give
us a little help?"

One night I had to listen to a fat major pontificate on Anatolia's last
remaining Sufi orders and on the still-prevailing belief in the Mehdi; he
did not speak as if he'd gleaned this information from intelligence
reports but from his own most unpleasant childhood memories: Celâl,
he said, had tried to make contact with these "reactionary leftovers"
during secret trips into Anatolia and had, in the end, managed to meet
up with one such group of sleepwalkers, either at a car repair shop on
the outskirts of Konya or at the home of a Konya quilt maker. He'd
told these people that he would signal the Day of Judgment in his column and that all they had to do was wait. Those columns he'd written
about the Cyclops, about pashas and sultans in disguise, and about the
Bosphorus drying up—they were swarming with such signs.

When one diligent agent informed me that he had cracked the code,
proudly announcing that he'd found the key to the enigma in an acros-
tic formed by the first letters of the paragraphs in the column entitled
"The Kiss," I felt like saying, I know that already. I felt like saying the
same thing when they told me why it was significant that the Ayatollah
Khomeini had chosen to call the account of his life and struggles *The*

Discovery of Mystery and what I should find significant in its photographs of the Ayatollah in the dark streets of Bursa during his years of exile in that city. I knew as well as they did that there was a lost man, and a lost mystery, hiding inside Celâl's columns on Rumi. I knew this already! I wanted to cry out, when—laughing heartily—they told me that Celâl (who hoped that, in dying, he might help restore the mystery that should always reside at the heart of life) had been seeking his own murderer; I wanted to say the same when they told me "he must have been out of his mind," when they spoke of his memory lapses, and when I saw among their photographs a face that called to mind one of the lost and mournful souls I'd found among the photographs in Celâl's elm cabinet. I wanted to tell them that I knew the identity of the beloved he summoned in his piece about the Bosphorus drying up, and the phantom wife to whom he addressed the first paragraph of "The Kiss," and heroes he'd met while wafting off to sleep. I was wary of believing anything they said, but still, when they told me that the ticket scalper Celâl had mentioned in one column as being madly in love with the Greek girl who worked in the ticket booth was, in actual fact, a plainclothes policeman and in their pay, I wanted to tell them I knew *that*, too; and the same words came to me another night, when I was being forced to study yet another ruined, vacant, sleep-deprived face, disfigured all the more by the one-way mirror that stood between us; upon hearing that I had failed to recognize it, they had told me the things Celâl had written on faces and maps meant nothing, that this was "just another of his cheap tricks"—he'd been sending his readers secret signs to keep them happy and con them into thinking they had a common cause.

Perhaps they already knew what I didn't know (or what I knew without knowing); perhaps they knew they had to kill off Celâl's dark mystery, kill off every mystery still lurking not just in my own mind but in the minds of all his readers, and everyone else in the country too; perhaps they knew they had to kill any doubt still languishing in the dregs of our minds before anything took root.

Sometimes one of the hard-boiled detectives would lose his patience, or a general I'd never met before would sweep into the room, or a scrawny prosecutor I'd met months earlier would make a return visit and offer up an entirely implausible theory, conjuring up clues like a detective in the last chapter of one of Rüya's murder mysteries. As the scene progressed, the other officials in the room would sit on the sidelines like the teacher's jury in a school debate, proudly jotting down their prize students' fine words on stationery stamped with the words STATE SUPPLY OFFICE. The killer was a pawn, dispatched by foreign powers wishing to "destablize" our nation; smarting from the shame of seeing their secrets ridiculed, the Bektaşis and Nakşibendis, along with a number of poets writing classical verse that contained acrostics and a number of contemporary poets best described as voluntary Hurufis, had become the unwitting agents of foreign powers aiming to push our country into anarchy and even, some said, to the brink of the apocalypse. No, there was nothing political about this murder: This was clear to anyone who had read the outmoded, long-winded, bizarre, and idiosyncratic nonsense that the murdered columnist had been churning out, year after year. The murderer was either a Beyoğlu gangster, who'd sensed ridicule behind the grand legends Celâl made up about him, or else he was a gunman Celâl had hired himself. There was one unusually busy night when a number of university students confessed to the murder—but just to make a name for themselves—and the officials found themselves obliged to subject them to torture, in the hope that this might help them change their minds; on the same night, a number of innocent men were picked up in a mosque and forced, upon arriving in the fortress, to make confessions; in the midst of all this commotion, we were suddenly joined by a professor of Classical Ottoman Literature, who had grown up in the same back streets and under the same trellised balconies as one of the highest-ranking MİT directors; after clacking his false teeth, ignoring the sniggers in the audience, and giving us a short but boring introduction to Hurufism and the ancient art of word games, he had listened to the story I was then forced to tell him, and then, affecting the air of a two-bit fortune-teller, he informed me that the "entire matter sat easily inside the framework of Sheikh Galip's *Beauty and Love*." Throughout this same period, two other men at the fort had been busy going through the mountains of letters of denunciation sent in by frenzied fortune hunters to the newspaper that had offered the prize, so no one paid much attention to the professor who claimed that the solution was to be found in poetry written two centuries earlier.

Not long afterward, it was decided that the murderer was a barber who'd been mentioned in one of these denunciations. It was after they showed me their photograph of this sixty-year-old man, and after they realized that I was not going to identify him as the culprit, that I stopped being invited to the fort to play mysterious games with other people's lives. For a week, the papers were full of stories about the barber, who first denied the crime, and then confessed to it, only to deny it again, and then confess to it once more. Celâl Salik had first mentioned this man many years ago, in a column entitled "I Must Be Myself." In that and a number of subsequent pieces, he'd described how the barber had come into the newspaper offices to ask him questions that, he claimed, would explain what it meant to be "us," while also illuminating the deepest mysteries of the East and life itself; the columnist had, by his own admission, answered him with jokes. Publicly humiliated, the enraged barber had then seen himself ridiculed in column after column. When the first column was reprinted under the same title twenty-three years later, he felt the full sting of the original insult; encouraged by various friends and acquaintances, he had resolved to seek revenge. The names of his accomplices were never discovered, however, for the barber (borrowing a phrase he'd heard bandied about the police station) claimed his crime to be "an act of solitary terrorism." The picture they ran in the papers showed the barber's ruined, tired face to be devoid of letters and empty of meaning; he was tried forthwith, and duly sentenced; having proven they could dispense swift and efficient justice, they ordered its swift and efficient execution, so early one morning, when the only creatures daring to break the curfew were the stray dogs roaming the streets, the barber was hanged.

While all this was going on, I was setting down all the Mount Kaf stories I could remember and gathering up any others I could find; I spent a great deal of time listening to everyone who came to my law offices with theories about the murder, though I had a hard time keeping my eyes open and did not offer these people any help. I was visited, for example, by an obsessive young man from a religious high school who had deduced from Celâl's own columns that Celâl was Deccal—Satan—and that his murderer had taken on the role of the Messiah or, to put it more succinctly, God; to prove his theory he brought out a handful of newspaper clippings that were, he said, full of stories about executioners; but his explication of their letters' second meanings meant as little to me as the story I heard from yet another visitor, the tailor who had made Celâl's historical costumes. His face was familiar but as difficult to place as a face from an old and half-forgotten movie, so it took me some time to work out that he was the same tailor I had met in the snowy streets on the evening of the day Rüya had disappeared. I was just as sleepy and unresponsive the day I was visited by my old friend Saim, who was hoping I could tell him just how detailed the MİT archives were, and who also thought I'd be happy to hear that the innocent student had been released following the arrest of the real Mehmet Yılmaz. As I pretended to listen to Saim's views on "I Must Be Myself," the column now viewed to have provoked Celâl's murder, I let my mind wander until I had floated far, far away from this black book in your hands, until I was no longer Galip, no longer myself.

For a time, I gave myself over to my law practice. At another point, I neglected my work, looked up old friends, and went to restaurants and taverns with a slew of new friends. Sometimes I would notice that the clouds hanging over Istanbul were unusually yellow, or that they had taken on a shade of gray I'd never seen before; I would look up at the sky and try to convince myself that it was the same sky as I'd always known. Some nights I would write two or three columns in one sitting—just as Celâl had done during his more productive periods—and then I would rise from the desk, sit down on the chair next to the telephone, prop my legs on the table, and stare at the objects that surrounded me until they had turned into signs, and stare at these signs until they had become objects in another world. Deep in the recesses of my mind, a shadow would come to life; I would watch it cross the garden of memory to pass through a gate that led to a second garden, and then a third, and a fourth; and as I watched this familiar sight I would feel my own self passing, too, from garden to garden, gate to gate, until I had become someone who could share life with that shadow, even know happiness with that shadow—but before I let myself speak in this other person's voice, I would stop myself.

I had to be careful: there was always the danger of stumbling across something that reminded me of Rüya when I least expected it, and I was always trying to evade the grief that continued to descend on me without pretext or warning. Two or three times a week, I would go to

Aunt Hâle's for supper, and after we had eaten I would help Vasıf feed the goldfish, but I never sat on the edge of the bed with him to look at his newspaper clippings. (Though I must have glanced in their direction, for one evening, I happened to catch a glimpse of one of Celâl's columns to see that someone had replaced his picture with a photograph of Edward G. Robinson—and I thought I saw a distant family resemblance.) When it was getting late, either my father or Aunt Suzan would tell me I should hurry home before it got even later—and you would think from their tone of voice that Rüya was at home in her sickbed, waiting for my return—I'd say, "Yes, I'd better get back before the curfew."

But I wouldn't walk past Alâaddin's store as Rüya and I had done; instead I took a roundabout route through back streets, always passing the home we'd once shared before walking on to the City-of-Hearts Apartments; and to avoid following the same path Celâl and Rüya would have taken after leaving the Palace Theater I would again change streets, and so find myself back in the dark maze of the city's back streets, surrounded by strange walls and stranger streetlights, letters, and mosque courtyards, buildings that looked like grimacing faces, and windows whose curtains were shut so tight they reminded me of a blind man's eyes. As I walked among these dark, dead signs, I felt so outside myself that when I arrived in front of the City-of-Hearts Apartments, with only moments to spare before the curfew began, and I saw the rag still tied to the rungs of the balcony on the top floor, I'd almost believe that Rüya was up there waiting for me.

After taking my long walk in the city's dark and empty streets, after seeing the sign Rüya had left for me, I would remember a long conversation she and I had had one snowy night in the third year of our marriage; for once we had talked like old friends, never needling each other, never letting the conversation drop into the bottomless well of Rüya's indifference, and ignoring the silence that still stood between us like a phantom. It had begun when I'd wondered out loud what we'd be like together when we were seventy-three; the idea had appealed to Rüya's imagination, and we'd sat there for hours, dreaming up the details.

When we were seventy-three, we'd go out together one winter morning and set off for Beyoğlu. We'd take the money we'd saved up

and buy each other presents: either a pullover or a pair of gloves. We'd
both be wearing our favorite coats; they'd be old and heavy and carry
our own scents. We'd wander aimlessly down the streets, talking and
glancing vacantly from time to time into the shop display windows, but
only to disparage them, to complain how much things had changed, to
remind each other that clothes in the old days, shop windows in the old
days, people in the old days, had been so much better, so much more
beautiful. Even as we spoke, we'd know that we only spoke like this
because we were too old to expect anything from the future; but that
wouldn't stop us. We'd buy two pounds of marrons glacés, paying
close attention to the way the boy weighed them and wrapped them
up. Then, as we continued our meander through the back streets, we'd
happen onto an old bookstore we'd never seen before; amazed, we'd
joyfully congratulate each other. Inside we'd find it to be full of detective novels that Rüya either hadn't read or couldn't remember reading.
As we browsed through the shelves, an old cat prowling among the
piles of books would hiss at us, and the old bookseller would watch us
with an understanding smile. We'd leave with bags of bargain books—
enough, Rüya would say happily, to keep her busy for at least two
months—but as we sipped our teas in a pudding shop afterward, we'd
have a little argument. We'd lash out at each other simply because we
were seventy-three, and because we knew—as do all people when they
reach the age of seventy-three—that we'd wasted the better part of
our lives. When we got home again, we'd open all our packages, and
take off our clothes, and, exposing our flabby, white old bodies to each
other without a moment of shyness, fall into bed to make love; we'd go
on for hours, pausing from time to time to feast on marrons glacés and
syrup. Though our bodies were old and tired, our skin would be the
same translucent white as it was when we'd first met as children, sixty-
seven years before. Rüya, whose imagination was always more vivid
than mine, predicted that halfway through our wild bout of lovemaking, we'd stop for a cigarette and a good cry. But I was the one who had
started our game, for I hoped that by the time we were seventy-three,
Rüya would have run out of other, better lives to long for and would,
at last, have come to love me. Though Istanbul would continue—as
my readers will have noticed—to be its old miserable self.

From time to time, when I'm going through one of Celâl's old boxes or searching through my office files or sitting in a room at Aunt Hâle's, I'll suddenly see one of her belongings—something I somehow missed and so did not throw away. A purple button from the flowery dress she was wearing when we first met; a pair of "modern" glasses with pointy corners that you saw European beauties wearing in all the best magazines in the sixties, and that Rüya wore for six months before discarding them; the small black hairpins she liked to put in her hair, using both hands but always with a spare in her mouth; the tail of a hollow wooden duck in which she'd kept her needle and thread, mislaid many years before but sorely missed and never forgotten; and, among Uncle Melih's legal files, a homework assignment for literature class—that she'd copied straight out of the encyclopedia—about the simurgh, the mythological bird rumored to live on Mount Kaf, the many adventurers who had gone in search of it; strands of her hair on Aunt Suzan's hairbrush; a list of things she'd asked me to buy on my way home (smoked fish, a copy of *Silver Screen* magazine, butane for her lighter, and a bar of Bonibon nut chocolate); a picture of a pine tree, drawn with Grandfather's help; a lone green sock I recognized as belonging to the pair she was wearing when we went out for a ride in rented bicycles nineteen years ago.

Each time I found one of these objects, I would carry it around in my grubby pocket for several days, sometimes several weeks—all right, it's true; sometimes I carried it with me for several months. But sooner or later I would take it outside and place it gently, respectfully, on top of some trash can in front of some apartment house or other, somewhere in Nişantaşı; even after saying my last farewells, I'd still dream that these sad mementos would, like all those things we'd thrown down the air shaft over the years, find their way back to me, trailing my memories behind them.

Today all I have left of Rüya are these words, these bleak black pages. Sometimes, one of the stories related here will come back to me—the executioner's tale, say, or "Rüya and Galip" as Celâl told it to us for the first time on that snowy evening—and it will remind me of another story in which the hero discovers that he can only become himself by first becoming someone else or by losing himself in someone else's stories; and as I dream of putting all these stories together in a single black book, I'll think of another adventure, another love story;

and as I wander through the garden of memory, through gate after gate, I'll remember the story of the lover who lost himself in the streets of Istanbul only to become himself, or the story of the man who believed life's meaning and mystery resided in his face, and with each story I embrace I become all the more enamored of the task I have set myself—which is not to invent new stories but to set down the tales we have been telling each other for many centuries, to gather them together in the black book whose last scene I am now ready to write. In that final scene, Galip is rushing to meet his deadline, and because Celâl is no longer the talk of the town these days, this column will be the last ever to appear under his name. Toward morning, beset by painful memories of Rüya, Galip rises from his desk and looks out over Istanbul's dark streets. Beset by painful memories of Rüya, I rise from my desk and look down on the dark streets of Istanbul. Together we think of Rüya and look out onto the dark streets of Istanbul; together we go to bed to drift between sleep and wakefulness, and whenever I see some sign of Rüya on the blue-checked quilt, we are both plunged into misery and surprised back to life. Because nothing is as surprising as life. Except for writing. Except for writing. Yes, of course, except for writing, the only consolation.

1985–1989

Translator's Afterword

There is no verb *to be* in Turkish, nor is there a verb *to have*. It's an agglutinative language, which means that root nouns in even the simplest sentences can carry five or six suffixes. ("Apparently, they were inside their houses" is a single word.) There are many more tenses—you use one mode for events you have witnessed with your own eyes, for example, and another for anything you know by hearsay. There is a special syllable you can add to a verb to emphasize the active role someone played in whatever you are describing. The passive voice is as graceful as the active voice and rather more popular, with the result that a fine Turkish sentence may choose to obscure exactly who did what. It may also decline to be precise about gender, there being only one word for *he*, *she*, and *it*. Add to this the vogue among Turkey's leading writers for the *devrik cümle*. This is a sentence—usually a very long sentence—in which words appear in an order different from that ordained by custom and practice, and cascading clauses create a series of expectations that are subverted by the verb at the very end. The poet Murat Nemet-Nejat has described Turkish as a language that can evoke a thought unfolding. How to do the same in English without the thought vanishing into thin air?

The accepted view, especially among bilingual Turks, is that the translator should pay close attention to the sentence's "inner logic." This might also be described as its architecture—the elegant way in which the various parts reflect one another and, together, reflect the mystery that must never be coarsened by words; the games with voice and tense and the imaginative melding of different epochs and places in sentences that may be admired at length like pictures in a museum. For those who feel at home inside the traditions of Turkish thought, the virtues of this approach are manifest. A translation that is utterly faithful to that inner logic will, in their view, open up like a flower to reveal its inner truth. Translators of poetry have often worked such miracles, but translators of Turkish prose have had a harder time of it. All too often, the grand, allusive flourishes are lost on readers accustomed to the simpler and more straightforward logic of English. The passive voice becomes cumbersome and even obfuscating—why won't this writer tell me who is doing all this? Mesmerizing lists of verbal nouns (the doing of . . . the seeing of . . . the having been done unto of . . .) begin to grate on the nerves. The tenses are robbed of their nuances, and the graceful unfolding of cascading clauses becomes an ungainly procession of non sequiturs. The verb that should have been the twist in the tail appears so early it robs the long sentence of its suspense, so that, instead of gaining momentum, each sentence seems to double back on itself. It's not just the meaning that gets muffled, it's the music.

And it's the music I love most in Turkish. This comes from my time as an American child in 1960s Istanbul, listening and not understanding, but catching the emotional undercurrents that words can so easily hide. So when I sat down to try my hand at translating Turkish, it seemed I should begin there, with the music. I would start at the heart of the sentence and work my way out, rather than the other way around. The challenge was to reorder the various parts of the sentence in a way that allowed it to unfold and reveal its heart. I was not done until I had managed to order them in a way I felt to be an accurate reflection of the author's original intentions. Because I came, with time, to understand how his long sentences contributed to the narrative trance, I tried, wherever possible, to keep them at their original length. But I also wanted them to be clear—or clear enough.

With *Snow* and *Istanbul*, the author and I worked out a system whereby I worked straight to the end without consulting him. He then went over the finished draft, measuring his Turkish against my English and inserting his praises, curses, and exhortations in the margins. Only then did we sit down together and go through each manuscript, sentence by sentence, hour after hour, no matter how high the sun in the sky, or how hot.

The Black Book (our third collaboration) was published in Turkey fifteen years ago. It first appeared in English in 1995; the translation, though ebullient and faithful to the original, was also somewhat opaque. My hope is that this new translation might bring the book to a generation of readers who know Orhan Pamuk only from his later works. For *The Black Book* is the cauldron from which they come.

The novel takes place at one of the darkest moments of recent Turkish history, but it is lit from within by the more innocent Istanbul we knew as children. The city was dusty and dilapidated in those days, and ringed by ruins. In every square stood a pristine statue of Atatürk, the father of modern Turkey. His portrait hung in every school and office. Sometimes he was dressed in a greatcoat, sometimes in a topcoat; whatever he was wearing and however he was posed, his luminous blue eyes were fixed on the horizon.

A quarter century after his death, Turkey was not yet the prosperous, Westward-looking republic he envisioned. The economy was all but closed, to protect its fledgling industries. We all used Omo detergent, İpana toothpaste, Job shaving cream, and Sana margarine. I remember a man on a donkey delivering milk straight from the farm. Another man with a horse-drawn cart delivered water. We bought glassware from Paşabahçe, Turkey's only glassmaker. Our shoes came from the dozen or so shoe shops lining İstiklâl Caddesi, and our silk scarves from Vakko, Turkey's only department store. There was almost no ready-made clothing, but the city's seamstresses, rumored to be the best in the world, were slavish and resourceful followers of Western fashion. The city's mechanics needed to be just as resourceful, for every taxi in the city was a 1956 Chevrolet.

Hollywood films came to Istanbul years late, if they came at all. There was no television in the 1960s, and the radio was state-controlled. It catered to all (respectable) tastes, keeping to a rigid schedule: Every evening there was a half-hour "advertisement program," during which the same actors did the same skits for the same products every day, and at 8:15 there was a forty-five-minute "light Western music" request program that was, for most of us, the only time we got to hear the Beatles. The news programs offered a single version of the news, reflecting the views of the army, which saw itself as the protector of Atatürk's republican vision.

Any government that seemed to compromise that vision could expect swift and decisive action. And so it was in 1961, when a group of generals removed Menderes, the prime minister, from office; their pretext was that he was secretly plotting an end to the secular state.

They put him and two of his ministers on trial and in due course hanged all three. The same generals drafted a new constitution that brought more freedom to the country than it had ever seen; it also gave more powers to the military. Though the press was less muzzled, certain topics remained taboo. It was unwise to discuss Turkey's minorities in public. Ideas could be crimes.

But by the late sixties, Turkey's students had drifted leftward, just as students had in Europe and the United States. Anti-Americanism was rife and fueled by the belief that America was pulling the army's strings. Marches turned into riots, and boycotts into pitched battles; Molotov cocktails gave way to bombs and high-profile kidnappings; on 12 March 1971, the army stepped in once again to "restore democracy." Within weeks, many thousands had been imprisoned.

By the mid-seventies, most had been released. But by the end of the decade, violence had again erupted, with leftists and rightists now fighting each other daily in the city's streets, and no one doubted that the army would soon be stepping in again to restore its version of order.

This, then, is the Istanbul we meet in the first pages of *The Black Book*. It is a cold morning in January 1980, and the brutal coup that will end "the anarchy" is nine months away.

—Maureen Freely
Bath, December 2005

ff

Faber and Faber – a home for writers

Faber and Faber is one of the great independent publishing houses in London. We were established in 1929 by Geoffrey Faber and our first editor was T. S. Eliot. We are proud to publish prize-winning fiction and non-fiction, as well as an unrivalled list of modern poets and playwrights. Among our list of writers we have five Booker Prize winners and eleven Nobel Laureates, and we continue to seek out the most exciting and innovative writers at work today.

www.faber.co.uk – a home for readers

The Faber website is a place where you will find all the latest news on our writers and events. You can listen to podcasts, preview new books, read specially commissioned articles and access reading guides, as well as entering competitions and enjoying a whole range of offers and exclusives. You can also browse the list of Faber Finds, an exciting new project where reader recommendations are helping to bring a wealth of lost classics back into print using the latest on-demand technology.